Y0-DBV-911

Radiance

BOOKS BY N. RICHARD NASH

Novels
APHRODITE'S CAVE
THE LAST MAGIC
EAST WIND, RAIN
CRY MACHO

Poetry
ABSALOM

Plays
ECHOES
GIRLS OF SUMMER
THE RAINMAKER
SEE THE JAGUAR
THE YOUNG AND FAIR
SECOND BEST BED

Nonfiction
THE WOUNDS OF SPARTA
THE ATHENIAN SPIRIT

Radiance

N. RICHARD NASH

Doubleday & Company, Inc.
Garden City, New York
1983

All characters in this book are fictitious,
and any resemblance to actual persons,
living or dead,
is entirely coincidental.

Library of Congress Cataloging in Publication Data

Nash, N. Richard.
Radiance.

I. Title.
PS3527.A6365R26 1983   813'.54
ISBN: 0-385-14295-1
Library of Congress Catalog Card Number 81–43726

for

DUFFY EDES

old friend and young poet
with much love

Radiance

I

She should have hung up instantly. And would have, if she hadn't had the feeling that she knew the voice. She couldn't exactly identify it, but the diction, the meticulous measuring of words, were tantalizingly familiar, and she had the nettling sense that she had worked with him somewhere, in a play or film, or in an acting class, long ago. So she kept him talking, certain that any moment she would know, or he would tell her who he was.

It was not by any means an obscene call. No objectionable words were uttered, not an innuendo; nor was it like the hate messages she used to receive.

But it was creepy. The peculiar part was how much he knew about her—yet didn't know. Like a Peeping Tom, he seemed to be squinting through the blinds of her naked thoughts, intimately, no stranger to any sensibility. Still, he apparently didn't know some of the stuff that had been in the newspapers for the last fifteen years—when she won the Oscar, for example, or when she was arrested. And he was wrong on easily available statistics: she had made fourteen films, not twelve; she was thirty-nine, not thirty-seven.

"Thirty-nine—really? I've lost a few years. . . . Do you feel that you've lost some years?"

"No. Where?" He didn't answer. "When?"

"When you were a Communist."

Carefully: "When was I a Communist?"

"In the Vietnam days."

"Are you sure I was a Communist?"

"You said you were."

"I never said I was."

"No, not publicly."

The son of a bitch.

She was on the verge of hanging up, when an echo came to her. She knew something about that voice. In a minute she would recognize it. It was British—an Englishman pretending to be an American, and doing it extremely well, dropping the final r's and broadening the vowels but not too much. A literate voice, as polished as satin, oddly sensual. Yes, a Briton—someone she might have read with when she had auditioned for the Osborne play. Not Tony Quayle—younger; nor Eric Ramsey. The tall Yorkshireman she had met with Alan Bates— what was his name? No, not that one. She felt that any minute, any minute now . . .

"Tell me something, Calla," he said. "Why do you think you're so unsuccessful these days?"

"Who says I'm unsuccessful?"

"Nobody—that's the point. Why do *you*?"

He was like an insect squirming in her clothes. With all the indices saying whammo, boffo, big-star-bankable and artist-come-of-age, why did she see herself as a failure? And how did he know it?

Edgar or Edward Something. No, not quite.

"Is it because you're not a firebrand any longer?"

He could be the man from *The Times* of London, or was it the *Telegraph*? The smarmy one who kept blathering about the alchemy of art, while groping under the table. No, he didn't talk with such dry silkiness; too much spittle.

She laughed. "Oh, I'm still a firebrand."

"What causes? Baby seals? Gerbils?"

It was a kidney shot. Written and played as a giddy comedy, her last film, *Gerbils Have No Germs*, had turned into a runaway success, and the more ponderous critics, like Stanley Kauffmann, had perceived significances in it. The story of a little boy who goes to a progressive private school where everything is permissible until he sets free a hutchful of gerbils, the reviewers had dragged into question a number of embattled democratic principles, including free speech and due process. The gerbil-child's mother was played by Calla, and her best scenes were with the dean of the Central Park West school. One of the critics hailed the film as the return of the good old American days—updated, by way of feminism, so that Calla Stark could play the Jimmy Stewart part and the dean could be Jean Arthur. At the end, the two—guess what—get married. And the movie marches on heartbeats to box-office glory.

"There are many such weighty causes crying for standard bearers," the telephone voice said. "Like the deplorable plight of the left-handed lacrosse players."

"I'll be in the vanguard," she promised.

"Good. Vanessa Redgrave will be chair-personing a committee."

Angry. "Who are you?" She had asked the question three times, and again he ignored it. Maybe it would be better not to sound so belligerent. "What did you say your name was?"

"I have a number of names."

"You're English, aren't you?"

"No, American."

"I think you're lying."

"What difference does it make? Why don't you ask me what I look like?"

"What do you look like?"

"I'm breathtakingly handsome."

She laughed.

"You have a sexy laugh," he said.

Perhaps she had been wrong; the call had obscene possibilities. Again, about to hang up, she felt the flick of recognition.

"Of course," he continued, "you know the sexiest part is your smile."

"Keep smiling."

"Oh, you do. It's your stock-in-trade these days, and you trot it out whenever you're a bit short of invention. A sexy smile will sell nearly everything, won't it?—even *Gerbils*. . . . I'm told you have a delicate stomach. How did you manage to read through it?"

"I don't read with my stomach."

"Nor act with it anymore."

"We do the best we can."

"On the contrary, we do the worst that we can get away with."

"What should I have done?"

"Hated it a little. You could at least have made a wry face."

"Or screamed."

He was silent, then: "Wouldn't a scream overplay it?"

Scream. The word had been a presence recently; a nighttime word, when she was sleepless. Like a bat, the term had come crashing at the window of her mind. Now she had vented it. She hated him for having gotten it out of her.

"What the hell do you want?"

"Nothing, really. Only to tell you that it's time."

"Time for what?"

"For something terrible to happen."

A tremor, but she shrugged it off. "Something cataclysmic?"

"No. Only terrible."

"Ah well," she said, staying with the light tone. "We all die."

"Worse than dying."

"I've heard that before. Threats don't scare me."

"I wasn't threatening," he said quickly. "Only prophesying."

And he hung up.

With the phone still in her hand, she hesitated, then replaced the instrument. She tried to put the conversation out of her mind but the words clung to her like Styrofoam packing pellets.

It's time, he had said. She did not know what he had in mind. Screw it, it was always time for something. Time for a new hairstyle or a medical checkup or a change of cars, time to do a play again or go on a trip, or find a lover.

Time for dinner, that was all. It was turning to dusk and she was alone in the house. She walked out of her study and into the living room, a vast chamber of glass where people were mute reflections and only the windows talked to each other. She hated the room. Sliding open the glass doors, she slipped out onto the cantilevered balcony. She could see down the valley and beyond, the lights of Beverly Hills just winking in, and Los Angeles starting to glimmer out of the smog.

The August day had been hot, and it was already cooling off; barely evening and she was chilled. She realized it wasn't the cold air—the breeze was balmy—it was the man's echo, coming insidiously alive.

She thought of Sharon, her smile adrift on a vapor of melancholy, and how she and those others had been murdered, her pregnant body tortured and mutilated. Not far from here, on Cielo Drive; you just follow Benedict Canyon Boulevard. Follow it more than a dozen years back, for God's sake, into another era. Yet, only last week, there were the two old people strangled; and on Monday, three children clubbed to death. With such blissful reveries, no wonder she couldn't sleep these nights. If she wanted to count cataclysms, why not the Ice Age, Hiroshima, the birth of television?

Not cataclysmic, the man had said, only something terrible. Only.

Why did I answer the damn phone? she thought. It was the public number, the line for producers, writers, directors, agents, lawyers, accountants, the thousand screaming summonses to which she seldom personally responded. Let Willi do it. Most of the time she flipped the switch on the recording machine, hardly heard the bell and never heard the voices. Later, coming back from errands or after finishing her desk work, Willi would write down all the messages and respond to every one of them. Willi was wonderful, a Siva with four arms, laying strong hands on everything. Occasionally, however, Calla would not turn on the recording instrument, but merely let the phone ring and ring. She would go on reading or planting an azalea bush, listening to the jangle and enjoying it, remembering the times, long past, when it was silent. Not a soul to call and say: Come and read for a part, we're sending a script, why don't we talk about it? Nobody, for months on end, and the telephone like a dead rat with an endless tail. So, these times, when she heard the clangor, she would tilt the watering pot or turn the page and smile, or talk back to the foul instrument: Go fuck yourself, she might say, not with any raging choler, more like a social comment about ruffled petunias or how Sartre and Montand got on with their respective Simones, ring, ring, go fuck yourself.

That was her apostrophe to the noisy phone, the beige one. There was a quiet phone as well. It was white. Willi alone knew the number, so when she was here with Calla, the white one never rang. If Willi was out and the private bell sounded, Calla always answered it, generally opening with: Where the hell are you?

Where the hell was she right now? She loved Willi, always felt safe and sustained in her presence, and chafed when she was away too long. The woman had started as her stand-in and double, fifteen years ago, and was now her secretary as well. When "secretary" was superseded in the hierarchy of credits by "assistant," Willi had adhered to the old title. Assistant what, she had asked, what's an assistant to a star? Willi was untainted and unbought. She didn't stockpile manure; her goal: to clean Augean stables.

Honest but laggard. It was nearly seven and she should be back. If she had been here a half hour ago, Calla would not have gone into the dusk-dimmed study and blindly lifted the beige phone. And she wouldn't have talked to the man with the slippery voice, Mr. Satin.

Why did she keep thinking of Sharon Tate, and why was it so damnably cold in here? She decided to go outside.

It was a schizoid house. Calla had described it, in a *Newsweek* interview, as early Cape Cod and Late Vitrine. Why she had bought a house that had such a glassy glitter she never knew, unless it was another instance of what her father called her "frenzy." What she really bought, and what she loved, was the view from the street-side, the approach, an old Colonial remembrance, modest and benignly disheveled, with too many vines and too many creepers. As she had entered on the first day, six years ago, there was a large study on the left, book-filled and with a huge outdated world globe that still showed Persia and Peiping and Petrograd, and Zanzibar not yet Tanzania; world unchangeable. On the right, a spacious kitchen-dining room was redolent of condiments and spices although the house had been empty for a while, as if some plumpish woman had just flavored a zesty stew with fennel and rosemary. Then she realized that the scent came from a tiny herb garden outside the kitchen door, everything dry and dying, and from a Connecticut lilac tree, exiled to an alien climate, also on the wane. Sometimes she believed she bought the house to save the lilac, which at last she had succeeded in doing. But that was the part of the building that rested on solid ground. The newer part was out in space, suspended over a chasm of canyon, nowhere.

There was another reason for her purchase. It was the only house in all the high-hilled, high-priced neighborhood that had no swimming pool. What kind of plus is that, Willi had asked, when you love to swim? Calla didn't know the answer, except as a quixotic, last ditch scramble to the barricades—against what? Certainly not against conspicuous consumption, since the house was situated in the posh-and-power zone. Then, where's the riot, the relentless Willi had demanded. The riot was in the doubleheadedness that made Calla want to be here and not be here. For Hollywood was a prison, and she had committed stardom.

Yet, she *wanted* to be a star, even as she wanted to be a fine actress, knowing that the two wishes were not always consonant. Also, perversely, she wanted to be a thirty-nine-year-old Hollywood winner and a thirty-year-old loser, bloody and maligned, fighting ill-fated causes. Or, best of all, far best of everything, to be in her young twenties once more, and understudying all the women's parts in *Lear*.

Then, poor Cordelia!
And yet not so, since I am sure my love's
More richer than my tongue.

More richer in those days—when I didn't know I was hungry—than I am now, hungrier.

"You'll starve out there," her father had said.

"Anyway . . ."

"Anyway, my foot. You've never had an empty stomach in your life, and you don't know what it's like. Finish your thesis."

Her master's paper was on an aspect of the American Revolution—"Roots of Rebellion," she called it, and she was getting her higher education free, on scholarship. She's scholarly, her mother said; her roses and emeralds are all in her books. It was more or less true. She spent most of her time in the library of what was then called the Connecticut College for Women, studying history in a stuffy carrel where history never happened.

Her father didn't believe that history *had* to happen to women, or that they would notice if it did. Calvin Starkenton liked the fact that his only child was called Calvina; at least some part of his name would be carried on. He regretted, however, that his daughter would not help to perpetuate his pharmacy—business was not a woman's business—especially since it was the only one in New Forge, Connecticut, and doing better every year.

Calvina's mother said everything would turn out all right; that was the pith of her philosophy. She wasn't bright. Her husband said of Rilla Starkenton's mentality that she enjoyed being left behind to look at things until they separated; when she thought too quickly, everything jumbled into one big mess. She had no objection to others racing ahead; let them run along, she said, let them fly. But she wasn't without principles. One of her doctrines was: "Everything on earth has disadvantages, except blueberries." She still had reveries about the day when she might have been accepted in the ballet school in Hartford if she had extended her right foot at the right time, and she now had a dream of embroidering all the characters in *The Tempest* onto a lovely bedspread for Callie's trousseau; she wouldn't include Caliban, however, because he was nasty.

Sometimes Calvina tried to be like her father, sometimes like her mother. Her father did everything in its season. He never stumbled on a stair or missed a train, his gutters and downspouts never clogged, his car never heated up in summer or froze in winter. The world was a reliable pharmacopoeia, and he had a drug of choice for everything. Her mother, on the other hand, was cloud-borne, and often unreachable. Rilla did not hold with cruel things, she said, and didn't want to know that Caliban—or cancer—existed. So she paid no attention to the lumps and swellings, told nobody about them, not even the pain, until it was too late, and died at fifty.

Long before Rilla slipped away, when Calvina was not yet in her teens, the girl noticed that it was not her strong father but her whimsical, airy-voiced mother who determined how her parents treated her.

They programmed her for happiness. Although she never asked for much, she could have anything she wanted. All she had to do in return was to be clean and mannerly and be a good student. As a student, she didn't have to learn anything specific, not a trade or profession or business or art, nothing, all she had to do was learn. Be bright, her mother said with the desperation of a have-not, be happy. Without some career to fashion or goal to reach, Calvina didn't know what she had to *do* to be happy; Happiness 1 and 2 were not courses in the curriculum. She felt as if she had wandered into the wrong apparatus, like an undiscovered error in a computer, an extra zero that might never be resolved. A superfluous symbol, she was not part of any calculation: nothing.

So she pretended to be something—somebody else. To be Titania or the woman on the shampoo box, or Amelia Earhart. She was Little Dorrit, suffering, or Estella Havisham, being suffered; she was Beauty in love with the Beast, or the Beast himself.

Then, hurting at home on the first evening of her first monthly period, she saw Kim Stanley on television. And, while falling in love with the actress, Calvina came to a stunning realization: she too had been an actress in her mind. Except that she had been doing it all wrong. If she wanted to be beautiful or bewitching or pathetic or luridly wicked, she didn't have to pretend to be someone else. All she had to do was to project an aspect of herself—as she was sure Kim Stanley had done—for she *was* all those things. Almost simultaneously it occurred to her that Kim Stanley was not pretending at all, that when she cried, her heart was really breaking. The possibility that acting could be so deeply painful was too scary to think about.

One night, she was awakened by a fearful racket in her parents' bedroom. With a start, she sat up to listen. Her mother was laughing at the top of her voice. She was shrieking with an abandoned hilarity Calvina had never heard. Exhilarated and curious, the eleven-year-old girl jumped out of bed, rushed out of her bedroom, hurried down the hallway. As she was about to knock on her parents' door, she stopped. Her mother wasn't laughing. She was crying, a heartbreaking wail that the girl could not bear. On the verge of tears herself, she hurried back to her room, and flung herself into bed, pulling the covers up over her ears, trying to shut out the sounds. But she couldn't get her mother's crying out of her mind. As with Kim Stanley, her mother's weeping was indistinguishable from laughter, except that here the confusion was worse: it was a trouble at home, a stranger lurking under the stairs.

Suddenly she had the sense that her door was opening and the stranger was softly walking into her room. With a moan, she tore herself out of bed, rushed into the hallway, down the stairs and into the darkness.

Outdoors, in the chilliness of fall, she ran and ran, and the presence pursued her. The wind, sweeping the autumn away, blew the leaves into her face. She hated November, when everything that had seemed so brave and beautiful was running for cover. As she was doing, trying to catch up with the retreating, dying season, trying to put miles between herself and the danger.

But there it was again, the confusion, pursuing her, like a ghostly smoke, rushing to envelop her.

You're afraid, it said, because you're lost. You're lost, it said, because you're afraid.

She ran from the thing, kept running, crying she was not lost, not frightened, not confused, she knew the difference between laughter and tears.

You're *lost*, the creature said.

All at once she saw nothing that she recognized. Her home town, New Forge, where she was born, where she was going to school, where her father owned a drugstore . . . the drugstore was not where it should have been, the goose pond had disappeared, the streets were going in the wrong direction.

You're lost.

No, I'm not. I know this corner, I know the names of people in this place, I know where I am.

Then find your way home.

Home . . .

Go home, it said.

But she couldn't find her way. Nothing was as familiar as she told herself it was. There was too much of the night. Nowhere to hide from it, no well-known door to open.

Lost. I'm lost.

I mustn't cry, or something worse will happen.

Help me, she cried to the empty place—I'm lost—find me. Somebody, find me!

She stopped where there were bare trees and a cobbled walkway. She stood there, frozen to the bone, not knowing which way to go.

Find me!

After a while, wandering one way and another, she saw the distant grayness of the public library.

At breakfast, she looked at her parents and they seemed unchanged. Her father did not appear to be angry, nor did her mother appear to be hurt. Her face was as composed as ever. They both looked the same. But she knew they were not.

Nor was she. They treated her as if she were the daughter of the day before. But she was someone else this morning, someone who had been lost. . . . The awful thing about the whole experience: Nobody had known that she had gone astray, and nobody had found her. The worst part about being lost was that nobody was searching.

Another concern remained. She felt there had been a kind of betrayal in the similarity between weeping and laughter, a trap to catch people not yet grown up. It made her deeply sad that henceforth she would have to question her mother's smile.

Yet it was also something to learn—how to make them seem alike. When nobody was within earshot, she practiced laughing in such a way that it sounded like crying. She did it as a physical exercise, trying to keep her thoughts away from her mother, from that unbearable sadness. Sometimes she became confused, as she had been while viewing Kim Stanley, between the pretended and the real.

As she got further from adolescence, there were some things that were unconfusedly real. Hunger, her father pointed out, was not ambiguous. Earn your daily bread. She decided to put her education to a useful purpose: be a teacher of history.

How, in her early twenties, she escaped the dust-laden, stifling carrel, she never knew. It was as if she smashed through the walls in an access of lunacy.

"It's a frenzy," her father said. "She's infected with a frenzy." To him, it was a toxic state, like being maddened by snakebite, and in all his pharmacopoeia he had no drug to counteract the venom.

"She'll get over it," her mother assured him, although it was unclear whether she wanted her daughter to get over it.

"She better come to her senses. Pass the marmalade, Callie," he continued. "She's no more an actress than I am. When she was a kid, she had one elocution lesson with Mrs. Newsome and ran out in the middle of it, yelling down Locust Street. No, the *marmalade*, Callie."

Besides, he pointed out, she hadn't the makings of an actress. She wasn't exactly beautiful, he said, adding charitably, except to her family. She had nice red hair (actually auburn) and good honest eyes, and she stood up straight; that was about the best of her, the rest was ordinary. Rilla had to admit that their daughter's voice was low and gravelly for a woman. . . . A damn frenzy, he repeated.

"No, Calvin," his wife said. "A fancy. That's all it is, and it'll pass. Everybody's entitled to one passing fancy in her life."

Calvina went to New York. She did all the banal things, starved in all the banal ways, worked in all the banal jobs. She sublet a tiny apartment in a loft building south of Canal Street, had a living room that was really a bedroom, a kitchen that was really a bathroom, and cockroaches that were really dinosaurs. To pay for food and lodging, she sat behind a switchboard, a typewriter, a reception desk, one job after another, lasting longest as cashier in a restaurant on lower Broadway where, for the first time, she had enough to eat. Her nearly achieved master's degree did her little good in the matter of employment for she was too ethical to accept a permanent job—to do research on a new magazine, to be a production assistant in an advertising firm—because, as she put it: Any day now I may be in rehearsal.

Rehearsal was a far way off. She tried to get into Lee Strasberg's acting class but he said the waiting list was long and hinted that she was short—of talent. The best she could manage in her first year was the Y on 92nd Street, which she joined in order to get a cheaper rate on the night classes.

She started to make the rounds, but getting a job on Broadway, or Off Broadway, was so beyond her experience and skills that she never made it past the producers' secretaries. Whenever she was so deeply despondent that she was about to give up, she wrote home to say how bright her future looked. In a letter from her father, there was an afterthought: "P.S. You mentioned a class at the YM and YWHA. Does the *H* stand for Hebrew?" In her next letter, she replied: "P.S. Yes." A query was as far as her father would go toward anti-Semitism—Jews were still a moot issue.

At the Y, she had a teacher named Bill Lieber, who predicted she would learn more than the others because she had more to learn. With the start of classes, she had one congealing fear: that when emotion was demanded, and emotion would inevitably be part of her tuition fee as a student actress, she would have to pay it with counterfeit. She worried that in her first classroom scene, she would look patently like a phony. But she discovered that emotion was the least of her problems; under stress, she could laugh and cry like any talented idiot. She had a worse misconception: That the art of acting was, in essence, the faithful and forthright expression of thought and feeling; and since she was a genuine, bright, hardworking, sensitive, strong-willed person, and since it was her intention to approach the craft with respect, willing muscles and all her pores open, she would not too laboriously master it. It would be a joy.

It was torture. The craft was a spiteful monster that didn't want her to be imaginative too soon, only to be real. It distrusted her emotions, their verity, and their right to be represented. It subjected every sentiment, every feeling to the restrictive screening of her mind and senses. She discovered that the quest for the most meagerly self-satisfying result was through a maze of perceptions and memories and traumas so impacted that she was certain she could never extricate them or make her experience useful to her. She did not know how to touch anything as if it were *there*, not only when it was imaginatively there, but even when she actually held the tangible object in her hand; she could not give it a firm presence, her fingers were boneless. She discovered that to act meant to *act*; an action was not merely a movement, it had to have intent and purpose; it had to be charged with energy, otherwise it was only a twitch . . . and she was a twitcher. Not all her memories were useful; some were too formless to be summoned, some were enervative; and frequently old tears remembered had no greater dramatic potency than to dampen the pages of the script. She discovered, mournfully, that prose precedes poetry; and finally, in an art that demanded a dossier of specifics, that the most insupportable lie was the generality.

And she saw that she was no good at it. She was the worst in the class. She was failing.

Late one night, when all the others had gone home, Lieber confronted her. "You don't work hard enough," he said.

"I work all the time."

It was true. She was in the rehearsal room every night until it closed; she labored at her voice and diction; she did concentration and memory exercises until her head reeled; she stretched and strained at calisthenics until she could not pick herself up off the floor.

"But you're not really working," Lieber insisted.

"I work harder than all the others."

"No, you only sweat more," he said. "You're actually lazy—in your gut, you're lazy. You ask for an effect without dragging anything out of yourself. You give me attitudes, not feelings. You imagine that because you're smarter than the others, you can trick me into crying or laughing. What makes you think you don't have to invest anything to get that kind of emotion out of me? What makes you think that an amateur has a *right* to all that effectiveness? Well, you haven't—and you're not effective. In any other art, you wouldn't expect to just come off the street and *be* effective. If you were a ballet dancer or a violinist, you would slave for years, you would break your ass, you would tear your heart out before anybody would watch or listen. But you just slide out of your reference room and up on the stage, and talk nice and smile pretty and wipe a tear that's absolutely irrelevant, and you expect me to jump up in the aisle and clap my hands, when all I want to do is beat the shit out of you."

"Well . . . you're doing it."

Her throat was dry. So were her eyes; she was too despairing for tears.

"What shall I do?" she said.

"Work harder. Dig for it. Or quit."

For him to have flayed her so unmercifully—a man of kindness, a teacher who never uttered a ravaging word—indicated what his advice really was. He knew she could not work any harder than she was working. As to digging, he probably suspected that she could burrow into her heart and soul, and come up with none of the riches of an actress. Maybe the deeper she went the less she would find; maybe there was nothing there.

It was grievous enough to fail; but, more of an anguish, she had at last found what she wanted to do with her life. She wanted to act.

She had no notion why she needed it so desperately. Lieber was wrong in saying all she desired was applause. There was something else, some other hunger that acting would satisfy, yet the ache, though all-pervasive, was unidentified. In some way she knew without the faintest doubt that a life on the stage would lay its hand upon the hurt and heal it.

Now the hope of the lifesaving remedy was gone. No talent. She must go back to the dusty shelves and the dry, silent ruin.

She was writing a letter of resignation from Lieber's class when the phone rang. Calvina was to come home at once, her father said; her mother was ill.

She was home for five weeks, watching her light-headed, light-hearted mother die. The pale-eyed woman had wasted away suddenly, but she lay as cheerfully in her hospital bed as if she were in utopia. She gave nobody any trouble; she spoke about cancer as though it were no more pesky than thrips on her daffodils. Aware of how close death was, she would not put up with the solemnity of it; it was boring.

There was something about her mother that Calvina had never noticed. Rilla had a secret. She held something in reserve, some riddle that she alone knew the answer to; there was a skeleton in a closet, perhaps, or a private place to which nobody had ever had admittance. Since the whole notion was amorphous in the daughter's mind, she had no way of getting to the source of it, nor did she want to bother the suffering woman with questions.

Not that anything in her mother's manner had changed. Rilla still made airy gestures, rearranging clouds like summer curtains. There were still no periods at the end of her sentences, only question marks. Most particularly, she went on believing that everything would turn out just fine. The secret lay not in any alteration in the woman, but only in Calvina's sense, for the first time, that it had always been there.

On her first day home, she lied to her mother. How was she doing in her acting work? Splendidly. It never occurred to the young woman that Rilla did not believe her. If the patient was not in pain, and frequently even when she was, the student actress delighted her mother with tales about her classes, recounting silly moments and serious ones, improvising with a pillow or a bedpan or the chart at the foot of the bed, illustrating exercises in which she had to be a skillet full of frying meatballs or a broken pinwheel or a drunk with a live lobster under his shirt. She told the story of *Phaedra,* she read a sonnet, summoning up remembrances of things past as if she were whispering to her lover in a dappled woodland. Sometimes her mother cried and enjoyed crying, sometimes she laughed and held herself and begged her daughter to stop, only to beg almost immediately for encores. Oh, Callie, her mother cried, oh, Callie, how happy you make me! . . . And it was at such despairingly lovely moments that Calvina, with a hurting heart, made her best pretenses, dug most deeply into her being and her dis-

sembling, and desperately ached to be an actress, ached for her mother
to live so that she could continue to make her happy.

One day, out of a clear sky, Rilla said, "You've given up, haven't
you?"

"Given up? No."

"Nearly, then. . . . Don't lie, Cal—there's no time."

". . . Nearly, Mom."

"I wish you wouldn't."

"It's not that important to me." She had to make the lie work.
"You once called it a passing fancy—and maybe I just better let it
pass." She began to cry.

"You have to go back, Callie."

"I'm not very gifted, Mom."

"What difference does it make?"

"What difference?" Her mother was being silly again. "If I don't
have the talent, it doesn't make sense."

"Good!" she said, smiling. "Good—I'm glad it doesn't make sense
—good! It's not worth anything if it's not a bit crazy. You've got to
have a foolish dream."

"Mom, please—"

"No, I mean it. They told me not to have any babies because I
would die. But I had a foolish dream. Then you were born too soon and
you were sickly and weighed only three pounds, and they said *you*
would die. Everybody said it—all the doctors—it wasn't wise for me to
get my hopes up. But I believed that you would live. And you were my
foolish dream, and see how beautiful you are."

She had heard the story of her birth a dozen times, but never in
this context, and suddenly she felt she might be on the verge of knowing something more about her mother, might be on the border of this
beautiful woman's secret, and she couldn't stand that there was so little
time to love her, so little time, and she felt she was losing hold of everything, and desperately alone, and—

"Don't die, Mom!"

"Oh, Callie . . ."

"Don't die!"

"Cal . . . Cal."

"I've got a foolish dream . . . that you won't die, Mom. *Please*
don't!"

"Dear Cal, dear Cal . . ."

Her mother died two days later. And she realized that grieving was all regret. Regret for the word unspoken, the hand touched too late. Regret that she had not learned her mother's secret until the end. The secret? Simple: She was a woman foolish by choice.

Foolishness was not her frailty but her strength. She had clung to the follies of high courage. And Calvina regretted that she had not been able to love her enough, to love her for what she was.

It also occurred to Calvina that she had within her all this capacity for loving that she had not given to her mother, nor to anyone as yet; this fearful pain and power of love which was dammed within her, ready to burst, to flood, to inundate the world.

I *will* be an actress, she said, and not care whether they clap their hands and shout from the aisles. I will not care whether they think I am good or bad or graceful or clumsy; I will not care whether I am rich and famous, or whether the crowd decks me with flowers and meets my plane and wears my portrait on its walls. I will not even care whether they love me.

But I will love them.

No, she said, I will not wait for some mother-feeling in my heart to die. I will show my loving while it lives. I will not spend my life in regret that I did not love enough, or soon enough. I will be a fool, I will allow myself a foolish dream, I will be an actress, and show them how much I love them, how much I love the world!

She went back to class and Lieber was monstrous to her, and she hated and idolized him. It was not an erotic attachment—he was a busily married man with a bustling wife and two energetic children—but a sibling devotion expressed in scrimmage, sweat, flirtation and encounter. She was tied to him and constantly gnawing at the bond.

As he gnawed at her. He forced her to start her work all over again, and this time he brandished a mace, crashing it down on her head whenever he detected her "partial presence."

"What have you got in your hand?" Lieber might say.

"An umbrella."

"Looks like a candle."

"It's an umbrella."

"No, it's not—it may not even be a hand. Or maybe there's nothing in your hand. Why do you say it's an umbrella?"

"Because it's raining."

"I see. The umbrella's supposed to tell me it's raining—the um-

brella's doing all the work, is it? How about you? Are you getting wet?
Where? How? What's wet about you—your spit?"

So she learned that an umbrella might just as well be a pogo stick
if she wasn't convincingly, to others and especially to herself, getting
wet in the rain.

"What are you crying about?"

"I'm unhappy."

"Any infant can cry because it's unhappy. What are you crying
about?"

"I don't want him to leave."

"Then keep him from going. You look like a mess, with the snot
running down your face. If I were he, I'd get the hell out, just to be rid
of you. Is crying the only way to keep him?"

She learned how not to cry, so that others might cry for her.

"Why are you so mean to Lövberg?"

"Because I think Hedda is mean."

"Does Hedda think she's mean?"

She learned that there was no such thing as a villain—not to the
actor who plays the part; and that self-justification was the least of the
instruments she could employ to humanize a heavy, that there were
even better devices for vindicating Shylock and Medea and Mephis-
topheles; there were tools to break the heart.

"You're drunk."

"I'm supposed to be drunk."

"Your legs may be drunk, your mouth may be drunk, but are *you*
drunk?"

"I've had five martinis, for God's sake."

"You've indulged yourself as the character, but don't indulge yourself as an actress. You're about to talk to your seven-year-old daughter.
Do you want her to know you're drunk? Now, do it right, and don't be
a slob."

She learned that a drunk isn't a drunk, and a lunatic isn't crazy,
and a villain is not wicked, and labels to identify destroy the identity,
and the best way to express pain is to have trouble getting rid of it. She
learned, too, that she was in love with learning how to act, not with
learning to be an actress. Also, no matter how hungrily she looked forward to giving performances for audiences, she knew they would never
be as rewarding as these skin-tearing classes.

At the end of her first year with Lieber, she managed to enroll in
one of Lee Strasberg's acting groups. He frightened her. While he de-

nied that the Method was anything more than a design for acting, he behaved as if it were acting itself. The thinking seemed more than the doing. Even as he glorified the instinctual aspects of the actor's craft, and appeared to derogate the intellectual as being the least competent midwife of art, his language, his manner, his deepest preoccupations were intellectual. She thought him too scholarly, too clinical. And always afraid to slip back into her carrel of bookishness, she felt as if he were seducing her with encyclopedias.

Particularly worrisome was the way the man allowed, even encouraged, an absorption in the minutiae of one's self. Trying to avoid the clichés of the fossilized acting conventions, Strasberg's students wound up recycling the clichés of their own private behavior. They seemed in love with the commonplace. Enslaved by the process of *being*, they were forgetting how to pretend; forgetting that to bring joy to a play, they had to *play*. They made no journeys into imaginary lands, they were not—as actors were meant to be—perennially new to themselves, the children of strangers, the wards of astonishment.

How real they were! However, she had not come to the theater for the real old world, but for a fantastic new one. Strasberg's acting lacked a foolish dream. Without the dream, it wasn't worth the torment. So she hastened back to Lieber.

That winter, more confident than the year before, she tried harder and harder to get a part. She had no agent and went unheralded from producer's office to producer's office, from agency to agency, as religiously as if they were the Stations of the Cross. Obdurately she kept her spirits up, wary of self-pity. On the mirror in her bathroom was the legend: *Don't cry over Callie.*

But she could not help crying over others: the young and untrained, the blindly hopeful, the elderly. One day, in a producer's office, she saw a seventyish-looking man, bald and bent, trying for the part of a forty-year-old husband. He was tactfully told, twice, that he was too "mature" for the role, but his courage was unflagging. He pointed to his hairless head. "I work with a piece," he said. "I have two of them—one gray and one blond. They make me different people."

Different people. Younger, in his case, and more attractive. All of us more attractive if we get the part, she thought, more glamorous, more exciting. I work with a piece too, she said of herself, with a mask, another voice, another set of bells. With another person, whoever she may be.

Toward the middle of her second year in New York, she got her first job. It was only a one-act, Off Off Broadway, but it was a good role in the last third of what was called the *Tribeca Trilogy*. The theater itself was a nothing place, had been a warehouse for Indian spices, and the single dressing room smelled of curry, which was fine, it fumigated the body odors. The Tribeca was so far downtown that the stage manager said the Statue of Liberty's torch would ruin the blackouts. Of course, none of the critics went to the distant outpost to review three one-acts, except the *Village Voice*, which gave the plays a favorable notice. And for Calvina it was smashing, a full and flattering paragraph, nearly half the entire column.

Two agents came to see her then, two women. The first was all thinness; tall and thin with a high thin voice, smoking through a long thin cigarette holder. Overdieted and overstyled, she gave pinched opinions through thin lips. Callie, intimidated, scarcely uttered a word. The woman had "come all this harrowing distance, down from Darien, sweet plum, and down from Darien is down." Calvina regretted that the woman had made the trip, and wanted to put an end to the meeting.

"You were excruciatingly good," the emaciated agent said. "You were funny-to-heartbreak. But do you have to wear that drudgy blouse? And about that strange voice—do you have polyps?"

Not certain what polyps were, the actress mutely shook her head.

"Well, then, it's diction—and Christ, do something with your hair."

The arrows kept coming until Calvina felt like a dart board.

"You'll need some personal refurbishing, but I absolutely adored your characterization. That lisp, that inspired lisp. It was agonizingly funny. Did you make it up, or did you actually hear somebody lisp like that?"

Calvina's revenge: "Lithp?" she said, unsmiling. "Wath I lithping?"

The already pale lady went as white as cold cream. She pulled the cigarette out of the long holder, didn't see where to throw the butt, and on the pretext of going in search of an ashtray, decamped to Darien.

Megan Farris was a different story. She had just been fired by Tedley-Famous and was starting her own talent company. Unsettled after being discharged, she was tentative, generous without being effusive about Calvina's performance, careful not to fawn for favor. But Megan couldn't hide how deeply she had been moved; in fact, she had no gift for hiding anything; as an agent, honesty was her besetting sin.

"You're quite good," she said, only half-looking at the actress. "And—I'm never really sure about these things—you may be very beautiful. I'd like to have some people see you in this part. When do you close?"

"You mean you want me as a client?"

"Not until I'm sure I can do something for you."

In the next three weeks, Megan saw Calvina three times in *Tribeca*, and often at opposite sides of a secondhand desk in a scantily furnished office in the West Fifties. Then they walked together, went to the Modern Museum, ate shish kebab. It was the year after Calvina's mother died, so Megan, only in her thirties, took on motherhood. She was a health nut and prescribed vitamins for all ills and adversities. Nothing like Vitamin B, she said, after a funeral, an abortion or the pink slip. A combination of E, acidophilus, and Alka-Seltzer had burped her through her divorce.

What touched the actress most deeply about her agent was Megan's outstretched hand. Once she had extended it, the hand was available forever. She had imperishable loyalty. Remembering only the best of past relationships, she spoke admiringly of the man who had fired her, of clients who had deserted her, of the husband whom she had divorced. How can I have lived with him and loved him all those years, and suddenly, because of a legal paper, not love him anymore? She did not fret the past; grudges, regrets, nostalgias made no sense to her; she had little use for eyes in the back of her head. Only the future was functional, and she saw nothing but good in it. And Megan was certain that Calvina would be a star.

Two weeks after *Tribeca Trilogy* closed, she got her new client a part in another Off Broadway play. It closed in three nights, unreviewed, unlamented. Calvina thereupon auditioned for a dozen things, and landed nothing. Then she was cast in an Off Broadway melodrama, followed by a comedy that opened cold in a midtown theater, the Booth. She had a tiny role but an impish one; she was onstage—Broadway!—for less than a minute and got four lusty laughs. The play lasted three weeks.

Unlike most players, who are mortally depressed by closing nights, Calvina was not discouraged. Much as the actress had loved classes, she loved rehearsals more. In many ways, she felt they were more invigorating, more deeply nourishing than performances. And for a young woman who had been a single and lonely child, an escapist bookworm, she had at last come to the hearthstone of friends. Quickly, her fellow actors became the companions of the best that she could do, the best that she was. They were friends of her most vivid make-believe, they were friends of her growing happiness and her ripening talent to make others happy; they were friends of her courage to expose herself, to strip her spirit of all the screens and shields, all the cotton wools of self-consciousness so that the world—and they, particularly—could see her more nakedly than she saw herself. They were friends, in sacred trust, of her vast and intimate dream.

One day, cuckoo with rehearsal happiness, she found herself galloping down the street, larruping the air with her arms. "I'm in rehearsal, I'm in rehearsal!" She was the first day of spring; any minute she would burst into leaf. "I'm in rehearsal!" The subscript was: I am loved.

But the rehearsal ecstasy was brief, and the friends were temporary, as if created in improvisation. When the rehearsals were over, the clasp of friendship slackened, the embraces became perfunctory and the ties were severed, sometimes slowly, but often with such suddenness that it made her want to cry. She did cry. But it was weeping without theatrical potency, it did not project; nothing she could use in her next rehearsals.

At the start of her third year in New York, Calvina got a good part in *Ferris Wheel*. Although Off Broadway, it was an estimable production with an excellent cast and director. She loved the role though she felt unsettled about the play. Megan recommended it because, she said, the subject matter was stylishly morbid. The four D's popular that year were disease, dementia, deformity and death. Calvina's part had a hefty share of each. The character was an osteomyelitic victim afflicted with a paranoiac certainty that her husband is feeding her poisoned yogurt. In her last scene, she upsets her wheelchair and expires in a diatribe of obscenity.

The play had everything. Calvina was splendidly daring in it. There was, however, a misunderstanding. The drama had been written with sober intent; the audience obstreperously presumed it to be a comedy. This presumption—and the play—lasted for three evening performances and one matinee.

For the last performance, however, Megan dragged somebody down from Lincoln Center. The next thing Calvina knew, she was understudying Cordelia, Goneril and Regan in *King Lear*. Even if she never got to play any of the parts, it was her first employment in a

Shakespearean production, and at a prestigious theater. She was ditheringly happy.

On the Sunday morning before they opened, the woman playing Cordelia came awake with a golden glory of hepatitis. Tuesday night— Calvina Starkenton—Cordelia!

She wasn't that good; she knew she wasn't that good. But she was now aware that her weird voice was an advantage, and that when she walked she gave an illusion of flight. She had also learned to touch things so that when she handled an object, it was *there*, no nonsense. And she could at last make a statement so directly and so simply that it sounded unchallengeably true. Thus, when she told the blighted old king that she could not heave her heart into her mouth, that she loved him according to her bond, no more, no less, there could be nobody in the audience who believed that hypocrisy might ever tarnish so shining a character.

She gleams, a critic said. Another also saw the light: phosphorescent. They were not, however, the important papers. Then, one evening, there he was, Walter Kerr, and the next morning he politely hated everything about the production, everything except the lithe girl who reminded him of Katharine Hepburn, using up all the air there was, leaving the audience breathless. In such wise, Kerr's valentine went on, lacking only rhyme.

It happened in a whirl: she was signed to make a film. Only one, she said to Bill Lieber, only one, I promise, and I'll be back for more classes, and home on the stage, Shakespeare, Shakespeare, my God, I'm hungry for more Shakespeare.

On the day she arrived in Los Angeles, she almost had a battle with Jay Sindell, the producer-director of the film. Constrained and tight-jawed, Sindell talked through locked teeth as if he had a pipe in his mouth. His youngish eyes were watchful, never seeming to blink. He was a "mental director," as Megan had described him, with an excellent background at the Guthrie in Minneapolis, where good things were being done, classically and experimentally.

His companion, Lou Espinosa, a free-lance publicity fellow, was always busy with his hands, wringing and dry-washing them, cracking the knuckles or clapping the palms together in silent applause.

"We think you should change your name," Sindell said.

"Really?" She could feel herself rising a foot taller; high dudgeon. "Is anybody changing names anymore?"

Sindell made a snap revision. "Not change it, shorten it."

Without a sound, Espinosa clapped his hands. "Calvina Starkenton," he said. "Seventeen letters. You'll fall off the marquee."

"If I ever get on it."

"I saw you do Cordelia," Sindell said. "You'll get on it."

Abruptly, from nowhere, Espinosa produced an eight by ten cardboard. It had lettering on it, vividly inked and colored:

DUSTIN HOFFMAN

in

ALIVE BUT ANXIOUS

with

CALLA STARKE

"My God," she said ecstatically, "you have Hoffman?"

"Uh . . . Dustin hasn't said no," Sindell replied. Then, pointing to Espinosa's card, "How do you like it?"

She didn't particularly like the title of the picture, but she wasn't being asked about that. Her new name? "Well . . . take the final e off. If I'm going stark, I won't wear pasties."

She had said yes to the name, Dustin Hoffman said no to the picture. The young man who played the part was, like Calla, a new face. Which would change the film from a presold, relatively sure thing at the box office to, they hoped, a sleeper. The budget was decreased by four fifths, the number of shooting days slashed from sixty to twenty-three.

Alive but Anxious was one of the first of those comedies of neurosis later elevated to a fine art by Woody Allen. Neither funny nor serious, more a wince than a smile, it was a whack on the crazybone. It told the story of Susie McCord and Reuben Felderman, who were married, although she insisted on keeping her maiden name because, she said, what if their love turned into gray string beans? They pretended that every caress was an illicit experience, and that sex in marriage was punishable by law. Soon they had their differences, like burglars fighting over swag. Constantly interrogating each other, they posed prickly questions: Why, for example, did Reuben, who did not have pimples, behave as if he had them; why did Susie whistle through her teeth whenever she watched him eat a runny egg? Presently, they started to talk massively not only about sex but during it. They muffled their laughter as if to keep wardens from hearing them; they began to kiss as if they had cold sores. Even their pets became neurotic. The canary engendered a hatred of their friends and, whenever guests arrived, took to lying down on the floor of its cage, stiff as an ashtray; their female dachshund developed such a dread of being sexually assaulted that she would not run free in the park, but insisted on a leash—her chastity belt, Reuben called it. Susie considered this remark a cravenly oblique insult.

They talked a lot about ambivalence, which was the word that year. They were ambivalent about their parents, the pill, blacks, whites, Burt Reynolds, Leonard Bernstein, sixty-nine, Andy Warhol, Zabar's and the New York *Times*. The only subject they were not ambivalent about was the necessity to terminate both the war in Vietnam and Richard Nixon. But since none of their friends felt differently, this made them feel ordinary, "like walking platitudes," Susie said. The fact that Nixon was the only person in the world they could agree about suggested to them that there might be something out of kilter in their marriage.

Calla, describing the film to her father, said it was a Kvetchy Komedy, a bit too Kute. Calvin Starkenton didn't understand what she had written in the letter, and when later, on the phone, she gave him a dissertation on the delicatessen language of the film industry, he said he had never in his life tasted chopped liver, and didn't feel under-nourished. Finally, she said it was a picture in which the characters, instead of sharing love, shared anxieties. Don't scoff at that, her father answered.

On the last day of shooting, she met Barney Loftus.

Susie McCord, the film's heroine, had a foster father. Dudley was a rowdy old man in his late sixties, described as still full of juices, gutsy and lecherous. He would feel and fumble any savory creature in sight, especially his foster daughter. The Dudley role was tiny, but it was noisy and bawdily funny, one of the best miniatures in the screenplay.

Barney Loftus was Jay Sindell's friend; they had known one another at the Guthrie. The old character actor arrived on the morning of the final day, costumed and made up for his two brief scenes, one with Reuben and one with Susie. The assistant director beckoned him to where Calla was standing. This is your foster father, Dudley, the assistant said. She thought how perfect the man looked for the part, except that his manner was too reticent, too shy, hardly the lascivious goat he would have to play. But he was an actor, they had said, a stage veteran who had played Polonius and Willy Loman; and Sindell was excellent at casting.

In a little while, however, watching Loftus rehearse with Reuben, she had the qualm again. The man was not only bashful, he was nervous.

Then the lights bumped up to full, they heard the word "action," and bang, the top of the set blew off. The old man exploded. He cavorted around in a drunken delirium, he galloped all over Reuben, he belched and hooted, he guffawed and wept, he blew words out of his mouth as if it were a police siren. In two takes, a difficult scene was done, and the crew applauded.

That afternoon, preparing to work with Calla, the same painful diffidence set in, as though he could not do what was expected. When it came to the moment when they had to rehearse the so-called lecherous kiss, he barely touched her. This time, after the lights flashed to the top and they heard Jay Sindell call for action, Loftus did not hit his marks, didn't remember when to make the movement to the bookcase, fumbled his lines. Jay called the cut.

"Anything wrong, Barney?" Jay said.

"No. . . . Just stupid."

It was a tricky, demanding sequence and he had to carry it practically alone; all the action and most of the dialogue were his. The old man was distressed and Calla felt sorry for him, but didn't know how to help.

The camera rolled again, there was an instant of latency, then Dudley shot out of the cannon. He twisted Calla around, the lines came tumbling out in precisely the way they were written, he shoved her against the bookcase as directed and exploited all the ruttishness of the scene. She could feel his hands on her breasts and his enormous cock like a granite rod against her, his tongue making a foray in her mouth, a raiding party, reconnoitering and marauding.

Calla felt a surge of anger.

"Cut!"

The director was silent.

In the quiet, she turned sideways to the old man and whispered hoarsely, "Don't do that."

"Can't help it," he said. "Playing the truth."

"Lie a little."

Jay, smiling with his teeth clenched, barely opened his mouth. "Barney . . . it's a little overstated. Take it down a bit."

She couldn't contain herself. "Down a lot."

Barney Loftus grinned. "Too up, huh?"

The next shot was exactly the same, and she burst out of it, hissing at him: "You do that again, and I'll kick you right in the balls!"

"Cut! Print it!"

She turned. "Print what?"

"Everything."

She was horrified. "Even what I said?"

"Everything."

"It's not in the script."

"It's in the film. Kill the lights, Andy."

"But, Jay—"

"Don't fuss, Cal—it was great."

The director was suddenly out of reach, and the crew started to light the final shots of the film, close-ups of Calla and Dudley, and an entering shot of Reuben. While she was still shaken by what had happened, the pickups were completed, and shooting on the film was finished.

Sindell raised his arms and called, "That's it. It's a wrap. Thank you. I think we've got a funny picture. There's food where the park set used to be, and drinks on the picnic table. You were all wonderful—thanks."

She needed a drink and had two quickly. The wrap party was noisy, they all shared Jay's confidence; it was a good picture. She got hugged a lot and kissed a lot, and lots of liquor was spilled on her Susie dress. She also drank a lot. By the time she got to her dressing room, she was airborne. She had shared the room with the woman who had played her mother, long departed from the filming. Alone, she started to get out of her costume. There was a knock on the door, so discreet that she wasn't sure she had heard one. She listened for a second. Another tap. She was standing in Susie's slip, décolleté.

"Come in," she said.

A nice-looking young man stood at the door. He was in his thirties, perhaps, sand-colored hair, attractive in a rough-hewn way, with an appealing carriage that could have been stallion grace or coltish awkwardness.

"I—uh—came to apologize."

"I don't know you," she said.

"Yes you do—I'm Barney Loftus."

"Barney . . . ?" She couldn't make the connection.

"Your foster father—Dudley."

It was impossible. "You?"

"Uh—yeah—I'm—urr—kind of a character actor."

He walked in tentatively. Hardly looking at her, and mortified: "I don't generally stick my tongue out at women."

"Or other things."

He laughed, grateful that she wasn't going to be sandpapery. He was so abjectly apologetic that she laughed too, and liked him. Be careful, she told herself, you're a little squiffed. He had strong, long-fingered hands and a temptingly greedy mouth. She wanted him to kiss her . . . the way he had done in the scene. She wondered about that other thing, whether it was a character prop, or real. Careful, she said again, you're drunk.

"But I have to confess," he went on, "if I had to do the scene again, I couldn't do it any differently—ever."

How could a man be so shy while telling a woman he had a perpetual hard-on for her, how could he be so seductive?

"As an actor, you should take things for it."

"Yes. You."

The cornball idiot, how beautiful he was. Could she be *that* drunk? Silly Putty drunk, happy as a merry-go-round drunk, love at first sight drunk.

Crocked. Go easy, she said.

She started to put on her dress.

"I think I've had a bit too much bourbon," she said carefully. "And I may be *non mental campus*, if I've got that right. So go away."

She couldn't make the dress come together.

"You're putting the second button into the third buttonhole," he said, without seeming critical.

Her hands didn't work. He started to do the buttoning for her. When he got to the bottom button, it was strategically placed, and for some reason he had to take extra time with it, which she couldn't stand, so she tried to do it herself. But she couldn't manage. Her hands were now quite useless, she realized, and if he were to take her in his arms, she wouldn't be able to push him or punch him.

He took her in his arms. He kissed her in much the same way he had done before, and his cock was as impressive and as hard, and she thought, holy mackerel, he's the same as he was this afternoon, what prejudices we have against the elderly, and she reached down and touched him with her hand, and it was exactly as prodigious as she had thought.

They locked the door and as he was helping her off with her dress, she said something about all that waste of buttoning, and they were on the day bed, and he had her breast in his mouth and she didn't know whether she wanted him to continue doing that wonderful thing, or whether she wanted him to come inside her immediately, or—third possibility—whether he was flexible enough to do both things at once. In a moment, she saw that he was, and even before he seemed to be reaching his destination, she had come, and it was the quickest advent of her life, and he came later, trumpeting his approach like an elephant rampant.

"My God, you're noisy," she said afterward.

"A well-supported tone," he replied. "I fuck from the diaphragm."

"I fuck with one . . . generally."

There had been more bourbon than prudence and she worried for a week. But when her period came, and she told him so, he asked whether she would consider screwing him without apparatus, in a sober state. He wanted her to move into his shack on the beach, and to marry him and have children, everything at once. Today.

She almost did it, almost said yes. Then she held back. Something restrained her, something about herself, about him, she didn't know what. Wait, she said. He was going much too fast.

Outdoors, in the garden, thinking back to her first meeting with Barney, she thought what a different person she had been. There were no terrors then.

Fifteen years. In the interval, she had been a success and a failure, a number of times in each category. She had been loved and despised, honored and vilified. She had received mash notes and hate communications, hundreds of them, threatening letters, sick telegrams, dirty chits of paper in her purse, obscene phone calls in the middle of the night. And there was a period when she was constantly afraid to turn the key in the ignition of her car.

But that was in the old days. Not recently, not in years.

Until this afternoon. The voice on the telephone.

"It's time," Mr. Satin had said.

Time for what?

Time for the monstrous messages to start again? But why? Whom had she recently antagonized? She did not think she could stand another wave of hatred. How she had endured it in those early years she could not now conceive, but . . . younger then. And it had left its token in her mind. She still listened for ticking sounds in packages. She still lay sleepless, nighttimes, and imagined prowlers. She still heard footsteps that seemed closer than her imagination.

Like the footsteps now, this minute.

It might be the other side of the eugenia hedge. She walked around it. Nobody. Listening, she did not hear the footsteps anymore. But she was certain that they had been real, she had heard them. Perhaps indoors . . . Maybe Willi had returned.

Inside again, she saw no one. Nor any sign of an intruder, and the doors were securely locked.

She entered her study and looked through the front window. Evening, toward night. Wasn't this the time of day when Sharon had been murdered?

There was a shadow on the pavement. She saw it materialize: not a shadow but a dog. The neighbor's beagle, sweet and harmless, loping down the street—and a boy, fifteen perhaps, stalking him. . . . Stalking? An odd word to describe a boy after his own dog. Prey are stalked.

Nothing is stalking you, Calla told herself, so don't run thrashing down an alley of terrors, all your fears are groundless . . . except for Mr. Satin's call.

It's time. . . . Time for what?

She wondered where Willi was, and why she wasn't back.

Barney said "marry me" so often that the words should have become monotonous. But they didn't; he varied the readings.

She put him off, remaining at the Chateau Marmont, a homey but tacky apartment hotel, with clunky furniture and a comfortable bed. Calla suspected that she loved him, but what did that have to do with anything?—she hardly knew the man. His house on Trancas Beach was a dilapidated shingle-sprung shack he had purchased with money raised by selling the farm his dead parents had owned in Minnesota. Reared as a farmer, with only two years of college training, he had gone to the Guthrie as a stagehand and had become an actor. He knew nothing about acting, only how to do it, and was afraid to learn more, so he never mastered the hardest task: how to play himself. He could not play a straight part. Vibrant and physically attractive as a person, he could never be that person on a stage. Whenever he was given the role of a young man anywhere near his age, if he had to perform in a scene that came close to Barney Loftus, his ego wilted, he was in an agony of self-consciousness, his voice went tight and unnatural, and he developed extra arms and legs. But the minute he wore a wig or a beard, or if he blacked out a tooth or packed his cheeks with absorbent cotton, the very instant he hid behind a mask, he was all truth, quickened with vitality.

To his continuing distress, however, he longed to be a leading man, to enact the roles of the romantic rogue, the racy detective, the derring-doer, the sexual dilettante—and get the girl. It was a bitter line for an engaging and virile actor of thirty-two to say that he was destined to play old men, Hindu swamis, pompous senators, creeps, hoboes, paralytics. And it was particularly difficult in Hollywood, where actors were cast according to what they resembled. Barney did not look like the parts he could play; he looked like a leading man.

Calla was in awe of his talent. He never knew what the hell he was doing, and it always came out right. She ached for his unhappiness as an actor, for his yearning to be Robert Redford, for the natural, protean genius that made him everybody but himself.

She loved him, wanted to be near him all the time, and did not know why she refused to marry him. It wasn't as though she distrusted sexual pleasures. Her virginity had not been a closely guarded treasure, but there was something in her soul that was still virginal—she had never been in love. She had no way of appraising love. Her affairs had lasted, typically, from the first run-through until the last performance when the stage was struck; on strike night all illusions were disassembled. And she played the farewells without tears. She didn't carry faded flowers through the stage door, but left them in her dressing room. Yet . . . she felt that Barney's flowers would never fade. Then why not marry him? He was vibrant, he was kind, and he gave her the most precious gift of all: her selfhood. He didn't intrude upon her secrets or her solitude. He knew instinctively how to be there and not be. Even sensing that she tended toward reclusion, he didn't allow her to be lonely. He never missed a cue for an exit or entrance.

And Barney was fun. A loud burlesquer, he could shatter the little shack with noise, fall down steps, imitate animals and give them human personality, do bawdy takeoffs on strait-laced characters, choke on chocolate pudding, get inextricably stuck in the bathtub, flop around in the ocean like a demented, drowning walrus. Essentially serious, however, he knew how to make her talk, and how to let her cry. He might pretend drunkenly to bump his head on lintels, but he was sober about thresholds; he never crossed an unwelcome one.

On the evening of his thirty-third birthday, when he was feeling somewhat depressed about life and the war and work, she enumerated his virtues.

He smily wryly. "Then why don't you marry me?"

". . . Because I don't know who you are."

"You just described me."

"Oh, I can describe you well enough. But those are only qualities. It's as if I'm outlining your . . . characterization."

"Well, isn't that enough? I'm an actor."

"But that's not who you are. It's all those other people you're playing. It doesn't identify your . . . self."

"My self is an actor."

"Is that all the self you want to be?"

"What self do you want to be?"

It was a poser. She wished he hadn't asked it. She had an illogical feeling that if she knew what she wanted to be, in addition to being an actress, she might know how she really felt about marrying Barney.

Anyway, she wanted urgently to know him better, so she moved in. She transferred her clothes, books and record player to his house, and he created what he called a painting, a mural seascape. Breaking through the wall of the downstairs bedroom, he installed a huge plate glass window, which revealed a wide panorama of the Pacific. The large balcony became their bedroom, the seaward room became her private study. But they slept on the floor of the study the first night and many nights thereafter, to watch the waves come crashing at the window.

They were becoming happier all the time, and one night, on the terrace, looking out at the ocean, they started to dream of futures.

"But the big one," she said. "The great big whopper of a dream—what do you want most?"

He didn't hesitate for an instant. "A crazy, wild, side-splitting, heart-breaking, terrible, wonderful—*part*."

"My God—just a part?"

"Didn't you hear all the adjectives?"

"But the noun, Barney—the thing you want most to be—"

In a rage—violently—he turned on her. "Don't *do* that to me."

"Barney!"

"I'm an actor! That's all I am—an actor!"

He jumped over the low brick wall, and rushed away, toward the water's edge. She could see him striding—running, almost—along the foam of the incoming tide.

She hadn't realized how deeply she was wounding him. Miserable, she wanted to retract the whole conversation. She started to run after him, but as she got to the wall, she saw him returning.

"I'm sorry," he said.

"No—my fault—"

"Listen—Calla, listen. I love you very much. But I may not be enough for you. I've been facing that. I may not. Still, I don't want to pretend I'm more than I am. An actor—that's all there is—what you see —what I am. But being an actor, it's not just an occupation to me, it's everything. It has saved my life. When I was a kid, working on the farm —I was nothing. In school I didn't exist, I was a zombie. In college, I kept wanting to die—to disappear. Then, when I went to the Guthrie, the first time I walked on the stage, the first words I spoke—it was as if I found my tongue, I learned how to speak. And with that audience out there—believing me—believing I was what I pretended to be—! That first performance—I was born, Calla, I was born!"

He twisted away to face the sea. She thought he might be crying.

"The only time I'm really alive is when I'm acting." He slowly turned to face her. "Don't expect any more of me than that, Callie. I love you and want you to marry me. But it'll be theater—I don't deny it —it'll be movies. And for me it'll be the greatest show on earth. I'll play your husband, and I'll play the part so well, you'll never doubt a single scene or a single line. You'll *believe* me. And oh, Callie, you will feel so *loved*. And when I die, you won't break down in tears, Calla—you'll give me a standing ovation!"

She tried to quiet her concern. Unlike a Strasberg actor, there was no being in him, only pretending, and it frightened her. Yet, she thought, that night as they were making love, he was more than merely the actor he claimed to be: He was a bit of a poet, and that was enough to identify him. At least, it told her why she loved him, if love had to be bolstered by reasons.

She decided to take Barney to New Forge, to meet her father. She wanted to see whether, in the presence of an ordinary man, Barney could be an ordinary man.

Her father was at first suspicious. Barney was one of those Hollywood people, ergo he might be afflicted with any number of quirks, deviations, abnormalities. He might be in a frenzy like his daughter.

The day after they arrived, while in the drugstore, Barney got into a discussion with a Mrs. Hillis, one of Mr. Starkenton's customers. The subject was liniments and what a puzzle they were: whether their burn was a comfort, a counterirritant, a bit of psychological hokey-pokey or a real remedy. Barney and Mrs. Hillis judiciously examined each possibility.

"He was sensible about liniments," her father said that evening. "He's very plain."

Plainness was a good thing.

"Yes, he is, Dad."

"Mrs. Hillis said he looks like he's got freckles. And I said, 'He does have freckles.'"

Freckles also were a good thing.

"I told you, Dad. He is what he looks like."

The instant she said it, she knew she had lied and wanted to change the words: He always looks the part. Right now he's playing Ordinary Man. And getting good notices.

Her father liked Barney and Calla loved him. They were married in the Presbyterian church in New Forge.

Calla had told Barney that it was never her plan to stay in films; she belonged, in her heart, to the theater. However, his stage technique was not nearly as secure as hers; he had managed to perform at the Guthrie where the run of plays was short, but was nervous about sustaining and growing in a part through weeks and months of what might be, with luck, a lengthy run. So he had committed himself to films, even to the extent of buying the house at Trancas. Still, New York was always a temptation to a talented performer. . . .

They had decided, after the wedding in New Forge, to rent a car, drive to New York, find an apartment and scrounge for work. Megan had a number of play scripts for Calla to read, and Barney thought he had a good chance for the Ephraim Cabot part in a revival of *Desire Under the Elms*. The day before they were to leave for Manhattan, on a Sunday afternoon in late October, Barney got a call from Ken Friedling, his agent in California. In the living room of the house Calla had grown up in, a mellowed colonial surrounded by maple trees, Calla was playing chess with her father while Barney stood near the big bay window, muttering almost inaudibly into the phone. When she looked at her husband he was haloed by autumn, with the westering sun blazing through everything, red and gold and amber. He hung up the phone and came to the chess table.

"Callie . . ."

He stopped. She looked up at him. He rubbed his cheek as if to feel whether he needed a shave. "I'm sorry, honey, but you'll have to go to New York by yourself."

"By myself? But we agreed . . ."

"I know," he said unhappily. "But Ken has set me up to read for Huston on Wednesday."

"Is it that important?"

The wrong thing to say. Even if it weren't John Huston, it was the wrong thing to say.

"It's important to me, love."

For the rest of the day, longing to be in rehearsal for a play, Calla planned to go to New York alone. Barney, if he got the film part, would join her when his shooting was over. Then, at noon the following day, she got a call. She was being summoned back to California for some cut-away shots and dubbing. They flew to Los Angeles together.

Alive but Anxious was scarcely out of rough cut when everybody from Culver City to Santa Barbara said that he/she/it had seen the picture and it was ravishing. The first sneak preview, held in Pasadena, was actually a good one, but the word went out that it was the hilarity of all time, that the audience had become ill with laughter, that untold numbers had been slain. The advertising campaign took the cue: See *Alive and Anxious* and die laughing.

It opened nationally, and the modest, low-budget, maybe-sleeper came bright-eyed and awake. A smash. Weekly *Variety* ran pages of Wow, every producer in the film factory town looked for a screenplay that would sedulously ape the "neurotic love story" and a trend was born.

So was a personality. The public had discovered a beloved kook. With a few hints from Espinosa's press releases, everybody was convinced that Calla Stark, in real life, *was* that way, with her neurasthenic aches and pains, halting speech, her habit of using the dog's-leash-chastity-belt to hold up her oversized slacks, her insistence on wearing a dirty, torn canvas rain hat, rain or shine. Overnight, teenagers were girdling themselves with chrome chains instead of leather, and Bloomingdale's sold rain hats in two models, "clean and simulated-dirty." When the wife of a Republican senator arrived at a Democratic White House dinner party wearing a red velvet version of the rain chapeau, the ditsy Susie McCord had jumped the barriers of age, class and party affiliation.

Calla Stark was a star.

But not to herself. One night, alone, when Barney was working, she entered a small Santa Monica theater and, for the first time, watched her performance in the presence of an audience. She hated what she saw. It was a passable exhibition, but she had gotten away with murder, and didn't deserve the critical confetti showered upon her. There was something vital missing. It was as if she had played the part in another country, or, as the show biz expression went, she had phoned it in. Yet, and this was what most deeply perturbed her, though she had worked hard and acted honestly, with faith in the character and in each of her intentions, though she had done nearly everything she had learned to do, Bill Lieber would have said that she had turned up absent. It made her ill to see herself. When Barney came home, she pretended to be asleep, not wanting to talk. She lay in bed wondering:

if she was rewarded for mediocrity, would she be punished for excellence? Or would she ultimately not know the difference?

Whatever misgivings she had, she was a success. Offers flooded in. At first the parts were all copies of Susie McCord, the adorable whacko; in one she collected poisonous spiders, in another she had a gift for the cello and a nose-picking problem. Megan dismissed them all; cloning time, she said; wide yawns.

Then *Not War, Not Peace* arrived, and the agent stayed awake reading it. "It's chancy," she said. "But I cried."

It was a love-in-war story, as gray-bearded as *Random Harvest* or *Waterloo Bridge*, but the talk was timely—drag races, rock and rut and Saigon bar girls, and puffin', droppin', snortin', grass, acid, speed, and where'd you get the tattoo, Shit Boy? But under the hard-pressed, doomsday talk there was a sad and genuine sweetness, and a terrible, dry despair. Best of all, the girl's part was unsentimentally written, flinty, sometimes a little mean, often witty, and it had the finality of heartbreak.

On the third day of shooting *Not War, Not Peace*, still troubled, Calla had a revelation. She saw that the camera, the technological instrument, the central impersonal mechanism, was not that at all. It was *alive*. It was a vigilant, pulsing *character* in the scene. Suddenly she realized why she had lacked presence in her first film, why she had been so remote. Cleaving to all the canons of acting she had learned, she had played the scenes closely with the other actors, scarcely taking her gaze off them, hanging on their words, pondering every eye blink. She had not allowed herself to be distracted by anything, not by lights or crew or camera. Especially not by the camera.

Mistake.

By not playing to the camera she distanced herself not only from the audience, but even in a paradoxical way, from the other actors. For the camera was the major *consciousness* of the medium, and it could be ignored only at great peril. She had to learn to play to the instrument itself. Especially in the close-ups. If the most significant part of screen acting was reacting, then she had to relate to the most searching stare that was upon her, to the single Cyclopean eye. She had to confide in it, tell it all her secrets, ask its advice, promise it her undying loyalty, get jealous of it, hate it, seduce it. She had to make love to it.

And never let anyone know that that's what she was doing. It was a violation of her faithful vow to conjugal acting in the theater; she and the camera would have a clandestine love affair.

She was so certain that she had come upon the hidden solution of her film acting problem, that at the end of three more days of work, she asked to see the rushes. That evening, when she came out of the projection room, she felt that she might be on the verge of understanding the medium, and had found something in her work that she must not reveal to anyone. Not even to Barney.

While she knew she had discovered an effective technique, she was a little ashamed. It somehow sullied the purity of her artistic intentions, and she couldn't go to the rushes anymore, couldn't bear to be in the audience that saw her making love to a mechanism. It seemed perverted.

During that year in Hollywood, two wonderful things happened.

First, she hired Willi as her secretary. She had met Wilhelmina Axil during the shooting of *Alive but Anxious*, in which the Dutch girl had worked as Calla's stand-in. Willi had been educated in Baltimore, where her widowed father, now dead, had been a doctor on the staff of Johns Hopkins. She had come to movieland to be an actress and had evolved, by stages, into Calla's stunt woman, double and alter ego. She was an athlete who could perform any feat demanded of her, and compete in any sport as if she had medals or ribbons in it. As Calla's stunt woman, she was required, in one film or another, to jump from a helicopter, get caught in mortar fire, and vault across a broken bridge span. It was all adventure to her. Gutsy as a lioness, Willi impudently defied danger. It was her one insanity; all the rest of her was common sense and freedom from self deceit; as for deceiving others, it was as if Willi's brain had been created without humbug cells.

Except for the difference in hair color, a discrepancy that Willi casually corrected as the need arose, they resembled each other remarkably. The first time Calla saw her, she thought enviously: We look almost like twins, except for one minor detail: she is beautiful. Then a heartwarming thing happened. Calla became so fond of the lively, magnanimous woman that she stopped being envious, and felt as if Willi was sharing her beauty. It never occurred to Calla that Willi's loveliness and generosity might be reflecting her own. Their affection, their trust in each other, was almost instantaneous, and within a year Calla felt that she had found her first inalienable friend.

The second wonderful thing began badly. During the last shooting days of *Not War, Not Peace*, Calla became violently ill. She threw up all through the wrap party, and Barney spirited her home.

The instant they knew and agreed they wanted the child, Calla's nausea was miraculously over. Her pregnancy was a total index of her happiness; in fact, they were both so gladdened by the news that they selfishly wanted to keep it private. To prevent Hollywood from measuring Calla's girth interview by interview, they went away for a while, to Hawaii, swimming, snorkeling, overeating, lying under pandanus trees or in the smogless sunlight. She was more lighthearted than she had ever been in her life; Barney said the same about himself, and they hated to go back. So they decided to protract their vacation, and went westward.

They arrived in Manila when there was talk that President Marcos would unprecedentedly run for reelection, amid charges of fraud. Violence and repression were everywhere. People disappeared in the night, secretly arrested; there were rumors of terrorism and martial law.

One evening, when they came out of a restaurant and walked in the gloom of an impoverished neighborhood, they saw four policemen expertly and unhurriedly, as if in slow motion, clubbing a man to death. As they were finishing, a woman appeared on a second-story balcony. She saw them across the street, and cried out. One of the policemen pulled his gun, drew a bead on her and fired. After the blast, they concluded their work on the dying man, and the street became still. The police got into a car and drove away.

Calla thought she would shake to pieces. "What shall we do? Can we call anybody? What shall we do?"

"Nothing."

"My God—nothing?"

"We're leaving in the morning."

In bed that night, she couldn't stop trembling. "What shall we do, what shall we do?"

He gave her hot tea, he gave her a sedative.

"What shall we do?"

They left Manila, went to Hong Kong, continued to Singapore, and decided to spend two weeks in India, then return home. In Calcutta, one afternoon, while standing under an awning and waiting for the rain to cease, they saw a man take a butcher knife into his right hand and hack down upon the fingers of his left.

Later, weeping: "I don't know what you're saying!" she cried to her husband. "What do you mean, it makes begging more effective? What the goddamn hell do you mean?"

"You know very well what I mean. You've seen the poverty in the streets—you've read about the beggars. Now, for Christ sake, stop talking about it."

Hysterical: "Cut his fingers off! I don't believe it!"

"Calla—honey—please."

"No. No!"

"Callie—you'll make yourself sick."

"I won't have a child in this world! I won't!"

"Calla!"

"I won't!"

He grabbed her and held her to himself with all his strength. She struggled, but he would not let her go. Finally, succumbing, she whispered: "Barney . . . how can we have a child in this world?"

"This isn't our world, Callie."

"Then what? Are we just on a goddamn tour? Is that all this is?"

"Yes."

"No! I *live here!*"

"We do not live *here.*"

"This world is where our baby's going to be born."

"No, Calla. We are not having a baby in this world, we're having it back there—back home." He made every word separate and deliberate. Then he softened. "Now, please, honey, if you go on like this, you'll be ill, you'll have a miscarriage. Do you want that? . . . Now, come on, sweetheart—Calla—honey—come on—you've got to shut your eyes to it."

She was weary, altogether spent, and confused. "We'll . . . go home?"

By the time they got to Trancas, Calla felt as if she had come through a hallucinogenic experience, out of which she now emerged feeling she no longer recognized the world she lived in. A few days at home, and she became quiet, almost comatose. No matter how Barney ascribed her trancelike state to the disjunctions of pregnancy, Calla knew she wasn't separating herself from the world, but reappraising it. Something dynamic was happening to her, some massive rearrangement, not only in her belly but in her brain. She knew she had to accommodate to her species, but she felt like a mutant with an incompatible nervous system, or defective senses, or limbs joined in the wrong places.

One day, by accident, she ran across her unfinished master's thesis, "Roots of Rebellion," and was appalled. Erudite, footnoted, annotated, not a single statement undocumented, it exposed how little she had known about the wellsprings of revolt, the rages that might be the primal cause. And how little she still knew, three years later, having been so naïvely shocked by the self-mutilating poverty of Calcutta, the political butchery in Manila—and the war still raging in Vietnam.

Three years, and she had been totally out of the world, becoming a stage actress, a screen actress, a star—inhaling none of the smoke from the burning of draft cards, barely hearing the gunshots that had killed John Kennedy and Martin Luther King, unaware of the pickets and placard-bearers who had paraded with Spock and the Berrigans, or the housewives and hippies and professors who had marched to the Pentagon to stuff flowers into the guns of the guards.

And there were still the maimed hands of India and torture in Manila and napalm on the Ho Chi Minh trail.

Without knowing what to think about any of it, she felt that she had unconsciously nurtured her ignorance as an alibi for inaction. She began to read everything about the war that she could lay hands on. Not satisfied with what she found in the American papers, she made trips to the library and read the foreign papers as well. She scoured the Manchester *Guardian* and, with her college French and Italian still serviceable, she pored over *Le Monde* and *Corriere della Sera*. Trying to reconcile the discrepancy between what was said at home and what the foreign press was reporting, she became convinced that Americans were wasting countrysides, torturing prisoners, dropping napalm, allowing B-52 bombers to cast loose their leftover cargo on non-combatant villages.

The time came when she could feel the first stirring of the baby. It was a bad day for her. She still questioned whether she wanted the child, whether she had a right to have a child in the midst of a cosmic struggle in which she was not engaged. She felt like a sluggish parasite being sustained by all those other anti-war workers and marchers.

So she went into action.

It was 1968 and a presidential election was coming up. Johnson had declared that he would not run again. Nixon would undoubtedly be the Republican nominee; as for the Democrats, the Las Vegas bookmakers were betting it would be either Hubert Humphrey or Robert Kennedy. While in college, she had admired Humphrey, but had become disillusioned with the Vice-president, who still remained loyal to what she saw as Johnson's pro-war position.

Robert Kennedy, however, had come out unequivocally against the war, and was now barnstorming the nation with the inflamed desperation of a man trying to halt a madness. One afternoon, she watched him being interviewed on television, and even before the program was over, she was in her car, en route to the Kennedy-for-President office in Santa Monica. She wrote out a check, got a pile of literature, stowed it in the car, and that very day started campaigning for him in the territory that had been assigned to her, from Zuma Beach to Oxnard.

Flushed with the spirit of the cause, she arrived home at midnight to a worried husband whose anxieties she routed in a flurry of excitement. The following morning she was out before breakfast and again did not return until late in the evening. Her pregnancy was showing and, although she had begun to hate the hampering ponderousness of it, she suddenly felt light-bellied and light-headed. She had inexhaustible energy and was stirred by accomplishment.

One day she came to a thrilling realization. All through her life she had been trying to cast herself in one role or another, trying to find her place on the program, her position in the dramatis personae. It had made her an actress, this search for an identifiable part. And she had not been able to find it. Now—! This revolt, this anger against injustice, this loving pity of humankind—! She had at last found a role that she felt perfectly suited for, and that she was proud to play—not in pretense but in truth, with heart and soul. It made her deeply happy.

A few weeks after she started to work for Robert Kennedy, on June 5, 1968, he was shot.

Her bright new existence went into blackout. To compound the misfortune, Calla took the news in an aberrant way. She began to imagine, in some twisted fixity of mind, that she had contributed to the climate of catastrophe. She suffered the guilt of Kennedy's death as if she had killed him, telling herself that if she had not come too late to her human responsibility, the great hope of a man might still be alive. It was a craziness, Barney said, and she knew it was crazy, but she could not shake it. She had never been to a psychiatrist and, in the midst of her pregnancy, she decided to go.

But just as suddenly as the neurosis seized her, it set her free. She went into a tempest of activity. Like millions of Americans, she was leaderless, so she reached out to carry any placard or banner, she shouted any slogan that demanded a better world. She joined everything. Donating her money faster than she had earned it, attending any meeting that promised peace, reform, ethnic equality, civic betterment,

the parity of women, clear air and water, anything that strove to elimi-
nate the hardships and handicaps of the destitute—she gave and gave,
she lavished love, money, work, rapture. She labored feverishly, as if she
were being clocked, days, nights, weekends, holidays. She had a time
limit, she felt, only the few months until her baby was born.

She answered her phone and opened her house—Barney's house—
to everyone. During the weeks that preceded the Democratic National
Convention, the cottage in Trancas became a way station for pacifists,
feminists, hippies, Third World subversives, gay activists, the emissaries
from dissident American Indians and Black Panthers, environ-
mentalists, gun controllers, radicals, revolutionaries, the peaceable and
the militant left. Barney threaded through the rallies of guests, walked
over the bodies of bivouacked strangers, his humor leavening his resentment. All he clung to was that he was a Democrat, as Calla was, and if
Humphrey got nominated, he would vote for him. It was certainly not
Barney's inclination to go to the convention in Chicago and heckle his
own party. Not heckle, Calla corrected, merely make a sound and join
an action.

"I'll do my action in the ballot booth," he said.

"Come on, Barney, is that enough?"

"It's enough for me."

As convention time approached, she began to have what she took
to be premature labor pains, and the doctor advised her to spend the
last month in bed. She tried, but couldn't. There were too many
demands on her attention, and she had no desire to ignore any of them.
A week before the convention, the local chapter of the two-year-old National Organization for Women added her name to the committee they
were sending to work the caucuses in Chicago. Calla needed to go; it
was compulsive. The doctor took her to task and Barney pleaded with
her to be sensible. Finally, at wits' end, her husband yelled:

"I forbid you, goddamn it!"

"Forbid? Barney! Forbid?"

It was the most inapposite word to hurl at a NOW delegate. He
smiled sheepishly, at a loss, as if onstage without rehearsal.

They started to pack. Unthinking, she lifted a full suitcase, felt a
sharp pain, a flooding, and fifteen minutes later was in the Santa
Monica hospital.

The baby was born healthy, although a month early, of moderate
size and weight. And the mother was splendid.

Three days after the infant was born, Calla read headlines about the bloodshed at the Democratic Convention in Chicago. She was upset, but she was quiet about it; a week earlier she might have smashed things. Although her activism was by no means over, her most ardent emotions were for her newborn child. If she had been asked to play a mother-and-baby scene, and had been touched to tears by the feelings that welled up in her when nursing the tiny creature, she would have squelched them as being too hackneyed. But now she was the stereotype: Blissful Mother.

She thought the notion that babies were born funny-looking was a canard. Her child was beautiful.

"Beet red," Barney said.

"Beet red? You're color blind," Calla retorted. "Her skin's like cream."

"Sour cream, with borscht."

Megan sent presents but said she did not want to see any pulpy infants. Childless, and convinced that the world's population should be stringently restricted by birth control, euthanasia and the sterilization of rapists and casting directors, Megan was anomalously devoted to other people's offspring—after they got rid of their birth fuzz. Calla, huffy, said her baby had been born without a hair anywhere; she was smooth and sweet as unbaked bread. Fine, the agent said, when she's baked, I'll come and see her.

Unlike Megan, Willi looked at the child every chance she could. She did not try to hide her yearning. In the hospital, one morning, she listed her "here-to-stay-and-gone-tomorrow men," and wondered aloud which of them she should choose to knock her up. Deciding she didn't like any of them, she said so long and drifted out into the corridor. Calla, who was to be discharged the next day, followed her into the hallway, to watch her go. The beautiful blond woman stopped in front of the plate glass window of the nursery. She simply stood there and stood there, gazing at the infants. The imperturbable, strong-muscled Willi did not cry, but rubbed her face a good deal.

That evening, watching the child being nursed, Willi said, "I know it's not the class-act thing for me to suggest, but if it's open casting for godmothers . . ."

"Oh, Willi, yes! If it's all right with Barney—and I'm sure it will be. Yes!"

Willi didn't even smile her thanks, just nodded, tapped her foot.

"There's another thing," Calla continued. "We were certain it was going to be a boy, and none of the names will work. So we've been thinking—how's Wilhelmina?"

Willi blanched. "Oh Christ, don't do that to the poor thing."

"I kind of like it."

"You don't have to live with it."

"Not necessarily the whole name. Just Willi."

"She's a *girl*, for Pete's sake!" Then, reservedly, "But I've often thought about the other end . . . Mina."

When Barney said he loved it, the baby became Mina Loftus. Willi, never having been a godmother, insisted on a bona fide christening, the whole white, water-sprinkling spectacle, with both mothers to be given billing. And she arranged all of it. Barney looked at the two doting women and said, in the presence of the Presbyterian minister, that he would have to break the kid's dolls and tear up her comic books so that she wouldn't get the false notion there was all that love floating around. The minister took him seriously and intoned that God's love should be enough for anybody. Calla and Willi, meaning no disrespect, exploded with laughter, and Barney was embarrassed.

Within three weeks, Mina was not red but she was growing a fuzz. Luckily, it was all on her head, and the hair was blond. Since her mothers looked like each other, and the child's hair favored Willi's, by the axiom of things equaling the same thing being equal to each other, it might be true that Mina would look like her godmother. Calla, seeing how beautiful Willi was, thought: Please, God, let it be that way.

On the day that Mina was a month old, *Not War, Not Peace* was released. There had been problems with the film; it had taken longer to edit than they had expected, and the distributor was not enthusiastic. Nor were the notices. The reviewers made a patronizing effort to like the picture, but in the end they dismissed it.

Except for what they had to say about Calla. Nearly all the comments on her performance were exclamations of surprise. The critics, watching her first film, had discovered a delectable weirdo; now they had come upon a film star who could act. At the least they were respectful; some were awestruck. In a few cases, where the journalists felt their voices had not been heard in the general acclaim, they went back and did special pieces on her. One of these, an article she cherished, came from a university magazine. The writer celebrated but one thing: her bravery. He pointed out the leaps and plunges she had taken to find what he termed the ultimate uses of emotion, and how she had risked being called ludicrous in comedy, melodramatic in emotion, and ugly in the final scenes of the film. Valor, he said, could not be taught in the drama schools; it was one of the qualities inherent in great artists. The review was entitled "Calla's Courage," and it was signed J.E.H. She never tried to find out who J.E.H. was; she wanted to keep the article anonymous; she didn't think of it as a tribute alone, but as an exhortation—courage!

Calla's likeness appeared on the covers of a number of film magazines, and talk about her began to animate the box office. Just as the exhibitors were about to yank the film, business took a spurt. They held the movie for one week, and another. It was never Whammo, Wow or Socko; in business conversations it was a success or a failure, depending on what point the speaker was trying to make.

Still, the consensus was that if the film did turn out to be profitable, Calla Stark had made it so. She was therefore "bankable." No longer just an actress, nor just a star, she had reached that exalted state: a fiscal security, a precious collateral which would induce financing institutions to invest or lend money. She was a good risk. Of course, Calla Stark was not "solo bankable," as the boardroom saying went, but if you put her in a "good package" with a "money director," or coupled her with another star who was a "hot ticket," you could start "buttering the popcorn." One Boston banker expressed the entire process in terms of food. "Stark is edible," he said. This comment was neither affectionate nor pornographic, it was pecuniary. He meant he would take a bite of the next Calla Stark project. "Not a whole mouthful," he said, "only a nibble." National Home Loan promised that on her third picture they would not ask for only a snack, but go the whole hog. She was now consumable, and could be cannibalized.

She didn't care what they called her as long as the producers offered good scripts and good directors. And they did. Meanwhile, the hands clapped and the phones rang and the fans shouted, "Look—look, there she is!" She was prime copy for the film and news journals, of course, and presently the literary periodicals were interested in the delightfully eccentric champion of lost and leftist causes. What a charming incongruity!

They hadn't, as yet, started to get angry.

3

The neighbor's dog barked. The boy pretended to bark as well, which made the dog bark louder. There was no stalking anymore, but running, both of them, back and forth, running and racketing.

Watching through the window, she was so absorbed by their fun and noise, she scarcely heard the telephone. Not Willi's but the beige one.

Whether to answer or not? It might be Mr. Satin again. She turned up the volume on the monitor, heard the directive Willi had recorded, so professionally friendly, please leave a message, we'll get back to you, wait for the signal . . . But there was no voice, no message, only a click.

Him, them.

No, why him? Lots of people hated machines and refused to be taken down on message tape.

. . . Waiting for Willi. Seeing things in the room she scarcely saw anymore. The enameled tea box Barney had given her in Singapore, the Oscar on the mantelpiece, the tiny silver-framed snapshot of Willi and Mina, taken thirteen years ago, on the child's first birthday . . . the little girl and her godmother sitting in the sand on Trancas Beach, with the woman blowing up a rubber goose, the two of them so alike as to be mother and daughter. . . .

She knew where Mina was, but where was Willi?

She heard the squeal of tires a block away. There was only one driver who so recklessly took that turn from the canyon road. Calla hurried to the window. Her own Alfa, black and obsolete, purchased long ago in Rome, sat hunched in the driveway like an elderly Italian widow.

In an instant, another lesser screech and Willi's bronze Audi was there. She scrambled out of the car, rushed across the lawn, then too quickly onto the wooden deck, and tripped.

"Goddamn that step."

Calla smiled. Willi had been promising to call the carpenter. Served her right.

She heard the front door open, heard Willi slam her keys onto the foyer table and, even before entering the study:

"Calla, you bastard!" she yelled. "You creepy crud!"

"If you're going to beat my bones, go home. Or come and have a drink."

Willi entered, went straight to the bookshelf where the bottles were kept, poured herself an inch of Wild Turkey and took a gulp.

"Where the hell were you?" she said.

"You know where I was—right here."

"I told them you were coming."

"I told *you* I wasn't," Calla replied.

"I said you would change your mind."

"I didn't. Anyway," helping herself to a drink, "they had you."

"They can't use me for the close-ups—only to get rained on."

There was no self-pity in it, just vexation. She was wearing the tie-dye dress for the scene they had been reshooting all day. The color of the sleazy costume had run, as it was designed to do, and it was still damp. Calla wondered why her stand-in had not changed her clothes; perhaps she was in a rage to battle it out, wanted her anger to steam through the dress. She was wrong.

"You lost a lot of weight on the picture," Willi said. "They want you to get into the dress, and I'm to pin it where it needs to be taken in."

"Why? I'm never going to wear it again."

"You mean you won't do the close-ups?"

"I *told* you, Willi."

"One day—one damn day of retakes—and you won't do it?"

"It's not the day, it's the ending of the picture. They promised they would sneak it with the original fadeout—the way it was written, with some salt. Now they want to finish with a lollypop. The hell with them."

"They only want to have the new ending ready—on film. But they'll try it both ways. Can't you believe them?"

"No."

"Can't you compromise a little?"

"I compromised. I made the picture."

Always a compromise these days. Every script she read required some concession of mood and mind; there were none she had a passion for. But *Tie-Dye* had seemed one of the better ones. It was a story of a husband and wife, and their seventeen-year-old daughter. Time: the late sixties—agitation for peace, civil rights, ethnic equality—a period no longer considered commercial. But, defying the trend analysts, and with Calla's name above the title, the producers had gone ahead. Now that it was nearly finished, all hands were trembling.

In the screenplay, the daughter has flown out of the family orbit, a lift-off into drugs, a flight into radical life. Unlike most scripts about the period, the husband becomes the feminist libertarian. As the woman keeps defending the conservative institutions, she realizes that the institution in most danger, especially since her daughter's defection, is her marriage. The parents separate, the adolescent goes further into space, there is a violently cruel street demonstration in which the daughter is seriously injured. Then the mother marches in the young woman's place.

In part, the script was a bargain counter of outdated merchandise. But the screenwriter was bright, too inexperienced to be jaded, a woman who wrote as if all her words had just come dewily off the vine, and she had natural, free-handed humor. Sometimes she mistook bathos for pathos but the script was an honest piece, and Calla enjoyed doing it. She thought the finished film would be successful in the way *An Unmarried Woman* had been successful, by nibbling at a morsel of truth, biting at a hangnail of reality without cutting too bloodily into the quick.

In the last scene, the daughter is in the hospital, a victim of social savagery. The mother sees the girl's tie-dye dress, a token of the daughter's disdain for bourgeois things. It is a cheap hand-colored sack. The mother looks at the emblem somberly, takes her modish clothes off, puts on the tie-dye dress and joins the demonstration. As she marches with the others, it starts to rain and the colors of the tie-dye begin to run. The mother has predicted that they would; she smiles—it is wry and courageous—and continues marching as the picture fades to its end.

The producers were insistent about tacking on a happier ending: The woman sees her alienated husband; they wave, forgiving each other, and as they start to close the distance—fade out, finis.

Willi was pouring herself another drink. "Why do you have to hassle all the time? Why don't you shoot it, make things a little easier for yourself?"

It was what Willi always said: Don't fight *every* windmill. "Don't chew the pit, Callie—eat the peach."

"Rotten center."

"You know what they'll say?"

"Of course. 'She doesn't want to share the tag with her husband— she's a selfish pig.' Or: 'Doesn't believe love is the answer to anything— an icy bitch.'"

"'A cunt-bitten feminist' was how one of the lads put it."

"Adorable. Who?"

"Name of Cephis. He's the new film editor."

"That means he'll cut straight to my left profile."

"Frig 'em all," Willi said. "And frig their friggin' suntans."

"A sensible sentiment."

She could see that Willi was not going to press further; she had accepted the resolution. The woman was more relaxed now, what with drink and decision; and Calla thought, as she had often thought, how beautiful she was. Her blond hair had been dyed with more flame than usual this time, like red-brown autumn leaves. She wondered why her double's hair, even dyed, was more alive and seemed more natural than her own. How could they look so much alike, and Willi be so exquisite?

And so unwaveringly attuned to the measures Calla played. This moment, just passed: it hadn't been so much a disagreement as a testing. The woman's private phone line to Calla was, in a sense, symbolic: nobody else had the number, or the power it entailed. Yet, Willi had not used it once today, hadn't phoned to say where the hell are you, not a single ring of pressure. And Calla knew why. Secretly, the woman was always glad to see her stand firm. Most of their differences were simply bustles of clarification.

"You didn't call me," she said.

Willi grinned. "No, I didn't."

"Thanks."

Willi went to the beige phone, and started to jot down messages. She pointed to the instrument in her hand. "Did you answer this today?"

"Twice."

"You did? Why?"

"Once pure dumbness, and the second time I thought it was the white one."

"Anything?"

"The *Reporter*, asking for an ad. . . . And a hate call."

"Really?"

"Well, not really. Some guy with a silky voice. He wanted me to beware."

"Of what?"

"The world. It's full of germs."

"Is that what he said?"

"No, what he said was—it's time."

"Time for what?"

"Wouldn't say."

"Was he a creep?"

"Creepy, but not a creep. Very good voice—cultivated. English, I think."

Recounting the conversation, she became aware that Willi was only half listening. How long the old conditioning persists, she thought. When the hate warnings were arriving in the old days, Calla never got used to them; but Willi, sterner stuff, learned how to turn a deaf ear to them.

As she was doing now, attending to realer voices on tape. The cost of repairing the front step and part of the deck would be $1,200, Calla was due for dental prophylaxis, the garage would have time for the Alfa Romeo's new muffler and brakes at nine tomorrow, the schedule for the public relations tour on *Tie-Dye* was not ready so they were stalling Dick Cavett, the name of the woman who did the fingernail hardening was Mary Janowitz, B. Dalton had the new Elizabeth Hardwick book, Megan called to tell Calla to quit taking the enzymes she had recommended because they would give her hives; also, she was sending over three scripts, one by Bill Goldman that she particularly liked. And:

"Three calls from Lucas O'Hare."

"Tell him to go to hell."

"I think you should read his script."

"I won't, Willi."

"Don't be a goddamn mule."

"Willi," she said quietly, "this subject doesn't require a lot of back-and-forth. I won't read it. Even if he had only *written* it, I wouldn't read it. But to think of having him *direct* me for two, three, four months—I can't imagine anything more loathsome."

"He's a brilliant director."

"He's a thug."

"He—is—a—brilliant—director."

"He—is—a—reptile."

"How can you object to that? You were willing to work with Preminger."

"Preminger may be revolting, but he's not a reptile."

"He's also not so talented. . . . And O'Hare's in trouble."

"I weep."

"Well, when a director makes three beautiful pictures, and then has a run of tough luck—and the town says he's finished—someone ought to weep a little."

Calla had seen only the second of O'Hare's pictures, hoping it would be terrible, and decided not to see any more; it had been too good. His first and third were said to have been better. She didn't want any of them to be good. O'Hare was a vandal and a redneck. Years ago, she had been permitted to address the Screen Directors Guild on Vietnam, to get them to pass a stop-the-war resolution. She had made an impassioned speech, to rousing applause. As the acclaim was dying away, O'Hare, who had just had his first *succès d'estime*, took the floor. He had talked about an artist's right to privacy, which could be trashed by political gangsters. Telling the story of a Russian poet who, in a figurative sense, had had his tongue cut out, he cautioned against Americans who waved red flags. Then, after having made as serious an attack upon her as she had made on the warmongers, he had craftily inflected toward caricature. You could clock the laughs, the Hollywood *Reporter* had said. The vote that day wasn't even taken; she had been put on a stool in the corner, with dunce cap. Ever since, she had thought of the man as a fascist, and, not incidentally, an offensive womanizer whose life was a macho insult.

Willi always said Calla overreacted. Perhaps. She couldn't help it. She dated many of her Hollywood misfortunes from the day he had attacked her; he had become an irrational symbol of the worst years of her life.

His last picture had been a failure and she had read the rotten notices with satisfaction. Even his few good reviews did not help at the box office because, unlike *The Deer Hunter*, where war was Russian roulette, in O'Hare's film the Vietnam War was not a game but a sadistic reality, and the audience had stayed away as if by edict. Whether good or bad, the film had come in a wrong year, and some wit had administered the death blow by calling it Apocalypse Later. If his early films cost practically nothing, the last one cost most of the money ever minted. It was a leviathan disaster. The promising young man, now forty, was to Hollywood no longer young or promising. Cheers.

"It won't hurt you to read his screenplay," Willi said. She went to the cupboard, opened the lowest file drawer and pulled out a green-bound manuscript. "Called *The Fabulist*. It's about a magician."

"Fabulist doesn't mean magician, it means liar."

"It also means storyteller. Can't a storyteller be a kind of magician?"

Calla could see Willi luring her into the valley of chat. It would be a seduction into the manuscript. "Stop it."

Undeterred: "It's really about two whites and a black. He'll shoot it in the South."

Calla was shocked. "Am I hearing you right? Do you imagine—can you possibly imagine that I would go on *location*—with Lucas Bastard O'Hare?"

Willi studied the question. "Yes."

She put the script on the coffee table, near Calla's drink. Noting that the glass was empty, she took it to the bookshelf, added ice and bourbon. "O'Hare was on the set today."

"Was he? Why?"

"He tried to reach you on the phone five times. Then he got wind of the reshooting, thought you might be there, and showed."

"Showed what?"

"He doesn't always have his thing out, Callie."

"What did he have out this time?"

"Only the script. He seemed almost—demented—how badly he wanted you to read it. I wish you wouldn't close your mind, Cal. No matter what you say, he's an artist. He's one of the few men I've ever met who has a . . ." The word seemed too much, but she managed it. ". . . passion."

"Passion! It's amazing about the sons of bitches, isn't it? They can be mean, stupid, dishonest, cold, heartless—but when they start to talk about film, they become The Anointed."

"*Please* read it. You won't be sorry. It's quite beautiful. It's a magical love story. And strange—you don't believe half of it—and suddenly you wonder why you didn't. Because something has happened to you that's haunting. As if he's defending you against . . . the dark things."

Calla looked at her. This was not an ordinary script report. Willi was not behaving like a screening device, sifting out the bad ones and recommending a creditable one, but was recounting a personal experience. Perhaps frightening.

"Please, Calla."

"Aren't you pushing me a bit hard, Will?"

"Maybe . . . but I won't stop."

"That has its dangers."

"I know. I've already done something risky." Then, tentatively, "I promised him you'd read it tonight and—"

"You didn't!"

"—and I invited him to have a drink with you tomorrow at six."

She was appalled. It was as if Willi had been disloyal, had violated a trust. Calla was angry, and hurt. And restrained.

"Call him off, Will."

The quiet lasted.

"You mean it?"

"Yes. I don't want him here."

"And you won't read it?"

"I can't."

"You mean you won't."

It was getting worse, and Calla did not know what to do. There was the hazard, too, that it might lead to other things, to recriminations.

Willi would not let it happen. She flipped through the Rolodex, found the number and dialed. She waited, then replaced the receiver.

"No answer," she said. "I'll phone him when I get home."

She paused only momentarily, as if to say something else, but seemed not to have the courage. She had a solemn distant look, a sadness. "I'll leave my car, and take the Alfa to the garage in the morning."

"How'll you get back?"

"The man in the showroom—what's his name—Guariglia."

They tried to smile and couldn't make it. Willi went out and left her shadow in the room. Calla heard her open the front door, heard her footsteps on the deck, on the unmended tread, on the gravel.

She didn't hear the car depart. Wondering how Willi would spend the evening, she hoped the woman would not be alone, and guessed there would be somebody. Tomorrow she might say she had gone to dinner with a George or Stan or Simon, and had beguiled the night with one of them, and the names would always be changing; and never, even after a first meeting, would there be a noticeable afterglow. She had been married once, ages ago in college, and even been pregnant for a while, but as Willi had miscarried, so had the marriage. One man having been too much, she had had many.

Or none at all. For her crowded calendar was, in all likelihood, fiction.

A lesbian. How opaque a word when describing Willi. She had had affairs with women; Calla was sure of that without knowing what satisfactions Willi had derived from them, or by what scales she measured the sexes; certainly the physical could not be all of it. There was always the question—not asked aloud—whether Willi would ultimately commit herself to a woman or to a man, and with whom she might be happier. It was a taboo subject. They didn't talk about it, and didn't have to. They both knew the only significant answer to all the questions, and neither of them wanted to spoil what they had. Willi was in love with Calla.

It was tacit, and it was an ache. Worse. Calla adored the woman, and could do nothing about it. Because the fact was mordantly simple: there was no sexual ambivalence in Calla, there never had been. She could think of a dozen men she had slept with, scarcely remembering them, never loving them as much as she loved Willi. No male in her life—Barney excepted, of course—had ever seemed as beautiful as Willi. Certainly there was nobody with whom she was so delicately attuned to the music of daily sounds, nobody with whom she had freeze-framed more moments of felicity; there was nobody who was so blessed with— what?—pure goodness.

Why, then? Why couldn't she go to bed with her? Why, when she had done so many unorthodox things in her life, why was this impossible? Simple, if she could dismiss it as a malevolence of sex, a hormonal mischief, a missing penis; but she knew it was more than that. If only for Willi's sake, why couldn't she? Especially since they were both so lonely?

It wasn't as if she hadn't tried; or at least, tried to put herself in the frame of mind. They had shared lodgings on location a half dozen times—a cabin in Wyoming, a bungalow in the Caribbean, the same double bed during a hotel room shortage in Vancouver; they had been naked together in bathrooms—one soaking in a tub, the other showering; they had felt the warm intimacy of wearing each other's clothes, eaten the remainder of each other's food. They had stood in the other's shoes, hit the same marks and glittered in the same lights. They had *been* each other. Why couldn't she cross the narrow breach? So that Willi would not have to go to her own apartment every night, and Calla could stop thinking that the twilight was her enemy.

Calla's loneliness, which used to be only a void, was becoming substantive; it was there, it had to be dealt with. Partly, it was a curse of this isolating town. Hollywood, for a solitary woman, was a place of quarantine. To acknowledge loneliness was to have contracted leprosy. For a woman to admit she was companionless was to divulge that she had a rotten spot in her character, that she was insatiable or as cold as aspic. Such women were rarely invited to a party, and when they were, they arrived alone and generally went home alone, or in the presence of a sloth.

Nobody imagined that such bleakness could happen to a star. Even when an invitation did come, it arrived with so many strings attached that the anticipation was strangled. Queen that she might be in the public eye, she was nearly always a pawn in some party-giver's gambit, an object to be manipulated into a deal, used as a showpiece, set up for a free ride, touched for a contribution. She could not wear a dress, only a costume; her hair could not be combed, it had to be coiffed. She was not spoken to as a person, but invoked as an institution. People produced special effects: they postured, bragged, genuflected, angled, sold goods and posted bills, whined, kissed ass, propositioned; they did everything but talk.

So, secluded, she was living her existence on camera and in dressing rooms, vamping until ready, inert between takes. And acting itself, which had been a joy, was becoming a frustration. She never felt good enough, and even when she was at her best, felt a dread that she was enacting a lie or a madness.

Nor did she trust stardom, for she put little faith in the critics who had helped confer it upon her, or in the writers and directors; or, most particularly, in the public, who were all too ready to love her, as they had loved Marilyn Monroe, for loveless reasons. She did not trust anything about the company enclave she lived in; treachery was the local art form. There was even something duplicitous in the locality itself, in southern California's climate and geography. The sunlight seemed hypocritical through the smog; the beautiful summer dazzle too recreantly became a conflagration of homes and hillsides; the first relief of winter rain turned into flood and calamity down the canyons; and there was always the threatened trickery of earthquake along the fault of the land.

She too was riven by fault. A decade ago, she had had a clear picture of what she dreamed, and knew specifically how much she would be willing to give for it: All. But being willing to give all, she wanted all —to be a loving wife and mother, to be a great actress and to live a life of moral splendor. Moral splendor—Barney's term, spoken with a taint of derogation, as if her dream came through some biblical sunburst. But, still sickened by injustice, she wondered if she might have become a parody of her younger self. The loss of illusion—was it the sclerosis of success?

She still espoused causes, contributed money, made a speech when called upon, went on the stump for decent candidates. Yet, it was not the same. Being a social reformer in socially acceptable ways was not at all the same.

But, goddamn it, she told herself, when a woman's pushing forty there has to be a corner of her mind that opens to the other person's point of view. Nothing was as simple as she had seen it, nothing. Even Vietnam was different in a decade's perspective. Not that she had changed her conclusions about it, but there had been a time when she would have considered it reprehensible to mention the fact that the Vietcong, as well as the Americans, dropped napalm; that where torture was considered, both sides were expert.

Her feminism, too. Although she would never weaken, she was not as clamorous as she used to be. She had never seen the principle from a narrow sexist purview, but had made a broader commitment to campaigns against prejudice or enslavement of men, women or children. That outcry of no was the obbligato to her voice shouting yes to life. And it seemed a paradox to Calla that she should be arraigned against those who called themselves pro-life and anti-abortion. Even if she had always voted, and always would, for a woman's right to abort her child —she couldn't, without real distress, say that she was for abortion. She could not champion the trauma that abortion meant to a woman, to say nothing of the unknowable meaning in the destruction of potential life. Nowadays, whenever she helped win a victory for a woman's right to choose, there were no longer hurrahs in it, only pity for the beset ones who might feel guilty or bereft. What had one day been a right that she had fought for with crusading certainty was becoming a poignant ambiguity.

Ambiguity. A gray word. As her life became less precious to her, she had less courage to risk it. Yet, she had never been so alive as when she had risked her life for something she believed in. Now there was nothing to give her life for. And she had the gray feeling, gray, that not being willing to die for something was in itself a kind of death.

That, for Calla Stark, was the heart of her thirty-ninth year. She was losing—or had lost—her nerve. Even in her work—perhaps the telephone voice was right—she had no stomach for the scene.

About a year ago, someone had written that Calla Stark had lost her scream. Her social outcries, like her socially conscious films, the article said, were now comfortably within her vocal range. No strain. Reading the criticism, she had been angry at first, then pained. Recently, the remark had begun to frighten her. She knew it was true; she had lost a part of herself, and if she did not find it . . . she had forfeited one of her vitals.

What a strange thing to be, she thought: a woman in search of her scream.

Was that what kept her awake at night, lying in the dimness, listening for a lost outcry? Seeking herself in old photographs, in bleached-out remembrances . . . and in the refrigerator?

Food.

How many times, in the last few weeks, had she opened the refrigerator door and found nothing to whet her appetite? Hungry, hungry all the time, and unable to find that one kind of food she wanted. Living on snacks, on unsatisfying tidbits, losing a little weight, not enough to worry about . . . but worried about it. I'm not anorexic, she told herself, I really *love* to eat, I'm hungry . . .

She wondered about a psychiatrist. She had often considered going to one, but had said, I can solve my own problems, I always have. But perhaps the time had come. Maybe that's what Mr. Satin was referring to: time for a soul doctor. Soul . . . what an odd, archaic word.

It was evening now. She had not turned on the lights; the room was going to black. She had an overpowering need to be with someone —not to be alone again tonight—to speak with a friend. Had Willi not yet driven off? She hadn't heard the car. The Alfa, noisy now that it was aging, left no doubt about whether it was starting.

She hurried to the window. Both cars were still in the driveway. Willi was in the Alfa. The dashboard light was aglow, and she sat behind the wheel. This puzzled Calla; abruptly she knew why. Willi was crying. Her head was hunched over the wheel in a posture of heartbreak.

"Willi!"

She hurried out into the hallway, tore open the door and rushed across the lawn.

"Willi!" she cried. "Willi—don't . . ."

The door of the car was open—that's why the light was on—but Willi did not notice. Nor was she crying.

Her head was pitched forward on the wheel. She was still.

"Willi!"

As her friend failed to answer, Calla lifted her head a little. The blood came in gushes. Her face was slashed across the cheeks, the forehead, the mouth. Her head was an obscene disfigurement. And she barely breathed.

4

After nine and a half hours, the surgeon came out, said he had done some work on her face but most of it would have to wait for later. The laborious part had been the brain. There was some cortical damage; how much would affect her functionally he didn't know. There might be a necessity . . . to go inside again, was his expression.

Brain damage.

Calla paced the long corridor toward the end where the tall pane of glass was turning opal. When she reached the floor-length window, she looked down at the nearly empty parking lot, and up at the sky. The sun was still hiding below the horizon, but hinted that it was rising, turquoise, gold.

The laceration of the face—she had already braced herself to what that would mean, plastic surgery, reconstruction, pain and operations and more pain. But miracles of facial sculpture had been accomplished; there was that girl in the explosion, May Loring, and the Watts children, and Montgomery Clift—he had even made some films after that, *The Misfits* was one. Whatever it would take in time, money, agony, it could be done.

But brain damage. Oh God, please not.

She saw them wheeling the bed out of the recovery room and into the corridor; she stepped alongside it, walking abreast of the nurse and intern, neither of them sending her away. At the elevator, however:

"She'll be in intensive care," the intern said.

And the nurse, more gently: "Go home, Miss Stark."

She took another elevator to the floor where the intensive care section was, and caught the same intern as he was coming through the archway. She inquired about other doctors, used words she did not know the meaning of and decided to stay in the hallway until it would be a decent time to call her own physician. Get some rest, he said, there's nothing more to do right now, I'll call you later.

She had not remembered the blood inside the car. The seat was dry, but as she drove, her foot was in a puddle. And she had forgotten altogether that, driving Willi to the hospital last night, her own dress had been covered with it.

When she got home it was nearly eight o'clock. Two men were waiting for her. The plainclothes detective, followed by a uniformed cop, got out of the squad car, and held her door open.

"I'm Lieutenant Reuss," he said. "This is Officer Molinas."

"Can it wait?" She pointed to her soiled dress.

The lieutenant nodded. "Please change as quickly as you can, Miss Stark—and don't throw anything away."

She had been questioned last night and did not know whether she could face another pair. "I haven't been to bed at all. If you can come back . . ."

"We've been up too, Miss Stark," the lieutenant said.

"All night," Molinas added. He had just had breakfast. He held a length of dental floss, which, as he turned away, he used furtively.

In her bathroom, she slipped out of the bloody mess, and left it on the floor. She showered quickly, got into a seersucker robe and went downstairs.

The policemen were in the study. Lieutenant Reuss was writing in a notebook; Molinas was sucking his teeth.

"I was questioned at the hospital for two hours," Calla said.

The detective nodded. "Yes. We've been apprised."

He used the word as if he were offering his card, to identify him as an interim cop, marking time—law school at night, perhaps, or a clandestine screenwriter, a potential movie mogul with a twenty-page film treatment in his glove compartment. The costume fitted the studio picture, a shiny beige broadcloth shirt, expensive, with a monogrammed pocket; Gucci loafers with flapping tassels; the trousers carefully tailored, pocketless, to show the trimness of limb. A trim face as well, as neatly tailored as his pants, no extra flesh anywhere, and a tidy buttoned-down mouth.

She wanted some coffee but didn't offer to make it. Nor did she sit down. They, however, did. He asked somewhat the same questions as she had answered the night before, as if to catch discrepancies.

"You made an odd statement to Lieutenant Savitz," he said. She knew what was coming, and braced herself. "You said the attack was meant for you."

"Yes."

"Why did you say that?"

"I told him why."

"She's your double, she was wearing your costume, she was about to drive your car, etcetera, etcetera." He sounded indifferent to the dully circumstantial things. What he was really interested in: "Why did somebody want to kill you?"

She had said it before. "Nobody wanted to kill me."

"She's got a cracked skull."

He was saying it brutally to shock something out of her.

"She probably fought back. She's very strong—and she has guts. If she had just let it happen . . ."

"What happen, Miss Stark? Rape?"

"No."

"What, then?"

"Disfigurement . . . my face."

"Her face, you mean."

"No—they meant to disfigure mine."

"That anonymous call—did he say he would disfigure your face?"

She had never suggested to Savitz that he had. The lieutenant was purposely trying to confuse her, she decided, and he was succeeding. She felt as if she could not make sense in anything she might say or think. She suddenly lost chronology. She was walking with Willi—when was it?—on a beach somewhere, with Mina between them. There was a telephone call—it couldn't have been on a beach. A mobile bed was being wheeled into an operating room, and the face was bloody, but it didn't matter because it was the wrong face. Read *The Fabulist*, someone was saying, and it had to be Willi. We may have to go inside again, the doctor said, as if it were a cave. Or was it Mr. Satin?

"Try to remember the whole telephone call," the detective said. "All of it."

She went through the conversation again, trying not to think but to hypnotize herself into accuracy.

"And you don't consider it a threatening call?" Reuss asked.

"He said it wasn't. He called it a prophecy."

"With violence predicted."

"Not necessarily physical violence. But something worse than dying."

"Murder in the mind."

She saw that he liked his phrase and was probably making a mental note to jot it down. "Yes, murder in the mind," she said.

"What did he want you to do about it?"

"Nothing—that's why I didn't think it was threatening. He wasn't blackmailing me, and he didn't order me to do something or stop doing anything. It wasn't a hate call—nothing like that."

"Only he said something terrible would happen, and it did. And you don't believe he made it happen?"

"It wasn't that kind of . . ." She felt foolish saying it. ". . . voice."

"He didn't have to do it himself. He could have caused it."

She suddenly *needed* to be foolish. "Effigies, you mean?"

He was annoyed. "It was a knife, Miss Stark, and something like a blackjack." Then he added, "She's strong, you say—it might have been two people, one on each side of her."

"Yes."

"Do you get a lot of anonymous calls, Miss Stark?"

"No, not anymore. I used to get them all the time."

He said quietly, "The war days."

She nodded.

"But now you're not so—active, are you?" He was trying to be circumspect. "I mean you're more active as an actress, and less in other ways."

". . . Yes."

"You know . . . we may be making a mistake about this. That attack might not have been meant for you at all." As she was about to interrupt, he went on hurriedly. "Did—does Miss Axil have any enemies?"

"I've never heard of any. I can't imagine anyone not liking her."

"Have you been in her apartment?"

"Not recently, no."

"When?"

"A long time . . . Two films ago."

"Do you know who's been occupying it with her?"

". . . Occupying?"

"Her companion."

It took her so unawares that she turned to him. "I didn't know she had a companion."

"Yes, there's been someone living with her."

She felt a twinge. Willi had not confided in her. Which meant it was something her friend could not bring herself to discuss. But what in the world could that be?—simply that she had at last committed herself to a woman? Poor Willi—how sad for her to think Calla would not approve. Or did she think—and this might be the reason she had kept it secret—that Calla would be jealous?

"Are you sure she's living with someone?" she asked.

"Yes. There are two sets of toothbrushes—two tubes of toothpaste —different brands. One's Pepsodent and the other's Crest."

"People change brands."

"There are a pair of men's bedroom slippers in the closet."

"Men's?"

"Size eleven."

"You mean she's been living with a man?"

"Does that surprise you?"

Off-balance, she had already shown her surprise, and was annoyed that he was trying to exploit it.

He said it quite directly. "There are rumors around that she's a lesbian."

"There are rumors that I am too."

"Yes."

"Why? Because I'm a feminist? Some of us are Presbyterians." He smiled too complacently. "Talking about rumors, Molinas tells me you're a fag."

Molinas was so surprised that he stopped worrying his teeth. He grinned and showed them, as perfect as dentures. Reuss was also good-humored about it; he seemed pleased with his power to get a star angry, even if today she was an easy mark.

"Willi's friend . . ." she said. "Do you know who he is?"

"No. Savitz believes he's not living there anymore. But we're looking."

Apparently he did not wish to add any information. With her permission, he sent Molinas upstairs to collect the bloodstained clothes. He had a few more questions. As they heard the uniformed officer clumping down the steps and leaving the house, the lieutenant's manner changed. He was now hardworkingly charming.

"I have to admit—like anybody else—I'm interested in the secret life of a famous person. But I don't go around prying unless I have a very good—"

"—excuse."

"—reason. And the reason is obvious. If the butcher who carried that knife was out for your stand-in, maybe that's the end of it. But if he was out for you, he'll try again. You can help us prevent that. If you learn something about the man she's been living with, I'd like to know. If you learn anything at all, I'd like to know." He winked. "And I'll stop making passes at Molinas."

Leaving, he pedantically raised his finger and instructed her to keep the doors and windows locked. He had already arranged for an extra patrol car on the street, he said; it would be there for a while. Not until they were gone did she wonder how long "a while" might be.

She didn't mind locking the doors, although she would have to give up her easy freedom in and out of the garden. But now, locking the window, her hand fumbled at the latch.

Not a wink last night, and she longed to be insensible. She was afraid of sleeping pills. But if ever she had a right to call the doctor and ask for a sedative . . . No.

She thought she heard the telephone but she was wrong. In that startled moment she had imagined it was the white phone. But Willi alone had that number, and right now she was not dialing telephones. Nor might she ever again. A picture lightened in her mind: Willi's beautiful face. . . . Oh, the destroying ghouls!

A man in Willi's life. There was some incongruity in her not having said a word about him, no excited confidences, no request for free time so they could be together. Within the last year, Calla could not recall Willi's mentioning a single masculine name that had quickened the tempo of her life.

The blur suddenly focused: a name Willi did not want her to hear.

Lucas O'Hare.

Calla discarded the thought. She was ascribing too much importance to Willi's ardor for his screenplay. The woman had been relating the writer's passion, not her own; if she herself had any, it was not for the man but for the manuscript.

Yet, Calla mused, that might be enough. How many times in her own life had she been infatuated not with a man but with the work he had created? Once, with a baritone, she had gone to bed with his vibrato; another time, with an Off Broadway director, she had floated through the ecstatic public performance of an opening night and through the private performance afterward, to a lesser ecstasy.

Was Willi having an affair with Lucas O'Hare or with *The Fabulist*? She recalled the intensity of her friend's voice when she had spoken of it. She had been haunted by the love story. Strange, she had said, you don't believe half of it, and suddenly you wonder why you didn't. He defends us against the dark things.

The script lay on the table.

She tried to remember whether Willi might have had the time to cancel his cocktail appointment with Calla. No, she couldn't have; she had had only time enough to be mutilated.

What did O'Hare know about it?

Well, he would be here later today. Six o'clock.

She picked up the script and took it to her bedroom.

5

She read *The Fabulist* and hated it. It was strewn with gratuitous violence, an occultism she did not understand, and its love story started with a rape and resolved in a reconciliation she neither believed nor wanted to believe. She definitely would not do the picture.

But she would not quickly forget the script. It would keep her wondering what this meant and that, and whether she fully understood the character of Kono. And there was the surprising sensitivity to the anxieties of a woman, beautifully observed. She would not forgive the bastard for having written it so shrewdly. The screenplay would stay in her mind, it might bedevil her.

She could understand Willi's bedevilment, and tried to imagine how much of her stand-in's feeling extended to the man. Well, he would be here in a few hours. Perhaps she would catch some hint of it.

She still had not slept and the afternoon sunlight had started to fade. She kept calling the hospital, but there were no changes, they said, and little likelihood that Miss Axil would be conscious for the next few days.

Or ever, Calla heard herself saying. It was sickly pessimism, she must not give way to it. Comfort . . . She wished she had Barney's address or phone number in Rome or Paris or Madrid, or wherever the hell he was. Surely he must have finished the Italian film. His shoulder was the best of shoulders to cry on . . . Comfort . . .

Thirty seconds before six o'clock, which meant that Lucas O'Hare would arrive in roughly ten minutes. In the canon of Hollywood meetings, ten minutes was the permissible margin of tardiness. On-the-dot punctuality was tight-muscled, it revealed one's insecurity; and if she knew anything about O'Hare, he would go to great lengths to display his self-assurance.

He arrived at the stroke of six.

She watched him through the window. His ancient, red MG convertible had chipped paint and a fender in need of repair. His clothes were slovenly: a battered baseball hat, a gray shirt, army surplus perhaps, old-style wrangler pants. And sneakers. She wondered what size they were.

She must keep such thoughts in close rein. The possibility that O'Hare had been living with Willi was only a conjecture. All the police knew about her "companion," according to Reuss, was that his bedroom slippers—not sneakers—were size eleven. And that he used either Pepsodent or Crest toothpaste. These amounted to something less than a definitive description of O'Hare, or anybody.

The doorbell rang. She went to the door. He did not say hello.

"How's Willi?"

She was surprised by his peremptoriness. Also, by the question itself. It had been in all the papers, even the name of the hospital, and if he were really concerned, he would already know how she was—a visit, a telephone call. Perhaps he was trying to disarm suspicion by implying he did not know her all that well.

"She's about the same," she said.

"Meaning?"

"Still unconscious. At least she was when I last called."

"When was that?"

"An hour ago."

"You look awful."

To a star he was wooing, it was hardly the canny thing to say. He too looked awful, like a Bowery bum, needing a haircut and shave. In the study, she gave him a drink, straight rye. He let himself flop into an armchair, his head back, his rear resting on the edge of the seat, his legs sprawled halfway across the room. She wondered why he was playing the sluggard, what he was hiding behind all that slouch and stubble. She recalled a scene in a picture he had directed: A winter's night, bitter cold. An elderly woman is lying in bed; she is asleep and seriously ill. Her gray-haired husband enters the room, gazes at her, feels under the bedcovers to see if her feet are cold. He brings her a hot water bottle, slides it under the covers next to her feet. She opens her eyes and smiles. He lifts her chilly hand, holds it in both his own, blows his warm breath on it. He moves a stray lock of hair off her forehead. That was all of it. O'Hare had chosen unoriginal illustrations of an old man's tenderness, and had infused them with such simple belief as to make them seem uncommon, and touching. There were other things in the picture, just as gentle. She could not believe that this lump had created it.

"Have they found the guy who did it?"

She watched him. "Not yet."

"No clues—anything?"

"I don't know."

"The scum," he said. "The motherfucking scum."

She hated the expression. And knew she could never work with the man. No matter how much tenderness he might generate in a scene, his climate was brutality. The sadistic war film, and how he appeared this instant, those were the nature of the beast, the true Lucas O'Hare. She wanted to be rid of him. But she needed to find out how close he had been to Willi, so she could call Lieutenant Reuss.

"What size shoe do you wear?" she asked.

He seemed surprised. "Why? Do you get off on shoes?"

"What size?"

"When I was a kid, we used to say, 'Large Ked, large cock.' Which are you asking about?"

"About eleven, I would think."

"Close. Eleven and a half."

"How well do you know Willi?"

Though he did not move, something changed. There had been a noisiness in the man, a din in the air around him. His whisper, she had thought, could make a racket. But now, as he didn't answer the question, he was enveloped in a cocoon of quiet.

"I know that she's talked to you a lot," Calla said with studied innocence. "She even saw you on the set yesterday. And she loves your script."

"I've seen Willi perhaps a half dozen times," he said at last. "I never had a special thing with her. Is that what you want to know?"

"Yes, that's what I want to know."

She did not believe him. She wished, for the sake of clarity, that her prejudice against the man were not a cluttering factor; still, clutter or not, he was lying. She pretended to believe him, to keep him talking and learn what she could learn.

"But you do like Willi."

"Yes, very much. And it means a great deal that she likes my script."

"How much is a great deal?"

"You're a great deal."

She pretended to smile at the pun. "But I'm not Willi."

"You mean you don't like the script?"

She cautioned herself not to end the discussion too soon. "I think I might like it better if I understood it."

"You really don't understand it?"

"Well, it's certainly a bit abstruse."

"On the contrary, it's a simple story. A woman loses track of her son. He's a philosophy student who's been studying myth and mystics. He goes on a trip to the South in order to get a closer look at a cult leader, a black man who is probably a charlatan. The boy disappears. She goes in search of him. She meets the cult leader who helps her in the quest for the young man, and she is perversely attracted to the black man even though she suspects he has murdered her son. It's an adventure love story. That's all there is to it."

"That's all?"

"That's it."

"Do you really think you've just told the story you've written?"

"Did I get something wrong?"

"Well, it's like telling *Hamlet* from the viewpoint of the gravedigger. You tell it to a female star as if it's a woman's picture. But it's really the story of Kono, the black leader, isn't it? He's even the title— *The Fabulist*."

"But the fabulist might be the woman."

It had not occurred to her. The idea was certainly not explicit in the scenario. But the script was dense with double meanings. "Whether he's the fabulist or she is—Kono is the active one and Rachel's quite passive, isn't she?"

"Really? You think she's passive?"

"Yes," she responded. "She doesn't do a thing—doesn't initiate a single major action."

"She doesn't have to. She's the catalyst. She's the Big Catalyst."

It was con. He was using the cant words, the pseudo-intellectual pap Hollywood fed on, mother-mash.

"Horseshit," she said.

He grinned. She was giving him permission, even daring him, to be as vulgar as he needed to be, so long as he avoided the phony argot of the story conference.

He rose to the challenge, literally. Getting up from his chair, he looked taller and deeper-chested, and physically stronger. He walked with an animal vitality, and his wranglers seemed too small for his thighs.

He started honestly enough. "It's not easy to write a script where half of what you want to show on the screen is below the surface, hiding in your gut. It's not easy to read that sort of script either. I don't want to talk about the hidden part, mainly because I can't. But the part you can see in the pages—the adventure, the love story, the excitement of the hunt—that's all I can sell. There's a hell of a lot more, but that much I'll guarantee—a wild, sexy, lurid melodrama. It'll get an audience angry and excited and horny. I'll show the black world exploding in a white woman's face, and in her belly. It'll be beautiful and violent—and it'll throw people into shock. I'm sure of it. Because it's got everything —headside, heartside and cockside."

The hogwash after all. Having begun his spiel in a straightforward way, he had fallen into the claptrap. Too bad. While she did not like the man, she felt sorry that he had been around so long, and had adopted the easy hypocrisies. Yet, there was something ingratiating about the fact that, at the start of his pitch, he had tried to be honest. She wondered if she could sift the genuine out of the spurious in him. If she could, she might discover something about Willi.

"Who's going to play Kono?"

"Sidney Poitier."

"Has he agreed to do it?"

"I just got off the phone with Marty Baum."

The slippery answer. The script promoter goes to Barbra Streisand and says, "I've got Redford." Streisand, interested in doing a film with Robert Redford, agrees to read the screenplay. The promoter instantly goes to Redford and says, "I've got Streisand." Like two negatives making a positive, two lies made one tinseltown truth.

"Have you *got* Poitier?"

"What do you mean, got? Has he signed a contract?—no. Who signs a contract until all the pieces are together?"

"Would you give Sidney a message?"

"Sure."

"Tell him I'm not doing the picture."

He deliberated. "It's not only because of the script, of course."

"Not only."

"You hate my guts."

"Not only your guts. Your clothes, the way you sit in a chair, the Hollywood margarine in your mouth. I don't like anything about you—headside, heartside or cockside."

"And you don't like my politics."

"And I don't like your politics."

"Then don't vote for me—but do the picture. . . . Please."

"Crawling isn't even becoming to a snake."

She thought he was going to hit her. He didn't stir. When he spoke, he was lifting a burden.

"The odd thing is . . . you don't really know a goddamn thing about me, Miss Stark. You don't even *know* my politics."

"I heard you—years ago."

"What did you hear?"

"A reactionary, pure and simple."

"Not so simple, Miss Stark. You know who I voted for in the last election? Nobody. And from now on, that's my political ticket."

"Good for you, you idiot."

"I may be an idiot and I may be a snake, but I'm not a reactionary. . . . You are."

"Me?"

"Yes. You still cling to the notion that the human race is worth the bother."

"Yes, I do."

"That's reactionary. A traditional idea that's been dead a long time. Don't you know that? Don't you get any message from the ruins? Hasn't it occurred to you that ruin is exactly what the human race wants?"

"I understand that's what you said in your last picture—and it was a flop."

"We're talking about failures, are we? You've had a few yourself. Can you always put your finger on the fault?"

"Pictures start with words."

She pointed to the copy of *The Fabulist* on the table. So did he. He was angry. "That's a goddamn good script!"

"You have a scene in there . . . The woman gets raped by the black man, and two scenes later they're a couple of lovebirds. Straight out of *The Sheik*, which was a half century ago. Do you really imagine that women secretly yearn to be raped?"

"She brought it on herself."

"Ah yes, I forgot—women bring it on themselves. Always."

"I didn't say always."

"All you said was that women like it."

"This one does."

"She's that sick? Do you go for women only when they're sick?"

"Listen, Stark. I like women a hell of a lot more than you do. I take them seriously, I take them the way they are, and I love them. But you're always nagging at them to be dissatisfied with their lives and with themselves. You torture them to be better than they are, you lie to them and say they *are* better. You even seduce them with promises of success and higher status and an equality with men that's not worth a goddamn. Well, some of them make good on the pledges. But many of them don't. They come up with nothing—they don't have the big fancy office, and they've lost the double bed. They're stranded—they don't know what the fuck ever hit them. You and your kind have done that, Stark. You've wrecked a lot of confidence, a lot of self-respect, and you've spoiled a lot of beauty that women felt about themselves. You've crippled their grace! . . . Well, I don't do that, Stark. I've never hurt a woman in my life. I don't lie to them, I don't rape them and I don't tear down their self-respect. I've never been to bed with a woman and let her go away thinking she was a failure—never. Whatever I may feel about myself, women feel they succeed with me. You know why? Because they *do* succeed—I genuinely love them. You don't. And if you make women afraid that they're incomplete—they've got something missing—being female is insufficient—I call that cruelty. It's worse than rape."

There could be no meeting of minds and they both knew it. She could see that it depressed him. He put his glass down and took a few steps toward the door.

"You know, Ms. Stark, we're all looking for a place we can't see— it's off the map. And our lives depend on finding it."

It was the first accord they had had: on a nihilism. And such a minor concurrence; they barely agreed that they lived on the same planet.

At the threshold, about to leave, he turned. "Just one thing. You said the screenplay was abstruse. Did you really mean that?"

"Yes."

"Well, I'm glad of that anyway."

"Why?"

"What you don't understand—that's the best part of the script."

"What's not in it, you mean?"

"No. What you know is there, and can't see."

She smiled. "Aren't you taking credit for something you haven't written?"

"Don't laugh. That's the magic."

"Someday, someone will explain that to me."

"You don't need it explained. You're a fine actress. You've done some of your best acting when you weren't even there."

He was becoming more arcane, yet she was getting a sharper perception of him. "If I wasn't there, who was?"

He didn't answer; merely smiled. It was a smile she had not thought him capable of. She had an unexpected intimation: he's teasing me. It had a contest in it, a game. And an oblique excitement.

"Do you really believe in magic?" she asked.

"Of course I do—I'm in the business. So are you."

"You do the show and the show does you."

"Yes. The ritual takes over. The lights go down in the theater—the Catholics celebrate the Mass—the Jews carry the Torah—"

"Voodoo," she said watchfully. "Witchcraft."

"Yes, that too—all of it."

"You believe in everything?"

He extended his arms to embrace the world. "Everything!"

"In other words, nothing."

For an instant, his eyes darted for escape. He started to speak, and held back.

So: an accessible man. With a quickening of pulse, she felt she was onto something which might lead her, by some path she couldn't predict, to his relationship with Willi.

"Would you take a small risk with me?" he asked.

"How small?"

"At worst, you lose an evening."

"Doing what?"

"If we're talking about magic—I'd like you to meet somebody."

"Who?"

"Kono."

"Kono? You mean The Fabulist?"

"He doesn't call himself that. His name is Julo Julasto. Would you like to meet him?"

"Where?"

"I'll take you to see him."

"Who is he?"

He looked at her with steady eyes. "He's the leader of a cult."

"What sort of cult?"

"Come and see."

He had an appetite for mystery and the mystical. And had not at all been joking when he had said he was a believer in everything. Perhaps he could not have written *The Fabulist* without having a greed for fantasy.

"Will you come?" he asked.

She thought about Willi, and her own certainty that he had lied. In some skein of magic could she find a thread of reality that would explain the savaging of her dearest friend?

"Yes," she said. "When?"

"I'll pick you up around seven-thirty tomorrow night."

Through the window, she saw him go down the steps.

He had a sexy walk. A small ass and belligerent shoulders. Sexy.

Stop it, she warned herself, stop it. You have no physical interest in the man, none whatever. But recently . . . a randiness. Not about anyone in particular, but men in general. It humiliated her. She felt that she was falling into one of the worst folkways of the town: sex for every purpose. It was bait, bribe, weapon, speed. Sometimes, only an exercise in acting.

It was the aspirin of the business. The all-purpose painkiller.

She knew all that. But she was randy. You'll turn into a Hollywood slob, she said.

She took aspirin and went to bed.

"Where are we going?" Calla asked.

"You'll see."

He hustled his tired old MG as if it were a brand-new, souped-up Ferrari, full out, roaring south on the Santa Ana Freeway, somewhere east of Anaheim. He drove not as if he were trying to arrive but to escape.

There was a sting in the night wind, in the lash of her hair against her face. It had been a long time since she had ridden in an open car, and the sky was so electrically charged that she felt, if she reached up, she could complete a circuit with a star.

She was about to say as much, but sensed that he did not want to talk. At first she thought it was because the speeding car was clattery. But she played with deeper reasons, pretending to know something about him. Indeed, she did know that he was a hyphenate, a writer-director, thus she extrapolated that the director part must be awash with talk, and the writer must shrivel at mush-mouthing in story conferences. Maybe he simply hated talk. Well, she was enjoying the silence, the cool of the ride and the prospect of watching the practice of a cult tonight.

California was a carnival of cults. Reality hadn't turned out very well, the world over; it had promised a shining truth and delivered a shoddy illusion. Los Angeles offered plenty of other illusions: Spiritism and scientism and preternaturalism, wish-bringers and curse-makers, gurus, lamas, witches, street saints, exorcisers, prophets of God and the devil. Hundreds of sideshows. They worked their fascination upon Calla although she did not convert. She had not allowed herself to feel victimized in an *est* workshop, she had been signally silent in a primal scream meeting and had laughed herself silly at a session of ID. But she was not averse to going to such gatherings; she bought many one-time tickets. Tonight, this one, some way, somehow, might bring her a revelation about Willi.

It had been a hot day, and unlike most California nights, no relief had come. Now, as they left the freeway and started up a narrow road into the Santa Ana foothills, the air became chillier, with a sharp bleakness that cut to the bone. She was about to ask Lucas to put the top up when they started to descend, and as quickly as the cold had come, the heat took over. What happened was uncanny, as if they were sinking into a steaming cauldron. It was a huge basin in the hills, a great round pit, miles in diameter, with a wide flat floor. The slopes that descended to it seemed geometrically hewn, all even and equal, without trees or shrubbery to differentiate one incline from another; no grass or weeds, only a gray boulder here and there, caught in moonlight, glistening like roughly minted silver. It was a wasteland.

"Moonscape," she said.

"Yes. It's a crater. Volcanic. They say that after the flaming lava there was water. Like Lake Elsinore, not far from here. Have you been there?"

"Yes, it smells like sulphur."

"Buoyant—you can't drown in it."

The dust was settling in a fine screen on the windshield. As they descended and made a turn, she was amazed at what she saw. Hundreds of cars, in an unbroken stream, were descending by other roads and pathways, moving downward to the crater's floor; pedestrians, too, she could not tell how many nor where they came from, continuing steadily down the trails of the distant hill.

The MG made another turn and another, and they were at the base of the crater, parking, as other drivers were doing, on rough gravel, rocky here and there, rutted by erosion, jagged.

They got out of the car and walked. Joining the movement toward the center of the flatland, she saw that much of the throng was black, but there were white people as well, poor for the most part, or middle class, locking their car doors prudently, wondering aloud whether the sharp-edged lava would cut their tires. And still they came, streaming down the boulder-strewn hillsides from every direction, down the narrow roads and trails, toward the crater's center.

She saw it: a high hill of wood nearly as large as a sound stage, rough logs and timbers, dead branches and tree stumps, and, at the base of everything the shavings and fagots of brushwood. It was to be a bonfire.

Carpenters were still working on the wooden mound, adding tinder to the base, hammering at a stairway that arose from the ground to the apex of the conical hill.

It did not seem that the flow of arrivals would ever stop. As the floor of the basin became crowded, the outer circle of the horde pressed inward, drawn by the centripetal pull of the wooden mountain. With decreasing room to spare, people pressed upon one another, so that they had to stand narrowly, arms folded, scarcely expanding their bodies for breath.

There was no downdraft of air; the heat became more oppressive, damp heat full of night humidity and the moisture of human closeness. Moment by moment, Calla began to notice a vibration among the multitude, an inner motion. She tried to put a name to it: the same buzz and oscillation, the same expectant thrill as she had noticed in second-night audiences after the newspapers have called the play a hit; but there was something else, something she had witnessed in church, a mode of conduct ritually determined, decorous and hushed. The normally rich laughter of blacks, the cadenzas of gaiety, were muted. Attendance here tonight was not a function of sound, but sight; they were going to observe a spectacle, perhaps a wonder. And they would wait softly for it.

Bit by bit, the hush became even quieter. Finally there was only the stir of the waiting. In an undertone, the other sound began. It was faint at first, barely identifiable as something humanly made. Then it grew into a humming, the gentlest murmur here and there, without particular pattern. Still growing, it became a droning vibration like a swarm of bees, coming closer and closer, and louder as well, swelling into a musical note, sustained and unchanging. A message? A mantra?

Calla heard the sound as a warning. It agitated her. She turned to see O'Hare smiling as if he knew every cue; all of it was going as he had expected; none of it daunted him. In the humid heat, she felt the sweat on her forehead and bursting from every pore of her body, but O'Hare seemed cool. Yet, she sensed that he was excited, and she envied his excitement since it seemed so utterly without alarm. Or was he pretending?

She turned toward the mass of wood and saw the man. He was standing on the ground, at the base of the hill. He did not look like a man but a radiant colossus in a flowing cape of feathers that were glitteringly white, a voluminous mantle with a train that followed him as he walked to the stairs of the wooden eminence. As though he were not tall enough, he wore a towering headpiece made of silver, more a helmet than a crown, which was crested with longer white feathers than those that made his cloak. He had a flair for costume, she thought; an excellent showman, he was dressing his production vividly. . . . He started to mount the stairs.

She felt a vague alarm. "What's he going to do?"

"You'll see."

As the man moved upward, he was a mammoth of whiteness, like a cloud ascending a mountain, a pale mist except for the gleam of ebony, his black and lustrous face.

Abruptly, as if on signal, the crowd shouted:

"Gorá!"

She turned to O'Hare. "What does that mean?"

"It's a Bantu word—it means fire god."

Her alarm was beginning to have a name. They were watching not only an act, but an act of divinity. This was more than an audience: a congregation. The show was a mass—fanatical, perhaps—celebrating a deity or a devil.

She had an urgency to flee, yet she felt compelled to see how it ended.

He was ascending slowly. As he got to the fourth or fifth tread on the staircase, the crowd began to echo the soft slur of his footsteps. They moved their feet lightly on the gravelly sand, like brushes on a drum, *shsh*, silence, *shsh*, silence, as the man mounted the stairs. When he was about two thirds of the way up, some of the spectators began to sing—a wordless song, without consonants, long sustained notes. It started with the thin and fluting voices of the young, then the full-bodied women's tone like cellos and woodwinds, finally the proclamation of the men's brasses. They sang together on an open syllable of rapture.

The man had reached the summit.

The music held for a moment. He raised an arm and there was silence. As he raised the other arm, it seemed the token they had been waiting for, and the crowd let out a sigh.

Suddenly, from all directions, torches burst aflame as if by spontaneous combustion, any number of them, twenty at least, high above the heads of the crowd, in the hands of the torchbearers. Pathways opened for them and they moved sedately, their fires blazing, toward the wooden mount. They came to a halt at the perimeter, and, as the man at the pinnacle slowly let his arms descend to his sides, the torchbearers set their flames to the kindling.

Almost simultaneously Calla could smell the burning of an essence, kerosene perhaps, with which the outer timbers had been drenched. An instant. Then, a detonation. With a clap of sound, like thunder, the flames took flight, running, darting around the bottom of the wooden hillock, and the whole base of the pile burst afire. Then, still running, the flames started upward.

They had not reached the apex where the man stood in his white and flammable feathers. Slowly now, without the slightest sign of haste, as if to reveal the combustibility of all he wore and all he was, he started to divest himself of his garments. His crested crown went first; raising it, he held it high above his head, then tossed it with a wide gesture into the flames. The slightest flicker of feathers, like eyelashes ablaze, and they were gone. Still unhurried, clasp by clasp, he began to loosen the cape. When all the clasps were free, he threw the mantle open, lifted it from his shoulders, swept it around to the front of him, held it aloft as he had held the crown, swung it once in a full circle around his head, like a white-feathered bird winging a halo around him, and tossed the plumed mantle out into the flames. There was a momentary maelstrom in the air, a whirl of fire and whiteness, and all at once it was gone, its ashes lifting in a flurry to the sky.

The man was naked. It seemed impossible that, without the huge cloak and towering crown, the black figure should be more mammoth than the white one had been. But so it seemed to Calla. Perhaps it was the wooden mountain he stood on, perhaps it was the titanic pride with which his outstretched arms seemed to support the sky, his head thrown back, his legs spread wide, his genitals hanging free like a great triad, his body like an unchained Prometheus.

What a magnificent physique he had, she thought, and how shrewdly he displayed it. He stood there—unmoving—waiting—challenging the flames.

There had been no wind. But the heat made its vacuums, and the flares of fire sucked upward, raging one direction, then another, the conflagration whipping and slashing and rampaging at the wooden mountain, upward and upward, toward the pinnacle where the man stood, immobile.

Then the flames were all around him. Sometimes the fire was like a pack of furious beasts clawing at his flesh, plucking at his limbs, leaping at his throat and his face, trying to destroy him as much by tearing as by burning; sometimes it was an animal washing its young, licking at him with a tongue of flame, licking and lapping and caressing. Soon the flames were rage and quarrel, snarling with anger, cracking and thundering in explosions of spite. He was engulfed by them. And he stood there, he did not move, he simply stood there, burning, burning. The man was burning!

Well, it was a stupendous show, she decided, with intensifying suspense and a fulfilled climax, but she certainly hadn't been taken in. A trick of some kind, a device in the deception of distances, an illusion expertly done—but nothing to send the shivers down her spine.

Something went wrong.

The man was gone. There was no sign of him. It clearly was not supposed to occur in this way. An accident had happened.

The instant he vanished, the crowd let up a cry, calling his name. Where is he, they cried, what happened, oh God, what happened to him? A woman screamed. Someone started a high and mournful wail. As if the shock and heartache were separating from a world aflame, another wail echoed from a hilltop far away. Then all the throng began to lament, where is he, oh, he is dead, where is he, like a people who had been betrayed, who had been lured here to rejoice and left to mourn.

The hill of fire was settling, collapsing. Old wood that had dried out and been oil-soaked, the tinders and timbers were burning themselves out in a fury of impatience. The multitude did not stir but continued to watch the dying conflagration, as if to consummate the ritual. It was no longer a hill but a pool of fire, all red embers like molten metal, with only a gray chaplet of ash circling the scarlet lake. They watched the lambent redness, fire-hypnotized, and did not take their eyes from it. A tall tree had fallen, a mountain had vanished. Some wept aloud, some lamented silently.

Then suddenly—

In the midst of the pool of flame, a shadow arose, a fire figure.

It was he, the man again, as if resurrected out of flame.

As they saw him, they could not believe what they were gazing at. Nor could Calla believe it. She was as still as the others.

An instant, and a cry went up, the whole cry, everyone.

"Gorá!"

Abruptly it happened to her, what she had not dreamed could happen. "Gorá!" she cried. She began to shake. She almost wept with happiness to see him alive. "Gorá!"

"Gorá!" they all exulted, and Calla with them. "Gorá!"

O'Hare smiled.

6

As they drove northward toward Los Angeles, in a slower and more pensive mood than on the southward journey, Calla tried to make some sense of the unbelievable event. Astonishing as the fire exhibition had been, she could scarcely believe that she had been taken in. A theatrical device. True, actors and actresses were reputedly the best audiences, the most unrepressed and available, but she had shouted a word she had never used before, a religious word in fact, an evocation of a fire god. Who was this man Julo Julasto, why did O'Hare write a screenplay about him, and how could he have accomplished the incredible fire trick?

It was clear enough *why* he had done it. Directly after the stunning demonstration, dozens of minions, young and old, black and white, had appeared from all quarters. They wore African caftans, beautiful ones, long and flowing, in bold patterns of vibrant color, and they swept through the crowd with their printed tracts—*Gorá, the Life Resurrected, the Soul Everlasting*—and passed their collection plates. She had heard the clink of coins all around her, and the crackle of bills; here and there she had seen people writing checks. Pay to the order of Gorá, they must have written, the order being religious.

It was a fraud, of course. Deliverance from the raging flame, and from death. The promise of reincarnation. Immortality, packaged in magic. Give, brother, give, money is temporal, but Gorá is eternal.

But how had the man accomplished the fire feat? The show, how had he rigged the scenery, how had he played the lights to make the illusion? Who was he? And why was O'Hare so evasive about the questions?

Later, the director said. As before, the timing had to be his own.

The big question, the one that stirred her most troublingly, was how had she allowed herself to become, in a symbolism too apt, inflamed by the black man's stupefying stunt? Just as she had decided that the crowd was being deluded into the acceptance of a divinity, just as she had begun to recoil from it—*Gorá!* . . . How could she have joined the outcry?

"Are you having a rough one?" he asked.

"Yes."

"I was the same when I saw him the first time."

"The same? In what way?"

"The sense that I was being tricked, disgust with the crowd, and then—Gorá!"

"Did you feel you were helping them create a god?"

He looked at her quickly. "Who says they were creating a god?"

"You did. Fire god—you said that's what Gorá means."

"It's only a word. Who cares about a word?"

"I do. If you say a word means 'god,' I don't read 'radish.'"

"But the *word* doesn't count. They weren't creating a god any more than you were. They were having a theatrical wingding. It was a wonderful fable—the most elemental kind of folk tale—with an epic conflict. Man against his terrifying friend, his beloved enemy—fire. And man triumphant. It's bigger than Beowulf."

"They shouted 'god.' So did I—so did you."

"I shouted Gorá, but what I meant was Bravo. I didn't deify anything, except as people in the theater deify stars. Bravo!"

"Only an audience . . ."

"Don't say 'only.' A great audience is as holy as a congregation."

"Holy? Do you really mean holy?"

"Yes—religious." He leaned forward over the wheel. He was excited. "An audience—when they're touched beyond what they're seeing and hearing—when they're capturing something beyond thought, and feeling something deeper than emotion—then an ecstasy lifts them into one single marvelous spirit—and the theater is a temple."

"And the performer is a fire god."

"No, not a god, but he's just as sacred—a poet, a fabulist. Oh Christ, if I could catch that ecstasy on film—if I could catch one sacred moment of it—!"

He looked more alive than she had seen him. Hungrier. If theater was a church to him, she understood now what he meant when he told her that he believed in everything. Ritual was raw material to him, grist to his theatrical mill. Faith, any faith, could be fabulized. Writing about Julo Julasto, he could also be writing about himself. A character in a separate world, perhaps, in a flaming illusion. A pantheist who found a god wherever he needed one; divinity service stations were everywhere. But when he had to pray, he went not to a church but to a theater.

The man had lured her into a deeper interest than she had intended, and it was all speculation; she did not know him. But of one thing she felt certain: he was a romantic. She wondered if it was easier to be what he was, a romantic fighting in a made-up world, than to be what she was, a realist who had done battle with things-as-they-are. Well, in one respect he had it easier; he had only a single world to fight, the inner one; the outer world probably did not exist. She had them both.

Too soon, it appeared to her, they turned off the main highway. Instead of continuing toward the city, they seemed to be going west.

"Where now?" she asked.

"The beach."

"I forgot my swimsuit."

"No swimming. We're going to see Julasto."

A wave of anticipation. Although she had expected to meet the man sooner or later, it had not occurred to her that it would be this evening. The night air seemed headier.

"How does he do it?" she asked.

"Go through fire? I don't know."

"Have you asked him?"

"Yes. He won't tell me. Perhaps he'll tell you."

"Why would he tell me and not you?"

"Because I don't need to know. You do."

She wondered if he was really so confident of his intuition that he had no need to dig for reasons. Or the reverse: afraid to put his intuitions to the test.

At a marker that said they were going to Redondo, they turned again and were soon riding along a beach road dotted with small boatyards, tackle stores, clam and beer bars, the land's edge enterprises of a raffish seacoast. They rode through an unlighted section, slowing down alongside an enclave of shanties, a tiny store called Flotsam, which sold shells and sea debris, and a place called Summertime, whence came the low, sullen beat of a band and heavy laughter that suggested mango and papaya, overripe.

They stopped at a narrow store, separate from the others, with a plate glass window silver-misted by sea spray. The illumination inside was murky, like candlelight, scarcely enough to outline the gilded legend on the window, *Arts Afriques*.

Inside, the merchandise was novelty junk, tourist African, dried pods strung into beads and necklaces, bracelets of elephant hair, badly carved figurines of tribal warriors in basswood stained to look like teak, safari animals of soapstone and papier-mâché. But there were beautiful things as well: a metal mask of an impala's head, coppery-bronze going to green sulphate; a looming witchman made of tattered rags and wild hair, a batik sunset of clamoring reds.

A half dozen customers milled around in the store, with nearly as many salespeople. The latter were young and of both sexes, two of them white, and they wore caftans, more subdued than those at the fire demonstration. Everything, in fact, was subdued; the lamplight flickered through pinholes in black lanterns, the music—drumbeats and soft ululations—distant, muted. An exotic muskiness pervaded the air, an incense, unidentifiable, as tantalizing as a shadow that refuses to cross a threshold.

One of the salespeople approached them, an old man with grizzled hair, the whites of his eyes shining like mirrors.

"Lucas." He bowed with a measured decorum.

"Darra, this is Miss Stark," the director said. "Darra is the buyer for the shop."

"No," the old man said quietly. "Only the good things I buy. The rest is arrive by himself."

His African courtliness made his English seem correct. "You want to see him Julo?" He drew out the name of his employer as if invoking a spirit.

Darra escorted them through an unnoticed passage, out to a garden. They were under a colonnade of greenery, a narrow pathway between tall columns of bamboo interlaced with ferns and clinging lianas. At the far end, a light glimmered. It was a pavilion or a summerhouse, she thought, but as they approached, she saw that it was totally enclosed, substantial, with an old brick facade, overgrown with ivy. The door, with a nicely handwrought knocker and iron strap-hinges, was wide and massive.

The door was opening . . . slowly, inch by inch, it seemed. For no reason at all, she had the uncanny sense that it was opening by itself, mechanically, without human assistance. The bizarre notion was fortified when the doorway was simply a rectangle of light, and nobody standing in the glow.

Then there was. A silhouette at first, a silent and powerful presence, filling nearly all of the doorway, as motionless as a mountain. Even when they were within arm's length, he did not move. At last, vacating the doorway, he made a slow and graceful gesture, inviting them to enter.

Indoors, he stepped back in the shadows as if to allow his visitors to accustom themselves to their environment. It was a large room with a huge fireplace, and a lively flame in the oversized logs. The hearth was the sole source of light, except for a glow through the smoked glass shades of wall sconces. In the far corner of the room lay a pallet, piled luxuriantly with pillows, wine-colored and maroon and ruby. It was a handsome, high-ceilinged room, yet, except for the softnesses in the sleeping place, rigorously austere, with a few pieces of African statuary, primitive, beautiful—a lean-faced woman with head tilted as if listening to a wind or summoning a memory; an arrow-stricken gazelle with a question in its eyes; a child asleep.

"I am glad you came."

The black man said it with formality, like the start of a ceremony. His voice was suitable for ceremony; it had resonance and an echo. With a wave of his arm, he indicated where they could sit. There were no chairs, only benches around a heavy oblong table, and drum stools half-circling the open fireplace. Now, seeming to stage every step of the proceeding, he stepped out of the shadows and into the brighter area of the fire: it was time for her to see him.

He walked with feral grace, a black leopard. His male-blatant costume should have looked silly, but didn't. Shiny black leather trousers so skin tight that she could discern each member and muscle, a red silk shirt very full and billowing like sails, and a silver headband, low-lustered against the shining blue-black skin. And barefoot.

"I was sorry to hear about Willi," he said.

Something happened in the room. In the silence it seemed as though a siren had shrieked. An unspoken warning between the two men: move warily. Once, years ago in a plane, the air pressure had become unequalized, and she had felt a similar threat—implosion at any moment—and the same panic.

As evenly as possible she asked the black man: "You know Willi?"

"I know Willi only because I know you, Miss Stark."

"What does that mean?"

His smile was ingratiating. "I know everything about you—your friends, your family, all the films you've made. If something happens to someone close to you, I read every word about it. I've followed every milestone of your career—your troubles, your triumphs."

A wonderful melody in his voice, cello tones, aloft. He was an eminence.

"That's . . . quite a tribute."

"You don't believe it, do you?"

She matched him, smile for smile. "You're not exactly the stereotype of the film fan, are you?"

"Film fan?" he protested. "I'm a Calla Stark fan. Not Calla Stark, the leading woman, but Calla Stark, the *woman leader*."

With a long stride, he went to the table and picked up a large Manila envelope. Out of it he pulled a number of photographs clipped from newspapers and magazines. He handed her one clipping at a time. They were all shots of the actress taken years ago; making speeches and demonstrating, carrying placards, waving banners, quarreling with policemen and getting arrested.

"There she is!" He sang her praise. "Calla Stark—marching! Calla Stark, with her fist raised! Calla Stark—thumbing her nose at all the bastard badges of the law! Calla Stark—telling the world to go to hell!"

Quietly: "I never told the world to go to hell."

He didn't hear her. "Calla Stark—fighting the sons of bitches! Tearing their eyes out! Drawing blood!"

"I hardly made a scratch."

Unexpectedly, he turned angry. "Then don't tell me about it!"

"Since you were kind enough to—"

"Don't turn your back on that woman!"

"I wasn't doing that."

"You're running her down! You're spitting on her accomplishment!"

She was stunned.

"Don't tell me who she was!" he raged, his mouth turning ugly. "She was a fighter. She took on the whole sonofabitching universe. 'Come on, you murderers,' she said. 'Come on, you cocksuckers, I'll beat the shit out of you!'"

"That was never—"

"Don't tell *me*! You don't know who the fuck she was!"

It was demented. One minute he was a man of grace with a well-modulated voice, the next minute a gutter rat. She couldn't understand him, how he could change his mood so suddenly, even his personality. Everything about Julasto had altered. His voice had lost its cello resonance and become a rasp. His speech, so meticulous, was now a bloody clot in his throat. How could he sound so educated, and suddenly be toilet and alleyway? Did he want to be taken as a man of elegance or as a mugger in the streets? Even his looks were indecipherable—handsome in one light and ugly, mean in another. He repelled her, he fascinated her.

She looked at O'Hare. Smilingly attentive, he was taking no part in the meeting. He did not even return her glance. He seemed totally detached.

Julasto, however, was watching her. Clearly, he saw her unease, and was humiliated by his outbreak. He had a stricken look, as if he wanted to flee.

"I'm sorry," he said. "I am very deeply sorry." His fastidious speech had returned; he was in polite society again. And guilty. His attack on her had wounded *him*. Oddly, she felt sorry for the man as she watched him tug at the tatters of his pride. Still, he couldn't capitulate. "Please don't tell me how you've changed." He tried to smile. "If you're not the Calla Stark I've got in my head, then mine is better than yours —and the hell with you."

She made an effort to fall in with his pretended good humor. "It's all pictures, isn't it?"

He took it as forgiveness, snatched at her sentence as if it were a life preserver. "Yes—exactly—we make our own pictures. Thank you— you've said it perfectly—pictures! You can be the wolf in the forest, but if I love you, you're Goldilocks! Pictures!"

He had hitherto been unable to alight anywhere, but now sat down on a stool, very close. In payment for the pardon, he wanted to make himself available, open his heart to her.

"Sometimes—in my mind—I paint a picture of myself and then can't recognize the portrait," he said. "Who is this? Is this Julo Julasto? I've never seen him before. I'm too many people, too many passions. I lose my temper, I lose my head. But those pictures of *you*—they remain constant in my mind. And I can't bear to have the portrait changed. She's beautiful, that woman—my God, she's beautiful! That's why I want you so badly to do *The Fabulist*." Then, quietly, almost a whisper: "You are going to do it, aren't you?"

"I'm still thinking about it."

"Don't think about it, Calla Stark—do it. Please do it." He turned to the director. "Lucas, make her do it. Woo her—seduce her—make her do it!"

"It's up to you, Julo."

Julo turned back to the actress. "It's a beautiful script—don't you think it's a beautiful script?"

"What do you find beautiful about it?"

Again he had difficulty. "It's as if he discovered a . . . secret."

"Whose secret?"

"Kono's."

"What is it?"

"I don't know—and that's what tantalizes me. I have the feeling that the writer does know, and will reveal it only on film." He was in their professional territory, unfamiliar to him, and he looked from one to another. "Is that possible?"

"Yes . . . it's possible," she said.

"I hear terrible reservations."

Not wanting to get into trade talk, she resorted to a bromide. "Every production is a risk."

"Of course," he said quickly. "But just think of *my* stake in the film. If it's a bad picture, you'll do another and another. Not me—I'll never recover from it. Whoever plays Kono plays *me*. If he portrays me foolishly, I'm the one who'll be laughed at. Even my virtues will seem ridiculous. Gorá will be a silly joke, and will die in a little suburb of Los Angeles."

"Instead of?"

"I want to hear Gorá in many places."

"Where?"

"All over, all over."

"All over the country?"

"Yes."

"The world?"

"There's a rebuke in the question."

"Is there? Perhaps."

"Why? Are you any different?" he asked. "It's a matter of radiance, isn't it?"

"Radiance?"

"Don't you want your radiance to shine all over the world? If it doesn't, the blaze of it will consume you. You have to share your fire—or perish in it. . . . And I am the same."

He was a spellbinder. His eyes glowed, his skin gleamed as if he were in a corona. She had no understanding of his cult, but whatever it was, he had the intensity and the zeal to spread it. Could O'Hare's film capture the fireworks of the man?

"Are you really the character in the script?"

"I must be. I hate him and love him—as I do myself."

"You're truly Kono?"

"Truly Kono."

"Are you as complex and selfless and noble as the script says you are?"

He smiled quite simply, not needing to be modest. "Yes, I am."

"The Fabulist."

"Teller of tales. Fire—and the deliverance from dragons."

"I think you're a fake."

Surprise: he howled with delight. "I am! Yes, by Christ, I'm that too—a fake! I'm the worst fake that ever fakulated!"

He leaped to his feet. When speaking to her, directly to her, she had sensed a warm, comprehensible human being. Intricate and histrionic, perhaps, and probably a bit deranged, but in some way reachable. Now she had lost him. He was laughing too loudly, dancing in twists and turns around the room, kicking away the props of accountability, singing what a fakulating fake he was, having a mad and marvelous time. Still another role. She had seen him as eminence, gutter rat, contrite sinner, spellbinder; now he was Julo the Clown, a black man hiding behind clown white.

When he had finally simmered down, she asked, "You don't mind my calling you a fake?"

"Mind—why should I mind? Call me any name you like. Call me fake, call me thief, call me motherkiller, call me nigger!" He stopped and spun on her, eyes flashing. "But when you see me burn, call me Gorá!"

She said it softly. "I did."

"Ah." He executed a bow that was ornately graceful. "Did you really say Gorá?"

"Yes. It was a wonderful performance."

"You're taking back your compliment."

"You don't like 'performance'?"

"Not at all. It sounds like a cheap trick."

"I have a great respect for good performances."

"You're in the acting business—I'm not."

"What business *are* you in?"

He looked at her fixedly. "It's not a business, Miss Calla. And not a trick."

"What is it?"

He tendered the word carefully: "Resurrection."

Again she looked at Lucas, and again he was inscrutable.

Julo snapped: "Don't look at him—look at me! When I offer you a gift, don't take your eyes off me. Me—I offer the resurrection—*me*. The Gorá who burned to ashes and arose in flame! The man of life and life again! The spirit of the reborn! The body regenerated, and the soul eternal!"

"And pass the collection plate."

It stung like an antiseptic; it also delighted him. He laughed again. "Wouldn't you give a buck for a second life?"

"You'd be taking me for a buck."

"Wouldn't you give a buck to *believe* in a second life?"

"Even if it's not true?"

"Suppose it was possible to believe in something—no matter how false—that made your life endurable. Suppose it was possible to believe in something that would bring you joy everlasting. Suppose you could find a love that would drive out hatred. Suppose—if you cannot drive out hatred—you are given a rod to smite your enemies, to smite them until they are indistinguishable from the dirt under your feet. Suppose you could live again and again, and make each life better than the last. Suppose, instead of being condemned through all eternity, you could be admitted into a vast mystery, and have a vision of God's face. . . . Suppose you could believe all that—even if it might be a lie—would you give money for it?"

"I can get that with cocaine."

"No! Cocaine will let you down, and heroin and booze—they all dump you in the pit." He laughed once more. "And my price is cheaper."

"What is your price?"

"Take what you need, give what you can."

"It's a higher price than that. Lies are expensive."

"Not lies. I'm selling an illusion. What are you selling?"

"I call myself an actor. You call yourself a god."

"You ask for more worship than I do."

"Perhaps. But I'm not a liar or a cheat."

"Which is what you think I am."

"Let's start with the assumption that I know that about you."

"White lady, you don't know me for shit."

"Is that what I should know you for?"

A peal of laughter. "You're witty, you know that? Miss Calla, you are tit-wit-witty." Abruptly the laughter ceased. His face was grave. "But I ain't shit."

"What are you?"

"I'm what you said—a liar and a cheat. I'm the black Paul Bunyan and I'm Father Divine. I'm Jesus on a white mule."

"Do you lump Jesus with the others?"

"No. You do."

Mercury. He was too quick, too changeable, she couldn't lay hands on him. Even if she were swift-footed enough to keep up with the man, he would trip her while running.

"Where do you come from?" she asked.

"Born, you mean?"

"To begin with."

"I was born in Harlem, I was born in Watts, I was born in Montgomeroodles, Albumen." He grinned broadly. "You don't like my playful pigshit, do you?"

"No. Why do you do it?"

"Obfucksation."

"Whom do you want to obfuck?"

"Anybody who talks in numbers. Anybody who asks me to kiss the ass of a mortal statistic."

"Money is a mortal statistic, isn't it?" As he looked at her sharply, "All that phony crap you sell in your store—where does it come from?"

"It's not phony, it's reproduction. And it comes from my country— Gorá."

"That's an all-purpose word, isn't it? Where's Gorá?"

"Africa."

"What latitude, what longitude?"

Angry: "What the hell are you, a cop? Don't push me into a lineup, white lady. Don't zap me with a fuckin' club. You want to get answers out of me—you *talk* to me! Don't beat my skull open. *Talk to me.*"

Having exposed a wound, he quickly covered it up, went back to japeries, did a little dance, a gleeful little caper. But as he was finishing, it became an ominous gaiety, like Hitler dancing at the fall of Czechoslovakia.

Apprehensively she backed away. "In your audience tonight, a lot of those people were well off. But many of them were poor. Doesn't it bother you to take money from them?"

"What do you think it means to be poor, Miss Calla?"

"Poor is poor."

"Poor is hungry, right? Poor is bedbugs, poor is sores that won't heal. Right?"

"Right."

"Wrong. I've had all those things and they don't matter a damn— you get over them. *Poor is fear*. It's a sickness of the soul that's with you night and day. It's a rat eating at your brain. It's a disease of the tongue, so you can't speak. It's a cataract, so your eyes can't see the sun. If someone speaks a word of love to you, you can't hear it, because you're afraid to believe it. *Poor is fear*."

She could see him trying to stop himself, to keep his hurt hidden like an unsightly scar. And his smile did not mask the pain. "Fear turns to hatred," he said. "Every day of your life, you hate yourself. Every day of your life, you cry out, 'Oh God, don't show me your face—I'm afraid!' . . . That's what poor is."

"And you don't mind taking the nickels and dimes of frightened people?"

"A nickel in my collection plate buys a million dollars' worth of courage."

"Courage to do what?"

"Defy death."

"I am the resurrection and the—"

"Right, right, right!"

"You pays your money and you gets your bingo card."

"Wipe the snot, Miss Calla."

He produced a handkerchief and tossed it to her. It fell in her lap. She felt as though he had pulled a flaming brand from the fire and thrown it in her face. For an instant, the insulting white thing lay in her lap. She snatched at it and threw it into the fireplace. A latent moment, nothing happened. The handkerchief started to smoke. The black man reached, plucked it out of the fire, and held the smoking thing in his hand. Abruptly, with a puff, it burst aflame. He let it stay there, on his outstretched palm, allowing the fire to burn his skin. He did not stir, did not flinch, he did not take his eyes off the actress. The flame grew and dwindled. At last, when it was all but out, he closed his hand, made a fist, opened it and tossed the ash away.

What an exhibitionist little antic, she thought. In the silence, she saw the man's intent: not only to show, up close, as he had in the distance, that he was the master of fire, but that there was a touch of madness in him, and danger. She had sensed the threat all the time, even while he was pretending to be a clown, the complicated, bridled power, the need to conquer or to avenge or to destroy; and, perhaps, be impervious to pain. He frightened her. And she sensed that his power to frighten was, perversely, a part of his sexual energy. While it intimidated, it hypnotized.

He was the first to break the silence. "I'm sorry we could not meet tonight," he said. He had written off the encounter as something that had not taken place.

O'Hare said, "Another night, perhaps."

"Yes," the black man replied. "Another night."

They both seemed to be asking for Calla's concordance. She knew it would be pointless to meet again; she could never come to terms with the man.

"Yes, perhaps another night," she said.

She started toward the door; the black man moved, in a mock gallant gesture, to open it for them. As she edged by him she saw that he was not giving her much room, as if he wanted her to brush against his body. She was careful not to, but felt that they had indeed touched one another. Even when she was a number of feet away, walking along the colonnade, she still felt the contact.

About to reenter the store, she couldn't help herself. She had to look back to see if he was still there. He was. The light of the outdoor lantern cast a glow upon him, and he was standing splendid and tall, his head inclined backward, as if he were gazing through the canopy of creepers overhead, watching for a motion in the sky.

Then he did an unexpected thing. He worked the hand as if it gave him pain.

There was a kind of scrutiny that a director concentrated upon an actor or actress that Calla called The Naked I. It did not signify that the director was naked, but that his eye stripped bare the actor's ego. Actually, it was a probing examination not by his vision alone, but by all his senses, by all the powers of his mind. His object was to x-ray everything, to peer through clothes and camouflage, defenses and pretenses, hangups and resistances and blockages. The Naked I denuded her of all physical and spiritual clothing. She hated it.

She hated it not only for personal reasons but for professional ones. The search and seizure ripped through her occupational safeguards and stole her trade secrets. A trade secret might be any kind of private, precious device she had found or invented, something not necessarily real, and frequently irrational, that she relied upon to catch a character or vivify a scene. It could be an intimate memory tripping an emotion, a gesture she had kept in mind but did not offer, an image of the other actor as a silk scarf or a pig or a mosquito bite; or it might be a conjured costume of rain or itching powder or curiosity. Inalienable secrets, all of them, at the heart of her player's mystery, that dare not be divulged. She was enraged at a director who exposed her. Paradoxically, The Naked I was an x-ray possessed by only the best directors; the worst had no rays at all. Sometimes, and only in this regard, she preferred the worst.

Tonight, driving home from the meeting with Julasto, she felt that O'Hare was turning her clothes to cellophane. Without even looking at her, with his eyes focused only on the road, the director saw her secret: she was sexually attracted to Julasto. She wondered how soon, and in what way, he would exploit this insight in getting her to do the film. On their first meeting, she would have said: he'll jump the gun. Now she wasn't certain.

"Intrigued you, didn't he?"

She must find the precise reading. "I found him interesting."

"I could see that."

What would disarm him? Thesis talk. "He's a societal danger."

"And rough in the clinches."

A gibe. The academic stuff had fizzled. He was on to her. She felt a sting.

What particularly provoked her was her conviction that the director had intended her to be attracted by the black man; he had staged it. Suggesting that she see a fire demonstration and meet a man of magic, what he meant was: Come and meet a strikingly well-favored male, see him virile and nude, larger than life, running a little rampant, with a dangerous cast to him and a promise of excitement. O'Hare could not be a good director if he did not know the uses of libido. Bringing her here tonight was devious. A tricky manipulator. Take care.

She stopped. The thoughts she was entertaining were just short of paranoia. He had done nothing unprincipled. Why did she feel the director was plotting against her? This irrational resistance—against what? Attraction? Was she being drawn to O'Hare as well as Julasto?

Two men in an evening? What an idiot I'm turning out to be, she thought. Here it is again, the need to be with a man, the demeaning horniness—and why am I blaming him for it, erecting a defense against a man who might never attack me?

Attack.

It was his relationship to Willi that had made her so nervous. She wasn't being so damned irrational after all; she had a right to distrust him. That instant of warning between him and Julasto when the black man had mentioned Willi's name. . . . There was some knot of relationship among the three of them.

"How well does Julasto know Willi?"

He was quick but guarded. "You think he knows her? He said he doesn't."

"He was lying."

"Why would he lie?"

"Why would you?"

His response was shrewd: no words, only a glance that said she was getting unhinged.

Still, she persisted. "Why *would* you lie?"

"I really have no answer to that." He was unruffled. "You'll have to supply one yourself."

In a while, they drove up Benedict Canyon, then off onto the side road. The street she lived on was underlighted and deserted; it was hours past midnight; no sign of the extra patrol car that Reuss had promised. Ever since Sharon's murder, Calla was always sure someone was lurking behind the next eugenia hedge; the shadows of pepper trees were always ready to leap from the ground. And since the attack on Willi, and the telephone voice, she was terrified to enter the house alone.

They arrived at her driveway, pulled into it, and sat in the motionless car for a moment. When she glanced at the unlighted house, he must have seen her apprehension. He offered to come in and look around, and she had a surging impulse to say yes.

"No—thanks. I'll be all right."

"Just a quick look around?"

"No, really—I'm not uneasy."

"You sure?"

"Absolutely. Thanks."

His offer had been considerate, and her response, politely grateful. Yet, she was certain he felt as she did, that they had just had a quarrel.

A question of trust had arisen, whether she could risk having him in her house tonight. If they had spoken further, she might have admitted that she distrusted not only him but herself. That, however, would have seemed a coy challenge in the sex game, and an invitation. So she said nothing, nor did he, and the tacit battle was over, both sides losing. She thanked him tersely for the evening. Getting out of the car, she could feel the wave of anger following her.

She hurried, fumbled in her purse, found her key and shoved it into the lock.

Calla didn't hear him leaving the car. As she opened the door, she suddenly caught the sound of him, on the path behind her, running. He streaked across the lawn and gravel, and rushed past her into the shadows of the foyer.

She was in a panic. She had no idea what was in his mind. She could not speak.

She heard him in the hallway, blundering about in the blackness, slapping at the walls to find a light switch, fumbling and cursing.

The foyer came ablaze with light. He looked to the right and left, not knowing which way to go. He rushed into the study. Again, she heard him smashing about for lights, and again saw the flare of whiteness. Almost instantly, he was out of there and across the hall, into the kitchen-dining room. Lights, everywhere the bungling and anger, cursing for the light, followed by electricity, a shout of it. She heard him thrashing through the garden, falling all over his strangeness and vexation, enraged at the indignity, coming in again, rushing past her, not acknowledging her presence. The downstairs bathroom then, and lights, the living room and lights, and out upon the terrace. Back again, he took the staircase three steps at a time. She heard him ransacking the dark, sweeping through the second floor, opening doors, bathrooms, bedrooms, closets.

He came down the stairs almost as swiftly as he had ascended them. She still stood in the foyer, motionless.

"You're safe," he said. "There's nobody here to bother you."

She could feel his fury like a gust.

In an instant, he was gone. She heard the car pull away. Then, silence. She had never, in this place, felt such a shrieking vulgarity of light. And everything, wherever she went, was open—doors, French windows, closets. He had left her house unbuttoned, and herself as well.

Slowly, switch by switch, she turned down the lights.

Still she felt unclothed, felt he had seen her temptation to have him come inside. And once indoors, for all her fright, she had been excited by the man, by the sheer muscularity of his search, the animality of his anger. That spurt, that gush of wild energy—if he had let her share it with him . . .

Even now, with the lights nearly all extinguished, she could still feel his swift, hot motion in her house.

She did an impulsive thing. Hurrying into the study, she found the script of *The Fabulist* and, as if to exorcise him, threw it into the wastebasket.

A few more lights and she was in the dimness of the bedroom. But even the bed lamp was too much; it hurt her eyes. She had a headache.

Aspirin.

She awakened in the night to the ringing of the phone. When she answered it, nobody was there, the line was dead. She hung up, had a random thought about Mina, years ago, toddling, learning how to walk. Getting out of bed, she made herself a hot toddy, with bourbon. There was rather more whiskey than usual in it and because it cooled the tea, she was able to drink it fast. It made her a little whoozy and she liked the feeling, so she had another bourbon, a small one. It was more than enough and she regretted she could not drink a great deal without getting sick.

The telephone rang again. She answered it and began to shake.

"Oh, Calla, I'm sorry," he said. "I can't tell you how terribly sorry I am about Willi."

"Who are you?"

"Do be careful, Calla. I warned you, didn't I? It was time, I said— I warned you."

"You did it, didn't you?"

"Come, now."

"You did it!"

"Do be careful, Calla. Terrible things—do be careful."

"You did it! You did, you did!"

"You're diddering."

"Just tell me—why?"

"Don't be stupid. I couldn't go at anybody with a knife."

"You're lying!"

"I'm not. And you're behaving like a hysterical idiot. Even if I had done such a hideous thing to Willi, do you think I would admit it? Would you?"

"I don't have to admit anything—I didn't *do* anything."

"Who knows?"

"Who knows what?"

"Exactly—who knows what? Who ever knows who did anything?"

"What the hell are you talking about?"

"A catastrophe like this—it's a murderous tangle. Who knows who's under suspicion? Who knows who's in danger? Who knows what errors are made—and what plans are designed to *look* like errors? Even you, Calla—it's not likely you mutilated your own friend with your own hands. But who knows how responsible you were?"

"You son of a bitch, you son of a bitch!"

He hung up, and so did she. She stood there trembling, not knowing what to do. She tried to keep hearing the voice so that its familiarity would strike recognition in her brain. It was familiar, even more so tonight than it had been the first time. Yet, oddly, there was a new shading she had not noticed before. Perhaps she was making it up, perhaps it was the bourbon still at work. But she could have sworn that there was another cadence in the British voice. Was it a black man pretending to be white?

7

In the morning she telephoned Lieutenant Reuss. He was not impressed.

"Just a voice on the telephone," he said.

"Not just a voice, but a voice disguised in a special way."

"You had a few drinks, you say?"

Annoyed: "Look, Lieutenant, I was not drunk. And I have a well-trained ear."

"But you can't actually say it was Julasto."

"No, I can't. I've only spoken to the man once. And he's . . . variable."

"The fire trick—did he tell you how he did it?"

"No."

"It had to be phony, of course."

"Well, they certainly didn't incinerate him." He was passing over the importance of the phone call, and it provoked her. "There was another thing the man said on the phone."

"Yes—what?"

" 'Who knows what plans are designed to *look* like errors?' "

"What do you take that to mean?"

"That they actually *meant* to harm Willi—and not me."

"Why?"

". . . I don't know."

Nor could she guess. Because . . . she didn't know Willi as intimately as she had thought. If the woman had in some way consorted with O'Hare and Julasto . . . But what hard evidence was there that she had consorted with anybody? A pair of bedroom slippers, an extra tube of toothpaste?

"Could I have a look at Willi's apartment?" she said.
"Of course. I have the keys. Can I pick you up this afternoon?"
"Yes—any time."
"Say three o'clock."

He picked her up in an ordinary Buick without police insignia. Wearing a bright foulard scarf in the open throat of his raw silk shirt, he smiled as if they were going on a weekend.

As he drove to Willi's apartment, Reuss asked, "Did you know that the director—Lucas O'Hare—came to see her on the *Tie-Dye* set?"

"He came to see me."

She said it impulsively, not meaning to offer an alibi for the man.

The lieutenant nodded. "That's what he said."

"You've seen him?"

"Yes, right after your call. How come he came to see you when you weren't there?"

"I was expected. They had scheduled some retakes. I didn't go."

"Exactly what he claims."

He seemed disappointed not to have caught the man in a lie. "How well does he know Willi?"

"How well did he say?"

"You mean you don't know?"

"No, I don't," she replied.

"He says he hardly knows her at all."

"Well, then."

"You don't believe that, do you?"

"I don't know." After a moment. "Did you ask him about Julasto?"

"And Willi, you mean?"

"Yes."

"He gave me a big stare on that one. Didn't know a damn thing." Reuss was being quite open with her, and she wondered why; there had to be some method in it. "Whoever the fellow is—black or white—he hasn't been around for a while and isn't coming back. He's certainly not stepping forward to be recognized."

Reaching into his inside breast pocket, he pulled out a blue leatherbound address book. She recognized it as Willi's. "This thing isn't very helpful," he said. "Damn near everybody's in it. Would you like to look?"

"I've seen it lots of times."

"I mean, if you saw any names that were strange . . ."

She took it. "Any number of them would be strange. She does everything for me—publicity, house, car—there are people whose names I never hear. Do you really want me to go through it?"

"Just on the ride. Give you something to do."

She went through it quickly. There was no point: half the names were unrecognizable. She returned the book.

"O'Hare's quite a guy, isn't he?" he said.

She didn't know what he meant. Director, writer, cocksman? She rather suspected he meant the last.

They turned up Laurel Canyon and approached the condominium. Willi's residence was a first- and second-floor duplex, with a large kitchen and living-dining room downstairs, and an iron spiral staircase to two bedrooms and a bath. As they came within sight of the place, Calla was certain that this trip would be wasted. She knew precisely what she would see inside Willi's apartment. Years ago, she had stayed in the smaller bedroom for a month and, later, for a weekend. In all the times she had been there, hardly anything had changed. It was a quiet and airy retreat, sparsely furnished, a haven of serenity. Willi decorated not with ornament but with space. Like the woman, her domicile was devoid of phony excess, unencumbered, bare to the wood, and sensible.

When the detective unlocked the door, Calla gasped.

It was a macabre museum.

The downstairs rooms were jammed with stuff. An enormous plant dominated everything, flattening its branches against the ceiling, its leaves as large as tennis rackets, a voracity of growth, spongy and rank. It hovered over everything in the room—the artifacts, the primitive urns and shards of pottery, the huge bone-colored phrenological head, and the tarot card mural depicting a man's torso, lightning struck, with the words *Le Feu du Ciel* written across his bare chest, and flames blazing out of his eyes. Next to it there was a hood mask on a plinth, stiff with incrustations of clay as if it had been unearthed, the hair made of shredded raffia, twisted, worked into tendrils, black, brown, gray; it had horns so that it was as much an antelope as a man, the curl of the antlers exquisite and real, at odds with the horrifying totality of it. And everywhere in the room, in every corner, on every bookshelf and windowsill, were pieces of statuary, all primitive, hewn in a primordial exaggeration, heads small and bodies voluptuous, gargantuan breasts and thighs and penises, all with the hint of covert African laughter. The odor in the place was something fainter and more sensual than the incense in the Arts Afriques shop in Redondo, but it had a similar muskiness.

It was as if she had stepped into a haunt, a black coven with amulets and madstones and caps of darkness. It couldn't possibly have anything to do with Willi, the rational, commonsensical Willi. Yet, this place was her home. It was frightening.

"Want to go upstairs?" Reuss asked.

She did not want to but she did. There was the room Calla had slept in, seeming about the same, but Willi's bedroom was beyond recognition. It had been full of sunlight, as she remembered it, a smile of yellow. Now, however, it was all somberness and shadow, with heavy curtains lapped over one another, permitting little light, and the bed canopied with the kind of netting that might be draped to shut out flying, crawling, poison-bearing things.

She saw the mobile. It hung from the ceiling at a distance from the bed. The rings suspending it were made of black wood, ebony perhaps. And the two figures were the same material, except that there was a low-gleaming luster to them. The man's hands were on the woman's buttocks and the female's were lovingly on the sides of his head as if to cover his ears and give them a gift of silence. They were black people not only in the wood that made them but in their features, inexpressibly beautiful. Yet, like the figures downstairs, their thighs and buttocks were too enormous for reality, and while the woman's breasts were not so immense as to seem unreal, they were distended to the point of bursting, so that one could almost feel the surging rush of blood. The heaviness, even the grossness of the individual figures should not have combined to make such a perfection, such an aerial float of lightness as to take the breath away.

Then, as Reuss opened the door to a closet, disturbing the stillness of the air, the mobile moved and suddenly there was an illusion. The figures, stirring in the faintest current, seemed to vibrate in an act of loving—delicate—almost imperceptible. Their bodies were in motion with one another, their limbs no longer wood but flesh and bone articulated. He seemed to move inside her, her arms seemed to tremble and her legs to writhe and thrust into the open space. Calla could not stand to watch, it was the most provocative lovemaking she had ever seen in art, and while it first seemed a thing of erotic beauty, the very act of viewing turned it into pornography. She looked away.

Reuss was gazing steadily at her. His stare compounded the pornographic act, and she averted her glance.

Later, in his car again, she realized why the man had been so seemingly candid. He had had that surprise ready to spring on her, and observe her reaction to another Willi than she had known. He was observing shock.

"Was it like anything you saw in the African shop?" he asked.

"Yes and no."

He smiled. "We can build an airtight case on that."

But it was the best she could do. Not one of Willi's objects was like anything Calla had seen at Arts Afriques or even in Julasto's cottage. Yet, they might all have had the same African source. There had to be a connection. The black man's claim that he had never met Willi was obviously untenable. He and O'Hare were perpetrating a weird lie about the whole relationship. What was the truth of it?

Calla was shaken. She couldn't assemble the two women into a single comprehensible Willi Axil. She had never had a friend whom she had known so well and so intimately, and now she didn't know her at all. Two different people, yin and yang, and a mystery. Willi had been her rock of reality, the basic no-nonsense of her life, and she had abruptly become a bizarre stranger. The actress had the sinking sense that because some part of her double had been kept from her, perhaps the most revealing part, she was thereby losing part of herself. She felt betrayed, cheated by a friend. She ached, and couldn't bear the loss.

"You think she bought all that stuff herself?" Reuss asked.

"I don't know."

"Or was it given to her?"

"I don't know."

"Well—whatever—it must've come from the black man's place," he said. "We're following up on it."

"Yes," she said, hardly listening. "Could you drop me at the hospital?"

Yesterday, when Calla had gone to the hospital, Willi was still in intensive care. Today she was in a private room. Nothing of her face was visible through the mask of bandages, except her nostrils and a lacuna of flesh around her mouth.

"Could I sit with her a while?" she asked the nurse.

"She won't know you're here, Miss Stark."

"Could I just sit with her?"

The nurse murmured something about pressing the bell button if she was needed, and went away.

Calla sat on the chrome chair beside the bed. She didn't do anything, she simply gazed at the mound of Willi. Helpless, she wanted to be comforting or healing, or simply a presence that her friend would subliminally recognize, and warm to. She wanted to be Willi's stand-in in a moment of pain.

The largest area of naked flesh was Willi's hand, so she took it in her own. It was limp, totally inert and a little damp. Calla wiped it on the sleeve of her blouse, then held it awhile. She tried to make it warmer, and couldn't. She held it to her cheek and rocked as if she held a child.

"Oh, Willi," she said softly.

Then she said it again, oh, Willi, not because she hoped her friend would hear her, but because it made her imagine they were talking together.

After a time, she asked a question, emptily. How are you, how are you? Suddenly, not meaning it, the "how" became "who," and Calla began to cry. When she stopped crying, she resumed talking to the woman in the bed, simply because she needed to talk to her, to talk to someone, she needed comfort, she, the conscious one, she had no one to love and to weep with, not Megan, a continent away in New York, nor Barney, lost somewhere in Europe, there was nobody . . .

"Barney . . ."

She hadn't meant to say it aloud. Bad enough to think of him; worse to utter his name. She hadn't cried for him—how long was it? But she needed him now, she wanted him here beside her—she needed him.

Oh, Barney, she cried again, how did we make such a mess—!

. . . It was toward the end of 1969, the year after Mina was born, when everything went wrong. Barney lost a film part he coveted, then a picture he was almost signed for was abruptly called off, and for months thereafter he did not go to a single meeting or audition. Calla too: overnight, it seemed, the wind was out of her pennant. *Not War, Not Peace*, which had had its fades and flashes, had finally paled away into disappointment. She made another film, *Private Entrance*, a failure. The flow of manuscripts began to dwindle. The bankable star was overpriced, they said; she was too distinct a type and hard to cast; she had lost her audience. Some said she had been only a fad.

"They're scared of you," Barney said. "Why the hell do you want to get mixed up in politics—you're an actress. You go out into that arena—and we can get killed out there."

He had said "you" and then "we." If they were scared, so was he.

Truth to tell, she was as frightened as her husband.

But she had returned to the barricades because she had needed cleansing. The very air of Hollywood gave off a fetor of corruption. The place was ridden with hypocrisy. It preached the pieties of a decent, healthy liberalism, and lived in baronial decay. Its films inveighed against the narcotic peddlers, yet there was scarcely a Hollywood party where drugs were not openly available, served as amenities. The producers mounted the fables of the new feminism on the screen, and continued banging the little ingenues in return for littler parts. They talked about every new film with the spirituality of holy men on mountaintops, but they slithered down into the wallow with any venality that sold a ticket.

She wanted to flee. But she could not leave Hollywood because she loved Barney, and their marriage was in it. Also, it would be too painful to depart as a failure. She had started with a bright success, and perhaps her next film . . .

The only recourse was action.

Nixon had been in office for nearly a year. All his resourceful schemes to bring a quick peace were nothing more than the increased bombings, the mounting waste of lives, the deadlier deceits wrapped in patriotic catchwords. And as the war escalated, there was talk of escalating it still further, into Cambodia.

With thickening dread, yet with her old exhilaration, Calla became an activist again. But the battle had changed; there was more gore and less glory. The infighting had begun, not only against the advocates of the war, but among the pacifists themselves. The range of rebels was broader than it had been; the carnage had made strange marching companions—liberals, conservatives, socialists, Communists, intellectuals, lovers, haters, crazies. And while they fought together against the Administration, they also wrangled with each other. Calla found herself in the middle of one of these quarrels.

One night she received an anonymous phone call from a woman who complimented her on—gallantry, was the word she used. She in-

vited the star to attend a cell meeting—an "inner dynamics group."
Calla politely declined, saying she did not want to be considered a
Communist. A few days later, an unsigned note arrived, repeating the
invitation, giving the time and place of the meeting. She ignored it. An-
other phone call, this time from a man, also anonymous. Angry now,
Calla hung up.

Overnight, she became the subject of bad-mouthing. The activists
said she was available for fancy luncheons and dinners where money-
raising for the cause was incidental to being seen, that she was a cock-
tail-party rebel. Radical chic, others added; a celebrity who chose her
shots, close-ups generally, with full camera coverage. She could be
called upon for only selected performances, Cameo Calla.

When she heard the slur, Calla allowed herself an evening of tears,
then once more—furious and fighting—took to her battle station. Thereafter, she stayed away from Beverly Hills dinners and Bel Air garden
parties as if they were under quarantine. Instead, she spent her time
with bail bondsmen and in magistrates' courts, getting people out of
jail; she attended all-night meetings, planning and bickering and chop-
ping logic; she typed stencils and ran Addressographs; cadged free space
in meeting halls and movie theaters and granges, and gave speeches in
schools and churches and synagogues and lodges; she paralyzed her
voice and her brain and her telephone ear. One day she fainted. There
was no damn reason to do that, she said, until she realized she had been
going for thirty hours, with no sleep, too much coffee, too little food.

Then she gave her speech at the Directors Guild, where Lucas
O'Hare reduced her to rubble. If she always considered, not altogether
accurately, that his attack was the start of her public misfortunes, there
was reason. The troubles began with the trade paper report of his assault, and for the first time she read the hint that she was a Communist.

The second reference came in early spring, after America invaded
Cambodia. There was an anti-war demonstration in the plaza outside
Union Station. In a modest meeting, without fanfare, there were low-
key speeches by representatives of a dozen civic organizations. A group
of perhaps fifty Mexican-Americans marched eastward out of Olvera
Street and joined the audience. Whispers said that there were Weather-
men and Black Panthers interspersed among the crowd. Whoever was
there, it still seemed a common cause, and everything was going on
peacefully when, out of nowhere, there was a gunshot. It looked as

though there would be a panic—a woman was lying on the ground, wounded.

As if on cue, the cops started pouring in from all directions—motorcycles, squad cars, forty or fifty policemen on foot.

People ran, people fell. It became a shrieking riot. There were bludgeonings, there was herding by horses and there was blood. Calla, starting to run, saw a policeman bearing down on a boy, fuzzy-bearded, hardly more than seventeen. As the club came down for a second time, she rushed at the cop and pushed him. He struck at her and missed. She heard a siren, a warning shout quite close, and suddenly she was in handcuffs.

At the police station, she called Barney, and by midnight she was out. She had paid a fifty-dollar fine and gotten a ten-day suspended sentence.

The morning papers had her picture. One headline read: *Calla Conks a Cop.* Written like a theatrical review, it was unfavorable, untrue and had more than a touch of acid in it. Pinko, it said.

She had been booked and convicted; now she had a record. The newspapers could call her lawbreaker, criminal, even without the word "alleged." She was a dissident—one of the more polite terms—a troublemaker, a radical, a red. The lead article in a trade paper, concurring, called her a dirty Communist. So did others.

One evening she had her first hate call. The following day, as her car was halted by a traffic light, a man rushed to her open window and sloshed a container of coffee in her face. The anonymous calls never stopped, morning, daytime, in the dead of night. On her birthday, she received a present, a beautiful beribboned package, and as she lifted it out of the mailbox, she heard a fluttering sound, like bird's wings. On reflex, she tossed it away. The instant it hit the ground, it exploded, ripping a grave-size pit in the lawn. From that time onward, Calla and Barney never parked their cars outdoors, but only in the garage, fitted with heavy locks and an alarm. But in her car she was terrified every time she turned the ignition key. And it worried them that their Trancas house was so isolated.

The hate letters were insulting, threatening and obscene. One of the most frightening ones, however, did not come from an enemy but "A Friend." It read:

Watch out, Calla. You're on three lists—one of them is Nixon's.

And there were no film offers. For a while she had been getting marginal scripts from marginal producers; now even those stopped coming.

"Barney's right," Megan said. "The producers are afraid of you."

"Probably. But it's because I've had two failures."

"Only one. You can't call *Not War, Not Peace* a failure."

"That's what *they're* calling it."

"I'm not saying it has nothing to do with it, Cal. But the point is, we're at war, and the studios think you're a . . ."

"Traitor."

There were a lot of people using Nixonian epithets. Lyndon Johnson, hating opposition to the war, had considered it a maddening aspect of cantankerous democracy; to Nixon, it was treason.

"Do you think I'm a traitor, Meg?"

"Calla—no. But what difference does it make what I think? I bring up your name and they have a convulsion."

"Millions of people are saying what I'm saying."

"But not so loud. You're overprojecting, Calla. Hollywood's a tiny theater."

Calla could see that the woman had been battling for her more desperately than she had suspected. And had lost. She felt sorrier for Megan than for herself.

"You want to cut the knot, Megan?"

"Don't be stupid."

"It's not stupid. Tear up my contract."

"Like hell I will," she said. "But you know what you have to do, don't you?"

"Go back to New York."

When Megan departed, Calla remained on the terrace, looking westward across the Trancas beach. It was June, but such an unseasonably gray and fogbound day that she could barely see Point Dume. The sea was turbid, resentful, as if it had a grudge against every wave.

New York . . . Was there a chance, the vaguest possibility of a chance that Barney would agree to go?

She heard Mina awakening from her nap. Entering the study, which now doubled as the child's bedroom, Calla lifted her out of the crib, let her half toddle and half crawl into the kitchen and fed her a few spoonfuls of what Barney called fruit goosh. She watched the baby eat it, then bang on the empty pewter dish with the spoon. Mina was over her post-nap frettishness now and jabbering happily; some burbles sounded like words. The little girl wanted more goosh, which she received and appreciated, but did not eat; she slapped both hands into the stuff, slushed it about the kitchen and told it, in effect, that she had won. Calla smiled a little and swore a little and smoothed the child's beautiful blond hair and called her slob, and Mina giggled.

Calla made her decision. If Barney said no to New York, she would not make an issue of it. Their marriage was not as certifiably strong as it used to be; there were fractures, widening. He thought the public image she was making of herself, obviously harmful to her, was a dissipation. Winning the moral argument was an ego luxury at a prohibitive cost. And she was not only blackening her own bright career, she was besmirching his. Like Megan, he was guilty by association. One of the studio executives, recently forgiven for padding a payroll, pontificated that he who touches pitch will be defiled; Barney's agent thought he meant bitch. Whatever the man meant, the actor's career was suffering.

Since that was the case, why wouldn't Barney also want to leave Hollywood? His misgivings about Broadway were neurotic, she thought. He had worked on the stage in a fine theater, and the difference between a short run in Minneapolis and a long run in Manhattan was not the difference between a good actor and a bad one. . . . She would talk him into it.

She started rather well, she thought, that night at dinner. Genuinely taking the blame for their predicament, she said that the misfortune might turn into a blessing. Even financially it was not too wild a risk.

"This house, for example," she said. "If we put it up for rent, we'd get more than we'd have to pay for an apartment in New York."

"Calla . . . I can't do it."

"We won't have to commit ourselves forever, Barney. Only a little while. At the most, a year."

"I can't, Cal. I got a part today."

She put down her coffee cup. "You got a part?"

"Yes."

"And you didn't tell me?"

"Well . . . it's a script I don't think you'll like."

She laughed hollowly. "We can't exactly be choosy, can we?"

It was a little eccentric, the delayed announcement of his good luck; so was her reserved response. Yet, she had merely fallen in with his mood. She hadn't cheered over his getting the job because he was not too happy about it, and his manner discouraged jubilation.

"I'd like you to read the script," he said.

Getting up from the table, he brought the bound copy to the living room. He muttered some imprecation upon the cold nights in June, lighted the fire with the gas jet, and puttered with the logs. The script lay there, on the davenport, saying more to them than they said to each other.

She watched him play with Mina, talking as if the child understood every word, and Calla thought: How loving he is with her, how kind and strong. She trusts him to hold her in the air and pretend to let her fall; babies are afraid of falling and loud noise, the books said, but not Mina, not with her father. There was an emanation from him that gave the little girl her extra courage. And gave him courage as well. Perhaps the role of father was his greatest part, perhaps this was where the actor and the man were most lovingly at home with one another. Maybe with Mina and Mina alone he was the real Barney, playing no part at all. He was allowing the child, only his beloved child, to have access to *himself*. With her he was not afraid, he was valiant.

It saddened Calla to realize that he retained his courage only with Mina, and was losing it everywhere else. And maybe she herself was at fault. His life, since they had met, had been built around her. In their first and only film together, he had been her supporting player. It was a role he was still playing. Only with Mina was he a leading man, nowhere else. Not in his career, not with his wife, whose star, even while blighted, shone brighter than his own. She was the potent one. No matter how deeply Calla loved him, no matter that she loved him with all her life, she had not allowed him to *change* her life. She had not altered any of her convictions for her own comfort or her own success . . . nor for his. Guiltily, she realized she had been asking him to spend as much of his life for her persuasions as she was willing to spend of her own. And he had been trying and couldn't.

She was frightened that he was scored for failure, worried that she might contribute to it, and did not know how to go about preventing such a catastrophe. There was nothing she could do to assist him, nothing. If changing the tenor of their honest marriage into a lie of some sort would help him, she would play the falsehood to the last deception; but she knew she had no talent for such trickery, and he had a great talent for detecting it. Christ, she thought, how can I love him so much and help him so little? . . . And what if all I have for him is harm?

When Mina and Barney were both in bed, she picked up his

script. The summer night was getting colder, and she was at odds with herself and the unseasonable chill. She added a log to the fire. The blaze seemed to come from a fake fireplace on a stage set, a trick display of light, showy but lifeless, offering no heat or comfort.

Turning off all the lamps except one, she sat and read the screenplay. *The Beer Hall* was the love story of an American nurse and a German intern in Berlin just prior to the ascendancy of Hitler, and through the war. It was a touching story in many ways, but there was one thing that gave Calla the shivers. When she finished reading the script, she felt that Nazis were extremely decent people who had no choice but to go with Hitler, wherever his perverted cruelty led them. In fact, the American woman, hideously destroyed in a concentration camp, was made to seem priggishly insensitive to the pitiful German dilemma, not wholly undeserving of her horrible fate.

Calla was upset by the script, and could not imagine who in this film community, with its strongly Jewish feeling, pro-Israel, anti-Hitler, would ever want to make such a picture. She looked at the title page again; the names of the producer, writer, director were all unfamiliar, so she assumed the production would be done at the fringes somewhere, on a small budget. Who might these people be, neo-Nazis? . . . and her husband?

She could not believe he would take the part. True, times had been leaden recently, but they had never been golden for him; he had always played what he called pickup stuff, second parts, third, fourth, surplus roles often left on the cutting room floor.

But this was the hero's role, his first . . . warm and poignant.

Too poignant, the brave, lamentable, sympathetic Nazi.

In the stillness of the chilly, dimly lighted living room she sat with the frightening screenplay in her lap. Surely, he didn't need her opinion of the manuscript; he was always more instinctively right than she was about plays of every kind. He knew that this was a vicious instrument. And she must stop imposing her conscience upon him; he had his own.

When she went to bed, hoping he was asleep, she tried to make as small a stir as possible. He was awake.

"Did you read it?" he asked.

"Yes."

"What do you think?"

"I'd rather not talk about it."

"I want to hear what you have to say."

"No, Barney."

"Is it that bad?"

"Barney, please."

"I want to hear you say it. Is it that bad?"

He was pressing her too hard. "Are you really going to do that script?"

"Yes, I am."

"All right, then—let's not say anymore."

"You've already said plenty."

"My God, why do you want to do it?"

"Because it's a great part."

"It may be—but who would want to play it?"

"If you mean that everybody has turned it down, I'm sure you're right."

"I didn't say that."

"Whether you did or not, it's probably true. I'm not a great actor, Calla—I'm not as good as you are. If I'm offered a part like this, it's only a fluke. I have to take it."

"But there will be others. You're better than you think."

"Quit that," he said.

It was as if he had finally come to face a truth about himself: Whatever his talent was, it had no built-in destiny for glory; whatever chance for success he had, it would come by luck alone, and he must snatch for it.

"I'm taking the part, Calla."

She lay in bed, unable to sleep, loving him and hurting that he should have to do such a thing. She wanted desperately to soothe his distress, to give him back something he had lost, his faith that he was a fine actor, any hope that once had given him the courage to walk across a stage.

Much later, still awake, feeling adrift from him and getting frightened by the widening distance, she touched him. She knew that he too was awake, and she wanted them not to lie in the same bed, so many rooms apart. Gently she kissed his shoulder and put her hand on his arm, caressing it; then she let her hand move to the front of him. Although their love life had faltered in the last few months, they had nearly always had a mutuality of wanting, the degrees being uneven perhaps, and the timings not necessarily simultaneous, but never, to her knowledge, had there been the indignity of a deception. Now, however, as she was touching him, he made a sleepy noise, a slurry moan of displeasure at being awakened. She knew he hadn't been asleep. She removed her hand and turned away.

During Barney's first two weeks of shooting, the lie continued. But he was indeed working hard, seven days a week and long hours, rising before dawn and often coming home at midnight. He could have been too tired to make love, or talk, or smile.

Yet he never seemed too fatigued for Mina. Always, when the teething child awakened in the night, he would be the first out of bed. He would lift the baby out of her crib, change her diaper, give her warm milk, walk with her to the window and, holding her snugly in his arms, wait until the sea sounds lulled her back to sleep. Calla pretended not to notice, but it filled her with dread. Not that she was jealous of the child, far from it; his love of the baby was the one unifying thing they could count on right now; it was as if they had lost their common language, and could not summon a single word that would reaffirm their love.

One night he returned quite late from location shooting. He had barely had time to catch the company bus back to the city, and was still wearing his uniform. Calla was in bed, but hearing him in the living room, she called to tell him she was awake. He knew what a pall the swastika would cast, so he told her he was dressed in his horror suit, and for her not to come see him. Too late. She appeared at the doorway and saw the chilling regalia. She pulled her robe tighter. With no wish to be hostile, and anxious to avoid confrontation, she flew to a silliness.

"Heil, handsome."

He was very still.

"I don't think that's funny, Calla."

She was ashamed of her inanity. "What I meant—you look very handsome in your uniform."

"My Nazi uniform, you mean."

"I wasn't being specific." Then, lamely, starting to give up, "I merely commented on the way you look."

"Do I look like Hitler?"

She was cautious. "I wouldn't say the resemblance is striking."

"Do you think every German looks like Hitler?"

"Not every man, woman and child, no. They don't all have mustaches."

"If you can stop being clever, I'd like to ask you a direct question. Don't you think—man, woman and child—there were any decent Nazis?"

"No. There were decent Germans, yes—but not decent Nazis."

"What if you had to be a Nazi?"

"I don't have to be a Nazi. I will never have to be a Nazi—I will always have an alternative."

"Death, you mean."

"No. I don't think death is the inevitable alternative. I don't think you necessarily have to die the death of a hero in order to be courageous. There are a thousand kinds of daily courage—ordinary courage—"

"You can talk about ordinary courage, but you can't talk about ordinary fear, can you? The part I'm playing—"

"He's a coward."

"He's not."

"And he's cruel."

"What choice does he have?"

"Tell me about the command scene, Barney—how are you going to play it?"

"Which command scene—there are a number of them."

"The first one. When the adjutant tells you to load the wagon with the second group of Jews, and you suddenly realize where they're going."

"I'll play it as it's written."

"But how? 'This hurts me worse than it does you'?"

"Of course. There's no other way to play it."

"Sympathetically."

"Always play villains sympathetically—you taught me that."

"Not a Nazi."

"Your politics are muddling your art."

"Not really. If you play a villain sympathetically, you have to find ways of justifying him, don't you?"

"Well?"

"Can you find any justification for sending a wagonload of people who have committed no crime—men, women and children—to a gas chamber?"

"Justification—?"

"Justification."

"Justification isn't everything, Calla. How about extenuation? How about a little empathy? Can't you feel a little sorry for a German who *has* to do it? Can't you feel sorry for a whole nation that—"

"In that script, I do feel sorry for them! That's what's so terrible about the picture—I feel sorry for them! He sends them to a gas chamber—and I excuse him. The adjutant throws them into a pit of quicklime—and I excuse him. I excuse all of them. Which means I'll excuse them a second time. And that is terribly, terribly wrong!"

"Wrong? What has wrong got to do with pity? Don't you pity the poor bastard for having to do it? Where's your pity?"

"Pity? Christ! Ask the Jewish lampshade about pity!"

"You're not a Jew!"

"*Yes I am.*"

He was silent, and she thought he was taking her literally, he had forgotten who she was, where she came from, who her parents had been. Utter estrangement. He tensed and made a strangled sound, as if he were choking. She was frightened—he looked ill—a stroke, perhaps—but all at once he seemed to smash through his suffocation, his arm swung wildly, his fist struck, and the glass of the front window shattered.

"Barney—no!"

He stood there, perplexed, his eyes glazed, unable to connect his act with the wind gusting through the jagged opening, and his hand, bleeding.

For some time, while she was bandaging his wound, he was in a daze. He didn't seem to know what she was doing, or what he himself had done. He watched the bandaging process with detached interest. Luckily, the heavy uniform had protected him; the wounds were not on the arm or wrist but across the knuckles. She bound them tightly, and he thanked her with quiet gratitude, as if she had ministered to nothing more unusual than a cold. And he went to bed.

She tacked a blanket over the window frame to keep the wind from blustering through the house, and remained awake.

She hated herself for not realizing how desperate he had been. He felt as guilty about playing the part as she needed him to feel, but he had had to accept the role, for nobody else wanted him. Acting was all he could do; he was not a versatile man, only a versatile actor. But he was not unthinking or unfeeling; she did not have to point out to him that when he animated certain sympathies in an audience, he was responsible for them. She had no need to give him lessons in integrity, and had vowed to herself that she would not be his conscience. Why had she torn him down?

She knew what she had to do: Stop being his rebuke. Hands off.

Later, when she entered the bedroom, she saw the glow of his lighted cigarette.

"Barney . . ."

She started quietly, and stopped. I'm not going to be able to make it, she thought, I'm going to fall apart. Still, she continued:

"I want you to know that I love you very much. But I think I ought to go back to New York for a while—at least until you finish this picture. I'm afraid if I stay here, I'll do worse and worse things to you—to both of us."

"Yes . . . I think you're right."

"You won't mind if I go?"

"Of course I'll mind."

But she had the feeling that he wouldn't, he would be relieved. Seeing it was so, she had the sense that she was disassembling her life, and every separate part of it was in pain. Her hurt was even worse when she realized that the only time his distress seemed to equal hers was when she mentioned taking Mina.

"You're working and I'm not," she murmured, "so I can take care of her."

He didn't answer. He took a deep drag at the cigarette and for an instant there was more light, but not enough for her to see his expression. Then he turned, crushed the lighted thing into the ashtray and remained in the turned position, facing away from her. She felt that he might be pressing his ache into the pillow.

"Yes," he said. "You better take her with you."

"It won't be long, will it? If you get another job immediately, I'll come back. Or a part in a play—if I get one, you'll come to New York . . . won't you?"

They both knew it was more likely that she would get a part, and she saw his hesitation. "You will come, Barney—won't you?"

"Yes, I'll come."

She said to herself: Don't cry. One of the curses of being an actress was that people suspected your emotions came too easily; she suspected it herself. You didn't dare to show too much, so it was better not to feel too much. Learn to say: I don't give a damn. But suddenly she couldn't help herself, she was crying and rushing to sit on the edge of the bed, beside him, saying Barney, over and over, Barney, Barney, and fumbling in the darkness to touch him, his shoulder, his face, and she did not feel him reaching for her, and she kept weeping, and the scene got out of hand.

Two days later at the airport, however, they had a dry scene, a cold reading. Take care of yourself, he said. Yes, you too, take care of yourself. And call, will you? Of course I'll call. Good-bye, Mina, he said. Say good-bye to Daddy, she prompted, but the child wouldn't. Mina, he kept murmuring, Mina.

She borrowed Megan's East Side apartment for a few days, while the agent was in Philadelphia with a tryout, then she rented a largish studio-bedroom-kitchen in the Village. She got a part almost immediately, and barely had time to hire a baby-sitter before she was in rehearsal.

It was a loony and satirical melodrama that had been enormously successful in London—called *Death Rattle*, and the title was literal. The lethal weapon was a child's rattle filled with poison gas; the murderer, an infant who has been trying unsuccessfully to kill his father, instead sends a number of innocent bystanders to oblivion—the first and second nannies, a cheek-pinching aunt and a harrumphing uncle from the Home Office. The child, a non-speaking character, is seen briefly at the very beginning and ending of the play. The father is a pompous dough of a man who cannot even mouth a bromide accurately, bumbles away at woolly idiocies, does everything wrong, cunningly captures any number of murderers, always the wrong people, and barely escapes his own asphyxiation. Offstage, he victimizes the child and onstage he victimizes his wife, played by Calla in a state of shock and outrage with a horror of falling bodies.

In the cast of nine, eight were Americans, speaking with British accents, and only one was English—Eric Ramsey, in the father role.

Calla, as Ramsey's wife, was amazed at the actor. A comic star in London, he was the darling of the West End theater, and she could not imagine why. He was pure ham. Handsome, pomaded, lint-free, foppish and fortyish, he was as tightly corseted as his acting. He did everything with the measured gesture, onstage and off. His performance address was late Victorian, formalized and elocutionary. He carried in his theater bag an old book called *Delsarte System of Oratory*, which prescribed all gestures and vocal intonations for every emotion and state of mind. He often referred to it and to a Mrs. Pembrilly, a brilliant and unsung teacher of declamation in the dairy country near Shrewsbury.

The rehearsals were little more than a military drill, with Eric Ramsey as sergeant. The director was merely a stage manager, for it was the English star's show. Ramsey knew precisely where every movement should start and end, he could graph the inflection of every spoken line, he knew where every laugh and titter would occur, and how many seconds each would last. Don't stir an eyelash on my cross, dove—there's a bit of a chortle there. Speak up, dovey, this Shropshire lad can't hear his cue. What bloody difference if the audience is American—do you want to sound like obstructed plumbing? Pride of mouth, dove, pride of mouth! Count, dove, comedy is counting—count. Do it Delsarte, dovey darling. Gesture, speak, gesture, turn—then-wait-for-laugh-and-turn again. Go Delsarte!

She thought wanly of the truths of Stanislavsky, Lieber, Strasberg, and contrasted them with the fakery of this corseted poseur. Several times she thought she would have to hand in her notice. But she had to pull this together, she prodded herself, because the other departments of her life were falling apart.

She missed Barney and was wretchedly lonely. She took to calling him far more often than he did her. Then, one morning, she read in a gossip column that it was rumored they had separated. She phoned instantly.

"Well, we *are* separated, Calla," he said evenly.

"Only by distance."

They both laughed; it sounded like such an obvious yet equivocal thing to say. He kept asking about Mina, and she realized he was more forlorn than she had imagined. Knowing that his film was about to finish, she suggested with extreme care that he might like to give New York a try.

"I'm up for a few things," he said vaguely.

"I see. . . . Anything good?"

"I don't know." He sounded depressed again. "I'm up for stuff and up for stuff, and at the last minute, I don't get the part."

"Well," she said with a defensive laugh, "if they see that column and get word that we're separated, maybe they won't hold your wife against you."

"Neither will I."

It was ambiguous. She started to pursue it, hoping he would say he missed her, but he pretended to misconstrue what she meant. She decided not to flirt with the subject anymore, but to meet it head-on. "I could come home," she said.

She didn't know how she could manage it since she was signed for the run of the play, but somehow, if he wanted her . . .

"Hang on awhile," he said.

He meant, of course, that *he* had to hang on without her, make his way on his own, undeterred by her influence, political or personal, or both. Their voices started to sound strained, like a bad mix in an echo chamber. But one thing was clearly audible: His pain was preferable to her presence.

The phone call was a jolt. She decided that she needed a stronger fixity in her life, a hard fact that would act as a counterirritant; she had to find it in her work. As an exercise, as a challenge, she determined to adopt a whole new technique of acting. Not forever, only for this one play. With no faith in it as a permanent way of working, especially since she was never going to use it again, she had to see if she could learn it, master it; she had a need to prove herself again.

Taking Eric as her mentor, she perseveringly studied his aloof and mechanical method, and without imitating it, adapted it to her own use. She practiced not calling upon her emotions, but only upon the outer objectivizations of them; not what they felt like, but what they looked like; not how to cry, but how to pretend to cry. As an actress, she had always been the slave of her Self; now she made herself the master. She compelled every movement, every utterance to serve her mind, her will, the result she intended. And she discovered what a disembodied craft she was acquiring, what a skilled comedienne she could be. Eric Ramsey no longer worried her; he was no longer telling her how Charlotte Iverson had played the wife in the London production. Indeed, he was directing her less and less as they approached the end of the rehearsal period.

The night before the first preview for a New York audience, he came to her dressing room. "I feel I must say, dove, you're better than Charlotte." Then he added, "You're colder."

She felt as if he had insulted her. Then she realized that to him it was an encomium. No heart, no soul, only crystalline technique. Capital.

The following evening—she had never played to such an audience. The laughs came like bombardments; she thought the prop glasses would shatter with the shrieks of merriment. Of course, Eric slew his audience and tossed dead bodies into the aisles; as for herself, she did not lose a single laugh, not a giggle's worth. During one of the convulsive hilarities, when the dialogue had to be halted, he touched her elbow and led her upstage to where the cocktail scene was to be played. As they faced away from the audience, and vamped until the laughter could subside, he said, sotto voce: "The customers love it, ducky—pissing in the pit."

He meant to crack her up, but she didn't even smile; her defense against anything lifelike was impenetrable; her technique was a polished steel shell.

The previews were sold out and the opening night was a triumph. Even before the rave reviews appeared, they knew they had a success. Eric, with a nosegay, came to fetch her after the first-nighters had thinned away. She had been invited to a party to be given by one of the backers.

"Nonsense," Eric said. "You're too good for the Americans. Come with me."

The party he took her to was in the scrubbiest house on the least prepossessing street in the East Twenties. It looked like a rooming house, and in a way it was. That season, with a number of British productions on Broadway, the English actors had banded together and rented this run-down brownstone, which they had converted into a dormitory. They called the place the Gaiety Club, and to it every migrant English actor was invited. The main floor, where there were no sleeping quarters, was reserved for the common rooms—the reception hall, as it was called, the dining room, the little tucked-away nooks and alcoves for quiet talking and quiet drinking. Where they had gotten the typically English furniture was unimaginable, but the place was a total translocation of a London pub cum club, with tacky leather furniture, bronze floor lamps and wooden wainscotting; and, off the pantry, a sideboard with meat pies and bangers, ale and bitters. It all seemed a single step from Piccadilly.

Although many people attended the party, the common rooms were almost silent; everything low-lighted and low-keyed. Those who had seen *Death Rattle* tonight complimented the two actors with half phrases and half-open lips, saying it was rather a bomb, you know, signifying a hit, and telling Calla she was quite as good as Charlotte, quite, but in an odd sort of way—American, what? You gave me a bit of a chuck-chuck, one of the women said, a chuckle.

A recently knighted Shakespearean actor came in, with Hotspur hauberk clanking, told Calla she was almost acceptable in the part, kissed two of the actresses, honked into an enormous handkerchief and departed. A famous avant-garde director entered, seeking an empty space to cast a spell in, found only a congestion of chat and chips, took Calla's hand, said how do you do, Miss Strook, and also departed. A music hall comic said he had heard that the producer's charwoman was playing the Charlotte Iverson part in *Death Rattle*; it was a joke, of course, but nobody laughed. Laughter, Calla noticed, was not to be squandered but to be meted out sparingly, as sweets are to children, to prevent blotches. They hardly seemed like actors at all, they were as austere as judges. They obeyed a rigid set of rules: One must speak not quite loud enough to be heard; no laughing or talking with the mouth open, no praise without reservation. Perhaps they were all tired, or perhaps they hated playing in the shoddy, barnlike New York theaters and longed for their sweet, smaller ones, with the gleaming brass and the woodwork smelling of lemon oil; or perhaps they simply yearned for home. It was all a little sad; a forlorn black humor, she thought, to have called the club the Gaiety.

"Nice party, what?" Eric said.

"A revel."

He smiled without wrinkling his face.

After a bit, even this wild spate of jollity ended. Everybody disappeared. The room, as if on carefully timed cues, was emptied. People simply drifted away, muttering little politenesses, vanishing into shadows. By theater clocks, it was still early.

"What happened?" Calla asked. "Where did they all go?"

"They're fucking," he said.

She had not noticed it before, but the softest sounds were drifting from behind the curtains of the alcoves and the dark nooks and niches. And like everything else at the party, it was all performed in undertones, with decorum.

She turned to meet Eric's eyes. He was appraising her, evaluating the texture of her skin, the low cut of her dress. He made a gesture to a stairway, a slow unfolding of his arm as if conducting the *lento* movement of a symphony. "I have a room up there," he said.

She smiled pleasantly. "I think not."

He continued, however, apparently by rote. "I want you to know that I've been married twice—and twice divorced—the first time for reacting too much, the second time, too little. Which is the unabridged and unexpurgated story of my life. I played at Stratford for nearly eight years. Laertes, Andronicus, all the Henrys, Richard One and Two. I was very good in the sadder parts—I could cry very easily."

It seemed her cue. "And now it's difficult?"

"No, it's always easy," he said. "But crying's quite outside the question, don't you think?"

"Well, it certainly doesn't *answer* any question."

"Such as?"

"Where did everybody go?"

"Fucking, I said."

"Is that anywhere?"

"Not really. But if you're nit enough to ask where everybody went—"

"—fucking will tell me."

Again he indicated the stairs. "We could find out."

"No, Eric. . . . Thank you."

He nodded and reached across the table to touch her. She thought he was going to pat her head patronizingly, but it was the gentlest caressing of her hair.

"I haven't told you," he continued. "I believe you've done a remarkable thing in the last month. Extraordinary. I didn't think it possible—I was quite sure we would have to let you go. To toss out everything you ever learned, stifle every emotion that came naturally to you, learn a whole new acting language—God, I'd've become a mute! . . . How did you ever do it?"

"It wasn't as hard as I thought it would be."

"Must've been, dear girl, to discard everything . . . ."

"Maybe it was because nothing I had—as an actress—was all that precious to me."

"Poor Calla."

She had not said exactly what she meant, that acting was not all of her life. Right now she wished it were. She knew he understood her meaning, he had always had an accurate instinct about her, and he certainly understood the desolation. She saw that he pitied her, and regretted having told him.

She got up quickly. "Thank you, Eric—good night."

"Calla—I'll see you home."

"No, not necessary."

She did not wait for other considerations, simply got up and ran. Outdoors, she continued running.

Slowing down at last, she realized how much she had wanted to go to bed with him. Go to bed, it was the literal essence of her need. Not the sweaty tilt and tournament of sex, but the warm amity of lying next to a man, a closeness and a kindness.

She was truly fond of Eric. In the last weeks of rehearsal, they had developed generous perceptions of one another, onstage and off; they spoke the language of looks and glances almost at once. They were unworried and companionable. They laid hands upon one another easily, without tension, adjusting the other's vagrant lock of hair, removing a crumb from the corner of the mouth. It was so swiftly, so gratifyingly becoming a good friendship. Tempted to go back to the Gaiety Club and spend the night, she had a dread of ruining it; sex might be a spoiler. Come in as a rapture and go out as a spite. So she went home alone.

The next day was Mina's second birthday, and Calla had a fantasy. Barney, between pictures, would surprise her. All of a sudden, without prelude, he would appear in New York. He would be backstage, waiting in her dressing room, and they would both be giddy with happiness. He would throw his arms around her, he would have a present for Mina, they would go somewhere, have a family party, get a little drunk and make love until they were mackerels.

On Mina's birthday, a present did arrive, but Barney didn't. Calla opened the box and there wasn't even a card in it. She chided herself: A card for whom?—the child couldn't read. The gift was pretty enough, a yellow dress, the butter color of Mina's hair, but it was made for a smaller child. Mina was already walking with a stumbling air of great consequence, she could speak well enough to make every need understood and she was exceptionally tall. Calla had told him that; she always kept him in touch with the happiest of the little girl's changes. But perhaps, she reflected, he wants to keep her younger in his mind, wants to deny the growth that happened when he was not there, wants to put the clock back to when they were all together. There was some comfort in the thought.

The wrong-sized dress was all he sent. He didn't call. There had been no word from him, not even when the play had opened.

She made the birthday cake herself, no store-bought thing; there had to be a celebration, dammit, and work had to be done to enhance the pleasure.

Mina blew the candles out, ate the strawberries off the cake and decorated her face with pink icing. When the baby-sitter came, the child cried a little—she had started to do that lately—but went quickly back to the balloons and the brand-new pushmobile.

In the next few weeks, Calla and Eric went to the Gaiety Club a number of times. She discovered that the house in the East Twenties was the locale for a drawing room comedy, a travesty really, that the English actors were playing. They were not staid, not a bit as stiffly decorous as their understated voices suggested. They were actors first, willy-nilly, with flamboyant imaginations and hair-trigger tempers and high sexual combustibility. Particularly, they were accomplished pretenders. This house was their intimate, naughty, practical joke upon themselves. They made believe they were living in a stuffy gentlemen's club, the women as well as the men, and from time to time they would have their revenge on its leather-armchaired pomposity. And their reprisals were nearly always libidinous, since it was particularly pleasant to play a lewd game in safety, away from home.

Calla's presence made the charade all the more enjoyable to them. To shock an American woman—a whilom cinema star—added a fillip of excitement. She let them think that they *were* shocking her, playing her game as they played theirs, acting out her dismay with wide-eyed, wide-mouthed naïveté. She was their perfect audience when they talked in august subcommittee terms about whether the club should install a two-way mirror in the shower room, whether it was against their policies to purchase a communal sheep, whether whips might not be sanctioned as long as they were administered tidily, whether a member who steals bananas from the dining room in order to beat the whistle in their skins should be brought up on charges. They posted written rules, which she suspected they had devised expressly for her reaction, listing what would be prohibited: Those who talked through cunnilingus (either party), exhibitionistic coprolagniacs, belligerents with necrophilic intent, members who had it off in other members' wigs, gloves, panty hose, athletic supporters, cold cream jars. Whether voyeurism should be permitted was still a moot point; as actors who lived off box-office proceeds, they considered the complimentary ticket a questionable benefit.

Calla would have wagered that hardly any of the perversions were practiced, but there was a lot of routine fucking going on.

Not by her, however. She laughed a good deal at the Gaiety, but the place was not aphrodisiacal, only a quirky side-street house to go to, so outlandish that it had no relationship to what was going on along the main avenue of her life. It was an escape, as it must have been to the English actors, from the yearning for another place, another person, a distant home.

Whenever she went to the Gaiety, she could feel Eric's steady observation of her, as if he were closely scrutinizing a stripped specimen. Sometimes it bothered her and she was on the side of the club members who were against voyeurism, but sometimes she enjoyed it and wanted to tease him a little. At such moments, she wondered . . .

On a Wednesday, between the matinee and evening performances, Calla and Eric were in his dressing room, and he turned the lights out. There was only a single window, leaded with Shubert dust, so the room was in shadow. She was wearing her makeup smock, which had a lipstick smudge on the shoulder, and he was wearing a blue-striped dressing robe with a faint finger of greasepaint on the pocket; it would have slain him had he noticed. In the dimness, she watched him take off his robe, and his shorts as well. He had a better body than she had imagined; he needed no corseting; it was his discipline that girdled him. He carefully hung up his robe in the closet and crossed the room to where she was sitting on the couch. His cock was erect and as he stood in front of her, it was at the level of her bosom. He bent a little and opened her smock, moved closer and put his penis between her breasts. Then he caressed one areola with it until the nipple was as hard as he was, and caressed the other. Slowly he separated her smock altogether, so that he could see all of her. He did not kiss her mouth, but knelt and kissed her in other places, one and another and another. When his head was there, while he was sucking her, she slowly began to lie back.

"Come inside," she said.

But he didn't, he kept at her with his mouth, his tongue, his teeth, until she couldn't stand it. Just as she was about to come, she felt him move and hurry, and with a surge he was inside her, and came at once, and she came with him.

As they lay there, she thought how adroitly he had done everything, how perfectly he had synchronized every touch with every movement. He was so skilled, so technically flawless. Count, dove, count—comedy is counting. She felt that she had had a screwing by Delsarte. . . . If, for him, it was an acting exercise, for her it was aspirin. But the painkiller did not work.

8

In late winter of that year, there was an anti-war demonstration at Battery Park. Somebody said the first gunshot was fired by a Weatherman; others said it came from the hard hats. Like an army, from all directions, the police stormed in. Some of the marchers ran, some fought back, some threw bricks from a nearby construction pile. There were two more gunshots, there was screaming and bloodshed. The anti-war paraders, refusing to be routed, started to lock hands and arms, they would not move, they began to sing. When the police took to using their billies, many of the marchers fled. Then, with the tear gas, others ran as well.

Calla and a small contingent stayed. Suddenly the cops were upon her, with fists and nightsticks raised. Move, disperse, they yelled, get going, you Commie bastards, move. One of them hit her and she fell. Her mouth was bleeding. As she got up, a policeman menaced: "Get goin'," he said. "Move it—move!"

"No!" she yelled. "Lock me up, pig!"

In the First Precinct Station in Ericcson Place, they booked her for disorderly conduct, breaking the peace and—paradoxically—resisting arrest. Megan came with a lawyer, and Eric came too. It was the resisting arrest charge that gave the lie to the cop's complaint, because there were a dozen people to testify that she had dared him to lock her up. Everybody was dismissed.

The following day, a wire service picture of her appeared in most of the newspapers across the country. If she were in a breeze of good humor, she would have thought the photograph was funny. Her fist was raised and her forearm looked like a ham hock. And one of the New York papers used the screaming headline:

LOCK ME UP, PIG!

She had phone calls from all over. Her father from New Forge, Bill Lieber from Bermuda, Willi from Los Angeles.

And Barney.

"What the hell are you doing?" he said. "Are you crazy?"

"No, I'm not."

"Do you want to get yourself killed? Do you want Mina left without a mother? What the fuck's happening to you? Are you obsessed? Is it a goddamn obsession?"

Not a conversation, a diatribe. So she hung up.

An obsession? The question tormented her. What if it was a sick compulsion like someone driven to drugs or liquor or kleptomania? Maybe it had nothing to do with morality and her sense of justice, but only her need to roil the waters of her life, and the lives of others. Or even—worse thought—maybe her stage was too small, the theater and film and public make-believe, maybe they didn't give her a platform broad enough for the size of her histrionic art. With an actor's overweening vanity, maybe she needed to play a larger conflict in a larger drama in the great, vast colosseum of the world. Hail, Calla!

It was repulsive.

But not true.

No. She would be willing to play the same scenes anywhere, on the tiniest of platforms, incognito and masked. She would be content with a bit part or a walk-on if she felt that her playing would save some child —a Mina somewhere, unseen, unknown—from the horror of napalm. Yet, what a dreadful drama to play in, the same grim story all the time, the same action, never any real rehearsal, the denouement always the same—the lost cause. What a killing comedy.

But win or lose, what else could she do but play it? She knew what all well-read people knew, that the innocent were dying, the ghettos were burning, that the world was not becoming kinder but crueler. What could she do with the knowledge—file and forget it? If she did not use what she believed to help improve the world she lived in, wouldn't she become a hysteric or a coward or a dunce? If what she perceived about the mundane sickness just lay in her mind, undigested into life, simply rotting away like diseased food in the gut, wouldn't its wastes poison her brain, wouldn't she madden? Yes, and serve her right, serve her to extinction. And serve her child as well.

No, Barney, I am not obsessed, I am not crazy. I am *sane*. She started to write it in a letter to her husband, but three days later, not a sentence was composed. Instead, there was a letter from him.

"Dear Calla," it said. "I'm doing a four-day television job until this Friday. When it's finished, I'm going somewhere to file for divorce. I've written you long letters on the subject, all of which I tore up, and I've had lengthy conversations in my mind. I can't bear going through all that—and believe me, a quick over-and-out is best. Barney."

The letter fluttered to the floor and she was afraid she might follow it. When she could feel the blood coursing more rapidly through her body, she had the impulse to rush to the phone. But she refrained. I won't make sense, she said, I'll weep through every word, I'll be deranged.

She put a monitor on herself, like a mechanical safety switch, to shut down every feeling. She went through her evening performance under its control. After the show, she walked home, all the way down to the Village, through a misty rain. Dismissing the baby-sitter with scarcely a word, she looked in on the sleeping child, closed the sash against the dampness that had made the room feel clammy, sat in the window chair and looked out at the wet street.

Knowing she would not sleep, she didn't go to bed. She did things. She cut up the remainder of a leg of lamb, skinned an onion, found a jar of dried green peas, emptied everything into a pot, half filled it with water, then forgot to turn the fire on. While making peanut cookies for Mina, she wondered why the soup wasn't boiling, twisted the knob to the highest heat, watched patiently, standing there and standing there while the water boiled, then turned the light to simmer. She tried to read.

It was 3 A.M. and all the food had been put away, the pots and dishes cleaned, there was nothing left to do, and she was wide awake.

She called him.

"You shit!" she said. "You dirty shit, to do it that way, you dirty shit!"

"Slow down," he said.

"You shit!"

"I didn't think we needed the extra pain."

"Extra pain, extra pain! We could have talked!"

"There's nothing to talk about anymore, Calla. I'm seeing women and I'm sure you're seeing men. Let's give ourselves a chance."

Oh God, she thought, oh God. I won't say any more for a while, try not to fill an emptiness with another emptiness.

"I'll come home, Barney—if you want me to," she said. "Tomorrow—or the next day." She wondered if she could get a plane this minute. "We have to talk about it—we have to."

"No." He was firm. "We don't have to talk about it at all."

There was another letter in a few days, a very reasoned and practical letter in which he said he wanted to make the details easy for her. He had thought of a Mexican divorce, with him doing everything, arranging the foreign lawyer, making the trip, putting in a solitary appearance; no inconvenience to her. But he had reconsidered—he had been advised, was the way he put it—and decided that Mexican divorces could be contested, and he was sure neither of them wanted an inconclusive thing. So he had decided on Nevada. He would go for the six weeks required—since he wouldn't be working anyway—and do the dirty work.

As to Mina, they would come to some agreement about the child . . . later, when the hurt wore off. He was certain they would both be reasonable about her. Then he added a note that had hardly any relevance: The child had not been made in hatred or indifference, he said. Clearly it was as close as Barney could come to saying he loved either or both of them.

On a morning two months later, the legal papers arrived and the divorce was final.

That night, in a dream, they were playing a wonderful game, she and Barney and Mina. A large vessel, a beautiful old galleon, had been shipwrecked on the beach outside the house in Trancas. It was so splendid— It had golden decks, three of them, and many fores and afts, and they couldn't count the quarterdecks and forecastles, they counted and counted, they ran all over the marvelous thing, straight, slanty, gilded and golden, they ran, they ran, oh how they ran! Mina ran the fastest; she was older now, with golden hair like Alice in Wonderland, and a laugh like golden bells, the brightest. She discovered more than anybody, lovely things, precious, very precious things, glowing ones that rolled and recited and nodded, and round white marbles, and songs that had been left behind, and how to tell time, and long, long ribbons that had no beginnings and no endings, and golden things. Then they played the most delicious game called Hide and Seek, and if you wanted to hide you could go right on hiding, you had all the nooks and crannies, they were all yours, and if you wanted to be found, well, wonderful, somebody would find you, somebody would call out: "I see you —there you are!" And it would be full of coins. I found you! Oh, so happy—full of golden coins!

She woke up and she was cold.

Barney's last letter, before the divorce, had suggested, in the one warm sentence he had allowed her, that they would be reasonable about Mina. But Calla was aware that another letter about the child, a legal one, could come any day. It might be up there now, aloft in the airmail, descending, to zero down upon her head. Sometimes, for days, she didn't open her mailbox.

Tense and full of foreboding, she saw her work begin to suffer. One of the evils of her worriment was that her mind would wander. Her performances lost their precision, her timing would go off; she blurred the jokes. Worse, she did not properly set up Eric's laughs and often stepped on those that were delayed. You're changing yocks to titters, he said one day, not good-naturedly, and you'd better have that green dress taken in again. A bit more rouge in the makeup, dove, and you're walking a bit down the gizzard, aren't you, darling? It was his way of saying she was acting badly and looking like hell. Backstage, she started to throw tantrums. What the devil's the matter with her? the actors said. Soon they said worse.

She began to have stomachaches and occasionally was nauseous. She went to a doctor who spoke of incipient ulcers and gastro-this-and-that. He gave her a vial of capsules. She drank milk in the middle of the night, chomped on thousands of white, chalky, dead-tasting tablets, felt that everything was going paper-white inside her belly, and her brain was blanching.

"Don't go onstage like that," Eric said one night. "You've got a disgusting white tongue."

"White tongue! Who sees my tongue? What the hell do they care if my tongue is white or black, or if my guts are green! White tongue, white tongue!"

She hated her self-pity, it scared her.

After the show, she went to Eric's dressing room and apologized.

He was exceptionally kind to her. With genuine concern, he asked whether she was still having attacks of nausea and how she slept at night.

"Yes—and awake, mostly."

He nodded and opened his theater bag. Rummaging, he found what he was looking for, a small cardboard box with no label or writing on it. He lifted the flap and showed her about a dozen gray hexagonal pills.

"Here," he said. "You'll slumber like a nun."

"You're sweet, Eric, but I've got tranquilizers and sleeping pills and—"

"Poison—sheer poison. These are different—I get them in Switzerland. They're not habit forming and they're mild as milky tea."

He was being warm and dear, and they were a gift of affection; she couldn't refuse them. She thanked him, and ruefully they gazed at each other, hearing the warning cue of closing night.

"I want to get out of the play."

"Dear girl . . ." He sounded dismal. "But I suppose you should."

"Will they let me out of my contract?"

"If you say you're sick—which God knows you are."

She was touched by his unpretended sadness, no Delsarte. He said she would soon be herself again, once she got away from the neurotic theater and its sick muses, Euphoria, Aphrodisia and Hysteria. Then he kissed her gently, as though she were his daughter, and tearfully sent her home. The following day she handed in her notice. The night the understudy went in, she was out of a job.

For a few weeks she recuperated, then got frightened by her declining bank balance and tried to get another role. Two months, without success. She's a little strange these days, the casting directors said, she doesn't show up for an interview, or she comes late and says she was afraid to come at all. Once, when she walked in and walked right out again, a producer yelled after her: Who the hell do you think you are? She stayed with the question for days, and had no answer. But she had little doubt about one thing: she was turning into an unholy wreck.

Except when she was with Mina. Then a tranquility descended upon her. For all the temperamental fits she had thrown backstage, for all her hysterics and grouches, she had never had a temper tantrum with her child. With her, Calla had a calm and lucid sense of recognition, she knew who she was, and that she belonged to someone who also belonged to her. Mina was her sole serenity. Not yet two and a half years old, the little girl had gone through mumps and measles, through nighttime croup, through a temporary allergy to milk, fear of the dark, bed-wetting long after she had already ceased bed-wetting. The child had weathered everything, and so had the mother, always with the confidence that together they were invincible.

They laughed a lot. Mina talked all the time now, a steady chitter-chatter, asking endless questions and, when responses were overdue, telling herself the answers. It amazed Calla how easy it was to help the little girl through problems. The recent regression to bed-wetting had been solved by giving Mina a cuddly flannel puppy to take to bed with her. The gift was linked to a responsibility. From time to time, during the night, Mina had to awaken the cotton animal and take him peepee. In a week the puppy was toilet-trained, and so was its mistress.

Then, thumbsucking. The child was still doing it until two months ago, with Calla pretending not to notice. One day, while Mina was in-dustriously at her digit, Calla did as the little girl was doing. Not ridiculing her, simply joining in the game. Mina, seeing her mother per-form such nonsense, burst into laughter. Frequently, in the next week or so, they had thumbsucking parties. Mina's merriment never ceased; she could hardly suck her thumb for laughing at her senseless mother. After a while, the sight of Calla's thumbsucking was the main thing; if her mother didn't join, the child reached for the maternal thumb and stuck it into the maternal mouth. As Calla played all variations of the game, not allowing it to become too predictable, Mina became more and more conscious of the activity itself. In a month the joke was over, and so was the thumbsucking.

They had one game together that was not really a game, but the simplest ceremony of love. It was hardly anything at all, it had no con-tent, but a real and invariable form, and a lovely feeling. It might hap-pen at any time. It merely consisted of this: One of them would stop whatever she was doing, look at the other, and in a soft singsong voice—as if from a long distance—lightly lyricize the other's name.

"Meeeenaaaa."

Then the partner would also stop what she was doing and recipro-cate.

"Mommmmeeee."

That was all there was to it, nothing more. It simply said that the other one was there. No one was hiding from anyone. It was a gentle touch of the voice, a loving rite of presence.

The letter arrived on the last day of March. It said that Barney was suing for the sole and irrevocable custody of their child. A separate envelope, in the same mail, contained many pages of legalese.

That afternoon she was in the office of Simon Ehrenstein, a lawyer who specialized in custodies. He was an elderly man with a hairless head and a face so narrow that it looked as if it had been compressed between the covers of a book. He spoke in truisms, which he seemed to count as he doled them out, like thousand-dollar bills. But his concern was grave, and he was paternal, with attentive eyes. As he put down the blue-bound pages and looked up, Calla pointed to them.

"It's all lies," she said.

"So. . . . The truth matters only in morals, my dear. In the courts, the only thing that matters is what can be made believable."

"I am not—believably—a monster."

He lifted the papers. "It does not say 'monster.' It says you are no longer a fit parent. You have been under arrest a number of times, you have broken the peace, incited to riot and attacked a police officer. You are at present unemployed and possibly unemployable. Because of emotional instability, you have been fired from your last employment—"

"That's not true. I handed in my notice. I quit."

"—and you are an acknowledged Communist."

"I am not."

"I believe everything you say. But what counts is that there is an American flag in the courtroom, and your ex-husband's lawyer will point to it on every occasion. You are against the war effort, you are a dangerous revolutionary, a Black Panther, a traitor—"

"I'm none of those things."

"—you are indigent and unstable, you have fits of depression and temper tantrums, you should be in a jail or an insane asylum. And you will turn your child into a delinquent, a dope fiend and a public ward."

"He wouldn't do it that way."

"And worst of all, since you have received innumerable hate letters and threats—even a package that exploded in your hands—the child's life is not safe with you."

"No! He would never say that—he would never do that to me."

The lawyer tapped the blue cover. "He is saying it, he is doing it. Not your ex-husband—his lawyer. And it's exactly how I would proceed if I were his lawyer."

". . . What can I do?"

"Don't fight it."

She was stunned. "You mean give her up?"

"No." There were a number of antique glass paperweights on his desk. Except for Calla's papers, however, there was nothing to weigh down. He rearranged the weights. "It *is* true that you haven't recently done well in California, and now you're not doing well in New York—isn't that so?"

"Yes."

"Why don't you give yourself a new start?"

"Where?"

"Say—London. You've been in an English play. You probably have a good English accent."

"It's a good English accent—in America."

"How about Paris? There's this new thing—what do they call it in films?—the New Wave—with lots of American actors."

"You mean run away?"

"Yes, until your husband remarries. And I'm sure he will. When that happens, it'll shock you how quickly he will lose interest in total custody."

"Not him—he loves her too much."

He uttered a doubting sound. He was disenchanted with child-lorn parents. Love, like truth in morals, was useful only if it could be made believable in court.

She agreed to think about it, and just as she was about to depart, he said, without stirring the air too much, "Try not to let her out of your sight for a while."

"You're trying to frighten me, aren't you?"

"Yes, I am. When matters get to this state, anything can happen."

"Like what?"

"I had a client who was charged with being criminally unstable. She wasn't. But the husband's lawyer thought it was grounds for a writ. On a Halloween evening, the writ was served by a man dressed as a bag lady, and the child was taken away in her pajamas. Last week—an article in the *Law Review*—a man hired a school bus and a driver, and kidnapped his child."

In panic, she fled. Walking home, something she herself had said in the meeting stayed with her. *You mean run away?* She had uttered it in horror. Now she realized why the notion of escape was too difficult to consider. If she fled she would be acknowledging defeat in too many provinces of her life—in her marriage, in films, on the stage, even in her faltering causes.

As if to mock her contribution to the anti-war effort, there were pictures in the afternoon papers of families in war-bombed cities. She saw a child of ten, perhaps, up to her knees in bombed rubble, her fist against her cheek, with a blind stare in her eyes, mouth loose, head at a grotesque angle. She of course saw Mina in the picture, the child wandering in the smoke and debris, frightened and war-crazed, calling Mommmmeeee. She saw herself digging in the ruins, crying for Mina, searching for the child taken from her by war and writs and lawyers and judges, by bus drivers and bag ladies and actors playing Nazis.

The following morning, out of the blue, a special delivery letter arrived:

Dear Miss Stark,

I am a Baptist minister, a black man, with a congregation in Ashton, Mississippi. You may not remember me, but about two years ago we met at a Martin Luther King memorial dinner in Los Angeles. You were one of the donors, and I was asked to deliver the invocation and something of a speech. When the occasion came to a close, you were kind enough to tell me that you thought well of what I had said, and offered a helping hand. At that time I was not nearly as active as you have been, and while I was grateful for the gesture, I had no need to accept your offer, except in friendship. Now, however, I need your help in a more tangible way.

An event has happened here in Ashton that requires something further than local attention. This place, where I have my church, is a small city with a prosperous side of town and a black side, very poor.

Leon Hakes is a young black man, not quite nineteen. He works for the Wetherill Lumber Company—yard boy, they call him—he loads the gravel trucks and carries timbers. He is a quiet employee, some think him surly, and he lives alone. A native of Memphis, not of Ashton, Leon will offer no more about himself.

A week ago, he had a sore throat and took the day off. That afternoon, the Ashton Bank and Trust Company was robbed. Three men, all hooded beyond recognition, and wearing long plastic gloves, held up the bank and made off with $9,400.

Two days later, Leon Hakes, who had returned to work the day after the robbery, was arrested on the presumptive evidence that one of the bank tellers, a weekend customer at the lumberyard, recognized his voice; another teller, however, said that none of the holdup men had uttered a single word. Hakes had no explanation for his absence from work except that he was in bed with a sore throat and a high temperature. He had no other alibi, nor could anyone offer one for him.

Since the sheriff's office had only circumstantial evidence and an uncertain identification against Hakes, they tried to wring a confession out of him, and attempted to get the young man to name his accomplices. But Leon has steadfastly clung to his story and denied his guilt.

The blacks in our town have had some trouble with the county sheriff, whose name is Boone Rickert. Interviewed recently, Rickert said he was proud that the nigras were finally coming in shape now that the sixties were over. "I don't like to see young bucks drivin' cars," he said. "And a drunk who's black oughta be black-and-blue."

They were black-and-blueing Hakes in an effort to make him talk. A rumor came out of the courthouse jail that they were beating him every day, "giving him the hoses."

The night before last, two detectives, Leroy Wilson and Mel Averill, were working him over, and a gun went off. Averill was killed.

Wilson declared that Leon pulled the gun out of the officer's holster and blasted away at Averill, point blank. So Hakes was charged with murder.

Until that time, for three days, the prisoner had had no lawyer. Nobody in town would take his case. When we finally got an attorney to come up from Vicksburg, we heard Hakes's story of what had happened. It was quite different. It seems that Averill, in a burst of temper, raised his gun, held it by the barrel and was beating Leon's head with the butt, while Wilson had a stranglehold on the prisoner. As the boy tried to shove the gun out of reach, it went off, still in the detective's hand. There are disputed questions about fingerprints, whether Leon put them on the gun or the police forced him to put them on, and whether they are there at all.

In any event, the Vicksburg lawyer, Gus Mayfield, thinks that the boy will never get a fair trial unless there's a change of venue. He doubts there is any chance it will be granted.

I think there is a chance. Irrespective of Leon's guilt or innocence, the blacks in this town want him to have a fair trial, and they are on the verge of making trouble. By trouble I mean violence.

I believe, with all my heart, that we can achieve our end without violence. I am convinced, and I am sure Dr. King would be convinced, that Black Power is not the power of hatred, but the strength of God's love. I am therefore organizing a demonstration, a peaceful demonstration, with singing and chanting and marching, as we did in Martin's day. But I am not naïve enough to think we can sing ourselves into a change of venue. It will take a bigger noise than that. A national noise.

So I ask you, as I ask many other white and black people of distinction, to join our march this coming Sunday, in the hope that this local issue can become a national one, and non-violence can reawaken as the surging motion of our time.

I do not know how you are thinking nowadays. Perhaps you no longer trust that peace is achievable through peace, but only through violence—some of my dearest friends have changed to that thought, and will not join me. However, I cannot believe, despite what the papers say about you, that you can have altered so much. You had in you, as I recollect, a love of humankind that was your radiance, and this I call upon.

I will telephone you shortly after you read this.

John Emmet Tolliver.

She remembered Reverend Tolliver very well. He was a picture in contrasts, a gleaming mahogany complexion and prematurely snowy hair, a thin body and a heavy rich voice. Not by any means a rabble-rousing orator, he had a knifelike incisiveness of mind, and spoke to the best instincts of his audience, to the depths of thought and feeling they did not know they could reach. Whatever trials of doubt and rancor he had gone through, he had come forth an unavenging man, and talked of the freedom struggle as an exalted privilege to reconcile the dissensions in the human spirit. If he took joy in the struggle, it was because he was an optimist, not a fool.

Well before she had come to any conclusion about what to do, in the early afternoon the phone rang. She heard the deep, mellow timbre of his voice and warmed to the memory of the man. He told her there would be a Sunday morning service in the church, then there would be songs, the old songs, "We Shall Overcome" and "Climbing Jacob's Ladder" and "Ain't Go' Let Nobody Turn Me 'Round." There would be speeches and a march outside the courthouse, with the newspaper and television people all invited, and the presentation of the petition to the judge of the court, symbolically of course, since the man would certainly not be present.

As he spoke, it was not as if he were inviting her to a political demonstration with conflict at the crux of it, but a great celebration of love. She could see him in the pulpit of his church, fervid with faith and a lustrous vision (Yes, Lord!), and the uplifted faces, voices mounting, spirits transcending (Amen, Lord!).

She felt chagrined that she must respond to his exultant lyric with her own prosy caution. "I'd like very much to come. But I'm having a difficulty right now."

"It's only for overnight—just one day."

"But I have a child—I can't leave her."

"Not even overnight?"

"No . . . it's complicated."

"I know, Miss Stark, of course it's complicated," he said with ready sympathy. "But can't we simplify it, when we need you so badly? Can't you bring your child with you?"

"Would it be safe?"

"It's the essence of what we're after—safety—for everybody. No violence. In fact, there has been no violence in the streets, none at all. It isn't as though we've got a Klan's den in our town—we haven't." Then he repeated urgently, "It's the whole point of the march—non-violence. Miss Stark, you can't imagine what a wonderful power for peace we have."

As he was passionate, she was prudent. "Do you have a permit for the march?"

"Of course we do. To march without a permit would in itself be construed as an act of violence. It would be against our deepest spirit."

Almost convinced, she still wavered. "If it weren't for my child . . ."

"Miss Stark," he said quietly, "my children are also here."

She was certain he did not say it to hurt her, but she felt the twinge.

"Let me think about it," she said.

Later, when she managed to get the sound of his persuasive voice out of her mind, her qualm about going to Mississippi became even more oppressive. She started for the phone a number of times to say she would not be coming, but she could still hear his words.

My children . . .

She did not telephone. An hour went by, then another and another. She was already late in returning his call. And she had made no decision at all.

Toward sundown, as she felt a bit nauseated and took a pill, and as the expression recurred once more—losing her stomach—she faced the dismaying fact that she was no longer the brave woman who had engaged in battles that had endangered her marriage, her career, her life. Shaken, she was losing her toughness of muscle and even her health of mind, and she might indeed, as Barney pictured her, turn into an unfit mother. Like a snowman in the rain, she was melting away.

How to stop it? There was no passage in her life that she could recall without some poignance of regret, except the risks she had taken for what she considered the common decency. She regretted that she had stayed in the libraries too long, that she had made some bad decisions in her career; she regretted she had not tried to know her father better, and had not loved her mother comprehendingly; she regretted—sorely she regretted—all the unfinished splendor in her love of Barney. But she regretted not one moment of her devotion to the troubled issues of her time. She could not imagine how miserly, how thin-blooded her life would have been if she had not joined the outcries and the marches. If the sacrifices she had made had diminished her world, they had also enlarged it, and she herself had become magnified. All else she might want to change, but her foolish love of mankind—her radiance, Tolliver had called it—the love that gave her heart for the battle, that she would never regret. Then why, now, when all her habits of mind, when her whole being told her to join Tolliver in Mississippi, why did she so tremulously hesitate?

For Mina's sake? Could she run away, and blame Mina for it? Was Mina going to be the whipping child, and take the punishment for her own fears? If it started with the fright that her daughter would be snatched out of bed at night or harmed in a southern city, where might the terror end? With a craven mother and a craven child?

But she could not go. She was starting to the telephone to give Tolliver her regrets, when the instrument rang.

She answered it. It was the doorman of the apartment building. There were two men, he said, one with a legal paper. They wanted to come up.

Hold them, she cried, delay them, say I'm in the shower, say anything—don't let them come. But it's a legal paper, he repeated.

She hung up.

They were coming for her child.

It was the illogical logic of moral retribution. For her refusal to go to the aid of Tolliver's children, her own would be snatched away.

No. There must be no more thinking, she said, no more inner struggles, no moralistic debates. Action. Only action. Overwrought, she threw armfuls into a bag, bundled her daughter up, hurried out of the apartment, rushed to the fire exit. Carrying Mina and the suitcase, she scrambled down eight flights of stairs. When she got to the rear lobby of the building, she looked in all directions, then rushed out into the street and hailed a taxi.

On her arrival at the airport, she called Tolliver and told him she was coming—a day earlier. Delighted, he said she could stay with his family—no trouble, they would be honored—and informed her that the only flight from New York would be by way of Atlanta, arriving at Memphis in the evening. He would pick them up in his car and drive them from the airport to Ashton, Mississippi.

At sunset, carrying the canvas suitcase in one hand and leading Mina by the other, Calla boarded the plane for Atlanta. Although it was the child's fourth flight, this was the first one on which she was old enough to pilot the aircraft, and for a half hour of the flight she talked it exhilaratedly through the skies. Then, kerplunk, she was asleep, and on the second flight as well. When they landed at the Memphis International Airport, Calla started down the staircase toward the dimly lighted apron of the airfield. A photoflash flared in the night, then another shot, and she saw the photographer go scampering toward the terminal building. Her annoyance passed as it occurred to her that this was exactly what she was here for, and that Reverend Tolliver was quick to use the advantage of her presence—the press wheels were already turning.

It was an off hour for arrivals and departures; the waiting room was practically empty. There was no sign of Tolliver. She had expected him to be there ahead of her, and it was particularly odd that he wasn't since the plane had been nearly a half hour late. Calla inquired at two desks, and stared at the entrances for the arrival of the tall, white-haired black man, but he did not appear.

She had a peculiar sense—phobic, she told herself—that she was being watched. The man was heavy-set with a bullish neck and a mottled complexion, liver-spotted. He wore sloppy, shapeless chino trousers, a plaid shirt, and decrepit hunting boots that suggested he was not going anywhere, nor had he the watchful eye of someone on the lookout for an arriving friend. It was the very fact that he was clearly not on the lookout for anybody that labeled the newspaper he hid behind as only a prop; he was staring through the pages straight at her.

Something happened to verify her suspicion. Tolliver came in through the farthest entrance. He was rushing and out of breath, trying to make up for his lateness. He waved across the length of the waiting room. Just as he did, the fat man slowly folded his newspaper, left it in the plastic chair and ambled away, slipping through the nearest exit.

"Hello—I'm sorry I'm late—I'm sorry," Tolliver said.

His handshake was damp. Seeming to know this, and embarrassed, he quickly withdrew his hand.

He was as magnetic as she remembered, with eyes that were keen with regard. But there was something disturbingly different tonight. Calla could not tell what it was. Certainly not his bright energy—it was all there—nor the rich vibrancy of his voice, nor the sense that he held more laughter than his face could show. Everything the same, yet the film and sound track were out of sync.

Perhaps, she thought in a silliness, it was simply that he kept his hat on. While it was of no consequence to her whether or not he was bareheaded, it seemed odd. Even considering the change in the hatting habits of men, she would have expected that a southern Baptist minister would have clung to the courtlier manners of an earlier day.

As they started to leave the terminal building en route to his car, he offered to carry Mina, but Calla, with reflexive panic, insisted that she enjoyed doing it; any day now the little girl would no longer permit herself to be babied.

He grinned and she thought how much she liked him, and knew he liked her as well. It was surprisingly easy between them. She had a lovely freedom from guilt about being white.

In the parking lot, as they approached his car, an old model Plymouth that looked shiny new, he turned to her with studied casualness.

"Can you drive a car?" he said.

"Yes, I can."

"Would you mind driving?" he asked. "I'm not feeling up to snuff tonight."

There had been no sign that there was anything wrong with him. As she turned with concern, he allayed it. "It's nothing, really—only a slight dizziness."

He obviously didn't want to discuss it; she wondered what malady he was hiding.

"I'll get in first." He opened the door. "And you can hand her to me."

The child murmured during the changeover; he whispered comforting words to her and supported her securely. He seemed graceful in handling her, and pleased at having her to hold.

The car was a bit noisy but full of pep, and Calla enjoyed driving it.

Her mind went to the prisoner. "Tell me about Hakes."

He suggested delaying the discussion until they got out of the traffic of Memphis and the airport. Meanwhile, as a filler, he chattered about how grateful he was that she had come, and hoped she wouldn't mind spending the next two nights in the room he had grown up in.

She made a gracious comment on his wife's friendliness in making her welcome.

"My wife has been dead for nearly five years," he said quietly.

Then, compulsively cheerful, as if sadness were a sin, he switched the subject to his three daughters, all younger than twelve, and all delightful to him. And he talked about his mother, also a treasure, a woman widowed years ago, who had bought an old abandoned house, a huge wreck of a place, and converted it into an orphanage for black children, and a home for her two boys, the younger of whom was John.

"She's a sanctuary, that woman," he said. "Before I knew what a church was, I thought our house was it."

They had crossed the state line and were now riding along the farmland of northwestern Mississippi. The sky was a royal purple, a spangled mantle over the broad expanse of the cotton country. From the great wide river, not far away, there was a breeze so gentle that it seemed like a remembrance of other zephyrs, long ago, out of her schoolgirl reading . . . of a white boy and a black man floating on a raft. And now, here she was, a white woman with a black man, journeying another Mississippi pathway, and she was deeply grateful to be here, quietly joyful she had come. She thought: this is a blessed moment, with my child in a black preacher's arms; and we older ones, friends, conjoined to make a friendlier place for our children. Despite the storm and stress, she felt a promise of harmony. She felt good.

"Hakes," she said.

"He hasn't changed his story, not a bit."

"Which is?"

"Not involved in the robbery, and not at fault in the death of the detective."

"And their story?"

"It gets worse all the time. They now say that the criminals wore Klan hoods. And since they're certain that Ku Kluxers wouldn't use their own gear to rob a bank—and because the men wore white plastic gloves to hide the color of their hands—the robbers had to be black. It's useless to suggest blacks wouldn't use Klansmen's hoods either, and that gloves can conceal white hands as well as black ones. One of the bank tellers says the holdup men didn't utter a word, but another teller identifies Hakes by the sound of his voice. Oh, the discrepancies! But there's no discrepancy in the way Leon describes how the detective was about to hit him with the butt of the gun, and how the boy clutched at his wrist."

"Will he get a change of venue?"

"Who knows?" he said worriedly. "But we'll settle for a delay. We need time for people to know about it—everywhere."

"Well, you're not losing any time." She smiled. "The man who took the pictures—was he one of yours, or from the newspapers?"

He turned quickly. He was alarmed. "What pictures?"

"At the airport—a photographer."

"Dear heaven!"

"Is something wrong?"

"I'm afraid so." Perturbed: "Your coming was to be kept secret until you actually arrived. People change their minds—we didn't want to say your name and then be weakened by your absence. On the other hand, the news people would be there anyway—it would have been dramatic."

"But it leaked." He nodded. "How?"

"I don't know . . . and I don't want to know." His distress was deepening. "It's known that your name is on the lists—there was a call from a Washington paper—they had heard that you were coming. Luckily, the woman who answered the phone didn't know that you'd even been asked, and she said you wouldn't be here. But how did they hear about it?"

She could feel him getting more and more tense. A simpler man than she had thought him to be, he had no talent for connivance, and did not want to believe that duplicity existed, especially close to home. "How did they find out?" he went on. "Some say we have FBI people in our courthouse, and some say in the sheriff's office. And I've been told about a black man—one of our own . . . But I try not to believe these things, I try."

"Do you believe them now?"

He evaded the question. "We are so haunted by violence . . ."

He reached up and took off his hat. "Look."

Turning from her preoccupation with the road, she glanced at him. She couldn't at first descry the whiteness against the whiteness of his hair. Then she saw it. His head was bandaged. She made a shocked sound.

"This is the reason I was late," he said. "As I started to unlock the car—two men—I was lucky not to be killed. If I hadn't yelled—the children came running—and people from a café—and the hoodlums disappeared."

"Hoodlums?"

"I don't know what to call them. I was certain we had no Klan group in the town—not organized anyway. But now, who can tell? Then too, Rickert . . . who knows?" Still shaken by the attack, he turned his stricken face to her. "When I told you on the phone that we would be safe, I swear to you I believed it. I still believe it. We have a permit—we were promised police protection. I can't believe there will be any more violence, I can't believe it. The march will be peaceable—I am absolutely convinced it will be peaceable."

It was a tenet of faith he could not surrender. Without thinking too directly of the danger to herself and to her child, she thought pityingly of the man. What an illusion it was turning out to be, the dream of peace achieved through peace. Was that the only sermon that Reverend King's murder would finally deliver to his disciples—that peace was a forlorn hope in a forlorn world? Was it a homily that she too would have to heed?

She didn't see the other car coming. It approached, head-on, out of the blackness—without lights. Suddenly, when it was almost upon her, the lights sprang alive, the high beams a blinding shock in the dark night.

"Look out!" he cried.

She yanked at the wheel. The tires screeched; so did the other car's. The Plymouth skidded onto the soft shoulder of the road, and she yanked once more. There was a spray of sand. As the car zigzagged out of control, she clung to the wheel. She took a breath—they were riding safely again.

In the rearview mirror she could see the other car's taillights winking, disappearing in the distance.

"Speed up," he said. "They'll come again."

She had thought at first, in the habit of sanity, that it might have been a drunken driver or a crazy man. But she knew, as Tolliver now knew, that it was the calm, cold rationality of assault. The minister's faith that violence would not be repeated was grimly set aside: they'll come again.

They were thirty miles outside of Ashton. She pressed down on the accelerator. Sixty, sixty-five miles an hour. Going at this speed on the narrow blacktop, she was lucky that the road was deserted. Or unlucky; the attackers might not try anything if there were other cars.

"Faster," he said.

Seventy, seventy-five.

The old car could not be equal to any more, she thought, but he said faster.

Eighty, eighty-five.

At ninety miles an hour, the vehicle was shaking to pieces. Her hands quivered at the wheel; she had no control of the car; she was scared. She let it drop back to eighty, to seventy-five.

"Faster."

Again she fed the gas.

He was slightly turned and looking back. His voice was low. "Here they come."

It might be someone else, she said, another car, but as she saw how fast it was gaining, she knew it was the same.

"Give it everything," he said.

She looked at the rearview mirror. It was not a car but a monster with fiery eyes. Gaining more rapidly now, it was close.

"There are two men," he said, "two of them." As if it mattered how many. "I can't tell who they are."

The car was alongside, keeping pace—riding abreast of them at breakneck speed—a terrifying companion.

Suddenly it nipped in a little, its bumper barely grazing her left fender. Then away, and back again. Another nip, an animal snapping at a flank, another nip.

"Faster!"

It was at her once more, the gray beast, biting, clawing at her. Suddenly a sharper torque, a clatter of metal against metal, a flare of sparks. She twisted the wheel, yanked and twisted.

The shoulder of the road was not soft anymore. Something stubborn—concrete, steel—as hard as penalty. The car made a great noise and was no longer hers. It was in the air—turning, turning.

9

It was as if she had the pain in someone else's body. A distant thing, but close enough to touch. Yet, nowhere.

"Do you think you can stand up?" a voice said.

"Yes, I can stand up," she replied.

And she did, without a bit of trouble. In fact, the pain was gone when she stood up.

"Can you turn?"

"Yes, I can turn."

"Can you feel my hand? Can you reach out?"

She could do all those things, and more.

"Can you see me?"

She could see him very well. Young. White, and in white. A doctor, perhaps, or an intern. And a middle-aged woman beside him, also in white. A nurse. And there was a man wearing a dark uniform—gray, brown, blue?—a policeman, maybe, or a trooper.

"Mina!"

"Your daughter's all right," the doctor said. "You don't have to worry about her. She's had a bit of sedation and she's sleeping in the children's ward."

"Mina!"

"I said don't worry."

"The other one?" She could not remember the name. "The other one?"

"Reverend Tolliver?"

"Yes—him—what?"

"He's dead."

She said oh as if she were merely registering information, and then said it again, in a different way, not knowing what the syllable meant, simply crying it, because she had no other syllable in mind.

The nurse told her to be still. So did the doctor.

She knew well enough how to be still-silent but not how to be still-motionless; she could not keep from shaking.

She heard the doctor say something to the trooper, and could only make out that they were talking about sedation, and the officer said something negative about it, not until something or other was finished, as long as she's all right.

She heard herself talking about dying, not to anybody special, except perhaps to Tolliver, and what she said didn't connect with anything she was thinking. Then suddenly—

"Mina! You're lying about her, aren't you?"

"No, we're not," the doctor said.

"I want to see her—I want to see her."

The doctor looked at the officer, and the man nodded.

The doctor went first. Then Calla and the nurse. Behind them, the trooper. A long, long corridor. It was a parade, a slow parade. It's a death march, she thought. But quickly she crossed it out of her mind, slashed at it.

There were many beds in the narrow room; she didn't know how many. Everything was too clean and white. Even in the dimmed night lights of the place, the whiteness hurt her eyes. She looked in one bed, then another. This is not Mina, she said, and this is not, and this is not.

This is Mina, she said, and she is asleep. Let me touch her. Yes, warm, not cold. Let me see her body. Yes, she has all her limbs; her fingers move if I touch them; if I put my thumb in her palm, her hand closes as it used to when she was an infant. Let me touch her chest, her belly, let me feel her back, her ribs, her buttocks, yes, this is Mina, and she is all right. Oh God, yes, she is all right.

But wait a minute. "Is she all right?" she asked.

"Absolutely," the doctor said. "She has a slight bruise on her cheekbone—I'm surprised you missed it. But she's fine. The poor man took the impact on himself. He had her so protected, we could hardly pry her out of his arms."

She started to say oh again, in pity for him, but the nurse stopped her. Then the tears came, and she was back to knowing what things were and what they had been, and she felt her stomach distress again, and she could call everything by name.

"You're under arrest," the trooper said.

"I'm . . . ?" She didn't understand. She wondered if, after all, there was something she had not returned to. "I'm under arrest for what?"

"For reckless driving," he said. "And I don't know what else."

She couldn't tell what the room was, except that it was in the federal courthouse and it was full of people. There were only men in here, a sheriff and his deputy, two policemen, somebody they deferentially called Marshal, his assistant and two photographers. In the shadowy corner of the room a fattish man sat on a folding chair; he was familiar-looking: the hunting boots and the liver-spotted skin.

There was a yellow oaken table that the marshal and the sheriff sat behind, and on the table, a well-known object, her canvas suitcase.

The marshal who was the important man had a long narrow face and orange-colored hair; the sheriff had no hair at all except what was growing out of his ears and nostrils, but it was luxuriant. He also had one tooth missing, a canine. He held a thick rubber band in his left hand and his fingers toyed with it, making it slip from digit to digit; it was a trick.

"My name is Ingels," one of them said. "I'm the federal marshal. And this is County Sheriff Boone Rickert." He grinned hospitably.

The sheriff's laugh seemed to come through a thick paste. He made a show of friendliness. "We know who you are, Miz Stark. Nobody have to tell us who you are."

"You want to start, Boonie?" the marshal asked him.

"Nope. You got the precedence." He laughed; the paste burbled.

The man who had the precedence began. He pointed to her canvas bag. "This was taken from the car you were drivin', Miss Stark. Is it your property?"

"Yes, it is."

"You got anything that it's illegal to carry across the state line— like liquor or drugs or a gun without a license?"

"No, nothing."

"That's your statement, is it?"

"Yes."

Sheriff Rickert laughed. "We'll see that soon enough."

Her head swam. There was a terrible disorder in their orderliness, a well-conducted chaos. She turned, saw the trooper, then addressed the marshal.

"He says I'm under arrest for reckless driving."

The sheriff replied, "Well, you're not goin' to deny *that* charge, are you?" As if she had already denied a series of others.

"Yes, I am. I was not driving recklessly. I was trying to avoid . . . There was another car—it forced me off the road." Then, seeing their impassive faces, she made a vague gesture to the trooper. "He knows what happened."

"How does he know, ma'am?" the sheriff asked. Then, quickly, to the trooper, "How do you know, Parmie? Was you a witness to the accident?"

"I sure wasn't."

"He says he weren't, Miz Stark, so how does he know?"

Because she told him, she would have to say, and it would sound foolish. "I was pushed off the road by another car."

The sheriff looked at the marshal, then they both looked at the trooper, who shrugged.

"What other car, Miz Stark?"

"There was another— My God, it was gray—there were two men in it."

"What make was it?"

"I don't know."

"Did you get the license number?"

"No, of course not. . . . Oh Christ."

"Don't curse in the courthouse, ma'am," Boone Rickert said.

The deputy sheriff and the assistant marshal were emptying her canvas bag on the oak table. They took out her night clothes, her extra blouse and skirt, underwear, Mina's pajamas and cookies, toilet articles, everything.

She didn't know whether her tremors came from her unsettled stomach or the violation of her privacy. Every garment was opened, the pockets searched, the hemline of the skirt squeezed, the night clothes and sleeves turned inside out.

She was becoming increasingly nauseous. Looking off to the right, she saw the door with the word Ladies on it. "While you're doing that, may I go in there, please?"

"No, you may not," Marshal Ingels said.

"I'm not feeling well."

"You'll have to wait until we finish."

Sick, and afraid she might throw up at any instant, it occurred to her why they would not let her go to the john. They thought she wanted to get rid of something she had carried across the state line; ironically they were right, but vomit was not contraband.

"If you think I'm hiding something, you may search me," she said.

"We're not allowed to do that," the marshal replied. "We're waiting for the matron."

Her stomach began to heave, and she made a little sound in her throat. "Please let me go."

"Stay here."

"I'm sick—I'm going to vomit."

They looked at her quickly, then at each other, but the marshal shook his head. She suddenly felt dizzy and her insides began to give way. She ran.

"Get her!"

She heard a flurry behind her, and a curse, and someone running in pursuit. It was the deputy, she thought, as she made it to the door. She flung herself into the ladies' room and heard the rush that followed her. The man grabbed and twisted her body. The insult to her stomach happened. The vomit came, a great gush at the deputy and upon herself, and it did not seem stoppable. The man released her and hurried to the toilet.

"You bitch," she heard him say. "You bitch."

In the stall, Calla kept spewing and spewing, and sobbing. After a while, she was through with it. The man was at one of the sinks, washing the puke off his shirt and off his badge.

"You bitch," he kept saying. "You Commie bitch."

Calla cleaned herself as best she could, and preceded the deputy back to the other room.

The red-haired marshal pointed to all her belongings on the table. "You can put your property back in," he said. "All but these."

He was pointing to a small plastic vial that contained capsules of a stomach sedative, and to the little cardboard box that Eric Ramsey had given her; there were still four gray, hexagonal pills in it.

He pointed to the vial. "What are these?"

"They're antacid capsules—for my stomach."

It was obviously not necessary to prove her need for them. He lifted the small box. "And these?"

"I have trouble sleeping."

"Narcotics, you mean?"

"No, I don't mean that. I don't know what they are."

"It's a federal offense, Miss Stark," the marshal said.

"What is?"

"Bringing illegal drugs across the state line. And I'm charging you with it." He wrote something down, then looked up. "It'll take precedence over the county's charge against you."

His voice droned for a few minutes about her legal rights.

When he finished, the sheriff said, "And I'm chargin' you with reckless drivin' while under the influence of drugs. And manslaughter."

He too read her her legal rights.

Almost in unison, the photographers moved forward. Lights flashed. One of the cameras came too close and as the light blazed in her face, she threw her arm up to protect her eyes. The assistant marshal pulled it down and she struck at him. Another picture was taken.

"I want to call a lawyer," she said.

"Sure." The marshal smiled. "Phone right there on the wall."

She had forgotten the name of the man she wanted, and did not know any number for him. "Who's defending Mr. Hakes?" she asked.

"He ain't no 'mister,'" the sheriff said. "But who's defendin' him is Gus Mayfield."

"And he ain't no 'mister' neither," his deputy said.

All the men laughed.

"Mayfield's at the Ashton Arms Hotel," the marshal said.

She called Mayfield and told him what had happened. The men in the room pretended to pay no attention. But the fat man, at the farthest distance from the phone, got up and moved closer. Arms folded across his chest, he cocked an ear and openly listened.

Mayfield said he would be right over.

The cell in the federal court building was immaculately clean. Calla sat on the hard bench and waited.

She wondered how deeply Mina was asleep . . . and Tolliver. Odd, that his face was clearer to her than her child's. She wished that he had not smiled so much, that he had been more lacking in courage or had had less faith in his fellow man; she wished that he had been less worthy of a long, good life. As she recalled how sweetly he had held her daughter in his arms, she wished he had no children and no mother who would grieve for him. She wished . . .

Later than she had expected, Gus Mayfield arrived. He had been scurrying for a bail bond, relatively easy to obtain for a famous actress who could not jump it and just flee anywhere, but difficult in the middle of the night. He wore unruly, mismatched clothing, he had a pock-marked face and angry arms which were constantly in motion, wrestling wildcats. Almost the instant he met her, as if to give her his liberal credentials, he said he had been only fourteen when he marched in Montgomery to boycott the Jim Crow buses. She did not need his dossier to like and trust him.

Still youngish, he was experienced in every kind of red tape—bureaucratic ballbusting, he called it—and did not let the county clerk or the assistant marshal stall him. He did, however, countersign the proviso that the defendant was not to leave the state until the federal probable-cause hearing at which it would be determined whether Calla would be dismissed on the narcotics charge or be bound over to a grand jury.

When the cell door was opened and they were walking up the stairs to the main floor of the courthouse, Calla noticed that her nausea was gone, but her whole body ached as if the crash had stripped her skeleton of flesh; her bones grated against one another.

"Where will I stay?" she asked. "The hotel?"

"No." He pointed. The bleak corridor was lighted only by the entrance lamps at the distant end. Mayfield raised a hand of greeting to the woman. She stood against the remote light, silhouetted, and now she slowly walked toward them.

As they met halfway, Calla saw that the black woman was tall, with the same glow of mahogany skin as Calla remembered, and the same white hair. Lorena Tolliver, the dead man's mother.

Hardly had they acknowledged one another than Calla blurted, in an act of confession: "Mrs. Tolliver—I was driving."

"*They* was drivin'," she corrected. Then quickly, as if afraid there might be a reenactment of the tragedy, "I don' want to hear nothin'," she said. "Gus tol' me all I need to know—don' want to hear no more."

There were no tears in the woman, no lowering of her white head, no faltering in the strength of her stride. But suddenly she became aware that her need might be different from Calla's. She stopped walking and looked at her.

"You poor one," she said.

The woman opened her arms and embraced Calla, giving her an acquittance from fault, letting her weep for the death of her son. Then, having endured all she could, "Don' cry no more," she said. That was all she would allow.

There was no question where Calla was going to spend the night. "In my house," Mrs. Tolliver said. "Jus' like it was planned."

Just like her son had planned it, she meant of course, but already she was learning to exclude him from the conversation.

Mayfield drove them home. They rode in silence through the city streets, crossed the bridge over a rivulet, and as they approached the poorer part of town:

"Are we anywhere near the hospital?" Calla asked.

"Not far," Mrs. Tolliver replied.

"Could we stop there and let me off?"

"At this hour? It's goin' on four o'clock."

"If she wakes up in a strange place . . ."

The woman reached and touched her. "They won' let you see her this time of night, child. It's a mean little hospital. Real democratic— unkind to white and black alike. I been takin' my orphan kids there near thirty years, an' it seem to get meaner all the time. If they don' like you, they take it out on the children."

That was a deterrent; she didn't want her anxieties to work against her child. She realized that Mina was under sedation and might sleep later than usual, but she would take no chances. She determined to be there well before the child awakened.

Mrs. Tolliver understood her stress. "Now don' you upset yourself. I promise to wake you up at sunrise. An' if they's ready to discharge her, you take and bring her home."

Calla wanted to lie down; she felt that her bones were being racked.

They passed the hospital and when they arrived at the house, she realized that the distance between them was quite short, she could walk there in a few minutes.

The Tolliver house, an antebellum mansion without pillars, had once been grand. Its rich owners had tried to sell it when it had become surrounded by the black population, and had finally abandoned it to vandals and pillagers. Mrs. Tolliver, after the death of her husband, had taken possession of the place, and, with the aid of donations, had converted it into an orphanage, for her own two semi-orphans as well. It was enormous, with white wood and plaster now gone gray, a decrepit roof, an overabundance of vines, and hollyhocks thriving ahead of the season.

As Mayfield's car pulled away, the women walked up the creaking steps onto a rickety porch and entered the center hall. In the dimness, lighted only by a faint glow at the top of the stairs, there was a stir.

"Who's that?" Mrs. Tolliver called.

"It's us, Mamma Lorena," a child's voice said.

Barely discernible in the shadows, her three grandchildren were sitting on the staircase. Two of them were identical twins; the tallest was the oldest; under twelve, Tolliver had said.

"Lor', what you doin', this time of night?" the black woman said.

"Binnie was cryin'," the oldest one said. "She kep' us all awake."

Binnie was still crying. "It ain't true he's dead, is it, Mamma Lorena?"

"Yes, it's true," she replied with an unnatural flatness in her voice. "Now, go on up to bed, all of you, an' do some prayin' for him. Go on up now."

Two of them, whose fear had not yet turned to grief, went up the stairs. But Binnie, grieving, stayed. "I ain't goin' to pray for him," she said.

"What else you goin' to do, child?" The woman's voice was less steady than before.

"I ain't goin' to pray." The stubbornness did not shore up the flooding misery.

"Just goin' to cry, are you?"

"Ain't goin' to cry, neither."

"What you goin' to do, Binnie?"

"Nothin'," she said, weeping. "Just ain't goin' to do nothin'."

The only sign that Mamma Lorena was touched by her was that she walked up the steps, extended her hand to the child and led her upward.

Calla waited in the hallway. Presently, she heard the old woman coming down the stairs. But at the upper landing, out of sight, her footsteps halted. Mrs. Tolliver was standing up there in the shadows, simply standing there, unseen, not moving. It seemed a long time. Then, once more, the sound of her footsteps.

She was much as she had appeared before, unshakable. "Your room is on the first floor," she said. "I had it all ready for you. . . . The march tomorrow . . . I wonder is there goin' to be a march . . . or services, or anything?"

The room was small and orderly, with a wicker rocking chair, red calico cushioned, and a bedspread of red calico as well. When Mamma

Lorena had turned down the bed and gone, it would have been a comfortable place to spend the night . . . if Calla could sleep. But she knew she couldn't. Taking her shoes off, she lay down fully clothed, eyes wide, listening to the sigh of a tree somewhere, not close; still further away, the grumbling complaint of bullfrogs.

If only she could sleep.

The hospital was an easy walking distance.

Her mind raced against an ache. She was in the car, seventy, eighty, ninety miles an hour. Faster, he said.

Easy walking distance.

She saw the face of her daughter.

Sitting up, she put her shoes on, tiptoed to the door, opened it as quietly as possible and slipped out of the house.

She turned to the right, toward the hospital. The street was totally still, deserted. It was hardly a street, but a dirt road, rutted in many places. The dwellings were tiny and dilapidated, some were shacks, standing lopsidedly, so crippled by age that they yearned to fall. Everything appeared to be separating, crumbling away, a porch roof without shingles, stairs without treads. The few trees seemed like abandonments, remembered only by the faint breeze and by the Spanish moss that hung from their limbs, like lynchings.

She was on the city street with the hospital in sight. It was further than she had imagined. Approaching it, she saw the first hinted brightening of sky.

She had not remembered leaving the hospital, and now, as she walked up its front steps, the entrance was unfamiliar.

The lobby was empty. Only a black man with a barrel vacuum cleaning the pale green, rubber-tiled floor, and two women behind the reception counter. One was at the switchboard, nodding asleep; the other had her elbow on the counter, her head resting on her hand; she too was asleep.

The telephone woman was the first to notice Calla. She whispered to the receptionist who came suddenly awake.

"What is it?" she said to the night intruder.

"I want to see my daughter," Calla replied.

The woman, fully alert now, recognized her. "I—she—" Stopping, she looked for help from the other one.

The switchboard operator also seemed at a loss, but by this time the receptionist had recovered. "There's a doctor up there," she said. "The children's ward—second floor."

Calla did not go down the corridor to the elevator, but took the
stairs, which were closer. She needed to run. There was something
wrong, she knew, or they would have given her more trouble.

She remembered everything about the building now, the beige
walls, the diamond-shaped green tiles on the floor, the door to the children's ward. As she was about to enter it, the doctor and nurse came
out.

"You can't go in there," he said.

"My daughter—Mina—Loftus—"

The nurse barred the way. "The children are asleep."

"Your child is dead," he said.

"No."

"There were internal injuries."

"No!"

Violent, she shoved the nurse out of the way and ran into the
hushed ward. Two thirds down the room, one of the beds had a screen
around it. She rushed, she grappled with the unwieldly object, it
buckled, teetered, collapsed on the floor. The light was too dim, she
could hardly see anything. She tore at the sheet that covered the face,
kept crying no, no, touched the cold cheek, not certain it was cold, felt
the arm, lifted it, already too inflexible to be an arm, starting to be only
a thing, no, touching, touching the cold face. Internal injuries, he had
said, we all have internal injuries, but a child— The eyes were open because they were alive, she told herself, yet the mouth was rigid and icy,
everything going to stone. She embraced the dead thing, and could not
endure it.

She ran out of the ward, out of the hospital, ran one direction but
it was not the right direction, ran another direction and that too was
wrong, there was no right way, no right place for a child to die in. She
rushed down one street and another, and was lost.

Later that morning, Mrs. Tolliver found her, she did not recognize
the place, except that there were hallways, with telephones ringing. She
was taken to a room that had a window and a bed, and she had a sense
of calico and redness, and Mamma Lorena asking her barely audible
questions about people to call, about family and friends, and Calla did
not know the answers. The black woman rubbed her hands and her
head and gave her things to drink and said that she would feel drowsy,
but she didn't. She knew she had something important to do, and could

not imagine what it was. . . . Call Barney and tell him that his child was dead.

She could not do it, she decided, nor would she ever be able to do it. She started to say no again, repeatedly, and at last forced herself to say other words to rout the agonizing one, and the only utterance that gave her any comfort was Willi's name. If only she could see her, talk to her, get her on the telephone.

"You sure you can't remember the number?" Mrs. Tolliver said. "Not even where she live?"

At last, remembering, she called.

"Calla! Calla, is that you?"

"Willi . . ."

Willi, she kept crying, no more than that, as if she hoped it was the only word she would need to tell her suffering.

"Calla—for God's sake—what is it?"

"Mina—"

"Calla—what?"

"Mina—tell Barney. Oh no—don't! She's dead, Willi!"

"What? For God's sake—what?"

As she started to tell, and as Willi said she would be there right away, it became too much to relate, too impossible to recount to anyone she knew, impossible to talk with anyone she loved. Don't come, she said, please don't come, I can't do with anyone, I can't live it again, don't come, don't come.

The most she could manage would be with strangers, at best with Mamma Lorena.

How strange, she thought afterward, that she didn't want Willi there, because it was her godchild. . . . Her godchild, as if that were Mina's sole identity. The guilt of it came home, that she had killed not only her own child but someone else's as well, the child of others, of Barney, of Willi, the grandchild of her father. It was as if she had betrayed everyone; a traitor not to her country but to the more intimate countries of the heart.

For days, waiting for her probable-cause hearing to come up, she lost herself. She wandered in the town and in the woods nearby, she came to a moment of consciousness here and a moment there, found herself on a strange street or in a strange neighborhood where people had to show her the way to another neighborhood, and she felt as if she were in a foreign land and spoke the wrong language, and every word that came out of her mouth seemed to say, I killed my child.

Sometimes she ran from the self-condemnation for fear she would lose her clutch on sanity, and charged herself with lesser reproaches. If she had insisted on getting out of Mayfield's car and had entered the hospital on her first impulse, if she had, earlier, asked for x-rays and the opinions of other doctors . . .

But at last she forced herself to gaze at the hard, the real, the terrible blame she had to lay upon herself. Why had she indeed brought the child with her? Why, irrespective of Tolliver's disclaimer about danger, why had she not known in her heart that there was peril and peril, and nothing else? Why did she take her recklessness for courage? What good to lay a wreath of bravery on a child's coffin? What good was her foolish dream, her love of mankind and her mirage of peace, when the facts of life were rage and war, and the destruction of her beautiful child? Oh, Mina, she cried, come back, I need you, I need to see you and touch you, oh, Mina.

Sometimes she found herself speaking to Mina as if she were still alive, and growing up before her very eyes: Lacing shoes is easy, she said to her daughter, did you paint that sailboat all by yourself, what's the difference between a widget and a gadget, here are some pencils you can take to school, you're getting prettier all the time, stand up straight, you can find it in the dictionary, of course we're ticklish, it runs in the family, there are two e's in Shelley, do you really want to call her Winnie the Pooch? . . . It was the laughing together that made her cry.

She had read somewhere that a remedy for bereavement was the memory of the dead in happy times. So she recalled Barney with Mina in his arms, running toward her on Trancas Beach; and she recalled the three of them sitting in the soft twilight, watching and hearing the sea pound against the window. And she recalled Mina learning to count, and the little girl on the potty with a flannel puppy in her arms, and the silly thumbsucking game.

And the other game as well. The sitting and looking at one another, the incantation of one another's name, the touch of voices, the loving rite of presence.

"Meeeenaaaa," she said in a whisper.

Perhaps, Calla thought, I'm not listening carefully enough. . . .

"Meeeenaaaa . . ."

There was an incurable quiet.

She wasn't aware, at first, what was happening to her in Mamma Lorena's house. In the period before the hearing came up, the old black woman simply put her to work in the orphanage. Calla made beds, set tables, helped to serve meals, stuffed the two washing machines with children's clothes. At the beginning, she found herself counting the items she had to deal with—how many knives and forks, the number of socks, shirts, underpants. Then she found herself counting children, which was, according to Mamma, a vast improvement over counting things.

One afternoon, she became aware of John Tolliver's oldest daughter, Tilda, and how she was writing all the time, and hiding what she wrote. Then the twins, Binnie and Karinetta, and how Binnie was always crying and Karie was always telling her to wipe her nose. They took Calla for walks in the woods, and one day on a longer hike than usual, they showed her a creek, and Tilda said, "Why, it jus' surrender to the Ashton River, which surrender to the big, big Missipp'." She was not as pretty as the twins but she had a darting imagination. There were alligators in the marsh, called "croachers," and Tilda related tales about how they ate people's heads off, only their heads, and "if a good man git his head bit off by a croacher, his body fly off to heaven, but a bad man fall clunk like a stone." The twins squealed in terror, shrieking stop, Tildy, stop skeerin' us.

The other orphans, all twenty-two of them, seemed like nothing but shadows at first, except for their eyes, which stared inwardly upon themselves or outwardly at the sky's distance, either too close or too far. Then she saw how beautiful and hungry they were, and how some of the lonelier ones rubbed their glances on her, furrily like kittens.

"Don't spoil 'em," Mamma Lorena said, but her smile said go on and do it. "You sweet 'em up too much. You is part woman and part Hershey bar."

Calla couldn't help it. She had to love them and feel them loving her. She looked for someone small enough to hold in her arms, but the youngest was past five, and Calla was not sure of herself as yet, not confident she could manage anyone who might be old enough to know. Know what? she asked herself, and for a while she puzzled over the question. Then, by glints, by chance reflection she realized she was seeking the little blond white child in every black face, and finding a glance here and a smile there, and sometimes the lift of a head that reminded her of her young one. But despairingly she perceived she would never assemble the disparate reminders into the integral presence of her dead child.

The non-violent march that Reverend Tolliver had dreamed of

leading had indeed happened; it was his funeral procession. And Mina's. So also, in his absence, had his peaceful prayer meeting come to pass. But unfortunately, the attendance had been meager, for hardly anyone had wanted to be visible. Yet, everybody, whites and blacks alike, claimed a triumph, both sides agreeing that it had been an exemplary tribute to the peaceable spirit of the reverend, who had died so tragically —and inexplicably. Rumors that the car crash had not been an accident were muffled—too many people were afraid.

The march and the prayer meeting had not, of course, accomplished what the reverend had hoped for; no change of venue had been granted, and the day of Hakes's trial was fast approaching.

Calla's trial, however, had had two postponements. Mayfield thought the delays were a government harassment of Calla in the war of nerves. More and more she dreaded the probable-cause hearing, and tried to escape it in her mind. One day she found a refuge.

It was called the Bayou. Late on a summer's afternoon, wandering alone, she went further and further along the creek than Tilda and the twins had ever taken her, and step by unnoticeable step, found herself deep in a luxuriant woodland. The children had never mentioned any wooded area; a forest seemed contradictory to this marshy flatland. But it was a lovely wildwood, as thick as a jungle in places, full of scrub and underbrush and creepers, and the soft sounds of animals in the cover. She rambled through it, not worried by the sense that she was lost, when all at once she was out of the sylvan closeness and into the Bayou. It was a marshland, serene and beautiful, where the creek widened into the river. Millions of birds came winging in from all directions, making a market day of song and color. On this balmy afternoon, the little pools and the lagoons were dappled by an uneventful wind; the reeds and tall grasses billowed like a coverlet of silk. The benevolence of everything, the charitable seclusion of the place was such a relief from the turmoil that Calla felt as if she had wandered into a slumber.

She went there often, always alone. She spent hours wading in the creek, sifting minnows through her fingers, reading, dozing, trying to reassemble the routed parts of herself. She knew all the changes in the Bayou's day, its time-stopping noons and its rioting sunsets. Like the birds, she had found her sanctuary.

Actually, the place was not unknown. At one edge of the Bayou, in a crescent around a large lagoon, there was a cluster of houses. Elsewhere, such dwellings would be called shacks or shanties, but here they seemed so rightfully a part of glade and wetland that they were beautiful to Calla, not tainted with privation. In fact, the blacks who lived there—Gurries, they were called—seemed far removed from worldly values, riches or poverty. They lived on whatever the Bayou gave them —fish from the river, rice from the bogs, greenery from the woodland. As if not to disturb the wildlife, they were soft-spoken people, even their smiles were soft. When they first saw her, they were as diffident to approach as if she were a visiting bird.

One day, when she had been there for hours and had fallen asleep in the scrub grass of a dune, she was awakened by a delectable aroma. There was an earthenware bowl of delicious chowder—fish and corn in creamy milk, soothing and savory—and not a sign of anyone. But there were a child's footprints in the sand. She ravenously ate every drop of the comforting concoction, then started in search of her benefactors. But she thought better of it. Instead, the following day, she left a basket full of caramels and M&M's and Milky Ways, and cookies of a dozen kinds. Next day, the confections were gone. Thereafter, whenever she saw any of the Gurries, they all smiled together, and the children giggled juicily and everyone shared a secret. There were other exchanges. Someone left her a pair of homemade sandals made of reeds; she left a pile of children's coloring books, with crayons. And she thought: What an intimate moment I'm having with them, what a delicate embrace without words, with strangers. There was a soft, sweet entrancement in the plainness of it, as there was magic in the place itself, a hushed rapport of wind and water. It was an unspoken mystery, preciously guarded.

But the Bayou days came to an end. Gus Mayfield called to say there would be no further postponements in the probable-cause hearing; a definite date had been set. The day before the trial, the lawyer came to the house with news of Hakes. They sat in the little parlor, away from the clatter of the children, and Mayfield cursed at what had happened in the black man's case.

A deal had been made. Hakes had confessed to having taken part in the robbery, and had named his two accomplices—both Memphis men, both now on the run. And Wilson, the detective who had witnessed the shooting of Averill, had admitted that perhaps he had not seen the occurrence too clearly, and perhaps the black man had not in fact laid his hands upon the gun. The murder charge would be dismissed in a few days, and Hakes would be sentenced for the robbery.

Mayfield was disgusted with everybody. He had come up from Vicksburg to contribute his time and services without a dollar's com-

pensation, and now even his psychic compensation would be nil. There
had been no moral pleasure in the whole case—both sides had lied, both
had been criminally at fault and no decent issue had been served.

"Both goddamn sides—everybody guilty!" he exclaimed bitterly.
He pointed to John Tolliver's portrait on the mantelpiece. "The only
innocent one is dead."

"Two."

"Yes, two."

His primary purpose in being here was to go over the testimony she
would be giving at her own trial, tomorrow. He listened, for the third
time, to every detail of her life that was pertinent to the case, and to a
recital of every incident on the fatal evening when she was arrested.
Well after she thought they were finished, he still did not get up to go.
He took a deep breath.

"Now," he said. "There's the whole question of what you will say
if they ask if you're a Communist."

She smiled wearily. She had told the lawyer, Simon Ehrenstein,
that she was not a Communist, she had told Barney, her father, Willi,
Megan, the same thing, never hesitating to tell the truth, as a voluntary
confidence among intimates. But if faced with what she considered an
illegal demand, an invasion of her sacred privacy, she would have to refuse to answer. And, of course, no matter what she answered, they
would believe what they wanted to believe.

"It's funny," she said, seeing only bitter humor in it, "when a reactionary asks me if I'm a Communist and I refuse to answer, he's sure I
am one. When a Communist asks and I refuse, he's sure I'm not."

"I don't want you to answer it."

"I wouldn't—except to a friend."

"And don't tell *me*, either—I'm not a friend."

She thought he must be joking, but his expression was grave.

"I'm surprised at that," she said.

"Why? You think I ought to buy the whole package?"

"I don't know what you mean."

"Because I believe in civil rights and the parity of blacks, do I have
to be against the war in Vietnam?"

She was amazed. "They generally go together."

" 'Generally' is a goddamn stereotype! Listen here, Miss Stark, I
admire your coming down here. I admire your honesty and your courage and your good heart. But I've got to tell you, I hate your attitude to
the war. I think it's two-faced and unpatriotic, and I think you're more

loyal to the reds than you are to the red, white and blues—whether you're a Communist or not. And I can name you thousands of Southerners who feel the way I do—and they still feel that the blacks should have a fair break. Southern people, Miss Stark. On the other hand, I know thousands of Southerners who want the war to end, win or lose— right now—and they don't want the blacks to use the same toilets as they do, and they want them shoved to the back of the bus. Now, you don't believe that decent, honest, well-meaning Americans can agree with you on one issue and disagree with you on another. You want them to buy your package, the whole damn thing. Miss Stark, I don't believe in packages—I hate 'em! A lot of you Yankees put us southern people into packages—and that's another way of declaring war against the South. And I can tell you: for every white liberal who came down to fight for civil rights, I can name you a whole grange full of white southern conservatives who've been fighting for them since before you were born!"

"I'm sure you're right, but—"

"No buts. I don't want to make this a polemical discussion with a client I admire. But I had to be honest with you. I know where you are —and I felt you had a right to know where I am. Only one thing—if you publicly admit to being a Communist, I drop the case."

"Fair enough."

The following day, in the federal courthouse building, the probable-cause hearing was held to determine whether Calla Stark had in fact carried illicit drugs across a state line, and whether she would be dismissed or bound over to a grand jury.

The courtroom was not large, and there were no spectators. The tables, the chairs, the witness box, the judge's bench were of yellow oak so glossily varnished as to be blinding. The chamber smelled of official cleanliness—naphtha, perhaps, or chlorine, or both; as if by disinfection the court could be cleansed of crime.

Presiding over the trial was U.S. Commissioner Alvin C. Humber, who had suggested, about two years ago, that there was nothing about the Vietnam ailment that a small-sized hydrogen bomb would not cure. The man who presented the government's case against Calla was of somewhat the same opinion, which he expressed with a bit more attenuation. He was U.S. Attorney Hugo Stellmaker.

The government's attorney had only one witness against Calla— U.S. Marshal Ingels. The red-haired man was expert at giving testimony; nothing ruffled him. When Stellmaker turned him over to Mayfield, the defense lawyer found him unshakable.

"No, sir," he replied to a question Mayfield put to him. "There was absolutely no harassment of Miss Stark—none at all."

"You didn't prevent her from going to the ladies' room?"

"Objection," Stellmaker said. "The witness has already testified that he didn't lay a finger on the defendant. If the defense is attempting to create sympathy for a so-called sick woman—"

"So-called?" Mayfield interrupted.

The commissioner lightly tapped his gavel. "Sustained."

Mayfield started on another tack. "Marshal, were you given any previous information that Miss Stark was arriving in Ashton?"

"Objection," Stellmaker said.

"Sustained."

Mayfield continued. "Nobody in your Washington office informed you that she was arriving?"

"Objection."

"Sustained."

"Nobody in the office of the Attorney General—"

"Objection, objection!"

"—or in any other Washington office—"

Stellmaker jumped to his feet. "Your honor, I object. Counsel is simply trying to get an irrelevancy into the record."

"It is not an irrelevancy," Mayfield retorted. "Miss Stark's arrest had nothing to do with the possession of narcotics, but was clearly an exercise in political harassment. It was instituted in Washington—"

"Objection!"

"—to discredit her as a leader in the peace movement."

"Mr. Mayfield." The commissioner was vexed. "You'll have to desist from this, Counselor. Washington is not on trial here."

"I'm not suggesting that it is, Commissioner. I'm simply trying to disclose that an order was issued to arrest Miss Stark on whatever pretext—"

Humber banged the gavel again, sharply this time. "Mr. Mayfield, if you insist on developing this argument, you will have to find some way that is germane to the proceedings."

Stymied, Mayfield started back toward the witness, changed his mind, and walked to the exhibits table. On a marked board there were the two containers of medicament. He lifted the cardboard box, opened it and extracted one of the gray, hexagonal pills. He walked close to Ingels and showed him the open box.

"Marshal, have you ever seen these pills?"

"Yes, sir."

"When?"

"On the night Miss Stark was arrested."

"Before that night, had you ever seen these pills?"

"Well, I've seen pills like it."

"Exactly like it? This shape? This color?"

"Well, not exactly, no. That's probably a foreign pill."

Mayfield pounced on it. "Precisely—it *is* a foreign pill." Quickly he moved even closer to the witness and showed him the box. "Now this box—look at it closely—is there anything written on it?"

"No, sir."

"Right. Nothing written." He showed the box from every angle. "Anything written or printed anywhere? Inside—outside—anywhere?"

"No, nothing."

"Nothing—not a thing." He looked into the marshal's eyes in a most friendly way. "Are you a pharmacist, Marshal Ingels?"

"Objection."

The commissioner turned to Stellmaker. "On what grounds do you object?"

"He's ridiculing the witness, Commissioner. The man's already identified himself as a United States marshal."

With an innocent smile, Mayfield turned to his adversary. "You've identified yourself as an Assistant United States Attorney, but I happen to know you're also a specialist in commemorative American postage stamps."

The commissioner smiled and said to Mayfield, "You may ask the question."

"Are you a pharmacist, Marshal Ingels?"

"No, I'm not."

"A physician?"

"No, sir."

"Since there is nothing written on this box, is there anything in your background that could make you certain that it contains a narcotic of any kind?"

"No, sir, but—"

"Is there any reason for you to say that these pills—which you had never seen before—are an illegal drug?"

"Yes, sir. Miss Stark said they were sleeping pills."

"Are you sure she said that? Didn't Miss Stark say, 'I have trouble sleeping'?"

"It's the same thing."

"You think so? Some people who have trouble sleeping take aspirin, isn't that so? Some people take hot milk, isn't that so? Isn't that so, Marshal Ingels?"

During the last few interchanges, Stellmaker was on his feet again, shouting objections. But it was too late. Mayfield had won an important point. He had sighted his prey, and now he ran it down.

"Marshal, did you at any time ask the defendant whether she had a prescription for these medications?"

"No, I didn't."

"Isn't it a regulation that you must ask that question?"

"Well, in a way it is, but—"

"Then why didn't you ask it? Did Washington waive that regulation?"

"They didn't tell me that."

"They didn't tell you *that*. What *did* they tell you, Marshal Ingels?"

"Objection!"

Again too late. Ingels, the unflappable, had flapped.

Mayfield dismissed the witness, and turned immediately to address the commissioner. "I ask for an adjournment until tomorrow."

"Tomorrow?" Stellmaker said. "I was under the impression we were winding up this afternoon."

"I would like to bring another witness who is out of the state, and not available today."

The U.S. Attorney was irked. "May I ask who the witness is?"

Mayfield was under no compulsion to tell him, but he was enjoying himself. "I'll be glad to take you into my confidence," he said. "I'm calling William B. Connery—he's a photographer with the Memphis *Press-Scimitar*. He was telephoned by Marshal Ingels' assistant about three hours before Miss Stark's arrival in Memphis. He was told—quote —'Hang around the airport. Catch her comin' and goin'—there's goin' to be fireworks.'"

Stellmaker's face fell. The Washington complicity in Calla's arrest might be verifiable. But he could not prevent the adjournment. Humber granted it.

The federal trial was never resumed. Late that afternoon, at the

Tolliver house, the phone rang and it was Mayfield. The U.S. Attorney's office had sent him a hand-delivered letter giving notice that tomorrow they would move to dismiss the case.

The following morning, he called again. At Sheriff Rickert's urging, the county attorney had also dropped the charges against Calla. Now that they could not make a case for reckless driving under the influence of drugs, the manslaughter charge might also not hold up. Most important, they were panicky about Mayfield. He was a terrier who would worry their case to death. They were afraid of what he might uncover—an automobile riding murderously in the night, perhaps.

Calla was exonerated.

But the victory was the government's. There was hardly a major newspaper in the country that had not carried an account of the arrest. The headlines had said that she had been charged with driving under the influence of drugs, and she had caused the death of an admirable black minister and of her own child. Who could believe her cock and bull story of a spectral automobile that had never been found or credibly identified? In any case, she had skirmished with police, she had been sick when arrested and in nearly all versions of the tragedy, there was the innuendo that it was a drug-related illness. She was an addict, probably. So nothing she had to say about the war or civil rights need ever again be credited. No point in listening to the carpings of an unbalanced, dope-habituated woman.

There was only one grace that came out of all of it: her meeting with Mrs. Tolliver. Calla regretted having to leave Lorena without truly getting to know her. She had thought of her as an unassailable island of serenity, but had soon realized that Mamma's apparent calm was costly to her, and Calla suspected that the black woman had terrible night agonies. Nothing of this torment was ever revealed. She was in pain for Lorena; she had come to love her, and dreaded having to leave. So she delayed going, and delayed.

At last, one night, on a surge of bravery, she suddenly embraced the old woman and wouldn't let her go.

"When?" was all Mamma said.

"Tomorrow, I think."

"Calla, honey . . ."

The old woman had not shed a tear through all the rest of it, the death of her son and Calla's daughter, the funeral, the memorial service, never. Nor did she now.

The next morning, at departure time, the actress gave the orphanage a donation. The old black woman looked at the check. "A thousand dollars—it's such a lot of money."

These days, it was a lot to Calla as well, nearly all she had. "I'll send you more from time to time," she said. "This is my orphanage too."

Outdoors, waiting for the taxi to arrive, the two women embraced once more. Suddenly, in the midst of it, Calla felt a spasm run through Lorena's body. It was violent, like a seizure. With a lurch, the old woman wrested herself out of the embrace. She stood there, shaking, gasping for breath, in a paroxysm.

"Mamma—Mamma!"

Lorena's eyes rolled back, her arms reached up to the sky, her fists were clenched.

"Goddamn them!" she screamed. "Goddamn them!"

"Mamma—don't!"

"Goddamn them!"

She was cursing the human world but her fists were beating at the sky, assailing heaven. Goddamn them, she kept crying. Forcibly Calla took the old woman into her arms, held her, pleaded with her, attempted to console her.

In a flood, Mamma started to sob. She clung to Calla, shaking uncontrollably, weeping in loud outcries. At last, she became still. For the longest time, Calla continued to hold her. After a while, the worst of it had passed. The old woman moved slowly out of the embrace, and then, without looking back, she went indoors.

In the taxi, even though her friend was still with her and in some manner always would be, Calla thought: Good-bye, Mamma Lorena.

. . . Presently, she approached the plane. She had arrived with Mina and was leaving without her. Good-bye, Mina. . . .

Calla returned to New York on a rainy afternoon. Willi met her at the airport and would stay a while to comfort her. Her readiness to be comforted, at last, suggested an irony, like saying a patient was finally well enough to see a doctor.

One evening, a few days after Willi had arrived, they sat in the living room of the apartment in the Village. Calla had had a pale drink,

and the bourbon had not disturbed her innards. There had been another article about her in the Sunday paper, only slightly scurrilous, and
the actress commented wryly that she had been a short-lived star, an
outrage, a curiosity—and now she was a sneer. There was a thought she
did not express: In none of the follow-up accounts that she had read
was there a further mention of Mina. Perhaps the papers had forgotten
that there ever was any child, or perhaps they were ignoring anything
that might lend some clemency to the stern view the public had of her.
For whatever reason, she was glad Mina was no longer in the news; the
child had never been part of her controversy with the world. Yet, untrue: the child *was* the controversy; she had been battling more for
Mina's world than for her own. And now, no reference to her. It was as
if the dead one's name had been blanked out, and the space left empty. A
void should have nothing in it. Why did it hold such pain?

She looked at Willi across the room. The woman was calm and
steady, the last pillar of her security. How grateful she was to have her
as a friend.

"I'm sorry I gave you the terrible chore," Calla said.

"What chore? Barney, you mean?"

"Yes." A moment. "Was it as bad as . . . ?"

"Yes. As bad."

Willi got up and opened the window. It was a warm summer
night. On the windowsill there was a Japanese jasmine plant that she
had brought as a present for Calla. The smell of jasmine filled the
room.

"He wants to see you," Willi said.

Her heart sank. "He does? How do you know?"

"He called this afternoon while you were out. He's in New York—
en route to Italy to do a picture."

She felt buried under mountains. He was coming for the complete
report, the whole memorandum on how their daughter had died.

"Why does he need it?" she asked.

"Maybe to put an end to it."

He was coming the following morning.

She awakened before dawn, showered, dressed and walked in the
cool of the sunrise. When she returned, Willi gave her coffee, stinging
hot. She drank it carefully, in measured sips. She must be on guard with
Barney every moment, she told herself, must not burden him with her
feelings, but give him whatever he needed to bind his wound. As for her-

self, she dare not ask for a thing, not forgiveness or comfort; not even hint that she needed to cry with him over the death of their child.

When she heard the elevator door opening, then his footsteps in the hallway, her palms went damply cold. What if we shake hands? She beat them against her thighs.

There was no embrace or handshake. He simply stood there in the doorway of the living room, squinting a little, out of the sunlight. He does not look well, she thought; what used to be a shaggy, campus charm is now a little seedy; he needs a haircut, he needs a subtler capping for that tooth . . . he needs a job.

They both pretended. You look very well, they said.

Willi came and offered fruit juice, coffee, toast; neither wanted any; she disappeared.

You look very well indeed, they said again. Let's not lie, she thought, let me tell you quickly what happened, and then please go away.

But they talked of other things. He was selling the Trancas house and going to do this film in Italy; there were those spaghetti Westerns. Yes, and she would probably stay here in New York; she was just in time for the fall season. If they kept talking this way, she realized, they would soon be pretending Mina was still alive, and they would go further and further from the truth, and then, what a havoc to come back.

He cleared his throat. "This part in Italy . . ."

"She died within eight hours of the accident," she said.

"Go on."

He wanted everything. She recounted it. Internal injuries, autopsy and post-mortem, spleen and pancreas and kidneys, rupture and hemorrhage.

She did it very well.

He also did it well. He listened standing; neither of them sat. He could easily have turned away during the report of it, but he did not; he faced her for every moment. Once or twice he nodded, tiny inclinations of the head, barely perceptible, only to indicate he understood, and please go on. Like the mother, the father showed no tremor of emotion, no glimmering of the eyes, no unsteadiness.

When the account was finished, she said: "That was all."

Having used precise units to quantify the report, she had not totaled it with precision. He insisted on precision. "All what?"

"She was dead."

He had asked for it, but could not take it. He raised his shoulders inordinately high. It looked as if he couldn't breathe. He's going to die of suffocation, she thought, if he doesn't gasp or cry or suck at the air. She wanted to shout permission to him: *Cry, Barney, cry out!*

But the crying, whatever he had done, was over. He started to say yes—too often—not realizing it was the wrong word, that *no* was wanted for the occasion, and she had had experience with it.

Then she saw him notice that she was there. And she thought: How good he is, he's looking at me with kindness and compassion, with the understanding that he always had for everyone and everything— even, in the early days, with me. How kind he is!

"You killed her," he said.

10

On the morning of what would have been Mina's fourteenth birthday, the mother went to visit the godmother. Willi had been in the hospital for over a week. There had been no change in her condition. And a routine of acceptance had begun. That the patient's vital signs were stable seemed satisfactory enough for everybody, nurses, house doctors, neurosurgeons. Let time do the healing, they said; no radical procedures were needed or should be rushed. To accept the patient's unconsciousness seemed an expedient compromise between life and death.

But not to Calla. One of the surgeons had admitted that it *would* be better if Willi did come to some state of awareness, if only for diagnostic purposes. It was all Calla needed. Daily, she talked to her insensible friend in order to get some response. She spoke quietly in conversational tones, telling Willi the news of the day, describing her surroundings in the hospital—and asking questions. It was the questions that were most important, of course, and she did not surrender her hope for answers. How do you feel, should your pillow be higher, would you like your eyes uncovered? Did you know that you've been drinking through a straw—there must be *some* consciousness in that—did you know you were doing it? . . . No answer.

On this particular day, when the nurse and intern were accustomed not only to Willi's unconsciousness but to Calla's eccentric monologues, the actress began to lose hope. She had seen no change whatever, none. The mask of bandages had been immutable. And she was afraid that if any sensibility was alive beneath the whiteness, the patient might detect that her friend was starting to despair.

"I'm going now, Willi," she said quietly. "Do you want to say anything before I leave?"

"Kitten."

The bandaged mouth had scarcely moved, but Calla was certain she had heard the word.

"What, Willi? What did you say?"

There was no sound from the bed, no movement of the lips.

"Willi—you said 'kitten.' What about it?"

The body remained inert. The silence persisted.

"Willi, say it again—say the word again."

No sign of anything.

"Willi—kitten—what does it mean?"

Nothing further, not a syllable. She left the patient, to find the resident doctor. The latter was interested in the progress and wrote it down. He could not, however, suggest any change in procedure. So she returned to Willi, tried throughout the day to get her to talk again, but her friend did not say another word.

Kitten. She had never heard Willi mention a pet of any kind. It was unlikely she had ever had one, for she had had no mother and no real home since she was an infant, and had spent most of her growing years in boarding schools. Yet, she might at one time have had a cat.

Not knowing whether her friend had ever possessed a pet was only a minor blank, but still it bothered Calla that the small, human fact was unknown to her . . . as incomprehensible as the African objects in Willi's apartment. Much else about her closest companion was in question now, or misunderstood. And she recalled that the issue of Willi's identity had been raised years ago, when Calla had suggested that she join a women's organization.

"I'm not a feminist," Willi had replied.

"Forget the labels," Calla had said. "You're lonely—it's a way of meeting other women."

Flippantly: "When I'm sure I'm a woman, I'll join up."

"I hate that! You sound like one of the locker room boys—lesbians ain't women!"

Willi sobered. "I'm saying worse than that, Cal. I don't know whether I'm a woman or a man—or anything. Willi the zombie."

She had begun to laugh, and had drawn the actress into her laughter. Calla had perceived the hilarity as a diversion to change the subject. If the subject didn't seem important enough to pursue in those days, it now seemed vital to find Willi's identity. For Calla had the irrational notion: The mirror image of Willi, like a crazy reflection in a fun-house looking glass, might be the picture of her attacker.

Calla spent nearly all of that same day in the hospital, talking to her friend, giving her intervals of respite, talking to her again and again. But Willi had gone back to her stillness.

Late in the afternoon, the actress departed from the hospital and walked through the underground crossover into the parking garage where she had left her car, on C-level, three floors below. She waited for the elevator and waited. She didn't mind that it failed to arrive; stretched tight, she felt that exercise would loosen her. Yanking open the heavy fire door, she started down the stairway.

As she approached the first landing, she heard a sound. A door being opened. That was all. There was no stir of footsteps.

She waited on the landing. She listened. Still no footsteps.

Her heart began to race. She did not know whether the door had opened on the landing above her or below. She could have sworn that she was not imagining; she was either being followed or awaited.

A choice to make: whether to rush back upward, or hurry down the fire stairway.

Frightened, unsteady, she leaned against the wall and took deep breaths.

If she was being followed, he would have come after her by now . . . so he must be waiting for her down below.

Reversing direction, she started up the stairs.

"The other way."

A man's voice—very soft—above her—in the shadow.

In terror, she started to run down again, rushing, falling, racing down the stairs.

"Don't hurry, Calla."

She stopped, petrified.

"Take your time."

She screamed.

No sound came out of her.

She screamed and screamed. But still there was no sound.

Even before the attack on Willi, Calla had not been sleeping well. She was afflicted with an indefinable sense that it might be dangerous not to "be there." Where it was she had to be she dreaded to question. Also, she was hungry all the time, ravenously hungry—and could not eat. She tried in various ways to trick herself into eating by collecting recipes, stocking junk food, cooking herself a delectable meal. But the food got wasted. She was getting thinner all the time, and it distressed her.

She was more distressed by what had happened this afternoon, by the fact that she couldn't scream. In a chilling, clammy way it suggested a breakdown of her function. Loss of appetite and sleeplessness, those were nice, friendly, normal neuroses. But an inability to scream was freakish; it struck at her expertise as an actress. Whatever she lacked as an artist, she was a well-trained craftsman who had slaved at her exercises and could accomplish all her études perfectly, laugh, cry, snore, hiccup . . . scream. To fail at one of these tasks, in these days of her proficiency, could mean that one of her major faculties had turned against her: this afternoon she had been stricken mute. The failure was a sign that she was falling apart as an actress and as a person. So, just as she decided to call a psychiatrist—

She called Lieutenant Reuss.

He arrived toward sundown. They talked in her study; she gave him a Coca-Cola and herself some tea. When he wasn't sneaking glances at himself in the mirror (he was wearing a brand-new jump suit), he asked questions and made high-flown comments on her answers. The kitten he dismissed as a clue too "nugatory" to be useful; the voice on the stairway was too "amorphous" since she had not actually seen the man.

"And you're not even sure whether the voice was English or black," he said.

"It could be both, couldn't it?"

"Yes, but . . . The last time we spoke, you said 'black man' and we spent four days on Julo Julasto."

"And—?" she asked intently. "Yes?"

"Obscurity." His smile was troubled. "I don't get him yet. He's an impressive man, and suddenly he's a buffoon. He's got a great trick—he admits everything. When he lies, he tells you he lies. In one hour, he confessed to the murder of his father, his mother, twenty-one rabbits and Lyndon B. Johnson. I got a lot of laughs out of him—and almost forgot that he could be dangerous."

"How dangerous?"

"I don't know."

His smile was gone; his trouble deepened. He was studying her searchingly, as if wondering whether to trust her. "Look, Miss Stark, I have to admit—we're not making any headway. We've had a number of men on this case and . . . I'm going to need your help."

"To do what?"

Hesitating, he didn't answer her question directly. "Those three— Julo, Willi and Lucas—there's something bizarre among them."

"Bizarre—in what way?"

"If I could answer that, it might not seem bizarre."

"What do you guess?"

"I don't . . . But the one way of finding out is probably through Lucas."

"Have you questioned him?"

"Yes, but he lied. And he's not the kind who lies and tells you he's lying."

"What did he tell you?"

"That he's never seen Willi socially—only a few times on business. But we have indications that they've had quite a . . . connection."

"In what way?"

"That's the point—we don't know. . . . And we'd like you to find out."

She had an instinctive aversion. "I would rather not."

"Not for us, for your friend. She's a pile of bandages right now, and—"

"Don't tell me what she is right now—I see her every day." Her tea spilled in her lap. She got up, brushed it fiercely, then turned on him. "My God, you want me to find out if they had an affair. And since you consider her a deviant, you're hoping I'll turn up something kinky or perverted or—"

She stopped, and he said quietly, "I'm not prejudging. Why are you?"

She felt ashamed. After a moment: "What do I have to do?"

"I understand you're considering a film O'Hare wrote."

"No, I'm not considering it at all."

"Could you pretend to consider it?"

"Oh Christ."

"Just long enough to get his confidence."

"And then what?"

"Find out what they had together." Then, quietly, "Or didn't have."

It was getting dark outside. She wanted something stronger than tea, but didn't want to prolong the conversation. She looked out the window into the gathering twilight. Specters everywhere. She felt ghostly.

His departure was so quiet that she scarcely heard him go. The starting of his car, however, was noisy, and so was the crunch of gravel under the tires. She listened until there was no further sound.

Abstractedly, she went to the bookshelf where the scripts were kept. In the duskiness she could not find the screenplay. As she turned the light on, she remembered: she had thrown the manuscript away.

It was a good excuse for calling immediately. Finding his name in Willi's Rolodex, she dialed the number. When she got him on the phone, she didn't waste time on preliminaries.

"Lucas," she said, "I want to reread *The Fabulist*, but I find I've mislaid the script. Do you have an extra copy?"

The silence, she suspected, was to hush the excitement. "I'll see that you get one in the morning."

She had no intention of rereading the script, not a page of it, but she was anxious to have their meeting over and done with. "I was hoping to get to it tonight."

"I'll bring it right over."

She was sure he would.

When Lucas arrived a half hour later, he seemed surprised that she invited him in. Clearly, he had expected to deliver the script and go away.

In the study, she hardly gave him time to finish his rye and soda before she inconspicuously refilled his glass. She drank water with a slice of lime in it, pretending it was vodka.

"What made you decide to reread the script?" he asked.

"I don't know. It was shrewd of you to take me to see Julasto." Then, cautiously casual: "And I kept hearing echoes of what Willi said about it."

"Yes, she likes it very much."

"Well . . . that was what troubled me. Whether she likes the script . . . or you."

"Both. We're a unit."

He was looking at her narrowly. He had turned wary. She had, perhaps, driven too directly toward her objective. More circuitously, she said:

"Do you mind talking about the script before I reread it?"

"Not at all."

"You know, of course, what disturbed me most about it."

"The rape scene."

"Well, not the scene itself. But the rather cavalier acceptance of its aftermath—and a kind of incoherent attitude to sex itself."

"In what way incoherent?"

Again, the guarded defensiveness. She would have to disarm him in some way.

"Please understand—I don't want to vitiate the strength of the scene. Perhaps I'm too sensitive to events like that. Somebody once said I confused politics with art, and it didn't bother me any more than if he had said I confuse art with life—which might have been a sort of tribute. However, over the years . . ."

"You've changed?"

"Well, I've become more circumspect." She could see that she had momentarily allayed a suspicion.

"Was it really a political thing—your objection to the scene?"

"Well, it had to be, didn't it?"

"What issue? Male versus female?"

"You don't think it's at issue?"

"Well, I don't vote for rape."

"Because you don't vote for it does it entitle you to make it seem attractive?"

I'm too caustic, she thought; he'll get more wary. But no, he was enjoying her, perhaps excited by the challenge.

"When I shoot the rape scene, do you imagine I'll make it seem attractive?"

"The consequences will be attractive, won't they?"

"Nothing in the screenplay deals with the consequences."

"Rachel falls in love with him."

"Not as a consequence of the rape."

"As a consequence of his force of character."

"No, his strength of character."

She couldn't help herself: "Is there anything in the script that dramatizes the difference?"

He was unsettled. In the academe of logic, she realized, she had better credentials than he had; she could make points about navel lint. But he apparently considered it more important than that.

"I'll have a look."

Then, a dreadful thing: he got up to go. She had gotten nowhere, had discovered nothing of his relationship with Willi. She needed to trick him in some way. Quickly:

"By the way, I have regards for you," she said.

"Regards? From whom?"

"Willi."

He looked puzzled and—did she imagine it?—alarmed.

"From Willi? When did she send them to me?"

"This afternoon."

He paused. Slowly, deliberately, he reentered the room. "Are you sure?"

"Yes. She was conscious for a few minutes, and the only word she said was 'Lucas.'"

"You couldn't have been mistaken, could you?"

"No. She said it a number of times. 'Lucas.'"

"You're lying."

"I think it was you who were lying."

"About what?"

"You had an affair with Willi, and said—in effect—that you didn't."

"Don't call it an affair."

"What do you call it?"

"Willi and I lived together," he said quietly, "for a short time."

"You didn't tell that to the police, did you?"

"No, I didn't." Suddenly he seemed to understand that she was acting for the detectives. "And if you do, you'll only be hurting Willi."

"How?"

"Now that Willi's conscious, ask her."

"Were you in love with each other?"

"Ask her that too."

"Were you?"

He lost his temper. "You know damn well Willi's a lesbian."

"Didn't you know that when you met her?"

He paused a moment to collect himself. "Yes, I knew it—immediately." Then, smiling ruefully, "But it wasn't as simple as that."

"Even that wasn't simple."

He was apparently considering whether to confide any more in her. "Willi was ill," he said quietly.

"In what way?"

"Crazy."

"That's not true!"

"She tried to kill herself."

"I don't believe it."

"I was there—I saw it."

"I don't believe it!"

"For a minute—before I heard about the blows on the head—I even suspected she inflicted those wounds upon herself."

"Herself? You're trying to make it even more horrible than it was, aren't you? Trying to shock me. You know goddamn well there would be no reason for her to do that."

"You might be the reason."

"Me? My God! *Me?*"

"What if she was so identified with you, so integrally a part of you —hating and loving you—that the wounds were not meant for herself but for her other self—"

"No!"

"—and the slashing would be against the love that didn't love her enough."

"You bastard! You're making it all up, aren't you?"

It was over. Wearily, his shoulders dropped. He seemed tired of the whole thing. "Yes, I'm making it up. Just as you made it up about Willi sending me her regards." She started to say something, but he stopped her. "Don't shore up the lie, please. Willi hasn't been calling my name—or anybody's name. She's not conscious. I was in the hospital only two hours ago. While I was there, they were taking the bandages off her eyes. She looked straight at me—stared at me—and didn't know who the hell I was. She's no more conscious than a cold stone."

Once again he started to depart, and again he turned to stop in the doorway. "I don't suppose you're really going to reread my script. But if you brought me here to find out more about Willi, you brought the wrong person. I suggest you speak to Julo Julasto."

She did a rash thing. Instead of phoning Julasto for an appointment, she got into her car and drove to his store in Redondo. Halfway to her destination, she realized how foolhardy it was. He might not be there, and the whole trip would have been a waste of time; or, worse, he might be there, and surprising him—which was her intention—might be a reckless thing to do.

Although she had left her house immediately after Lucas's departure, and had not delayed for dinner, it was nearly nine o'clock by the time she got to the turnoff. On the beach road, passing the boatyards and clam bars, she heard the sensual beat of the Summertime band. Only a short distance now . . .

But the Arts Afriques shop was dark as the moonless sky, and there was not a soul in sight. As if the occupants had moved, even the windows were empty, nothing on display except shadows. What a long trip for nothing, she thought, annoyed at her impulsiveness. Then she noted, at the side door, an old-fashioned bell handle made of brass. Approaching, she pulled it; the sound responded far away, a low tolling too heavy for an effort so slight. In a while, through the obscurity of the store, a figure moved. At first it had no other quality than blackness, but when it got closer it was the old man, the store's buyer, Darra. He opened the door, muttered and squinted.

"I'm Calla Stark—do you remember me?" she said. "I want to see Mr. Julasto."

He started to demur, then stopped. Telling her to wait, he closed the door without inviting her in, and she heard him throw the heavy bolt. It seemed hours. At last he returned, reopened the door and murmured for her to follow him.

Darra led her through the store. Without illumination, the place appeared totally different. The thousands of smaller articles on the tables receded into the background; only the larger objects dominated the shadows. Great heavy carvings hung from the rafters, looming and threatening.

Again, as on her first visit with Lucas, the old man showed the way to the rear door, opened it and vanished. She was out in the garden, under the colonnade. But this time the distant door did not open to throw a welcoming light. She had to make her way in the blackness, and the cottage was more remote than she remembered it.

Even when she arrived at the door, and knocked, there was no immediate response. She waited, wondering if the delay was punishment for having appeared without an appointment. But when he did open the door, she saw the smile that she recalled, worn like a mask of comedy, twisted by mockery and mischief.

"Come in," he said. "You're late. I've been expecting you for days."

He was dressed ludicrously. He wore a metallic silver dressing gown, the gaudy robe a prizefighter might wear in the ring, except that it had a regal train which sparklingly swept the floor. He allowed the robe to gape open to the beltline at the waist—a hint of nakedness—

black skin and silver lamé. His slippers were silver as well, turned up at
the toes in harlequin fashion, with silver pompoms at the tips. The
flashiness, the glitter . . . she was disappointed in the actor and the costume.

"When Darra said you were here on the jump, I was a bit annoyed." He let the rebuke have its moment, then smiled. "But then it
occurred to me that good news always comes as a surprise."

"What good news?"

"You're here to tell me you're going to do *The Fabulist.*"

"I'm . . . rereading it."

"Well, that's not exactly bad news, is it?"

"That's not why I'm here."

"Go on."

Pausing, she remembered Reuss, and quoted him: "I need your
help."

With an extravagant flourish of benevolence—all I have is yours!—
he led her to the fireplace. Although there were ashes but no flames in
the firebox, he was offering her the imaginary glow of the hearth.

"Tell me," he said.

"How well do you know Willi?"

His eyes sparkled. "Truth or a lie?"

"Do I really have a choice?"

He grinned. "No."

Throwing herself on his mercy, "Please tell me the truth," she said.

"Willi and I were married five years ago. We have three children—
one white, one black and one pinkish-purple."

She was quite still and so was he. Then he exploded into laughter.

After a while, they were both silent. She studied him a long time,
making no stir. Barely above a whisper: "Is there any part of you that's
real?"

"Any part you can poke at, you mean?"

"Is that what you think I would do?"

He flew into a rage. "What the fuck do you want, white lady?
Where the hell do you get off, breakin' in here like this, tearin' open
my closet doors? Where's your warrant?"

"I'm sorry, but—"

"Sorry, bullshit! Do you know that a cop-eye was here for hours,
sweatin' me? Do you know that another one was here all morning,
pumpin' my employees and hasslin' my customers, wantin' to look at
my records and inside my safe and down my throat and up my ass?

'Come back with a goddamn warrant!' I said, and I say the same to you —come back with a warrant!"

She had an impulse to flee, but she didn't. "Is that all you told them?"

"No. I told them I never laid eyes on Willi Axil. That I wouldn't recognize her if she was sittin' in my lap."

"Lucas O'Hare says you know her very well."

She felt as if she had really gotten to him. He seemed stunned and incredulous. "Lucas said that?"

"Yes."

"I don't believe it."

"Call him."

Without hesitation, he strode to the table, lifted the phone and pressed the buttons. He waited. Frustrated, he put the phone down. "No answer." He was discomposed; she had drawn more blood than she had expected. "I can't believe he would say a thing like that."

"Why not—if it's true?"

He seemed suddenly impatient, and just as anxious as she was to get to the crux of the matter. "Do you think I mutilated your friend's face?"

"Did you?"

"No."

"If you admit to being a liar, how can I believe you?"

"You can't. What else would you like to know?"

"I've been getting anonymous phone calls—I was followed down a fire stairway."

"Do you think I've been doing those things?"

"You have dozens of people working for you."

He crossed in front of the fireplace, sat on a stool where he was near enough to touch her, reached for her hand and held it firmly in both his own. His face was intimately close. "Look, Calla, beautiful Miss Calla, let us be friends, let us try to know one another. I was born in a ghetto, I've been to college, I've been to jail. Don't ask which ghetto, which college, which jail—they're all the same. I've committed mayhem and I've had mayhem done to me. I've had my life stolen from me, and I've stolen it back. I've been married twice and had any number of women, and perhaps I have countless children somewhere—I don't know any of them. I don't hold names and places and departures in my mind, or I would die of guilt and loneliness. I *have* known Willi —yes, I have—but I've never harmed her. And I've never done a single act to threaten you or your peace of mind. Now, then . . . nothing that I've said is either true or untrue, because they're all *facts*, and there's not a ray of light in them. The only truth—Calla, please listen and take part in this—the only truth— Ask me what it is."

"The only truth?"

"Fear. . . . It's my truth—and it's yours as well."

"If you mean I live in fear—"

"We all do."

"My best friend has been butchered, I've been getting warnings that follow me and wake me in the night. Wouldn't there be something wrong with me if I weren't frightened?"

"There is something wrong with you."

She wanted to withdraw her hand from his, and leave. Instead: "What do you see wrong with me?"

Abruptly: "Have you had your dinner?"

"No."

"Would you like something to eat?" he said. "I'm a very good cook."

"No, thank you."

"No dinner and not hungry? You're very thin. Don't you eat?"

In ordinary times it would have been an easy social question. But now it was so close to the quick that she wanted to lie. "I don't eat very much."

"Or sleep, I'm sure. . . . And now your hand is shaking."

"I'm trying to remove it from yours."

"Why don't you eat or sleep, Miss Calla?"

"Please—I don't like cheap psychologizing."

"Would you like it if it were dear?"

She pulled at her hand; he tightened his grip on it. "If I release your hand, will you promise not to vanish in smoke, and answer a question?"

". . . I'll try."

Before releasing her hand, he lifted it to his mouth and kissed it gently, lightly, with a courtly deference. Then he let it go. He looked at her intently, as if to see whether she had remained present. He still did not ask his question. Curious, she wanted to hear it, and had a misgiving that he might not ask.

"When you can't sleep," he said, "what do you take for it?"

"Is that the question?"

"No—later. What do you take? Pills?"

"No. I used to—years ago." Then, hastily, "I was never addicted, if that's what you're asking."

"And now—you take nothing—no soporific of any kind?"

"Any kind?" She stalled. "I don't know what you mean? Hot milk? Counting sheep?"

"Please."

"Do you mean sex?"

"Yes, as a narcotic."

He had said soporific, and had changed to narcotic. She wondered if he was on drugs. It would shed light on his quicksilver changes of mood, his instability.

"Sex as a narcotic?" he asked again.

"Yes, I have taken it that way."

"And you still do?"

"No. Not anymore."

"How did you get over it?"

"Cold turkey."

"Did you really? Just like that?"

"Just like that."

"You're a strong woman, Miss Calla. . . . When did you give up fighting?"

"Fighting what?"

"The injustices. Black kids shot by cops, hunger in swollen guts, napalm in the face, cancer in the drinking water."

"I never quit fighting those things."

"Yes, you did. Shall I tell you when? When you took on The Big Injustice."

"Are you going to talk about death again?"

"Do you mind?"

"It bores me."

"Bores, but doesn't hurt?"

"Of course it hurts. But not my own death."

"Whose?" When she hesitated: "Whose death hurts you?"

"All those others—who left before it was time. All the people who never got an audition, or died in the middle of a speech, or got murdered in tryout, or never made it to New Haven."

"Ah, the new haven!"

"Stop it. I hate that double-meaning horseshit."

He did stop. When he resumed the conversation, it was with a totally unrelated subject.

"Which do you like better—movies or the theater?"

It was such a relief that she laughed. "I take calcium for my finger-nails, and I brush my hair a hundred strokes with each hand. I believe that sensible exercise and clean thoughts are the secret to robust health and a lifetime of stardom in the cinema."

"It was a serious question."

"Was that the one I promised to answer?"

"No, we haven't come to that. Do you enjoy doing films as much as the theater?"

"Strange . . . I always thought I loved the theater more. But now that you ask the question . . . films. I think I prefer films."

"Why?"

The continuing inquiry should not have disturbed her as it did. "I don't know."

"Can it be because, whenever you finish playing a play, it's over? All you created was consumed—nothing was left of you. But on film, you live forever."

"But I don't. Only the emulsion lasts."

"Emulsion—is that all those moving images are to you?"

She was not sure of her reply, not sure of anything. She could see that he sensed his moment of power over her. And that now he would ask his main question:

"What's your imperative, Calla?"

"What do you mean?"

"In my language—Gorá—"

"Please," she said quietly. "Can't we do without the mumbo jumbo? There's no such language and no such country."

"There is a country of magic, Miss Calla."

It was the most quietly fervid thing he had uttered, and she heard an entreaty in his voice. Please don't make a joke of it, his tone said; go along with me on a friendly supposition until we know one another bet-ter. He was begging her, not necessarily for belief, but a suspension of disbelief, a gift of pretending such as she might offer to a film or a play.

She prompted him. "In your language . . . Gorá . . ."

"In English, the imperative is only in the verb. But in the language of Gorá, it's in the noun as well, every living creature has its own imper-ative. All we do is simply place the accent on the last syllable of the name. For example, Gora means a fire god, but Gorá means 'Oh God—please—bring life out of the flame!' As to myself, Julo is my name, but Juló is my imperative—to resurrect myself." He hesitated, uncertain whether she would permit him to proceed without mockery. When he saw that she wasn't smiling, he continued. "I think O'Hare's imperative is to create a work of art, a work of great beauty. . . . What is yours?"

If she took the question in earnest, it was too difficult. Easier, far easier a decade ago. But these years—what? I'm a woman in quest of my outcry? Ridiculous. Against which injustice—death? Even more ridiculous. Her imperative—what an aching question, and how desperately she wanted to answer it.

"I'll think about it," she said.

"Yes—please. Think about it as you reread the script. There's magic in it. And there may be answers."

How shrewd he was. When he knew he had made his most emotional effect, he used it to sell the product: the film.

She had come to find out what he knew about Willi, and had discovered what he knew about herself. Perhaps more than she herself knew. Or perhaps that too was fakery. But one thing was certain: he would tell her no more about Willi, not tonight.

Then why didn't she quickly depart? Tantalizingly caught by him, she didn't want to go. She was no longer sitting, but standing in front of the fireless hearth and he was standing close to her. She seemed irresolute, as if she had forgotten where the door was. Once more, he reached down and took her hand, to kiss it, as if in farewell. But this time he gently and deliberately turned it over, opened the clenched fist, bent down and kissed the palm. His mouth stayed too long, and she could feel his tongue on her skin. Then, because she didn't withdraw her hand, he put his arms around her. His dressing gown was open, a vertical panel of blackness showed beside the silver cloth, and in the embrace she could feel the heat of his body. His mouth was close to hers, an inch away, and as they touched, she couldn't stand how much she wanted him. But she had a sense that his hands were tensing, his arms were tightening around her, he would give her no choice, not let her go, he would force her in some way, there was more anger than loving in him. With a moan, she broke away.

Minutes later, she was in her car, speeding along the freeway.

Whether she slept or not, she went through the ritual, every night, of undressing for bed. Then, if she didn't lose consciousness, she blamed it on the night disturbances: the distant traffic, a neighbor's dog, the soughing of the eucalyptus trees. But tonight the air was still, no sound. No noise, except wide-eyed wakefulness, a shout.

Staring into the dark, she felt his mouth on her hand, kissing the palm. Even more agitating, his words: What is your imperative? As if it were possible, in a world more ruthlessly real than his mythical country, to say what her single-minded action was, what part she must perform, not in a film, but in life itself. She could have answered him without hesitation in an earlier time, when the mind went straight to the muscles. But it should not be so difficult *now*, the black man would answer; just put the accent on the last syllable and—presto chango—your passive name is an action.

Callá.

Callá, Calloo, Callay—smash through the looking glass! See yourself and be yourself as you were, those years ago. Restore that old imperative! . . . How inane it was, how simple.

Yet, what if simplicity were the key to it? Just put the accent on the final syllable, the *end*, where end might mean not only the objective but the termination. How marvelous—life and death in a single accent—Callá! La was a nice syllable to end one's life on. A musical note, a dance, an insolent indifference. But she knew there was not a single cell of indifference in her. How, then, had she run out of passion for her causes, how had she lost her high and precious imperative?

There was some altering of the light outdoors. It was nearly dawn, she imagined, and it would not be a happy day.

She went downstairs and found the screenplay in her study. She took it, not to her own chair but to the one Willi generally sat in, and sank down to start reading.

The light outdoors changed even more; the dawn was gilding one of the panes of the mullioned windows. By the time it had gilded all of them, she had finished rereading the script.

Beautiful was the wrong word. Even magical might not be right. He's defending you against the dark things, Willi had said, and the dark things haunted the scenario. Bewitchment, good and evil. A mother's search for a young man and a meaning, a pursuit of black magic, with a play on words without playfulness. There were other aspects of the script, of course. The suspense not only in the bold dramatic action, but the change in feelings, how one character is the projection of another, and how . . .

No, don't fall in love with it, she cautioned herself. There were the bad things as well, too many questions left dangling. . . . She thought of Franco Notale, with whom she had made a successful film, and knew what he would say: Leave the questions in the air, where they belong. A work of art needs a little madness, as climate for the myth.

She was not long on myth, she had to admit. She felt it as a lack. Perhaps there was a great ganglion in her brain that she had never used, a major nerve—a myth nerve—a lobe of mysticism that she was allowing to atrophy. Perhaps that's what Julasto meant.

She had to be in the picture.

It might not be her lifetime imperative, as the black man demanded, but it was a part she had to play, a film she had to make.

Suddenly—a miracle—her spirits lifted. She felt as if she were on the threshold of a discovery, on the verge of finding a hidden treasure, a new meaning, a new Calla Stark with whom she could feel safe and whom she could love. She was the young actress running down the street—I'm in rehearsal!

But . . . there was one thing. It might be the single killing element that would make her afraid to accept the part.

Lucas O'Hare.

There it was again—her doubt about the man himself. She could not put aside her disquiet over his questionable relationship with Willi, nor her sense that it was shifty of him to use the attractive black man as star bait; but, even more, she had a nagging worry, not about O'Hare alone, but about O'Hare and herself together. They were an abrasion. Even her attraction to the man was based on it. She had been most excited by him—when? When he had run ransacking through her house, in anger.

She knew what abrasion could do to her as an actress. It could wear her down, it could grind away all the lumps and gnarls of individuality, scrape her smooth and slick as plexiglass. In the hands of a director who rubbed her the wrong way, she would be leery of taking chances, she would not feel free to be foolish or reckless or crazily imaginative. It was disturbing enough to realize that she had become more and more wary in her recent films; with him, a director who could intimidate her, she might be afraid to hazard anything at all.

What a mistake it was to reread the script, she thought. Something had happened to her that might be too important to repudiate. She wished she had the same admiration for the director as she had for the writer.

But why need O'Hare direct it? Would he absolutely insist on doing so? Was it an inalienable condition of the deal?

She knew that most screenwriters who had become hyphenates had done so not because they wanted primarily to be directors, but because they had had such painful experiences with the bungling of their manuscripts by hack directors. Putting aside the potential rewards of money and glory, they had taken on the second chore largely to protect their written work. This could easily have been the case with O'Hare. There was some question about his directorial talents; many people thought him excellent, but many said he was only a capable craftsman, not first rate. As a writer, however, he was brilliant, on the manic side, with a humor that was tickled, as Notale would have said, by the feather of a fool. Before directing his own screenplays, he had had dolts for directors—and failures. But what if he could be guaranteed a fine director, even a great one? Suppose, with the efficacy of her name, Calla could arrange it. For example, a writer might find it very difficult to reject such a director as Truffaut or Antonioni or Kubrick.

Or Franco Notale, who had just had two major successes, and an award at Cannes.

Franco . . . Why not?

She wondered how she would feel working with him again. It might be too strained, a second time. In actor's jargon, the text of the thought was pleasure, but the subtext might be pain. Still . . .

11

Franco. . . .

After Calla was acquitted of the Mississippi charges, Willi stayed on with her for nearly a month. It was a convalescent time, and with her sanative friend setting the mood of her daily life, she began to recuperate.

When Willi departed, Calla's money ran out and she needed work, for every kind of sustenance. She wanted a part in a New York play, but felt as if she were starting all over again. She almost got a role in another British importation, a Pinter work, but they finally turned her down. Megan summoned her to California, all expenses paid by a producer, to do a screen test, which was also a failure. She was about to fly back to New York when her agent called her once more, to her office in Beverly Hills.

She went that afternoon. It was a new establishment for Megan, her first branch office, in California. The woman had risked everything on the expansion, had even taken a new name for the company, Writers, Artists and Directors. "WAD," she said, "it's something you blow."

Megan sat behind her new desk, wearing tinted glasses and a huge sunhat, and cursing. "The bastards didn't send the goddamn drapes," she said, "to block out the goddamn sun."

There were pictures on the floor, not yet hung, all Eastern pictures —New England ice ponds and snowscapes. She was bemoaning her absence from New York, and sentimentalizing winter. "I want snow, goddamn it, and a blazing fireplace."

"It's August."

"Yes, here—always." In nearly the same breath, Megan said, "I've got a movie for you."

It did not seem possible. The agent was always herniating herself to lift dead weights. "Are you writing it this minute?"

"No, it's written, Cal. You can have it if you want it." Then she added, in an abstracted voice. "It's to be made in Italy—by Franco Notale."

That, of course, was the catch. Notale had a hex on him; in Italy they called it the *malocchio*. Still in his forties, his career as a director had started meteorically with a film called *Trappola da Topi*, which had played in America as *Rat Trap*, an austere but moving story about the rat packs of homeless children that swarmed in the alleyways of Rome after World War II. It had been successful all over Europe and had won a score of prizes. The second, *Aldo e Maria*, had been a violent drama about a half-demented girl and a brutish police informer, and some of the love scenes had been bestially sensual, yet the film lingered in the mind as a cinematic lyric. From that time onward, everything Notale touched had turned to failure. His last two pictures had not even been finished; one, because he had run so many months over schedule that the moneymen had fled; the other, because an injunction for invasion of privacy had stopped the production, and the case was still in the Italian court.

Notale had had another case in the court, a paternity suit. He had been acquitted, but some said he owed his victory to a technicality. Calla had once met an Italian stage actress who had played a Goldoni comedy that Notale had directed. Describing him, the woman raised both thumbs in the horns of the goat; he was always in rut, she said, *perpetuamente in fregola*. She added that it was something Italians said about females but not about males, and she smiled. "He is very man, but he touch like a woman." She said it piningly.

In practically every way—director, writer, producer, man—Notale's star was flickering. But Calla's was already out.

"What's the picture?"

"It's his—he wrote it. It's called *Grotto of Love*."

"You're kidding."

"No, serious. It's better in Italian—*Grotta d'Amore*. It doesn't translate well."

"Neither do I."

"You translate beautifully, Cal. You're everybody's language." Then she spoiled it. "Esperanto." She had the wit to know she had run over. "You see, I've learned the picture formula: the last word has to make you gag."

"He really wants me?"

"Yes, he does."

"Does he know I'm Typhoid Mary in America?"

"Stop that."

"Well, why is he asking me?"

Megan took the straw hat off but did not remove the sunglasses. "Truth is, he's been turned down by Streisand, Fonda, Burstyn, Bergen —I don't know who else. I wouldn't have told you, but it's been in the columns. Nobody wants to work with him, and besides . . ."

"The script is terrible."

"No. As a matter of fact, it's very good. Even in a dopey translation—honestly—it's really good."

"What, then?"

"Nudity."

"Oh." Too bad. "Others—or me?"

"You too."

"Everything?"

"Dorsal, frontal, north, south, east and west."

"Tell him I quick-freeze in the raw."

"I've already told him. He still wants you to read the script."

"I won't go buff, Meg. Is there any point in reading it?"

"Yes. We'll work something out."

Calla took the screenplay back to Willi's apartment and read it. There was very little dialogue. The translation, while slavishly literal, was comprehensible enough; yet, in the first fifth, she thought she was missing the point, that pages had been left out of the manuscript. And it started with maudlin sentimentality.

There is this idyllic couple. She's a water-colorist from America and her husband is an Italian automobile designer. They are on their tenth anniversary trip to Capri where they met. Arriving on the island, they go almost immediately into the grotto where they caught their first glimpse of one another. There is a disturbance in the sea around them—a seaquake, it is called in the script—and the cavern becomes entirely different from their memory of it. They are lost in a labyrinth of beauty—hanging crystals and walls of gleaming stones that shine like citrine and carnelian, and great stalactites that glint like diamonds. It is more than the grotto of memory, it is the grotto of their dreams. Step by step, they realize they have come here to capture a love ecstasy that neither of them has ever found, and here in the fantasy cavern they call upon the images of dream lovers, dead and gone, real and fictional: Héloïse and Cyrano and Petrarch and Miranda and Beatrice; and lovers of cruelty—Bluebeard and Henry VIII and Cain and Lilith and Jezebel. At first each of the spouses runs the course of idyllic love, the reveries of romantic gentleness that the fables promised them. But then the kindest lovers play them false; they become faithless or dull or misconstrued, or they become realities. They are not meant—and were never meant—to be trusted. But the ruthless lovers remain constant; they are what they have always seemed to be, selfish and brutally honest, and they inflict pain. But they will never change; cruelty can be trusted. To the husband and wife, this is such a perversion of their romantic picture of love that they cannot stand the grotto, the gems are too brilliant to behold, too hard, too sharp, there's too much fury in the beauty. So they try to destroy the granite-walled cave in a bacchanalia of rage. And they themselves are destroyed on the rocks of reality.

She finished reading it and thought: What glop.

But she wondered what she would have thought of the script of *Last Year in Marienbad*, or *Blood of the Poet*, which she had seen three times. Or the esoteric scenes in *Belle de Jour*, the strained reality of a husband serenely watching the torture of his wife—what would she have made of the script? Yet, as film . . .

Notale, for everything that had been said about his palate for women, was an artist. In *Rat Trap* there was a scene of an alley urchin walking in the gloom toward the rodent boys, his face war-shocked and bleeding, pretending courage he did not feel, hungry and terrified that the older ones would turn on him. It was a moment she could not get out of her mind. And there was the first love sequence in *Aldo e Maria* . . .

Notale was a bit of a genius; she had a yearning to work with him.

"And there won't be any nude scenes—not with you," Megan said the following day. "He promised it faithfully on the phone, and he'll put it in the contract."

"Why does he promise that?"

"He wants you."

How good it was to be wanted again, she thought, and how good to run away—to Italy, where the men would look like De Sica and the women like Anna Magnani. She would go to places she had never seen, Venice afloat and Florence, she would touch the sun-baked stones of Verona and Siena, and run to the sea everywhere. For the first time in a year, she felt a loosening of her tightened fibers, a warming in her bones, and a soft Mediterranean promise of happiness. And she would be acting again.

She was going to be met at Fiumicino Airport by Notale himself. As the plane descended out of the morning mist, she realized that sooner or later they would have to play the inevitable sex charade, so she practiced her lines and her actor's adjustments. Let's cut that scene right now and not even rehearse it, she would say, the one where you try to make love to me; a waste of time and footage. While I'm not a puritan, I don't like lubricious men—what was "lubricious" in Italian? —no matter how attractive they may be. By the look of his photographs, he *was* attractive in a vulpine way, but it would make no difference.

As she saw him coming toward her on the other side of Customs, she realized it was going to be easier than she had expected. He was not as well favored as his pictures. His foxlike aspect was hidden under too much flesh, he was running to adipose tissue, not fat exactly, but fortyish-rounding. Approaching, she did not see the dashing captain of the *carabiniere* she had expected, nor the wifeless, childless sly Lothario of Rome. She wondered why, after his wife's death many years ago, he had not remarried and comfortably stocked his life with *vino*, lucite furniture and *bambini*. That was certainly the bourgeois look of the man who was now greeting her.

"I am very pleased to see you," he said. Even his voice was not as resonant as she had expected.

He had a nice long striding walk, however, a reminder of what he might have looked like when he was slim. But he wore, of all things, American storebought trousers, when Italian tailors were so good, and the pants clung to the wrong places.

"Your flight—it was okay?" he said.

He went on that way, her flight, the quality of food, was there any trouble with her baggage? His opening stanzas, prosy. She thought: No Dante, this.

"My flight was fine," she said, "just fine."

He had a dusty Alpha Romeo into which her bags, few as they were, could barely fit. He drove with middling efficiency, and on the ride to Rome they talked of other sublimities like airline schedules and the subtle differences between Pan Am and Alitalia. The only reference to anything of interest:

"You read my script, I understand."

"Yes, I did."

"And you think—?"

"I'm afraid I don't understand it."

"I don't either."

If he had said it as a joke, it would have thawed the frost. But he was terminally serious. Suddenly she had an appalling insight: he has no sense of humor. Murder, she thought, how long is the shooting schedule? Eight weeks with a man who cannot laugh? She would be ready for the morgue.

"We will leave tomorrow for Capri," he said. "Your clothes are already there."

She looked at him unbelievingly. No sketches, designs, fittings?

He understood her worry. "It's all right," he said. "We received all your measurements from your agent. And I have seen your films." He turned to her with disarming honesty. "I have to admit to you—I have a trouble. I cannot waste time, I cannot waste a cigarette. Everybody thinks now I am an incompetent. So I have to do everything economically. Help me if you can."

It was the first sign of emotion in the man. He was in a box, fighting his way out. She warmed to him a little.

"Don't worry," she said. "If there's a good seamstress . . ."

"Yes, the designer is also a seamstress. . . . My sister-in-law."

She had another accession of the horrors.

They drove down to Naples in the car; *lire* were being saved in every possible way. During the lengthy drive, and on the boat to Capri, she realized a simple fact. There would be no carnal relations with this man. He was not interested in her sexually, nor she in him. He was a non-event.

Relieved that *la sensualità* would not be an issue, she was also puzzled. This man who talked of schedules and budgets and the cost of lunches for the crew did not answer the description of the man who had bedded his leading women and the leading women of many another man. He was not an erotomaniac, his hands were not prehensile, his zipper was securely locked. No stallion this fellow; a middle-aged gelding a bit too fond of food who, when they stopped at Pavese, a restaurant in the middle of the highway, had eaten two orders of pasta and said that the wine was not so bad in such places, considering the price, and would she wait for him a little while, because he always took some extra time in the men's room. The poor constipated Romeo.

When they got to Capri, the clothes were gratifyingly not too awful, and his sister-in-law, a dumpy mustached lady, was quick and accurate. Before Calla knew what had happened, she was being photographed on a dinghy, a *singolo*, and on the terrace of an old hotel. Her husband was played by Erno Tiglo, who kept squeezing her arm on and off camera; Notale seemed not to notice he was doing it in either circumstance. It was all happening so offhandedly, so casually, as if they were shooting home movies.

The picture really got started on their return to Rome. The sound stage was an abandoned factory on the outskirts of the city, and a huge grotto had been constructed on a floor that once had had rows of machinery. When she saw it she was disappointed. For all its inlays and overlays of colored glass and glistening rhinestones and plastics, it had less atmosphere than the black, sea-tortured grotto in Capri.

Notale saw her disappointment. "The real grotto in Capri is too exactly what it looks like," he said. "Too honest." He smiled conspiratorially as if to impart a secret. "You have in English two words— 'illusion' and 'delusion.' One word suggests a deception, and the other suggests a sickness. In Italian we have the same word for both of them —*l'illusione*. There is some point in having only one word. That is one of the reasons for the picture."

It was the only statement she had heard him utter that might not have been spoken to one of the grips. And no more comprehensible to her than the script. Moreover, she had a suspicion that he himself had not understood his own comment.

It was one of his rarer utterances; he hardly spoke to anybody. In the first days of shooting, she was amazed that he was able to get anything done with so little instruction to his assistants and his crew. There were no tirades, no flashes of temperament. Yet, the grips and gaffers and prop people went about their business as if he were a stern taskmaster whose orders were explicit. Unlike him, they were not quiet. Exuberant, excitable, they craved pandemonium. They pulled practical jokes on one another, goosed the women extras, ate their lunch in high decibels, sang in and at their *vino*, fortissimo. They were Italian, but he was not. Italian as his parents and films had been, Notale was like a taciturn New Englander, reserved and undemonstrative. He had no Italian flare, none of the jauntiness of a Venetian waiter or a Roman haberdasher, none of the white-gloved flash of a traffic policeman. He seemed to plead for anonymity.

His reticence worked a hardship on her. The set itself was hardship enough. A maze that she occasionally got lost in, and making no pretense to reality, it suggested a nightmare grotto, a labyrinth of shocks and surprises, murky tunnels opening into palatial luster, steep ascents and sudden plummets, a painted wall that looked like a bleeding retina, soft recesses into obscurity. Before it became a magical cave to work in, it was treacherous; a quick movement and she could impale herself on stalagmites made of long spears of glass; a wrong step and she could fall into emptiness.

Notale himself was the most besetting affliction. Unable to understand his script, Calla expected he would illuminate it for her. But every question was answered with an evasive technicality—take the shot full camera instead of three quarters, walk partly in the light and partly out of it. Nothing—ever—that had to do with her intention in a scene or her relationship to her husband, played by a man who, if he found his light and squeezed her arm, was as contented as wallpaper. As a consequence of her uncertainty and edginess, she began to fall back upon the securer tricks of naturalism, indicating susceptibilities she did not feel, making editorial comments on her external behavior. During her worst spell of this, about ten days after the Roman shooting had begun, Notale said quietly:

"I would like, Calla, much less detail and a bit more truth."

The generality unnerved her. "I don't know what that would be in this part."

"Not only what is written, but what you bring to it."

"I don't even know what's written," she responded. "All I know is that she's an American woman—an artist."

"That is not enough—and it is not even correct."

"It's what's written."

"No. What is written is an American woman—as seen through the eyes of an Italian. Why don't you at least start with that?"

It was as if she needed him to drive a nail and he was hitting it with a sponge. "I can't see through your eyes unless you tell me what to look for."

"Why don't you look for yourself?"

It was the end of the day and he had been totally evasive. Abruptly he was not there at all, he had literally slipped away, and neither his assistant nor Darola, the script woman, knew where to find him.

"Tell the son of a bitch I'm not coming in tomorrow," she said.

But the following morning she was as prompt as usual and ready for work, come what may. She was deeply depressed, however, certain

that her ten days of film were cheap, false and superficial. And she had
no notion what he felt about anything.

Before the day's shooting began, he arrived at her dressing room
and dismissed her dresser and the makeup woman. His face was
clouded, he scarcely looked at her.

"We will shoot yesterday's work again," he said.

"Why? Because I was terrible?"

"I did not say that."

"Well, say it—I was. Why don't you help me be better?"

"I do what I can."

"You don't do anything."

"Maybe it would be good for *you* not to do anything—unless you
feel it."

"Feel what, for God's sake? Who is she, what does she want, what
is she asking of her husband? What's her action in the scene I did yesterday?"

"I do not know."

"You *have* to know."

"You ask me questions as if I know the answers better than you
do."

"You should know them better. You wrote the script. What does
it mean?"

"You ask me what it means as if it were a blueprint. It is a dream!
A work of art is a dream. Do you know what your dreams mean? Go
and ask the dream."

"Bullshit."

"Go and ask the dream!"

"That's a pretentious cop-out. A work of art is not a dream, it's a
conscious creation. If you're an artist, a little of you can be ascribed to
accident or inspiration—or dreams. But the rest of you is *conscious*. You
know damn well what you're doing. And you're accountable."

"Accountable for what? Something you want me to know? Well, I
do not know it! Maybe I should not be a director. Maybe I am too stupid. In my class, I was always the foolish one—*Il Cretino*. It is because I
do not have clear ideas, only sensibilities. I am hurt, I am full of wonder, I am sad, I am happy. And a few intuitions—not many. I say a
grotto, but I do not know what a grotto means. What is it—a cave?
Is it something terrible in the dark, is it the inside of a woman, is it the
hope of a treasure, is it the fear of being born, is it a tomb, is it where

all my beasts are waiting for me? *What is it?* Suppose you ask me that, what will I tell you? Only that it is a dream—a nightmare—I do not know how to answer. And I am afraid that you will ask me, and again I will be *Il Cretino*. So stop asking me who you are—I do not know. Stop asking what the picture means. If I am lucky, maybe I will understand the film after it is finished. Maybe I will look at you—on the screen— and you will tell me what it means."

His face was burning red, his forehead was beaded with sweat. Awkwardly he wiped the perspiration away with his hand, and did not seem to know what the next step was, so he turned and left her dressing room, and the sound stage as well. He did not return for two hours.

She was unstrung by what he had said. Much of it, she knew, was the disclaimer of the artist who is afraid to be judged as a responsible craftsman, and wants to be excused as an errant genius. But perhaps, in his case, it was true that his mind was not a latchstring to his art . . . Yet, he had created beauty.

Go and ask the dream, he had directed her, as if she had written the script. Reared a realist, she had been brought up to ask nothing of a dream; ask it no questions, it will tell you no lies. Life had to be truthful and calculable. Accounts, in the pharmacy, in the household, in her master's thesis, had to be supported by facts and figures. As a star-gazing student, it had disheartened her that so much of her existence had to be cross-referenced with documents; even God was footnoted. She had yearned to keep her fantasy options open, but had had to subordinate her illusions of life to the labors of it. "The fact is the sweetest dream that labor knows," the poet had said, but maybe Frost had it the wrong way around. Hadn't she become an actress because she hoped the dream was the sweetest fact?

She needed the two hours that Notale was away to encompass the size of his injunction, of the creative contribution he was demanding of her: tell me what my film means. She had no notion how she could ever satisfy the need. But I want to, she told herself, I want to help him know what it means. The thought excited her. She had a yearning to sound whatever depths there were in herself that could enable her to feel and to reveal some truthful illumination of this effort they were making together. And perhaps cast some light on his life and her own.

When he returned, the surface patterns of their work were all the same. He spoke the same technical patois—wait until you are in the light, hit the marks, speak a little louder than your thought; but from that instant onward, she heard the professional cant only in the margins of her consciousness. The rest of her, the whole center of her being, was focused upon herself and upon his personal film, so that through it she could start to tell him deeply and unashamedly who she was.

Four days later, exactly two weeks after they had first started their major shooting, he paid her the first compliment. The lights were being killed and the men were shoving equipment to the perimeter of the sound stage. As nearly everybody was starting for home, Notale walked with her in the direction of her dressing room. He was talking about the sequence they had just completed, her scene with Cain.

"The script said for you to put your hand on his shoulder. But you didn't. How did you know not to touch him?"

"Oh, didn't I touch him? I thought I did."

She was teasing, and he smiled. "Yes, it was as if you did." Then, almost to himself: "You are excellent. Without moving, you can reach very far."

A number of feet from him, beyond arm's length, she again felt as if she were reaching far, touching him with her gratitude. But she sensed no answering response from him, nothing nearly so intimate. With regret, she withdrew her imaginary hand.

But he was really not that remote from her at this moment; he was preoccupied with the stirring change in her performance. "From now on, you can allow a little madness, if it happens. Don't be afraid—open the door as much as you like—maybe the myth will come in."

She cautioned herself to listen carefully but not try to understand him too well . . . just open the door a little.

He turned away. As she was entering her dressing room, he turned back again.

"Tomorrow . . ." And he stopped.

Something was balking him. She waited.

"Tomorrow Elsa Velletri will be here," he said.

She had forgotten about Velletri. She was the woman who would be her double in the nude scenes. It would be Velletri's unclothed body, substituting for Calla's, that would appear in the final film. Calla had recommended Willi for the work, but Notale had demurred. Watching every *lira*, he had pointed out that the few brief fill-ins the woman would supply did not warrant the expense of transportation, living expenses and a union salary. Calla had not pressed, for she was unsure that Willi, any more than she herself, would want to work in the nude.

"Elsa . . ." She affected a detachment. "I hope she has a beautiful figure."

"Yes, it is lovely."

He added no more; did not say that Calla's was more beautiful or that the woman with the beautiful figure was very like Calla. He simply produced the information, unadorned.

Still he was not departing. "I can phone her tonight, however, and tell her not to come."

". . . Don't."

"I will of course keep my contract with you, Calla—but can I not convince you that . . . ?"

"No."

"Then . . . *ciao*."

Ruefully he walked away. She felt more than a little regret, and was surprised how disquieted she was by the incident. Would she really mind so much if she went naked in the film? Or wasn't that the reason for her disturbance? . . . She wished that he had reached for her.

All evening she thought of him. She had noticed that he never ate anything during the course of even the longest day, and that he was getting thinner. The man was beginning to resemble his photographs, the gaunt look of a hungry, alerted animal; he seemed younger too, a bit feverish and troubled . . . and more attractive.

She must stop this restiveness, she told herself. No reason for it. In the last four days, she had done some of the best acting in her life. It was real and more instinctive than usual, sometimes catching the thing in a single shot, often profoundly and accurately touched.

She wondered why he had not touched her.

She had a shock the following morning when she saw her double.

Elsa Velletri was not beautiful. Not that she had to be, Calla reminded herself, for, after all, it was not Velletri's face that would be photographed, but her body. And in the blousy loose-fitting tent the woman wore, there was no telling what her body actually looked like. But Calla had expected, for no logical reason, to see a more striking counterpart of herself, as Willi was more striking.

However, when Elsa was brought across the set, in that first instant of introduction, Calla realized she had overlooked some active component of the woman, some vital part that could more than pass for beauty. She did not know what it was.

As if the woman divined that the thought of beauty was running through Calla's head, she said graciously, "You are more than your films—more beautiful."

"Thank you—I've never considered myself beautiful."

"But you *are*. Like an actress."

Perhaps she was giving with one hand and taking with the other. "Aren't you also an actress?"

"Ah no," Velletri answered. *"Una donna."*

A *woman*, as if it were distinct from every other career, a dignity of office. Velletri smiled. The irregularity of her white teeth was only a minor aspect of her smile; the rest was an irradiation of cheer and warmth. Calla thought, with a twinge: she is more beautiful than I am. But then, so was Willi, she told herself, and she could remember when she had thought nearly all women were more beautiful than she was.

What disconcerted her about Velletri was to see how Notale touched her. His familiarity was not only affectionate and friendly; when he laid his hand on Elsa's arm, Calla knew it had been other places. His eyes as well, and his mouth; and she faced the fact that she was deeply envious, and wanted him to make love to her.

Calla's second surprise with respect to Elsa came that same morning. They were shooting a scene in which the wife accuses the husband of falling in love with the night evil, Lilith. He denies this but finally, badgered, confesses that he does love the nocturnal demon. Cruelly he describes how the succubus comes to him and forgives his weakness, deadens his pain, extenuates his brutishness; and how she makes love to him, step by voluptuating step, with her mouth, her fingertips, and with the way she unclothes herself. As the husband is describing the other woman, the wife slowly imagines herself as Lilith, and sees a vision of a woman undressing; and she cannot be certain whether she is seeing herself or the woman of evil.

The quarrel scene had been played, and as the camera moved in closely on the wife undressing in the manner of Lilith, Notale said to print it. There would be intercuts to the wife's face as she disrobes, and to the husband's as he starts to see her becoming naked. These shots would be taken later, but now the continuity would not be broken. Notale was ready to photograph the scenes of the wife's body, nude.

Velletri was called. She appeared in a pearl gray dressing robe. Tightening the wrapper about herself, she stepped onto the set, was shown her starting point at the far end of the grotto's passageway, and the places at which she must discard one piece of clothing after another, and then her final mark.

The double was ready. The lights went up. Notale called the action. The camera rolled. Velletri, far in the distance, started slowly toward the camera, disrobing as she approached. And the closer she got, the more unbelievable it was to Calla that Notale had chosen Elsa's body to be the substitute.

It was not beautiful. Her form was no less ordinary than her face had seemed. The breasts were good enough and full without being pendulous, but they were far apart, and the nipples, because they were not evenly placed, seemed walleyed. As to the rest of her, she was pleasantly proportioned, her legs were good, but there was a kind of unevenness about her flesh, as if the clay had not been smoothly molded by the sculptor. A good body, perhaps even an erotic body, but not beautiful.

Watching Velletri as her double, seeing that those breasts and legs and arms, and the way the woman carried herself, were not Calla's alter ego, she felt waves of disturbance. She could not stand the thought that an audience would think this ordinariness was the unclothed reality of her self. She, Calla Stark, never face- or body-proud, was physically more beautiful than her double. She was certain Notale had deliberately—and despicably—chosen a second-rate image to represent her. He knew without doubt that Calla would not allow herself to be depicted by an unbeautiful physique, by a body not as well molded as her own, not as graceful in motion, not as voluptuous. Realizing how this discrepancy would upset Calla, he was counting on her to change her mind, and agree to let herself be photographed in the nude.

She would not do it. She would demand that another double be chosen, a woman whose figure she would have a right to approve. If he did not accede to her demand, she would quit—right now, in the middle of the picture.

Having made her decision, she went to her dressing room, changed clothes, did not pause to get out of her makeup, left the sound stage and returned to the hotel. She had a quick shower, got into a pair of old slacks and a slightly frayed T-shirt, went down to the hotel's outdoor café, drank three cognac baci in rapid succession, and wondered how soon she would be sick. It had been weeks since she had had any hint of nausea, and if she was going to have it again, this would surely be the time. But everything stayed down; she was somewhat drunk and more than somewhat elated. I'll walk, she said, I'll walk to every museum there is, she said, I'll float, she said, I'll talk to every child in Rome, I'll float.

Thinking of children, she went to the American Express office and sent half of her first salary installment to Mrs. Tolliver's orphanage, and enclosed an affectionate letter asking Mamma Lorena for pictures of all the new arrivals. Majestically, then, she strode out of the American Express office; like a princess she marched in solo procession from the Piazza di Spagna, ceremoniously tripped on the steps and fell flat on her face. She sat on the staircase, hilarious and unhurt, gazing upward, giggling at the topsy-turvy Rome. She had another *bacio* somewhere and the vague sense that she hadn't had any lunch, but was in an airy museum looking at a marble statue of either herself or Velletri, except that the figure was armless.

She was beginning to feel dizzy. In some disorganized cupboard of her mind, she had a memory of a hotel and a bed. But she did not want to go there, for she knew they would be phoning from the set, and she was not able to think about that. Let them fret for a while, she said. But finally she couldn't stand how her head was spinning, so she went back to the hotel. There were a dozen messages, from everyone, four from Notale. Calling the operator, she told her to hold all calls. She took a stomach pill, groaned and lay down.

Nighttime, the telephone. Damn them, she said, for putting it through when I told them not to. The operator was agog with apology; they were worried about her, *il signor* Notale was frantic, an emergency, the operator said. She heard his voice:

"Are you sick? Are you all right?"

"Yes. I'm all right."

"What happened? Where did you go?"

She did not answer. Her head still turned, but not as badly as before.

"Calla—what happened?"

"You know damn well what happened. Velletri happened."

"Velletri?"

"You know goddamn well I'm not going to allow that body to be mine."

He was silent. Then, with quiet gravity: "She has a very beautiful body."

She felt a twinge. "I don't find it so."

"Then you should see it on film."

"I have no interest in seeing it."

"You're being unfair to her, Calla—and to me."

"I don't give a damn."

"Calla . . . Come tonight, and see the rushes."

"I never see rushes."

"Make an exception. Only tonight."

"I don't care—go to hell—I don't care!"

She heard herself. She had been temperamental in her career, but this was the first time she heard a meanness in her voice, spoiled, selfish, the ugly star noises.

"Calla, listen—don't be miserable to me." His plea was unreserved. "Believe me—she photographs beautifully. I have used her body before."

"I'm sure you have."

Christ, she thought, can't I stop this bitchiness? "I'm sorry, Franco."

"Good. Then come and see her in the rushes. Will you?"

"No."

"Please, Calla. Tonight at ten. The garage office of the warehouse —the other door, not the sound stage. Will you come? Please." When she did not answer, he pursued it. "I have an appointment or I would pick you up. No, I'll put off my appointment until later—pick you up at nine o'clock. Calla—please—*carissima*."

It was the first endearment he had ever used; he wanted something.

"I'll pick you up," he repeated.

Since she did not say yes or no, he assumed yes, and picked her up at nine.

In his Alfa, still slightly hung over, she rode beside him the entire hour's distance without saying a word. Nor did he. When the projector was being prepared, and while the assistant director, the two cameramen and the script woman were chattering, Calla sat apart from Notale and the others, and did not speak.

There was darkness, a flare of white, of black, the clapperboard, a false start, the clapperboard a few times, then the Cain scene they had finished this morning. It was better than she had expected, and the husband was more real than she had imagined him to be. His emptiness as a human being was passing as an inner torment, and she wondered: Am I also in real life so much less than I appear on film? Am I a superficial woman, as shallow as my temper tantrums, as vain as my wanting to appear more beautiful than I am, as selfish as the stereotypical star who means to discharge a woman because . . .

No. Her work was her work, Calla told herself, and the image was all she had to live with, act with, dream with, and—yes—sell. Not Calla Stark the woman, nor even Calla Stark the star, but the image that others saw and that she saw in herself, an image of some beauty brighter than the looking glass could tell.

There she was, Velletri. Velletri's body.

And he had been quite right. What an eye he had, to have started the shot with the woman at such a far distance, so out of reach in the shadowy cave, coming to the husband out of his own doubts, the face totally unrecognizable, the clothes being shed image by image, then the nude woman coming, coming closer, the halt in the alcove, like a change of mind, only an arm and thigh visible, and she is there, still closer but seen through a veil, a filter of cave cloud. Then the intercuts to each of them as the husband moves nakedly to meet her, the shade of wavering recognition on his face, then the vision of her body, finally a shot of both of them as he moves near enough to touch her, the curve of her body to her hip, trying to recall her with his hands, his fingertips touching her breasts; now her hand moves slowly to his thigh, his penis, and the distance between their bodies closes.

The lights went up and the others talked about the day's work. She was still at a distance from them, and silent. She listened to Notale speaking softly to the first cameraman, questioning whether the filters were falsifying colors, whether he could change to paler ones. She heard him discuss matters she did not understand, neutral densities and circles of confusion and masking the halogen, all the code words in the technical cabal they belonged to, and jealously she felt out of it. Then the others left. The two of them were alone.

It was a makeshift projection room with rows of unmatched folding chairs. He sat in the second row, and she sat in the last one, diagonally far away. He did not come to sit beside her, he only half turned in his seat.

"Well?" he said.

"She's very beautiful."

She wanted to say that the beauty was not in Velletri but in him.

"I'm glad you think so," he said.

"Tell her to walk a little . . . higher," she suggested.

"Yes. You do walk higher, don't you? But . . ." Then, as if to apologize, "She will never walk exactly as you do, Calla. She is not a star."

"Thank you . . . But if she could only . . ."

Not wanting to sound captious, she did not go on.

She didn't have to. "Yes," he said.

He was still bothered by Calla's comment. "It's a long walk from the end of that passageway. Our eyes have nothing to do but study her body and the way she moves. I was hoping to keep it one single, unbroken shot—I thought it might be beautiful." He sighed heavily. "But perhaps I will have to intercut with shots of him."

She heard his disappointment. "Yes, it was a lovely . . . idea," she said.

A pensive silence.

"It is too bad," he murmured.

"Yes, it is too bad."

More silence.

"Well . . ."

"You could shoot it over," she said, "and tell her to . . ."

Again she did not finish. Nor did he respond until moments later.

". . . Yes, I could. But . . ."

A question was slowly forming in Calla's mind. Why, when the woman was not really beautiful, did she look so exquisite? It was, of course, the haze of unreality about her, the idealized beauty that could not strictly be held to terms nor even signally described; it was a vision in the director's dream. And it occurred to Calla that this was hardly nudity at all; very little of the woman's body could be clearly descried in that fantasy light.

"I'll do the nude scenes."

Still, he did not arise from his chair, he did not move to be near her. "I am very glad."

"I'm assuming that the dream quality—in the naked scenes—will continue through the film."

"Yes, that's right."

"If there are shots that are too clear—"

"There won't be."

"—or too explicit—"

"None. I promise."

"Will you let me see the rushes?"

"But you never want to see them."

"I will, this time—if you let me. Only the nude scenes. . . . May I?"

"Yes—absolutely."

"And you'll listen to my feelings about them?"

"I will not only listen. I will cut anything you want to cut. Or reshoot."

"You mean that?"

"Oh, we will have fights, and I will try to convince you. I will yell, I will weep—"

"So will I."

"But you will have the last word," he said. "I promise."

"All right, then."

She wondered fleetingly whether he could be trusted to keep his word. She had had warnings not to let herself be naïve about the man's pledges, that he was a Machiavelli. But she had also had warnings that he was a lecher, and God knows, she would gladly put up with one fault if the other one were true. As to his being dishonest, part of their problem had been his excessive honesty, his refusal to praise her when praise was not earned. No, she said, he was a genuine artist, a man to put her faith in.

If he was less than genuine when, in Calla's presence he called Elsa and lied to her on the telephone, it was a white fib, on the side of kindness. You were too good, he told the woman, too beautiful, and added the excuse that Calla was worried that the press might discover it was not the star's figure they were looking at but the lovelier body of a double. *Mi ne dispiace,* he kept apologizing, but Elsa must surely understand what trials one went through when a star was involved.

Their evening's work was over. Remembering his delayed appointment, he looked hurriedly at his watch and offered to drive her back to the hotel. She saw the rush he was in and said she would find a taxi, which he did for her. She went back to the hotel alone.

The following day they reshot the footage that had been done with Elsa. Calla had never played an even nearly nude scene before, and between shots she clung to her wrapper, twisting it tightly about her body, feeling ridiculously virginal, yet dissolute. At first, nakedness was simply too naked. No matter how true a confession she always hoped her acting would be, she had never meant it to be an exhibition. There had to be a difference between revelation and exposure, she thought; there had to be secrets, was the adage, and now there were none. But suddenly, midmorning, she came upon a secret even in her nudity; she let her body show itself as it was—bare, stitchless; but the rest of her being was fully clothed, her eyes were hooded, her mouth suggested it would never divulge the answer to a riddle, the pride of her head said she was retaining the precious privacy of selfhood, and nobody could share it.

She thought what she had found was her own personal trade secret, but Notale ferreted it out. "Your privacy is your seduction," he said. Then he added, "Now—do the opposite. In the scenes where you are fully clothed, walk as if you are naked."

Intriguing as his suggestion was, it was not typical of the way he directed the nude scenes. If he had previously seemed remote, he now became even more distant, measurable in linear feet, when she was unclothed. He never got close, but spoke from his platform beside the camera, glued to his chair, talking to her as if she were in another room. He would lay out the action, listing her cues for movement and business, setting up hand signals which she could follow out of the corner of her eye. Sometimes, when she did not understand what was expected of her, he would whisper to the script woman, who would hurry into the playing area and relay the director's message to the star. Nobody except Calla seemed to think his behavior was in the least bit unusual. The tenet was maintained that the director, with a nicety, was scrupulous not to invade the famous actress's *intimità*. But she was annoyed by his aloofness and felt she was being directed by transatlantic cable.

Toward the end of their third week of shooting, they had a quarrel. It was, as Calla had apprehended, about one of the nude scenes. In the rushes, one evening, she saw medium shots of herself, from the top of her head to just above the waist, and every pore was as explicit and klieg-lighted as if she were in a police lineup. She hated the footage and called a few seats over to say so.

Notale listened carefully. Then he speculated aloud whether she was actually objecting on the score that the shots were too explicit, which they had established as a legitimate area of argument, or whether she was objecting to the film because it was unflattering.

She winced. "I know that it's supposed to be an unflattering scene —it's the way my husband is beginning to see me. But everything else in the film is dreamlike, and this is too real."

"It's the shattering of the dream."

"It shatters right out of the film."

"The film is not finished. You have not seen all of it."

"What will I see? Hard porn?"

It was too rough, she wanted to take it back. He had threatened, if this issue came up, that he would yell and weep. She would have preferred it to the lethal chill in his voice. "It will not be pornography," he said. He turned to his assistant. "Throw it away. We will reshoot the scene tomorrow."

She had made him stick to his promise, and did not regret it, but she could have bitten her tongue for having been so acerbic with him. In the next few sessions of rushes, she objected more tactfully to two other minor scenes and he reshot them without caviling.

Her most humiliating moment on any film came about two weeks before the shooting was concluded. One afternoon, when the work was over, Notale came to her dressing room and explained that the following day would be an exacting one, and he hoped that he and Calla would not have any difference about the film that resulted from it. It was a sequence in the script where a wild and violent boy, a satyr, sees her naked for the first time. He stares at her eyes, her mouth, her throat, and his glance comes to rest on her bosom. It is a moment in the script where the story comes to a climax, not only the culmination of a pursuit through the mazes of the grotto, but the change from fantasy to reality.

She knew that Notale would say exactly what he was now saying: the images would have to be clear, there would be no further reliance on dreamlike gauzes, the force of the scene must not be dissipated, nor could they dare risk an anti-climax to what the foregoing minutes of the film have promised. So, in the instant when the camera would come to a close-up of her breasts—

"If you are naked, you must be naked," he said.

"The camera—how close will it be?"

"As close as I can get it."

"And not through a glass darkly."

"That's the point, Calla—no filters. We will disguise nothing."

"In the finished film . . . ?"

"It will be very fast—I promise. A flash shot of your breasts—no more than that—a few seconds on the screen."

She knew it was necessary; the crisis in the scenario demanded it. Grateful that he had been forthright and had not tried to double-talk her into anything, she agreed to waive her right of approval.

They got to the scene the following afternoon. When the time came to shoot it, Notale sent nearly everybody away. It seemed odd of him to do so inasmuch as the crew had attended the shooting of other scenes of nudity. The set was nearly empty; except for the head gaffer and grip, most of the workmen were gone, and, since it was going to be a silent shot, the sound men were dismissed; even the clacker boy was told to go. Darola did the boy's job, writing numbers into her script.

The camera was going to be in motion but Calla was not. She sat

on a high stool. There was no necessity for her to be totally nude, for
the focus would be only upon the upper part of her body; she wore
walking shorts and sneakers. Her bare bosom was only lightly made up
so that she would not perspire too much—the lights were close and it
was already very hot. Even before the camera was anywhere near being
lined up, the makeup woman was dabbing at the perspiration.

It was extraordinarily quiet. The only sound was the camera assistant, whistling through his teeth, making more sibilance than melody.
The assistant director glanced around; the microphones were off, there
was no need to ask for silence, but he did. Then he looked at Notale.

Seated in his chair, on his platform, the director was smoking,
holding the cigarette between his ring and middle fingers, letting his
hand cover his mouth, squinting through the haze of smoke. At last he
lowered his hand and looked at Calla. She had let her body relax a little, her head down, almost touching her bosom with her chin, her eyes
closed.

"Ready?" he asked.

She raised her head, opened her eyes, took a slow, even breath to
lift her breasts. She looked at him, then at the camera. It was closer
than it had usually been, and would be closer still. He was closer too;
she could smell his cigarette.

"Ready," she said.

The assistant cameraman waved his hand gently to clear the air of
smoke. Notale took one more drag, bent down, carefully put the cigarette under his heel, snuffed it out. The script woman glanced at him.

"*Azione*," he said.

Calla looked directly into the camera as if it were the face of the
satyr boy, a wildness of beauty and ferocity. She was fascinated by him
and terrified. But she must see something particular about him that was
appealing—his mouth, yes; and must find something fearsome as well—
the darting, feral eyes. He is going to leap at me, she told herself, I can
feel him at my mouth, my throat, my breast—

"Cut."

Notale said *momento* to nobody in particular, then whispered to
the cinematographer, who answered in the negative and shrugged his
shoulders.

"*Ancora*," Notale said to the others. And to Calla, "Again."

She loosened her shoulders, let them sag a moment and
straightened up while they were getting ready to shoot once more.

"*Azione*," he said again. This time, when she saw the satyr, he seemed more alluring, yet just as cruel, as ready to attack, and she wanted to flee and to stay.

Cut, he said, and again they conferred, he and the chief cameraman, but this time they brought the script woman in to join their sotto voce conference.

Just as they started to shoot the scene for the third time, it struck her: Their whisperings were not about a technical matter, not lights or interference or camera; they were talking about her. She was doing something wrong or unspecifically . . . or she was not beautiful enough.

Then the shooting stopped altogether, and Notale arose from his chair. He's going to approach me, she thought. But it was the opposite: he walked in the other direction, forty or fifty feet away, and called for Darola to join him. In a hush, they talked together for a while. At last, he walked back to his chair, but the script woman did not return to hers. Instead, she slowly approached Calla.

The woman was in a fret of embarrassment. She whispered *signorina* a few times, but could not begin.

"Yes, Darola, what is it?"

"Your . . . breasts."

Without sensing what was wrong, Calla felt a flush of humiliation. "What about them?"

"If you can . . ." In distress, she stopped. "If you can think of something . . . *appassionato* . . ."

The star's nipples were flat, and the director wanted them risen. Abruptly, she needed to run. The mortification was the more terrible because she knew she could not possibly satisfy the direction simply upon command. She felt rage at him for requiring it and rage at herself for being an actress and not being able to do what he asked. She sat there, trying to think of it as simply an assignment in acting, which it was. But no sense memory came to her, no emotion memory helped her recall someone kissing her breast, or thrusting inside her, or the first time she came. She was in a panic. It was in too many contorted ways a failure. She could not satisfy the director or the man; her body was not responding to the camera or the bed, real or remembered, or to anything that would make her seem more excited or exciting.

She began to sweat. The makeup woman was at her, daubing between her breasts.

And the script woman was suggesting: "I could bring you some ice for them. Sometimes if they are cold . . ."

"No."

"Ready?" the director asked.

She could not bear to look at him, only at the camera. But there was no satyr anymore. Only Notale—out of view—and she wanted her nipples to firm for him.

"*Azione.*"

She ran.

She did not know where she was—somewhere between a wild wing of scenery and a wall, in shadow. It was a tightly confined corridor, hardly wide enough for her to stand in, but no more space than she wanted. Burning with heat, she shivered as if freezing. Which way to go, she wondered, so she could get to her dressing room without anyone seeing her. She was frightened at herself for having panicked, for having gone berserk. Quaking, she did not know what to do.

She saw him at the lighted end of the long dark corridor. He stood there quite a while, it seemed, not moving. Then he said her name softly.

"Go away," she said.

Slowly, quite slowly, so as not to frighten her, he moved in her direction.

"Please . . ." But she did not know what she wanted him to do, whether to stay where he was or to come closer, or whether she should hold still or run away.

He was perhaps twenty feet from where she stood, still moving slowly, slowly, advancing upon her as if she were a young doe that might take flight if he were to make an alarming movement. And all the while he was stirring forward to her, he was murmuring, comforting an unnerved creature in a nest, a cavern.

"Please," she said.

Still he moved, still he murmured until at last he was close enough to touch her. But he didn't. He held his hands together, loosely clasped on his chest as if in prayer, and he did not reach to her.

All at once, she needed him to do so, with a rush of heat she needed so badly to feel his hands upon her flesh that she wanted to throw herself into his arms, or to run frantically free.

"Touch me," she whispered.

The space between them was so little, so close that they could sense the breath of one another, and yet he did not extend his hand to her. She hardly heard his murmured words; only saw the movements of his mouth, saw his lips trembling like kisses, wanted them on her breasts. And she could feel her nipples rising, tightening, rising.

"Oh, touch me!"

His mouth still moved, but now even the murmuring had ceased. She heard no sound at all, saw only the slow pursing of his lips.

"Oh, please," she said. "Oh, please."

Slowly he unclasped his hands, and reached forward to touch her breasts.

They performed the film scene in the afternoon and the real one in the evening. Both were satisfactory.

They made love that night and every night thereafter for the next two weeks, and early mornings as well, and whenever it was possible during the shooting days, as soon as he gave the signal to kill the lights. They made love as if it were their single, obsessional, monomaniacal mission.

Calla moved into Franco's apartment, a chaotic, spacious, wonderfully skylighted studio on one of the crooked streets in Trastevere. The actual shooting of the film, which continued at a workmanlike pace, became a secondary chore; their main employment, their pastime, their devout vocation, the exercise of their skills, the joint endeavor of their embodied beauty—their art!—was fucking. To this end they did everything to pleasure one another. They learned all the lines in the love script they were performing for and with each other, they spoke them with such a depth of sincerity, with such a transport of passion that they not only believed the lines were true, but that they had spontaneously burst forth as if from a new creation, a freshly made cosmos they had inspiredly brought into being. It was their very own dramaturgical production: Love Play, in Numberless Acts. The nighttime drama they performed was more exquisite than the daytime one, for they were simultaneously the players and the audience, performing the scene and applauding it. Between them, they created the Utopia of the theater, all passion and no critics.

But it could not last. In the soulless bromide of the entertainment business, they were deeply in love, but the show closed.

The shooting of the film was finished. It had been completed four days ahead of schedule, rare in Italy; for Notale, it was a record. And everybody talked well of it; even Franco, who was never certain at this stage what it was he had wrought, felt that the finished picture would have *demenza e compassione*.

Calla's work in the film was over, but Franco's had, in a sense, just begun. There were complicated process effects to be done, and editing and scoring. His working day lengthened. He would get up before dawn and return to the apartment late at night. At first she felt deprived by his absence, and longed for a return of the shooting days when they were constantly together. But soon she bought a car exactly like his, an Alfa Romeo, and took to driving into the country. She went to Tarquinia and became absorbed in the Etruscans; she drove to Volterra to watch them open a tumulus and dig for artifacts; she spent a weekend by the sea, alone, and enjoyed it.

One morning, as she and Franco lay in bed later than usual, she looked up at the skylight. Previously, the attic had been an artist's studio, and the slanting window overhead was immense. But the leaded glass was not entirely transparent; it presented an unpatterned chiaroscuro of bright sky and opacity, as if the artist had gone onto the roof and painted it in a pointillism of silver gray, cloudy white and varied tints of lavender. Perceiving the lovely mottled skylight this morning, she observed an odd thing: she had never had the slightest curiosity how the window had come to have such an exquisitely shaded surface, had simply accepted it as another gift of this romantic room and her romantic life with Notale.

But suddenly she had to know. "How did it happen?" she asked.

"What?"

She pointed. "That beautiful painting on the skylight."

"It's pigeon shit."

It was, of course, too trivial to give it further thought, but she could not stop thinking of it. It irked her that her mind could not have chanced upon a less bathetic, a more exalted symbol to foreshadow a sadness. She tried to find some aesthetic emblem that would betoken the end of a warmly satisfying love affair, any emblem, even a hackneyed one—a wilted rose, an empty perfume bottle, a fragile little finger ring—but she could find none, and she wanted to weep because nothing of the lyric still remained.

For Franco's sake, she pretended that it did. She was quite certain, during those last moments, that his love of her was genuine. And in a way, she loved him too.

When he took her to the airport, he pretended to be really concerned about the mundane things he was discussing: the need for an assistant film editor, the bad workmanship of the processing lab, the shipping of her Alfa, which he would attend to. But she could see that he was crying; it amazed her that his eyes were so full and did not shed tears. She realized that her own face was wet, there were spots on her Florentine kidskin purse, and she could not talk nearly as coherently as he was doing.

"Franco . . ."

"*Che bella, che bella.*"

It was what he sent her away with, how beautiful she was.

. . . And the words came back to her six months later, when the film was released. How beautiful, one of the Los Angeles reviewers said, and she wondered whether he was referring to Calla Stark, the actress, or Calla Stark, the nude.

Not everybody was ambiguous. The notices were mixed, between bad and awful. Some few critics were titillated, but pretended not to be. Those who were shocked refrained from labeling it obscene for fear it would attract customers, and called it tedious. Pauline Kael used every euphemism for dung that she could find, and Andrew Sarris, at the anatomical other end, disported himself on the subject of vomit.

The audiences, however, had no such alimentary squeamishness. They took to the film as if they had been hornily awaiting it; they loved it, they talked to the screen in many theaters, masturbated in a few, and threw kisses. They threw money as well; it was a box-office gold mine. Starting in the art houses, the movie quickly outgrew them and burst into the large commercial theaters with a roar of triumph. It was one of the prurient talk pieces, like *I Am Curious Yellow* and *Barbarella*, alternately called erotica and pornography. The Hollywood *Reporter* ran a headline which read *Stark Stark Wow*, and *Variety* said *Stark Buff Boff*.

Prophetically having taken the pasties off her name, Calla watched the world gawk at her unpastied body. Overnight, she became the lurid sex object and the radioactive subject of lunchtime conversation in studio dining rooms and commissaries. The executives read in the trade papers that "she draws the longest lines and the biggest numbers" and "she's a one-woman Torrid Zone in American pictures."

That quickly, they forgot that she was Commie Callie, who had at one time been charged with manslaughter and transporting dope. If they did remember, they leered as if they were having their revenge on her—they had stripped her naked. But they had to admit that whether audiences were paying money to see her in the raw because they loved her or because they hated her, the customers had rocketed her back into the firmament: she was once again a star.

The smaller independent producers were the quickest to send her scripts, every screenplay a nudie. She and Megan rejected all of them. Presently, the more important producers and the major studios were ringing her phone, carpeting her driveway with manuscripts. They were no longer leery of her politics; her radical knives were not so sharp when sheathed in greenbacks.

To rationalize their turnabout, they said that it was she who had turned about. They told their public that she was older now, and wiser, no longer an unwashed hippy. They excused her former rebelliousness by saying she was merely one of the whacky kids of the sixties; nothing more dangerous than a kooky girl, a guitar-playing adolescent, hanging a bit too loose. She had only been confused, politicizing license by calling it liberation, no more responsible for being caught in the current of the years than millions and millions of others. "Your own kids were like that," a middle-aged publicist said, adding that she was really a mild person, a good ordinary American, like everyone's sister.

The portrait they drew was, of course, belittling. And it was untrue down to the mention of the guitar, an instrument she had never possessed or played; and she had never been an unwashed hippy, she had been a clean-haired woman in her middle and late twenties, on a heart-wrenching crusade.

However, it was true that the political climate itself had changed. It was no longer shameful to be against the Vietnam war, especially now that it was coming to an end. And it was no longer treasonous to call Nixon a liar; he had been forced to confess an equivalence of it.

Moreover, it was true that she had changed. She had lost a husband by divorce and a child by murder, and a love affair had just died in an attrition that was endemic to her profession. Also, she had another loss: she was missing a few causes and a scream. So it all added up to a change by a process of diminution, where less is not more, but emptier and lonelier. . . .

. . . Since *Grotto*, there had been many pictures. Two of them had not been good, failures; one had been a moderate success; the others had ballooned in triumph, at home and abroad. These last years of immersion, when she had had time for nothing but films, had rewarded her with two Oscar nominations and, for playing the role of a holocaust survivor, one Oscar. She had been unable to accept the award in person because she was on filming location in the Andes.

Despite her good fortune, she had come to know that after every success, failure was more certain, not only because of the law of averages, and because the world wanted to take the winner down a peg, but because, with success at stake, it was becoming increasingly difficult to take chances. She was not so brave anymore.

She still lacked the courage to go and see her own films. However, she had made one exception to that rule. She had finally seen *Grotto*.

An odd thing had been happening to it in recent years. Since the film was now a decade old, people had forgotten how bad the notices had been. But some reviewers, notably in the professional and university journals, had taken up the movie as if it were a creed. They praised it lavishly, enthralled by Notale's genius for shadow, his world within worlds, and they talked with the admiration of discovery about Calla's performance. A cult was forming.

About six months ago, while on an errand in Beverly Hills, she had noticed that *Grotto* was playing at the Fine Arts. On impulse, she had bought a ticket and entered the theater. She watched the movie from start to finish, totally detached from it. She thought that some of the film was beautiful and some, silly. It did not deserve the bad reviews, she felt, nor did it deserve its current celebration by a cult. She thought her performance was all right enough, but sometimes mawkish. It did not embarrass her because that was somebody else.

The most curious parts of the film were the nude scenes. She remembered distinctly objecting to at least three sequences of shots— which Notale had faithfully pledged to excise from the picture. But every single one of them was in the final film. As to the close-ups of her breast, he had promised there would be only a flash shot—merely a few seconds on the screen. Well, only a flash shot, yes—but there were a half dozen intercuts to the breast. He had betrayed her.

Then why, today, so many years after having said a final farewell to Franco, was she considering him as the potential director of O'Hare's screenplay? It certainly could not be because, having seen *Grotto*, she agreed that he was right in putting the offensive shots in, that they improved the picture. How ironic it was that she forgave him his betrayal for exactly the same reason that the studios forgave her: success. He had made the film a smash—maybe he had even artistically heightened its tensions—ergo, he was morally forgivable. Perhaps even morally right. The morality of the business.

But the truth was that he *had* betrayed her once, and might do it again, and was not to be trusted. If she had the same objection to Lucas O'Hare, what was the difference?

The difference was that the *actress* in her felt safe with Franco. She was free to do anything in his presence. She understood his working methods, his moods, his silences. Even his perfidies were predictable and, she might say, quixotic and condonable. Best of all, she was deeply fond of him.

She picked up the script of *The Fabulist*, held it a moment, and set it down. She telephoned O'Hare.

"I've changed my mind about your script," she said. "I think it's beautiful."

The silence was full of disbelief, or was he simply taking time to get his bearings? "Do you mean it?"

"Yes, I do. And I want to play the part."

"Oh God."

"But there is one thing . . ."

"Anything, Calla—anything."

"Don't speak too soon." Even though she meant to demand his acceptance of Notale as a condition of the deal, she must put it to him without effrontery. Tactfully, gently. "I want to ask you an enormous favor," she said.

"Yes? What?"

"It's very difficult—I'd rather not talk about it on the phone. Could you drop over for an hour or so?"

Another instant of latency. When he spoke again it was as if he were making a totally new adjustment to her. He was no longer a courtier on his knees, begging a favor of the queen. He too was royalty.

"Would you mind coming to my place?" he asked.

She smiled wryly. It was the question of turf, the desperate dominance game. Who would sit on the higher chair, looking down at the other; who would answer the phone to whose secretary, who would choose the field of combat?

She did not mind going to his place. It might give her an opportunity to find out something more deeply personal about the man . . . and Willi.

"I'll be glad to come," she said.

12

Lucas hung up the phone.

She was going to do it.

Calla Stark was going to do his film!

The gummy brown stuff in his plastic cup began to taste like coffee, his dead geranium came to life and his hair stopped getting thin.

Calla Stark!

He smelled the chili burning in the pan, lowered the flame and he too simmered down a little. There was a hitch somewhere; she had said she wanted a favor. He was canny enough to know that in the language of stardom a favor might mean a non-negotiable proviso.

No, he said, don't worry. Perhaps she had her own production company, and would demand that *The Fabulist* be done under its aegis. Lots of stars had private corporations these days, and although he disliked dealing with actors incorporate, he knew she had made a lot of money, and perhaps even so dauntless a woman as Calla Stark might feel she had to cover her fiscal flanks. It would be all the same to him; let her make a mintful for her Inane Enterprises, Inc., or her Pisspot Productions, Ltd., he didn't care. As to himself, he had never been in it for the buck, and he would settle for his last salary, which had been modest, and even risk part of his income on the fortunes of the film. It occurred to him that she might do the same, that she was no more mercenary than he, but simply wanted to be the producer, the boss.

Well, let her be the damn producer. He needed no dominion that did not come out of his skill as a director. He felt that his potency was, in part, a talent to persuade. And if persuasion was difficult in a Hollywood studio, where a star was subject to the pulls and pushes of agents, coaches, managers, friends, lovers, lawyers, it would be easier on location, somewhere in the South, where she would be in a tiny zone of influence, his own. Whatever exalted title she had acquired in Beverly Hills—Executive Producer in Charge of Pomp and Circumstance—would be meaningless at a distance from hysteria-land. He would be in charge. The Director.

No, the *work* would be in charge. The fable. He would set up a magic cauldron, and out of the fumes of the hot creative brew would come all the enchanted, dancing images. Then, if his persuasion had been seductive, it would hardly be a question of who was the producer or director. What would matter would be the elation of making the illusion come true. Making the lie come true was at the heart of the maddening paradox.

This was what he wanted to say to her. But if he were to utter it now, at this stage of their appraisal of one another, she would consider it part of the pitch. And she would be partly right; he never knew where the hard sell ended and the heart-cry began. The trouble was that he operated in two worlds: A conscientious artist, he was also a cunning deal-maker who, anomalously, didn't give a damn about money; a hermetically private man, he made entertainments for the multitude he deprecated; he would go to the ends of fakery—to tell the truth.

He was two-sided, geminate in everything, even to his parentage. His Irish father had been an electrician on the studio stages, not a gaffer but a juicer, whatever the distinction was in those days. I'm a juicer in both respects, the man used to confess, but the fact was that he hardly drank at all; it was his alibi for being crocked on fantasy. He fantasized himself off a catwalk one day, and fell splat into a barroom scene with a dozen cowboys. With his dying breath, he lamented that if he had fallen a few seconds sooner he'd have been in the scene with Gary Cooper.

Luke's mother, still alive, was the head of a secretarial pool at a major studio. Frieda, a plumpish, cuddly woman, loved food and loved being Jewish, saying that her life, like her stuffed cabbage, was sweet and sour. But she was not The Jewish Mother, she hated the discriminatory and indiscriminate term, loathed the sentimentality it suggested, and fought her hunger to be maternal as if it were high in calories. Devoted to the decencies, she viewed them as dishes she had to prepare fresh daily—a kind deed, a word of praise, a slap at hypocrisy. She had a penchant for the disadvantaged, and staffed her secretarial pool with widows, divorcées and the sadly born. To discourage tear-jerking, she

helped them make a brave and bitter joke of their rotten job by calling
the pool the Dying Dream Department. Everybody, including Frieda,
knew the expression was cruel, but they forgave her for it, because they
knew that Frieda wasn't.

She was a woman not easily confused. Her husband's death grieved
her, but she was too sensible to let it wreck their lives, so she made a
compromise with mortality. Perhaps it would be practical for Luke to
shift from a high tuition school like USC to a state university like
UCLA, and move back from the costly dormitory to their home in
West Los Angeles where he could live rent-free.

Luke had majored in English—the Elizabethans, primarily—intend-
ing to teach while pursuing a career as a writer, which had begun, in
early adolescence, with poems, short stories, an unfinished play. He had
determined that he would never be involved in motion pictures, certainly not on the sidelines as his parents had been, for he had no interest
in what he called the industrial complex. But it was his lot to have been
in two California universities that were fervent with film, where a litter
of movie pups had been whelped, among them Francis Coppola, George
Lucas, John Milius. While he never tried directing in those days, writing
for pictures was inescapable, and suddenly he was burning with cinema
fever. His whole life changed. Not only did he find his career, but his
world, a chimerical region independent of objective fact, the realm of
the impossible possibility.

Every screenplay he wrote was a failure, however, not only in college, but during his first years in the industry. Either his scripts did not
get produced or if they did scratch their way to the screen, they looked
false or pretentious, at odds with the nature of things. At odds with
him, too, for he did not recognize them as his own; they were never
what he had written, let alone envisioned. Perhaps the directors were
not at fault, he told himself; he simply lacked the writing talent for
the screen, the wand that waves one illusion into another.

He was about to quit Los Angeles and apply for a teaching position elsewhere when, at the last minute, he determined to give himself
one more chance at writing a film, if he could direct it himself. He took
a job as assistant to a film editor, Charlie Wernick, a college friend, who
was employed at Paramount. Daytimes, Lucas learned how to cut and
splice, how to build a continuity, the difference between film space and
film time; at night, he shackled himself to the typewriter. Living in
a room no larger than a pocket, he ate sparingly, saved every nickel he

could. A year or so later, he gathered his small sinking fund, borrowed money from Charlie, his mother and her relatives in San Diego.

With a secondhand Arriflex 16mm camera and four amateur actors, none of whom ever became a member of the Screen Actors Guild, he packed off in an old station wagon to a deserted silver mine near Tehachapi. He was cameraman, director, gaffer and grip. He was the cook and social director, the doctor in charge of bruises, a broken arm and shingles, the psychiatrist in charge of anxiety.

The script he wanted to film was called *Silver and Gold*. It was an ingenuous story. A seventeen-year-old girl whose mother is dead has been living with her father on the edge of the western desert. He owns a general store, which is seeing its last days, for the town is disappearing. The girl, Abby, has quit school; she is plain-looking, painfully shy, and feels that she does not do anything well. One day a young escaped convict comes along in a dilapidated jeep. He is en route to reopen a nearly used-up silver mine in the Tehachapi area, to start a new life, and to deliver himself from the curse of violence. He sees the girl, who has learned to make do with short hopes, and helps her feel beautiful and beloved. The boy is tracked by the law enforcers, and seized. She remains behind, knowing she will never see him again. She is deeply shaken, but her view of herself has changed, and her demand upon life has magnified.

In contrasting the two main characters, Luke wanted to derive through moments of love and beauty the kind of excitement that violence and ugliness can generate. He was challenged to create in an encounter between two loving people the kind of detonation of the spirit that happens in war.

His major dread, as he started to shoot the picture, was that the technology of film-making would be beyond his expertise: specialized skills he had only academically studied, the choices in distance and exposure, the mechanics of the camera itself. In the first weeks of shooting, he got everything wrong. But bit by bit he discovered that the terrifying monster of technology might one day be conquered. The instruments were not inscrutable, not recalcitrant, they would do as they were told. Allowing him to make mistakes and to learn from them, they held no grudges.

The massive problem he would have to face as a director was not instruments but people. Although he had written an adventure story, he became more preoccupied with characters than with events. Notably the ill-starred girl, Abby. Isolated on the edge of a forsaken dust bowl, unloved and unlovely, she has made a companionship with nature, the changes in the desert, the language of wind and weather, the conversation of flowering things. Falling in love with a man has never occurred to her as one of her opportunities. The arrival of the convict upsets her contentment with the world, and quickens a hope of ecstasy she is not equipped to handle.

It was her quandary that fascinated Lucas. He had a need to go deeper into the pain and beauty of her dilemma. He wanted to feel her ache, wanted to understand the common sense of her effort to keep her old world from falling apart, and the lunacy of her joy in risking everything for love.

It would take a skilled and talented actress, perhaps a great one, to achieve not only the power but the intimate delicacies of the part. And it would take a director who had the skill to bring forth such artistry.

Lucas had neither. He himself knew little about film performance. He had taken courses in acting and directing, but they were schematic. He felt like an alien in a country where the language was Stanislavsky and Actors Studio, a stage parlance that was becoming the patois of film actors as well. And he was nervous in the presence of performers, feeling that they were wise to his inadequacies, viewing him as a boondock Californian, an intruder in their New York charmed circle.

The fact that all his actors were amateurs was a blessing. But it was also a curse: they knew nothing. The girl who played Abby was Millie Edland, the only child of a forgotten man who owned a one-pump gas station on a back road to the desert. Because she could expertly handle the physical objects of the place—gas nozzle, air hose, car hoods, oil cans—Luke changed the locale of his script from general store to gas station.

He changed another important element—the main character. Abby, in the screenplay, was ill-favored; Millie Edland, however, had a lovely face, a smile that was reticent, sad, utterly beguiling. But she had one defect that dramatized the essence of Abby. Millie Edland was crippled. One leg was shorter than the other, a birth defect, and she walked with a limp. But in personality she was perfect casting. The deformity had made her recessive; she was frightened of the world and wanted to hide; she spoke barely above a whisper. Of course, Millie had never acted in a play, not so much as a Christmas pageant; she had watched movies mostly on television, and had never seen live actors on a stage. The thought of doing a film terrified her, and she had to laugh and cry and run away before she agreed to do it.

Luke knew he had to take things easy with her. In the first few days of shooting, he had her do the simplest actions, which she performed none too well. Overnight, the girl who had been so adroit with all the gas station paraphernalia did not know how to open an oil can, and the gas nozzle became her enemy. At last the director realized that if he was to break through and give her courage as an actress, it was he —not she—who would have to take the greatest risk. So he decided to do her most difficult scene—not at the end of the shooting period, as he had originally intended, but now.

It was the moment in the story when she meets the young man and realizes she is in love with him. Even for a seasoned actress, it was one of the most difficult effects to create movingly—love at first sight. An amateur might never be able to make it believable, let alone touching.

It was a boiling day in desert summer. The camera was set up on an improvised track alongside Edland's filling station. The scene was straightforwardly written: A broken-down jeep pulls into the station. The unkempt young stranger drives to the pump, stops, honks his horn. The girl comes limping out, asks what he wants, fills his gas tank and collects the money. As he receives his change, Abby notes that the man has a bad cut across the knuckles. He is evasive as to how he got it. The hand is still bleeding and he starts to wipe the blood on his shirt. Quickly she says no, don't do that, I'll get you a bandage. She hurries indoors, comes out with a few Band-Aids, hands them to him. With one hand, he can't manage, so she does it for him. As she is ministering to the man, he comments on how kind she is, and how pretty. And— the touching thing to her—how quickly she does everything. She blurts that she has never thought of herself as quick, and unintentionally glances downward. He says he didn't notice that she was crippled. When he drives away, she has a moment of doubt; then she believes him. It is an instant of joy and revelation. And suddenly—!

It was the "suddenly" that Lucas had to capture on film. Suddenly she falls in love, suddenly something changes her whole world. Suddenly she shows it.

How?

He spoke to Millie quietly, then tried the scene. Once, twice, again and again. He suggested a number of devices, which she dutifully attempted. She ventured a few things on her own—sighing, putting her hands on her mouth to control her pleasure; once, she even managed a few tears. None of it was wrong, none right.

"Millie. . ."

"I'm sorry, Luke. I just don't know what to do."

"You're doing everything fine, honey—you really are. It's not your fault—honestly it's not—it's mine."

"No."

"Millie—listen—I'm not going to direct the scene anymore. Forget everything I've said. You don't have to come to any places that are marked on the ground—none of them. I'm not going to shoot it with the camera tied down—I'm going to carry it. I don't care where you are or what you do. Anything. When the car drives away, all I want you to do is . . ."

He knew, at last, what he wanted; knew exactly what he needed her to do. But how could he get it without expressly asking for it, thereby risking the almost certain probability that, if it happened at all, it would be too studied, and lack the spontaneity the scene required?

"Millie . . ." He started again, tentatively. "Do you know what love is? It's a dream come true."

She couldn't face him. "I . . . I've never had that dream."

"Then substitute another. Show me a dream come true, Millie. The most wonderful dream in the world—make it come true. Show me."

"I can't!"

But already he was loosening the camera. He had it in his hands. The jeep was back in position, moving away from the pump. The girl stood there, white, rigid as death, too frightened to move. Then suddenly she came alive. Her eyes followed the vehicle. She watched it disappear. Her face was filled with a fear of believing what she yearned to believe. All at once, she embraced herself as if to clutch his words to her heart. Something happened in her eyes—a hope—the joy of a dream come true—and then—

She did it! She began to run. She ran in one direction and another, everywhere at once, she ran as if she had never been crippled in her life, ran like a blissful filly, ran and fell and arose, and kept on running. She ran right out of the camera range.

For an instant, he thought he would race after her and keep her in the camera's view. Then another thought struck him: he kept the film rolling on the empty space where she had been. And he yelled at her:

"Come back! Run back! Millie, run back!"

The camera rolled—on emptiness. Directly, she came running

back, running. At last, spent, she fell on the ground, threw out her arms and embraced it.

At the first showing of the completed film, with an audience of strangers at a preview, there was that moment of empty space again. On the split second when Abby comes rushing back onto the scene, the audience broke into happy laughter, then an outburst of applause. . . . Years later, Luke believed that that moment started him as a director.

It did not, however, assure the success of *Silver and Gold*. The finished picture had cost $31,000, not counting two sizable bills for film and processing. In Los Angeles, he showed it to the studios and to any number of distributors, and nobody would have anything to do with it. Not that it was bad, they said; in fact, rather interesting. But it wasn't slick, it had no glitz, one of the professionals declared, and if the 16mm were converted to 35, the final film would be grainy, not worth the cost. So it was never released to the theaters.

Nevertheless, it was seen on TV. He sold all the rights to the network, and the television money paid his bills and reimbursed his backers with a respectable profit, and left $12,000 for himself. The actors also shared, and with her money Millie enrolled at the University of Colorado, where she studied art history, to become a teacher. He heard from her now and then, postcards from museums mostly. Occasionally, when he remembered, he sent her a present on her birthday.

Silver and Gold was good, he knew it was good. He might call the acting amateur and even embarrassing at times, but he could also call it raw and naked and often poignant. The story could be dismissed as barren, but it could also be accounted lean to the bone of truth. Some of the camera work, scenes of desert mystery and loneliness, he could never equal with all the fanciest equipment in the world. He was certain now that he was talented as a writer, and perhaps even as a director; and he was resolved never again to allow his written work to be transformed into film by anyone but himself.

Columbia Pictures allowed him to direct his next screenplay because he was a bargain, an eager young craftsman who could shoot quickly and economically. The film came in even more cheaply than they had expected, a week ahead of schedule, and made a small but creditable profit. In a community that had an awesome regard for directors but a barely concealed contempt for writers, he was earning an attentive respect among the studio overlords. But the vigilance was guarded—there was something eccentric about him, his preoccupation with the inexplicable, for example, even the supernatural; dangerous stuff. He was an oddball. Beware.

Still, they bought his next package. The main characters were an elderly couple whose story drew its quiet eloquence from their courage in the face of death. It was a tale without a hopeful alternative, but it had a valor about it, and a comforting note that mortality—and life— were never so hideous as the fear of them. The business experts said bad risk, don't touch it. The picture had a budget as lean as a knuckle, received excellent notices and showed a handsome profit.

In Hollywood, there was only one figure of speech: hyperbole. Whether a statement was a plaudit or a pan, it was always an extremity; a man was either a colossus or a pygmy. From this moment onward, in the industry's view, O'Hare could do only one thing: tower.

But the colossus crumbled. After three failures in a row, it was no longer possible for him to put together a package in which he was the sole luminary; he needed a constellation, with at least one acting star, preferably two. Calla Stark, rediscovered, three successes in a row, was all the nova he needed.

And she had said yes. Would he have been as elated if she had not been perfect for the part? Would he have been satisfied, at last, to get the picture started with just any star? Had he come so far afield from himself, through the nettles of failure, that he would have compromised *this* script? In any event, he had been saved.

The telephone rang. His ex-wife, calling from New York. Alma, née Orenstein. They had been divorced for a decade, and married barely long enough to have one child, a daughter whom they named Joanna but called Wendy for reasons nobody could remember. Because of the little girl, they had maintained a display of their affection, like a building kept in good repair by absentee landlords. Alma was currently an editor at Prentice Hall; privately, she wrote chastening letters to the governor of New Hampshire and assorted librarians on the subject of freedom from censorship in schoolbooks. Responses were routine and unsatisfactory. They made her lips thinner.

She didn't call often. He wondered what she wanted. "You sound wonderful," he said.

"I *am* wonderful and I *look* wonderful." She was jubilant. "My hair's out of my eyes, and I'm wearing contact lenses."

"Congratulations."

"And I don't start every sentence with 'however' anymore."

"New boy friend or new analyst?"

She giggled. "Both. The same man."

"Still efficient," he said. "How's Wendy?"

"She's fine. That's what I called you about."

"I know—Saturday's her birthday. What shall I send her?"

"I thought a silver bracelet—inscribed. But don't put Wendy on it. She wants to be called Joanna now."

"I'm glad she got around to it."

"Yes, growing up. She speaks seven languages."

There had to be a mistake. He had seen Wendy less than a year ago, on her eleventh birthday. The best she could manage in French sounded like, "Monsieur Gaston's pocket has an ankle which sells white teeth."

"What do you mean, speaks seven languages?"

"Computer languages." She tittered. "She's fluent in Significant Ratio and Double Aggregate."

"Do you understand her?"

"No, but I don't understand her in English either."

Neither did he. The words, yes. Not the quantifications. She had a quantum mind. He had never realized how alien he felt to the measuring mentality until he tried to comprehend his daughter. She knew the weight, amplitude and extent of all of life's propositions, and the number of everything. One of the geniuses of the Dalton School ($6,000 per annum—that was a number *he* knew), she made him feel as if all his thoughts had been filed in the wrong drawers. But she was always kind to him. Take your time, Dad, she would say, until you really know what you mean. He had stopped telling her fairy tales when she was two years old; there were no trolls or hippogriffs, she said. At seven, she handed him a critique of one of his films. It read as if it had been written with claws.

"Did she get my script?" he asked.

"Yes, she did. I hated it."

"I didn't send it to you."

"She didn't read it. I did."

"Alma, for Pete's sake, why do you bother?"

"I love to read what you write."

"You love to read it so you can hate it. Listen, Alma, why don't you save yourself some time? Just stitch me a sampler: *I Hate Your Work.*"

"I don't hate your work. I loved *The Runaways*."

"Because it was a failure."

"Not because it was a failure, because it touched me. I still cry over it."

"So do I."

"It was about real people. Why can't you write about real people again?"

"They are real people—in my mind."

"Good grief, you don't have a mind like that. The rape scene was disgusting."

That was it. After talking to Alma, he knew that the scene was precisely what Calla would confront him with. It was the "enormous favor" she was going to ask. He could see her demand in capital letters, a title filling the screen:

PROVISO: CUT THE RAPE SCENE

He had deluded himself into thinking the favor would have to do with such considerations as whose company would produce the film. No, it went to the jugular. The script. He dreaded that he might not be able to persuade her that the sexual assault was the symbol of the love-and-rage conflict, and vital to the story.

He was glad he had asked her to come here. Not for dominance; at this stage of the game, dominance was a useless card. He wanted her to see where he lived, and how. She had taken him to be an ignoramus, a boor, but she would view him differently here, surrounded by his books, his friends. If he was to be judged by his associates, these were his closest.

But what did his bibliophilia have to do with the rape scene? A book-loving man who considered the assault as heinous as she did—so what? It wouldn't matter what he read but what he wrote: a ravage sequence that had to be an affront to a raw-nerved, activist woman; to Calla Stark it would be the archetypal atrocity committed by the male.

How to convince her that his feminism was genuine? He could never write the patronizing "woman's picture." Films like *An Unmarried Woman* and *Alice Doesn't Live Here Anymore* made him ill. They were soft-centered, the women soft-centered, all sentimental flab. He could not demean a female by excusing a sick dependency or by cosseting a weakness he would not tolerate in a male. He was incapable of touching a woman with limp fingers, as Scorsese had done in *Alice*, or with cruel hands as De Palma could do, probing at them with the cold scalpel. Maybe that was one of his problems: as a director, he could not take the maudlin popular view or the voyeuristic detached one; he had to be intimately involved with every character, his camera in the heart. In his own heart as well. . . . And he knew that the rape scene was *right*.

He heard a car and, almost immediately, the doorbell. He nervously slapped his palm down on his cowlick and tightened his belt. Glancing at himself in the hall mirror, all he could see was that his hair was graying a little. He would never dye it, he decided, and opened the door.

She wore pale yellow slacks and yellow canvas shoes, meant to look inexpensive. From the waist down she was sport, but her shirt was silk, and he suspected there was no brassiere under it. It intimated that she was setting him up. Or soliciting: whatever favor she wanted, she wanted badly. Good, he thought, she's playing from weakness.

He motioned Calla to a chair but she paced the room, prowling, reconnoitering as though she meant to lay siege to it.

"Would you like a drink?"

"Please. Bourbon, if you have it."

Better and better. The auguries were excellent—her revealing blouse, her nervous restlessness, and not asking for the discreet white wine on the rocks or the guarded Perrier and lime. Bourbon: the hell with defenses—bonnet over the barroom.

"Ice?"

"Yes, please."

He pulled the tray out of the freezer compartment and snapped the lever. It made a nice crackle.

"The Breaking of Ice," he said.

"What?"

"Don't mind me. Everything's a title."

"The breaking of ice, did you say?"

She smiled. It was open, unaffected, yet why did it seem so sexual to him? There was nothing voluptuous about her, no luxury of ass or bosom. But there was that walk: the slatternly queen, in dawnlight, slipping out of the stable. And the mouth bruised from the busyness of the night, still hungry, unsatisfied, the teeth too large. Wonderful, what a stealthy sensuality she would bring to the picture.

"I don't know how I missed it the first time," she said.

"Missed what?"

"The script—how good it is."

"Does it bother you, that you missed it the first time?"

"Not really. Except an audience—"

"—gets only one crack. But I wouldn't worry about that. They'll get so much help—"

"—in sight and sound."

"Of course."

She nodded and was silent. She had stopped pacing.

"It's very frightening," she said. "And quite beautiful."

"Thank you."

"You've been to this southern town?"

"No."

"You're kidding."

"No. It's all made up."

"It's persuasively real, and yet . . . enchanted."

"That's what Julo likes about it."

"The enchantment, you mean?"

"Yes."

"Why not? He hawks it."

"So do I."

Trying to disarm her with his honesty, he saw that she did not need to be disarmed, she was confessing her defenselessness. Yet, he had better tread cautiously; perhaps she too was trying to disarm, pretending herself exposed. Any minute she might spring the trap, the "favor." Snap!—there goes the rape scene.

"And the script is surprisingly erotic," she said.

"Why surprising?"

"I mean in surprising places."

"Where Rachel's pretending to be asleep."

"No, that's an obvious one." Quickly, as if concerned that he might think the remark negative: "Not obvious-bad, obvious-good. . . . But it's the unexpected eroticism . . ."

"Where she's bathing the little boy."

She looked at him. Their eyes engaged.

"Yes." She let the moment breathe. "There's something so elementally stirring about a white woman bathing a black child . . . a little boy . . . soaping him, stroking him . . . Beautiful."

"Thank you."

She appeared pleased that she had discovered an erotic effect that had not been accidental but intended, yet hidden by the author.

"You've sketched the scene very briefly. Do you see it shot in any detail?"

She was testing his taste. "I don't know yet. What do you think?"

"If you only shoot the *fact* of it—without lingering or commenting —you may be able to get away with—"

"—doing all of it."

"Yes—doing all of it."

"And yet," he said, "if the audience doesn't *see* all of it . . ."

". . . it'll see more of it."

"Yes."

We're half talking and half diddling, he thought. Be careful, he told himself; he had not written this passage they were playing; it was she who was dictating the lines, setting the rhythms. She might be manipulating him, selling him the beauty of his work, so that she could sell him the revision of it.

"How I'm dying to play the moment with that little boy!"

Her eyes filled. For an instant he thought the emotion was faked, she was working him over. Then he remembered that she had had a child who had been killed, in the South somewhere.

It was all going to be easier than he had expected. And the rape scene—she had not brought it up. So be it. Let it alone. Let sleeping dogs lie.

"What about the rape scene?" he asked.

He could not believe that he had broached it. What damn compulsion to have it all out in the open? So that he could conquer everything? Hadn't he had enough approval for the moment? Dammit, he thought, dammit, when everything was going so well.

"I take it back, about the rape scene," she said.

"You . . . ?"

"I was wrong."

There had to be a trick. "You mean that?"

"Yes. The second time around, I realized why it had to be there. Not only because your plot depends on it—I don't care about that. But there's something painfully ironic in the fact that when they do fall in love, they never stop savaging each other. And the cruelty goes on— without a bit of physical violence—the cruelty becomes worse. And love becomes a punishment."

She had reversed herself too effortlessly, it seemed to him, and he wondered whether her new opinion was genuine. Perhaps she was better at seduction than he was. Take care.

"Are you sure you mean what you say?" he asked.

"Yes, I'm sure," she replied. "Anyway, the rape isn't what your story is about. In fact, part of my fascination is that I'm not sure what it *is* about."

"All the world is a magic show."

"What?"

"That's what it's about."

She looked disappointed. "Is that the whole screenplay?"

"The whole world."

"No more than a magic show?"

"Full of beauty and terror."

"I think the Greeks said pity and terror."

"That's tragedy—much tougher stuff," he said. "I'm not up to that."

"Can't make a great outcry?"

"Not so the audience will."

"So you try for lesser things."

"A furtive tear."

He grinned but she responded gravely. "Don't run it down. The script is very touching."

"Are you really being honest?" She had made him vulnerable. "It's such a turnaround."

"I had to get used to your extravagances. You're not exactly understated, are you? You're not one of those self-effacing writers who stops the scene so far from the brink that we're not even sure there's an abyss. You take us right smack up to it, and give us a shove."

"I'm embarrassed."

"No, don't be. I mean the fact that TV and the bad films have been so violent that they've killed everything vital— Good God, Shakespeare never understated anything. And if you've got to show and tell and tear a passion to tatters—then maybe the rape is, if anything, understated."

"I beg your pardon?"

"What I mean—I should hold off on any criticism at all—just wait —simply wait until your style is mine—and let myself fall in love with it."

He no longer had any doubt. There would be an ambush. She was luring him into it.

Cautiously: "Then you do have some reservations about the script, don't you?"

"No, only questions. There are things about Rachel that I can't keep track of. I get the impression she's doing things that are inconsistent with her character—and suddenly I realize I'm not sure what her character is." She paused. "But then it occurs to me—I'm not *supposed* to be sure what her character is."

"Does that bother you?"

"Not really. Still . . . if I'm *expected* to understand, I wouldn't want to seem obtuse."

"Well, if you need any meanings supplied . . ."

"Will you do that?"

"Of course."

"What if you're not directing?"

". . . Not directing?"

"That's the favor I wanted to ask."

He thought he had heard her wrong. "If I'm not directing, you said."

"Yes."

He wanted to have heard her wrong. "I don't know what you mean."

"Allow someone else to direct *The Fabulist*."

The proviso. All the other talk was parsley, this was the bloody meat. Her praise had been a well-turned rejection slip, written on fancy paper with deckle-edged words. How beautiful your screenplay is, erotic, touching, but I'll have nothing to do with the man who wrote it. She had tricked him, sweet-talked him into a false bonhomie, and lulled him to sleep with a rubber nipple. He felt foolish and betrayed. He wondered if she could guess how close to tears he was, and murder.

"Would you like another drink?"

"Don't be dismayed," she answered gently. "You're a far better writer than you are a director. *The Fabulist* is probably the best thing you've ever written, and you should give it the chance it deserves. You never *have* been given what your work cries for, have you? I'm sure you became a director out of self-defense—against the butchers. So being your own director had to be a compromise, didn't it?—when what you wanted, what you had a right to ask for was—what name can I choose—Bergman?"

"He writes his own," he said aridly. "And directs as well."

"Yes . . . well. In his case it's the other way around, isn't it? He's a better director than he is a writer."

"Perhaps you should advise him to get another writer."

"If we can avoid being recriminatory . . ."

"What if I think you're committing a crime?"

"Am I really? I love *The Fabulist*—I want to do it—I want it to be a success. Isn't that what you want?"

"I want to direct it. What have you got against my doing it? Or against me?"

"This will get bitter, won't it?"

"Let it. What have you got against me?"

"I don't trust you."

"As a director or as a man?"

"Are they separate?"

"Of course they are. Wagner was a bastard."

"As a man, then. Someone I'd be . . . afraid of."

It struck him what might be behind it all. Not those political differences of long ago; those were in another country, the wench a little dead. This woman was altogether different, he surmised, grown cautious, her banners carefully furled, finding it necessary, now that she was fortyish, to say "afraid of."

"It's Willi, isn't it?" he said.

"It's you!" She lost control. "I don't trust you—and I don't trust Julo—and I don't trust the two of you together."

"We're not together. He won't have anything to do with the picture—he won't even be allowed on the set."

"He *is* the picture!" she cried. "You told me to talk to him, and I did. And all I got was lies. I think you're both lying—and shuttling me back and forth between you. Well, if I have a feeling there's some sort of conspiracy against Willi and me—"

"There's no conspiracy. What the hell's the matter with you?"

"I—am—afraid."

He was quiet, letting her agitation subside. He knew she was ashamed of her panic, so he averted his attention. Then he said pacifyingly, "Have you ever started a picture without being afraid?"

"It has nothing to do with the start of a picture."

"I think it does. Do you think you're the only one who's scared? I'm as frightened of you as you are of me."

It caught her. "In what way?"

He might be on dangerous grounds expressing any uncertainties about her. So he equivocated. "Everybody's scared at the beginning, Calla. The producer is terrified that the director will run over schedule and ruin him. The director thinks the actor is faking laryngitis so that he can spend a weekend with his best friend's wife. The actress thinks the costume designer hates women and is trying to expose her sagging bosom and her bandy legs. It's fear and distrust—everybody's infected—they're the bacteria we breathe at one another."

"I've been in the business as long as you have, Lucas. . . . What frightens you about me?"

He would have to give it to her straight. "You're at a critical time. Your last few pictures were successful—congratulations. But you've been playing in the same old rooms. You haven't opened a new door in yourself for quite a while. I think that's what you're scared of—not of me."

"Opening a door?"

"Yes. Afraid you might not like what's behind it. Or . . ."

"Or?"

". . . find nothing."

"And you'll be stuck with a star who's . . . empty."

"It's always a possibility."

Smarting, she drew back. "Telling me that—aren't you a bit nervous I'll snap my bag shut and stomp out of the house?"

"Of course I am," he said. "Look, Calla, if we're not scared at the start of a film, we're playing it too damn safe."

"Aren't you playing it safe—going for a star?"

"No, I'm not. Look at the screenplay. Is it safe? Is it a nice little genre piece about the robbery of the First National—or infidelity in Westchester County? I've had three failures—all of them different. But they had one thing in common: they were all a little reckless. And this one—a film about a world that doesn't exist—it's the scariest of all."

"Why don't you do one about a world that does exist?"

"Because I've got a more beautiful one up here."

"In fact, you're not sure there is one out there."

"No, I'm not sure. Are you?"

Her voice was deadly calm. "That's what makes you wrong for this picture."

Another trap. He knew he had walked right into it.

"You'll ruin it, Lucas." She was pleading, and she sounded genuine. "You'll compound all the unreality of it. You'll make it unbelievable. I know the feeling you have for your own script—you love it. But perhaps you love it too much. Please—let someone else direct it."

"Preferably someone who hates it."

"That isn't the only alternative. We can find someone who loves it and can give it credibility."

"Ah, one of the credibility boys! A good solid, realistic, kitchen-sinker like Martin Ritt or Arthur Hiller or Sidney Lumet—"

"Further out."

"Like?"

"Franco Notale."

"You're making a joke. He's crazier than I am."

"Well, he's crazy in the *way* that you are, but he doesn't go the limit."

"How far does he go?"

His sarcasm made her defensive. "What I mean is, he would believe everything you wrote—and make it believable. He's like you—I can't tell you how much you're alike—and he's not frightened by the bizarre. But he makes it comprehensible. He may not have as much emotional vigor as you have, but perhaps the film could do with a little less. And to compensate, he has a surer sense of reality. He's closer to the audience than you are, Lucas—because he's part of it."

He tried not to seem envious. "What makes him part of it?"

"He's ordinary. He's a bourgeois, really. He enjoys the middle class pleasures—he eats too much pasta, he cries over Puccini, he worries about not going to church, he wears trousers that don't fit him—"

"—and he's wonderfully rooted in reality."

"Don't make fun of it."

"I don't, Christ knows."

The envy was plain, and she played on it. "You can have it . . . working for you." As he felt himself weaken, she was on surer ground and her voice became more soothing, to palliate the pain he was feeling. "And he'll be as much in love with your script as I am. Please—may I send it to him?"

It wasn't only that she believed every word she was saying, and loved the script, yearning for its success as he did. The vital thing was that he knew she would not do the film unless he said yes. And it might be well-advised to have somebody like Notale direct it; never, in the old days, had his work been in the hands of a director so talented. Let him do it, and walk away . . . while his baby was being born. But he understood the feelings of women who chose natural childbirth. They couldn't opt for unconsciousness, and absent themselves. They had to be there, doing it; they had to know what was happening, feel everything, the pain and the ecstasy.

"No," he said. "Don't send it."

He wished his voice didn't sound so weary and defeated. Afraid of pity, he didn't want to see his funeral rites in her face.

Not accompanying her to the door, he scarcely heard her departure. She left a void in the room, an almost tangible emptiness.

He had failed. He had not done his best to entice her, had not trotted out his shrewdest words, had not sung his sweetest song, had not performed his engaging solo dance that might have ended in a pas de deux.

Suddenly he was sick of all of it, sick of stars and blandishments, and producers to whom he had to lie and who lied to him, sick of the language, the pseudo-literary language, sick of the hypocritical pieties about art, sick of the protestations of sensibility in a tough, insensible business.

Perhaps he was glad that she was gone, perhaps he was better off. It would have been murderous to direct that woman. She was all rationality, and he was all intuition. He would have had to justify every flight, tie his wings in straitjackets. Reasons—she would ask for calm reasons—hold back the tempest. For all her talent, she was no longer an artist but a technician—no, a detective who would go to the source of his fault, and find him out. Find out that he was not at all reliable, that his art dwelt not only in the land of make-believe but in chaos. He couldn't help it. He was an oddball in the way that one of his eyes was brown and the other one hazel; he was born that way. His mother had called him a *meshuggener* for as long as he could remember. And perhaps what he enjoyed most in art was not its order but its anarchy.

Loving art, he hated being an artist. But there was nothing else he could do. When he was between tales, part of him perished, and part of him had not yet been born.

Without identity, and alone, he wondered at such times where all his friends were, always realizing with the same shock that he had never truly had any. Once, in college, he had a close associate, a younger schoolmate, Andy Littauer, who had become a Peace Corps volunteer and had disappeared somewhere, to spread the religion of hygiene, as one of the letters put it. Sometimes he wished he could see Andy again. Or talk shop with John Milius or Tony LoSarco, or with Coppola whose extra flesh always suggested extra generosity. But while at college, they had seemed friends first and competitors afterward, and now it was the other way around.

A friend to talk to . . . Willi. Someone to touch . . . when he was failing.

Oh, beautiful Willi, with the exquisite face, mummified. If only we could talk together, as we used to. If only there were something we could have changed.

It was just short of two years ago that he had met her, while finishing his last film. He had been trying to get some pickup shots on Redondo Beach, and had been delayed by a sea storm. In the late afternoon, when the rains had subsided, he took a walk along the beach. The coast was littered with the flotsam that the turbulence had cast up, great crabs and dying fish still thrashing in the scum and seaweed. There were dozens of kids around, with pails and wastepaper baskets and cardboard cartons, collecting seafood and debris. Many of them were gathering the shiny smooth stones, agate and flintstone and minerals as red as rubies, and he heard their outcries of discovery. As darkness came on, lanterns and flashlights appeared, and the search for seaborne treasure continued in the darting beams.

At the wharf where the beach disappeared into the high-risen ocean, Luke left the water and continued along the road. He came to the Arts Afriques shop. Since the shop was closed and the interior was black, nothing about the store attracted his attention until he passed the window. Then something, an afterimage, caught his mind. A glint of some kind, a double glint, shining. He turned back to the glass façade, looked through the window, but could see nothing. Using his hands as blinders to shut out the streetlight, he peered and saw twin points of brightness, glittering gold with a trace of viridian. Eyes in the small wooden statue of a cat. The wood was dark, with a patina that caught a glimmer from outdoors, and the animal was exquisitely carved. But its chief beauty was in the glow of the eyes, so illuminated from within that he felt as if the creature could see him. It was hypnotic, that glance, and it had a feeling of inner fire, tiger, tiger, but there were no forests of the night, only a deserted store, a plate glass window and a back street.

Suddenly Luke felt a compulsion—the statue spoke irresistibly to him—he had to own it.

But the store was shut and there was nobody around.

"Is very clear, yes?"

The old man passed behind him and, with keys in hand, went to unlock the door.

"Did you say 'clear'?" Luke asked.

"Yes—eyes—form—everything—most clear."

The statue did have clarity, but it had much more. The creature was unreal, like no cat imaginable, yet somehow seemed as lifelike as if it were going to spring through the window glass.

"Who carved it?"

"Somebody in village—jungle—who know?"

"What kind of cat is it?"

"Lepra."

If it was meant to be a leopard it was a black one, pantherish, in a shadowy woodland. But there was no saying what variety it might be; it was simply feline, the likeness of a kitten, not yet ready to be murderous, except for its eyes, which were.

"Is it for sale?"

"Yes, yes. Come in."

It was surprisingly cheap, only seventy-five dollars, and the man had more of them. But there was not another one truly like it; the rest were not badly made, but they were somehow unrealized, as if the one he had bought had been done by the master, the others copied by apprentices.

When he went to pay for it, however, Luke discovered that he had only sixty dollars. Offering to leave a deposit, he was pleased to hear the old man say he could take the statuette with him, and give him the balance at another time.

"I'll send someone tomorrow," Luke assured him. As if leaving him a security, he identified himself and described where they were shooting the film.

"Darra," the old man said, introducing himself with a nod.

Luke carried the thing away in a paper bag, and retraced his steps along the road to the spot, a mile away, where the Cinemobile and auxiliary sound truck were parked. The trailer he used was a hundred or so yards from the shoreline, closer now in the aftermath of the storm.

Indoors, he could hear the pounding of the surf, and through the narrow, plastic-curtained window, espied the last few gem seekers with their flashlights making lightning darts across the sand. The night, with the storm and spindrift and the unnatural lights of children, made him apprehensive. There was something extraordinary in the evening, especially his impetuous purchase of the cat, something irrational in the air.

It was still early, not yet nine o'clock, but he was dead tired. The film had been a tough one; the storm had made him tense and worn him out. He went to bed.

Later, when he heard the knock on the door, he thought the sound was in his sleep. But it insisted and, awake, he still heard it.

"Who is it?" But nobody answered.

The knocking continued, and irritably he called over the sound of the surf. "Who is it?"

He opened the door. A woman stood there. She didn't enter, didn't move, simply waited outside the door as if she had been directed to find her light—moon, palely filtered through greenish gel. She wore the wrong thing for the beach—not slacks or shorts, but something filmy and blowy, and whatever color it actually was, it looked like seaweed. But she was too tall and statuesque and real to be an undine; there was something strong and palpable about her, and she was fleshily beautiful.

"Mr. O'Hare—I'm Willi Axil. Could I talk to you?"

The name was vaguely familiar. "Yes. What is it?"

"You—Darra—at the African place—"

"Come in."

She hesitated an instant, crossed the threshold, closed the door. He lighted the lamp on the bedside table and buttoned his pajama shirt.

"Darra, you said."

"Yes, he tells me—" She stopped and her glance halted at the cat. "There it is."

"The cat?"

"Kitten, yes."

"Beautiful, isn't he?"

"She."

"It's a she?"

"Yes."

He grinned. "How do you know?"

She flushed. "Never mind. Point is, it's mine."

"Yours?"

"Well, not really—except by discovery. I saw it a week ago."

"And bought it?"

"No—I couldn't. The damn store was closed, and it kept being closed every time I came here. Then, tonight—it was gone."

"Then you didn't actually buy it, did you?"

"No, but that's a technicality, isn't it? Discovery, you know—like posting signs—hoisting banners—"

She was trying to make a gay thing of it, to bring it off in style, but he could see it was awkward for her. And important.

"But you didn't really buy it, did you?" he said.

"If you're talking about money, I'll be glad to reimburse you."

"Well, to tell the truth, I like the thing very much—"

"Come now, don't be sticky about it."

"Is it sticky for me to like it but not sticky for you?"

"I don't simply like it—I need it!"

"Need it? In what way?"

"We don't have to go into that—I'll double what you paid for it."

"No, thanks."

"Quadruple. As a matter of fact, you haven't entirely paid for it—it's not totally yours."

"Darra told you that?"

"Yes." Nervous, she rattled on. "And where to find you and who you are, but I didn't have to be told who you are, we met a long time ago."

"Did we? Where?"

"Columbia. You were casting a film—I was auditioning."

"Yes, you do look familiar."

"Because you remember me or because I look like Calla Stark?"

He remembered her distinctly now. That was why he had turned her down; the uncanny likeness. "As a matter of fact, you work for her, don't you?"

"Yes—stand-in—secretary."

"Double."

"Yes—double." She said the word reluctantly.

"But you're more beautiful than she is." Hastily: "That was a professional opinion."

"As distinct from a pass."

"As distinct."

"I noticed how quickly you put my mind at rest."

He smiled. She did too. She relaxed a little; it gave her body a more animal grace.

Abruptly, she unslung her shoulder bag and opened it. Swiftly, without rooting around too much, she found what she wanted: three one-hundred dollar bills.

"Here," she said. "You needn't bother giving me any change."

When he did not take it, she dropped the money on the bed and started toward the statue.

"Please don't do that," he said.

"You mean you won't let me buy it?"

"No. I'm sorry."

"You're just being perverse."

It was true; he was; and he didn't know why. He could dismiss it by saying it was wariness: he was being swindled. If the object was worth three hundred to her, it was probably worth three thousand to someone she would sell it to. But there was something else, less rational. The statue had spoken to him as few physical objects had ever done; not because it was any supreme example of the sculptor's art—he knew very little about that—but because it had touched some nerve in him he had not known was sensitive; it had completed some jointure in his nervous system, and gave him a mysterious pleasure. If she had had the same experience, she might be able to cast a light on the mystery.

"Why do you want it so badly?"

"I didn't say want—I said need."

"Do you really mean need?"

"Need, need!"

As though her intensity had revealed too much, she backed off, went silent. He waited her out.

"If not money," she said, "what do you want for it?"

Too bad, he thought. While it might be pleasurable to go to bed with her, all he wanted for the moment . . .

"You haven't told me why you need it."

"I . . . because . . ." Silence. "Do you believe in anything?"

"Anything?"

"Yes—like Yoga—or horns and hellfire—or no meat—or gnomes in oak trees? . . . God?"

"Yes, all of them. And the Bible as literature."

"They're only aesthetics?"

"Right."

"No prayer?"

"No knees."

"Then you won't understand what I mean."

"Try me."

She didn't respond immediately. He could see her distress. At last:

"I'm alive—and have been alive—in more bodies than my own. I've been in Blake, and one of the faces of a Caravaggio, and in a little boy that I saw get run over when I was a kid, and in Calla Stark, and"—she indicated the animal—". . . that."

As she pointed to the statue, her hand began to tremble, and like a child, she hid it behind her back. Then she started to quake all over, and he realized: She's spaced. Zonked out on something.

Seeming to divine his thought, she suddenly snatched at the statue, clasped it to her breast, tore the door open and ran.

"Wait!"

He ran after her.

"Wait, you lunatic—wait!"

She didn't stop but ran along the edge of the water, stirring the sea-smoothed sand. She ran as if she were part of the surf, indistinguishable from the spume. He sped after her, amazed how fast she was. At top speed he couldn't gain a foot, then started to lose yards. Winded and straining, he ignored the pain in his chest; he had to overtake her. She ran violently now, like the final spasm of the storm. And she was getting further and further away. At last, about to drop, he started to slacken and give up. But something slowed her as well. She came to a jetty and was clambering over the rocks, when suddenly he did not see her. He thought a wave had washed over her body, but the tide was farther out. She had simply fallen, and, rising, she looked one direction and another, as if in panic. She had dropped the statue and couldn't find it.

He quickened, called her name, ran full speed. He got to the jetty just as she found the statue and started off again. But there was no racing across these rocks, they were sharp and jagged, slippery, puddled with water and slime.

He lurched at her and grabbed her arm.

"Let go!"

He reached for the statue. "*You* let go!"

Again she slipped, the thing fell out of the crook of her arm, and simultaneously she lost her balance, her body twisted, she let out a cry of pain, and subsided, as if struck down.

Grabbing her foreleg in both hands, she pulled at the shinbone, kept pulling as if to counteract one pain with another.

He had retrieved the statue, but now his concern was the woman.

"What is it?"

"I don't know—I wrenched something. Oh damn, oh damn!"

She tried not to cry out. "Can you get up—stand on it?"

"Christ—afraid to try."

"I've got a phone in the trailer. I'll call for help."

He turned as if to go.

"No—please."

She seemed frightened of being alone. She made the same spaced-out, zonky movement she had made indoors. Sharply, with a shake, she attempted to pull herself together. Lifting herself from the rock, she tried to stand. He went to her quickly and put his arm around her waist, offering his body for support.

She eased the leg forward, straight out. "Hurts like a bastard," she said, "but I think it's only a twist."

"It might not be—take it easy."

"I used to get them all the time—track—the mile—but it's been centuries. Oh God—son of a bitch."

"Ease up. You don't have to run the mile."

She looked in the direction of the trailer. "Half?"

"Can you make it?"

"I'll try. May I hold on?"

He shifted the statue to his left hand so she could lean on his right shoulder. They walked carefully across the unevenness of the jetty rocks, then onto the smooth shining sand. She was doing rather well, and trying to make light of the pain. From time to time, she cursed a little, but allowed herself no other form of complaint. They were about two thirds of the distance when she asked to stop.

"Can you make it?"

"I'll have to, won't I?" She laughed. "Unless you carry me."

She was a tall woman nearly his own height. "Petruchio or piggyback?"

"What's Petruchio?"

"Slung over the shoulder, butt to the audience."

" 'And kiss me, Kate, we shall be married a' Sunday.' "

"Have you played it?"

"No. I'm a lousy actress. Calla's the actress in our family."

"Family? Are you related?"

"Intimately. . . . By identity."

There it was again. She was Calla and a face in a Caravaggio and a cat. He suddenly had an impulse. It was as if his infatuation with the animal was over, and he was more taken with the woman, and might not be allowed to enjoy both. But that was a nonsense thought; he routed it. Truth was, he felt compelled to make an irrational gesture in generosity.

And now, as they were indoors and she was sitting on his bed, as he knew her a minute or an hour more, he no longer suspected that she was trying to cheat him or con him or—

"Here." He handed the statue to her.

"Do you mean it?" She blinked a few times. "You won't snatch it back?"

"No—have it."

Almost shyly, again a little girl, she took it from him. "Will you take my money?" She pointed to her shoulder purse on the chair. "Pay yourself as much as you want. Just take it, please."

He shook his head and smiled.

"You don't want anything?"

"Nothing."

"Would you like to kiss me?"

"No quid pro quo."

"Not even if I want to?"

He sat on the edge of the bed, but did not kiss her. He put his hand on her breast, and simply held it there, calming one excitement and causing another. She slowly took his hand from her breast and lay it in her lap, more intimately, and leaned toward him with a hungry mouth. He kissed her and undressed her unhurriedly—almost, it seemed, one breast at a time, so that he could enjoy her without haste. He had thought of her body as being thin, athletically rawboned, and was amazed at how full it was in nakedness. He wondered where, under the guise of slenderness, she had hidden the lush abundance of her person, the bounty of her bosom; and how her thighs and belly seemed to offer themselves roundly and accessibly, while the soft triangle at her groin gave promise of unfolding a secret. It was a body the more beautiful because it so wantingly responded, the nipples erect to excite hunger and satisfy it, the legs opening to welcome and envelop, all the flesh quivering to be loved, to be consumed.

Suddenly she broke away from his caresses and, throwing her arms back on the bed, cried out for him to hurry, to please hurry. He lay on her a moment, wanting to prolong the hunger and put off the satisfaction, when he heard her murmur that if she couldn't with him, she couldn't with anyone.

"What did you say?"

"Hurry—please!"

Just as he was about to enter her, he felt a violent agitation in her like none he had experienced in a woman, then a convulsive movement, and she thrust at him in a frenzy.

"No—stop!" she cried.

She ripped herself out from under him, rushed away toward the sink where she clutched the porcelain rim with both hands, as if she meant to tear the object from the wall. Then she leaned over the faucets and he thought she would be sick. He heard her retching at nothing, weeping at everything.

"I can't!" She cried the words, I can't, I can't.

"With me?"

"No, it's not you—"

"A man?"

"—yes—and it's not just bodies—"

"Then why do you try?"

"Oh God."

"Why?"

"I *want* things! I want to get married and have children, I want a family—I want to belong to something that will *last!*"

He smiled ruefully and thought of his own marriage, and a family that had not lasted. "Are you hearing yourself?" he said gently.

"Oh, I know—I know. But in marriage there's at least the illusion."

He felt deeply sorry for her. Bright and blighted, she was willing to settle for any myth that would offer a makeshift happiness. She was unblessed and she hurt to the bone.

He reached a kind hand to her. "Come back to bed," he said softly. As she looked at him with worry, "Come on now, come back—I won't hurt you," he murmured soothingly. "I won't make love to you, but I'll try to love you, if you let me. Come on."

"No." But she wanted to.

"Come back, Willi. Lie here and be still a moment—come on."

For an instant he thought the beautiful frightened animal would respond. "No," she said. "I'm going to get dressed."

"No—please don't. Come back—just sleep with me—I mean really let's go to sleep—and dream—and wake up and have breakfast together. Come on, Willi—please—come on."

Slowly, as if hypnotized by his gentleness, the sweetness of his voice, she returned to bed. To give her more room, he moved closer to the wall than he needed to. She lay beside him, very separate, no part of her body touching his. Eyes wide, staring at the ceiling, she barely breathed. He too was quite motionless. After a while, he realized that his wakefulness might be something she was having to contend with, keeping her taut, making it impossible for her to sleep. So he slowly changed the rhythm of his breathing and, inhalation by inhalation, pretended to be asleep.

He was not certain how long later—and perhaps he had indeed

fallen asleep—he felt her hand. It was on his arm at first, then slowly, furtively, he felt the fingertips caress his cheek. After a moment, she let the hand move downward. It came to rest on his chest, and simply remained there. And in a little while, he knew she was asleep.

She was the strangest woman, and it was the strangest friendship, he had ever known. She had come along at a disillusioned time of his life. A man with a need to devote himself to someone, he loved to be in love. But at last he had given it up as men surrender tennis; at thirty-eight, he felt he was too old for it. Too disenchanted was what he meant. He loathed the careerist opportunism that had adulterated his recent love affairs; and in trying to avoid being vulnerable again, he had slithered into the rut of sex-as-catch-can. He hated the hassle. It made him like himself less and less each day, which became his definition of loneliness.

And since Willi was achingly in need of love, as he was always in need of giving it, they came together naturally, in an unnatural way. They were never, of course, sexually compatible, although at the beginning, with the utmost tentativeness, they tried to be. For the time being, he felt a great relief to be out of the churning millrace. He enjoyed abstaining from carnal pleasure, like a monk on a soul-purifying fast. It was not a hardship; there was an oblique kind of bliss in it. With a native talent for loving, he felt that he had found a new way to love someone, and he began to like himself again.

The heart of his devotion to Willi was a simple thing: It hurt him to see her in such pain. At first, before he realized that she was more seriously disturbed than he had imagined, he advised her simplistically: If it was Calla she needed, why didn't she simply pay court to her, seek favor as if she were a man?

But he soon saw that it was not only that she was in love with Calla; it was deeper and more tortuous: she thought she *was* Calla. She lived, breathed, dreamed as Calla did, and to make love to her would almost have been an act of narcissism, masturbatory. Yet her mirror-image identity was entirely Willi's secret, she thought, and she led not only the life of a double, but a double life.

On the few occasions when she was on the verge of telling Calla her obsession, she stopped herself. Her friend might be frightened by it, might talk about analysts and cures and getting over it. As if Willi had not tried to get over it. Once, on the pretext of having landed an excellent acting role, Willi had fled to Greece, only to return almost immediately. Another time, she had taken a position in her home town, Baltimore, and had come back to Calla within a month. Even now, during the period when Lucas was first seeing her, she was trying to forget her alter ego. The star had accepted a part in a film that was to be shot in Vienna. Willi, of course, was expected to go along. But at the last minute, with the ostensible purpose of making a new start on her own acting career, Willi had begged off. She had stayed behind to break the bond.

In the early weeks of Calla's absence, when Lucas realized how unhappy Willi was, he assumed that her heartache was the affliction of a woman who was fugitive from her homosexuality. If she were to commit herself to it, not secretly and haphazardly as she had done on a few irresolute occasions, but openly and permanently . . .

However, her relationships with women remained brief and uncommitted. It puzzled him that she was not a part of the feminist movement; she seemed only tangentially interested. Once, when he advised her to go to a NOW meeting, she replied irritably, "Please. Calla's been at me—don't you start."

"But—if for no other reason—you'll meet other women."

"And fight the good fight."

His urging her to a feminist association didn't seem as odd to him as her resistance to it. "Why *don't* you go?"

He asked a number of times until he saw how acutely the question distressed her. "I'm sorry I upset you, Will," he said.

"What upsets me is that I don't know why I'm upset," she replied. "Maybe I can't join any fighters because I'm not *against* anything. I don't have a quarrel with men—or with women—or with society. . . . I think my quarrel is with God."

It worried him, how this practical-seeming woman sought spiritual answers to substantive concerns. Her common sense was a veneer, she lived out of the world, in occult regions. The physicality of a love life was not important to her, and whenever she made a one-night concurrence with a woman, she came away miserable because it had been only a corporeal meeting, not a jointure of the spirit. Her spirit was joined with Calla's, only with Calla's. They were one.

There were other complications. He had thought, the first night in Redondo, that she was spaced out. But he learned that her hallucinations were not brought on by narcotics or amphetamines or drugs of any sort; not by liquor either—she drank even less than Lucas did. It was the enigma of all those other conditions of her existence. In addition to being the face in the Caravaggio and the kitten, she was the mother she could not remember, she was Hagar in the house of Sarah, she was a soldier on the eve of battle. She had a doomed belief that her existence was a miscarriage of creation, a blundering reincarnation as a person she was not meant to be, in a flesh that was hateful to her. Once, in discussing her failure as an actress, she had said self-deprecatingly that she was miscast in everything. Miscast in reality, she went elsewhere.

He was amazed at how she managed to conceal her alienations. In fact, at the beginning he considered them no worse than charming poses, fascinating eccentricities, until, at her urging, he moved in with her. Then he saw her response to the visions, witnessed her sudden awakenings at night, heard her conversations with the phantoms. Sometimes these secret nighttime meetings were like passionate assignations with a lover; sometimes, however, especially when she maintained a margin of sanity, the specter was an enemy, a blackmailer who knew something heinous about her, and she was terrified that the world would find her out . . . that Calla would find her out.

Lucas at last knew how disturbed she was. It worried him. He suggested that she see a psychiatrist; one night he begged her to do so. She flew into a rage:

"Why do you think I'm ill? I'm not. I merely see things differently from you, I have other images, other lives—but I'm not ill. I do my work, don't I? People can rely on me, can't they? I function as well as you do—better in many ways. How dare you say I'm ill!"

Two nights later, in a calmer mood, and with tongue in cheek, she told him she had done some "research" on people kookier than she was, personages of respectable estate. There was the famous columnist who had a collection of thousands of human teeth, the Westwood minister who couldn't deliver his Sunday sermon without a dead mouse in his pocket, the famous actor who prepared for lovemaking by smearing his member with anchovy paste, the congressman who went in drag to séances. She took a snippet of paper from her purse and read a list of organized crazies and cultists—psychophiliacs and theohedonists, blood votaries and urinolaters, wanga worshipers and obeah doctors, endless varieties of whackos who went to work for the Bank of America and NBC and Metro and Pacific Gas and Electric, and became executives with two assistants and nine telephones. Willi contended that by the standards of local psychic eccentricity, she was as normal as milk. And with justifiable pride, she pointed out that she was functioning without fault, as many others were.

But many weren't. And after a while, neither was Willi.

To begin with, while Calla was abroad, she had several minor mishaps. Her thoughts would wander in the middle of a sentence, she would forget her purse in a restaurant. She who had always been as punctual as a decimal point, now started to appear an hour after the appointed time. More seriously, she began to drive her car erratically.

One evening they were going to a preview of a Spielberg picture. Willi was to meet Luke at the theater, they would see the film and have dinner afterward. He waited outdoors for her, and when it began to rain heavily, entered the lobby. It was getting late. Finally, receiving word that the film had started, he went inside, sat in the last row and saved an aisle seat for her. She didn't arrive.

Worried, he called her number and his own, called them again, and there was no answer. He returned to the auditorium, sat down once more, but was too unnerved to remain in his seat. He would try to reach her just once more, he decided, and then give up. He dialed and heard a busy signal. Relieved, he waited in the phone booth. He tried it again; again the busy signal. He loitered, and whenever he attempted to reach her . . . busy. Abruptly it occurred to him: she had taken the phone off the hook to be alone with whatever she was doing, which might be anything.

He got into his car and went streaking up the hill to her apartment. It was truly storming now—blustering—her front door was open— the rain was pouring onto her living room rug. The lower floor of the duplex was dark, but there was a light in the second-floor hallway. He hurried up the stairs and entered her bedroom.

The room reeked of melting wax. There were lighted candles all around her bed as if she were a corpse. Although she was not dead, she was lying rigidly still, naked, showing no flutter of life, her eyes glazed.

She had shaved every hair off her body, including her beautiful blond head.

"Willi—for God's sake—what did you do?"

She murmured; he could not make out the words. Then she was silent.

He sat on the edge of the bed, but said nothing, waiting for her to speak again. After a while she began to talk softly, in a self-possessed way. Without any seeming aberration, as though she were discussing a matter of prudential wisdom, she said that lots of people, at different times and in different places—in the eighteenth century in England, in the twentieth century in Africa—had shorn their bodies clean of hair. It had to do with vermin, she said, sometimes on the head, sometimes in it.

She didn't leave the house for a few days, didn't put on a stitch of clothing, didn't leave her bedroom. He had to bring her food, and trick her into eating it, as if she were an ailing child. She did not complain about headaches, although he suspected she had them, and once she hoped aloud that she would not have another nightmare tonight. At last he prevailed on her to go to a doctor, not an analyst, an internist. She came back with a small package of Nembutal, and that night took an overdose.

She told the doctor who revived her that she had made an error, she had been befuddled, and had taken the extra pills by mistake. Later, she confessed to Lucas that she had taken Nembutal once before, a number of years ago, in an effort to kill herself. And, for the first time, she agreed to go for psychiatric help.

But she didn't go. She seemed, however, to be pulling herself together, looking for self-cures of one kind and another. She started to consult fortune-tellers, went to cryptic meetings, took to tarot cards and I Ching, studied palmistry; she went to a quack for scalp massage to make her hair grow in more rapidly.

Then, overnight it seemed, there was a dramatic change. She was able to sleep the night through, peacefully; hitherto a picky eater, she developed a lusty appetite. She stopped talking about visions, and Luke wondered if they had ceased. He was curious about what had caused her wonderful improvement, but she was secretive.

One night he insisted: "You *are* seeing a psychiatrist, aren't you?"
She seemed to debate. Finally: "No. I'm seeing a friend."
She has at last found a woman to be in love with, he thought. It was a pang and a pleasure. "I'm glad, Willi."
"Not a woman, Luke—not a lover."
But she wouldn't tell him who the man was.

He had a strong suspicion that whoever Willi's new-found friend was, he had something to do with Africa. In the past few weeks Willi had begun to load her apartment with wooden plaques, strangely carved heads and sensual figures of jungle art, some hideous, some beautiful.

One afternoon, when they were hanging an exquisite duo of lovers in her bedroom, he asked: "Is your new friend Darra?"
A startled laugh: "But he's ancient."

"Does a friend have to be young?"

"Darra rarely says a word."

"A friend has to be chatty, then."

"You'll meet him by and by."

"When?"

"At the fire."

That's how he came to meet Julasto—after a fire show—with Willi.

At first, he hated him. The man was a fake, and Luke was convinced the charlatan was conning Willi for money. She went on what sounded like psychiatric sessions with "my wizard," as she called him, and came back tremulously high, as if he had given her benzies or some special kind of uppers. She vowed that he never gave her drugs, but Lucas had his doubts. Moreover, she was bringing home African artifacts, not the cheap imitations they sold in the store, but original paintings and beautiful batiks and sculptures that could not have been reproductions. It was obvious that Julo had found an easy mark, and was dumping expensive merchandise upon her, taking her for all her savings. But, because the whole parcel was wrapped up with her recovery, and she continued to improve, Lucas did not dare to question anything.

One day, however, when she brought home what looked like a particularly expensive papyrus painting, he broke out, "How much did Julo take you for?"

"*Take* me for?"

"How much did it cost?"

"Nothing."

"Nothing?" he said in disbelief. "Willi, please."

"None of these things cost me anything. They're gifts."

"From whom?"

"Julo, of course."

Not for an instant did Lucas think it could be true. But, riddled with curiosity, he accepted one of Willi's invitations to join her on another trip to Redondo. He watched them together, and was fascinated. Soon, what had been curiosity junkets became pleasurable visits, and he went often. They became a threesome. They would sit outdoors under the garden colonnade or in the cottage with the fire blazing, and talk intimately for hours at a time. Luke would not have believed it possible: Julo was a healer. Willi had come to him on the verge of disintegration, and he had put her together again, with charm and incantation. They spoke a common tongue, a language of magic in which they saw no madness, where everything was credible and everything possible. The black man allowed the white woman to have her visions, without calling them aberrations. He had demolished the scarecrow, the fear that she might be demented. When she talked about her other selves, Julo saw them or pretended to see them, or wanted to see them better, asking questions, laughing at their idiosyncrasies, decrying an injustice, sympathizing with them or with her. To speak of herself as a cat or a Caravaggio was no more unusual than telling any good friend about her family—an aunt who brought her an Easter present, a brother who teased, how her mother wore her hair.

There was no longer any question in Luke's mind about the expensive presents; Julo had indeed given them to Willi. The black man loved her. She was his creation. He had taken the bits and pieces of a wrecked human being and had made a wholly new one. A beautiful, cultivated, wonderful white woman—who believed in him.

The fire demonstrations happened rarely and irregularly, but the small cult meetings—encounter sessions of twenty or thirty people—occurred frequently. Lucas paid his "free offering," as the others did. They were blacks, predominantly; they talked openly about life's trials and injustices, their frustrations and rages, their thwarted, heartaching hopes. They comforted and counseled one another, while Julo listened, speaking very little, offering no advice, except to promise that "the fires" would burn them clean as they burned him clean, and that they would be happily reborn out of the ashes. Most of all, he offered love. There was never any question about that: he loved them all.

He loved Willi best. More than any of his converts who continued to live their own lives, he adored Willi, who lived only in the magical realm of Julo. She was his child. There was no sexuality in their closeness. It was less carnal than father and daughter. There was a passion in it, but it had a strange, immaculate spirituality.

That was what puzzled Lucas about Julo—that this tough and raffish man, teeming with ruttishness, potentially brutal and dangerous, should be such a pure and tender complement to an ailing woman. It occurred to him that Julo's need might be as poignant as Willi's. A need for what? For giving kindness and a selfless love? Or . . . a need to believe in his own deceptions?

At the onset of spring, that year, Luke could tell that his own relationship with Willi was over. She no longer needed him—and unneeded, he began to feel estranged. It saddened him.

"I'll be leaving soon," he said.

"I know."

"In fact, today."

"Oh no, Luke—oh no." She started to tremble.

"Come on, now," he said softly. "It's not an ending—we'll both be around."

"But not together."

She rushed into his arms and clung to him as he stroked the curly stubble of her hair.

"Don't go—don't go!" she said.

She was crying and he wished she wouldn't. She looked up and tried to talk as unemotionally as possible. "I want you to know—it is very important that you know how deeply I love you, Luke."

Knowing, he nodded.

"And I know that you love me too," she said.

Again, because he didn't trust his voice, he nodded.

"Oh God, why did you make two kinds?" she cried. "We could have made do with one."

They both tried to laugh, and he started to pack. In the midst of it, helping him, she said: "Holy murder, do you have to take every damn sign of yourself?"

So he left her some things: his coffee cup, a first edition of *Androcles and the Lion*, an original Arthur Rackham illustration, a pair of bedroom slippers that were too small for him, and assorted toiletries, forgotten in the second bathroom. And, like the movie cliché he would never have written, she would not see him to the door.

He thought, as he was driving away: I left some souvenirs of me, but took none of her. The best memento, of course, was his continued love. And his memory of Julo and Willi together. He wondered if he and the black man would ever see each other again. He hoped they would, because they had become, in a strange concomitance, friends. He began to think of the possibility of writing about Julo, but the subject seemed too difficult. The knot of the difficulty was his suspicion of the man himself. As fond as Lucas was of his friend—there was hardly anyone with whom he felt a closer communion—he didn't trust him.

It was the fire trick. Luke could not believe that it was done, as Julo proclaimed, in an act of faith. There had to be some deception of the eye. Perhaps the fire did not happen to Julo, but to me, he speculated; the man hypnotized me into seeing him in flames. Flimflam magic. . . . And Luke fought a troubling realization: I do not believe in magic, yet—like Julo—I have dedicated my life to creating it.

It was a corrosive irony, this conflicting view of life and work, and it might be the cause of his last three failures. He was, perhaps, leading a duplicitous existence, the disbelieving man who sold belief to others—a charlatan like Julo—and failure might be his fitting punishment. He wondered if failure was the price of fantasy/fraud.

As a high school boy, he had thought the word "fakir" was a Hindu spelling of the word "faker." Even when he learned that a fakir was a religious ascetic who performed a feat of magic as a holy rite, he was not altogether convinced that the words were not related. He had said as much to Julo, who had burst into a fit of anger, and pointed out that the fakirs did indeed walk on nails and hot coals, they did climb ropes, they did allow themselves to be buried alive only to become gloriously revivified.

"There are astonishments!" the black man had said. "*Astonishments!*"

Perhaps. No matter how rationally the miracles could be dismissed, or even rationally supported—the explicable tidal wave that caused the explicable parting of the Red Sea of Moses—there was always the residue of the inexplicable that could be accounted for only by some phenomenon beyond the brain's imagining. Whatever the gap between knowing by the mind and apprehending by the soul, that was the realm of ultimate meaning, and it was the domain Lucas wanted to explore. In a sense, it was the place where he and Julo could meet, irrespective of how they disagreed about truth and falsehood. For they both clung to the romantic notion that life had a more beautiful significance than was described by the gibberish syllable, death. That Luke tried to find the significance in a theater did not profane it any more than if he sought it in a temple.

It was with the sense of starting on a mystical search that he began to write *The Fabulist*. To find where the tension broke between the truth of fiction and the lie of fact.

He knew, of course, that he had come nowhere near a discovery, certainly not in his pages. Even the recent occurrences shed no light. The attack on Willi had brought forth hardly any response from Julo. He had telephoned Luke once, and the hospital a number of times, but had not gone to visit the patient. His adored one, damaged beyond repair, and he did not go to see her! What feature did that draw in the portrait of Julo Julasto? Did the event mean horror beyond the black man's ability to cope, or his rejection of beauty defaced . . . or guilt? What disillusionments and betrayals might have happened between him and Willi? What might Julo know about the attack?

What was the essence of the man? It was an obscurity Lucas had hoped to cast light upon in his picture. He always learned more about his script while filming it than in the writing. And now the learning had stopped. Everything, in a sense, had stopped. With Calla's rejection of the part, the film would not be made.

Alma, on the day of their divorce, had said that he was doomed to failure because he had an irresponsible imagination, he was at war with plausibility. Perhaps she was right. He envied the clear-headed, rational people like Alma and Calla, who, after every war with the crazies, could find their way home-safe to reality. For him there never was a home-safe he could count on; he felt as if his spirit had no hearth. Maybe he had forfeited his right to it. Sometimes he couldn't stand how chilly it was out here, and yearned to go inside, just anywhere. Tonight, for example. He felt miserable. Erratically he thought: If I have to be alone, I wish I were alone with someone else.

Perhaps the star was right in rejecting him as a director. Wondering why he had ever had any hope for the whole project, for the original idea and the screenplay, he suddenly hated *The Fabulist* and hated himself, and wished he were worth crying over.

There was a ring of the doorbell. He went to the hallway and opened the door.

"May I come back?" Calla said.

13

Why did you go back?

She lay in bed, asking the question. With all those qualms about the man as a director, with all the unbridled anxieties about her safety, why did she reverse herself and return to his house? I went back, she said, simply out of impulse, out of sheer foolishness; I went back because I love the script, and didn't want to lose it.

Or lose the man?

Which man? Lucas or Julo? Or both?

No, she told herself, sex had nothing to do with it.

Then why didn't you wear a bra?

Caught. She was caught in the act of mixing all her motives, feelings, hungers, hopes, anxieties, sensibilities—all in chaos. And seeking—what was it Willi called it?—quickie sexual solutions.

But she no longer resorted to QSS, she told herself, not consciously at least; and while free of their delusion, she was also deprived of their comfort.

Why did she go back to Lucas's house? Was it the need to take a chance? To risk—what? To test her strength, professionally and personally, at a time when she was unsure of it? To see how woundable she was, how killable perhaps. Or how perdurable—a star must live forever!

A rat ran over her grave. Shivering, she realized she was echoing Julo. Why do you like films better than the stage, why do you need to perpetuate your image, why do you insist on living after you are dead?

She adjusted the pillow, straightened the storm-tossed bedclothes. Not sheep tonight, lambs; sheep were stupid, but lambs didn't have to be bright, they were children, all they had to be was young. But watching them grow was not sleep-inducing. Be satisfied with counting them, as sheep.

The telephone rang and, without turning the light on, she answered it. The voice was a woman's, high-pitched and shrill, asking for a Mr. Adams. There is no Adams here, Calla said, and hung up. She was again trying to sleep when the phone rang for the second time. The same voice, angry at being put off, certain that Mr. Adams was being kept from her, demanding that he come to the phone or she would summon the police. What number do you *want*, Calla asked. The wrong one. She lay in bed, staring awake.

Then she heard the noise in the garden.

It was a slight sound, no louder than the rustle of the eucalyptus.

She got up and went to the window. Tonight the moon was pale lilac, a distant floodlight with an orchid filter; the garden greenery was purple. But she could see only a corner of it from the window—the azaleas, a few herb frames, and a wide border of dichondra.

And nobody in sight.

Certain she had heard the sound, she debated whether to turn on the lights or call the police.

There was not a sign of anyone, and the noise had not been repeated. In the dark, she put on a wrapper, slipped softly out of the room and down the stairs.

She edged her way from one window to another, looking out on the street and the balcony. Slowly, more apprehensively, she sidled along the wall to the glass door leading to the garden. She managed to look through the glass but was not sure she could bring herself to go outdoors. At last, inch by inch, she did open the door and after a moment slipped onto the brick walkway.

The night was chilly. The illusion of lilac was gone; the moon was icy white, the greenery was black.

There was no one there.

She hastened back into the house and, as she entered, the phone rang again.

The shrill voice once more, asking for her husband.

"There is no Mr. Adams here," Calla said.

The angry woman began to laugh loudly, a bray. The woman was not a woman, but a man.

"Calla," he said. "Just making sure you're there."

The English voice. Mr. Satin. He hung up.

She checked all the doors and windows once more, and sat in her study, shaking in the night chill.

"Whose death hurts you?"

She was getting things mixed up. It was not the telephone caller who had asked the question, but Julasto.

The following morning, when she called Lieutenant Reuss to tell him about the call, he seemed less interested in the telephone incident than in the imaginary prowler. "Are you sure it was imaginary?"

"Yes."

"Anyway, I'll be right over."

After he investigated every square inch of the garden, he was convinced that the intruder had been a figment. But she could see that he was preoccupied, annoyed.

"You've done a damn fool thing, you know that?"

"Many," she said. "Which damn fool thing are you referring to?"

"You went to Julasto's place. By yourself."

"Yes. How did you know?"

"We've got him staked out."

"Me as well, apparently."

"Yes, you as well," he said. "And if you're going to risk your life with a man who may be vicious—"

"In what way, vicious?"

He retreated, apparently realizing he should be hiding behind his hedging-alleging words. "In the case of your friend, Willi Axil," he said carefully, "he's one of the major suspects."

"How did you arrive at that?"

"We discovered he had quite a relationship with her. And I don't know how freaky things can get, but it looks like it was a high temperature love affair."

"That's nonsense."

"Well, if you just want to call them good friends, that's all right with me. But there's something creepy about. . ."

"About what?"

"Not once—not ever—in all the time she's been in the hospital, has he gone to visit her."

"He's not stupid. He knows you've got him 'staked out.'"

"If he's got nothing to hide, why doesn't he go see her?"

"What exactly do you think he's hiding?"

"We're not sure, or we'd haul him in. But we are sure of his record."

"Police record, you mean?"

"Criminal record, yes."

He pulled out his notebook. Not looking at her, he referred to the entries. "From the age of twenty-two to the age of forty-one—nineteen years—arrested eleven times. In many places—Los Angeles, Detroit, Philadelphia, Detroit again, Knoxville, etcetera, etcetera. Among the charges, robbery, molesting a minor, forgery and murder. Shall I give you the details?"

"Murder, you said?"

"Yes. Knoxville—a young black woman."

"And he actually did it—he was convicted of it?"

"No, he was acquitted."

"How about 'molesting a minor'?"

"He was acquitted of that as well." Then he added. "But the man *has* done time, Miss Stark."

"For what crime?"

"Robbery."

"And the others?"

"He was acquitted."

"You said he might be vicious. Do you really think he is?"

"Yes, I do. You know very well how these things work, Miss Stark. It's not easy to get a conviction. If a D.A. so much as splits an infinitive, the case gets thrown out of court, or there's a mistrial, or a postponement until the witnesses disappear—and the prisoner goes free. He may be acquitted, but it doesn't for a minute mean he's innocent. A man like this who's been arrested eleven times for mean, vicious crimes has a mean, vicious streak."

She resented his presumptive sentence of guilt, even after the prisoner had been exonerated, but she should not have been as resentful as she was. In Julasto's arms, she had felt his potential violence, and fled from it. Reuss's documentation was not really unbelievable to her. It lent a formal authority to her fear.

"Please," he said, "don't go anywhere near him."

She had no intention of doing so again, she replied, and Reuss departed.

Peculiar. Thinking about the lieutenant's information, she was not so much alarmed by it as disappointed. The actual facts of the crimes—burglary, forgery, molesting a minor—seemed too tawdry for the splendor of the man. His crimes should not have been committed by stealth but on parade. Only murder had the proper dimension, and perhaps the murder of the black woman, if it had happened, was a crime of passion, equal in size to the colossus who had stood naked above the flames. If he had to be a villain, she wanted to see him a grand one, an Othello.

Well, she needn't feel so let down. The man might indeed have slaughter in him.

A number of days later, sitting at her desk, she read in *Variety* that she was going to do *The Fabulist* with Lucas O'Hare. How they got the item she didn't know; he had promised not to release it until they had a deal with a studio, and had said he would telephone as soon as he had any news. It was nearly a week and he had not phoned.

She was about to call him when Willi's day nurse rang.

Willi was conscious. She was awake—and seeing—and talking!

Every other thought flew from Calla's mind. She rushed to her car. Leaving it on a street three blocks from the Emergency entrance—she did not trust the parking garage anymore—she walked. It was a beautiful day, there was a fresh breeze, her friend was coming out of opaqueness—she hurried lightfootedly, exhilarated. Willi conscious—she couldn't believe it.

It was true. She was sitting up in bed, propped by pillows on all sides, to keep her from tilting. The bandages looked like a neat white cap with muffs that came lightly over her ears and under her chin. Only the oval of her face was visible; she looked like a nun, stigmatized. One of the lacerations showed angry and red, like a diagonal saber cut from the forehead across her cheekbone, and disappeared at her jawline.

The venetian blinds in the room were half shut; apparently the sunlight hurt the patient's eyes. She did not change the position of her head when Calla entered; she blinked a good deal, however, trying to recognize her visitor. But she didn't, quite. Yet, her failure to make any connection did not seem to trouble Willi; her face was pleasant, she smiled a little. Calla had the foreboding sense that she would smile at anything.

Entering the room, the actress said nothing, sensing it would make a demand; even a sign of recognition might wastefully spend the convalescent's energy. She simply sat on the chrome chair beside the bed and, after a while, inched closer. As she did, the casters made a noise on the floor and Willi's smile widened.

"Whistle," Willi said.

The sound was more like a squeak, but Calla rejoiced over the effort. "Yes, a whistle," she said.

She reached to the bed and lay her hand on Willi's. The fingers, feeling her touch, fluttered and were still.

"Is that your hand?" Willi asked.

"Yes."

"Calla?"

"Yes—Calla."

The woman's arm moved somewhat, as if uncertain how to accomplish what it meant to do. The hand drifted out from under Calla's, stirred indecisively for a moment, then tentatively passed its fingertips over the surface of the visitor's hand, exploring its formature, studying it by the sense of touch, learning every nail and knuckle. Then slowly, having committed all the digits to memory, Willi's fingers edged upward to the wrist and came to the cuff of Calla's sweater.

"Silk?" she said.

"Wool."

The word gave her a problem; her smile faded. The blinking of the eyes slowed, as if to transfer all effort inwardly. Then, in a bright flash, having satisfactorily finished the chore, she smiled again. "Yes—wool," she said.

Her fingertips kept stroking the cuff, caressing it as if it were alive. The pleasure of doing it seemed a reward for having recognized the word. Then:

"Did you bring me something?"

There was a querulous note in it; a child speaking to her mother.

"No, I didn't," Calla apologized. "What would you like? I'll bring it the next time I come."

". . . I don't know."

She was about to cry, and Calla said quickly, "It's all right, Willi—in a little while we'll find out what you want."

She took Willi's hand and put it on the sweater cuff again. Abruptly, the child's face changed, and became the visage of the grown-up Willi. The eyes had a past in them, old questions that seemed to go into the depths, like candlelight in a cellar.

"Was I in an accident?" she asked.

"They didn't tell you anything?"

"Accident?"

"A kind of accident, yes."

Troubled: "Will I remember it?"

"Yes, of course," she replied, trying to make it a reassurance rather than a warning. Would it be better or worse for her to remember? Seeing Willi distressed, she cast about for another subject but saw that it was unnecessary. A veil had clouded the patient's eyes, and she was drifting. It had happened that quickly, a sudden drowsiness, then deep slumber.

Calla waited a few moments, then rose. As she reached the doorway:

"Don't go."

Willi's eyes were open again and there was an entreaty in her voice. "Please—don't go."

Hesitant, Calla lingered at the doorway, then started back toward the chair.

"Don't ever go."

"But I always come back," Calla assured her. "I've been here nearly every day."

The voice turned petulant. "I don't care—I don't want you to leave. Never. Promise—never, never!"

Putting a child's meaning in the word, Calla promised she would never leave, and stood over the bed looking down at the beseeching face. Presently, Willi was smiling again. She had remembered.

"Kitten," she said.

There it was, repeated. "What about it?"

"When you come, will you bring me the kitten?"

Before she could respond, the veil gathered once more, and Willi was asleep again. This time the slumber was even more profound, and she did not notice Calla's movement to the door. On the threshold, she waited for another summons, but it didn't come, so she departed.

In the hallway, "She's been that way since last night," the nurse said. "She goes in and out. . . . Have you talked to Dr. Lurie?"

She had spoken to the neurosurgeon a number of times, and her own doctor had been in touch with him. But not in the last week or so. Told that he was in the hospital today, she waited in the corridor, and went to meet him at the stairway when she saw him coming down. He used words she would rather not have heard—hemorrhage and embolism—and while he heartened her in one sentence, he alarmed her in the next. When Calla talked about sleep, he talked about coma and stupor; if she said forgetting, he said amnesia. Yet he did give her the first hope she had heard in weeks, that there might be no necessity for further surgical access to the brain since there were no indriven fragments of bone, and no perceptible leak of cerebrospinal fluid. Most important, the patient was beginning to make a little sense.

"But she may never straighten out," he said.

"Straighten out—in what way?"

"Past, present—who she is, who the rest of us are."

"She asked me for the kitten again," she said. "I don't know that she's ever had a kitten. I don't know what to do."

"She just wants to stroke something, I imagine," he replied. "She wants to touch things. It was the first sense she recaptured." He had gray hair and wore gray clothes. He kept his hand over his mouth nearly all the time he spoke, and monitored his words through his fingers. "It would be good if you could come in a couple of times each day. You could help her exercise."

"Exercise?"

"Her head, I mean. Start her putting things together."

"Yes, of course—I'll come as often as I can."

"But don't stay too long—just a few minutes at a time."

"Yes," she said eagerly. "Yes, I will."

When she arrived later in the afternoon with a toy kitten covered with imitation nutria, Willi was asleep. Asleep too the following day, and the following. Then, on Friday of that week, Willi held the toy kitten in her hands, close to her cheek. She blew gently on the soft fur, then stroked it quickly as if to catch the current of her breath before it wafted away.

"It's beautiful," she said. "And when I blow on it, it comes alive . . . like the other one."

"What other one?"

She tried to remember. Apparently she had bits and pieces of memory and couldn't assemble them. She fretted. "Why can't I remember the other one?"

Generally, however, she was not unhappy; on the contrary, she drifted in and out of a pleasant childishness, without a single reference to how she happened to be there or here or anywhere. She noticed that Calla was too thin and reproved her. Recalling the sweater the actress had worn, she asked if it was new and whether it was cashmere. Soft, she said, how soft and smooth it was, and hospital sheets were so coarse that her hands were chapping. Weren't they chapping, she asked, and when she was told they weren't, they both laughed.

Willi's giddy moments alternated with surprisingly clear-headed ones. One afternoon she asked: "Are you going to do *The Fabulist?*"

"Yes, I am."

"I'm happy about that." Then, the shadow. "I hope you won't be mad at me for wanting you to do it."

"I promise I won't."

How strange it was, Calla thought, that she could recall their disagreement so distinctly. Now, as they talked about it, the dispute seemed bizarre against all the questions: the savaging of the woman, her relationship with Lucas and Julo . . .

"What made you change your mind?"

"I went to Lucas's house—and we talked—and he convinced me to do it."

Like any synopsis, oversimplification made it false, and without wonder. But not for Willi—she thought it marvelous. She laughed with glee.

She seemed delighted over everything in the next few days. No matter what her physical state, no matter what confusions of time and self, her mood was blissful. Living in a constant beatitude, she exclaimed over naïve pleasures: the sweetness of the raisins in the pudding, a ray of light that changed the color of a flower petal, the glisten of the night nurse's hair. Oh, look at that, she would cry, beautiful, oh, look, Callie, look!

Awakening to a new state of consciousness, she had fallen in love with surprising and delightful minutiae, which seemed all she could handle. Calla loved her in an odd, bittersweet, unaccustomed way; she was a different person, a child Calla had never known, a deliciously silly child, Gush-and-Giggles she called her, trying to rout all the sadder designations.

Willi had acute headaches from time to time, but they were beginning to "blunt off," she said, and become less frequent. Soon, even the headaches did not distress her. Almost nothing seemed to distress her deeply, not even her continued failure to fill the gaps in her continuum of time. Haphazardly, she was in college or having her fifth birthday party or an adolescent in Baltimore, going to the Alice Fellows School, a motherless girl with a distant but adoring father and a talent for sport, breezily competitive, skinny as a hockey stick, the best in everything, hey, catch it, you fool, time out, time out for dumbbells, I'll die if we don't win, I'll croak! It would start with memory and always wind up in the present tense, good shot, you sweetheart, we've won, we've won!

No real distresses except one. A woman who had been an athlete, a kinetic creature who sprang through life on a trampoline, she had lost her sense of balance. Willi was never altogether certain whether she was sitting upright or leaning. Sometimes she did not hold her water glass vertically, and would suddenly feel a wetness dripping down her arm. Always, if she set her cup down on a saucer, she had to guide it with both hands. This disability worried her so much that she would not discuss it, and often talked with her eyes closed so as not to behold a world askew.

In a few weeks, however, her sense of equilibrium seemed markedly improved. Calla noticed it before Willi did; the patient, who had developed the tic of tilting her head, had stopped doing it, and day by day she was sitting up straighter.

"Maybe you're ready to walk," Calla said.

Willi looked nervous but daring.

That same afternoon she took her first steps. The following morning, with Calla at her side, she walked halfway down the corridor. Toward evening, she went the entire distance to the waiting room.

The triumph turned to new misfortune. She had not looked at herself in the mirror. Now, walking with Calla to the waiting room, she saw the full-length thing, the defaced one, staring across the room at her. Step by measured step, she advanced to it and stood in front of the glass. For a long time, she merely studied the white apparition, the disfigured stranger with the bandaged head and purple gash from forehead to cheekbone. She made no sound as she gazed at herself, and barely blinked her eyes. At last, ever so deliberately, she raised her hand and placed its palm against the visage, eliminating the wounded creature from her sight. She held it there, then slowly turned her head away, started out of the waiting room and down the corridor, with Calla close behind.

Although the experience did not cause a physical relapse or impede her mental recovery, Willi no longer lived in a glow of delight. The cheery child had vanished through the looking glass. Perversely, she would not discuss the possibility that at some time, in an unspecified future, she might have plastic surgery done on her face. The subject upset her deeply, as though she had irrationally accepted the ordeal of living with her scars as a divine punishment for some fault she might never be able to articulate.

She seemed constantly apprehensive about tomorrow. One day, the lieutenant told her how she had become disfigured, and it was as though the report was precisely the calamity she had been waiting for. But she could recall nothing of the attack, not the place or time of day, and not the faintest glimmer of the assailant.

From that time onward, her anxieties increased. She went back to being frightened that Calla would not return from visit to visit. Do you have to go, she would say forlornly, do you have to?

As Willi regained more and more of her awareness, it became easier for Calla to go to the hospital. Besides, it gave her something to do while waiting for Lucas to arrange the production.

He phoned occasionally, progress reports. This studio or that producer was reading the script, but it was too early for any real offers to be made, or meetings to be held. People had to read it, he said, and mull over it, and the financial gainsayers had to hate the preliminary budget he had prepared. His tidings were sketchy because, she suspected, he didn't want to abrade her with the grit of merchandising until it was necessary.

He never asked to see her. She knew there was, as yet, no reason for them to meet in person, still it piqued her that he did not call to have a drink, or ask if he could drop in. But she didn't want to believe it bothered her too much, so she made an excuse for him. Busy for both of us, she said.

One day she got an unexpected letter in the mail.

"Dear Calla," it read. "I came back a while ago, after having been in Italy and Spain, among other places, and could barely recognize the town again. To get my bearings on something that might seem familiar, I almost went to Trancas to look at our old house, but hadn't the guts to do it. Then suddenly I saw a newspaper and read the date and realized this coming Friday would have been our fifteenth anniversary, if . . . Anyway, I thought I'd like to see you on that day, and perhaps have a drink. Unless it will trouble you, would you call me at 617-2121? In case I'm not there, please leave a message. Barney."

She tore the letter in half and threw it in the wastebasket.

Unless it will trouble you . . .

It did trouble her, more deeply than it should have, in ways she did not understand. Fifteen years. She had stopped noting anniversaries long ago, yet had a perverse satisfaction in his still keeping track of them. What a cruel streak I must have, she speculated, to be pleased that he still grieves a little. Or was it that she still nursed good feelings for him—not amatory ones, of course—and was glad that he had gotten over his cold rage. Or perhaps he wanted to get over it, at last, by replacing it with kinder memories . . . and she ought to help him do it.

But it was ages past the time when she had any obligation, she decided; if there had ever been an emotional debt, it had long ago outrun the statute of limitations.

Friday would have been our fifteenth anniversary, if . . .

Friday was today.

Fifteen years ago today I was supremely happy.

She recovered the scraps of his letter, found the number and telephoned. He was not there. It sounded like the switchboard of a hotel—she didn't catch the name. She left a message. A drink, she said, at five this afternoon.

It was nearly five-thirty when he arrived. He apologized for being late; it had taken him longer than he had expected to get a lift.

A lift, she asked, not knowing what he meant, until it occurred to her that he had hitchhiked from somewhere—downtown Los Angeles, he said—and that he had no car, no money for a taxi, he was broke.

He stood in front of the wall of window with the afternoon sky behind him, and she thought: he's purposely standing there, backlighted, so that I won't get a good look at him.

"Are you all right?" she said.

"Yes, I'm fine."

She knew he wasn't. When she offered him a drink, he still chose bourbon but asked that it be a light one, and she wondered what his caution signified. The glass was unsteady in his hand, but her hand was not all that stable either.

As the dusk came quickly, he was only a contour in the room, a shadowgraph against the dimming light, and she speculated: what would happen if she suddenly flooded the room with illumination—would he cringe, would he run?

She said as casually as she could, "I think I'll turn the lights on."

"If you must."

She did.

"You've lost a little weight," she said.

"Yes, I've lost a little weight."

"You've been ill, haven't you?"

"Yes."

"Seriously?"

"I had pneumonia a few winters ago, and thought I had it licked. But there was a spot on my lung."

"Is it still there?"

". . . I guess so."

Abruptly, she had an ache as if she had never stopped loving him; in fact she did love him, Calla realized, in another fashion. She couldn't imagine living with him again, or lying in bed and making love, but they were related as if by blood, by suffering. And now, his illness . . .

"Are you doing anything about it?"

"No, not really," he said. "I'm much better than I've been. At least I can work again, if I can get a part."

"If you need any money—"

"No—hell, Calla—no. What I need is a picture."

"Meanwhile, let me give you a check."

"No—please. . . . But I heard you're doing a new film."

"Yes."

"Is there anything?"

"Well, there are only two good roles for men. One's a black man, and the other is a hunter-guide who—"

Interrupting, "I'm a hunter-guide." He smiled. "I walk so softly, I never stir a leaf—and I can smell a lion miles away."

"I'm afraid they'll be looking for a name."

"Big?"

"Well . . . Nicholson . . . Sutherland."

"I can play Nicholson Sutherland." The grin was gone. "But I'm not a name."

She was feeling more and more miserable for him, and now he made it worse. "It needn't be *that* part, you know. I wasn't talking about a lead or anything."

"I'll see what I can do," she said.

But they both knew that would be the end of it. Then, evenly, trying to avoid the slightest inflection: "Barney, I'm going to insist on helping you with some money. I've got all there is, and it doesn't mean anything to me, so please—"

"No—don't, Cal." He looked up at the ceiling. "But just for tonight, if you've got a spare bedroom . . . I owe the hotel a bundle and I . . ."

He turned away. She sensed that he was having difficulty catching his breath, and she knew the desperation was worse than the ailment.

"Oh, Barney, of course!"

She hurried across the room, took him in her arms and held him, as he started to cry.

"It's nothing," he said, "this crying—it's just—I'm still a little weak —it's nothing."

"It's all right," she kept saying, "it's all right."

They made dinner together—an omelet—and he ate most of what she served him, then asked for milk, and drank the better part of a quart of it.

"I never used to drink milk—remember?" he said. "But now it's so soothing."

"Yes . . . that's right . . . soothing."

After dinner, he seemed his old self again, telling funny tales of spaghetti Westerns he had made, imitating one of the directors, a bottom-heavy Abruzzi with a thick *mezzogiorno* accent and a handclasp like cold lasagna. He waddled across the room with his feet a yard apart, and disgorged a torrent of mutterings that sounded like real Italian, and she marveled at how perfectly he had caught a type she had seen often when she had lived in Rome. Then he imitated the overdelicate actor who played the Pecos Kid as brutally as he was meant to be, but with a Venetian lisp. He did the Italian actress who sashayed as a Nebraska schoolmarm, and the slate boy who kept snapping the wrong scene numbers and thwacking his thumb with the clapperboard, and the drunken cameraman with the incontinent bladder, and she saw every one of them so clearly and so comically that she screamed with laughter and was nearly incontinent herself. . . . And she thought how extremely gifted he was, and what a talent was being lost, and how his life was wasting away.

She showed him to the guest bedroom and got him an extra blanket against the chilly night—he needed additional warmth these days, he said, except when he suddenly got roasty.

Through the night, concerned, she kept half listening in the stillness. When it was almost dawn and she thought he was asleep, she heard him wandering around the house, in the kitchen at first, then in the study, and at last, when there were footsteps in the hallway, she sensed he was going back to bed.

At breakfast, he seemed healthier and more self-assured. His complexion was rosy but without an insalubrious flush. There was, in fact, no ailing look about him, and his leanness made him appear handsomer than she had remembered.

"I hope you don't mind," he said. "I couldn't sleep too well last night, so I read *The Fabulist*."
"Did you? No, I don't mind."
"It's a hell of a thing."
"Hell of a good, or hell of a bad?"
"Exciting. The first ten pages, I thought: it doesn't make sense. The next fifty, I didn't care whether it did, and at the end, it hurt."
"Yes."
"I could play the spots off that hunter part."
"Yes, I know you could."
He looked at her quickly to measure her concurrence and it gave him confidence to see that it was total. He was grateful.
"I thought last night: I wonder if Calla would mind my staying here for a little while—until I get some work. But this morning, I don't need to do that. However . . . I will take you up on that loan you offered."
She had not meant it as a loan. But now he thought of it as an advance against whatever he could earn somewhere; he seemed genuinely to view it that way, and to know that he would pay it back.
She gave him a check for a thousand dollars, and told him he could have more if he needed it. Thanking her, he folded it carefully and put it in the outside breast pocket of his seedy sport jacket.
A little before noon, she drove him down to The Strip, where he had an appointment to see his onetime agent.
As he got out of the car, he repeated, "I could play the spots off that hunter part."
And again she agreed.
Turning the car in the direction of the hospital, she realized with a start: he had not even mentioned Mina's name. She wondered if the two of them could ever spend a quiet evening together, having dinner perhaps, and then, over coffee and the rest of the wine, talk healingly about their dead child. Reflecting that he had departed an enemy and returned as a friend, she pondered whether, with shared memories and a fire on the hearth, they might not be able to create an illusion together, that death was not such an irrevocable thing.

14

What Lucas had not told Calla was that prior to her reading *The Fabulist*, he had submitted the manuscript to all the major studios and to a number of important independents. All of them, without exception, had turned it down.

How the trade papers got news of Calla's agreement to do the film he did not know. Certainly not a word had come from him. But there were insiders who knew, Megan Farris, and his own agent, Arnold Gellman. Perhaps there was a memorandum here or there; and there were always assistants and secretaries. In Hollywood, he was aware, there were no secrets; as his agent had elegantly expressed it, a fart at Metro was a fanfare at Fox.

He wasn't altogether sorry that the item had appeared in *Variety*. The instant the paper hit the offices and poolsides, his phone began to ring. Studios where the script had been rejected, seeing Calla Stark's name, suddenly envisioned a totally different project, and begged for a resubmission of the screenplay. He reminded the president of Universal Pictures—tactlessly, but with a need to rub it in—that the man had already read and rejected it. *I* didn't read it, *I* didn't reject it, was what nearly all of them said, and perhaps it was true—the script had been discarded by some lower echelon executive, it had fallen into the wastebasket of an underling's mind. Besides, it was an early draft, wasn't it? a producer asked. Luke didn't tell him it was the latest version. Without changing a single word, he sent another copy over, and the man thought it was much improved.

While this was going on, in the first weeks after the resubmission of the scripts, he telephoned Calla sporadically and told her very little. He was never sure how studio heads would behave, and if there were further rejections he did not want to unsettle the star by giving her bad tidings. Besides, if a deal was to be made, it was a point of pride to make it on his own, without asking for additional help; the use of her name was contribution enough, the most potent one.

Waiting on the edge, he kept thinking that any day now his phone would ring, there would be an exciting offer and the flourishing trumpets of a deal; he would vault into his car, race to Calla's house and bellow the good news.

But the news was dilatory. Here was his worst disquiet, the delay in the response. The studios had clamored for scripts in a hurry and were replying at leisure. While he didn't entirely subscribe to the notion of the quick yes and the slow no, the procrastinations did give him concern. Besides, a few producers were requesting additional copies of the script, which meant they were soliciting opinions, and he knew that *The Fabulist* was not the kind of screenplay that would catch on at urinal meetings.

When he got really nervous, he phoned his agent. Gellman was glad to be consulted.

"You better drop in to the office," he said. "There's been interesting developments."

"Like what?"

"Come in, Luke—we'll do a little talk. And don't be antsy, kid—they're gonna take some time makin' up their so-called. After all, this isn't exactly a Staple—it's a Personal Vision. Right?"

Luke agreed, and the conversation was over.

Not a Staple, a Personal Vision. The current argot to distinguish between the safe and the risky. The Staple was usually a realistic story based more or less on a formula, and fleshed out with recognizable characters. If it had the semblance of originality, with a new slant or quirk or twist—not too eccentric—so much the better. It could be a commonplace account like *Ordinary People* or *Kramer vs. Kramer*, or an adventure tale with a soupçon of mystery-horror like *Carrie* or *Rosemary's Baby*. While some of the staple films were imaginative, and a few were the work of artists, most were orthodox in their objectives and conventional in technique. They were the bread and butter of the business.

The film of Personal Vision was usually the dream of a single artisan, commonly the writer-director, *l'auteur*. He would nearly always be a man who had had an enormous success—as Coppola had had in *The Godfather* or Cimino in *The Deer Hunter*—and who could thereupon be trusted with a chancy story, a flexible budget and nearly limitless freedom. If he could succeed so dazzlingly before, the moneymen reasoned, let's give him his heart's desires once again, and not meddle with his mystique. Sometimes the personal vision film became a triumph—2001; sometimes, a qualified success—*Apocalypse Now*; more often, a box-office failure—*1941* and *Heaven's Gate*.

To the studio potentates, the risk of the personal vision film represented not only the possible loss of Eldorado, but something far more precious, the loss of power. To the man who had been granted free rein and all that money, his personal vision nearly always was his *secret* vision. No matter what the script or budget said, the fiction was in his head. And it might be useless, even dangerous, to trim the artist's fantasy to fiscal reality; the dream might die. Even in those cases where the dream did not seem to be coming alive, they dared not fire *l'auteur*; for, however quick or dead, the thing was in the director's brain alone, and without him they could not even finish the picture.

So the studios were not, nowadays, jostling one another to underwrite what Luke called the *egauteurs*. And he was one of the least likely of them, with six years of failure and a hazardous script. A film company would have to be out of its corporate mind, he supposed, to risk $15 million on a picture that was going to be shot exclusively on location, beyond the borders of studio supervision.

But film companies *were* out of their minds, frequently. What usually sent them loony was a star. Luke had one star, and probably two. Then why wasn't he getting a quicker response?

He went to his agent's office that afternoon. He had been Arnold Gellman's client since the release of his last successful picture. In a sense, the failures of the two men had been concurrent. At one time, Arnold, an independent who hated the mega-agencies, used to be a prime packaging broker in Hollywood, but those were the days when film investment was a tax shelter acceptable to the Internal Revenue Service. When that well ran dry, Arnold went to the oil well. But the sheiks and emirs found that watching the shooting of a film was a costly tickle, that the dollar fluctuated too nervously, and the beautiful Hollywood flesh was purchasable more cheaply, and in houses of better repute. So Gellman lost his latest patrons of the arts.

Such setbacks never seemed to unman him. He was well into his sixties now, an old battle charger out of bygone jousts, and he had had what he called a friendly heart attack. This indisposition had left him a hint to slow down, which he did with an engagingly philosophical smile. He had been blessed with easygoing courage and three rich wives, the daughters of: First, a vice-president hatchet man in the days of Louis B. Mayer; second, a major stockholder in Technicolor; third, a merger-maker. It had been said that Gellman had married the fathers, not the daughters, but Arnold claimed it was not true; he deeply, genuinely and faithfully loved rich women.

For all his pelf, Arnold clung to the emblem of his Lower East Side upbringing: his Yiddish accent. It was like a phylactery that he would not profane. Yet, he derived pleasure from English well spoken and written, which was why he handled writers. He was, as he described himself, a sucker for similes. But he was merciful enough never to finish one, for they were all hackneyed.

"Don't worry, Lukey-boy," he said in his Canon Drive office. "You've got a sure deal somewhere. With Calla Stark and Sidney Poitier—what?—you're in like the proverbial."

"Did Sidney say yes?"

"What do I need Sidney to say yes? If Marty Baum says Sidney's gonna do it, his word's as good as his whatsis."

"Did Sidney read it?"

"What?—he has to read it?"

"How about the studios?"

"What are you worryin'?" he asked expansively. "The only thing, I need a new handle to bang with. If I could get a new handle, I'd be as busy as a one-arm-guess-who."

"What handle have you been using?"

"Sex-adventure in Dixie."

"Jesus."

"Well, maybe I'm callin' it wrong. But I figured, if you're talkin' to a Gulf and Western mind, you gotta talk sex-adventure. So I hock them with a great hot love story of a white woman and a black hunter—"

"The hunter is a white man."

"You changed it?"

"No, I didn't change it. Did you read the script?"

"What do I have to read it? You told it to me so graphic."

Arnold's need for a new handle was a tip-off. He was not getting an enthusiastic response. Even with Calla Stark, and the possibility of Poitier—no jumpers. And Gellman himself wasn't helping much.

"Tell you what, Arnie. Let's hold back—let's not push it for a while."

"You don't want me to follow up?"

"No. Let's wait for the calls."

"We could have to wait till the cows come marchin' in."

Lucas decided, however, that he would break the inertia; he would try to put the thing together himself. After his meeting with Arnold, instead of waiting for messages, he started to telephone. The responses were not really rejections, and all were friendly; nobody was headlong about turning down a Calla Stark project. But he heard an assortment of evasions: We're setting up a meeting on Tuesday. We're restudying your budget. We're doing a demographic on the subject.

Then it was over. Everybody had passed. The rejections were all in. Not in the tenor of the times, they said. It's a soft ticket at a hard price. We buy the talent, but we pass the project. A black film in a white market.

Lucas was not a quitter. He had slugged his way through one film while nursing a broken arm, he had kept a face of cheer in another when his actors had come down with hepatitis and the banks had foreclosed, he had gritted his teeth through bad reviews and the dead smell of empty theaters, and had gone on to make another picture. But this was a drawn blank. This was the film city telling him flatly that it did not want him.

Lucas didn't mind the loss of substance, that's not what failure meant to him. Nor did he mind the shame in a milieu where failure was disreputable, like body odor. What he hated about failing—what he feared, in fact—was that it would halt his search. He was not able to say, precisely, what he searched for, but occasionally he imagined it was something he had once had and lost, a radiance that had faded, something he had mislaid in childhood, or betrayed in growing up. Or, it was a search for something not yet lost but not yet found, somewhere around the bend of the world.

Sometimes, rarely, when the pages wrote themselves, or when the scene seemed to glide off the soundstage and flow of its own energy into the camera, he caught hints of beauty, scintillas of light that might flare into truth. They were a promise that led him onward, gave him hope and filled his work with joy. This was the heart of his optimism as a man, the bone of his courage.

It was a message that came to him only in his work. Not in any sensuous pleasure, eating or drinking or making love. Only in his work. Away from the white page, away from the whirring film, he could scarcely think or imagine, and even his dreams did not beguile him. And for him to fail in his work—blessed with the curse of being an artist—was for him to perish.

When one of his films came to grief, Lucas believed his allies innocent of blame, and should not be burdened with his failure. Now, regretting that he had ever approached Calla, he knew that his tarnish would taint the star. Her last success was a free ride, they would say, and the smart money is betting on her decline; she can't still be a powerhouse if her name can't launch a picture. He loathed such talk and wished he did not have to subject her to it.

"It's me they're rejecting," he said, when he reported to her on the phone. "It has nothing to do with you."

"I can't believe that everybody's turning us down."

"Not us—me. The script and the director."

"I'm in it."

"No. I do appreciate everything, Calla. But you're off the hook."

"I hate that expression. I never considered myself on any hook. I want to do the film—and we'll do it." It was the last wave of the flag, from a recumbent position. "Do you know Lily Westerson?"

"I've met her," he said.

"But never worked with her?"

"No."

"Would you mind if I sent her the script?"

"It would be useless, wouldn't it? She's unemployed."

Lily had been an executive at Columbia, Metro, Universal. One of the first women appointed to a high administrative position, she had been a standard bearer for females in the industry, but had been turned into a stalking horse. The mare, mid-foaling, had been aborted. All the films she had undertaken, still in their maturational stages, were terminated. Her contract had been "settled amicably."

"She's not unemployed," Calla said. "She's the head of Carmel Pictures."

It was a new company in what the *Reporter* had called an "absentee syndicate," which meant the money had come from sources outside the picture business.

"They really named Lily?" he asked.

"Yes. It'll be announced tomorrow."

"I can't believe they hired her."

"Why not? She's very bright—and she knows what a camera is."

"For that very reason. They want accountants."

"*They're* the accountants." With a laugh, "Refreshing, isn't it?"

"If true."

"Shall we see? Shall I send her the script?"

He said yes, though he held no hope. He was now on a treadmill of rejection. He had hardly put down the phone, it seemed, when, early the following morning, Calla called.

"She loves it!"

"What?"

"The whole damn thing—Lily loves it! She's crazy about the script—she thinks you're a genius—she says the casting ideas are wonderful—and she wants to see us right away."

"When is right away?"

"Are you dressed?"

"Only have to put my pearls on," he said, and was out the door.

The new company was in temporary quarters at the old Goldwyn Studios on Santa Monica Boulevard. They approached Lily Westerson's office by way of an outside stairway that took them to an anteroom. It was a raw, inclement day, on the edge of the rainy season, and the outer office was cuttingly damp, its heat augmented by a kerosene stove. Millions of dollars, he thought, billions, being kept warm by coal oil.

They were told to wait by a blowsy receptionist who ate a tunafish sandwich and licked the mayonnaise from the corner of her mouth. "Sorry I can't offer you coffee," she said. "The machine didn't get here yet."

Waiting for Westerson, Lucas reflected upon the tattle he had heard about her. He had come upon the secret by way of pillow talk with a woman who had gone to college with Lily. It was Westerson's closest guarded confidence, the skeleton in her attic.

She was a closet intellectual.

Not the commonplace variety of pseudo-savant prevalent in the film village, but a committed, card-carrying scholar: various cum laudes, a Ph.D. in philosophy and a monograph or two. That was Lily Westerson's "trip": she was addicted to thought. If she had been a phony, mouthing didactically what she had heard Sagan say last night about intergalactic destiny, or Alistair Cooke about America's manifest horizons, she would have had no need to hide her cleverness. But Lily's brain was not adept at showy calisthenics; it was a hardworking muscular thing that agonized and slaved for her. This weakness for thinking, this obsession with the thought behind the word, she seldom confided to her colleagues, for she knew that to be a woman elevated in the film business was suspect enough; to be a woman who harbored an elevated idea was to be branded an Intellectual with an "I" emblazoned on her breast.

She ushered them into her office; she had just moved in and the place was a hodgepodge. So was her hair. Almost coal black with streaks of gray, there was a comb and a pencil in it, and she seemed on the verge of tearing it out by the roots. Frustrated, she scrounged through the drawers of her desk.

"Does either of you have a typewriter ribbon? Those idiots gave me a machine without one. They think I'll feel demoted if the damn thing *works*. Hello, Cal—good God, you're aglow! Who's your long-limbed friend?"

Lucas grinned. "We met about two years ago."

"I know—I still talk Barbizon Plaza—is it true it's gone coed?—oh, brother, it's hard to keep pace with the parity—I love your script."

With a proprietary air, Calla said, "You're meant to."

"Meant to doesn't count, does it?" Lily said. "I'll bet there aren't many of us."

Lucas tightened. It was true enough. But if she knew that, why was she allowing herself to get interested?

"There aren't many who like the whole setup," Calla said. "The script, Lucas and me. Even the possibility of Poitier doesn't stampede them."

"Fuck 'em. Picture making isn't tests and measurements." Lily leaned forward. "Want to know what I love about the script?"

"Not really." He smiled. "Just tell me how *much* you love it."

"I didn't think I was going to like it," she went on. "It seemed only an antic fable at first. Then suddenly it occurred to me: this isn't a fiction, it's a documentary—it really happened. And then, the most chilling part . . . those implausible things happened to *me*."

He was touched and muttered a word of gratitude.

Lily continued. "And you had me imagining that it might, it just might be possible we could live forever."

The tribute was too much and he turned away. Calla was watching him. She too seemed touched, sharing his pleasure.

"There has to be a 'but' somewhere," he said.
Lily nodded. "There is."
"What?"
"Dyer Addison."
"What's that?"
"My boss. I don't know what rank to call him. Let's say he's the persona of Carmel Pictures. No, a persona's a facade, isn't it? He's *it*."
"And he doesn't like my script?"
She seemed to be disentangling a knot. "Well . . . he likes the elements—Calla, the script, the casting potentials—Poitier, Nicholson—maybe even Redford for the hunter's part—"
"Redford would be dead wrong."
Calla looked at him quickly. He felt certain she agreed with him, but was flashing the signal that he had spoken incautiously. Gear back, he told himself.
"I agree," Lily said. "Redford's too pretty for the part. It should be someone craggier. But I have to tell you—Dyer and I don't agree about everything. I think it's important for you to know that he and I don't *have* to agree on everything." She was in a new position, and having difficulty describing it. "What I mean is, we're good together not in *spite* of but *because* of our differences."
He thought regretfully: Either she protests too much, or she's not long for this job. "What sort of differences?"
"Oh, they can be minor. Take this office, for example. It's only temporary and I don't mind being here—I love this old dump of a studio. With all its bad ventilation, and linoleum floors and the plaster plopping into the water glass, there's old-time Hollywood in the place. I can see Mary Pickford down the hall and Chaplin on the stairs and Goldwyn getting up from his nap—well, I'm sentimental about all that. He's not. He hates being here, and can't wait for Century City, and perhaps . . ."
Her voice petered off. She was disconcerted. She had gone from one executive suite to another, downgrade. Recently fired from Universal and Big Business, perhaps she was frightened to be thrown back into the stainless steel, computerized Century City of cold commerce.
She was recovering quickly. "Now understand, I don't think being sentimental about old buildings can separate the lads from the lassies, but sometimes a sense of tradition is more a woman's thing than a man's, and . . ."
"Has that been your major disagreement?" Calla asked.

"Not really." Lily looked from one to the other. She was apparently trying to send them a message. She liked them and wanted her company to do their film, and might be warily on the point of disclosing inside information that could help to bring it about. It occurred to Lucas: she's having difficulty being clear without being indiscreet.

"Let me tell you an incident," Lily said. "The day before yesterday, we turned down a project we had been considering. It involved a novella, one thread of which was the story of a woman harassed by a flasher who stood at his window, across the courtyard, and masturbated so that she could see him. He did it a number of times and she reported it to the police. Whenever they arrived, he had disappeared. Then the molestations stopped until, one evening, she came home, started to undress for bed, and found a used condom on the floor of her bathroom. . . . Now, Dyer and I both read the identical story. When I read the bathroom sequence I thought it was obscene and terrifying. I was in a meeting with five people—all the others were men. Everybody in that room agreed with me that the bathroom incident *was* obscene and terrifying. Everybody except Dyer. He thought it was obscene and funny. He laughed his head off."

Lily paused. "Would you say Dyer and I have a major difference?"

"I'm afraid so," Calla said.

"Are you sure?" asked Lucas. "Couldn't the story have been obscene, funny *and* terrifying?"

Lily looked at him oddly. "You want it all, don't you?"

"If I can get it."

"But I haven't really told the point of the story." Lily's eyes narrowed. "In that roomful of men, none of whom laughed, Dyer turned on one of them. 'You laughed in my presence, but not in Lily's,' he said. . . . And that afternoon the young man was fired."

Calla was shocked. "For not laughing with Addison?"

"Oh no," Lily said quickly. "None of the others laughed with him."

"For hypocrisy, then?"

"Exactly."

"The point is a warning, isn't it?" Luke said.

"Yes."

"What?"

"Don't shit him."

"I hadn't meant to try."

"I don't think any of us can help trying—it's the *modus operandi* of the business. But, don't. He's too smart. If you try, you'll fail."

He felt ambivalent about Westerson, half admiring and half pitying her. She was in trouble because she wanted irreconcilable things: To be loyal, yet to suggest confidences that were not her own; to be devious, yet to be honest; to be a pure artist and a moneymaker; to be cozy in old Hollywood and a powerhouse in the new one. To be liked, especially to be liked. He did like her, but was uncertain how staunch an ally she would turn out to be.

When Dyer Addison came in, he was younger than Luke had expected—thirtyish. Luke recognized the type: One of the new breed who were sidewinding their way into the upper echelons. He was from the Bank of Boston, perhaps, or from a Main Line investment family, or the boardroom emissary of ITT. He would be a Wasp in ethnic country, and although tightly wound, he would affect an easygoing role. Tempted to wear Rodeo Drive sportsclothes, he would stay with the Brooks Brothers button-down collar and foulard tie, knowing there was an edge of intimidation in a three-piece suit. To show that he had quickly learned the cipher of the trade, he would speak in the Hollywood vernacular—the Vegas talk, the Yiddish raciness, a sprinkling of polysyllables, the glitz and glitch. But the relaxed good fellowship of such a man was nearly always a disguise; he was high-strung, hyped up, adrenalin his drug of choice. Yet, he could never become the usual Hollywood *hondler*, the old-fashioned wheeler-dealer who trafficked in the phony, for the lie would be, to him, the recourse of the lesser brain, and his was the greater. If he was a graduate of the Wharton School or Harvard School of Business Administration, a life of accountancy and money stewardship had not offered exciting rewards to his ego. He had needed to take more personal risks, and to be somebody else.

A gambler. Not a stumblebum gambler, but a counter-of-cards who had the educated skill to computerize the odds, the exposure against the opportunity, the downside risk against the upside gain, the catastrophe against the insurance, the exotic accidents against the norms of common business practice—but a gambler nonetheless. The quick-eyed, single-minded, bet-the-limit, play-to-the-last-hand gambler. The lustful one.

With no lust left over for anything else. No time for social chat or lolling in the Caribbean or going to the polling booth; and little enough time for sex, unless it was a vital part of the action. The action was the game, to win. Yet, money was only a token, a counter, a petty chip, never cashed in; it was even, sometimes, the object of contempt, worth nothing more than to be risked. As everything must be risked. If the odds were right.

The odds, then. "It's a chancy piece, isn't it?" Dyer Addison said.

"It's always chancy to go for a killer," Luke replied.

"What's going for it?"

"Calla Stark, to begin with."

Addison nodded. "It's a hell of a beginning. That's the big one, isn't it?"

As if she were neuter. And not present.

Luke smiled. "Yes, that's the big one."

"And Lily says the script is good."

"Haven't you read it?"

"Yes, very carefully. But I don't know about such things." Then, narrowly: "You, however—you're not an odds-on favorite, are you?"

"No."

Addison was not trying to belittle Lucas; he studied the director impersonally. "Maybe you're due for one," he said. "But it's hell to play the averages."

"Yes, it's hell."

"How will you sell it?" he asked.

"You mean when it's finished?"

"Yes—tickets. What'll they buy besides Stark?"

"You mean what sort of film will it be?"

"Yes. Identify it."

"Well, basically it's a love story."

"You mean Calla and the black man."

"Yes."

He turned to Lily. "Miscegenation—how are we on that subject these days? Long or short?"

Lily smiled equably. "Well, people aren't saying, 'Goody, let's go out and see a miscegenation flick tonight.'"

He had no time for the facetious. "You mean it's not selling."

"Not really."

"Guess Who's Coming to Dinner—when was that?"

"The late sixties," she replied.

"That's the last time it paid off?"

"I think so."

He turned to Lucas once more. "What else could you sell?"

"Well, it has to do with myth—the liberation from the curse of mortality—a kind of fable—"

"Curse—you said curse." Seizing upon the word, Dyer returned to Lily. *"The Exorcist*—when was that?"

"Seventy-two or three, I think."

Calla said dryly, "There have been others since that time."

"But no curse picture was quite that big, right?"

"I think that's right," Lily said.

Luke could feel his skin tightening. "Does it have to be sold as if it were something that's been done before?"

"No," he answered. "But it's good to know what we're betting on."

"You're betting on a script and on people. On Calla Stark and Sidney Poitier and—"

"Poitier turned it down."

Lucas was stunned. He didn't look at Calla but heard her stir. He wondered if some slyness was being perpetrated. The last he had heard was an enthusiastic report from Sidney's agent.

"Baum said he liked it, and that Sidney would do it."

For the first time, Dyer smiled. "If agents were actors . . . I didn't speak to Baum, I spoke to Sidney."

"When?"

"A half hour ago."

"What did he say?"

"Well, he's a civil man. Tactful. Loved the script. Thinks you're a fine director—an artist, he said. But he's looking for something else these days—doesn't want to play a trashy black."

"What does he want to play?" Lily asked. "A noble black?"

"A noble white."

It was dirty. Besides, untrue. Luke had met Sidney and admired him. He knew that Addison was trying to show his loyalty to the script, defending it against a choosy actor and a black, to demonstrate he was on Luke's side. But the director did not want him there.

Calla, embarrassed, was counting the ridges in her corduroy skirt.

Lily filled the gap. "There are other actors for the part." She mentioned James Earl Jones, an actor she liked, but added that his name had no pulling power, and Addison said he had gone through the lists and his secretary had scoured the directories, and there wasn't a black actor around, aside from Poitier, who could sell a ticket to Christ riding a bicycle.

Calla glanced at him quickly, and away. "Maybe it's just as well to be satisfied with only two stars. Three makes the budget awful fat, doesn't it?"

Luke agreed. "If we can get Nicholson for the part of the hunter—"

"Nicholson turned it down," Dyer said. "So did Sutherland."

There was a feeling of collapse.

"You work fast," Luke said.

"I didn't send it to them," Addison replied. "They read it weeks ago. The studios have been peddling it all over. Your script has been around."

"Yes, I know."

"Aren't you interested in why Nicholson rejected it?"

"He thinks it's the third part," Luke said.

"It *is* the third part, Lucas. But it needn't be. Maybe if you built it up a little . . . Personally, he's the one I go for in the script. He's tough and he's the true hunter-guide, and he's white. Lucas, I tell you, if you could make a real starring part out of it, you might even get Redford."

"Enlarging the part of Titus wouldn't change his nature," Luke replied guardedly. "And Redford's too shiny."

Addison was undeterred. "How about Newman?"

"Same thing, really, only a bit older."

"Couldn't the part be written older?"

Before Luke could respond, Lily suggested, "Well, if it could be written older, I'd go for George Scott—he's meaner, more abrasive—"

"And fatter," Dyer said.

"He can lose weight," Lily said. "And is there any reason—if you're not making him the romantic interest—he can't be on the portly side?"

Even from Lily the writer was getting it. Although on the surface it looked as if Westerson was disagreeing with her boss, basically she was on Addison's side: change the script. She was different from the woman she had been before Dyer's entrance; now she was the employee he had hired not for her taste and intellect, but for her lingo and savvy. The screenplay which had been a work of art that had "happened" to her was now something to manipulate. Write the part older or younger, skinnier or portlier, write it any way except as written.

"Portly?" Dyer said. "You want a portly leading man?"

"Why not?" Lily was defensive. "Titus doesn't wind up with the woman—why does he have to be an Olympian? Why can't he be a little strange, a little odd?"

"Strange—odd!" Dyer retorted. "That's what's wrong with the

script—it's too odd. I want things more even. What if the hunter *is* handsome and likable—is there anything wrong with that? What if he *doesn't* hate animals—what if he loves them and it hurts to kill them—is that a crime? What if he's a nice guy—why not? *Why not?* Is it terrible if she falls in love with someone I'm rooting for? Will it be a motion picture disgrace if she marries him and it all turns out even? Why does it have to be odd? *You don't get good odds on oddballs."*

Title: Writing in Conference. The paradox was that nearly everybody, in one way or another, made sense. They were not, for the most part, stupid people, as the intellectual periodicals occasionally made them out to be. Nearly all of them were bright, shrewd; some were even educated. But, making sense, they had little faith in the sense of their fellow human beings, nor in their intuitions or readiness to be stirred. The worst shortcoming of the conferees was the lack of an imagination that can assemble the unassemblable. They were diarists, not prophets; they followed the directive of the single day that had just passed, and were frightened of the future. The last twenty-four hours could be trusted; there were box-office figures to certify them; the next twenty-four were the hours of the fools and crackpots. They were mortally terrified of the illogical. Thus, in a meeting, they went obsessively to the task of ironing out all the unconventional lumps in a story, until the texture was smooth, credible and flat; so that every sense, perception and emotion was safely close to the comfort station of everyone's experience. Then all hands would approve it. With all the highs now muffled, the spices sugared away, the bird now a pedestrian, the script would be sent to mimeo or multigraph or Xerox, as if it weren't already a copy of hundreds like it.

"We'll have to give this a second go-round," Addison said.

Nothing had been resolved, and no offer had been made. Luke saw the shadow of another rejection.

But for Lily it was not over. Intimidated as she might be by her boss, she picked up her desk calendar. "When would you like the next meeting?"

Dyer turned. A nip of annoyance. Using candor as a whip, he snapped, "I wasn't going to have another meeting. There's not enough here, not for me. I'm not saying there can't be. It's up to you, Lucas. You're a creative man—create! Put a big package together. Get a Reynolds, get a Redford, get a Newman. It's all in the package—pearls won't sell in a paper bag. Package them. Package this thing, Lucas—package it!"

The meeting was set for Friday, the same time. The director would have three days to be, as Dyer put it, creative.

Leaving the office, Lucas was not at all certain what Calla was thinking. As for himself: Pearls won't sell in a paper bag—package them. No matter how—with a gimmick of some sort, with another star who would sell, irrespective of whether the star threw the wrong light on the picture. Package was everything. The soap could blister the skin, the cereal cause diabetes, the hair dye rot follicles, but if the package was right, there would be a market.

As they got to their cars, she said: "Would you like to talk?"

"Yes—where? Is it time for lunch?"

"Probably. But I hate restaurants." She unlocked her car door. "Would you like a banana sandwich?"

"A what?"

"Banana, lamb and hot chili peppers."

"Sounds lethal."

"To suit your mood. Drive slowly and let me clean the kitchen."

Riding toward her house, he surprised himself by his impulse to buy her a bottle of wine. He stopped at a liquor store, almost purchased a fine Montrachet, then desisted. It bothered him that he wanted to give her a present; it bothered him that he had inhibited the impulse. It bothered him that it bothered him.

They ate at a counter in the kitchen. The sandwich was delicious, but so spicy hot that he felt it burning through his skull.

"A little fiery?" she said.

"Singeing my hair."

"Have you always had red hair?"

"It's brown."

"I know it's brown. Your brown hair is red."

"Only when I rub chili peppers in it."

"There were no peppers at the meeting."

"Was my hair red? I thought I was surprisingly cool."

"On the surface."

"He's an asshole."

"What'd you think of Lily?"

"She knows the words. If she weren't so scared, she might be marvelous."

"If he knew the words, he might not be an asshole."

"He knows the words."

"Not the writer words."

He put down his coffee and dabbed the napkin at his suffering mouth. "You mean our difference was simply a matter of trade vernacular? And if I were a better listener, I would hear that he was right?"

"I didn't say he was right."

"He was talking sense, then."

"I didn't even say he was talking sense. He was simply trying to express a feeling—a discomfort that others may have felt."

"Others? You too?"

"Me too."

"About what?"

"The character of Titus."

"What's wrong with him?"

"Nothing's wrong with him. He's just not as fully written as a major character might be."

"What's missing?"

"Complexity, I think." She was treading carefully. "If he's just a hunter who enjoys the kill . . . But I don't think you're the sort of writer who'd be satisfied with saying he's mean and cruel, and the hell with him. You don't write that way. None of your people are that uncomplicated. Rachel has twists and turns in her—and secrets—and I'm never sure what she'll think or do. And Kono—an entangled black man —he's wonderfully mixed-up. But all I see in Titus is a man who likes to see animals die."

"He doesn't like to see them die. He suffers over it."

"You haven't written that."

"My camera will write it."

"Close-up: Titus: He suffers."

"Don't make fun of the camera—it's a vengeful beast."

"I don't make fun of the camera, Lucas. I merely mean that when the rest of the story searches so restlessly, so painfully for some answers to complex questions, a close-up showing that the man suffers when he kills a young deer is goddamn shallow."

"You want me to go deeper—"

"Yes."

"—and broader—"

"Yes."

"—bigger—"

"Yes!"

"Big enough for a star."

"You louse!"

Error. Blunder. Stupid goddamn mistake.

He pulled back. She might be right that he wasn't listening sympathetically.

But then again, this might be just another of those story conferences. She might be wrong. Her criticism, which she had not expressed before, might simply come from panic. When the studios all compete hotly for the same screenplay, everything about the project is wonderful, especially the script. The pages are inviolable. But when the rejections come, the first thing that needs revision is not the star's voice or the director's sense of timing, but the manuscript; it's too long and too wordy, there's not enough action, the scenes lack humor, the hunter's part needs beefing up.

He tried to restore the peace. "Sorry, Calla. You may be right—but it's not the major part. The picture's not *about* Titus. It's about Rachel and Kono. I think the hunter's part is strong and colorful, and it should attract a star. But even if it doesn't, it won't matter terribly to me, because the key to the casting is not Titus, it's Kono."

She seemed relieved to abandon the subject. "Yes, I agree."

"And there's only one man I know who can play Kono."

"And he's turned it down."

"I wasn't thinking of Poitier."

"Who?"

"Julo."

She blanched. He thought she would be ill. "You don't mean that?"

"Yes, I do."

"I won't do the picture if you're serious."

"Calla—listen—before you back yourself into a corner—listen."

"I won't!" She lashed out. "My God, he's not even an actor!"

"He's nothing *but* an actor."

"The worst kind. You'd never be able to get one honest word out of him."

"Let me worry about that."

"While I worry about *him*."

He could see her getting more and more upset. He started to say something to ease her mind, but she interrupted. "I've been dreading this—that the two of you—"

"Don't say that. There aren't 'the two of you'—we're not a set. There's Julo and there's me."

She pulled herself together and spoke more calmly. "Lucas . . .

you'd be betting everything on a man who is, at best, unstable. Lieutenant Reuss thinks he may be dangerous. 'Vicious' was the word he used. And he *is* a criminal. He's been arrested eleven times."

"I know all about that. Julo told me."

"And yet you would take a chance—"

"Do you—in your heart—do you think Julo is dangerous?"

"In my heart? What kind of ridiculous question is that? I don't ask my heart about dangerous people, I ask my head."

"Well, I'm not a match for that. But do you think I'd risk your life —and mine—or a fifteen-million-dollar picture?"

She seemed incredulous. "You mean you'd really take a chance on him?"

"Yes, I would. Do you know why? Not only because I think he'll be magnificent in the part. But because Julo Julasto is the safest choice."

"Safe? Are you crazy? Safe?"

"Yes. To you and me—no matter how important this film is—it'll be only another picture. But to Julo, this will be his life. Fiction or not, we're doing his *life*. He'll want so desperately to do it—he'll want so desperately for it to be good—that he'll give everything. He'll be the kindest, the most tractable, the hardest-working actor on that set. Nobody will get hurt when Julo is around. He'll be the *guardian* of this picture."

"My God, you're slick."

He winced. He had meant every word. It wasn't a new idea to him, Julo in the role. He had hidden the thought like a sin. But he was convinced that the black man would be superb. As to the menace in him, while Lucas did not discount it, he had also seen the other side, his kindness, his sweetness with Willi, his love, and most of all, the intensity of his yearning.

"I'm sorry I said that, Luke."

"I have a strong feeling about this, Calla. I think he'd be exciting in the part—and unique."

"Who'd ever back the picture with him in it?" she asked. "Julo's not exactly a name to enrich a package, is he?"

"That's a reasonable worry, and if films were made on reason . . . But this is better than reason, it's a second sight. It might be the risk that would kill us. On the other hand, it might bring us to life—quicken us—so that the picture *will* be made, and made better than we dreamed." He paused, seeing that she was not going to respond. "However, if I don't have you to back me up, it's useless—nobody will accept him."

It would be ill-advised to press further, he decided.

"Let me sleep on it," she said.

"All right. But I want you to know, I won't push and shove. I won't try to maneuver you—I promise. If you're really frightened of the man—"

"I'm sick to death of my goddamn frights!"

An outcry. Full of fury, full of pain.

He wanted to take her in his arms, to comfort her.

"All right, Luke," she said. "Give him the part."

He was amazed, not sure she meant it. "Don't do it on impulse."

"Impulse is the only way I can do it."

"Are you sure?"

"Yes."

"Shall I call him now?"

They were sitting at the counter in the kitchen. She silently slid the phone along the tiles so he could reach it.

He dialed the number. In a moment, someone answered. It was Darra. The old man was barely audible.

"Julo isn't there," Lucas reported. "Darra says he'll be back in the afternoon."

He thanked her for the lunch, got up from the counter and murmured that he would call later, after he talked to Julo. She was distracted, her mind on the black man. The worry in her face had not passed. And he realized, as he departed, that he had talked her into something. Both of them might regret it.

15

A wonderful thing might be happening, Calla thought. Perhaps her courage was coming back. She had agreed to do a risky film . . . and today she had accepted Julo as her leading man. She felt a stir of pleasure. An old, friendly sensation, the exhilaration in the gamble. How euphoric to realize that her backbone had not entirely withered, that she could still take chances, that excitement could neutralize dread.

It was almost sunset when Lucas called. Hearing his voice, her own voice lilted. "Did you reach him?"

"He turned it down."

"What?"

"He turned the part down, Calla. He said absolutely he won't play the picture."

"I can't believe it. Why?"

"I don't know."

"What did he say—what reason?"

"He wouldn't give a reason."

"Well, what did *you* say? Did you tell him what trouble we're having casting the part?"

"Yes, I did. And I told him the picture would probably not be made if he doesn't play it."

"And?"

"And there was a long silence . . . and a click."

Hanging up, Calla kept thinking how incredible it was. She would have wagered anything that the man would stake his life to play the part.

She watched the sun disappear. It had all been so useless, such a waste of high resolve. Just as she was conditioning herself for a hazard, Julo Julasto was no longer a threat.

There was also no longer a film, so far as she could see. The "package" had not materialized. If it hurt her this much, how could Lucas stand it? She called him back to offer a drink.

"Thanks, Calla, but I'm afraid I'll blubber," he said. "Now, don't you worry—I'm going to make this happen. *Happen.*"

The valiant unflinching idiot, she thought. Doesn't know when he's beaten, when it's time to strike his colors and get drunk.

She did. Not purposely. She just wanted a little brandy to lift her spirits. But the first snifter did nothing for her, and the second was gone before she knew it. Even when she was on her third, she could still taste the bitter irony of the day. Nothing was left but brandy.

Not that brandy was to be sneezed at. It made her recall other valors of the past, the days when she was daring ridicule and joblessness and failure and cops. Come to think of it, Julo was a toy pistol compared to the artillery she had been up against. And with the liquor whipping up a daring she currently had no use for, she felt as if she could wage war against a war once more, alone.

And I could wage him too, that bastard, Julo What's-his-face. I could take him on myself and beat him, bust his chops, exterminate the goddamn Gorá, Goray, Gorúmm!

She called information and got his telephone number in Redondo. Speak slowly, she told herself, speak carefully, you may be—what was the decorous word for pissed?

"Hello," he said.

"This is Calla Stark."

The silence was so long that she thought they had been disconnected. "If you're calling about my playing Kono, I've already said no to Lucas."

"I know that. Why?"

"Do I have to give you a reason?"

"Well, you didn't give Lucas a reason, and you have to give one to somebody."

The alcohol lent logic to her statement. But he asked: "Why?"

" 'Why' is not a fair response." Her voice was lofty, but her speech was thick. "Could we discuss it?"

"Aren't we doing that?"

"I mean in person."

Long stage wait, she thought, his pace needs speeding up.

"When will you be here?"

"I'm leaving now."

Am I sober enough to drive? Shall I take a cold shower or have a cold thought? I could wash my face in snow, if it were snowing. She opened the freezer compartment of the refrigerator, got two ice cubes and rubbed one on each eyelid.

Three quarters of the way to Redondo, she pulled over onto the safety lane, and parked. What an idiot I am, what a damn fool thing to do. The man is dangerous; Reuss said so. But then, looking back on some of the reckless chances she had taken . . . No matter . . . her valor muscles needed exercise.

When she arrived at the beach road, she looked up at a heaven so theatrically hung with stars that she wanted glorious lines to speak, but the best she could manage was, "Starlight, star bright . . ." *You* be star bright, she instructed herself: watch every word you say.

Darra was waiting for her. So was Julo. The handsome man was fully dressed this time; no silver nakedness. He wore subtler clothes, the expensive window-wear of Beverly Hills haberdashers, a beige cotton shirt with a muted, silky gloss, the trousers carefully tailored to look perpetually pressed, and soft leather half-boots that had a deep, warm glow of amber. He gestured her to a seat, but didn't speak. Poking the fire a little, he watched the sparks, more intent on where they went than on whether she had arrived. At last, he turned.

She saw why he had not faced her. He was angry.

There were no preliminary courtesies. "I turned Lucas down."

"Yes, I know."

"Why don't you let it go at that? Why do you have to push things?"

"Why did you turn him down?"

"Lucas is my friend—I trust him. If I wouldn't tell him, why would I tell you?"

"Does it have to be a mystery?"

"It's none of your business."

"Look, I've come all the way from the city—"

"Go back."

She didn't get up to go. Instead, she shifted her attention to the fire. The intoxication was passing, but the warmth of the blaze made her a little dizzy.

"Are you drunk?" he said.

"I was, but I'm sobering up."

"Go home."

"The first time I met you, you told me how much this film would mean to you. More than it would mean to Lucas or me—and I believed it. Has anything changed?"

"Yes. He asked me to play a part."

"I should imagine that would make it mean even more to you."

"Are you telling me what it would mean? You don't have the vaguest goddamn notion."

"If you say no to this, the picture will probably not be made."

"Don't hang that on me. I hate it that it won't be made—hate it! I'm always getting it that way—somebody gives me red roses, and they turn into shit."

"Maybe if you agreed to—"

"I can't!"

It was not all anger; desperation. "Why can't you?"

"I told you to go home—didn't I tell you to go home?"

"Why are you angry?"

"What do you want me to be? Polite—happy—comical? Shall I do my showbiz nigger for you?"

He began to strum an imaginary banjo, laughed a phony yach-yach and started to sing "Swanee River" in a high falsetto voice. She felt ice down her spine.

"Would you please stop that."

He stopped instantly. "Why? Scare you?"

It's what he wanted her to confess. "No, you don't."

"You sure I don't scare you? Didn't that cocksucker Reuss tell you enough to scare you shitless?"

"He told me some things."

"Did he tell you I killed somebody?"

"He said you were charged with it."

"Well, I did kill somebody. In Knoxville. A woman. I took a jack-knife and sliced her heart out, and held it dripping in my hand until it didn't beat any more. In Atlanta, I molested a nine-year-old, and stuffed her in a culvert. When the culvert began to stink, they dug her out and locked me up. I've sold dope to kids in schoolyards, and I'm still doing it. You want me to go on?"

"Those are milk and water. Have you got any bloody ones?"

The soft crackle of burning wood. A log shifted in the grate.

"You never killed anybody, did you?" she said.

"No."

"Or molested a little girl."

"No."

"Or sold dope."

"No, not even that. A dull life. During a riot in Watts, I ran off with a TV set."

"And assorted con jobs."

"Nobody hurt—except in the pocket."

"Then why should I be afraid of you? You're not dangerous."

"Wrong."

He was no longer acting, nor was he tense. Loose now, he was unmasked, real. He might have been harmless when he bore false witness against himself, but simply standing there, with his powerful arms dangling free, and the look of truth on his face, he was frightening. All the prancings and caperings, all the clown's motley he wore were meant to disguise only one thing: fury.

She wished she weren't sobering so quickly.

"You haven't even begun to use it, have you?" she asked.

"Use what?"

"Your rage."

A glance at her. "Not yet."

He was losing his easiness, returning to a tension he felt more at home with. Even his smile tightened. It became a weapon, with her as target. "You haven't seen it yet."

"Will I?"

"Is that a request?"

"No. Just asking."

"If you don't get out of here, I might use it."

"Why?"

"Because I want to fuck you."

"Would that be an act of rage?"

"With you it would be."

"Why?" she said again.

"I hate your guts."

"Why?"

"Because you're a white Hollywood whore."

"The first time we met you treated me like a queen."

"Queen whore."

"But I'm not."

"That's what you're here for, isn't it?"

"Whoring? I don't think so. What would I get out of it?"

"A leading man, white lady, a leading man."

"You don't mean what you're saying. You're shrewder than that."

"In your business, women sleep with men to *get* parts. You're a star—you'll sleep with me to *give* one. It's pretty much the same."

"You really think I'm here to sleep with you?"

"If you're not, you're here for something worse."

"Like?"

"Cocktease."

Then he said, without emphasis, "Do you know that half the time a black man's up for raping a white woman, it's because she teased his cock. Do you know that?"

"I haven't any statistics on the subject," she said. "In any event, it's not applicable—I'm not here to tease you."

"Then take your clothes off."

She had thought they were playing abstractions, a game of insolences, where indignities were swatted around like badminton birds. Suddenly the winged words were bullets. He had armed himself years ago with rancors; he had murder on his mind.

"I said take your clothes off."

Escape. She got up and started away from him.

Suddenly, like an animal, he was at her. A predator with prey, he was clawing at her, ripping her clothes.

"Stop," she said. "Stop!"

She heard the rending sound before she saw him tear at it, her blouse. She struck back at him, at air, his face, at nothing, shouting, crying *stop, stop,* and kept striking at him. The blouse was gone and he was twisting her, turning her, his strong arms at her and around her, twisting as if she were a toy, pulling at her skirt, and as she tried to break out of the dizzying orbit, tried to run, he struck at her face and struck again. She fell, she rose, fell tripping over him, and he continued to tear at her clothes. She bit at something, his hand, his arm, crying *stop,* and bit again and felt the hard fist crashing at her face. Then she lay on the floor, not altogether naked, yet bare enough to be ashamed and angry and weeping, and ashamed, ashamed.

He stood over her, looking at her semi-nudity, the disorder of being not one thing or another, the ignominy, the ugliness of half-clothing, neither woman nor chaos. And she thought, what do I do now, what do I do when he comes down on me?

He was in no hurry. He stared down at her body, slowly from head to foot, lingering, abusive, at her breasts, her thighs. He stared her more naked than she was. And the staring was worse than the ripping at her clothes had been, less escapable. Still, he did not fumble at a button or a belt, did not touch his own clothing. That too was an injury—his clothes in order, a self-possession, and her half-nudity, a shamefulness.

"Get dressed and go away," he said quietly. "Show them your torn clothes and your beat-up face—and tell them you've been raped. Tell them a black buck nigger raped you. Get out of here."

He turned and walked slowly to the fireplace.

Her impulse was to take a knife to him, her impulse was to snatch her clothes and run outdoors somewhere, dress in darkness, do everything in darkness, no light on her fury and her shame. But as she started to gather her things, she said: It's over, the worst is over. The rape didn't happen and yet the rape was done, and I must try to understand the difference. She felt the sobs coming, the racking cries like vomits of heartbreak, and she could have killed herself for giving him the satisfaction of the sound.

All at once the miracle happened. She had herself under control. It was as if her brain had been irradiated with a terrible and wonderful vision:

She would not run away. She would fight. He—not she—would be the loser.

She had all her clothes under her arm. Only a shoe was missing, and she found it. I may look like a ruin, she told herself, and there is no dignity in torn underwear or the blood that's dripping from my cheekbone, but his hardly mussed clothes would not cover him any longer. She would strip him bare.

"Bathroom," she said.

He pointed. She went into a black hallway, fumbled for a door, felt a knob and turned it. Inside, she patted at the walls and flipped the switch. The white light stung like antiseptic. She washed her face and hands. She put her clothes on. The rip in the blouse would be unmendable; the swelling, the cut lip, the cheekbone would heal in a few days. She had no comb, so she wet her hands, dampened her hair and coiffed it with her fingers.

She must remind herself: The victor, I am the victor. Tell yourself you're strong. Use it as a key word, Strong.

Taking a long deep breath, she reentered the room. He was staring in the opposite direction. When she approached the lighted area, he still did not look at her.

"There's some stuff in the medicine chest," he said.

An added affront: without looking at her, prescribing Band-Aids. "Never mind," she said.

"Go home." His voice was low.

"No."

He was surprised and gave her a glance, then looked at the fire again. He waited, and when she didn't say anything or do anything or depart. "You want to see me crawl? I won't. Go home."

"You have to tell me why."

"Why I did that? Jesus."

"No. Why you turned down the part."

"I won't tell you that."

"You owe it to me."

"Crawl, huh?" It was a growl. "You want to see me crawl."

"If that's the way you get around."

"What do you want to hear, white lady—some more lies?"

"No."

"Everybody wants lies."

"Not me."

"You too. It's the only language people understand. Fabulisms, Lucas calls them, but that's bullshit. Lies."

"I'm beginning to know you, Julasto," she said. "If you lie to me, I'll see right through it."

She was bluffing. She didn't know him any better now than she ever had.

She felt a drip of blood coming downward on her cheek from the cut on her cheekbone. She had an impulse to wipe it away. But he might see the gesture. Either way she would be wounded—weakened— and she must not let him see the slightest sign of it. Strong. Keep saying it: Strong.

She challenged: "Are you afraid to tell the truth about yourself?"

He looked at her. He handed her a handkerchief. This time she did not toss it into the fire. She wiped the blood briefly, then returned his property by dropping it on the table.

She persisted. "The truth . . ."

"You wouldn't know it if you heard it."

"That excuses all the bullshit, doesn't it?"

"What if I were to tell you . . ." He stopped.

"Go on," she said.

"What if I were to tell you that the fire you saw me flaming in— that was no trick."

"If it's not a trick, what is it?"

"Ha! I'm standing up there on the fire mound. The flames are beating around me in a roar. The heat is enough to twist an iron bar. I feel it. I feel it on my skin, in my blood, in my bones—and it doesn't hurt me. It doesn't hurt me, white lady—and it's not a trick. No trick, Miss Calla, no double shuffle, no abracadabra, no junko-bunko. *No trick.* And the only thing that burns are my sins. For one moment of fiery hell I am burned clean. I am seared of all my thievings and whorings and all my murderous hatreds. I come out pure and saved, and it's all done by faith! By faith in God and resurrection! By faith alone!" His voice had risen in defiance. Now he asked quietly. "What if I were to tell you that?"

"I wouldn't believe it."

"And you're right, Miss Calla. You're absolutely right to disbelieve it. It's a lie."

But he didn't speak with his usual bluster. Not a hoot of derision, no mocking laughter over having fooled a gullible idiot. Perhaps he himself, in the bitter half smile, might be the butt of his ridicule.

"You tell me you go through fire by faith alone. You say it's the truth, you say it's a lie. Which do you believe?"

"Both." Perhaps his laughter was not at her. "You think I'm a little crazy, don't you?"

"Maybe more than a little."

"White lady, you—are—right. The nigger's deranged. The black baby was born with stars in his head and fire in his belly. He got dreams of sleepin' in the lap of the Lord."

"And he has terrors."

"Even the Lord had terrors."

He was back in his serious mode, and she wanted to keep him there. "You know . . . I think you do believe in magic."

"And miracles, yes."

"And life everlasting."

"Oh yes!"

"And even God."

"How can you say 'even'? Don't you believe in Him?"

"God today is lobotomy tomorrow."

"Don't be smart, white lady!"

He said it in a rage. Not as if he were talking about a God of goodness but a Fury of murder. He was dangerous again, and she recalled her catchword: Strong.

She went back a step. "We've gotten away from the film, haven't we?"

"I haven't been away." He halted, measured her. "Would you believe that once—just once—I did go through those flames without a trick?"

". . . No."

"Would you believe that I *will?*"

"Is that your dream?"

Quick suspicion. "Are you making a joke of it?"

"No. What would we do without our illusions?"

"Exactly," he said. "I would be dead without my illusions. All my life I believe in nothing—*nothing*. And suddenly one of my own fabrications becomes so believable to me—"

"—that you won't perish in the flames."

"No—I won't! I will *live* in them. It's the first and only passion of my life! *I will walk through flames, Miss Calla.*"

"And come out alive?"

"Life resurrected!"

"And it's real to you?"

"So real that if I were to do it in a film, it would become another lie. I would be playing a part—another part. I would be the same goddamn liar I have always been."

"Do you have so little faith that you're afraid to test it?"

"Don't tempt me, Miss Calla. There's the mammon side of me that says Gorá will prosper if the film is made. But there's the God side . . ."

"When does the truth become a lie, Julo? When the camera rolls?"

"Perhaps."

She had a picture of him: An unsteady colossus, astride a chasm. Afraid to raise either foot.

"I don't want to be a showbiz nigger! I want to be a great black man who consorts with the Lord!" He looked upward for help. "Oh murder, what do I do?"

In trouble, he went silent. She too was still. At last:

"You know what you've done?" he said. "You've conned me into confessing a weakness. You forced it out of me—you forced it!"

One rape deserves another, she thought.

16

Lucas was not an early riser, except when shooting a film. He was not altogether awake when Calla called, but felt as if he were hearing one ellipsis after another, she was deliberately leaving out the important words.

"When did he say he would do it?" he asked.

"Last night."

"You saw him last night?"

"Yes."

"Where?"

"In his cottage—Redondo."

"You mean you *went* there, and convinced him?"

"Yes," with a bit of annoyance. "I've said it three times. You're being thick-headed this morning."

He wasn't thick, he was simply trying to hear what she was not telling him. "You did a good job."

"I didn't do a job on him," she said defensively.

"I didn't say 'on him'—I said 'good job.' Congratulations—and thank you, Calla."

"That's better." She went right on. "And I got a call from Lily. Dyer Addison is changing the date of our meeting."

"To when—next year?"

"No. He wants to move it up. Can you pull yourself out of there in a half hour?"

"Now?"

"As soon as you can."

". . . Julo really said yes?"

"Julo said yes."

"Someday you'll tell me how you did it."

"I didn't sleep with him, Lucas."

She said good-bye, then had an afterthought. "By the way, I look like hell. I had a little car accident and bruised my face. I'm going to be inches thick with makeup."

"An accident? Are you all right?"·

"Oh yes," she said airily. "I'm fine."

Julo. How did she do it? Why did it rattle him, why was he looking in the wrong drawers for socks and underwear? She owed nothing to Luke, and was doing the director's work. If she and Julo were sexually attracted, so much the better. There were two difficult love scenes in the script, and if Rachel and Kono were not erotically excited, he could lower the lights and trick the looks and leers but in the inquest of the tight two-shot lies would be told. Emotion in the audience came from emotion between the players, and it was no fluke that the leading man and woman of many a film found themselves in bed together, off screen as well as on. I should feel lucky, he told himself; I won't have to synthesize that sexual ion, that electric charge that ignites the theater. Action!

Then why wasn't he crowing? Surely, it wasn't as simple as jealousy. Not once in his career had he fallen in love with his leading actress; not once, the between-takes diddling with the star. The hell with them.

He burned his scrambled eggs and spilled coffee on his leg. The hell with breakfast too.

He rushed, hating to be the last arrival at a meeting, always certain that the most important statement had been uttered the instant before his entrance. When he got to Lily's office, the others were all there, and apparently the important statement had been uttered. Calla was grave and quiet, considering whatever it was that Addison had propounded, zeroing her concentration down to the head of a pin, counting angels. Lily was eager, and Dyer was epiphanous.

"It was lightning," he said. "When I got the idea, it was lightning. Didn't I say 'create'? Wasn't that the word I used—'create'? Create the package, that's the whole kumquat, create the package. Well, if others won't do it, I will! If the river won't flow to Mohammed, let Mohammed flow to the river. Do you get my drift?"

He laughed at his wit, and Lily, hiding her chagrin, joined him.

"Do you flow with the current, O'Hare?" he cried. "Do you flow?"

"I float along a little way, but I'm not sure where we're going."

"I told the others—now I'll tell you." Dyer paused as if to unveil a work of art. "I've thought of the perfect man for the part of Kono."

"Yes? Who?"

"He's a name. A big name."

"A black actor with a big name—whom we haven't considered?"

"Well, not a picture name."

"Theater?"

"No. TV."

"You mean Lem Dorcas?"

"First shot!" Dyer exploded with delight. "Lem Dorcas! First shot!"

Lucas fought an impulse to hide. "He's a saloon singer."

"Let's start from a more creative angle, Lucas. His television show —what's the name of it?"

"*Clifford's Club*," Lily said.

"It's way up there, isn't it?" her boss continued. "Number three, number four? The man can't walk down the street without the kids ripping him apart. He's one of the biggest names in show business. Right, Lily?"

"One of the biggest, yes."

"He's not an actor."

The instant he said it, Luke realized he had blundered. Neither was Julo.

"What do you mean, Dorcas is not an actor?" Dyer said. "What's he doing in *Clifford's Club*?"

"It's a door-slamming farce," Luke replied. "All he has to do is come in on cue."

"Who was it that said farce is the hardest thing to play? Who was it, Lily?"

"Let me think," she muttered.

"Now, you know, Lucas—if a man can play farce, he can play anything. Ask Lily—ask Calla, for Pete's sake. Am I right, Calla?"

"No, you're wrong."

"Then you're not flowing with me." He was aggrieved. "Perhaps you can't read the whole *terrain*, but you should know how the *river* runs. What do we need in the part? First instance, we need a name— nobody's going to deny that, I hope. Second instance, we need a handsome black—and Lem Dorcas is the image of Sidney Poitier."

"He's nothing like Poitier," Lucas said.

"Of course he is. He looks like Poitier, walks like Poitier, acts like Poitier. My God, he's even married to a Jewish girl."

Calla said quietly, "He's a nice man, but he has no grandeur."

"He's two inches taller than Poitier. Right, Lily?"

Lily pretended to be rearranging things on her desk. "About two inches, yes."

Dyer stopped, realizing that nobody was looking at him. Even Lily, embarrassed, was no longer meeting his glance. He reddened and didn't know what the next step might be. But he forged ahead. "I think we've got something in Lem Dorcas. He's a name that'll draw the kids. We need the kids. We can't simply have a middle-aged picture, you know—there are fifty million adolescents in the country. Right, Lily?"

"About thirty million, I think."

"That was yesterday." How differently he told a joke now, as if he no longer needed them to laugh; in fact, forbade it. Then he concluded:

"Will you consider him, Lucas?"

Calla looked at the director; he knew she was telling him to be tactful. "I'll tell you why I can't consider him, Dyer. No matter how popular and attractive Dorcas is, his quality is thin and pinched and miniature. Most of his success, I think, comes from the fact that audiences feel superior to him—tall as he is, he's smaller than life. That makes him funny and pathetic, but he could never make you angry or outraged or afraid. There's no tragedy in him."

Dyer turned to wood. "That's only words to me, Lucas. I sent the script to Dorcas and he loves it. Point is, if you take him, we've got a picture. If you don't, we don't."

The ultimatum was distinct.

"Then we don't, I guess," Luke said.

Dyer's hands went up in the air. "Okay, the picture's off."

"Yes, I guess it was inevitable," the director said.

He would have to advance at a tangent, he admonished himself, but he was not certain how to start. "We never could have made it, could we, Dyer? Too bad—you're a very shrewd man."

The flattery heightened interest in the room. He could see Calla's puzzlement. Perhaps he should not have used the compliment so quickly, it sounded fulsome. But probably not to Addison, who would be quick to accept an award. Yet, I must be specially cautious not to underestimate him, Lucas speculated. Fatuous as he might be, he was

craftier at deal-making than Lucas was. Don't shit him, Lily had
warned, and Lucas was about to try.

"Now that it's over," the director resumed, "I wish you would tell
me something, Dyer. Just as a matter of self-education, I'd like your
opinion."

"On what?"

"Let's say you own this project—with a problem script, which I
grant you it is, and a director who's not an asset but a liability—but
you've got Calla Stark. With all those minuses, she's the only plus.
What sort of budget would make this picture . . . viable?"

"None."

"Come on, Dyer—with Calla Stark?"

"You mean playing it close?"

"Close, close."

"Five million. How about it, Lily—five? Six?"

"Six, tops."

Luke pretended worry. "That's all, huh?"

"Six at most, Lucas. And understand, that setup wouldn't interest
me in the least."

"Oh, I know, I know."

Now that he was being flattered as the wise adviser, and would
have no responsibility as a constituent, Dyer relaxed. Generous with expert counsel, he became a cautioning parent. "And it shouldn't interest
you either, Luke. First instance, with only Calla to sell—excuse me,
Calla, no offense—this film would limp, foreign. And it would die in the
boonies. And—second instance—the script can't be *made* with only one
star, it *demands* a second one."

"Well, there I have to disagree with you, Dyer. Now believe me, I
think you're mighty smart about all the rest of it, but on that point, I
don't think you're being . . . creative."

"I'm not?"

"In packaging, I mean."

"How so?"

"Well, let's suppose you could get an actor that nobody's seen
before—a new face—a new excitement—somebody you could call . . .
the Fire King."

"You mean the actual guy?"

"Julo Julasto."

"Not worth a nickel at the box office."

"You think not, huh? Well, it's only hypothetical, you'd never get him. The first thing he tells you: 'It's a real fire—no trick, no performance.' He hates people to think he's only a performer. But if you could get him—hypothetically, you understand—*if* you could, what a build-up you could do on him. A film king is a real king! It's a cult epic."

"And a cult flop."

"You're right, Dyer—if you're only making a picture. But you're creating an *event*. You're originating a myth! When that great, massive, wonderful figure walks through those roaring flames—"

"The audience won't believe it."

"But he *does* it—Julasto actually does it!"

"Tell it to Peoria. They're used to movie flimflam. Special Effects. Even if it's real, they'll call it fake."

"That's exactly what you sell in your advertising, that it's not a fake. That a man actually walked through fire to make this film—and he's alive to tell it."

"Never—you'd never make an audience believe it."

Luke pretended to give up. "Okay, it doesn't matter. We couldn't in a million years get Julo to play it."

"Good, then nobody's fighting."

Luke was quiet. So were the others. Calla sat with her eyes averted, one hand covering her mouth. He wondered what she was trying so hard not to disclose. Certainly the news that Julo had accepted the part was no longer a useful secret. The project was cold.

"Does he really do it?" Dyer asked.

Luke pretended not to know what he meant. "Do what?"

"Walk through fire?"

"You see? Everybody will want to know the answer to that."

"Well, does he?"

"Yes, he does."

"It's not a trick?"

"Define 'trick.' "

"I don't believe he does it."

"He would probably perform it—in the flesh—on the release of the picture."

"Really? As a side show?"

Dryly, "Well put."

"It would be good exploitation—I have to admit that."

Luke went into reverse. "Forget it, Dyer. We could stand on our heads and never get him for the part. Forget it."

"Will you please stop saying 'forget it,'" Dyer said irritably. "I have absolutely no interest in your picture. I'm simply curious about the man. What's he like?"

The director was about to describe him, when he was struck with a god-sent notion. "Ask Calla."

Addison turned to her. "You met him, didn't you?" As she nodded, "Did you like him?"

"Well, you don't simply 'like' Julo Julasto—you're bedeviled by him." She spoke her lines with a bit of bravura. Nothing she said was factually untrue, yet it was conference hype, which made it all a deception. "You can't take your eyes off him, and every word he says—by the time it reaches your brain, it has a hundred meanings. In his presence, you find yourself believing the incredible. Without performing, without being an actor, he's a star." Then sighting Dyer perfectly as her prey, she gunned him down: "And he's a great big black tower of sex."

She glanced at Luke as if to apologize for her meretricious description. But the portrait had done its work.

Dyer smiled; gambler with a buried ace.

Lily, also smiling, said, "Calla Stark, in *The Fabulist*, featuring the Great Big Black Tower of Sex."

"Wish we could put that on a marquee," Dyer said.

"Forget it." Luke turned away. "You'll never get him."

"Why the hell do you go on that way, Luke?" Dyer erupted. "What makes you think he'd turn down the part?"

"He's the head of a cult, for Chrissake. He's a king! Would you ask King Carlos to play himself in a film, would you ask Queen Elizabeth? Christ, would you ask Ronnie Reagan?"

"Sure I'd ask—why not? And if you don't ask, I will."

Luke didn't dare look at Calla. "You'll get turned down, Dyer."

"Well, perhaps. But before anybody does any asking—can you do this film for six?"

"Never."

"What, then? Give me a figure."

"Ten."

"No deal. You're out of your mind. . . . Seven."

"I couldn't possibly transport a whole company, shoot nearly every scene on location, and come in under nine."

"Only one star, Luke—you don't have much above the line. What do you think, Lily, can we stretch to seven and a half?"

"It's spooky," she said.

"Exactly—spooky. I'll tell you what, Luke—I'll go for eight, if you cut above the line."

"The only big salary is Calla's."

"Yours."

Luke had been expecting it. "I'll defer half my money until payoff."

"Well, that's a start." Dyer turned to Calla.

"Half," she said.

"And Megan won't renege?"

"I won't renege."

"Well, it's eight million—but we're not committed without Julasto," Dyer warned.

"I'll do my best to get him."

"Your best won't start the camera, Luke. The deal's off if you can't deliver him."

"I'll deliver him."

Dyer Addison let go. He grinned. The contest became a celebration. "Congratulations, Lucas. You know what you did, my friend? You had an overpriced product, and what did you do with it? You put the damn thing into a smaller package, and you reduced the price. Well, goddamn it, you turned it into a bargain! It's a bargain, Lucas—it's a sale! A fire sale!"

They all laughed.

"Cheers, everybody!" Lily cried. "It's Carmel's first picture!"

Dyer bestowed the chaplet of laurel. "You're a hell of a packager, Lucas!"

"Here's to *The Fabulist*," Calla said.

Lucas wondered whether the *f* was small or capitalized.

17

She watched Luke conning the producer into accepting Julo in the role, she watched in fascination. He had lured Calla into contributing her widow's mite, but it was his show. And he had played it deftly, turn by turn. Originally, when she had first met the director, she was struck by his abrasive candor; his honesty had seemed a vice. Now, she had seen signs that he had another reed to his flute: cunning. And observing the flutist hypnotizing the cobra, she was not sure which was the more insidious, the musician or the serpent.

It was disquieting. What tune will he play for me? What if he performs a similar or subtler melody, will I shimmy to his music? Well, what would be wrong with that? Doesn't an actress yearn to fall under the spell of her director? Wasn't acting the place where remoteness was dangerous, where distance lent disenchantment?

He was paying no attention to her these days. Now that the Carmel Pictures deal had been set, Lucas was hard at it, reworking the budget, hiring staff and crew, casting the smaller parts, designing the production. He called even less frequently than before, and spoke in half sentences, edgy, distracted. She hadn't realized how she looked forward to their conversations on the phone.

One morning he came for breakfast. He was tightly drawn. His besetting worry was that they couldn't find a suitable location. The second unit people had gone to a number of places—Tennessee, the Carolinas, Louisiana—but were unable to find a river village close to a fair-sized town, one that seemed misleadingly peaceful, with an atmosphere that might suggest an eerie, ominous beauty.

"The Bayou," she said.

"Which bayou?"

"No—never mind."

It was a blunder. As the name passed her lips, she felt a shiver of cold remembrance. What a terrible thing it would be to have to return to Ashton, to relive Mina's death.

"A bayou sounds like a good idea," he said. "Is it an actual swamp?"

"It's a beautiful marsh," she said compulsively. "But I don't think it's suitable."

She wanted the subject finished.

Luke pursued it. "Is there a river? We need a river."

"There's a river."

"Where is it?"

"Near Ashton, Mississippi." Then, quickly, "I would rather we didn't go there, Luke. . . . It's where Mina died."

"I see." Instantly, he was contending with restraint. His manner was considerate. "Calla, I don't want to stir things up for you. And if you say no, that's the end of it. But the place does sound like a possibility. And we're stuck. Would you mind if I just sent one of the second unit people down to have a look?"

She minded acutely. Yet, she had to face the fact that, with the passage of all those years, she still had not exorcised the guilt of Mina's death. The details were as clear as if they had happened yesterday. Would she have to go through life without laying her child's ghost to rest? Might this not be a heaven-sent chance to free herself of the aching memory?

"No, I don't mind."

But when he departed, the apprehensions returned. She had to rout them by telling herself that he would reject the Bayou, there were too many things about the place that would not be acceptable.

The Bayou, she heard from Luke a few days later, was perfect. What was most beguiling was the little village of Gurries. The place was the precise background for the otherworldly mood he needed. He would have to make a few changes in the script, he added offhandedly, but the "aura" was worth it.

The rest of the day was full of petty accidents. She placed a coffee mug too close to the edge of a table; its contents slopped all over the rug. You could have prevented Luke from going to Ashton; why didn't you? She burned her fingers on a pan she thought had cooled. Because you *wanted* to go to Ashton, you're *drawn* to it. She mislaid her house keys. You *have* to go back. You have to measure the size of your grief, then and now; the depth of your culpability, and will it never end? You have to make peace with the memory of your daughter.

She saw Mina—this very minute—playing on the kitchen floor.

Yes . . . return to Ashton.

While Luke was busy, she tried to fill her waiting time by spending longer periods with Willi. However, even if the patient was improving steadily, her memory was still faulty, and she was in many ways unreachable. It was odd: Calla missed her more when she was partially present than when she had been comatose.

Erratically, she began to miss her father as well. More often than before, she telephoned him, and was wistfully amused at his annoyance. Is anything the matter, he always wanted to know, why are you calling, are you all right? Once, she let it slip that she was lonely, and he didn't hear her. What did you say? Never mind, she replied. As for himself, he was healthy and happy, still running the drugstore at seventy-four, and none too communicative with a daughter who talked too eccentrically for his taste, and who no longer knew the names of his customers and neighbors. Ah yes, he might say, acting in another movie, are you? Good, good, keep working. Thanks for the shearling slippers, he repeated for the third time. No, thank you, Callie, nothing else. I'm just fine and dandy, don't need a thing.

Unneeded.

Then she got a present from him. That is, she thought it was from him. She found it on her doorstep and had no notion how it had been delivered. It was about the size of a glove box and the outside wrapper was addressed in quavery handwriting. She opened it.

It was a jackknife with a long blade, covered with dried blood.

She couldn't hold on to it; it clattered to the floor.

Reuss arrived immediately, asked if she had touched the weapon, took it away, sent a man to get Calla's fingerprints and called back the same afternoon.

"There's nothing but you on it," he said. "Not a single fingerprint."

"Brainprint."

"Did you say brainprint? Whose?"

"Mine."

Hanging up, she had a new dread. Funked-out images. Brainprint on the knife, or the knife on the brain? Garbled. Illogical.

Illogical too for the incident to awaken Julo in her mind. Where was he?

He still had not visited Willi. Once, two weeks ago, he had phoned the patient to say he would be there, but had never arrived. Lucas had the explanation. Directly after Julo had made the deal with Dyer Addison—a phone call that lasted five minutes—the man had disappeared. His African shop was still open, but all his encounter meetings had been canceled, and his cottage, emptied. This was on Reuss's account. The detective had been hounding the cult leader, setting a man on him around the clock. Julo had been planning another fire demonstration, but the constant surveillance had worn him down. He dreaded that the detective might, at the last minute, arrest him on a trumped-up charge —anything, fraud, swindling, embezzlement—just to make the headlines. Reuss might even raid the fire demonstration. Whether Julo's anxieties were well founded or not, he felt that to be charged with fakery just before the shooting of the film would be catastrophic not only for the picture, but for Gorá itself. So he had canceled the demonstration, and vanished.

"Will he show up for the picture?" Calla asked.

She could see Luke had a doubt but wouldn't plague her. "I'm sure he will."

It did plague her. Julo was a fugitive by nature, and she was committed to do a picture with him. The electricity he would bring to it might cost . . . what?

Every good thing in her life seemed to cost more than it was worth. She began to sleep for longer periods than usual, and had bad dreams. She began to eat better, and had stomachaches. She caught a cold, then developed a strawberry rash. A strawberry rash, for God's sake.

Stage fright. Don't fret over it, she said. You always have stage fright before the shooting of a picture and before rehearsals for a play; it means nothing.

Bad dreams began to hang on even when she was awake, nightmares in the daytime, a disembodied telephone caller. Or she would run in the bright sunlight of New Forge and not recognize a street or house or tree. Nothing was familiar, and she was familiar to nobody. She was in the night of her childhood. . . . Find me.

As if to prove nobody was looking, two days went by and the phone didn't ring, not once. A famous woman, a major film star on the verge of doing a new film, and—who would ever believe it?—all lines to the outside world were dead.

On the morning of the third day, the phone rang.

"Did you miss me?" the British voice asked.

To prove herself unshaken, she did not mention the knife. "Where've you been?"

"I've been to London to visit the Queen."

"What did you there?"

"I frightened a little mouse under the chair."

"I'm not under a chair. Your knife didn't frighten me."

"I sent it as a warning."

He paused. She gave him no cue to continue. But he did:

"Don't go to Ashton."

Her composure was gone. His power was more awesome than she had imagined; not only to terrify, but to madden.

"But I *am* going to Ashton."

"I think you want to be hurt." She couldn't tell whether it was anger or apprehension. "You court danger to prove you're not a coward. Don't do it—please."

The plea was genuine. It was such an earnest appeal that she had a dazzling thought: *He doesn't want to hurt me. But if I expose myself, he won't be able to resist.*

"Please tell me who you are."

"*Do not go to Ashton.*"

"Who are you? Are you calling for someone else? Who are you?"

He hung up. She phoned the lieutenant. He sounded discouraged; the knife had added nothing useful to the dossier.

"You didn't find out anything new about him, did you?" he said.

"Only that he's under pressure."

"Whose?" When she said she didn't know, he continued evenly. "About the knife—the hospital tests show the blood was probably Willi's. But it doesn't help us very much, does it?" Worse than discouragement; he was vexed.

"Are you closing the case, Lieutenant?"

"No, not at all," he replied. "It's always open. But I have to admit, we can't afford to give it much time, Miss Stark. It wasn't, after all, a murder."

"Well, maybe the Englishman will supply you with one," she said acidly.

He lashed back. "And if he doesn't, you will."

"How?"

"I warned you not to go to Julasto's. You went there and came out with torn clothes and a bleeding face. I told you the man was dangerous—and you found out. Well, you haven't found out the half of it, Miss Stark—and neither have we. If you want to do things on your own, I wash my hands."

He was deserting. She felt deserted by everyone. Lucas was getting further and further away, Megan was in New York, Willi was hardly there, her father didn't need her, and Barney, who had seemed more in need of her than anyone, hadn't put in an appearance or telephoned since the day she had lent him money.

The next day, Barney, unannounced, arrived. He looked healthier than the last time, and was in work clothes, overalls.

"Is it a costume?" she asked.

"It's a uniform—I work for Kleenstrip."

"Porno?"

He laughed. "No. We strip furniture, not people."

"Bare wood, not bare skin."

"Right. Kleenstrip lifts the paint right off your coffee table."

"And puts it where?"

"It's what a lot of people want. Haven't you heard the commercial? 'We'll get your wood ready for paint or for stain—No sanding, no scraping, no blisters, no pain.'"

"What's wrong with your hands?"

"Blisters and pain." He flexed the bandaged hand and grinned. "Kleenstrip keeps the customer from getting them."

"Is it bad?"

"No, not really—most of it's gone. My hands are toughening."

He coughed.

"Fumes too, huh?" she said.

"Some, yes. I have this mask over my mouth and nose. It's a muzzle—no biting, but I bark." He kept on grinning. "I'm okay, Cal, honest. . . . I brought you something."

He reached into his pocket with his left hand and brought out two one-hundred-dollar bills and a fifty. He was embarrassed, but proud. "This is part of it. In about a month I can pay all of it."

"Why don't you wait a month?"

"Because if I pay in installments, I get to see you."

"You could get to see me anyway. You want some dinner?"

"Really? Yes, I'd love it."

It was cold cuts and leftovers. They sprinkled curry powder over everything, and drank three bottles of wine. She ate heartily and so did he, and they laughed together again.

Later, sitting on the verandah, looking down at the lights of Beverly Hills, she asked, "Is it better than acting?"

"It pays well, and it's steady."

"Have you tried?"

"The other thing? Well, yes. I've seen Ken Friedling a few times. But his agency has gotten so big and he's so successful . . . He asked if I'd mind being taken care of by Bill Sohmers. So I met Sohmers, and he looked like he just flunked geometry, and he called me sir. So I got. . ."

"What?"

"Scared." She could feel him shoring himself up. "I'm scared, Cal . . . of everything."

She realized that he needed more help than she was giving him. "That hunter part . . . The film is going non-star, except for myself. Do you really think you can do it?"

"Oh, can I!" Then, clouding. "But getting it is something else."

"Shall I call O'Hare?"

"Would you?" As she got out of her chair. "You mean now?"

"Well—to make an appointment—go and meet him."

Clearly, he was dying for the part, but would not let himself believe he had a chance. "It'll be the same thing, you know. They say they don't want a name, but Jack Lemmon gets it."

"It's not a Jack Lemmon part."

"Everything's a Jack Lemmon part."

"Shall I call?"

". . . Yes."

She rang Luke's number. It was still midevening, but his voice sounded sleepy.

"Not a bad idea," he said. "How come you haven't thought of it before?"

Starting to equivocate, she told the truth. "Too close to home, I guess."

"Will he be?"

"No, I don't think so."

"You're sure? I don't want an old relationship on the screen."

His tone was tough. He didn't have to tell her that making a picture was not a dalliance. "I know what you want," she said.

"No, you don't, but you will." That too was rockier than it needed to be, she thought, but he quickly went ahead. "Can I meet him tonight?"

"Shall we come over?"

"No. I'd rather go to your place, if it's all right."

She had guessed accurately; he was in bed with someone. "Yes, it's all right."

"I'll just get some clothes on."

The moment she hung up, Barney was a different person. While his nerves were as jangled as before, she could see him mustering his nervous energy. He looked at himself in the mirror. His hair was too neatly combed for the part; he tousled it. Glad to be wearing overalls, he said they gave a rough-hewn look to the character he was to play, an outdoors man, careless of appearance, not a button's worth of vanity. Pacing and fidgeting, he suddenly halted, remained stock still, took note of who he was and how he must appear. Then he walked on firmer feet, as though his toes could grab the earth.

"What if he asks me to read?"

"Then you'll have to read."

"But I *can't* read, Cal—you know that."

His panic had returned, with good reason. He was the world's worst sight reader. Even on the set, when he actually had the part, his first walk-through was always tight and withheld, and showed little of that dazzling talent.

"There are only two long dialogue scenes, Barney—and they're both with me," she said assuringly. "I'll go over them with you."

"Wouldn't my chances be better if I tell him I won't read?"

"Not if he wants you to read. Come on, Barney."

Her voice was curt and she walked into the study. They sat on the couch with the script between them and read straight through without interruption or comment.

When the reading was finished, she said, "Let's try it again."

"Didn't have him at all, did I?"

"Well, start with this. You don't like women, especially this one. She's rich and spoiled, and she's a Yankee to boot. You're a hunter, not a cheap backwoods detective, and she's offering you a job—to help her find her son and a black man. You want to spit in her eye and walk away from it, but you're broke, you need the money. So you pretend to be polite, while the subtext of everything you do is your hostility to the woman."

They read through the scene twice. On the third reading, Barney grabbed the part by the scruff of the neck and shook it angrily. It was a retained anger, like the smoke before the blaze. Calla was awed by how much violence he could bring to the role.

They had no time to do the other scene. The doorbell rang. Considering it had been Lucas's suggestion that they meet tonight, he seemed brusque and hurried, as if going through the motions, doing the star a favor. It struck her that the audition would go badly, he wouldn't like Barney at all, and her ex-husband would sink still lower.

"You look great for the part," Luke said. It was a calculated graciousness, the kind proferred to an actor likely to be rejected. "How would you look if you had a stubble of a beard?"

"It comes in lighter than my hair," Barney answered. "A reddish-brown."

"Good."

"Why? Want to hide my weak chin?"

A bid for a compliment; she wished he hadn't said it. However, the compliment came. "You've got a good chin. Just a little stubble, right?"

Luke pointed to the script, which was open, face down on the couch. "I see you've been looking at it."

"Yes," Barney said uncertainly.

"Which scene?"

"When they first meet."

"How'd you like to read it aloud—the two of you?"

"Well . . . I hadn't exactly expected . . . I'm a lousy first reader."

"Good—read it lousy. Don't do anything. Just feel around for it."

He spoke offhandedly, as if he were offering a cashew. Wandering around the room, he read the titles on the bookshelves.

"These O'Neill sea plays—was this the original Modern Library edition?"

"Yes, I had it rebound."

"Holy—! Modern Library in morocco." He plopped down on the linen-covered settee and threw a leg over the arm. "Who says first?"

"I say," Calla replied, and started to read aloud.

The instant Barney spoke his first line, she knew she could relax. He wasn't reading, he was performing. Not ostentatiously, never losing the character, never straying from the intention of the script, every line informed by his contempt for Rachel. As the audition progressed, Luke relinquished his studied casualness, sat upright, then forward in the settee, nodded once or twice and listened.

At the end of the scene, "Terribly interesting," he said. "Both of you—interesting. Now tell me, Barney, what were you going for?"

Encouraged, Barney expanded. He reiterated Calla's analysis of the hunter as if it were his own; indeed, having read the part with such authority, he spoke as if the interpretation had always been his private property.

Lucas kept nodding, occasionally repeating "interesting."

"He really hates her and her kind," Barney concluded. "And he's too honest to conceal it."

"It's interesting," Luke repeated for the last time. "But it's bullshit."

Barney reddened. Calla saw the trembling of the hand that held the screenplay, and inconspicuously relieved him of the manuscript.

"Let me tell you about Titus—some things that are in the script, and some that aren't." He didn't look at Calla, only at Barney. "He used to be a hunter—in the days when there was game in the woods. Now, it's nearly all gone—there's very little that's worth hunting in this part of the South. So he kills alligators and sells the skins. It's against the law. He used to have a kind of sportsman's status, but now he's a poacher, a thief, a waste product. He's embittered—not only at women, at everybody. The only thing he loves is his gun, and even guns could be outlawed if Yankee women like Rachel have their way. Well, how does he adjust to all this failure and loss and anger? He's a shrewd man, he's cunning—and he's got one weapon that's almost as powerful as his gun. His southern charm. He uses it like a rifle. He guns Rachel down in that first scene. She wouldn't know—the audience wouldn't know— that he hates women, that he hates everybody in the world. It's all southern hospitality. And they may even fall in love before the end of the picture. And—Barney—if you show one little shadow of hatred in that first scene, you've blown it."

Before Barney could utter a word, Calla spoke. "I have to take responsibility for his reading, Luke."

"Why you?"

"He didn't have much time with the script—so I gave him my feeling about his character. I told him all that contempt-and-anger stuff."

"Don't direct the actors, Miss Stark."

He said it with a smile, but the needle pierced the skin. He turned quickly away. Having damaged something in the actor, he had mending to do. "You're a good actor, Loftus—you don't have to prove that to me. But I'm wondering how 'honestly' charming you can be when you know what a bastard this man is."

"May I try again?"

"Please."

They started from the beginning once more. For a number of speeches, Barney stumbled and couldn't even manage the words; in his effort to relax, he was playing nothing except his effort to relax. Bit by bit, however, he began to find the track of the scene, and halfway through Lucas murmured that it was good. Now they were almost to the end of the sequence; the dialogue was seemingly easy:

TITUS

Have you ever fired a gun?

RACHEL

I've already told you—I hate guns.

TITUS

Have you ever held a gun in your hand?

RACHEL

No.

As they went through those speeches and a few lines that followed, Lucas interrupted. He got into a chair that was more upright than the settee, leaned forward, his elbows on his knees, his hands tightly clasped. Without unclenching his hands, he gestured to Barney. "You've come through the superficial charm now, you're finished with it. You're going to talk about something that has a heartfelt meaning to you—hunting. There aren't any game animals anymore, but you've got a new kind of prey—a black man. And there are things that you love— guns. So what you say to this woman is going to be intensely personal. You're going to ask her an intimate question. For you, it's the most intimate question you can ask a woman."

"Have you ever fired a gun?"

"Yes. And to Titus, it's as if he's asking if she's still—"

"—a virgin."

"Exactly. And his next question, 'Have you ever held a gun in your hand'?"

"If she's ever touched a man."

Luke nodded. "Now—let's forget the script—the hell with the actual words. Let's improvise, you and I. You ask me those questions and

I'll give you the answers. Let's keep them seemingly objective, but the subtext is not objective, it's deeply personal—it's erotic. However, we've got to hide the lovemaking—don't tell it, only let it *be* there."

They started to improvise the remainder of the scene, supplying their own words, inventing as they went along, yet faithfully expressing the writer's meaning. It was a many-leveled encounter the two men were playing, carnal by intimation, removed from reality, slightly out of focus, and strangely disturbing.

She felt totally out of it. Lucas was enticing the actor, making love to him. And the performer, sensing how rich and right the improvisation was, responding to the excitement of its intimacy, exposing himself with pleasure and without shame, began to fall under the spell of the director as if he were a woman succumbing to a man.

The scene was over, and they did not return to the script. They didn't need to, Lucas said.

"You've got the part."

The odd thing was that Barney did not make a display of his happiness, no nip-ups of pleasure, he didn't even pretend to be surprised. He was still under the spell of the love scene that he and Lucas had woven.

The director, finished now, was hastening to depart. Calla had a twinge of loss, and wanted to detain him.

"Would you like a drink?" she said.

"No, thanks."

He was going back to bed, she felt quite sure.

When he departed, Barney expressed his pleasure in getting the part by snatching up the script and ensconcing himself in the study. Munching apples, he pored over the pages of the screenplay like a monk over vellum.

Calla had a worrisome thing to tell him, and didn't know how to broach it. At last, unable to put it off, she interrupted his concentration.

"The film is going to be shot on location, you know."

"Yes, you said that. In the South."

"In Ashton."

It took him a moment to make the association. She saw the specter in his eyes. "Mina . . ."

"Yes."

"Oh God."

It wasn't only that his face changed; his whole body became frailer. All the improvement in health he had made in the last weeks seemed to have been lost. He was a sick man again, his hands unsteady, his eyes frightened.

Then, by main force, he routed the apparition. He had another presence to deal with: Titus. The actor went back to perusing the script. He could make the hunter more real than the dead child. She envied him.

Willi sat in the second-floor solarium of the hospital, basking in the golden warmth, and smiled to all comers. The change in the patient had been amazing. There had been a succession of a few weeks when, conscious of her scars, she had been in and out of melancholy. Then, as if summarily deciding not to think of them anymore, she had shed her gloom like a dirty cloak. A roseate cheer enveloped her.

Calla saw her mood change overnight—in one afternoon, in fact, when Lucas had brought her a small wooden cat that he had once given her as a present. Calla considered it an exotically beautiful thing, but its eyes worried her, they were so glintingly alive. It was a weird companion to the furry little kitten that she herself had bought for her friend. They were Willi's counterparts, two complementary aspects of herself. With one creature under each arm, she would promenade from her room to the solarium at the head of the stairs, nestle herself into the cushions of the white wicker armchair, and with her pets in her lap, beam at the revolving planet.

At first, Willi conversed very little with anyone, not always trusting herself to speech; but after a while, she progressed to greeting people— not vocally as yet, but with a small wave of the right arm, a gentle half circle, regal, like a beneficent empress. This phase lasted only a few days, then suddenly Willi bloomed. She became giggly and talkative. She had kind words for everyone who entered the solarium, as if she were the inducted hostess for the hospital, its goodwill committee. To the patients, how are you, she would say, I see you're up and moving, or, well, well, no more bandages, what a lovely color in your cheeks. To the visitors she gave only the most gladdening bulletins, the most buoyant gossip she had been told by nurses or overheard from doctors: Your brother's doing very well, his blood count's going up; your father's walking, and I hear they'll soon be putting him on solid food. To everyone she promised faithfully, with well-secured pledges, that good health would be universal.

Since what she looked like did not apparently bother Willi anymore, she didn't seem to notice the unsightly shower cap she wore to cover her unbandaged head. One day, however, Calla caught her fingering the cap from time to time, touching it unpleasantly, and she thought Willi might be in some discomfort.

"Is something wrong?" she asked.

"This damn cap—they've given me a plastic head."

Clearly it was a note of vanity. The wounded woman did not sense the incongruity that it didn't matter what sort of cap she wore; the scars on her face were her most noticeable aspect. However, that afternoon Calla went shopping for another head covering. The best she could find was in an antique shop. It was an old French mopcap, pure creamy cotton with eyelets and embroidery, and faded ecru ribbons. It was charming but ridiculous, and Calla had qualms when she bought it.

Seeing the cap, Willi shrieked with laughter and had to hold her head because her racket made it ache. She discarded the plastic shower cap, and put the antique thing on her head. To Calla's delight, it did not deride Willi. It was such an eccentric frippery, so quaint, that it made her scarred face seem not so bizarre as it had appeared to be.

"It's pretty," Calla said. "Willi, you look sweet."

"Sweet? Old Sneakers Axil?"

The instant she spoke her name, her smile froze. She went white. "Axil—did I say Axil—is that my name?"

"Yes, of course it is."

Willi gripped one of her hands with the other, tightly, as if to cause herself some pain. "For weeks . . . Wilhelmina Axil . . . I've been hearing the name . . . I've been called the name . . . Maybe I've even answered to it. . . . Have I?"

"Yes."

"And I never said, 'It's me.'"

Calla nodded. She had noticed how strange it was, Willi answering to a name, without having an identity. And now she had it.

But there were still gaps in Willi's memory. They could be having a seemingly normal conversation, and suddenly her friend would jump backward a sentence or two, or forget the word for a familiar object, a pencil, a window, a chair. Her memory was capricious; it did not seem to go out of gear in any predictable pattern, or on a course toward deterioration or improvement. And she could not remember a single element or instant of the attack.

At Lieutenant Reuss's suggestion, Calla engaged her in an association game. *Day*, she would say, and Willi would answer *night*. *Red* would elicit *blue—hunger, food—up, down.* But whenever she got anywhere near the attack—

"Car."

"Person."

"Hurt."

"Person."

"Knife."

"Person."

Always the same word, not whether it was a man or woman, tall or short, known or unknown.

It wasn't only the loss of memory that worried Calla, it was Willi's regression to childhood. Lean-minded as she used to be, with a personality that went to muscle, she was now going to marzipan. She was sentimental about the flowers that were sent to her; when they died, she wrangled over having to throw them away. She would not allow her kittens out of her sight; she would not allow the cap that Calla gave her to be washed when it was soiled. When the hospital authorities forbade her to fondle the pigeons on her windowsill, she refused to believe that they might be carrying psittacosis; how could birds be harmful? She watched treacly TV programs and sighed over old ballads; "I Love You Truly" could make her weep blissfully. The only evidence of the erstwhile woman of strength was her undaunted good cheer, her refusal to admit she was often in pain and that her life might be irremediably damaged.

One afternoon, when it was late enough for Willi to have worn down, Calla found her holding court in the solarium, as nippy as ginger, dispensing her panaceas of good cheer and taking huge doses of her own medicine. There was particular cause for her happiness today. The doctor had left word that she was well enough to be discharged, and could go home on Friday.

Home, of course, would have to be Calla's house; who else could look after Willi? Although the patient scoffed at the notion of being tended like an invalid, she did not hide her gladness that Calla wanted so unconditionally to take her in. I won't be any trouble to you, Willi kept saying over and over, I promise I won't be any trouble; and you'll see how soon I'll be back to work.

It was not easy for Calla to bring her home. The actress had long ago made the distinction between loneliness and solitude, and had accepted one as compensation for the other. Even when she could afford to have more help around the place, she preferred to do her own house-

work, put up with her own periodic disorderliness, so as not to have a
stranger underfoot. If there was a servant in the house, it was impossible for Calla simply to take another person for granted. It was not that
people meant too little to her, but too much; loneliness was a trade-off.

Thus . . . much as she loved Willi, she had apprehensions about
having her here twenty-four hours of every day. She didn't mind giving
her guest her own bedroom, for it had a southern exposure and the heat
could be better regulated than in the guest room. Nor was it any great
chore to cook the meals and occasionally, when Willi was having dizzy
spells, carry them upstairs and eat with her friend in the bedroom. In
fact, they made a picnic of it, got silly over sloppy sandwiches and
strange ice cream concoctions with guavas and macadamia nuts and cin-
namon. Sometimes they did not talk at meals, but simply turned up the
music full blast, having Bach and indigestion.

But there was always a subliminal worry. Now and then, Willi forgot where she was; sometimes she wandered around the house, looking
for things that had never been there. Once, a little frightened, wanting
to return to bed, she could not find the stairs, and cried like a forsaken
child. Since Calla always slept with one ear awake, she could hear
whether Willi was wandering again or simply going to the bathroom;
the flush of the john was always a reassurance.

What particularly worried Calla was that she could not always be
at home with the convalescent. There were costumes to be fitted,
hairdo and makeup tests, all the experimentation that had to be done
here, not on location. She returned home one day to find that Willi
had not ventured down the steps to get her already prepared lunch out
of the refrigerator; she had gone to the head of the stairs and gotten
dizzy. That afternoon, Calla employed Grace Lattimer as a live-in assistant.

To add validity to the fiction that Willi was as well as she pretended to be, Calla did not call Grace Lattimer a nurse, although that
was the woman's training. Past sixty-five, she had worked for years as an
RN. While still vigorous, she had been forced to retire from hospital
employment, and had a reluctance to talk about her Social Security status. If she was getting money from the government, she said evasively,
it was her own and she certainly wouldn't lie, for she was a reborn
Christian—thrice reborn, she said, and it had worked every time. Grace
didn't mind having the tiny maid's room, and loved to labor, rabid for
it. If she had been a bit less austere, the other two would not have

made a private joke of her, but she was a caricature of severity and bitterness, as if she brushed her teeth with alum.

Calla imitated the pursing of Grace's lips. "That tight little mouth —do you suppose she put a few stitches in it?"

"A tuck."

"And elsewhere."

They got hilarious and called each other cruel. But they treated Grace quite well and before long developed a fondness for her. Oddly, instead of invading their intimacy, Grace brought them closer, and gave them another, brighter color they sorely needed.

One evening, after a guffawing moment, Willi was suddenly grave. "I know why you hired Grace."

"Of course you do."

"No, not only because you have to go to meetings and fittings and tests. . . . She's for when you go away."

"Yes." Calla admitted it had been uppermost in her mind. "But that's only temporary, Will. I won't be away forever."

"Maybe three months."

She was a child again, unable to judge duration, a week sounding like a year; three months was beyond reckoning. Sometimes, when she noticed these reversions to childhood, Calla gently tried to lead Willi's mind back to a more adult view of things. But latterly she realized that the effort gave Willi too much distress, and it was just as well to treat her as a child, and make a game of it.

"How many days in three months?" Calla asked.

Willi sulked. "I know how many."

"Ten or a hundred?"

She lashed out. "Don't treat me like an idiot!"

For the moment she had had enough of the childhood games. Calla did not know whether it was a good sign, or bad. She tendered an apology of sorts, and Willi too made penitential sounds. But the regrets they expressed were a cosmetic to hide a painful sore. For the rest of the afternoon they were too self-consciously friendly with one another; things might get worse.

Toward evening, Willi said, forlornly, "Do you suppose Julo will ever come and visit me?"

"Of course he will, honey."

"I wonder where he is these days?"

The question, unanswered, lingered in the house like the scent of dying flowers. After a while, Willi asked, "Do you suppose—before you go away—Luke might come and visit?"

It puzzled Calla that the convalescent could recount her remembrances of Julo and Lucas with so many empty spaces in her recollection, yet no uncertainty that she loved them both. Lucas had come to visit Willi the day after her discharge from the hospital. He had stayed long enough to show his affection, but not so long as to tire her. After that time, he had not come again. His visit had set Willi talking about him, piecing together more fragments in the broken chronology, how she had met the director, how they had tried to make love and failed, how they were left with a friendship Willi could not quite describe. It was not enough to say simply that she adored him; there were mystic overtones to her worship of the man. To a woman who sought the occult reason for the most mundane phenomenon, a true artist was touched by an arcane power. He was a medium between the worlds of material and essence. Lucas was, to her, the poet of what she had always considered inexpressible. Having written *The Fabulist* as a direct result of his relationship with her and Julo, he had, in effect, conferred a wonderful gift upon them. It made him a progenitor in her eyes, an archetypal father in a myth. Although it saddened her that he came to see her so infrequently, she was commonsensical enough to realize that mythical figures did not materialize at will.

"If you want him over," Calla said, "why don't you call him?"

"I'm shy about it."

"I'll call him . . . for you."

"Thank you, Calla."

On his visit, Lucas brought good news. He had heard from Julo. Where the fugitive was phoning from Luke did not know, nor had he tried to pry the information out of his friend. The black man's assurance that he would be in Ashton on the first day of shooting was enough for the director, and an occasion for relief and celebration.

Except for the news of Julo, Luke's visit was a disappointment to Willi. He was loving enough with the woman, hugging and kissing her, but his mind was elsewhere. He was full of the film, of course, and it was only natural for it to be his sole subject of conversation, especially since he was leaving for Mississippi tonight. He would go ahead of the cast, he said, to complete the final location details before shooting time. The next few weeks would be a madness of work, with sets to finish, and logistics and schedules, and the battle of revised budgets. As his picture palaver continued, Willi faded and went quiet. Then suddenly her voice—clear and cool:

"Why are you going to Ashton?"

Calla and Lucas looked at her, then exchanged a furtive glance. She was out of touch again. Neither of them filled the silence.

Willi repeated the question. "Both of you—why are you going to Ashton?"

Patiently, again as to a child, Calla said, "To make a film, Willi."

"Is that all?"

"What did you think, Will?" Luke asked gently.

"I . . . don't know." Disturbed, she put her hand to her forehead. "I thought . . . a quest . . . Julo too . . . a quest."

This time, Calla spoke to an adult. "It's always that, isn't it?"

Willi's perplexity became pain. "Yes . . . but for what?"

Luke leaned forward. "Yes, Willi . . . what?"

"I . . . don't know."

Abruptly she didn't seem to know where she was or who they were. Her features appeared to collapse. Calla, concerned, moved swiftly to her. "Willi—Willi!"

That quickly, the woman recovered. "Don't worry—I'm all right. But . . . could I speak to Luke, please?"

Calla was embarrassed that it had not occurred to her: Willi wanted to be alone with him. She placed the used glasses on a tray and beat a quick retreat from the study.

In the kitchen, busying herself, making the room excessively neat, disordering it and neatening it again, Willi's question—and her condition—upset her. She was agitated, too, by what her friend might have to say so privately to Luke.

He appeared at the kitchen door. "I think you're in trouble."

"Trouble? How?"

"She wants to go with you."

"To Ashton?"

"Yes."

"Oh no."

"I tried to talk her out of it," he said.

"And . . . ?"

"I'm afraid I wasn't very good."

"Can it be let alone? Will she get over wanting it?"

"I don't think so."

"You mean it won't . . . ?"

"Go away? No."

"Good God. . . . Do I really have to deal with it?"

"Yes, Calla, you do."

"All right. I'll talk to her tomorrow."

"Not tomorrow—now."

The urgency in his manner alarmed her. She left the bright light of the kitchen and entered the dimmer illumination of the study. She felt as if she were entering a dungeon.

Willi sat on the couch and was refilling her glass with bourbon. Drinking had been on her forbidden list.

"Do you think you ought to have that?" Calla asked.

"Yes, I do."

"Why didn't you tell *me* that you wanted to come along?"

"Christ, did I have to tell you?"

Calla flushed. "No . . . you didn't."

"It's all right, Calla, don't worry about it."

"You know why I can't take you along, don't you?"

"You think I'm too sick—which I'm not."

"That's not all of it. I'll be totally occupied with the film, I won't have time for you—and you'll be more hurt than if you weren't there."

"It's all right—never mind."

"Willi," she pleaded, "we won't be away forever—at the most three months."

"I know—I know."

"And Grace will take care of you."

"Go to hell!"

Calla was silent.

Willi started to cry. "Oh God, what a bitch I am. I'm sorry, Calla —I'm sorry I said that."

"But you do understand, don't you, Will? Please say you do."

"I said it's all right—what more do you want?"

"Willi . . ." Gently she reached her hand to Willi's shoulder.

"Don't touch me!"

Spilling her drink, Willi got up and hurried to the door. Her gait was not up to the speed she demanded of herself. She stumbled. Calla hurried to steady her.

"Don't touch me, I said! Don't touch me!"

Her face was purple, her hands shook as if she were palsied. "What for? What are you going for?"

She didn't wait for an answer. In a rush, she crossed the foyer, made her way to the stairs, and started upward to the bedroom. Calla stood at the doorway, hesitating until Willi had disappeared, feeling culpable of everything, and wretched. Looking back into the study, she saw the spilled glass on the floor. She picked it up, uncertain what to do with it. Or with herself. She poured herself some bourbon. Drinking alone, she didn't notice that Lucas was on the threshold, watching her.

"She's not going?" he asked.

"No."

He poured himself some whiskey and stood in the middle of the room, not drinking it. "What did you say to convince her?"

"Nothing really. She just came to her senses, I suppose."

"Do you think she ever will?"

"Come to her senses? . . . Oh God."

They stood in silence, with glasses in their hands, neither of them drinking, but needing the theatrical props to help them pretend that the moment was not real.

"What can I ever do for her?" she said, half to herself.

"You talk as if she were your child."

"She is."

Before he had said it aloud, she had had the same thought: My child, yes, brain damaged. Possibly she'll get better, possibly worse. What do I do for her?

They heard a strange rupturing noise overhead, then the banging of a window in the wind. Crash, and crash again, and he was ahead of her, racing up the stairs.

By the time Calla got into the bedroom, he had rushed across to the French windows that led onto the tiny balcony. She could see what Lucas must have seen immediately. The rope was not a rope but a strip of bed sheet. It was tied around the metal banister, and the body hung from the other end of the sheet, only a few feet lower than the balcony.

"Help me!" he cried.

As he raised the hanging form, Calla tore at the knot, untwisted and scrabbled at it with her fingernails.

The woman lay on the floor now, her head bare; the bandage on her skull was a tight cap. Her face was ashen, her lips twitched but not in the spasms of death; she was trying to breathe, sucking at the air.

In a little while the doctor came, and said it was safe to lift her from the floor and put her to bed. The damage was superficial, he assured them, predicting she would have a sore neck for a few days; and there were abrasions on her arm where it had scraped the metal railing of the balcony. He detected nothing wrong with her lungs or trachea, and her respiration was already normal. Giving her a shot of a heavy sedative, he told the others she would be all right.

She'll be all right, Calla thought, all right for what? She locked the window securely so it would not bang open in the night, left Willi's door ajar, and her own as well. Away from Willi, standing in the guest bedroom, she felt like a stranger in her own house, and where wouldn't she be?

She had not heard Luke leave, but assumed that he had gone immediately after the doctor's departure. Neither of them, nobody in fact, had said good night; people and events were just drifting away.

She saw him in the semi-darkness of the hallway, gazing in at her. He opened the door wider. "Are you okay?" he said.

"Yes . . . okay."

"Good. Then stop chewing at your mouth."

It was sore and bleeding; she hadn't noticed.

"I'm taking her with me," she said.

"Calla—don't."

"What can I do, what can I do?"

I'm flying apart, she thought, in a minute I'll be all over the place. Stop it. "She did it for me," she cried. "She did it for me!"

"Did what for you?"

"That attack—that wreckage—it was meant for me! Her face—her beautiful face—she did it for me!"

"Quit that!"

"She took it—she took it for me!"

She could feel the hysteria taking hold. She tried to wrest herself out of it, as if out of a maelstrom, but she couldn't.

"For me!"

"She did not consciously do anything for you, Calla! It happened, that's all—it happened!"

"And now I'm going to kill her!"

"How? For God's sake, how?"

"By taking her with me!"

"Stop that!"

"It's Mina all over again! It's Ashton and Mina—all over again! I'm taking her with me—I'm going to kill her!"

"Calla—stop—Calla!"

"It's Mina! It's Mina!"

He grabbed her and tried to hold her together. She knew she was bound tightly to him, but it didn't help, she could feel her body trembling apart. After some time, she sensed a stillness, a terrible stillness. He was holding her in one arm, ministering to her with the other, his hand brushing the hair off her forehead, caressing her cheek to comfort her. She half sensed it and half didn't, and wished he wouldn't do it. She wanted to cry out, as Willi had done, don't touch me, don't anybody touch me. She didn't recognize him or herself, and didn't want to; wanted nothing, really, no human contact, no voice in her ear, no messages, only to be alone, to lose the consciousness that was too painful to endure. . . . A while later, he seemed to know about her. He hesitated a few seconds longer, with the futile look of a man who had no alternative than to leave, and he departed.

When he was gone, she thought comfortlessly: how tender he was with me . . . and how nothing came at the right time.

Oh, Willi, what a cruel thing to ask—why am I going? I'm going to find a scream, the one I lost.

18

There was nobody to meet them at the airport in Memphis; the company had expected them by a later plane. Calla hired a taxi, and directed the driver the long distance to Mamma Lorena's place.

Before going to the location area, Calla wanted to get it over with: her meeting with the old black woman. She had not seen Mamma Lorena in all these years. There had been many letters, and checks in the mail, and occasional telephone conversations. But she dreaded the face-to-face moment. Time and distance would be nullified; they had a common sorrow which had never been completely put to rest, but lay dormant and threatening, waiting to be reawakened by their reunion.

"You're nervous, aren't you?" Willi said in the taxi.

"Yes, I'm nervous."

"Don't worry. It'll be all right."

It was better than all right. The embrace was like a homecoming, Mamma Lorena's welcome was all the easiness of mother-warmth and food. She had baked an enormous ham as if to feed all the orphans at once, and the three of them sat in the alcove of the kitchen with the smell of cloves and glazed crushed pineapple, slightly roasted and sweetening the air. Mamma had paid little attention to Willi, so as not to notice her disfigurement, but now, in the familiar domain of her kitchen, she kept pressing food upon her, sweet things mostly, pawpaw confiture and sassafras jelly, as if they would act as unguents to her scars.

She hasn't changed, Calla reflected, hasn't aged, hasn't faltered. Well into her seventies, she had no new lines on her face, nor frailties in her motion. She forgot things from time to time, neglected to turn the water off in the kitchen and left her cooking ladle on the phone table in the hallway. "I startin' to forget only the dumb things, thank the Lord," she said. She still ran the orphanage herself, with only one extra cleaning woman these days, and a Mrs. Ebby Tibbott to help with the Sunday dinner. And she wouldn't need *them*, she said, if the twins weren't off working in a beauty salon in Biloxi, and Tildy in the state college, learning literature.

"You're stayin' here with me, the both of you." The old woman assumed her bossy voice. "While you're doin' the picture."

It was a temptation to Calla. But there was always the hazard of memories. Besides, impractical. She needed all the privacy she could get while shooting a film, and it would be difficult enough to have Willi so close.

"The company has trailers arranged for all of us," Calla said.

"Trailers?" Mamma scoffed. "That's like livin' in a towel dispenser."

"Well, it'll be convenient," Calla said. "Close to the set."

"You'll come and see me, won't you?"

"Oh yes, Mamma."

"If you don't, I'll come lookin' for you. Eat your greens."

After lunch Calla went into the parlor and sat alone for a few minutes. It was the room in which she had had her meetings with Gus Mayfield, and she thought of the lawyer and how fond of him she had been. On the mantel there was still the picture of Reverend Tolliver. Walking closer to it, she wondered if it was indeed the same photograph; he seemed so much younger in this one. She had a feeling of losing the past as it was gaining on her.

Later that afternoon, Hubie, the slate boy on the production, arrived in a jeep. He apologized for not bringing the limousine, but it had gone to Shreveport on another errand, and there were temperaments on the set.

"Is anything wrong?" Calla asked.

"I don't know what's right or wrong—it's my first picture." He was only in his teens, twenty at most, and tentative in his job.

It was odd, driving through the woodland where she had always walked. The place was the same and not the same. She tried to pretend it was the vehicle that made the difference, and the gravel road, which had been only a narrow footpath as she recollected it, but she suspected that the difference was deeper. It had been a covert place in those days, a haven of concealment, and now it was, somehow, exposed. Part of its mystery had gone, and she regretted it.

They came out of the woods, onto the Bayou. There were more

Gurrie houses than she recollected, many more, but they had not changed their nature, they were still shacks and shanties, poor without suggesting poverty, and blurrily removed from the world, as if filmed through filters.

What puzzled her: There was no sign of the picture company. No trailers or cottages, no cameras, lighting equipment, nothing.

"Where's everybody?" she asked.

"The picture won't be shot here," Hubie said.

"Not here? Where, then?"

"Mr. O'Hare is building a copy of the village."

The inexperienced boy did not understand how these things were done. "Just a few houses, probably, so he can break the walls away and do interiors."

"No, not just a few houses."

She felt that Hubie had it wrong. But they hardly even stopped at the Gurrie village. Instead, they continued through and past it, about a mile along the creek to where it joined the river.

She heard the hammering before she saw the site. Shacks, forty or fifty of them, were being built. Perhaps a hundred laborers, black and white, with the company's carpenters working alongside them, were constructing a partial copy of the beautiful village. It was startling how exact the replica was: meticulous duplicates of cabins and lean-tos, of fowl cotes and truck gardens, of a particular shanty that tilted out of the way of a cypress tree, of the inlet where the fishing rafts were moored—all here, scaled one to one, painstakingly detailed, shaded by air gun to catch the precise degree of age and the fading by time and weather. What was finished was punctilious in every detail and nearly perfect. It had only one fault.

It was fake. No matter how the scene was to be dressed and decorated, no matter how the Gurries and city blacks and whites might be directed to verify the habitat, the people would look like extras on this set. Something intangible was missing, some quality of the human spirit had been inadvertently left out, overlooked somewhere. It convinced the senses but remained, betrayed and betraying, untrue to the heart. The village shacks, the paddies, the lagoon, the very air had been alive, but this was sterile, dead.

She had seen such early disasters happen too often in films, the first adulterations for economy or expedience, then another makeshift and another, until the dream was corrupted. She felt a sinking worry.

They were out of the jeep. She noticed, sideways, that Hubie was glancing in another direction. The sensitive boy had left her alone with her disappointment, to get used to the set, and mourn silently over it.

"You hate it, don't you?"

She turned and saw Lucas. He had been working with the men, and held a curved saw in his hand. In the three weeks since she had seen him, he had become rail-thin. His clothes hung on him; they were dirty. He needed a shave, and his eyes were bloodshot as if he had not slept for months.

"Yes, I hate it," she said quietly.

"It's not finished."

"It's too finished."

"It has to be dressed, it has to be lighted."

She pointed back to the real village. "That didn't."

"Everything does."

"Why did we come here if we're not going to film it?"

"The people, the ambience."

"What ambience?"

"You won't know the difference when we're finished."

"You could have built it on the Metro back lot—"

"Calla—"

"—the Warner ranch."

"Stop it."

"I hate it—and so do you."

Wounded, he did not answer immediately. "Yes, I hate it. But I wouldn't be able to shoot in the village."

"Why not? It's all *there*."

"So are they. They don't want us here. We're invaders. They'd like us to clear out."

She felt sure he hadn't told her all of it, and might not. He was tired, his nerves were raveled, and in all likelihood he hated the fake village as much as he said he did. At the moment, he probably didn't like her very much either, especially since she was confirming his own sense of deficiency.

"I've had a rough time with the Gurries," he said. "At the beginning, they were delighted with the whole idea—and the money we would pay them. But when they saw the size of the changes they'd have to make—moving out of their houses—doing things on order—pretending to be what they aren't— They're not like city blacks at all. They're totally unsophisticated. Half of them can't read—most of their kids have never been to school. Some of them have never been to a movie theater—they haven't the slightest idea what this is all about. And they couldn't care less. They don't like what's happening out there—in town. And they don't want to be part of it."

"That's why they're here."

"That's why they don't want *us* here."

"There must be some way to help you understand one another."

"Only if I leave them alone. Which I want to do anyway. I like them—they're good people. But one day I heard myself ordering them around—getting angry at them. I wanted to be considerate and kind— but I didn't have time."

"Does kindness take any longer?"

"Try not to lecture, Calla." Then, in an outburst: "I couldn't push them any further—I don't want them to hate me."

She felt sorry for him. "Do they have to love you?"

She had said it in kindness, but he looked as though she had struck him. That was it, then. He did need them all to love him. If they didn't, he couldn't compromise—love was not negotiable. So he left the real village, and built his own, a fake.

She could see that he was disturbed, perhaps angry at the question. "You've got me wrong, Calla. They don't have to love me. . . . Do you?"

"To do what?"

She could have bitten her tongue. It was a stupid lapse of mind. He had been speaking of work, only of work. There had been no hint of the sexual about it, not the slightest innuendo. Her libido, playing a nasty trick, was exposing her in a combustible area.

Clearly, he was not going to let the question pass. "To do whatever," he said. "Do you have to love me?"

"To work with you—no, I don't."

"To work with me or sleep with me."

She tried to keep her voice level. "I can do both without loving you. But you'll get a better performance—in either activity—if I don't dislike you."

"That's where we differ. So far as I'm concerned, we can film and fuck—and hate one another's guts."

"It would be a bad film and a bad fuck."

"Give it a try."

"I'm trying the film."

"I'll settle for that."

They were interrupted by the arrival of Abel Gould, the director of photography who had been a second assistant cameraman on Calla's first picture. She recalled him as a talented but wishy-washy invertebrate who needed an affectation, and had found one: a monocle dangling from a silver chain. Then she saw a veteran boom man, Alan Greenstone, who used to ruin his own sound track by laughing in the middle of her comedy scenes; she went through the crowd of carpenters and electricians to greet him and give him a hug.

The generator truck trembled, the motors started up, two electric saws shrieked with power, the gaffers yelled that their lights were working, and what had been handwork clatter turned into electrified bedlam. Another truck moved in, an obsolete Cinemobile that the company had purchased and re-equipped. Then a mammoth vehicle, a flatbed International with many sets of double tires, lumbered slowly back and forth along the improvised main street, compressing the earth until it was hard as concrete. Finally, the company minibus arrived, carrying a load of palmettos and grass plants and serpent creepers, and the set decorators started imbedding the greenery in the barren soil.

The percussion of the generator had been like an air raid, blasting the last vestige of naturalness out of the replicated village, making the place more explicitly a movie location, clamorous and anxiety-ridden by workmen under the pressure of a deadline:

Tomorrow would be the first day of shooting.

The man and woman on either side of Calla were nagging at her. They were Dennis Ziemert, the line producer of the film, who was Dyer Addison's watchdog, and Feona Carney, an assistant. They wanted Calla to disappear into her trailer, safely out of the path of vehicles, and of a crane bucket that could come crashing down on her head.

The trailer was like all the others she had ever lived in on location, stainless steel, Herculon upholstery, chemical toilet, sanitized comfort. The Formica table and plastic curtains on the windows were as stiff as rigor mortis. But the beds were surprisingly soft yet firmly sprung, and Willi, with all her clothes on, was already in one of them. She dozed frequently these days, and while she was improving in lucidity, she tired quickly, and her life was a succession of slumbers.

Suddenly, a disturbance. Somebody was cursing outside the door. A man's voice, rough as a rasp, with a gamy southern accent. "Goddamn Yankee hookers, they got the world by the acorns!"

The door opened with a burst and a stranger stood there. He was rangy and unkempt, with a ratty, ginger-colored beard. The plaid shirt he wore was threadbare, with buttons missing; his hunting breeches were stiff with old grease, his boots were scuffed and down at the heel. He looked a bit drunk, and his eyes were red.

"Barney!"

He had done it again, he had dressed the character, had totally invested himself, the look, the sound, the whole being, down to the musk of the man.

"Goddamn stars—wait to the last minute to show up. Ta-*ra!* Calla Stark! Bugles, banners and bullshit!"

"Is that Titus Macauley?"

"After the charm's worn off—when he shows what a crud he is."

"Barney, it's wonderful!"

For an instant he stopped acting. "Is it? Did you see him that way?"

"No, not at all—you've got something better. More fun and more balls."

"Three."

"At least."

"No, I mean it," he said seriously. "That's the image I'm working on. No brain at all—his head is his third testicle."

Willi laughed loudest. She stopped being drowsy and got out of bed, as Barney pretended to notice her for the first time. It was clear to Calla that he had been aware of her immediately upon his entrance, if only as part of his audience; he needed time to get over his shock at Willi's appearance. Now, able to dissemble, he pretended there was no difference in the way she looked, she was the same as ever. He hugged her and asked when the hell she was getting back to work again, and told her that idleness would make her fat.

"I've gained fifteen pounds," she said with a laugh.

"I see it—right there." He slapped her lightly on the bottom. The suggestion of lewdness got him back to Titus Macauley. He did a turn and struck a pose. "How's the costume—good?"

"Marvelous," Willi said.

"Praise me! How's the beard—perfect? Praise me, praise me! Tell me I'm wonderful!"

The women laughed. "You *are* wonderful," Calla said. "And Macauley's a bit of a drunk, isn't he?"

"I'm not drunk—he is. How'd you know?"

"The red around the eyelids." With a start, it struck Calla that the redness might not be makeup. "Or is it real?"

"It's greasepaint, idiot."

Willi turned away. She thinks he's lying, Calla supposed. Perhaps he was. Had he really been drinking a great deal? Or crying?

There was a pall. As if he had been exposed, Barney quietly confessed:

"I couldn't find it. Nobody seemed to know where it was. But this morning I did find it . . . and put flowers on her grave."

Calla, trying to speak, nodded instead. As she was about to regain her voice, he seemed in a panic that they would be talking about the child, and he forestalled it:

"I'm not sure I like Titus in a beard. Do you like the beard?"

". . . Yes, I like it."

"It's so scruffy-looking, but I was afraid, if I trimmed it, I'd lose the backwoods feeling—you know—the river rat."

"Yes. I think you're right."

"Ho-LA!" He made a trumpet noise. "Opening shot—tomorrow!"

"Tomorrow, yes."

"Titus Macauley—the terror of the alligators!"

Abruptly, as if the asbestos had rung down, his clothes were a costume the surprise of which had worn off, and he was an actor for whom no more words had been written. Without them, even the beard seemed fake. Having no further scene to play and nothing to be, he had to get offstage, quick exit.

When he left, Willi gave her a glance and seemed to know: whatever her friend was thinking, she could not bear to discuss it. So Willi went back to bed.

Calla felt cheated. She had been on the verge of giving and getting a comfort, of consoling away an old heartache with her ex-husband, and he had forfeited the moment. Unplayable. The poor man, if he could only *play* it, he would give a fine performance. He had never given a bad one.

The total actor, as he had once painfully confessed himself to be, he was an empty vessel into which he had poured one fictional existence after another, without filling the container. Nothing real to fill the empty spaces, always a little hollow. All those people he had pretended to be, all those roles . . . and he was less than the sum of his parts.

The thought dismayed her, for she realized that the same might be said of her.

Less than the sum of her parts. Ever since she had stopped being an activist—or was it since Mina died?—she had been a series of fictional character, many shadows combined to make an apparition.

No, that was not true, she said; that was Barney, not Calla. Not one of the parts he had ever performed was really Barney, but she had dug inside herself, into heartaches she had not known she had, every role an agony of discovery. For each lovely aspect of herself she had uncovered, there was a failure or a wound unhealed, a Mina she thought she had buried long ago. All the anguishes were Calla, they were her *material*. She was paid to suffer the pain of finding herself.

With the help of the script, of course. And the director. Help me to search, was always the cry—help me!

She had an appalling realization. In her last films she had needed the help of directors more and more desperately. It should have been the opposite: as her skills increased, she should have become more self-sufficient, not less. And the dependence had nothing to do with her expertise or lack of it, but with her growing need for love. Her hunger for affection had become a craving. Like a narcotic, love had to be taken in larger and larger doses if she was to be adorable in The Scene.

"Do you have to love me?" Lucas had asked.

Yes, but most of all I need *you* to love *me*. Not forever, I don't ask that, but for long enough to see me through the picture. What about that other high expectancy, her vision of love's permanence? Now she would settle for less, the transitory romance, no more time-resistant than the breakaway sets. Love, like the leasing of camera equipment, on a rental basis.

How ignominious it was.

And if she had been honest enough to ask for such a provisional love affair, Lucas would probably say no. She suspected, for all his bluster about filming and fucking and hating each other's guts, that he always hoped that *this* love, whichever it might be, had a chance to last, to fill a dream. He went about creating perfect fantasies, constructing illusory villages.

The trouble with us, dear Lucas, is that we cannot lie and love each other. So we settle for insolences . . . and wanting. Oh, this miserable candor! Who needs honesty, for God's sake? The whole art is built on lies—who needs honesty?

She foresaw failure. Without offering love or the pretense of it, he might not be able to find a Rachel in her. The filming would be conflict after conflict. And both sides, losing.

She began to feel ill. A dizziness and a pain somewhere, an indefinable pain. She tried to stop the ache, but it was getting worse, spreading from nowhere to nowhere. She would be too ill for the first day of shooting. . . . Please . . . no . . . don't let me be sick . . . please . . .

She flayed herself: None of this would be tolerated in an ordinary woman. If Ms. Jones behaved like this she would not be trusted with the children or the customers or the telephone; she would be called a hysteric, and sent hungrily to bed. But a star gets Oscars. By what right, by what ill-gotten right? Shape up, goddamn it.

The pain was backing away into the corners. The dizziness was going too, drifting over the horizon of her mind. Her hands, her mouth were steady. If she had to learn a speech right now, she might manage to speak the lines. Five minutes, Miss Stark. That's all she would need, five minutes. She'd be able to go onstage any moment now. There! There's a good girl, a real trouper, there's a great little pro.

Christ.

"Where's Julo?" she asked.

"He hasn't arrived as yet," Lucas replied.

"Have you heard from him?"

"Yes, he called again, a few days ago."

"Where was he?"

"He said he was in New York, but the operator's voice was southern."

"What can we trust about him?"

He meted out the words like figures of measurement. "That he will be here—as he said he would—tomorrow—on the first day of shooting."

He was trying to sound confident so as not to start rumors in the company, whispering to prevent anybody at the afternoon coffee break from hearing him. Nobody did, because there was the clatter of cups and saucers, and the preoccupation with pie and cookies and ginger cake. Anyway, outdoors, by the tail-gated chuck wagon, everyone had other concerns, whether shooting in the South would be as hot as today had been, and would there be iced drinks instead of hot coffee, and what idiot had blundered in not having ordered enough diet colas?

Behind her, Calla heard a loud noise and a disgusting laugh, and she felt the sharpness of a stab. I know that awful sound, she thought, and I don't want to see who's making it.

It was Boone Rickert, the county sheriff who had had her arrested

years ago . . . reckless driving, drugs, manslaughter. If it had not been
for the laugh, the burbling through thick paste, she wouldn't have recognized him. He had been bald, years ago, but now he wore a well-
fitting toupee in various tones of dead-leaf brown. And where he had
had a canine tooth missing, there was now a false one, and other false
ones besides, in a gleam of whiteness that did not seem unnatural.

He came forward, straight to Lucas, with a number of sealed envelopes in his left hand and his right hand extended for a handshake.

"Luke, m'boy, I got ya everything your little heart asked for." He
ritually transmitted the envelopes one by one, as if they were sacra-
mental. "This here now, it's your general permit. This one—it's police
pertection. And this one here—it gives you the right to use the waterway."

"Thank you, Sheriff."

"A pleasure, Luke, a real pleasure. And I don't want you to think
this here's the end of it. We are goddamighty proud to have you here,
we are so tickle silly that you chosen our neck of the woods, that anything you want—if it's within reason—we'll be happy to help you out."

He looked at Calla, had a moment of indecision, then pointedly
looked away. He was having a difficulty about her, and she was certainly
having one about him. Nothing except the sheriff's laugh matched her
recollection, certainly not his appearance. With his new hair and teeth,
he seemed like an ordinarily pleasant man, not the simple creep that
she remembered.

He's not a simple creep, Gus Mayfield had said of Rickert in
those days. Nothing about the sheriff could be labeled simple, the lawyer warned her; he was a complex man, not to be underestimated. He
might walk like a slob and talk like an idiot, but it was part of his cunning: to disarm. Boone Rickert pretended to be thick-skinned, fawning
for favor, toadying, insensitive to insult, seeming to welcome insolence
as a test of his good nature; but don't let it fool you, Gus had said, the
fellow's pride runs deep, he won't forget an injury. All of this might
paint a picture of a man who was dishonest and hypocritical, but the
sheriff was one of the least hypocritical men Mayfield had ever met.
Boone Rickert believed in God, the law and his country; he honestly
believed in them with all his Boy Scout and Sunday school faith, and
he would do nothing—ever—to betray any of them. That night, in the
courthouse, when Calla had used a profanity and Rickert had scolded

her—don't curse in the courthouse, ma'am—he was not being falsely pious but expressing his genuine shock. He was a Bible-believing fundamentalist, his God was stern, and the closest he got to profaning His name was "goldamn." People knew this about him, and he never had trouble at the polls. Even many of the blacks, whom he professed to like (his sole hypocrisy), voted for him. But the main reason he was generally popular was that he talked like a caricature of his constituents, he was a grits-and-cornpone cartoon of a Dixie-dolt, and it was an advantage. Now he had two more advantages: a hairpiece and false teeth.

Rickert, having walked away from Calla, now stopped and reconsidered. Turning, he overcame his difficulty, and slowly advanced. She could feel every muscle tighten. When he was within conversational distance, he turned to the director.

"Lucas," he said with a smile, "I'd like you to interduce me to your leadin' lady."

"As you know, we met many years ago, Sheriff," Calla said.

"If we did, miss, I clean forgotten. And I hope you forgotten too. We live and learn, we start all over. Now you say howdy-do to me and I'll say howdy-do to you. Howdy-do, Miz Stark."

He extended his hand. She ignored the hand but murmured a greeting.

He was clearly disappointed by the rebuff of his hand, but shrewdly made the most of the greeting. "Goldam, Miz Stark, you're a good, forgivin' woman—and I am much obliged for that, I am much obliged."

His spirits lifting, he turned to the others. "I want you all to know —Luke, I want your whole company to know how happy I am this day. Happy to have you here—and happy to be here with you. And I got somethin' else to be happy about. This mornin'—at ten o'clock—I went before the justice and I married me the sweetest, the purtiest girl you ever laid eyes on. Ellasue Hendley, that's her name. Louisiana girl— come from a fine family in Shreveport."

There were shouts of congratulation, and people started to pump his hand. He cut it short by laughing and waving his arms. "You know what she said?" he bellowed over the din. "You know what my Ellasue said to me? She said, 'Boonie, I want me a great big weddin' party tonight. I want a gran' ol' time Louisiana weddin' party—a shivaree! An' I want the whole darn world invited.' So I'm invitin' all of ya, every God-lovin' one of ya, with your dogs and cats and chickens—come to my shivaree tonight—the ol' landin'—a mile down the river."

There was another outbreak, applause, laughter, hollers of acceptance. Boone Rickert vibrated with happiness.

When the cry subsided, it was not lost on him that Calla had not joined the boisterousness, nor had she accepted his invitation. He spoke more quietly:

"I didn't hear you say nothin', Miz Stark. I'd be honored to have you come."

She was careful. "Thank you, Sheriff, but we're starting tomorrow, and I'll be . . . preparing tonight."

He saw through the excuse. It bothered him. "Miz Stark, times has changed a lot. I changed too, Miz Stark. Would you believe it—there's goin' to be nigras at the shivaree tonight, and they're my guests. And would you believe it, thirty percent of the folks that voted for me last election was nigras—would you believe that? Well, it's true. And you notice I don't say nigger anymore, you notice that?" He laughed self-deprecatingly. "I ain't to the point of callin' 'em blacks yet, but I *ha'* been changin'. . . . How 'bout you?"

"I haven't changed very much."

"Well, could you change a little tonight?" There was a plea in his voice. "My Ellasue is so goldarn movie crazy, she knows them Hollywood stars better'n she knows her own family. She is so wild for pitchers—why, when the lights go out in the theater, she has herself a conniption." Then, with a canny instinct for lulling opposition, he made himself vulnerable to her. "You could sure make me a big man in her eyes if you was to come. A big man, Miz Stark."

"I'm afraid you're going to have to stay your size, Sheriff."

He laughed uproariously to hide his humiliation. Then he made a number of chummy remarks to his general audience, shook Luke's hand again and departed.

As the coffee break was ending, Luke said, "I wish you could come tonight."

"I can't."

"He's obviously a scum, but he's done us a number of favors. I'm afraid we'll need him."

Deliberately: "I'd like to kill him."

"Take a ticket."

She could see how hard it was for him to pretend affability with Rickert. And she realized that she, as well as all the others, was the beneficiary of his compromise. It hurt her that he had to do it.

Because there was going to be a shivaree tonight, dinner was early. The company dining room was a large round tent, rented for the duration of the filming, set up between the trailers and the outdoor shooting location. On the eve of the first filming day, the meal was more festive than it usually would be, with a liquor bar around the center post, and cold beer on tap from a huge aluminum barrel.

Dinner was Willi's most open exposure since the attack—she had slept all afternoon—and Calla wondered how her friend would fare. She fared magnificently. Instead of hanging back, she did the rounds of the tables, greeting people she had known on previous pictures, making her professional hail-fellow noises. But when she returned to her place at the table, Calla noted that she didn't open her napkin or touch her food.

"You're great," Calla said. "Now eat your dinner."

The social task had taken its toll and Willi was unsteady. "I want to go to the shivaree."

"Haven't you had enough for your first time out?"

"No." She gritted her teeth. "I need to do it all at once."

"Then go, honey."

"I won't go without you."

It was not an expression of dependence but of loyalty.

"Willi, we don't have to do all the same things, you know."

"Don't we? I thought we did." Willi laughed, but she was serious.

Later, when it got dark and the first sounds of the country music band were heard from the wedding celebration, Calla decided to go for a walk in the other direction, toward the Bayou. She wanted sorely to be alone, to sit on the deserted side of the lagoon, take her shoes off, dip her feet in the water and invite the starlight. After the hubbub of the day, she needed the solitude to prepare for her first camera exposure tomorrow. But of course . . . Willi . . . so they walked together, her companion gave her a blessed silence, and she was grateful. Nights were generally cool, as Calla recalled them, but this was a hot evening, with a steamy mist off the river. Ambling along the moonlit waterway, sometimes one of them would stop for no important reason, simply to pause and stare or to pick up a piece of river flotsam or a shiny stone; sometimes they walked together, sometimes separately. When they arrived at the lagoon, Willi was the first to go barefoot. They sat in the scrub grass on the bank, with the water so warm on their feet that they scarcely felt it. The peace of the night was a sedative. Even the beat of the country music, fainter here, was not a disturbance but a sound from a world they had no part of. And the soft tremor of a breeze was like the wafting of a silken curtain.

A noise, a shout. They arose in a spasm, and grabbed their shoes as if to run. A figure was charging at them, bearing down like a great dark beast, shrieking in a mad assault.

"Julo!" Willi yelled.

He came bellowing across the sand, thundering. He ignored Calla and made straight for Willi. Seizing the woman in his arms, he lifted her off the ground, wheeled with her, roaring and laughing, spinning round and round, whirling as Willi sang out with happiness, Julo, oh, Julo, Julo!

The whirling over, he held her at arm's length, to gaze at her. With no concern that he might be disconcerting the woman, he turned her toward the moonlight and studied her marred face. At that instant, as if in affinity, his own face seemed just as damaged. With delicate fingertips he touched the scars on her cheeks, on her forehead. Then, overcome with what he saw, he started to kiss the blemishes, he kissed each one, the long slashes from forehead to jawbone, the cicatrices on her head beneath the stubble of hair, kissed every injury to make it well, a parent kissing away the pain. And as he was doing it, all Willi could say was oh, Julo, Julo, and she began to cry, not for her distress but for his.

"I'll make them better," he said. He held both hands on her face, his palms covering her cheeks to conceal the scars. "I promise you, beautiful Willi, I'll make them better. I'll wipe out every scar, I'll smooth them all away, I'll make them disappear. I promise, Willi honey, I promise I'll make them better!"

Calla had a catch in her throat. The great-hearted liar believed it, every word; he would create a miracle out of his love for the woman, he believed every pledge he uttered.

When he was more aware of Calla's presence, she welcomed him to the film and asked where he had been these last few weeks. Affecting not to understand the question, he was evasive. He had just arrived, he said, as if that answered everything, and had found hardly anyone at the company compound.

"They're at the party," Willi said.

It struck him funny. "Holy Judas, a cop's party."

"Sheriff," Willi corrected.

"Cops—they're all cops—all the mother-humpin' bastards."

Willi said, "It's called a shivaree, and you're invited."

"Fuckaroo! That's what they told me—I'm invited—me!" A disorder of laughter. "Me, goin' to a pig's party. Ain't that enough to make you shit?"

It tickled him more and more. He started to shake with laughter, his eyes filled with tears, his breath couldn't keep up with his need for it. At last, he yelled:

"Come on, white ladies—let's move ass!"

"Where?" Willi said.

"To the party, goddamn it—to the shiverin' shivaree."

"Calla won't go," Willi said heavily.

"Won't go? Why not?"

"She . . . had a bad experience with Rickert years ago."

"Chrissake, I've had bad experiences with those shitheads all my life!"

"Then how can you go?" Calla said. "Why?"

"Because he don' want me there! And I'll have a better time than he will if I go. So—I—am—goin'! I'm goin' to the bastard's party, I'm gonna eat his vittles and drink his licker and dance to his music and piss right in his eye!"

His laughter was a trombone in the sky. He grabbed both of them, one in each arm, and hustled them to the party.

When they got to the shivaree, Rickert and his bride had not yet arrived. His deputy said the newlyweds were delaying in order to make a big Hollywood entrance.

Hundreds were there. Whites and blacks from Ashton, Gurries from the Bayou, Creoles from Shreveport, civilians and police and the people from the federal courthouse and employees from Rickert's county jail. If the mix of blacks and whites at the wedding party of a man like Rickert seemed odd to Calla, it became logical when she realized they were all voters, and it was rumored that Rickert was going to run for lieutenant governor. In addition to pleasing his new wife, the shivaree was a campaign investment. Quite a sizable investment too. There were ten musicians playing country music, and three huge cookeries—a fish fry, southern chicken, and a barbecue of the ugliest, most behemoth hog Calla had ever seen. The tables were heaped with delectable side dishes and relishes, with puddings and candies and layer cakes. Liquor flowed like the river, straight corn brew and juleps and whiskeys and Cuba libres in foot-high glasses; and what somebody called widow's ale, on tap, ran unstoppably onto the sand, dribbling its yellowness down to the creek.

There was a specially decorated table for the picture people, draped in the city colors of Ashton, green and gold. Most of the upper echelon staff were already seated, although many places were still vacant, and Calla noticed that neither Lucas nor Barney was anywhere in evidence.

As Calla sat down with Willi and Julo, the country music, amplified to bedlam, beat a madness on her skull, and she wished she hadn't come. To escape, she tried to imagine she was a teenage girl again, and this was a campfire cookout in the Maine woods where soon they would sing "Old Macdonald"; she tried to imagine it was a farce with Hope and Crosby, *The Road to Dixie*, but the din of the music was unforgiving, and the dancers moved with grim expressionlessness, like a ceremony in resentment. And she was too close to the roasting hog. When the barbecue spit turned somewhat eccentrically, the beast seemed to quiver, still breathing, then fall, quiver and fall.

In the middle of a number, the music stopped. So did the dancing. Silence, then a trumpet blared. Drums rolled. And out of a mile-long limousine the married couple appeared.

They had been wed in street clothes this morning, but now they were in nuptial regalia. The sheriff wore a frock coat and satin-striped trousers, but his tie was green and gold, to honor the municipality, and so was his breast pocket handkerchief, with enough showing so that the city seal was visible. Unfortunately, as he came through the doorway of the vehicle, he didn't stoop low enough and his toupee was tipped askew.

But his bride's blond hair was perfect. It had been lacquered and perfumed and star-flecked, and the straw was sculpted into a round, stiff, wavy, molded crown. Ellasue was a generation younger than her husband, certainly no older than thirty, and without being overweight she had a luxuriance of flesh, of breast and bottom, and she had been overpoured, like an excess of cake batter, into her bridal dress of peau de soie and eyelet embroidery. For reasons unknown, sentimental no doubt, she wore a bridal veil, which obscured her face, but her lush red mouth burst through the lacery.

Moving among the crowd toward the table of film celebrities, the wedded couple went from clot to clot, erupting each one with a grenade of laughter. The loudest laugh was Ellasue's. It was a shriek that ended in a cadenza. Actually, she was a well-favored woman, but the louder and closer she got, the uncomelier she seemed to Calla. To Boone Rickert, however, she was exquisite. He kissed her often and bumped at her with his shoulders and thighs. In his happiness, he seemed to need physical connection not only with his bride but with everyone. He kissed as many women as had mouths, and shook the hand of nearly every man, but Calla noted that the handshakes with the blacks were quickly terminated, as if he wanted to wipe his palm.

They arrived eventually at the table where Calla and the movie people were seated, and the explosions of laughter became volcanic.

"Goldamn, this has been a happy day!" Rickert shouted. "Ain't it just been a happy day, Ellasue, sugar?"

"And gonna be a happy night." She wiggled her torso.

A few people laughed. Unsure how her humor was being interpreted, Rickert also laughed, but guardedly. "Meet everybody, Ellasue, sugar," he said. "Miz Stark, I sure do appreciate you changin' your mind and *bein'* here tonight—and I want you to meet my new-wedded wife. Ellasue, shake hands with a big lumisary from Hollywood. My little girl here is a bit of a lumisary herself, Miz Stark—come from a fine family in Shreveport."

Ellasue gave her laughing screech. "What he mean, fine family, is nobody got th'own in the pokey. Ain't that what you mean, Boonie-lover? Fix your hairpiece, honey."

He squeezed her into an embrace. "Beautiful, ain't she beautiful? And made *me* beautiful too." It seemed to occur to him that immodesty mightn't garner votes, so he added quickly. "She sure done wonders with a ugly ol' man."

"I don' know about ugly, but I sure know about ol'," she said without ill feeling. "I says to him, 'Boonie, if you want to marry me, you better lose some years.' Well, son of a gun, if he don' show up with a new setta teeth and a new heada hair. And I just wet, laughin'." He looked at her quickly, and she sensed she had to modify her vulgarity. "Well, I *nearly* wet." Somebody laughed and she appreciated it. "And that was the first damn night I let him get the weenchiest bit personal with me. Fix your hairpiece, lover."

Laughs, polite and otherwise. Giggles and gales. The crowd was liking her; she was going over as a wit. Rickert relaxed.

Seating herself directly opposite Calla, Ellasue leaned across the table and spoke intimately to the actress. "I certain'y admire you, Miz Stark, I jus' admire the hell out of you."

"Thank you."

"I jus' can't tell you what it means to have you right here in the center of our midst. I jus' can't tell you."

"That's very kind—thank you."

"I saw every pitcher you ever made, an' I cried th'ough every one— even the funny ones."

That did it. A solid laugh from everybody. Calla smiled. The sheriff held his sides.

"An' if you can use your influence, I'll be grateful to my grave if I can take a part in your pitcher." Ellasue was serious. "Now, I don' mean no big talkin' part, hear—jus' a kind of be-there part, you know what I mean?"

"Yes, I know what you mean."

"Oh, you *are* nice, you jus' naturally are. Last time I saw you in a pitcher, I says to Boone, 'She's just naturally nice, she looks like a governor's wife—don' she look like a governor's wife, Boonie?' And I see that I was right—you *are* a governor's wife."

"Thank you very much."

The sheriff, still on his feet, busily working the table, handshakes everywhere, paid his quick and uneasy respects to Willi, then came to Julo.

"Now, then," he said, smiling expansively to the black man, "you must be Mr. Julery."

"Julasto."

"Julasta, is it? Well, sorry, Mr. Julasta," he said, "I musta read it wrong. Musta been a misprint. You know how them teletypes are, don' you?"

Julo had started to rise, but now he stopped the motion. "What else did they get wrong on the teletype, Mista Sheriff?"

"I don' know and I ain't askin'. I don't give a goldarn what they say about you in L.A. or Knoxville or any dump-hole town in the U.S.A. To us here in Ashton County, you are a visitor. You are a pitcher star to us, Mr. Julasta, and I won't forget it . . . and don't you forget it neither."

He extended his hand.

Julo's face lighted. He was enjoying himself. The black man rose and reached for the sheriff's hand. And didn't let go. While holding it, he made a reciprocating speech.

"I want you to know, Mr. Rickets—"

"Rickert."

"I want you to know, Mr. Rickert, that you have just made a wonderful expression of the fine old anti-belly South. You make me feel that the nice warm harmony we all had together is gonna all come back to us, black and white alike, with the bright lights burnin' in the big house, and the darkies singin' soft and low, and the magnolias bloomin' the whole year 'round. You make me feel that those of us black folk that fought on the side of General Bob Lee and Cap'n Bill Yancy did not—after all—shed our blood in vain—and—"

"Leggo my hand, Mr. Julasta."

"—and I can't tell you how happy I am to come back to the hills o' home, to the booooosom of you and your beautiful wife."

"Leggo my hand."

"Leggo my husband's hand."

Julo bowed to Ellasue. "I would certainly do anything for you, Miz Rickert." He released the sheriff's hand.

There had been no merriment for a constricted moment, and now Julo restored it with a laugh. "A helluva party, Sheriff!" he yelled. "You have got here one helluva party!" Then he left the table and disappeared for a while.

A guest complained about the heat and Rickert apologized as if it had been a bungle in his party arrangements. He sat down beside his wife, and everybody at the table of honor became an actor, even the civilians; they're playing us, Calla thought, and we're playing them. They all pretended to be having a good time, all convincingly seemed to enjoy one another. The food, even the pork, was excellent, Willi said, but Calla had none of it. Someone brought her a drink which they called Bayou punch, made with corn liquor and persimmon juice and limes and whatnot. It had a lovely color and a delicately tart flavor that cleansed her mouth and throat. She didn't know its potency and didn't care. The music wasn't sounding too loud anymore. And the wedding party had a staged gaiety that was not altogether unpleasant. It reminded her of the wedding party of the grape-grower—what was the name of the film?—*They Knew What They Wanted*. Even the characters were a bit similar, the older man and the young woman. Hollywood does it all, she thought vaguely, what a lovely drink this is, and every-one's a star.

Out of nowhere, Barney appeared. Seeing him, Ellasue jumped up as if she had been waiting for his arrival, and ran to greet him.

"Mr. Loftus, I gotta tell ya," she gushed. "I've seen you in a hun'red pitchers, and you been hidin' behind a hun'red *dis*-guises, but I swear I'd know you if you was closed up in a cardboard box. Because you have got—what shall I call it—*personality*."

"Thank you," Barney said, with a manner. "Thank you very much."

"Havin' said that, would you kiss the bride?" She puckered up.

As he put his arms around her, she remembered to be tactful. "Boonie, it's all right if he kisses the bride, ain't it, Boonie Boonie?"

"It's all right with me." He showed his white teeth, but it wasn't a smile.

Barney pulled her closer. "But before you do," she said, "I want you to know, Mr. Bernard Loftus, that I saw you in *Ordinary People* and I'm not goin' to forgive you for the way you made me cry."

"That was Don Sutherland," he said.

"It wa'n't you? Oh, I know—it was that other pitcher I saw you in— *Five Easy Pieces*."

"That was Jack Nicholson."

"By damn, I'm gonna kiss you anyways."

She went at him with her mouth open and he gave her a long kiss, moving a little as he did, crushing her bridal dress. When it was over, while she was still in his arms, she leaned back, flushed. "Holy smokers, you kiss like Burt Reynolds."

"Have you ever kissed Burt Reynolds?"

"Every goddamn night."

"Don't curse, sugar," Rickert said.

When she walked back to sit beside her husband, there was a hiatus in the evening. The band had taken time out for refreshment, and the first high of the drinks had worn off. Calla asked for another Bayou punch, and got it. The shivaree seemed to be wavering in indeci-sion, the night itself in a kind of suspension. Suddenly, at a distance, there was a curious sound. It was not a human voice, yet it was; it was not a wail, yet there was an almost comically overstated dolor in it.

"What's that?" Willi asked.

"It's the song of the croacher," the sheriff replied.

"What's a croacher?"

"Alligator."

"I looked all day yesterday and most of today," Barney said. "I didn't see any alligators."

"There's alligators," the sheriff said. "There's some in there that's twiced your size."

The sound again, more sustained this time, more mournful.

Barney tilted his head to listen. "It does sound like a song."

"You know who they singin' to? . . . Snakes."

"Come on," Barney said.

The sheriff was in earnest. "Yeah—snakes. They open their mouth to sing. The snakes come glidin' along to hear 'em, then slippety-slip, right in the croacher's mouth—snap, snap."

The information had a singular effect on Barney. If Calla was wrong in supposing him drunk this afternoon, she felt more certain now. The liquor and the alligator talk had excited him. "Does it really happen?" he asked. "The 'gater sings and the snake gets hypnotized?"

"Right into the mouth."

"It's kid stories," Ellasue said.

"How do you know? You come from Shreveport. It ain't no kid story—it's a fack."

"Tell it to your shinbone," she said. "Them croachers ain't harmful to nothin' and nobody."

"They ain't, huh?" He was annoyed. "Well, there's records in my office—last year, a fella from Me'phis—got swallered up without a ripple in the water. And two years ago, a couple of grown men—cousins—the croachers come from all directions. White water, white water, and the poor suckers were gone."

"Fix your hairpiece."

"I fixed it as good as I can. I ain't got no mirrow—I can't see without a mirrow."

Barney was watching their altercation with a tipsy grin, enjoying it. "Why don't you fix it for him, Ellasue?"

"Don' give her no ideas." The sheriff was getting angrier.

"Stay out of it, Barney," Calla murmured.

"Straighten his rug, Ellasue," Barney said.

Challenged, Ellasue reached to her husband's toupee, and the sheriff struck her hand away. "Keep your pickers to yourself," he said.

In a sweat of temper, he got up from the table, walked fast and joined a group on the other side of the bandstand.

Ellasue, a bit uncertain of what she had done, laughed with nervousness. "Well, I guess we know a sore-ass when we see one." Without waiting too long, she went to find her bridegroom.

Calla turned to her ex-husband. "Barney, for heaven's sake, why did you do that?"

"I don't like either of them. And if they want to squabble—"

"You provoked it."

"No I didn't. It was there."

"They've just been married."

"Oh Promise Me! She hates the son of a bitch."

"Where did you hear that? At the punch bowl?"

"There you go again—you think I'm drunk." He was ruffled. Leaning across the table, he blew his breath in her face. "Smell that. Do you smell any liquor? Do you?"

She did not in fact smell any liquor. But there was another odor on his breath, dense and a bit fetid, an aroma she could not name. It was faintly familiar and brought a vague, unpleasant sense of the past.

"Smell liquor, smell liquor?" He taunted her.

She noticed that his speech had gone sloppy. The superbly articulated southern accent had been displaced by a twang that was not southern, and had no definition. "Your drawl is slipping."

It was the most chastising thing she could say.

"Your fault. You've wrecked my character." His eyes were blazing with anger. "Don't ever do that again."

As he twisted away, she realized that Barney too saw the shivaree as a film. But, unlike her, instead of standing apart as a spectator, he had engaged other actors, he had entered the scenario to play his role. And she had ruined it by insisting on reality. Spoilsport. Why couldn't she too enter the fantasy? Find a character that she herself could play. Better get into the fiction, or something terrible might happen. . . . She wished she hadn't had the second drink.

Willi had disappeared. And Julo hadn't returned. Calla wanted to get away; she was apprehensive about something, she didn't know what. She began to recall the odor she had smelled on Barney's breath. It went back to the sixties, a drug, an incense—was it India, the Philippines?—a pungent essence, animal and musky.

The music had resumed, so had the dancing. At a distance, she caught a glimpse of a swiftly moving pale dress, and it was Willi. He was putting her through things, Julo was, making her do steps she had probably never done before. She had regained her equilibrium nearly totally in the last few weeks, but this was difficult—dancing—whirling in a way that could have made her dizzy. Yet, she was enjoying it, her face aglow with trying and succeeding.

Drawn to them, Calla walked to the edge of the dance floor. The music was different now, not country and not rock, she couldn't identify it. All the instruments in the band were the same, yet the rhythms had altered. The wooden floor, laid down especially for the occasion, had been silent before, responding hardly at all to the dancers' steps, but now it was being drummed by the pounding feet, and it made a beating pulse.

The measures were becoming more exotically sensual, as if there were human voices in the instruments. And the dancers changed as well, conscious of a leading spirit on the floor, someone fashioning the figurations of the dance, interpreting the night. It was Julo they were following, as he guided Willi around the floor, gliding and coiling, entwining himself with her, stopping to drum with his feet and clap with his hands, reeling in patterns Calla had never seen before. And how beautifully Willi was following all the twists and turns, how the bird grace of the woman complemented the feral grace of the man—Willi, the athlete again, the creature of litheness and speed—how beautiful they were together!

Now, change to change, like an acceleration of the phases of the moon, Julo seemed to become someone else. No longer an ordinary man, he was the Gorá again, out of a fantasy country in Africa, a chieftain in a woodland somewhere, the minister of deities leading the prowl for prey. The man who had probably never been out of America was dancing to the beat of another continent, playing another passion. His fever became everyone's. There were no longer any separate dancers; they were all one. He had made a ritual, and they followed him. So did Willi. Transported, the scarred white woman and the black man moved in a single motion, dancing out of their bodies, as if lifted on a flame. Calla burst with pride in her friend, felt that the ecstasy was happening not only to Willi but to herself. Exalted, she felt as if she could *become* Willi; any moment it might happen.

Envy overtook her. I wish I could dance like that, she said, I wish I could feel like that, I wish I were Willi!

The music pounded louder and faster, and beat itself to a wild death. There was a flickering of lights, the melee of an interval, and Willi and Julo vanished. As suddenly as they had disappeared, they appeared again, standing beside Calla, hot and perspiring, their faces gleaming.

Willi could scarcely catch her breath. "Dance with him." She threw her arms wide in generosity. "He's wonderful, Callie—dance with my Julo!"

Offering his arms in invitation, Julo moved toward Calla.

She had an urge to rush into his embrace, a yearning to be rhapsodically in motion with him. But just as the band struck up:

"Thank you," she said. "But I think not."

"Oh, Calla—do it," Willi begged. "Feel the way I felt. Do it!"

"Please," he said. "I want to dance with you."

She pretended to make light of it. "You've danced with the best. The rest is anti-climax."

Willi and Julo glanced at each other and back to Calla, with looks to console an ailing friend. Then they glided away among the dancers.

Envy, more acid than before. It ate at her. Jealous of the friend she adored, of the true beauty that came alive in motion, the radiance that transcended scars. She envied her right to say "my Julo" as if he were her husband or lover or father, envied Willi's anything that gave her the sense of someone belonging to her, to whom she could belong. Christ, she thought, I wish for one moment, for one breath of being, that I were Willi!

The whites began to depart, but the blacks—mostly the Gurries— remained. Someone built a bonfire. It blazed at a distance from the dance floor. Many of the guests who had been caught by the charisma of the black man were imitating his movements around the flames. There was a new ardor in the air, a religious zeal for hotter action and wilder contest and more fervent feeling.

The liquor struck Calla's forehead like a mallet. An image: Mina, growing up before her eyes, five, ten, fifteen years old, like sped-up film, growing horribly, switching roles with her mother, taking over, don't drink so much, urging guilt, be guilty, Mother, I dare you to run to Ashton and get rid of me, I dare you to run, don't drink so much, be guilty . . . Oh God, I'm flipping. . . . *Run, Mother!*

"Stand there! Don't move!"

A light flashed. A picture was taken.

It was Lucas. He shoved the tiny still camera into his pocket, and swung his 16mm motion picture camera off his shoulder.

"Marvelous shot," he said. "With the fire behind you, your hair will be in flames."

He turned the turret of the movie camera from lens to lens. Close on his footsteps, Al Czarnis, the still photographer, was trying to reason with him. "Let me give you some light," he kept saying, "let me throw a flood on it."

"No." Lucas was irritable. Pointing to Julo, he muttered about not spoiling a ritual.

"What ritual, for God's sake? Without light, you won't *get* anything!" The photographer turned to Calla. "I think he's buggo. Picture doesn't start until tomorrow, and already he's whacked out." He took his leave.

Luke said: "Your leading man—I heard him ask you to dance. Why didn't you?"

"I didn't want to dance with him."

"With her, then."

The impulse to slap his face was trivial, she decided; she walked away.

Whacked out. Al was right, they were all whacking out tonight. With most of the white guests gone, the black members of the band had taken over. Abandoning the country music, the players were improvising, letting time and place run free; they were in Africa. What an old scenario, she thought, the jungle drums driving the white folk crazy. Everything according to the cliché continuity. Was there nothing new in it? Where was the twist?

The drumbeats didn't vary. Unbroken, unrelieved rhythm. Meant to derange.

When she got closer to the bonfire, she saw Lucas, threading snakelike around the blaze, filming, spying, recording everyone's unwontedness, her own as well. She hated candid shots, resented being captured by a director turned voyeur.

But wasn't that always his function? She could feel herself inventing charges against him, one grudge after another. Nothing he did seemed to fill her with anything but rancor. Worse, she knew that her wanting to go to bed with him—and loathing herself for wanting it—was roiling her fury against the man.

In the heat, the male dancers were tossing their shirts away, and the women were divesting themselves of whatever clothes they could. Teasing one another, they bet their bodies in the gamble of lovemaking, they touched and clutched and broke away. The drumbeats shook the night, quickening the current of the river.

There had to be some twist, some difference in the scene, a gimmick. What she was seeing was a terrible picture with a tacky title, *Jungle Passion* or *African Madness*. She could predict every banality. The drums, the erotic dancing would drive Lucas crazy, he would be unmanageable to himself, a rapacious animal on the prowl for Calla. He would find her, they would quarrel—a titillating tussle—insults as aphrodisiacs—then bang!

No. No bang. She had found the gimmick! *She would reject him.* Thus, she would conquer two enemies at once, his male-and-directorial dominance, and her own disgusting, self-degrading horniness. Calla, the winner!

Yet . . . she might have danced with Lucas, if he had asked her. Even now she would like to whirl around with him. But he was no longer taking pictures, he was gone.

The music was in her feet, her hands. She started to beat her hands together, to beat them until they hurt. The heat was suffocating—should she have another drink?

Aaaaa, the dancers sang, *aaaaa*, and she yearned to join them. She wanted to run, in pursuit of breath, and for Lucas to catch her. She wanted to be in his arms, reel around the fire with him, join the wild blaze of the blacks, get scorched by the flames. Craving, she felt she had to dance or scream, had to run smashing through her inhibitions.

Afraid. Beware of the real feeling. Stage it. Don't do anything you haven't rehearsed; don't dance until you've learned the steps; don't look awkward or foolish or miscast; don't be the wrong person in the wrong part.

Afraid. Of what? Of being in Ashton with Mina? The grown-up child was back again, blaming, challenging, terrifying:

Run, Mother.

No. Go away.

I don't have to run, I've got some status here, I'm the star, I play the part of mother and woman very well, I don't have to live and love by some inferior script—I don't like this demented going-and-coming scene. Stop the action!

Cut!

Quit, she said. Walk off the picture. Take your makeup off, get rid of the costume, go back to bare skin.

Cut.

Cut and run!

She had to get away from the dancers and the drums and the sounds that dared the lovemaking.

Run, Mother.

She was running as fast as she could, leaving the landing place, racing, falling, out of breath, here and gone, there and elsewhere, fleeing along the river.

She was back in the false village now, the one Luke had built. Nobody in sight. Deserted. They had left the fake place to the floodlight of a fake, all-purpose moon; the gaffers had done it well; a good effect. How real it looked, juiced up like that, as real as the other moon she had just run away from, how beautiful this thing that the director had counterfeited. Much more useful than the other place—he was right after all—because she could not play a scene in the other place, only here. . . . God, was this falsity all she could handle? Had she come to this?

Cut.

Call Lucas, she told herself, call Lucas. She barely whispered his name. Like a shy one at a first reading, she mumbled it. Call him out loud, she said, project.

She heard a plashing sound. It came from the river. With a start, she thought of croachers. She twisted sharply toward the moonlit water.

There were no alligators tonight. Lucas. He was down at the river's edge, unloading a rowboat, carrying a cardboard carton full of scripts and cassettes and desk junk.

"What are you doing?" she asked.

"Getting my house in order."

"Is it out of order?"

"If I don't do this tonight, it will be, tomorrow."

"Tomorrow . . . I can't start."

"What?"

"I can't start the picture. . . . I'm scared."

"First day. Why shouldn't you be?"

"I'm scared, I'm scared!"

He put the box down on the scraggly grass at the riverside. "Is there something really wrong?"

"Yes—you."

"Oh, that."

"Don't say oh that, you bastard," she said. "I want to go to bed with you."

No. Wrong twist. The script said for him to be the aggressor, not her. Wrong.

"No," he said evenly. "You don't want to go to bed with me. You suggested you dislike me, and I believe it."

"That's right. I do."

"You want to have it over and done with."

"Yes."

"Sex as an act of hatred. Didn't we talk about that?"

She was confused. "Talk about what?"

"Rape. Wouldn't you like it better if I raped you?"

"What are you trying to prove—what you wrote in the script? Women want to be raped?"

"Don't be a damn fool."

"You think that, don't you?"

"Go to hell."

"I want you—now—tonight."

"In the hope I'll be a dud. That would be more satisfying to you than an orgasm, wouldn't it?"

"Yes—no."

"Lucas exorcised."

"Yes!"

She started to take her clothes off.

"Don't do that," he said quietly.

She knew she was playing against the scene, and it would look terrible on film. Perhaps they would have to reshoot it, but meanwhile she was nearly naked.

"Quit it," he said.

"You want me to go on wanting you, is that it? It's a great power to have over an actress, isn't it? It keeps her going—like the carrot in front of the jackass."

"The jackass never gets the carrot."

"And I'll get mine."

"If you're good."

She was totally naked now. Suddenly he stopped, picked up the carton and started to walk away from her.

"You bastard!" she cried. "You bastard!"

She felt a rush of reality, a rush of shame. She was burning with humiliation. Her skin felt hot, her mouth was dry, she was ablaze to the roots of her hair—and dirty. She turned from him and looked at the river. Running to cool herself in the water, to hide in it and get clean, she rushed into the wetness.

"Come back!" he yelled. "You stupid—! Come back!"

She was a good swimmer but she flailed tonight. She struck at the water as if to tear the river apart.

"Come back! It's dangerous!"

She kept ripping at the current, slashing at it.

"Come back!"

He plunged in after her. Enraged, he threw his fury into every stroke. She was beyond the rocks now, in the full flood of the river. He swam downstream a little, avoiding the boulders. He reached her. She thrashed, swimming away from him. He grabbed her.

"Let go," she muttered.

He tried to encircle her body with one arm, but she struck him off. When he tried once more, she smashed at him.

At last, as if rescuing a drowner, his fist shot out. He hit her once, and again.

She saw the blows but scarcely felt them. Then she felt nothing at all.

When she revived a little, she was still naked, lying on the river-bank, and so was he. He was kissing her awake, kissing her roughly to bring an awareness to her, a sense that they were continuing with the night.

"My breasts," she said.

He did as she wanted, kissing them, hurting them.

"Don't wait," she said. "Please don't wait."

She felt that the water had not cooled her, that she had a fever, that nothing could ever cool her except a burning, the blaze of his body.

"Please," she said.

Gradually, without haste, he came closer and closer, and she could smell the brackish zest of the river water on his skin. And at last he was inside her.

Later, when he had gone, she thought how mixed-up the lovemaking had been. She had never been brought abed by anyone where the antipathy, on both sides, was so clear. She would have thought herself incapable, drunk or sober, of engaging in it. Yet, his antagonism had lent a strange high tension to the act, an unpredictability at being touched by a man whose hands were naturally gentle, using his body in a rough and angry way, and his actual coming as if it were a penalty.

Perhaps he was right after all, she thought: we can film and fuck, and hate each other's guts. She wouldn't have guessed there would be any real satisfaction in it, and was surprised that there was so much. There might even be something salutary about their not liking each other. No strings attached. When the film was over, they could go their separate ways. No need to look back with bitter regret, no danger of turning into a pillar of salt.

Meanwhile, unfortunately, she would want him more and more, and there would not be enough of him. Starting tomorrow, he would no longer be a man but a director, driven. All his juices would be drained, sucked out of him by the film he was making; and nothing for her. She resented that every director she had known, even Notale, could have his sexual hungers satisfied by work, but that performing only whetted her appetite, and she was ravenous. Doubtless, Luke would be no different, and it would be another reason for hating him. If sex was a pleasure in hatred, what might that say about rape? Perhaps the bones of her morality were softening, and her brain as well.

She wanted him again. Right now, wanted him. She resisted the hunger and thanked her stars that it was only a physical distress, not the aching dependency of love. Truth was, however, she ached because she didn't ache. And she longed for that day, long gone, when love and lovemaking were inseparable, and could hurt her to the soul.

19

He lay in bed, contemptuous of himself, contemptuous of his gonads for betraying him. This afternoon, after their argument about the fake village, he had determined on a course of sexual action with Calla: *None.*

He had resolved that he would treat her no differently from all the other leading women he had never made love to. Same distance. And here he was, the director before the first shooting day, and he had already fired a shot. A blank too, so far as his truest, most self-respecting feelings were concerned. He had simply gotten his gun off. Incontinent bastard.

Point was, he could easily—no, painfully—fall in love with her. And might be in love right now. If so, what a suicidal rashness. Dependent on her in the deepmost ways, he could let her dominate the film, and that would be the least of it. She could dominate him, take over his entire life. Knowing what prodigious needs he had for loving and giving, he could squander his whole existence on the woman, give her all his time, subordinate his hopes, let her into all the locked-up, vulnerable places, and toss away every badge of pride and selfhood.

Well, why not? Because she was a strong woman going through a weakened state, a moment in her life when she could not take her potency for granted, and had to be testing it all the time. Uncertain of her courage, she was frightened enough to commit an act of destruction. . . . Dangerous.

Jesus. Don't fall in love with her.

Fall asleep instead. Fall asleep right now, because it's almost dawn, and in a few hours the camera will roll; fall dead unconscious and forget that the thing exists, don't fall in love with her, it isn't there.

For Lucas O'Hare there never was such terror as there was on the first day of shooting. Always, in every picture he had ever directed, it was the same; no matter how much expertise he acquired, he never grew calmer or more self-certain. He didn't dare eat breakfast for fear he might not keep it down, he didn't shake hands lest someone notice that his palms were damp.

For Lucas O'Hare, there never was such hope as there was on the first day of shooting. Always, in every picture, he would be on the verge of solving some riddle of his life, discovering a panacea for the ache . . . or at least might fabricate some summer night's tale that would make him forget the toils and searches.

If pity and terror were the essence of Greek tragedy, Luke told himself, then hope and terror were the essence of his small comedy. These were the two emotions he lived by, and to him, a man who did not dwell in a state of morality but in a morality play, comedy was the triumph of good over evil; therefore, he felt certain that his hope would vanquish his terror.

Today, hope and terror were at a standoff.

He looked at all the people, blacks and whites, uncomplicated Gurries and sophisticated artists and craftsmen, and saw his battalions in the confusion before the march, waiting for the call to arms. All the vehicles and equipment were taking their battle stations, the flatbed truck to the farthest reach of the riverbank, the Cinemobile at the edge of the woodland, the sound truck midway between the water and the woods, the camera on its track from the forest pathway to the shoreline, where the rowboat would come upstream to make its landing; and hovering over everything, the silver blue helicopter, which would come to earth on the stretch of sand where the river made a cove.

He was responsible for all this, he had set it all in motion on that first day when he had written: Fade In—A Clearing in a Forest. But if he had started it, he could not stop it; the thing had its own flux now, as irreversible as the river. It was his unborn child, but he could not prevent its birth; his pregnancy, unlike a woman's, could not be aborted; if he were to quit, another director would be hired to give the offspring its bastard existence. He could only hope that when the calamities struck, as strike they always did, he would be ready for them, that his yearning would give him courage, and his brain would not go blank.

The excitement was not in him alone, of course, it was in everybody. The scene was a small landing stage on a grassy bank. It was not the very opening of the screenplay that he was shooting, but the first meeting of the three principals, Rachel, Kono and Titus. He had chosen to start the work partway into the script so as to set the personal tone among them. He felt that if he caught them all together while everyone was a bit nervous there would be an excited tension in the scene, and a lucky accident might happen; he always prayed for lucky accidents.

It was not a backbreaking shot, but difficult. It involved the synchronized landing of a boat and a helicopter, and the union of three groups of people. Moreover, he wanted the sound to be natural, not dubbed, and the camera to move in, without a cut, to the dialogue. If he got the scene by lunchtime, he would be ahead of schedule; if he got it by nightfall, he would not be behind.

He looked up at the sky. There was the barest wisp of a cloud, directly overhead; upriver, beyond the rise of ground, the heavier cumulus did not seem to be coming in this direction. There would be no lighting problems; it would be a good, even day; the gaffers would compensate for the changing sunlight.

Two arc lights were being tested, on, off, on, off; the older one was noisy, hissing. His assistant director, Harry Fellows, was on a public address microphone, shouting to a group of blacks at the edge of the clearing. Another assistant with a walkie-talkie was directing the helicopter pilot, Manuel Garcia, to ascend a few hundred feet and slow down his rotors for a moment; then Luke called the motorboat where Elsie Rush, the second assistant camera operator, would be double-covering the shot with a hand-held camera. There was going to be full sound on the first shot, he said, so the motorboat would have to kill its engines. Full sound, the motorboatman shouted, is he crazy, what's he going to do about the chopper? Mind your business, said the assistant.

The shot was nearly ready for rehearsal, but a painter was still aging the rowboat with an airbrush. The main camera was being trundled back and forth to trace the squeak in the track. Alan Greenstone, the sound man, said he needed more height for his boom, and somebody muttered, "Christ, he's got the whole sky."

Luke said to the walkie-talkie man, "Get Barney."

"He's already in the chopper."

"I know that," Luke replied evenly. "Get him."

"Barney in the chopper, Barney in the chopper." He heard Garcia, the pilot, responding. "Put Barney on," Luke said irritably.

"Yeah? Yeah?" Barney answered.

Luke took the walkie-talkie. "When you land, stay in the wind of the chopper for a few instants—count to three."

"Will it blow my hat off?"

"Carry it."

"Right."

"Then, when you see her—instead of speeding up your walk, consciously slow it down. Don't do it gradually. Let's see the moment you *decide* to slow down."

"Yeah—gotcha."

He heard the man's appetite for playing the affront. He was an actor who solicited abrasion. "Don't overdo it, Barney."

"Who, me?" And he laughed.

Luke turned and saw Julo join his group of cultists at the edge of the clearing. He took the PA mike from his assistant.

"Julo," he said. "Julo, if you can hear me, please wave your arm."

Julo smiled and made a broad gesture.

"Good. All you have to do is wait until the door of the helicopter opens, then start to walk toward the landing. Tell the others to walk a few paces behind you. When you see me raise my hand, stop walking and watch the two white people greet one another. That's all—nothing to act—just walking and watching. Okay?"

Julo now raised both his arms, waved and was still.

The director heard a stir at the water's edge, and laughter, and turned to see the grips and assistants making a fuss over her, Calla, the star. She was getting into the rowboat, careful of her well-aged boots and of the khaki riding breeches, which also looked the worse for wear but fit her perfectly. She tossed her denim cap into the boat as the costume woman offered her a choice of sunglasses, holding a hand mirror up to the actress so she could see herself.

How beautiful she is, he thought, dressed and naked, how beautiful right now with the suntan makeup darkening her pale skin, her eyes brighter through the glow of bronze.

She waved one pair of glasses at him, then another, trying them on, then calling across the distance, "Which?"

"The wide ones," he yelled.

She laughed. "Want to hide my face, huh?"

Lucas felt a rush of extra excitement, and wondered if she did.

He called for a rehearsal of the vehicles, to get the timing right, the landing of the boat and the chopper. The walkie-talkie squawked again, so did the PA system. They tried the landings once, told the rower to delay the boat a little on the second rehearsal, to speed it up on the third, and then they had it right. The assistant asked if they would rehearse the actors, but Luke said no, that Julo had no lines, and the other two had only a half dozen each; they would wing it on the first shot.

"Stand by for action," Lucas said.

"Stand by!" the PA system called. "Quiet. Quiet, please. Stand by."

"Stand by," the walkie-talkie told the boat and chopper.

"Roll 'em," the director said.

"Speed."

Stillness. Only the birds might be in motion now, and none of them were heard. The quiet was rigid. Luke felt the heat, the chill, the hope, the dread.

"Action!"

"Action!" the assistants echoed.

The sound boom descended. The camera moved slowly on its dolly track.

The rotor of the helicopter reverberated, loud and louder, as the aircraft came in from the distance. A dog barked somewhere, far away. The plash of the oars became more present, but the sound was smothered under the rotor noise as the boat came upstream along the riverbank. The blacks appeared on the fringe of the woods. They separated to make a path for their leader, and Kono came to the forefront. He waited. He looked one way, then another, saw the helicopter in the sky and watched; then he saw the boat and his eyes stayed on it for a moment. He was quite still.

The rowboat started to land. The helicopter began to descend. Kono looked up at the aircraft and held upon it.

The camera had to ride to where its track divided. It stopped and turned somewhat, to take in the landing from the sky. It stayed upon it then, and waited for the craft to come to earth. Slowly the camera turned again, moved ever so slightly backward, following focus.

The boat came to ground; so did the chopper. As the woman was debarking at the water's edge, the door of the aircraft opened. The ginger-bearded man got out. He started to walk, saw the woman, consciously slowed his pace. She noted the provocation, had not expected it, and tensed a little. The black man began to walk, his followers close behind him. Even with her dark glasses on, the woman raised her hand and shielded her eyes from the sun. She looked at the white man approaching her, and at the black. She hesitated. There was no question that the two men unnerved her, but she was a strong woman exactingly controlled.

The director raised his hand and the black man halted. But the white hunter did not. He kept approaching the woman.

The camera moved and kept moving closer, closer to the two white people. The sound boom continued to lower. The white man said her name, and she nodded. She spoke softly so that the black man might not hear. But the hunter did not care whether they were overheard; in fact, there was a certain truculence, as if he wanted the cult leader to know what they were saying. It vexed her. But the black man's presence also provoked her . . . she was frightened. At last, to cope with her alarm, she left the guide and slowly started to approach the waiting black.

"Cut!"

The director called the word, and then added:

"It's a take."

The first assistant lowered his PA microphone; the other one switched off his walkie-talkie.

The assistant director asked, "Shall we set it up again?"

"I said it's a take," Luke repeated. "Print it."

"What did he say?" someone whispered.

"He said it's a take, it's a print."

For a moment no one could believe it. Then there was a shout of delight. Somebody yahooed. A prop boy started to jump up and down.

Feona Carney yelled, "One shot, one take, one print!"

A grip embraced a gaffer and kissed him. Someone started to dance. The Gurries had not understood what was going on, but dancing was familiar. They started to dance as well. People sang, people clapped their hands, people beat on the light pans.

Calla, Julo, Barney, the soundmen, the camera operators, dressers, decorators surrounded Luke. Do you mean it, they said, one shot, one take, one print, do you mean it, is that it?

"That's it," he said.

The company's joy was boundless, it was giddy-brained. They all

sensed, everybody knew in an inchoate way, that what they were celebrating was more consequential than a single shot, a single take. They
were jubilant because the man who had directed the scene was sure of
hand; he was a leader who knew what he was looking for, recognized it
when he saw it, and, without a hedging shot, had the courage to commit himself. We've caught it, he had said, we've captured the elusive
thing, at least the start of it. It's a take!

All through the day, the shooting was excellent. The crew was a
fortunate meld, the electricians were swift, the set decorators had an accurate sense of place, the sound man was not pesky about distractions,
and while Lucas could not positively predict what the day's film would
look like, he had a sense that the camera was catching the starkness of
white heat and black shadow. Best of all, he felt certain that he had not
made a single mistake in casting; the actors played with assurance and
skill. Even Julo, who, in his daily life, made every entrance with flares
of fireworks and discussed even the weather histrionically, played his
scenes with modulated reservation. He listened to direction eagerly, and
responded instantly. If at times his voice did slightly tend to recitation,
it was his own voice, and honest.

By nightfall, although no one-shot-one-take miracle was repeated,
they had done two more setups than the schedule called for, and Luke
was pleased. When the chuck wagon pulled up to the dining tent, he
went inside. He could hear from the noisy babble in the large dining
place that everybody felt as he did, buoyant. Surveying the four oblong
tables, he chose to sit at the largest one, between Feona and the film editor, Norman Arnold. The dinner was a succulent fricassee of lamb and
chicken, and he had his first full meal in days, leaving the table just in
time to miss the rice-and-prune pudding.

He wanted to be alone a bit, so he walked along the river as the
sun was setting behind him. He had been told by one of his assistants
that whenever he went below the lagoon he must carry a gun, for there
was talk of croachers on the bank, also copperheads and water mocca-
sins. Still, when he got to the lagoon, he did not turn back. Not that he
was witless or foolhardy, he told himself, but that he had to risk something tonight.

Although everything had gone exceptionally well today, he felt
that he had not as yet caught—in the three weeks he had been here—
any intuition of the place, the shadow place of a cult. Perhaps he had
been too insulatedly safe, had guarded himself too carefully, allowing
nothing of its menace to touch him. He needed danger; it brought new

meanings to him, it lit a fuse under the complacent reliance on experience. He had to avoid getting too cozy with his skills. He was afraid that his talent, like love in a smug marriage, would die of habit. And he always felt that a locale was not dramatic unless it coupled beauty with peril.

Yet, there seemed no danger in this dusk, it was all beauty. He saw no signs of croachers or serpents, only the silliness of newborn birds trying to take to the sky, and the jumpy nervousness of frogs. Then a flight of odd-looking, pink-tailed birds, drinking, one at a time, as if queuing up to a single faucet. A heavy gray goose hovered and descended to wade a little, grunted and honked; with a whir and whoosh, heavy no longer, it lifted like a winged balloon into the blue.

It was all lovely, yet nothing exotic, nothing to match the sense of unearthliness in the script. Still, the Gurries had seemed strange to him at first, and in some way, haunted. He had to find the special thing that made a cult possible down here, but he mustn't rush it; first day's shooting, that was all; hardly more than establishing shots. He must, however, be on the watch, keep himself vulnerable, carry no guns, be available for what Julo might call enchantment.

There was, of course, that one form of enchantment he must beware of. Don't fall in love with her. If you do, you'll get no love in return; she's made that clear from the beginning. . . . Yet, last night she had wanted him, even more hungrily than he had wanted her. But there was no significance in it, he warned himself, none that wouldn't be true of frogs or geese. Still, people like us—can we be satisfied with . . . ?

Knock it off. Just satisfy the rudimentary hard-on. Make the arrangement an exercise in discipline, screw and forget, incorporate it into the shooting schedule. It was what many another director would do; the cast and crew would think you were doing it anyway. There was nothing exceptional about location romances, routine transactions, all washed up on wrap-up day. Rigidly conventional. Procedural, like the clicking of the clapperboard, take one, take two . . .

Returning, he passed an edge of the Bayou. The Gurrie village was asleep. He heard a small child crying; that was all the sound there was. Then a quick swishing into the water; so he made his way more inland than before. Now his own footsteps on sand or gravel were the only disturbance he could hear.

The location compound was also hushed. The generator truck had been turned off, saving fuel, and it was silent. From the trailers, a guitar somewhere, country music on a radio, the mumble and occasional laughter of men playing poker. Through the doorways, in narrow oblongs on the ground there were spills of light from oil lamps, since electricity was made by generators, and rationed. He wondered how the cast and crew could manage with so little illumination. They would need more light if the film went badly, he thought.

He had an urge, an almost irresistible urge to go to her trailer. But he remembered that Willi would also be there, and his mind thanked her for her presence. He was glad that Willi was with the company, even if she had no function. He had given her his director's chair today, seating her on the sidelines, telling her it was her place, she could always have it. She had been pleased, totally satisfied to be a spectator, touchingly grateful for the privilege. Now he was grateful to her for being a chaperone. Thank you, Willi.

When he entered his own trailer, Calla was there.

Many nights, however, she wasn't. Whether she would be present or absent was unpredictable, nor could he discern why she made one choice or the other. At first he did not discuss it with her, not wishing to admit how much he wanted her company. But one night, after lovemaking:

"Why do you stay away?" he asked. "Do you think we have to make love every night? Can't you just sleep with me?"

"Never mind."

"No. Tell me."

"I don't know why." In the dark, he sensed that she was consciously lightening her voice. "I'm whimsical."

But she was not a feather tossed by whims; she was putting him off. She did not want to share the warmth or tenderness, or any of the intimacies that would make her more emotionally dependent. He didn't believe she was using him only as a stud, or as a soporific; he felt he was fulfilling a deeper function, an anodyne. Not a cure, certainly—even with love, nobody could cure anybody of anything. A palliative.

One night, mulling over the obstacle between them, it occurred to Lucas that she might still distrust him, might have some lingering suspicion that he had had something to do with the assault on Willi.

"Nonsense. I stopped suspecting you long ago," she said. "Mr. Satin did it."

She had told him about the anonymous caller, but this time she gave him more details about the voice, what little more she knew. He tried to comfort her. "Perhaps it's over. You haven't heard from him in over a month, you say. Maybe you'll never hear from him again."

"No, I'll hear from him. Any time now."

She had spoken with the cold fatalism that people speak of death. While he had not for a moment thought she had concocted the tales of Satin, he had the intimation that she was magnifying their significance, allowing them to storm in her mind. He wondered whether a realist's relief from reality might be hysteria.

But he might be seeing her all wrong. She might be more stable than he imagined, more ready to put aside her fears of Satins and O'Hares, more ready to be loved. If there was any plausibility to the hope, he had better be patient. Wait her out.

As he was waiting her out in daylight, on the set.

Her acting had begun to disappoint him. It was dispiriting how good she was in the part, without being good enough; how much she brought without bringing herself. He had no real complaint against her. She was scrupulously faithful to the intentions of the script, fulfilling every nuance. A generous listener, she followed his directions minutely; she said yes, I'll try that, even before the words were out of his mouth; she thought up illuminating bits of business, and praised his inventions. To the actors she gave far more than they gave her. When she had to speak off-camera, throwing lines for close-ups, she never let up on her vitality or feeling, but played as fully as if the camera were solely on her face. Everyone adored her and thought she was wonderful in the part.

But Lucas didn't. Something at the heart of her performance had never come to life. The most terrible aspect was that he did not know how to name it. He had seen evidence of a pallor in her last two films, and had ascribed it to scripts she had no passion for, or to insensitive, anemic directors. But here it was again, as if her blood were thinning, her soul sickening. Having no cure, he did not dare to speak openly for fear she would panic. So he dealt with the more obvious craft problems, the mechanical staging of her scenes, the interpretations in terms of readings and business and camera. Yet, his inability to deal with the heart trouble of the woman-in-the-part made him morose.

One day, after two weeks of shooting, he lost his temper. "Don't treat him as a prop, he's a person!"

"What?" She was shocked by his tone.

It was an intimate scene between her and the hunter. Barney, sensing a crisis, moved apart from the confrontation and started to mutter his lines to himself, as if to lock them in memory.

"What do you mean, treat him as a prop?" she said coolly. "I haven't even touched him."

"Then touch him, for God's sake."

"I'm supposed to be quarreling with him."

"Then quarrel. Don't discuss, don't reason—quarrel!"

"I don't think she would lose her temper, do you?"

"I don't know—let's find out. I see a lot of skilled acting, but no *behavior*. Do something. Get angry—throw something at him."

She looked around the set. It was bare, without ornaments or knickknacks. "There's nothing to throw."

"Throw a fit!"

She smiled. "Do you want me to behave like a hysteric?"

The word, which had been in his own mind, stopped him. "No. I want you to be an emotionally available woman."

"Are they the same?"

"Maybe to you, not to me. Women do lose control of themselves, you know."

Still quiet-spoken: "I don't want to lose control."

That was it. Afraid of losing control. It was true even in lovemaking. For the most part, she was passionate, but sometimes, on the verge of orgasm, he felt that she held back, resisting as if sexual satisfaction made her a victim not only of him but of herself. No wonder she talked so possessively about control; she was terrified it would be wrested from her. On the set, he had thought they were arguing some generalized feminist issue, but what they were discussing was the dismay of the star.

The paranoia of stardom. She must hang on to her Self, for everyone was out to snatch it away. They were out to *get* her, in two senses: capture and kill. She trusted nobody anymore, not even the man who caressed her in the dark; better keep the watchlight burning. And take extra precaution against falling in love, especially with her director, the man in charge. She could not unguardedly give herself to the scene or to the bed, for she was frightened, this side of panic. He had a surge of pity; what a shining talent she was blighting.

In the next few days of shooting, he had a sense of failure about the whole film. He dreaded seeing the rushes, which were delayed because Dyer Addison had quarreled with one lab and haggled with another, and Luke had a foreboding that the first weeks of work would reveal a parallel of Calla's performance, craftsmanlike but spiritless. He found himself doing the duller scenes very well, with security. It angered him that there was so much authority in the commonplace. Would he ever be able to find the tension between the banal and the bizarre?

The sorest spot in all this, he realized, was the character of Kono. And the fault was not in the way Julo played him. The actor, without any training at all, had a protean talent, he could do anything, pretend anything. Moreover, he had such trust in Lucas, he was so devoted, that he would unquestioningly follow any suggestion in any way he was told. But what to tell him?

Lucas had the sense that some major element in Kono had been left out, or badly written. It was as if he had painted a man and given him no eyes, or had drawn someone else's mouth upon the face. No matter how he agonized over a picture that was wrong, he could not tell what was missing or distorted.

But he did know *why* he was failing. Because he could not comprehend the actual man upon whom the part was based. Julo was still a mystification to him. He was a mass of inconsistencies. The leader of a growing cult in California, he now scarcely mentioned his ambitions for it; he was currently an actor, totally an actor, worrying about makeup and costume and movement and motive, and how do I make my exit? There were other inconsistencies, the old ones, the crude speech against the carefully articulated thought, the cynical gutter-brute against the spiritual man of God. Even in his spirituality he was inconsistent. Sometimes he was a pantheist, seeing divinity in trees, snakes, a well-cooked meal, the lifting of a mist. Sometimes he was a resurrectionist, believing in the reincarnated body and the reborn soul.

One night, as he and Julo were walking along the river, seeing the moon as a boat on the water, Julo cried:

"Look! Look!"

Further down the river, where the lagoon emptied into it, a family of badgers were drinking at the water's edge.

"The first one—the buck badger," he said. "Look at the big one— the buck!"

"What about him?"

"He's my cousin."

Lucas laughed, enjoying the man.

"Stop laughing."

Surprised, Lucas turned to see if he was serious. Yes, and annoyed.

Lucas didn't know what to do with the instant, how to interpret the vexation.

"Julo, when you do that, I get lost—which may be what you want. But I don't like it. If you say a badger is your cousin, I can smile and enjoy it—it's funny and even poetic. But if you actually mean it . . . I can't believe you're a fake or a fool, so what are you?"

"Go fuck yourself."

"What are you?"

Julo got over his anger and, grinning, pointed to the sky. "You see that yellow star that's blinking over the Bayou?"

"Your brother-in-law?"

"No, it's a thought I had when I was a child."

"A thought?"

"Yes. When I was thirteen or fourteen, around this time of year, it was my opinion that a star should be right there. That star is my opinion."

This time they laughed together. It was clear to Luke that the man felt he had unbalanced something that had been steady in their friendship, and wanted to restore the equilibrium.

"Don't ask me for sensible answers, Lucas." It was a plea.

"I'll be grateful for any answers, Julo. You're my friend. Why don't you trust me? Why don't you tell me who you are?"

"I'm the Gorá."

"The hell with you!" He started away.

"Wait! Lucas, come back!"

Half turning: "No! I'm sick of this double-talking crap! If you don't trust me enough—"

"I'm a Watts nigger!"

Slowly Luke returned. "Are you?"

"Yes—I was born there—Watts. I lived in ugliness that was so authentic—! My God, it was so incontestably real—! That's the only way I can describe the hopelessness and the shit and the squalor and the dead end—it was *real*. But right next door—an hour's walk—"

"Hollywood."

"That's right. Now, do I have to tell you how I was hacked into two pieces? Do I have to draw you a picture of a schitzy nigger? Man, I was a schizophrenic from the day I saw my first picture show! But that wasn't the heart of it. Me, the college student—Howard on a scholarship—me, the Andy Young, the Adam Clayton Powell—me, the first black president of the fuckin' United States—but that wasn't the heart of it."

"What was the heart of it?"

"God."

"You, the Martin Luther King."

"Oh no! Martin was a well-connected man—he had influence with God. He was in the inner circle of heaven. But not me—I was a ravin' demon—wrasslin' with the Holy Ghost! I was strugglin' with all my might with my Almighty. I was sayin' to Him: You ain't gonna get away with it. Love me! Believe in me! I ain't gonna believe in you until you believe in me. Love me! Give me somethin'—show me somethin'— let me into your confidence! *Love me!* Why can't you fuckin' well be my friend? Why can't you love me like I love you? LOVE ME!"

"Did He answer you?"

"If He did, I didn't hear Him."

"Did you see Him?"

"I saw Him at a distance, goin' away."

"Is He gone?"

"Yeah. . . . But I'm gonna bring Him back."

"How?"

"In my image."

"Which is?"

"Flames."

"What does that mean, Julo?"

"I don't know—how the hell do I know? He didn't give me the slightest hint. I'm in this God business by myself. By myself, Lucas— and I've got to make a go of it. I've got to find something to believe in. I've got to find something to believe in, or the world is Watts. Oh, Lucas, my friend, the world is Watts!"

Angry and aching, he hurried away.

The following evening, Lucas had an appointment to work privately with Julo on a difficult scene scheduled for the next morning. It was well past dinnertime, getting dark, and Julo didn't show up. Luke sent an assistant to the actor's trailer; he wasn't there. He hadn't been in the dining tent for dinner, and Willi had had no word of him.

Lucas got into one of the company cars and drove into town. The streets of Ashton were deserted; the stores had all closed for the night.

It occurred to Lucas that Julo might be on the other side of the river, in the black section.

However, the black section was also shut up for the night. All except the poolroom at the far end of an alley so narrow that Luke had to leave the car and walk. It was a long, dismal, dirt-paved passageway. The light at the remote end of blackness was like a frail ghost; the music was weary, the tired beat of used-up jazz.

As Luke approached the poolroom, something struck him as odd. Although the doors were wide open to the summer night, no noise issued from inside, not a sound except for the soft jazz, no voices, no laughter, no click of billiard cues or the racking of balls. It was a disquieting quiet.

Slowly he went to the open doorway and gazed in. Nobody was shooting pool. Very few of the green-shaded table lights were in use. Those that were alight were angled up to throw a flood of illumination on the man who stood on one of the billiard tables. Julo.

He was talking to the crowd. Not many people, twenty at most, the riffraff of the black side of town, mostly men, a few disheveled women . . . all listening, spellbound.

He was not haranguing them; his voice was scarcely a whisper, so that they had to strain to hear. What he was saying could not be spoken loudly, it was too intimate, a personal message to personal friends, his family in fact, the family tidings of God, a message He had sent to them, a greeting of good heart, a promise of better times, a vision of the benign hereafter.

The somber half light of the poolroom shone on a magical moment and made it a magical place . . . while the enraptured congregants at the ceremony listened and nodded, smiling but grave, rejoicing silently at the tidings of the god-messenger.

Suddenly, mid-syllable, Julo stopped speaking. He had seen Lucas at the doorway. For an instant, the black man seemed almost catatonic, as if all his life processes had ceased. It was as though an icy actuality had frozen his spirit. Then, after a bit, his muscles relaxed, and he continued to speak. But the magic was gone. He talked with a dry voice, from a far distance.

It bothered Lucas, as it bothered everyone, to watch Willi slip into a depression. The euphoria of the shivaree had lasted only a few days for her, and then she began to see her disfigurement everywhere, the world had turned into mirrors. She rarely came to the set anymore, for she felt that everyone was staring at her. She spent her time in the trailer, reading, sleeping, watching television.

One day, however, when she could no longer stand her solitude, she came to observe a scene being filmed. Lucas was rehearsing Barney and Calla in a short sequence, a nearly silent incident in an abandoned shack where they cook a meal together on a two-burner spirit stove. Immediately after the rehearsal was over, the principals left the set so that it could be lighted, and Lucas called, "Second team."

That meant stand-ins. Just as Feona, the script woman, was about to take Calla's place, Luke called again, "Willi—places!"

Instinctively she got out of her chair, then arrested the motion. She hadn't done a stroke of work in months, and certainly in that time she had never functioned on a set. In fright, her eyes darted for an escape.

Luke's voice was peremptory. "Come on, Willi, don't waste time."

Slowly, like a sleepwalker, she moved onto the set. As Feona prompted her from position to position, and as the lights were focused, she began to walk with greater confidence. Toward the end of the scene, when Feona directed her once too often, Willi smiled. "I know—I remember." The script woman slipped away.

Calla stood on the sidelines, watching. Her hands covered her mouth as if she were afraid to utter so much as a whisper that might interrupt Willi's concentration. Halfway through, Willi saw her and they smiled, and Calla could not stand how happy they were.

When it was over, Lucas approached Willi. "Good girl, you got all your marks."

"You got the marks, Luke," she said.

She was back at work from that day onward, and for nearly a week her spirits were up again. Then they began to slip once more. Expression by expression, her features started to droop, her shoulders sagged and the listlessness returned.

This time it was Julo who brought her back to life. It happened in what they called the green room, a double trailer as wide as it was long, which was used during the day as a sort of operations office. At night it became a lounge, with coffee urn and teapots, and machines for dispensing drinks, cigarettes, candy bars. One evening, when there was a carnival in Ashton, the green room was practically empty. Lucas was there, working, dictating instructions into a mini-recorder which he constantly carried, Willi was reading, and Calla and Barney were running through a dialogue scene that would be shot tomorrow.

The door opened and Julo came bursting in on a gust of enthusiasm.

"Willi! Look what I've got for you! Look what I've got—look where we're going!"

His voice rang loud, the energy of his excitement shook the trailer. Barney was irritated. "We're working."

"Sorry," the black man said.

They had a strange relationship, those two. There was respect in it, but reservation. Since they had to be enemies in the film, by an odd, unspoken work ethic they had stayed apart from one another, as if afraid that any warm regard they might develop might soften their hostility on film.

Julo had a large envelope in his hand and he waved it at Willi. "Come here," he muttered in a stage whisper. "Let me show you."

Drawing her into a corner of the room, half hidden by a bank of vending machines, he sat her on a chrome and plastic couch, plopped down beside her and opened the envelope. It had a mass of clippings from magazines, pictures in bright color, mountains and forests and savannas, people and wild animals.

Luke, who had clicked his mini-recorder off, watched them. He heard the black man in a flood of words, high-spirited, buoyant with happiness, as he turned from one brilliant photograph to another.

"It's Gorá, honey," he said. "It's my country—it's Gorá!"

"So beautiful," she said.

"And we're goin' there—you and big Julo—we're goin' there, Willi."

"Dumbhead." She touched him affectionately. "Sweet dumbhead."

"No, I mean it. Look at that. Look at that savanna there—you know where it's goin'? To the start of time! Right to the first startin'-up, wakin'-up, open-eyed minute of time! Look at the way that hilltop's makin' passes at the sky. Look at that beautiful hartebeest—that's a hartebeest, Willi—we make home for the hartebeest. Look at the giraffes, look at them—they're like wallpaper in a kindergarten. I love you, giraffe, I love you!"

"I love you, Julo." And she hit him.

"You don't believe me, do you? You don't believe we're goin' to Gorá."

"Oh, Julo."

"We are! Goddamn, we are! When this picture's over, I'm goin' to take and buy us two airplane tickets, and I'm goin' to take and lift us up into Gorá! We're goin' to Gorá!"

"Why?"

"Why? I'm goin' to tell you why. I'm goin' to fill your pink-white ears with the golden reason why!" He was a pitchman selling paradise. "Why is because Gorá is beautiful, why is because Gorá is heaven for the beasts of the field and birds of the sky and black folk lookin' for the face of God. Gorá is the end of cryin'. Why, you say? Why is the women with signs on their faces."

He gently touched her cheek.

"Why the women with signs on their faces?" she asked softly.

"Because—look, Willi—look." He had kept the best, the most important pictures for last.

"Look at that black woman, Will. She's a princess of Gorá. Look at her face—slash marks. Look at that. She's got scars from her forehead to her cheekbone. And look at this one. She looks just like you, except she's black—and her scars are just like yours. Only they weren't done by a hatin' monster, Willi—they were done by her father, in an act of love. Scars are beauty in Gorá, Willi. Scars tell how you're loved by your father and loved by your tribe, and you are the favored of the gods. Scars are the mark of heaven, Willi. Beautiful Willi, they are the mark of heaven!"

The man was so ecstatic but so patently fabricating that Luke could not believe Willi would credit a single word he was saying. But she wasn't hearing the words, only the melody of the dream, and the resonance of the man's love.

"Julo," she murmured, "Julo, how wonderful you are."

"It's Gorá that's wonderful. Gorá is the holy land of God and beauty!"

Barney said: "Gorá's a load of shit."

The room went dead.

Barney continued. "I saw that picture—the one Willi's got in her hand. I was in a dentist's office, and I saw it in a *National Geographic*. Gorá, my ass. You know what that is? It's either Somalia or Uganda, I can't remember which. Those are pictures of the way a tribe looked thirty years ago. But now they don't look like that, they're starving, they're diseased. I forgot the name of the tribe—some asshole place in Africa."

"That's not true." Julo got up from the settee.

"Don't tell me! You're selling her a lot of bullshit."

Calla said, "Barney, don't."

"Barney, stay out of it," Lucas said.

"No, I won't! Doesn't she have enough to handle without him giving her a load of lies to carry around with her? What happens if she believes him? What happens if she goes there, and finds those women are sick with hunger, and their babies have blown-up bellies and—"

"That's wrong!" Julo cried. "They're beautiful!"

"Beautiful? Read the article. Read the back of the picture!"

He snatched the picture out of Willi's hand, turned it over and was about to read the article aloud.

"Give me that!" Julo shouted.

"I'm going to read it to her."

"I said give me that!"

He reached and Barney stepped away. "Hands off, you son of a bitch!"

Julo's fist struck out. Barney reeled, then started forward to the fight.

"Quit it!" Luke shouted. "Quit it, both of you!"

The men were exchanging blows. Luke rushed between them.

"Stop it!"

He shoved them apart. "Stop it, you dumb bastards!" There was a silence of glaring rage. "Don't do that! Never! Don't do that!"

Barney hurried out of the trailer, slamming the door after him.

Then . . . as if nothing had happened . . . as if their idyll over the pictures had never been interrupted, Julo and Willi sat down once more, and returned to the fantasy. It was muted at first, too sober for the words to sing as they had sung before. But in a little while: Look at this, he said, look at that endless plain, look how far that horizon is, look at this beautiful face, look how proudly she holds her head, look, look . . .

And Willi looked and saw her vision.

Lucas had a visit from Rickert. The sheriff appeared one afternoon as the company was doing pickup shots with stand-ins. When they were finished, and setting up for a new scene, the sheriff beckoned the director apart from the others, so that they could talk confidentially.

"I got a little favor to ask you, Luke."

"What is it?"

"It's about my Ellasue."

"What's the matter?"

"Nothin' the matter, everything jim-dandy. Except . . . You know how crazy gone she is on movin' pitcher stuff. Well, she got it in her head she'll shrivel up and die if you don' let her take a part in your pitcher."

Luke tried to be genial. "Well, the larger parts, of course—"

"No, no, no—goldarn it, no. She don' expect no big part. Hell, that'd just scare her to shivers. All she wants . . ." He was embarrassed.

"I'm sure I could find her a small part—keep her working a few days."

"Well, it ain't the work, Luke. She don' need the money nor nothin', come from a fine family in Shreveport. But . . . She wanta be —you understand me, Luke?—she wanta be kinder part of the pitcher."

"As I say, it would only be a few days' work . . ."

"She wouldn't be around all the time, huh?"

"Well . . . no."

He snickered through the paste, but the laugh failed to conceal his discomfiture. "And wouldn't be here for the . . . uh . . . special stuff?"

"What do you mean?"

He dodged the question. "You know, she read your—what do you call it?—the story-like."

"The script? Where'd she get it?"

Again, the pasty laugh. "Heck, Lucas, there's lots of ways."

"I hope she liked it."

"Oh yeah, she sure did. She pitchered in her head just like it was already up there on the silver screen. . . . Especially the ornery stuff."

"What ornery stuff?"

The sheriff was caught between his lurid interest in the lascivious, and his righteous objection to it:

"R—a—p—e."

". . . I see."

"What she really want—now, Luke, you understand me, hear?— she's her and I'm me—and I'm embarrassed to say this."

"Well?"

"She want to watch you when you're takin' pitchers of that."

Luke didn't reply immediately. The sheriff's position was uneasy, so was his own. A young wife to whom he had to prove himself had put Rickert in a thorny place, and Luke didn't want to make it more uncomfortable for him. "Sheriff, it's a little difficult. There are certain scenes that are troublesome to the actors—and they demand such privacy that they're done on what is called a closed set. But really closed— no visitors permitted. Even the crew is often pared down to only the most essential people. And the rape scene will be one of them."

Rickert flushed. "Luke—believe me—I see your point. I see it right good and well. But she's only one person, you know—she ain't a crowd. And she's smart, Ellasue is, she's mighty smart. She's loud when she has to be loud, and quiet when she has to be quiet. And if you was to let her in, she'd be the quietest little mouse—hell, nobody'd know she was breathin'."

"I'm sorry, Sheriff, I just can't do it."

"You don't know what it'd mean to me."

"I do know, and if I could—"

"It's like—if you do this for me—well, hell, I'd be a man of power in her eyes. And if you don't—"

"You're still a man of power, Sheriff."

"Don't lard me, Lucas." All the slack was out of his voice.

"I don't know how I'm doing that, but—"

"Don't lard me, I said. Don't tell me I'm powerful while you're cuttin' my balls off. You can do this little thing for me, after what I been doin' for you. You can do it if you wanta do it. And if you don't wanta do it, you better tighten rein."

"What's that mean?"

"Pull up your big nigger."

"Why?"

"He's bustin' windas."

"Whose windows is he busting?"

"He's out on the town. Rabble-rousin'. He's got his arm up like a big black Jesus, and he's claimin' the word of the Lord."

"Is there anything wrong with that?"

"He's sellin' a bill of goods."

"It's religion, Sheriff. You're not against religion, are you?"

It was the wrong question to a self-appointed deacon of the Lord. Unlike rape, gospel was a subject on which he needn't hide his emotion: righteous indignation. "Don't you question my religion, mister!"

"I won't. But you can't question his, either. You've got black voters, Sheriff. How will it look on election day if you've come out against a black man who's preaching the word of God?"

"It's not God—it's voodoo! He's gonna light a great big fire somewhere—and he's gonna walk through it like an angel of the Lord—and he ain't gonna singe a hair on his head. He's been tellin' that to all the niggers—he's been roilin' 'em up—he's been sayin' he's pertected by the hand of the Almighty God. Now you know and I know, Mr. Lucas O'Hare, that that is a big goldamn con job—and he's gonna take them niggers for every black nickel they've got!"

"You've got it wrong, Sheriff. He's doing what I asked him to do. We need a big crowd for the fire scene at the end of the picture. It'll take hundreds of people—mostly blacks. He and the second unit men are trying to get them together."

It was true, and the sheriff saw that it might be. He was taken aback. "It ain't smart of you to cover for him, Lucas."

"I'm not covering."

"You know who you're coverin' for, don't you?"

"I am not covering!"

"The man's got a record goes back twenty years, and clear across the country. He's gonna get in trouble here—no chance in the world he won't. And when he does, you'll be sorry you let him piss in your toilet. So don't you do it, Lucas." Circumspectly, he decided not to leave on an angry note. "Will you try to remember that I gave you a piece of good advice?"

"I'll try."

The sheriff went away.

20

Calla was having difficulties with the telephone in her trailer. It had been installed as a convenience, so that she could be paged when needed on the set, and not have to hang around. But the instrument was turning into more trouble than it was worth. It would ring at odd times, for the wrong person. Sometimes it would ring and no one would be there. It was particularly spiteful on long distance; there were interruptions, disconnections, clicks, buzzes, high whistles.

One day she heard the assorted noises of long distance and the Bronx voice of a telephone operator. Then it was Mr. Satin.

"Hello! How are you?" he chanted cheerily. "How are things going?"

She made a discomposed rejoinder.

"Well, I'm glad to hear it's going better than the gossip has it."

"What does the gossip have?"

"There's a rumor up here that the film's going to shut down."

"Shut down? For what?"

"Rewrites."

"The rumors are wrong," she said.

"What else is wrong?"

"I'm going to ruin your afternoon. Nothing."

"Wait. Trouble isn't always prompt, you know."

"I'll be patient."

"I told you not to go to Ashton, didn't I?"

"Yes, you did, and everything's fine. What are you telling me today?"

"Pretty perky, aren't you? Wouldn't turn a hair if I gave you another warning, would you?"

"No, I wouldn't. Your warnings are suspect."

"Everything should be suspect to you, Calla—everything."

"It's a counsel of paranoia."

"Paranoia in a cutthroat world—ah, normalcy indeed!"

"Any particular cutthroat you have in mind?"

"Beware of fabulists."

"Why? I was beginning to like them."

"Some of them are fanatics."

"What kind of fanatics?"

"Religious. They would kill their mothers in a sacrifice to God. They would slash a woman's face—as a kindness."

". . . A kindness?"

"To exorcise her devil."

"I'm going to hang up now."

"Julasto's a lunatic, Calla—be careful!"

She shouted go to hell, go to hell, which should have been coupled with the hanging up of the phone, but she found herself clutching it tighter to her ear, compulsively attached to it.

"He's not a lunatic, he's not!" she cried.

"That's because you think a lunatic has to tear at his skin or eat babies or open his fly in public. But read the newspapers, Calla. A perfectly normal greengrocer stabs a customer twenty times, a perfectly normal college student shoves his best friend off a roof. And God knows, Julasto isn't even perfectly normal. So watch it, Calla—or your sweet white belly will have cutlery in it."

"I won't let you frighten me anymore—I won't!"

"I'm not trying to frighten you—I'm trying to keep you safe. . . . That's why I'm sending somebody down there."

"You're what?"

"A friend, Calla—you need a friend. I'm sending someone to look after you."

"Don't you dare!"

"You won't even know he's there. But he'll see that you don't get hurt."

"Don't you dare, don't you dare!"

This time she did manage to hang up.

The tremors. Never mind, she said, he won't do it. The man is always warning and threatening and making ominous noises. Then he gets things wrong. She didn't know whether it was a relief or more alarming that he had made those mistakes: how old she was, how many pictures she had performed in, whether the current film would halt for rewrites . . . which woman to mutilate. Deadly misconceptions. And now he would be sending an emissary, to commit what fatal blunder?

She stood at the bedside table where the phone was, hardly aware of Willi in the trailer. She wasn't sure about her friend's concentration, whether she hadn't heard Calla on the phone, or was pretending. Whichever, Willi seemed singlemindedly intent on her diversion. She was pasting pictures of African scenes on Bristol board. On the wall alongside her bed there already hung a framed photograph of a Masai warrior; beside it, a blowup of an Akarra tribeswoman with beaded ear-rings and a glittering necklace of colored stones and painted pods, her exquisite black face scarred from hairline to chin. On the table there were books on Africa and travel brochures that Julo had brought from Memphis. They were indeed going away, Willi and Julo, when the pic-ture was finished, going on safari, not only to see savannas and wild beasts, but to find Gorá, whatever it might be.

Calla asked, "Did you hear that call?"

". . . Yes."

"Can you guess who and what?"

"Yes."

"You want to talk about it?"

"No."

"Just for a little while? I won't heckle you with questions this time, Will. Why don't we free-associate, the way we used to do?"

"No."

"Car."

"Person."

"Help me, Willi. Night."

"Person, person, person!" She raged. Almost instantly, she was calm again. "I'm sorry, Cal. I can't find anything. There's nothing there."

"You've remembered everything else."

"No, I haven't. There are people on the set who know me and I haven't the vaguest recollection who they are."

"If you really put your mind to it—"

"You think I haven't?"

Calla didn't answer. Willi put the photograph and scissors down.

Not looking at Calla, she picked the dried paste off her fingertips. "You think I'm hiding something from you, Cal?"

"Maybe from yourself."

"Hiding what?"

"Or whom?"

"Julo, you mean."

"Yes."

Willi pointed to her marked face. "Do you think I would protect someone who did this to me?"

"No . . . unless it was Julo."

Willi nodded almost imperceptibly. Without reproach: "If I believed it was Julo, do you suppose I could live with that? What excuse could I make for him? How would he and I agree to ignore it? . . . And why would he have done it?"

"If you've asked yourself those questions, why won't you talk about them?"

"It hurts!"

She looked at her hands as if they were important. "Calla . . . do you really believe he could do such a thing? You think he could love me so much and hate me so much?"

"Even in marriages—"

"Please. Do you think he could hate me like that?"

"I don't know. I don't understand him at all. Some religious fanatics are . . . The man on the phone thinks he's . . . unbalanced."

"Of course he is. So am I. . . . So are you, Cal."

"You think we're all in the same goofy-bin?"

The flippancy delayed Willi. "You don't believe it, do you?"

"No, I don't," she said hotly. "And the idea makes me vomit. It's the catchall excuse for everything. Madness, the big mitigation. And the new aesthetic, too. Crazy is beautiful. Bullshit!"

"You want to know something, Calla? I think you're sicker than I am."

"I am? How?"

"You're locked up in the way things are."

She was going to say more, but Calla could see her stopping herself. "Go on," she said.

"No, that's enough."

"No—please—get it out of your system."

"*My* system? *Mine?*"

She laughed in an unhappy way, and went back to Africa.

As in the old Mamma Lorena days, so many years ago, Calla frequently went to the Bayou to find release from the jangles in her mind. She went alone, and sat on the other side of the lagoon from the Gurrie village, watching the wading bitterns, listening to the cry of the river gulls, part lullaby and part lament.

In an early twilight, two days after Mr. Satin's call, she was sitting there, but the Bayou, this time, was not soothing to her spirit. She hadn't been able to get Willi's words out of her mind.

Locked up in the way things are: what a stupid thing for a bright woman to say, as if one had a choice of prisons. You, Willi, are locked up in things as they're not, and I dare you to break free of them. I, the champion of free choice, I dare anyone to make a volitional decision that'll tear loose from . . .

Why can't my head stop aching?

Why can't I play this goddamn part with some freedom from myself, with . . . courage?

Why can't I love Lucas when he so patently loves me? How good he is, how decent!

He was all awareness, not only of her but of everyone. He spoke everybody's language now—the Gurries, the Ashton blacks and whites, the artists on the picture and the crew, all those diverse tongues. He had an idiom of affection with Julo, a communion of friendship. And with Barney, a silent vocabulary of looks and glances. A nod from Lucas, and the actor would change from sobriety to laughter; a frown, and he would probe into aches and angers.

Then why, when all the others were inspired by Lucas, was she letting him down? He was now allowing her almost total liberty in interpreting the script, so that she often forgot he had written it. She knew that the freedom was granted in the hope that she would *become* Rachel, not merely play her, so she could lift the character off the page, and soar. But she was earthbound. For fear of falling, she was apprehensive of every step she took in the role, as if it were a leap across a bottomless chasm of her being. And she remained bound—body and spirit—to Calla Stark.

Locked up in the way things are.

This miserable headache. Why don't the packaged remedies work for me anymore? Twenty grains of anything are no more potent than five used to be.

Getting sicker. Thinner than I've ever been before, even than on *Grotto*. Sleeping less, eating less. Ill. I can't be. I've never been really ill on a film, never missed a single day of shooting, and I won't on this one.

I won't.

Oh, Lucas, if I could only love you as you love me. If I could only be the first to say the words—what a gift I would be giving both of us!

The hell with sitting here, by this lagoon, it doesn't work.

There was no sunlight left, yet it wasn't night, it wasn't anything. The shortest way back from the Bayou was across the neck of the marsh and through the woodland. She entered the woods. The summer foliage was at its densest and the sweet wildwood had turned into a jungle. It had become more difficult to get through it these days, and easier to get lost. She had better hurry before all the light was gone. Things were not as familiar as they used to be; even the bird sounds were different.

"Calla!"

She thought it was a man's voice, shouting to her from a far distance. But when the sound was repeated, she realized it was an animal noise, a winged creature, a parrot or macaw. But there were no parrots in the Bayou woods, and surely macaws were also not native to these latitudes.

"Calla!"

A bird's voice, no question of it, too guttural to be human, and with a note of mockery.

It was the mockery that frightened her. It had to be a human sound, and when it was repeated—

"Yes?" she called. "Who is it?"

"Calla, Calla, Calla!"

A bird, an animal, a man, and she began to run.

The voice echoed after her, then ceased. There was a laugh, a hollow one, distant and eerie, as if the creature was retreating, coming closer, retreating again.

She continued running. She knew the way. Dense as the undergrowth had become, she knew the pathways in this wood, and which ones led to the compound. But—running—she didn't arrive at the great cypress that was a landmark, or at the stand of water alders.

"Calla!"

The voice was nearer than the last time, the woods were deeper, the brush thicker than she remembered.

"Don't run, Calla!"

The warning was so sharp that she stopped dead still.

Then the laughter, as if he knew he had halted her in her tracks, and he was getting closer all the time.

She changed direction, struck inland, parallel to where she took the compound to be.

"Go back!"

The sound was no longer behind her, but directly in her path, straight ahead, she was going to run into him. Again she changed direction. I won't get lost, she told herself, I know these woods, I won't get lost.

"Caaa—laaa!"

Then quickly, a mechanical toy, "CallaCallaCallaCallaCalla!"

The sounds were before and behind her, to the left and to the right. There was no sense to it, she said, the same voice could not be coming from all directions at once. Run, she said, run, run.

Her breath was coming fast. Her heart pounded. The pain in her chest was hot.

"Caaa—laaa!"

Closer, closer, the laugh punctuating everything, the laugh being closest of all, as if it came from another source, a second voice, a mimicry, an echo.

"Calla."

Oh Christ, don't stop running, she said, keep running.

"Calla!"

Something caught at her foot. She tripped and fell. Getting up, she couldn't extricate herself from the creeper. She turned one direction, then another. I'm getting more tangled, she said. She yanked her leg with all her might, and instead of freeing herself, she fell. Lying on the ground, she snatched at the tough tendrils and twisted them, pulled, ripped leaves off with torn hands, tore at the ropy thing, still not freeing herself.

"Calla!"

He was close, close enough for her to hear him beating at the brush. It was the sound of someone cutting a path, slashing with a knife or a machete, a threshing sound.

"Calla!"

She couldn't run, she couldn't move. The tendrils wouldn't tear or snap or let her free. He would be here any moment. She heard the mocking sounds again, the bird noises, the laughter too wild to be altogether sane. Closer, closer.

She waited while the demented cries continued closer, Calla, Calla, Calla.

Waiting.

"Calla, Calla". . . Waiting.

But he did not come. The threshing sound stopped, and the maniacal laughter became softer and more distant. So did the calling of her name.

For a long time she remained there. By slow degrees, she severed the tendrils and broke herself free. Then, catching her breath and regaining her composure, she thought: The deranged man could have killed me if he wanted to, but didn't. Perhaps it didn't happen as I thought it did.

Perhaps it didn't happen at all.

Nobody could make those noises come from all directions, nobody could be here and there and all around her. Nobody could do it except herself. *She* could do it, she could imagine it, she could imagine anything if there was something terribly wrong with her. . . .

She could remember Mr. Satin's first phone call, every word of it. He had predicted—threatened—that a terrible event would happen. And she had answered:

"We all die."

"Worse than dying."

This might be worse.

She called Lieutenant Reuss in California.

"What do you mean, you heard him all around you?"

She tried to explain, and abruptly stopped. He thinks I'm flipping, and so do I. I'd better be quiet now, I'd better hang up.

"I'd like to help you," he said, "but I don't know how."

The last time they had spoken he had sharply reprimanded her. But now his voice was gentle, softer than she had imagined it could be. The voice of a man humoring the sick.

"Besides, you're in Mississippi," he continued. "It's not exactly my precinct."

"Help me!"

She heard herself, distraught. Pulling herself together, she murmured a vagueness and a good-bye.

Good-bye, Lieutenant Reuss, you're off the case now, and I'm still
on it. Alone. . . .

There is a danger, Calla told herself at dawn the following morning, that I won't get through the picture.

My hands shake, I feel faint, I can't remember lines. There is a real
danger I may not even be able to get through this particular day . . .
with the rape scene on the schedule. A rape scene, for God's sake, how
can I play a rape scene in this condition?

By playing it, she said. If you're sick, use it. If you're freaking out,
freak out in the rape scene.

No, it never works that way. It takes cool rationality to play insane.

She would go to the infirmary trailer and get something. There was
a young doctor there, a movie-struck kid—what was his name? Fuhrman,
Joel Fuhrman. He was fresh out of medical school, he would know all
the newest junk, all the specifics for a thirty-nine-year-old star who was
falling to pieces.

She walked across the compound, got within twenty feet of the
infirmary and stopped. It would be brainless. She knew what he would
prescribe. One look at her jittery hands and trembly mouth and he
would give her a sedative. Valium, Librium, something to calm her
down, when what she needed, if she was to play a rape scene, was salt
on her raw nerves . . . to welcome insanity and fight it.

Mid-morning, she got to the location, about a mile from the compound. A Dark Place in the Forest, the script called it. The "set" was
nearly ready, with extra shrubbery, and wild things used as lighting
baffles, the camera track all in place.

She saw Julo and felt a flutter. It had been three days since they
had worked together, and she hadn't seen him since the Satin call.
Every instinct told her that the caller's charge against the man was untrue; he couldn't possibly have had any complicity in the damage to a
woman he loved so deeply. It was only a measure of Calla's instability,
she told herself, that she had this feeling of dread in his presence. Use
it, she kept saying, use it as emotional material in the rape scene.

The instant she saw Lucas and Julo huddle together, she had a
sense of what was in the director's mind. He was going to throw the
whole scene to Kono. The length of his whispered conversation with
the cult leader, and his cursory greeting of Rachel, convinced her that

this was so. The director had lost confidence in her, certainly in her ability to do the scene, or her freedom to make herself available to it. He was giving it all to the dynamic character, he was playing it safe.

All her terrors of the sequence returned, all her quakes and shudders. She tightened every muscle and let go, tightened and let go. She breathed deeply.

The two men were walking close together, away from the camera, in the density of woods. From time to time their voices would rise in a mock playing of the scene, and she could hear the word "rage" more often than any other, and occasionally "revenge." She wondered which revenge they were discussing, the black against the white, or the man against the woman. With a pang, she realized she was thinking of reaction, not action; she was not going to play but be played upon. Murder, she thought, what can I do to dynamite myself? Bleakly she realized she meant "dynamize."

Lucas and Julo returned to the set. The director explained the technical structure of the work to be done. He broke the sequence into three stages: First, the moment of encounter, when she realizes that while she has been hunting for him, *he* has been stalking *her*. Then, terror, flight, and the struggle. Finally, the aftermath. Luke choreographed the movements as if they were a dance, and, like a drill sergeant—since the violence would be dangerous—he made them repeat, word for word, the steps he had outlined. Then, slow motion, he rehearsed the action once, twice, many times.

"All right," he said. "Let's shoot it."

The camera had hardly begun to grind.

"Cut," he said.

He took Julo apart again, and she heard the actor mutter in an agitated voice, "But I'm afraid to hurt her."

"Of course you are—and I don't want you to hurt her. But your face mustn't betray that that's what you're feeling. No matter how your hands and arms don't hurt her, your face—your emotions—have to kill her. It's rape, Julo."

"Yes." He understood, but understanding didn't ease his qualms.

They did the sequence again and again. Instead of getting better, Julo got worse. She recalled the time in his cottage when he had beaten her, and might have raped her. But that was in hot rage, not in the controlled deliberation of picture making. He could not coldly commit the violence.

They started the scene once more, and suddenly, in the midst of it, Julo stopped acting, turned away from Calla and the camera.

"I can't do it," he said quietly.

"Yes, you can." Luke was also quiet. "In fact, you were just beginning to perform it."

"I was not performing."

"Good. Whatever you were doing—"

"It had murder in it!"

The woods seemed as still as if they had been caught on film.

Lucas said evenly. "I don't believe there's murder in you, Julo, and I don't believe—"

"I don't care what you believe!" he raged. "I know goddamn well what's in me! There's murder—"

"No."

"—and ugliness—"

"Julo, listen—"

"—I can't bear to look at it—"

"Julo, it's not true!"

"—ugliness, ugliness—"

"Stop it! Goddamn it, stop it!"

Luke started toward him. As he did, the black man twisted away, throwing his arms up in a spastic gesture, as if shielding himself from view. When the man was still, Luke stood beside him and said:

"You are not ugly, Julo. You are the most beautiful man I've ever known."

On impulse, without reservation, Luke put his arms around his friend and held him in a close embrace. They did not stir from one another for quite a while. The black man's tension loosened and he turned away. Presently, they moved together, quite closely together, out of camera range, back into the shadow of the woods.

Calla knew that in the lore of the theater, such painful encounters between director and actor were supposed to bring forth performances of great splendor. It was a romantic notion not often substantiated. When the two men returned, the scene did not go much better than before. The man was simply lacking in expertise, and, afraid to parade his emotions, he had to falsify them. Time and again they did the scene, until he began to forget his movements and his cues. If he continued to miss his marks, someone might get hurt, so he started to be too cautious and to retard his actions, making the conflict look as if it were being played in slow motion. It weakened everything, and Kono himself appeared weak. At last, when they almost had it, just as they were approaching the brutality of the scene, Julo faltered, reached for Calla too late, slipped and fell.

Somebody laughed.

It was a strange sound, loud and shocking. A woman's voice. But the only women on the set were Calla, Feona Carney and Willi. None of them had laughed.

They saw her. She was standing behind a wild wall that was used as a light baffle. It was Ellasue Rickert, somewhat drunk, and shrieking with laughter.

"Can't do it, black boy?" she yelled. "Can't you th'ow it on her, boy?"

Julo whirled to look at her. He was too off-balance to speak.

"Give 'im some bull juice, Luke!" she shrilled with hilarity. "Give the black boy some bull juice!"

"You bitch!" Julo shouted. "You dirty bitch!"

Luke started for her. "Get out of here!"

Drunkenly she waved her arms, shouting taunts. "Hey, black boy, white folk water your gism? Water your gism, did they?"

Julo rushed at her. Men ran in from all directions. They grabbed him and he flailed, trying to free himself. Two grips bore down on Ellasue and hustled her out of the clearing.

"It's my woods!" she screeched. "It's my woods more'n it's yours!"

They could hear her shrieking even when they couldn't see her anymore.

Julo, held by the men, was still trying to break free. At last he wrenched himself out of their grasp, and ran. Not after the white woman, but in the other direction, through the woods.

"Julo!" Luke called. "Julo, come back!"

But he was gone.

The clearing was still. No leaf stirred in the woods. No one breathed.

"Print the third one," Lucas said to an assistant, "and the next to last."

"Are they good enough?" the cameraman asked.

"They'll have to be."

Calla had cut her hand during the last shot, not more than a scratch but it was bleeding. The real blood, combined with the fake blood of the fight, were starting to soil her clothes. Two makeup assistants arrived with wet cloths and antiseptics. They were about to go to work on her, when Lucas said, "Don't clean her up."

Calla looked up at him. "Are we going on?"

"Yes—the last section."

"What's the last section?"

"You—alone—afterward."

With a start, she realized that he hadn't thrown the whole scene to Kono, not at all. Nor had he lost confidence in her. On the contrary, he had saved the most important sequence of film for Calla, for the emotional reaction to the physical horror.

"What do I do?" she asked.

"Whatever you want."

"What do you mean?"

"You've been hurt, you've been mutilated. You try to get up, you can't. When you do, you walk one direction, then another. You try to catch your breath—a bit of strength returns—you're as enraged as he was. And then—it's all yours, Calla. Do whatever you want."

"Aren't you going to stage it?"

"No."

"Nothing?" She felt scattered.

"You know all the movements—where you start, where you finish, where the camera is. And you certainly know the emotions—rage, shame, loss, terror, whatever. Take all the time you need—as fully as you like. No limits—everything. Go."

"Tell me what to do, Luke." She didn't mean to plead; she wished she hadn't.

"Go crazy."

"What?" As if she had a doubt.

"You heard me. Go crazy. Tear the woods apart, tear yourself apart."

"Help me!" She was crying to him, to Reuss once more, to everyone.

"Go on."

"*Help me.*"

He shoved her as hard as he could, and she fell.

"Roll 'em," he said.

She realized the camera was on her, and was dazed. Going back into the action of the scene, she tried to reconstruct her feelings when Kono was there, but it was used up, useless. I must make a scenario for myself, she said; but words had no place in it. She tried to get up off the ground, to pull herself together, as the character and the star, and was at a loss. Something told her: you can't do it, stay here on the ground, disappear, bury yourself. Starting to sob, trying to rise and unable to do so, she searched for Rachel and couldn't find her. She got up at last, stumbled one direction, another, not knowing where to go, enraged at him for not having staged the scene, enraged at Kono or Julo, or both. She started to tear at things, at saplings, at her clothes, then began to run and run.

She was doing very well, it seemed to her, filling every acting need, satisfying every demand of the story, yes, doing very well.

But she did not go crazy.

"Cut," he said. "It was good." He paused. "You want to try it again?"

"Was something wrong?"

"No. . . . But you didn't quite get there, did you?"

I didn't take off, he means, I didn't go insane. "I'll try again."

She did it three times, four, five. Let go, he said, don't hang on to anything, let go. "Again?"

Six times, seven. He didn't, as he usually did, give her images to play, ifs and what-ifs and supposes. All he said, mulishly repeating himself, was let go, leave it all behind, don't carry anything with you, give it up, let go. "Again?"

Eight times, nine. She was on a trapeze this time, and if she could *let go* she would fly through the air and smash right through the membrane of the great wide hoop of the world—and be out on the other side of sanity, flying free!

But she could not let go. She clung to the bar . . . until, at last, the trapeze hung motionless.

He walked away from the camera, then back. "Again?"

"I—can't do any better than that," she murmured.

"Yes, you can."

"I can't!"

"Do it again."

"No! You're not helping me, you son of a bitch! I don't know what you want!"

"*Let go.*"

"Let go of what?"

"Of sanity! Go crazy! Scream!"

"I can't!"

"Scream, goddamn it!"

She was going berserk and unable to play berserk. She was dying of fatigue, and had no breath left in her.

"Could I have ten minutes?" she said.

"We're losing the light," he replied. "Yes, take ten." He turned quickly to the others. "We'll do the covering shots. Willi!"

Willi came forward. Her costume was an exact copy of Calla's, soiled and torn in the same way, but the blood patterns had to be altered quickly.

"You know the run?" Luke said to her.

"Yes, I know," Willi replied.

"You need a rehearsal, or shall we shoot it?"

"Shoot it, I think."

"Roll 'em."

"Speed."

The action started, and Willi ran. She ran and screamed at mutilators that had ravaged her, at rapists that had violated her beauty, she screamed at a heaven that had deprived her of some of her womanhood, she screamed and ran and beat herself against a tree, in an insanity of destruction, to devastate herself and the tree and all of nature, she beat herself, she beat herself against the tree.

And Calla could not stand how right it was, how ugly and beautiful and bone-chilling and fitting to the horror. Silently she slipped away from the shooting, drifted deeper into the forest and deeper, hoping she would get lost in it and never be found.

After a while, she heard a thrashing in the woods, and they were calling her name.

When Calla got back to the trailer, Willi was Scotch-taping a map of Africa on the wall. She was elaborately busy, making a show of being undisturbed by the other's presence. For an instant, the actress thought it would be better that way, neither of them seeming to be there. But it couldn't last.

"You were very good," Calla said.

"I don't know what I was."

"I'm telling you what you were—you were chillingly good."

"Were you chilled?"

"Yes, I was. I saw all the things I should have been, and wasn't."

"You didn't want to be."

"You don't really think that, do you?" Calla replied. "I'd have given my eyes to have played the scene that way."

"You never really tried."

"Yes, I did! How can you say that? I did!"

"Not for a minute."

"How can you know? How the hell can you be so sure of that?"

"Because it's *me!* That character is *me!* Lucas wrote the character of Rachel about *me!*"

"He wrote it about somebody in his mind."

"*Me!* He watched us together—Julo and Willi—us! He watched us in love. Not your kind of love, not anybody's but our own—he wrote it about us! And the Rachel that excited him to write the part was *me!*"

Her face was purple and her scars were white. "Why are you so angry?"

"Because I wanted you to *be* me in the part. I wanted you to love me so much that you'd understand everything about Rachel, you'd know everything, you'd feel everything. There'd be no difference among us—you and the part and me. We would be one person—Calla and Willi and Rachel—one person. One flesh, one spirit. And you would make such an outcry for my sake—! You would make such a madness—!" She made a terrible sound, trying to shout, choking, the cry of a woman in anguish. Then, the lament: "Oh, Calla, why couldn't you do it?"

The torment was too much for Calla to console. She barely stirred. "I'm sorry . . . I didn't see you, Willi. . . . I didn't see the character as you."

Willi became more calm. "You've never seen any part as someone else, have you?"

"You think I haven't?"

"No. You've never gotten into someone else's skin."

"I've played a variety of parts in my life, Will."

"Always Calla."

"You're not going to tell me that the only way to be a good actor is to put a mask on, the way Barney does—be someone else in every part."

"Someone else and still yourself, yes."

"I try to do that."

"No, you don't, Calla—you don't even try anymore. I used to think, 'She's got a spark of genius in her, and one day it'll burst aflame.' But it never did. Year by year, you've clung to yourself more and more. You stopped being an actress and became a star. You started to play the image of your fame. A personality. And after a while, you never allowed yourself out of your reflection—Calla Stark, the celebrity."

Calla tried to speak with utmost control, to hide the hurt. "If you felt that way, why didn't you ever say so?"

"Because I never did feel that way—not in the old days. It never occurred to me that you were self-centered. My God, you were so generous, so honest—and oh, you were so brave—risking yourself for so many causes! How could I think of you as an egotist? But the truth is, Calla, that you could give yourself to causes but not to people. You may have loved Barney, but you were never a part of him. Or of Mina—or of me. And that's where loving begins, Cal—when you become someone else. And it's where great acting begins as well."

"Which totals me up to a dead failure."

"I didn't say that."

"It sounded pretty clear to me."

"No. I didn't say that at all!"

"I'm an egotist and self-centered, and I've thrown away my talent and my birthright, and I'm incapable of loving anyone—"

"I didn't say it, I didn't!"

"—and you didn't add that you're trying to hurt me because you're jealous."

"Of course I'm jealous! Isn't that what a star wants? To be loved and admired—and *envied?*"

"Would it surprise you that I was jealous of you this afternoon—that I've often been jealous of you?"

"I don't believe you."

"It's true."

"Jealous, for Christ sake—of what? Do I have as much as you? Do I have as much of *anything* as you do? What have I got now? Julo? I don't even have him completely—I can't even sleep with him! You want to do that? Is that why you're jealous—because of Julo? You want to sleep with him, Calla? Do you? Well, you certainly can. He'll make room in his bed any night you appear. Any man will. You can have anybody you want—anybody! You want me, Cal? You can sleep with me any night in the world! Do you want me, do you want me?"

"Willi, stop it!"

"Oh God, why don't you want me?"

She was weeping and hysterical. She kept crying oh God, oh Christ, and Calla kept trying to comfort her, whispering pleas and endearments, and begging her not to tremble, not to weep. At last Willi had control of herself, her feet tightly together, her hands clasped in an iron grip of one another.

Slowly, silently, aware of every movement she was making, Calla started to undress. Willi's gaze was upon her but her eyes were glazed as if she didn't see what Calla was doing. There was no haste in the actress' movements. Each button was deliberate. When she was nearly naked, she saw the turmoil in Willi's eyes, and the need to flee. But Calla went to her and held her firmly, then started to undo the fastenings of her skirt. In a little while, when they were both unclothed, Calla got into Willi's bed, but her friend simply stood there, her hands covering her scarred face, her most terrible nakedness.

"Come," Calla said.

". . . No."

"Please . . . come, Willi."

At last, she removed her hands from her face and got into bed beside Calla's naked body.

They were quite still. Then Calla caressed Willi's hand, her face, her breast. Soon they were kissing passionately, touching and fondling and murmuring their names. And at last they were making love, trying to find one another, trying to be one another.

Nothing they did together was remarkably different from what Calla had done with men, except that there had been no male member to do it with; nothing was strange or unnatural, and certainly not "queer." Yet, nothing was the same.

It seemed like a dissimilar variety of human concourse, gentler than she had experienced with men; yet, she had never made love with sexual vandals but with men of kindly touch, Lucas one of them. Perhaps it was a more delicate sensibility to one another's bodies, to the thresholds between pain and pleasure, since a woman could know with greater certainty the intimate secrets of another woman's person. More likely it was something else: there had been no contest in the lovemaking; it was as if the main effort had been to give comfort to one another, for the longings that men customarily ignored, for the slurs and scuffs of being secondary people, for the wounds of womanhood. Neither of them had any battle to win, no point to prove, no superiority to maintain. And, since there was no separate victory for either of them to score, when it was over Calla felt as if, together, they had had a com-

mon triumph; an enemy had been conquered, at least the outside world
had momentarily been kept at bay.

Neither she nor Willi had felt a need—which had always seemed
present in lovemaking with men—for seas to part or mountains to deto-
nate; there was no need for each thrust of the body to annihilate an
enemy, for each outcry to be heard in heaven.

There was another need, for a miracle as unrealizable as the parting of the seas, unattainable in the amorous act of men and women, no
matter the combination of the sexes. Still, no matter how unattainable,
people who had no belief in miracles sometimes believed that a miracle
could happen in the act of love. It did not happen. Willi and Calla did
not become one entity. It was an ungratifiable hunger. Whatever physical cravings had been satisfied, Willi's yearning for identity with Calla
would always have to go unconsummated. It saddened them that this
hunger would always persist. But they were both wise enough to know
that their felicity during the lovemaking was an ecstasy of The First
Time, and it would be futile to try to recapture it. . . .

. . . Later, when they were dressed again, there was a knock on the
door, and it was Lucas. Calla could not tell the state of his mind, his expression was impenetrable. He made no mention of her defection in the
rape scene, and was playing the fiction that it was all in the day's work;
tomorrow there would be another scene to shoot.

"Did Julo get back?" Willi asked.

"Not yet."

Calla saw his worry. "Can you shoot around him? Is there much
work for him still to do?"

"Only the fire scene."

Only. It was probably the most important scene in the film, certainly the most difficult. "He's bound to be back," she said. "When did
you expect to shoot it?"

He smiled grimly. "Tomorrow."

Summarily, he appeared to rout the trouble. "The first batch of
rushes has arrived."

"Rushes?" Calla said.

"Yes. I'm running them tonight. Would you like to see them?"

"No," she said. "I hate to look at rushes."

"I know. But these may be helpful."

"See them, Cal," Willi said.

"Rushes freeze me up—you know that. After I see them, I get
worse."

"I think you ought to risk it," he said.

"You mean I couldn't possibly get worse."

"I didn't say that."

"Then say it. I'm a disaster."

Willi didn't want to hear any more, and left the trailer. The word "disaster" stayed.

"You could never be a disaster, Calla," he said. "But whatever is wrong—or missing . . . Point is, I don't know how to help you. And I thought—if you saw yourself—"

"I'm too terrified, Luke."

"Maybe you're not terrified enough. Maybe you're not anything enough."

She flinched. "Yes. I've made a note of that."

"You're taking it wrong. I don't mean *you're* not enough, I mean you're not giving enough of what you are. Christ, Calla, I'm not trying to diminish you—I'm in love with you."

She wanted him to say it, and wanted him not to. But if it had to be said for the first time, couldn't it have been whispered in the darkness, when they were making love? Or watching a change of light, a night going to morning. She smiled grimly at herself; the realist asking for a love less real and more romantic, so she wouldn't have to deal with it.

She felt a bitter taste. Both of them loving me, Luke and Willi, and both cutting me down to size. Yet, she knew that neither of them did it painlessly, without stabbing at themselves. She could see the self-wound he was suffering, and wanted so desperately to be in love with him that she too ached.

"That doesn't make it easier, does it?"

"It should," he said with a gray smile. "It should make you surer that I won't hurt you."

"I'm sure you wouldn't do it purposely. I may be sick in the head, but I'm not crazy enough—"

"You're not crazy at all."

"Oh, Lucas, you don't know!"

"*Then play it.*"

It was his outcry, and if only he knew, it was hers as well. But surely he had to know how desperately she wanted to play the ecstatic madness that Willi had given to that one scene.

He saw how desolate she was. "We could look at the rushes and be all wrong, you know."

"Don't be too kind, Luke."

"I'm not. Maybe your performance is enough. Less is more, isn't it?"

If he had to resort to platitude, she thought, he did not believe what he was saying. She could imagine him praying for a gift of wonder he knew he would not receive, and she felt worse than ever.

"Luke—I'm sorry—"

"Calla—please—come and see the rushes."

Miserable, she agreed, and he departed before she could change her mind.

She went to the green room that evening to see the rushes. The work table had been shoved into a corner, the desk had been pushed against a wall, and leaning against the opposite wall there stood a plastic screen that had been pulled out of a long map case. The projector was already set up and alight when she arrived. Feona, two assistants and the camera operator were bringing folding chairs from other places, and Norman Arnold, the editor, was arranging them in rows. When she entered, Luke waved to her and went back to his mini-recorder, dictating notes.

She looked around for Julo, but he had not appeared. Nobody mentioned his name. Noticing that Barney too was missing, it puzzled her that he had begged off. She wondered why he had done so, since he had not evinced a single quiver of insecurity in the playing of the part.

The rushes would cover only the first few weeks of shooting; the last weeks would arrive, they said, in a few days. But there would be enough material, she thought nervously, to make judgments.

The battery-run lights were dim in the room, and somebody turned them out. Fellows, Luke's first assistant, went to the door, gestured to the man in the generator truck, and the motor started with a whine. The operator switched the projector from battery to generator juice; the light stopped flickering and brightened.

"The sound won't be very good," the boom man warned. "The generator's bleeding a little."

So am I, she thought. She felt someone press her shoulder reassuringly, looked up, saw Luke smile down at her, then pass and sit on an isolated chair against the wall. He gave a signal to the projectionist and the viewing began.

Calla knew it took an experienced eye to read dailies with a vision of the finished film, and she had seen too few of them to trust her opinions. But she did know enough about acting and direction to detect falsity in a scene, and she saw nothing that struck her as a lie. She was impressed by how good some of the performances wcrc—Julo, for example, who seemed so undisguised and yet so many-leveled, a frightening man who oddly caught one's sympathy; and a Gurrie's short scene of anger when his boat is taken from him; and the terrible moment when Kono strangles a defector from the cult.

As to her own performance, she could not come to any conclusion. She had been right, and Lucas wrong, about the quarrel with Titus. She did not feel that her aloofness from the hunter had diminished her feminine appeal; on the contrary, it suggested an interesting concealment of her womanliness. Luke's reaction, she was now sure, had not been to the playing of the role, but to the woman playing it. He, the man more than the director, needed her closer and more revealed.

She was not bad in the rushes, not at all bad. She simply lacked one thing. Singularity. She was not any particular woman. She had held her privacy too close, allowing her uniqueness to be too precious; she might not pique an audience, whetting its curiosity. Again she envied Willi's solitary identification with the part.

The real star of the dailies was Barney. She had expected him to be good, but she could not have imagined the size of his conception. It was staggering. His technique was prodigious. He had invented the slovenly speech of a once self-respecting Southerner who has allowed his jaw, his diction, his morals, his whole life to go slack. He had the hulking walk of a man no longer agile, yet the swift, shifting eyes of a jackal; and he had an ugly beast's mouth, snarling, gnawing, devouring. There was an even greater dimension to his characterization: he was the primordial hunted hunter who is being run to earth, the killer and the kill. There was something wonderfully wrong about his interpretation of the role. He was false to the script. He did not play the recognizable man that Luke had written; he played an original, a primitive archetype, the hairy Esau, neuroticized. The paradox he brought to the part was the strength of his weakness: brutality that could be taken for fortitude, dementia that expressed itself with the logic of the reasonable man. The power of the performance was its sickness of spirit. Calla was proud of him; he was brilliant beyond jealousy.

When the lights went up there was a round of confusion; people milled and said extravagantly noncommittal things, for few of them had any more skill at viewing rushes than she had. So they praised too much and exaggerated their feelings, and waited for the skilled ones to talk. But the most skillful one had slipped away. She looked for the director. She had not seen him depart, and wondered where he had gone. Where he always went to think things through, she suspected—the riverbank. She too went away, in search of him.

He was at a distance, downstream; if the moonlight had not been mid-day bright, she might not have seen him. When he caught a glimpse of her, he made a reflexive movement, and she thought: He wants to escape. But the instant passed and he slowly advanced toward her. His face was drawn; his trouble went deep.

"Is it so bad?" she asked.

"*You're* not."

"I'm not bad and I'm not good—I'm just not anything."

"It's not you, it's the film."

"They're only rushes—the first. It's early to say, isn't it?"

"Not when it's so clear."

"What's clear, Luke?"

He hesitated as if reluctant to share his depression. "What I just saw is nothing I ever imagined," he said. "It has a different look, a different sound—I don't recognize anything about it."

"Does that mean it's not good?"

"I don't know," he said cheerlessly. "It's someone else's."

"Can't you make it yours?"

"I'm not even sure I want to. It's so damn prosaic. And predictable —I know every shot before it happens."

"Of course you do—you shot it."

"But that's the point. How can I have done it, how can it be so predictable, yet seem to be somebody else's work? I kept looking for myself in it, and I wasn't there."

He was in a rout; she pitied him. It was probably like the bad days, years ago, when his scripts were in the hands of other directors, strangers who alienated his work, detaching it from life, deadening it, as he felt he was doing right now. She had thought that the worst trouble was her own; now she glimpsed what he was going through day and night.

He seemed to regret that he had confided his worry. Hastily, "I've got to go," he said. "I'm going to run the rushes again."

He hurried away. In the stillness, the chatter in the green room came faintly around the bend of the river. She heard his voice as he entered the lounge. It was the loudest of all, and the cheeriest. His cheer was, to her, the saddest sound in the night.

Slowly she returned to her own quarters. Barney was there. Declaring that Willi had gone for a walk, he made the simple statement sound like a historic pronouncement. He was exhilarated. His eyes were too bright, his body would not alight anywhere, his speech couldn't keep pace with his thoughts.

"Christ, did you see them?" he said. "Did you see the rushes?"

"Yes. Why didn't you come?"

"I did come. I snuck in when the lights went out, and left after my scenes were over. Have you ever seen such a wonderful picture? Have you ever seen such a fantastic film?"

"You think it's that good?"

"Good? We're all going to win Academy Awards. There'll be a thousand Oscars in this picture."

The actor, first and last. The picture was going to be great because he was great. "Barney, you *are* wonderful in it."

"Wonderful? I'm more than wonderful. I am *epic*. I am the first word—no, the final word that will ever be said about a hunter! I am the manner and the man! I am the single character and the whole goddamn breed! Nobody will ever dare to play a hunter again—nobody! The part is mine! I claim it, I own it, I'm the king of it!"

She had never seen him in such euphoria. On first glance, he seemed drunk, but it was an elation beyond liquor, an unholy sickness. His arms slashed at the air, as if to destroy it.

"Sit down, Barney," she said quietly.

"Don't calm me down," he shouted. "Why the hell do you want to calm me down?"

His voice reverberated, and other trailers were close. "You'll wake the dead," she said.

"What do you expect me to do—talk in whispers the way you do? If you lifted your voice and your goddamn skirt, you'd be better in the part, you know that?"

"Yes, I know that."

"Take something, for Chrissake!"

She turned to gaze at him. "Take what, Barney?"

"What I'm taking. The place is loaded with it."

"Loaded with what?"

"Stuff like this."

He reached into his pocket, pulled his hand out and showed her what he had on his palm. The pellets were uneven, a grayish brown, some as tiny as peppercorns, some as large as peas.

"What is it?"

"It's called *narco' di follia*—I got it in Sicily. They put it in a dish, set fire to it and inhale the fumes. But I take the kernels—they're made of jimson and grass and some other shit. It's the residue. Look."

He took one of the pellets, held it up and popped it into his mouth. Then he laughed. "Presto chango, I'm a star! I'm a galaxy!"

He popped another one into his mouth.

"I wouldn't take any more of those things, Barney."

"You wouldn't, huh? Go look at my performance, and look at yours—and see if you wouldn't. You think I could have gotten hold of Titus Macauley without these things? You know what this does for me? It makes me reach back. Not to what I was last year or the year before, but to what I was a generation ago. A millennium—a goddamn millennium! Do you know what this stuff does? It gives me birthdays— not every year, but every century! I'm an aeonic man!"

She tried to ease things. "Well, Aeonic Man, I think you better go —it's getting late."

He laughed excessively. "It's never too late for me."

Suddenly he seemed steadier than before, and his voice was kinder. "Here. I'll leave you some of these, Cal. Take a few. You'll get your crazies back."

It was pitch dark outdoors, and she heard someone's footsteps. She looked up from her reading, put the book down on the table by the chair and wondered if it might be Willi coming back from her walk. Then she heard the skidding of a car, the loud honking of a horn and a bedlam of voices.

She tore the door open and hurried out. There was a crowd forming around one of the company station wagons. Someone was calling for Lucas. Then she saw Willi running to the vehicle, yelling, "Where? Where is he?"

Calla rushed to the confusion. "What is it? What's happened?"

"Julo—"

"What about him?"

"He's been arrested."

"Arrested? For what?"

"Rape."

21

There were three of them sitting in the front seat of the station wagon —Calla, Willi and Lucas. Nobody knew anything except for the rumor that one of the gaffers had brought back from Ashton, that Julo Julasto had been arrested for the rape of Ellasue Rickert.

Lucas drove very fast. Willi barely said anything, and when she did, she skipped words and didn't complete sentences. Approaching the federal courthouse, they saw that the red neon sign saying Sheriff's Office had the last *c* missing. There were going to be gaps in everything tonight, Calla thought.

They went indoors, not by way of the federal entrance, but into the county wing of the building. It was an exact duplicate of the other wing, years ago, and Calla had a chill of remembrance. The corridor, beyond, would lead to a stairway, and, one floor below, the cell she had occupied. The place was as spotless as it had been in that other time, and again she had the sense of an orderly chaos.

There were four men in the sheriff's office—Rickert, his deputy, and two state troopers. As the motion picture contingent entered, Rickert looked up from his desk. He put one index finger in the air and counted the arrivals. "Three of you." He didn't laugh. "How many's it take to run a useless errand?"

"We're here for Julo Julasto," Lucas said.

" 'Here for'? What the hell does that mean, 'here for'?"

"To arrange bail for him. Just tell me the charges and—"

"There's been no charges."

Lucas looked at Calla, and she could see that he didn't understand any more than she did. The sheriff continued. "We ain't booked him yet."

Rickert arose from his chair. He was in trouble, and unsure. His eyes were bloodshot. His anger was like foul breath. "Look, mister, he was locked up three hours ago in another county and brought across the line. We don' want to do nothin' irregular. We're goin' to do everythin' jus' exackly right—the dead perfec' letter of the law. We're goin' to crucify this black bastard with legal nails. So we're waitin' for another sheriff."

It didn't make sense to Calla, but she could see that Lucas had already understood the situation, at least his anger had encompassed it. "What's he going to be charged with?"

"Rape—the sport of niggers—rape."

Calla said quietly to Lucas, "Let's get out of here and call a lawyer."

"You call, Miz Stark," the sheriff said. "You go and call Gus Mayfield. But he ain't goin' to get the best of me this time. You bastards know who the victim was? You know who it was? It was my wife, it was my Ellasue!"

He did a weird thing. He made two fists and beat them together, as if to hurt his own knuckles. Seeing the man's havoc, Luke mitigated his anger. "Would you mind telling me what happened?"

"I do mind—goldamn, I do mind! But I'll tell you. My Ellasue went to watch your pitcher shootin' this afternoon, and she made some unfortunate remarks to your leadin' nigger. We ain't denyin' she made the remarks—she had a little licker in 'er—an' she did make 'em. But then she lit outta there in her car, and as she's comin' to where the shortcut comes outta the woods, there's your nigger standin' in the middle of the road with his arms stretched out and yellin' curses at my Ellasue's oncomin' vehicle. She slammed her brakes, and the car skidded onto the sand shoulder of the road. And that filthy eight-ball coon, he pushed her out of the driver's seat, he took over the car, he drove her to Pedlar's Point, he beat the hell out of her and raped her."

The story was packaged—short, neat and conclusive. And for that very reason, unbelievable to Calla.

"You've had him locked up for how long?" Luke asked.

"I tol' you how long—three hours."

"You kept it a big secret, didn't you?"

"You mean we shoulda paid you a social call and tol' you the gossip?" His eyes narrowed. "Did *he* pay you a social call and tell you the gossip?"

"No."

"You know why, don't you? The son of a bitch is ashamed. The son of a bitch is guilty."

"I want to see him."

It was Willi. She had been totally silent, recessive, standing as far from the sheriff as the room would allow.

"Ain't nobody goin' to see him," the sheriff said quietly.

Luke's voice was deadly calm. "Look, Rickert. I'm going to ask you to book him or free him. If you don't book him and read him his rights—"

Rickert exploded. "There's no need! He made a full confession."

"You're a goddamn liar!"

"'I could lock you up for that."

"Lock me up, you son of a bitch!"

Unexpectedly, Rickert went slack. He suddenly seemed to be getting a bitter satisfaction from the proceedings. "I'm goin' to change my mind, mister. I'm goin' to let you see him—and you can ask him by your own sweet self. Go on—ask him if he didn't make a full confession."

With his deputy and a trooper, he led the way through the hallway, down the stairs and along the corridor of cells. There were only three cells, and the deputy unlocked the door of the last one. They entered.

Julo lay on a low bench, prostrate and still, one arm dangling loosely, touching the cement floor. His hand was bleeding and his head had a large gash in it. His hair was matted with blood, most of which had dried, but he still appeared to be bleeding a little. His face was swollen and he was breathing as if every breath was something he had to think about.

Willi rushed to him, knelt, threw her arms across his body. It caused him to stir in pain, and she made a moaning sound. He was barely able to turn his head to see his visitors. His eyes were witless, like the feebleminded.

"Go away," he muttered thickly. "Everybody, go away."

Willi started to sob.

"Go away," he said again. "Please go away."

With disgust Rickert leaned over the body of the prisoner. "They come to hear the truth, Julasta. Did you do it? Did you rape Ellasue?"

"Go away."

"You hear me, Julasta? Did you rape Ellasue?"

"Go away—go away—"

The repetition of the words sounded autistic, or like the hollow voice of a man speaking from hallucination. Then the sound—still an echo, still remote—became louder and stronger. "Everybody go away. Nobody got a ticket here—nobody can stay—nobody but the Lord!"

Willi murmured, "It's me, Julo—Willi."

"Nobody got a ticket but the Lord! Only the Good Shepherd! Only the good sweet Jesus!"

It was an eerie remembrance of a voice, a Holy Roller incantation, the resonance of a ghetto far away. Forlorn, uneducated, deranged.

Lucas wheeled on the sheriff. "You bastard, you've beaten him out of his mind!"

"He ain't out of his mind—he's fakin'." Rickert grabbed Julo's arm. "Did you do it? Tell 'em what you tol' me. Did you do it?"

"Let him alone!"

"Did you?"

"I don't know," Julo murmured. "I don't know."

"There!" The sheriff was triumphant. "You hear that?"

"You call that a confession?"

"He's already confessed in the presence of witnesses. And right now—if he didn't do it—why ain't he outright sayin' no?"

"Because he's senseless, you son of a bitch! You beat him!"

"Self-defense!" the sheriff said. "The nigger went at me—ask the boys—he hit me."

Julo's voice rose: "The Lord Almighty—He can stay!"

Willi cried, "Julo—Julo!"

Lucas reached for the sheriff. "That's why you didn't book him, isn't it? So you could beat him first!"

"Let go!"

"You son of a bitch!"

As Luke started to hit him, the deputy and trooper separated them. But Lucas, breaking free, started back toward the sheriff, and Calla shouted, "Luke—no!"

She and Willi dragged him away. They heard the boot heels of the sheriff clapping the concrete floor behind them, and the other two men trailing.

On the upper floor, passing the office, they saw a trooper at the door, vigilantly watching them. He did not follow them, however, as they walked down the corridor toward the distant exit.

Outdoors, they seemed to have lost their bearings, and hesitated, not recalling where the station wagon was parked.

Nothing seemed right and there weren't any solutions, Calla was thinking, when suddenly it all came to a too-easy turning, like the end of an old melodrama, complete with *deus ex machina.*

Dea, actually, in the person of Ellasue, and the *machina* was a shiny new white convertible with the top down. The car veered around the corner and came to a jarring halt outside the entrance. Its driver's blond hair, blown by the wind, looked like a yellow puffball. She was laughing at the sight of them, laughing and honking her horn; drinking had made her a tumult, even the car seemed drunk. Calla's impulse, and Willi's, was to avoid the woman.

"We got ya, di'n't we?" she yelled. "Hey, nigger lovers, we got ya, di'n't we?"

Calla and Willi were already halfway to the station wagon. But Lucas had stopped beside the convertible.

"Yes, you got us, all right," he said.

"Come on, Luke," Calla shouted.

She didn't want any more trouble. All she wanted was to get away to a telephone so she could call Mayfield. "Luke!"

Ellasue jeered at Calla. "We got you too, Miz Commie-shit, we got you too!"

"Yes, you did." Luke studied her. "You got all of us."

"Outsmarted ya!" she shrieked. "Hollywood smart-asses—I outsmarted all of ya!"

"Sure did, Miz Ellasue."

"You bet your poodies I did!" She hooted with laughter. "And you don't know the stinkin' half of it!"

"What's the other half?"

"I says to him, 'Get in, get in,' I says to him. 'Get your black butt into the goddamn car,' I says."

"Yes, he told us that," Luke said.

"'Get in,' I says, 'and I'll show ya how to play that scene. I'll show ya good, you black-balled nigger.'"

There was a shout from the entrance. Rickert came charging down the steps. "Ellasue, go home!" he yelled. "I tol' ya not to come here! Go home!"

"We showed 'em, Boonie," she crowed. "Goddamn, we showed 'em how to play a fuckin' rape scene, di'n't we? 'Rape me,' I says to him. 'Rape me, nigger!'"

"Ellasue, shut up!"

"'Get in,' I says. 'Rape me, black boy,' I says. Goddamn, I played my part real good. Di'n't I play my part real good, Mr. Director Man, di'n't I play it good?"

"You sure did, Ellasue."

"She's drunk!" the sheriff shouted. "She's makin' it all up—she's drunk. She was drunk then, and she's drunk now—and she's makin' it up!"

"I ain't makin' nothin' up!" she ranted. "Goddamn, I ain't!"

"Shut up! Shut up!"

"You shut up, you ol' sof'-cock. And fix your fuckin' piece!"

Rickert twisted to face Lucas. "She's drunk! If you get her in court, she'll deny every word she said. She'll deny she ever said it."

"And you'll deny you said that too, won't you?" Luke said.

"Everything! Every goldamn word!"

"You do that. I've got it all."

Luke reached into his pocket and pulled out his mini-recorder.

The sheriff was stunned for an instant, then he grabbed for it. "Gimme that! Gimme that, you bastard!"

Lucas shoved it back into his pocket and the man started to tear at the director's clothes. There was an entanglement of arms and bodies, someone lost his footing, the sheriff fell back against the hood of the convertible. He shouted for his deputy, who was at the glass door, the other side of it, and simultaneously reached for his gun. But he had left it indoors—gun, belt, holster.

"Come on, Luke!" Calla yelled.

As they got into the station wagon and sped away, the sheriff was shouting at his deputy and one of the troopers who was running down the steps.

Luke pushed the vehicle to top speed. It was late, the streets were practically deserted, and there was no sign of anyone following them.

When they got to the production compound, everything was quite still. Calla noticed that there were extra night guards around the shooting area, and extra kerosene lamps as well. The three of them hurried into Luke's trailer and, trying to reach Gus Mayfield, called Information in Vicksburg, Biloxi and Jackson. There was no listing for him in any of those places. They were about to call Meridian, when it was no longer necessary.

There was a commotion outdoors, one of the company guards shouted, then there were other voices. As the three of them tore through the doorway, they saw a car come roaring in, with the police siren blaring. The car came to a halt. Someone opened a window of the vehicle and tried to yell over the siren. What was shouted went unheard, but a door opened and Julo's body was thrown out.

When they ran to pick it up, it was not clear whether he was alive or dead. But as they started to raise him off the ground, he muttered in pain and weakly struck at them, fighting, waving them away.

"Let me be," he said. "Hands off—go away."

Awkwardly, like a drowning swimmer, he kept thrashing with his arms, pushing his rescuers away. "Nobody—don't touch—go away."

Weak and hoarse as his voice was, there was so much passion in his demand to be let alone, that they stayed at a distance. He still lay there, however, quite still. Then he started to grovel on the ground, trying to arise, but unable to do so without assistance. He tried once, twice, but his legs would not support him, and each time he sank ignominiously down again, cursing through his groans. Yet, when others moved nearer, he swore at them and warned them away. At last he rolled over on his hands and knees and pulled himself to a kneeling position, his fingers clawing at the dirt. Alone, like a crippled crab, he scrabbled at the ground as if to disinter himself from it, and finally pulled himself erect. He just stood there, trembling. Afraid to fall, he did not dare to move. Then he took a step, a single stride, and held the position in a ridiculous stance, motionless. Another step, and another—and he was going in the wrong direction.

Luke pointed to Julo's trailer. "This way, Julo—here it is."

"Go 'way."

He did turn, at last, slowly, like an automaton, and followed where Lucas was leading. A few more steps, and he fell. Willi, with a cry, ran to him. Enraged, his arm struck at her, and in the strength of his fury he was able to rise again. Once more, stumbling, he started for the trailer. Like a blind man he wavered through the atmosphere, arms out, thrusting, fingers grasping to get a hand-hold on the air. When he got to the trailer, Luke opened the door for him and the injured man hobbled over the threshold. Willi hurried inside after him, and there was a shout.

"Only the Almighty!" his voice thundered in the darkness. "Get out! Only the Lord of Hosts!"

Willi came outside again, and after a few moments, Luke shut the door. They could still hear him calling for the Almighty, but now his voice was a wail. "Where is He? Where is He? Where did He go?"

They kept hearing him cry, begging, lamenting for the Missing One. A crowd gathered, and someone sent for Fuhrman. When the young doctor arrived and went into Julo's trailer, the sounds of anger returned to Julo's voice, louder than before. Soon, the doctor came out and said it was useless; he had tried to inject him with a calmative, but Julo had driven him off. Only God would be admitted.

Hours later, when Willi and Calla couldn't sleep, they made some tea, and sat huddled in the semi-light of their trailer. They were static. After a lengthy nothingness, Willi said, "I've decided. He's going to get better."

She spoke with incontestable confidence. "Of course he is," Calla said.

"You say it, but I know it."

"How do you know, Will?"

"Because I'm the one who will make him better."

"Are you, Willi? How?"

"He said he was going to take me to Africa," she said evenly. "It'll be the other way around. I'll take him."

". . . Yes."

As if a heavenly vision had appeared to her, all of Willi's dreads lifted. The lightless space she had occupied seemed radiantly illuminated. With no more to add, she slipped out of her bathrobe and got into bed. Minutes later, Calla heard the deep regularity of her breathing. She was asleep.

How I envy the talented dreamer, Calla thought. Envy again . . . of the mind and resolution that can summon—what? Africa.

Sleepless, she went outdoors. The wind had subsided a little, but it was still a bit raw. She pulled her bathrobe tighter.

He'll get better, Willi had said, but he mightn't. It could happen either way; in the morning he would be there, in the morning he wouldn't. Even now, she said, I wonder if he's breathing, if he's unconscious or in pain, if he needs somebody.

She walked to his trailer and listened at the closed door. There was no sound. She turned the knob and cautiously entered. Leaving the door open for the moonlight, she stood on the threshold and waited for her eyes to overtake the dark. At last she saw him, still fully clothed, lying on the bed. He was motionless.

"Close the door," he said softly. His voice was unsteady, but there was no madness in it, and he wasn't sending her away.

"Don't turn the light on," he said weakly. "It too bright—it hurt my eyes." They were ghetto inflections.

"Do you want something?" she said.

"I called for the Lord, but He didn't come." A despairing whisper.

As if to a child: "Perhaps He'll come tomorrow."

He took a long time responding. Apparently he was weighing the thought. "No. . . . Could be He jus' don' come. Could be you have to go and git Him."

She thought it a mercy that his mind was wandering. "Isn't there something I can do for you?"

"Hot," he murmured. "I'm burnin' hot."

Calla shuffled about in the darkness, trying to find a cloth for a cold compress. She found a roll of paper towels. Making a pad of a number of sheets, she made her way to the sink and ran cold water on the paper. As she returned to his bed, the opaqueness was like a tangible substance she had to walk through. At last her shinbone touched the mattress and, sitting on the edge of it, she put the compress on his forehead. She felt him shiver with shock, then he relaxed to the pleasure of the cooling thing. When the pad was warm, she freshened it with cold water. Again and again she did it, but he still complained of being warm, suffocating. She saw him trying to take his bloodstained shirt off, so she helped him; helped him also to remove his shoes and trousers, so that he lay in only his shorts, breathing more coolly than before.

She simply sat there on the bed. After a while, she felt his hand groping for hers. He held it tensely at first, as if to keep her from departing, then more tranquilly. When he finally released her, she stroked his face with her fingertips, caressed his brow, touched his eyelids closed, coaxing him to sleep.

They were silent for a long time. She thought at last that he was drowsing, but then she heard him whisper.

"Willi . . . ?"

Her heart stopped. Was he calling the absent Willi, or had he confused her—even while hearing her talk—with her double? And should she correct him?

"Yes?" she said.

"Willi . . . If I'm not too ugly . . . would you kiss me?"

She hesitated. Then slowly she inclined her head and kissed him softly on the lips, and his mouth was as gentle as her own.

A moment later, he moved his whole body. Laboriously, painfully, he edged himself toward the wall. He was making room for her in bed.

Her heart pounded so loudly she thought he might hear it. He wanted Willi to lie beside him, and she wanted to comfort him. If the other woman's presence, if the closeness of her body would bring him some respite from his pain, she would gladly be Willi for the passing of the night. But she didn't know what Willi was to him in the darkness.

She started to undress. When she was nearly naked, she lay in bed beside him. For a moment she thought again, as she had before, that he was asleep. But his hand moved to touch her face, the fingertips lightly taking count of all her features, her forehead, eyelids, mouth. Then his hand slipped downward and lay gently on her breast. It did not move, simply rested there, as if for the breast's assurance and its own.

She wanted him. She sensed that if she touched him, no matter how bruised and battered he was, the man would awaken to her, and they could make love. But she also sensed that his need tonight was not for her but for Willi. So she lay there quietly, not stirring, with his hand on her breast, being Willi.

Soon there was no doubt of it: he had fallen into a deep slumber. As the dawn was breaking, she thought: I mustn't stay for the light, or he'll see who I am. So she got out of bed and dressed, went to the door, opened it as quietly as she could, and slipped away.

22

Early in the morning, Lucas thought he would be the first to go to Julo's trailer, but when he arrived, Willi and Calla were already there. They had brought the wounded man his breakfast. While he had left the scrambled eggs untouched, he had eaten one of the hot biscuits and had drunk nearly all the coffee.

The cheer in the trailer was not genuine. Lucas sensed that everyone suspected, as he did, that the black man was absent today as he had been yesterday. He was remote, his eyes were on inner visions and his voice resonated elsewhere. Willi, like a musician playing the solo part, carried the leitmotif of cheer. She was making a pleasantry of his forgetfulness. "He's joining the Amnesia Club," she said. "He thinks I was with him last night."

"I could have sworn . . ." Julo said. He looked up at Lucas. "She cooled my forehead. I don't know how she did it. Her hands were damp, I think."

Everybody laughed, playing the measure longer than it was worth. Luke noted that Calla's laugh was restrained, and she contributed nothing to the topic.

He looked at the wounds Julo had sustained. The only bad one was on the head. "Are you really feeling better?"

"What?" Lucas repeated the question. "Oh, better yes."

The director turned to Willi. "Did the doctor come?"

"Yes. He left just before you arrived."

"And?"

"He said, 'Rubber hoses don't break bones.' "

"How about that—and that—and that?" Lucas pointed to the ripped hand, the gash on Julo's head, the cut over his eye.

"He said the concussion was probably mild," she replied. "As to the marks—collodion."

Lucas smiled but he was annoyed. The young doctor's infatuation with movies was sometimes cloying. He didn't think in terms of bandages, but of makeup. "If you're in pain, I hope he gave you something."

"I don't want anything. . . . I'm sorry, Lucas. I'm sorry it happened."

The director put a hand on his friend's shoulder and was about to say a word of comfort, when it occurred once more: Julo disappeared. Lucas watched him vanishing before his eyes. Preoccupied with another set of phenomena, the wounded man was like a figure receding into a shadow, into a cave. Seeing the evanescence, and helpless to stop it, Luke had a poignant sense of loss. He felt confused, hurt by a friend's abandonment of him, as the man had twice hurt him by running away. Yet, in an anomalous way, he had suffered the physical flights less than the flight of the spirit.

Quietly: "Julo, come back."

The man looked up without comprehension. "What, what?"

"Please don't go away again."

On impulse, Luke reached for Julo's hand, but it was the injured one, and the man cried out in pain.

"Julo—I'm sorry—did I hurt you—did I hurt you?"

I'm feeling this too deeply, he told himself, on the verge of a foolishness. The black man saw his distress. "You didn't hurt me, Luke."

Impetuously, as if it were the director's hand that had been harmed, Julo lifted it to his lips and kissed it.

Willi smiled and so did Calla. Abruptly, the sober moment was over, and Julo took the happier cue. "When do I go back to work?"

"Slow down," Luke said. "You won't be ready for work until—when did Fuhrman say?"

"Right away."

"He's an asshole."

"No, right away." Julo went on. "I hear the fire set is ready."

"Almost."

"When were you planning to shoot it?"

"Come on, Julo—"

"When?"

"This evening. Night for night."

"I'll be there."

Willi pointed to his wounded face and head. "What'll you do about that?"

"Just what the young man said—collodion." Then, mimicking the doctor, "It's a cellulose coating for wounds and when you put makeup on it—"

"—it hurts like hell," Luke said.

But they were all relieved by the resumption of life and work, and there was a motion in the room, a bustle about schedules and costumes, and Calla was starting for the door.

About to depart, Lucas noticed a damp paper compress on the drainboard of the sink. The connection struck him: Julo's wandering mind hadn't conjured up the cool hands ministering to him in the darkness. They were real.

Outdoors, walking with Calla, he asked: "Was it you who were with Julo last night?"

She took a moment. "Yes."

"What happened?"

"It was just as he described it."

"Tell me."

"*He* told you. He had a fever. I put cold compresses on his forehead, and I comforted him."

"How?"

"You can't imagine he was capable of lovemaking last night?"

He had conflicting notions. "If you had made love, he wouldn't have thought you were Willi. . . . Why did you let him think so?"

". . . I don't know."

"And why didn't you tell him this morning?"

He had the sense that she was having a tough time, pulling things together from all directions. "I can't explain it," she said. "It was a . . . precious secret. I don't know why it was so precious to me. Anyway, I didn't want to share it . . . until I had looked at it."

He had the regretful feeling that he had spoiled it for her by invading. It was like a performance secret, so intimate that no whisper of it dare be uttered, or the magic would vanish.

They walked on for a while, in silence. But her concentration hadn't eased. "What if I had slept with him . . . ?"

"Well, what if?"

"What sort of signal would that have sent you?"

"I'd have to know what signal it sent you." He found himself on the verge of invading again, and tried to avoid it. "We haven't exactly made vows of fidelity to each other, Calla."

He wouldn't have said it if he had realized he meant it as a cue. But she didn't take it. For minutes, for hours it seemed to him, he waited for her to respond. But all she gave him was silence. Don't you know your lines, he wanted to shout to her, you're supposed to say I love you.

The hell of it was that he knew she did love him. Perhaps she didn't know it herself. Or maybe she was simply wiser than he was, and had understood all along something he had discovered in the last few days:

He was in love with two women. Calla and Rachel. The real one was all he had ever hoped to find in a woman. She was the body and spirit of everything he wanted. She satisfied him totally. But the Rachel—

The Rachel that she played was only a shadow of his dream. And this was the heart of his unhappiness with her. Even more than that she had never said she loved him, was his sadness—his rage—that he was being cheated by her Rachel. Cheated of the rapture he could capture on film. It was not enough to film the fury and terror of a woman no longer young, bereft of husband and child, raped by barbarity, losing her beauty and success, and now starting to lose the valor of her talent. He wanted something more, the ineffable extra: to see the insane ecstasy that an artist demands as a recompense for all the loss. A fleeting ecstasy that his camera would immortalize. That was all he wanted of the actress, he thought wanly, a mere nothing—immortality.

And what would he give for the fulfillment of Rachel? He'd give everything he owned, which wasn't much, and everything he was, which might not be enough, for the realization of this film. It was not a measure of his bravery but of his priorities. He had to create something beautiful, or perish. Art or arsenic.

Calla, the woman—and Rachel, the dream. He loved them both. But what a crucifixion for a woman to have to *be* both. And if this was what Calla knew about herself and Lucas, perhaps the better part of valor was to resist falling in love with him. Well, she was certainly resisting it.

The fire scene would be the most daring and most costly sequence in the picture. The set would be built and destroyed. Only once. There would be no relighting, restaging or retakes. It was to be a one-shot. Get it the first time or not at all.

All morning Lucas felt a constriction of the throat; swallowing was painful. He tried to sound equable, but everyone knew he was edgy; nobody dared ask him a question that could be answered elsewhere.

The set was, as usual, taking too long to light. And there was too much equipment, which would interfere with the action. Too much; everything had cost three times as much as he had budgeted. At the last minute, a week ago, he had become nervous about getting the scene in one crack and had rented extra cameras, which came with extra operators. One of the cameras, an Astro-Vision strapped to the belly of a special helicopter, would be monitored from the ground but operated by remote control from the cockpit of the chopper where the cameraman would watch the action on a closed-end television screen.

The most expensive item had been the cutting of the firebreak. To the south of the shooting site, there was the safety of the Ashton River. But all around, in a semi-circle, he had had to mow a half-mile swath of cornfields, which had meant buying entire crops, cutting and carting the unripe stalks, and burning the stubble. In all, including the helicopter and extra cameras, he had added a half million dollars to the cost of the picture.

And he might not get the shot.

The scene was going to be filmed this evening, darkness for darkness. The actors had the day off, with an after-dinner call. Although they were excited to see the set being built, they were discouraged from crossing the river, tying up the busy motorboat and rowboats, and getting underfoot. Some of the Gurries managed to get across the water; some did get underfoot, but others helped by carrying things and banging away at something as soon as a hammer was free.

The sun was setting as the last nails were being driven to conceal the stairway and render it secure. Soon the actors started arriving.

Julo crossed the river in the largest of the rowboats, with Willi rowing. Watching them land, Lucas approached. Julo walked with an even more erect posture than usual, as if to deny he had a body, and that it was in pain. The denial went further. He disavowed his own presence. Someone else was walking in his stead.

"You can get into costume in the camera shack." Lucas pointed to a makeshift shanty about a hundred yards from the river. "But before you go in, I'd like you to look at the fire mound."

"Why?"

"In case there's something you want changed."

"I won't want anything changed."

"How do you know?"

Julo's attention seemed to drift. "It's not . . . I don't want to think about it as a set, Lucas."

"But it is a set."

"Not for me."

"You've done it I don't know how many times. There are things you're used to—things you need—"

Julo interrupted. "I won't need anything. Nothing. As long as there are steps for me to climb to the top—and someone to light the fire . . ." The remote look again. "It doesn't need staging, Lucas."

There was an awkward moment. "We only get one shot at it, you know."

"I know." Gently: "Don't worry."

He started for the camera shack, Willi with him. Lucas watched them go.

The people of the crowd started to arrive from the land side and by boat across the water. Soon there were hundreds of them, nearly all black, but there were many whites as well.

The landing lights had just been turned on when a larger rowboat appeared, and Luke saw Mamma Lorena disembark from it. She had visited the set a few times and he had met her briefly, but he did not know the three young women who accompanied her. They were Lorena's granddaughters, he surmised; the twins were beautiful, and the third was an unpretty young woman with a striking, tall attractiveness. From out of nowhere, it seemed, Calla appeared and went rushing to them, embracing them all together and separately, then all together again. Quickly, the black women got lost in the throng, and Calla disappeared as well.

Considering the size of the multitude, they were unusually subdued. The unnatural quiet had an ominousness about it, since news of Julo's arrest and brutalization had spread through the town. A large number of the people had been invited by the cult leader himself—for weeks they had been spreading the word—and inevitably he had made some personal mark upon them. Lucas wondered how deeply it went.

Out of old habit and nervousness, the assistant director was calling for everyone to be quiet. But the growing darkness was as hushed as it needed to be, and it was too soon to ask for total silence. The loudest noise was the occasional rattle of a gear or a ratchet, the zizz of an arc light, a random hammer blow. For the most part there was only whispering, the shuffle of feet, the call of a workman, the crackle of the dry torches which had not yet been set aflame.

It would be dark enough in a few minutes, Luke thought, and in what light was left he made a quick survey of the company. One of the assistants had a group of Gurries waiting at the pathway to the river. On the other side, Feona was ready with the second group. A third group was on the set. The regular camera operator was testing the dolly track; when Luke raised his hand, the movement stopped. The newly rented camera, which would move directly in on the fire, seemingly right into the midst of the blaze, was almost ready; its operator was asking for some of the debris to be moved from the borders of his track so that it would not catch any sparks. Two of the 16mm operators were right and left of the wooden hill; two others were on the river side, in boats.

The helicopter seemed higher in the sky than necessary. Luke thought its lights, large white and small red, were too distant. He walked to Harry Fellows and took the PA mike out of the man's hand.

"Manuel," he called. "Manuel, can you come down a few hundred feet?"

"Yes," the voice replied. "But Cooper's afraid of ash on the camera lens."

"To say nothing of the hotfoot," Cooper added.

"You can come down a little," Luke said.

He saw the lights coming closer, then the chopper hung there.

"Sound?"

Alan, on the boom, waved and grinned. A tiny screech of feedback, then quiet.

"Gaffer?"

A quick test of four lights, in succession. Six more. A barrage. Then back to dimness. The pilot lights, a dozen naked bulbs strung from wires around the set, went on to give general illumination.

Luke turned to his production assistant. "I see only two safeties."

"The other two are on the water side."

Luke turned to Fellows, on the PA. "I want to rehearse the safeties again."

"Oh Jesus," the production assistant said.

"Don't say oh Jesus to me, you little bastard. Call the safeties in."

The four safeties came in from all directions. They wore enormous fire suits filled with asbestos fiber, and huge helmets made of the same stuff. The lenses of their goggles were tiny and seemed mean, not large enough for a ray of light. Their mittens were bulky and made their hands seem like monstrous, one-toed hooves. They were terrifying animals—gray rhinoceroses standing on hind legs.

"We'll run through it once more," Luke said to the four beasts. Then, to one of them, "There's a drop-off on Julo's platform, the other side of the steps—be careful."

They hurried back to their positions and in a moment one of the assistants raised the pistol and shot off a signal flare, purple and green, and the safeties came barreling in from their positions, straight to the mound. Two of them disappeared; one ran up the steps; the fourth took the inside camera track, and he too disappeared.

Luke nodded to the PA man who shouted, "Safeties, okay—return to places."

From the background, the director heard a voice: "What are they doing?"

He turned. It was Julo. He was perturbed. "Those men—who are they—why are they there?"

"They're safeties," Luke replied.

"For what purpose?"

Lucas was set back by the question. "In case something goes wrong."

"Nothing will go wrong. Don't signal them to come in for me."

"But if something happens—"

"Nothing will happen," Julo said. "Promise me you won't send them in."

"Julo, it's a standard precaution."

"I don't want them. Promise you won't send them in."

"I can't promise you that, Julo."

"Then I won't go up the steps."

Without another word, he went away. A group of blacks followed him toward the camera shack. Lucas was confounded. The man couldn't possibly resist such a sensible safeguard. He'll change his mind, Luke thought, when he hears the scene proceeding; it's his picture as well as mine.

"Stand by," he said to the assistant.

The PA system squawked. "Quiet, please—stand by."

He heard the crackle of the voice in the helicopter. "What's going on?"

The man on the shortwave microphone said, "Garcia and Cooper —stand by."

There was a relay of directions to the gaffers. The new arc burst instantly into light; the old one made a complaint, fluttered, then brightened. The rheostated lights, in their final test, glowed to full, dimmed to darkness, then glowed again.

"Call Julo," Lucas said.

"Kono onstage." The intercom had an echo. "Kono onstage."

There was a silence. Everybody waited. Kono did not come. The helicopter churned overhead.

"Kono—onstage!"

The slate boy came running. "He says he won't come."

Luke looked up at the mountain of wood with the real and fake moonlight shining on it.

"Save the lights," he said.

Except for the pilot lights, the lamps went out. Slowly turning from the set, Lucas started for the camera shack.

It was not much more than a temporary shanty that had been constructed to shelter the equipment. Two kerosene lamps glowed in the dark. In their unsteady light, he saw Calla sitting with her hands folded in her lap and her head bent forward. Willi was poised in the middle of the empty space, absolutely still, as if trying to decide which way to move. Julo stood at the Lucite-covered opening that functioned as a window, looking into the distance where the black-blue sky met the blacker blue of the low hills. He did not turn on Luke's entrance.

In the glimmering of lamplight, two wardrobe women were tying the last few white feathers to the huge cape that the Gorá was meant to wear. With an apology, Luke indicated the doorway and asked the women to leave the shack. As they departed, Calla also made a movement toward the door.

"No—please stay," Luke said.

She looked at the men, then went back to the dark corner, to disappear. Willi did not budge.

"We're ready for you, Julo," Lucas said.

"I'm not going out."

"Please."

"Unless you promise me—"

"I can't, Julo. Nobody does a fire scene without safeties. My God, it could mean the difference between—"

"—life and death."

"Yes."

"I'm trying to understand the difference."

"You won't understand it until you feel the fire."

"I won't feel the fire. You don't believe that, but it's true. I won't feel the fire unless you send those men in for me. And if you do, the flames will burn me like a feather."

Lucas told himself: beware of the man's mystical talk; it was impossible to reach him through it. It'll be worse now, after his beating. Try to keep him reasonable.

"Julo, listen. It's only a safeguard we're talking about—an added one, that's all. I don't know how you've protected yourself in the past, but—"

"This time it's different."

"Different? How?"

"No more safeties. . . . Of any kind."

The man said it calmly.

Luke felt ice. It would no longer be a death-defying feat, but a death-welcoming one. Whatever fire trick had saved him from immolation in the flames, he would be discarding it. Whatever flimflam, hocus-pocus, whatever audience hypnosis he had ever used . . .

Double the caution, Lucas warned himself; measure every word. "Julo—listen—those bastards—they beat you sick. Forty years, they've been beating you sick. You've been through hell—I know that. But the answer isn't heaven."

Evenly: "What's the answer, Luke?"

"You need . . ."

". . . help." He smiled with faint irony.

"Yes."

"That's what I'm going for, Lucas."

"You're going to kill yourself."

"No! Oh no, you've got it wrong. I'm going to come out of this *alive!* I'm not putting a pistol to my head, Lucas, I'm not taking poison. That's not me. Don't send the cops up to the thirteenth floor to talk me off the window ledge—I'm not there, I'm not a suicide. I'm here, Lucas—and not about to kill myself. I want to *live.* And I will live, my friend. I'm going into those flames, and I'm coming out of them. And I'll come out stronger and cleaner and happier than I've ever been. I'll burn all the ugliness out of my body and soul, I'll burn out all the rage, all the loathing of myself and the world! I'll be re-created in an image of beauty and goodness! I will see the face of the Lord!"

It was frightening. The man's fervor made him blind to the peril; he did not see an act of self-destruction, only the image of beauty to glorify him, and the sanctity of a holy devotion. Luke felt powerless to deal with him, and he looked to Willi, to Calla, silently pleading for help. But they were transfixed, as terrified as he was.

Julo silently watched them. There was a sorrowing smile in his eyes. "You think I'm crazy, don't you?"

Luke replied carefully. "You're talking about miracles . . . and I don't understand them."

"You think miracle talk is the language of lunatics, don't you?" he persisted. "Or liars."

"I . . . don't know the language."

"You started to learn it at one time. What happened? Did you lose your courage?"

Luke watched him closely, unsure where he was leading. "I never had the courage to be a visionary."

"Yes, you did, Lucas. Before you began your screenplay. Remember our conversations? 'What's the difference between a faker and a fakir?' Remember that? Remember the wonderful questions we asked and the great spirits we stirred? How does the buried man remain alive? Who makes the leper's hand seem beautiful? What is the cure in kindness? Can hatred be the other face of love? Who is the deity in all this—God or the devil? Did you give up asking the questions?"

"Did you ever find the answers?"

"The answer's in the fire, Lucas. For me it is. I'll go through life a liar or a man of faith."

"Go through life, you said."

He smiled once more. "Eternal life, yes."

Lucas took a slow, deep breath. Then, quietly: "I'm not going to let you go into the fire—without the safeties."

"You're going to condemn me to a world of Watts, aren't you?"

"I'm not condemning you to anything!" He hurt, and he was enraged. "And I won't condemn you to death!"

"I won't die!" he cried. "Oh, my good friend, *believe me!*"

"Believe him, Luke."

It was Willi.

"I won't—I can't!" He turned quickly to the other one. "Calla—please—help me—talk to him!"

"I have to believe that *he* believes, Lucas," she said softly.

That *he* believes. Hence, Julo's choice, not his. If Lucas could only convince himself that his friend was not ill. . . . Or if he could convince himself that the man, being ill, would be curable and happier cured. . . . If he could convince himself that he had a right to make a judgment. . . .

He took a step toward the black man. He found, suddenly, that he was word shy with him, had lost an easiness with talk that they had shared together. Then, with difficulty: "I love you, Julo. If only I could believe you're not trying to kill yourself . . ."

"*Believe me.*" He reached and touched him. "Please, Lucas—*friend* —have faith in me! I'll come out alive. I beg you—don't send the safeties in."

Lucas nodded in assent.

"You promise?" Julo said.

"Yes."

Nobody knew what to say or do. Suddenly the men embraced, and Lucas, unable to stand it there, hurried away.

When he came outdoors, the director walked a few paces and halted. He wanted to rush back and rescind his promise. Then he wanted to run away. But he kept going toward the cameras, and when he arrived, he again gave the direction to get ready. Once more the calls went up. Stand by, the voices said, quiet, please, stand by. The arc lights burst aglow, the smaller lights winked in, the pilot lights went out.

"Roll 'em."

"Speed."

"Action, Group One."

The assemblage of people closest to the fire mound finished adding the last scraps of wood, the tinder pieces at the base, the dry brush and the corn silk.

"Action, Group Two."

From the distance, at the river's edge, there was a low murmur of voices, a strange, dull shuffling sound, and the Gurries began to appear. They had the night faces of people who dreaded what they could not see. As the signal was given to the third group, it started to join them. Their added numbers did not seem to give the others any added fortitude. On the contrary, it was as if they were verifying for one another the perils of the unknown.

He gave a hand sign to an assistant, who beckoned to Rachel to take her place. He saw Calla walk to her designated position at a distance from the wooden mound. The main camera swung leftward to catch her.

Softly, the instructed sound began. It was the same faint undertone as Luke had heard twice before, in California, scarcely identifiable as human; like the rising of the wind. The murmur seemed to have more pattern than he had asked for. Less improvised, the ritual continued to unfold with an unalterable certainty. Growing and growing, it was a swarm of bees, the flooding of the river, at last a great swelling into a musical note, insistent and sustained, a call, a mantra.

It was better than he had designed; it excited him. He knew every cue of the staging, every angle and movement of the cameras, he knew the steps that everyone would follow, the marks they would hold to, yet there was something so unexpected about the night, so deeply and resentfully felt by the blacks, that anything might happen—a tumult, a riot, a miracle—and he would capture it on film.

The mantra sound ceased. He heard the softer utterance of the blacks.

"Gorá!"

Lucas could see him now—Julo Julasto, the fire god—exactly where he was supposed to be, a hundred paces to the right of the looming hill of wood.

The main camera slowly rolled along its oblique track. The new camera moved into its more direct position. On cue, everything on cue.

How beautiful the man looked. His costume was a radiance of whiteness. The night wind lifted the feathers of his flowing cape; the voluminous mantle and its glittering white train followed him like a wake of water. His silver headpiece made him tower so high as to lift him skyward, its plume of feathers fluttering in the wind. Now the great cloud of whiteness started to ascend the wooden mountain, and the ebony of his lustrous face gleamed in the moonlight.

"Gorá!"

The furthest cameraman glanced at Lucas, who nodded, and the rolling, tilting movement started slowly. Slowly too the figure in white ascended. As he was halfway up the staircase, the cult people took up the rhythm of his walk, murmuring, echoing the soft slurring of his footsteps. Then they too stirred in their places, moving their bare feet on the hard-packed earth, brushing the ground, making the long drawn shush, like reeds scraping on drums, shush, silence, shush. They did not start to sing until he was nearly at the top, a song without words, and barely the clarity of consonants, long tones, no beginning and no end.

The man now reached the summit.

The music held until he raised his arm, then there was stillness, unbroken. Raising his other arm, he seemed to be proffering whatever they wanted of him, and the people made a low, soft sigh.

Now, from every direction, the torches came. Pathways opened and the upheld fires moved swiftly toward the wooden mountain. At the edge of it, they paused. As the white figure at the pinnacle let his arms descend to his sides, the torchbearers set their flames to the kindling.

Luke raised one arm, then another, gesturing to cameras on his right and left. One resumed its motion directly inward; the other, tilting upward, started to close in. The helicopter descended a little.

A clap like thunder, then a roar, and the flames took over, darting and enveloping, as the whole base of the pile burst afire. Then the flames raced upward. But still the man at the apex had not been reached; he stood white-clad against the night sky.

Now, unhastily, he started to divest himself of his costume. He raised his crested crown, held it high above his head, then tossed it widely into the flames. The slightest flare of feathers and the crown was gone. Unhurried still, he loosened his splendid mantle. With all the clasps free, he threw the cape open, lifted it aloft, swept it in a circle like a halo around himself and tossed the feathered cloak into the flames. There was a whir of fire, and it vanished.

The man was naked. Without his clothes he seemed even more monumental. He stood there in his titanic pride and, reaching out to the right and left, he held the whole sky in his arms. His head thrown back, his legs spread wide, his genitals like a great triad, his body was an unchained fire god.

Luke thought: How magnificent he is!

The man stood there—motionless—challenging fire.

The wind rose a little. The flares swept one way, then another, bursting in gusts of rage. The conflagration assaulted the wooden mountain, upward and upward, toward the apex where the man stood waiting, without motion.

The flames engulfed him, then they were gone and he was seen again. Once more they swept around him.

He did something he had never done before: He turned.

The flames seemed to give him respite. Then they too turned.

Again, they enveloped him, and when they separated for the third time—

The man cried out.

That too was something he had never done before. Not either time in California, no outcry, never a murmur, never a sound. But perhaps Lucas had heard it wrong; it might have been the sighing of the wind.

Again, the man's voice. No mistake this time. Lucas heard the agonized note, the cry of anguish.

"Oh God, he's burning!"

The third cry. Oh God, Lucas said, what shall I do? He reached for the signal gun. Oh God, what shall I do, he's burning, what shall I do? He pulled the trigger. The signal light burst upward, green and purple.

From all directions, the mammoth rhinos appeared, one and another, a third, a fourth. With forelegs raised in the air, they converged upon the flames.

The black man, tottering, saw them.

"No!" he cried. "Send them back! No!"

Only one of the gray-suited creatures was swift enough to get to the flames, and he was on the wrong side.

The hill of fire caved in upon itself. Darts of flame, like red lightning, leaped upward across the sky.

The multitude did not stir.

"Gorá!" they cried.

He's not dead, Luke told himself, he'll rise again as he always does, he'll appear in the pool of flame, unharmed.

But he didn't.

"Gorá!" they cried again.

Luke rushed toward the flames and started inward.

"Stop, you idiot!" someone shouted.

He felt the arms around him, his own arms flailing. "Stop, Luke! For Christ sake!"

"Let go, let go!"

When they finally let go, he knew it was too late, and he ran, his breath tearing at his heart, trying to outdistance himself.

He was in the camera shack. He heard Calla's voice behind him.

"Luke—oh, Luke!"

"I killed him!" he cried.

"No—no!"

"I betrayed him!"

He started to quake and to cry. "I betrayed him!"

"Stop—oh please—oh stop, Luke!"

But there was no end to his shame and guilt and self-rage and heartache. "I betrayed him, I betrayed him!"

No place was the right place for him, and he ran. He fled from the camera shack and rushed inland, seeking woods and shadows and hidden places. But he was exposed to everything, laid bare to himself as a man who had betrayed his friend. What good, he said, what good the thing he had been creating all these months, these years, what beauty could it hold if there was treachery at the heart of it, if there was the ugly death of someone who was, to him, so beautiful and beloved?

After a while, he heard a sound. It was Harry Fellows. The man approached him tentatively.

"Lucas . . . he's dead."

Luke said nothing, did not move.

"They can't even get his body out," Fellows continued. "What's left of it."

"Go away."

But he didn't. He could see the director's misery, and wanted in some way to mitigate it. "We got everything, Luke. It's all on film—every moment of it."

His heart withered. Every moment eternalized on film. He would see it again and again in the next months, he would run it on the Moviola, he would cut and splice it, he would match this track and that, he would have it scored with music. He could run his friend's death scene any time a projection room was free, any time for the rest of his life.

"Please go away," he said.

"What shall I tell them?"

"Them?"

"The crowd is still there. There's the rest of the scene to shoot."

"The rest . . . ?"

"The turnabout—when they all shout Gorá—the—"

The resurrection. The ecstasy.

He started to laugh and cry.

The ecstasy, the goddamn ecstasy.

"Tell them to go," he said.

"You mean dismiss them?"

"Tell them to go."

23

Calla stood at the outer edge of the crowd, waiting for Fellows to return. He seemed a long time away. Perhaps he hadn't found Lucas, or perhaps he was succeeding where she had failed, in comforting him.

She saw the man coming back, moving too slowly to be carrying instructions.

"You found him?" she said.

"Yes."

"Well?"

"He said tell them to go."

"Go? What did he actually say?"

"Go. Tell them to go."

"But there's the end of the scene . . ."

"I know."

"He has to shoot it, or . . ."

Or not. Don't *you* cry, she said to herself. Return to rules: Bad theater when both characters are weeping. Stay dry, a director had once said to her, stay dry. There must be a serviceable smile somewhere. Find it.

"It won't work without the rest of the scene," she murmured. "It just won't work."

"Yes . . . right," he answered. "But still . . . the director . . ."

They were walking back to the collapsible aluminum table on which Fellows had left the PA stuff. He started to fumble around in things, trying to find the microphone.

The people were quite still. Although none had departed, they seemed a smaller crowd than before, huddled as they were in smaller spaces. There wasn't any movement, and very little sound. There was smoke in the air, however, not stirring very much, for the breeze had died away. How quickly the flames had consumed the wood. A blanket of fire ash lay neatly on the ground, and some embers were still burning, glowing, but not too many.

Fellows found the microphone. He flipped the switch. The silence became a crackle of static.

"Don't," she said.

"What?"

"Don't dismiss them."

"He told me to do it."

"Please—no."

"Calla, if he tells me to—"

"Wait."

"Wait for what?"

"Luke. He'll be back. Just wait."

"It could be a year, for God sake."

"Please—don't send them away—please, Harry—please."

He put the microphone back on the table.

She wondered what good it would do. Wait, she had told him, and he was waiting, which she must do as well. As everyone was doing.

But their waiting was different from any she had ever experienced. The sense of it was not delay, but imminence. Anything could happen, and might even be happening right now. In the waiting there was a live creature, a watchful animal pretending to be asleep, but poised for a cue to spring.

She wondered what the nerve of the living thing was. She could say that the faces of the blacks were still, but they weren't, there was a clamor in them. Their mood seemed an acceptance of an accidental tragedy, but they knew it was no accident, and was not acceptable. For, latterly, the man had been victimized. Nothing was forgotten, nothing forgiven; they knew too little about the events to forget or forgive.

And hardly anything about the man. Only a few had met him. Even to those who had, he was not much more than a stranger, charismatic, a little crazy perhaps, and loving. But a stranger. Still, he had promised something, they did not know quite what, he had left a summons for them to come and find out, a question in their minds, a sign on their foreheads.

Waiting.

It puzzled her that they moved so little. Hardly at all, in fact. They were collected in small groups, their murmurs so soft that it seemed their mouths were trembling on the edge of sound. No sounds were necessary, perhaps, or possible, or capable of expressing what this time might mean. They didn't seem restless to do anything or go anywhere. Nor did they seem afraid of what had happened, or what was still to be.

But what were they waiting *for*?

They were actors waiting for a cue. They were real people waiting for a signal—to do what?

We need to mourn, they seemed to say, and don't know how or why. Some of us listened to what he started to tell us, and we need to hear the end of it. We need to shout out for him, or in his name. We need to see him alive—in some way, alive—in our memories, in our songs, in our sermons—we need him resurrected. We need, we need . . .

The need was terrible, and it was wonderful; it threatened, it promised to come alive. Rage could be stirring in it, and catastrophe. If only she knew how to think of it, what to do with it, how to feel it exactly the same way as they did, to make something of it, make anything, an action, a cry of pain, of beauty.

Then she saw Mamma Lorena, sitting quietly with her three grand-daughters, the daughters of John Tolliver. And Calla knew who Julo was to them. He was their son, their father. With no resemblance to any of them, he was Reverend Tolliver and Leon Hakes and Malcolm X and Martin Luther King. He was the minister and the thief, he was the guilty and the guiltless, he was the angel of peace and the devil of vengeance, he was their sweet kindness and their torturing insanity. He was a stranger who was intimately known to them, their son and father who had perished, and might, if their faith was strong, come alive again.

Not a movie scene, it was a memorial service. They were here to celebrate the dead, and to acclaim the reawakening.

He has to be alive to them, she said, he has to be alive!

Quickly, compelled by a force she did not try to monitor, she threaded her way through the crowd, toward Mamma Lorena. When she got there, she was breathless, she didn't know what to say, what to do. She looked at the old woman as if to beg her for lines to speak or an action to play. And when it was not forthcoming, she burst into it herself. She clapped her hands.

She clapped them again, kept clapping them in the air, not knowing what it signified, kept clapping. The old woman looked at her with
a scurry of panic. She didn't understand. But Tilda did. As if she had
heard a musical call, the young woman responded to it. Not only with
the clapping of her hands, but with a note of singing. *Aaaaa*, she sang,
aaaaa. And Calla sang with her. Suddenly Tilda found the words to the
old song.

> *I gonna see His face again,*
> *I gonna see my Lord!*

Someone else, at a distance, took it up. Then all the Tolliver
women, even Binnie, who had refused to mourn her father, they were
all singing it:

> *I gonna see Him in the night*
> *And see Him in the dawn.*

It was like the tinder of the fire mound. The song burst into a
blaze, and others were singing, lifting the hymn aloft like a flame. It became a bright burning, a conflagration of sound, with the clapping of
hands and the soaring of voices.

> *I gonna see Him while I live*
> *And on and on and on!*

They were no longer motionless. They were unable to contain their
grief and their elation. Some of them made movements where they
stood, some embraced, some danced separately, some together. A number of the younger ones ran to the fire and encircled it. Soon there were
more. And they danced around the embers of Julo's flame.

"Gorá!" someone shouted.

"Gorá!" Calla shouted too. "Gorá!"

Now she was one of the dancers. She danced from one cluster to
another, knowing she had to be everywhere, she had to join all of them.
She could feel her power growing as she passed among the throng. Say
Gorá, she said. And those who had been silent said the name. Her electricity, a chain reaction, flashed from group to group, and all the air was
charged with it. Say Gorá, she urged them, shout Gorá, Gorá. Suddenly
they melded into a single voice, calling for the resurrection of their fire
god:

"GORÁ!"

The lights started to come on again.

She heard Lucas's voice saying, quite softly:

"Action."

They shot it only once, and once was all that was needed. When it was over, people flocked around her, as if no calamity had happened to-night, as if it were an opening night performance, a premiere with floodlights blazing.

"Calla, you were wonderful!"

Wonderful, they kept saying, how she had galvanized the last scene. Inspiring, they said, throat-catching, heart-stopping, Calla, you were wonderful.

She could see that Lucas was barely aware of what was happening. He was stuporous, fulfilling his function like an automaton, walking in his sleep, in his nightmare.

But the others, the camera people, the crowd, the grips, the gaffers: Calla, you were wonderful.

As if a man had not died.

For Lucas he had died. When the shooting was over, Calla could not find the director; he had taken his grief away from the others, to walk along the river.

And for Willi he had died . . . but only temporarily. She went to Julo's trailer to spend the night there, as if to wait for his return.

There had been two deaths, Calla decided later that night, the death of Julo and the demise of herself as an actress.

No matter what showers of praise the company had bestowed upon her, she knew that the moment had not been—for *her*—what she and Luke had hoped for: ecstasy.

Not that she had performed badly. On the contrary, it was a per-formance of impeccable skill, the adroit use of all she had learned, the muster of her energies, the dynamic fulfillment of the action. And God knows she had played the *mask* of ecstasy superbly; anyone might have been fooled by it, even Lucas, perhaps, if he had been aware enough to notice. In fact, she was certain nobody could tell, nobody, that there was no rapture in it. Nobody but herself.

There was an excuse, of course. A man had been killed, cremated before her very eyes. A strange and wonderful voice, a spirit had been stilled. How could she play a scene against such catastrophe?

How could she not?

If her art was part of her life, and her life part of her art, as she had always believed, how could one not electrify the other? Did it mean that her work as an actress would from now on be insensate to what happened to her as a woman?

She grieved over Julo and despaired over herself.

It was well past midnight when she heard a knock on her door. It was Barney; he too couldn't sleep.

They tried to comfort one another by talking about objective things: Since Kono's scenes had already been committed to film, the shooting would be halted only briefly; they would try to reach Julo's family, although it was doubtful that anyone knew how; the sheriff had come and gone, and had "commiserated" over an unfortunate accident. The objective stuff was like the floral wreaths at a funeral, formal and dead.

She was relieved that no mention was made of her scene. She could not have stood another compliment on her performance.

Barney's presence was a solace and she regretted seeing him on the verge of leaving.

"What did you think of your performance?" he said.

Plummeting, she felt like a wounded bird that gives up flight.

"I don't want to talk about it," she said.

". . . I know."

There was never any way of fooling Barney. He always knew. He knew because he played everyone's part within himself; he was all empathy, alive in every spoken line. Especially in Calla's.

"Barney, I can't stand it," she said.

"And I know why it is," he said gently.

"Why? For God's sake, why?"

"We think it'll last forever—that vital throb. We think it'll go on beating, and never stop. Then suddenly we're in our late thirties and early forties, and the throb gets a little weaker. It dies a little. Then, all at once—in the middle of that great obligatory scene—it fails us. It's gone. And we can't ever bring it back again."

"No . . . please. Don't say that."

"I've had it happen to myself. Why not you?"

"Oh Christ. . . . What to do?"

"You either satisfy yourself with technique—and hell knows, Callie, yours is magnificent . . ."

"Or?"

"Narco' di follia."

"Not me. I won't take them."

"What did you do with them?"

"I wouldn't *consider* taking them, Barney."

He repeated, "What did you do with them?"

"I don't know. They're here somewhere."

"If you wouldn't consider taking them, why did you keep them?"

"I don't know. Maybe I did throw them out—I don't know."

She turned away from him. Despair. Nothing to hang on to. "Oh, Barney, I'm all gone!"

"Don't, honey." He took her in his arms and held her. "You don't really need that vital throb, you know. You're so damn good—nobody'll ever know it's missing. There aren't many people who actually look and *see*. And not a living soul who could *be* who you are. So who cares? Play it technically. You can play your whole *life* technically, for Chrissake. And nobody'd know the difference. You're so wonderful, you can get away with anything."

"And nothing."

". . . Yes."

When Barney departed, Calla looked for the pellets. It didn't take her long to find them. They were in a bobby pin box in the top drawer of the dresser.

She selected the smallest pellet, a grayish brown, like a peppercorn, held it in her hands, studied it. Then she placed it in her mouth. It was bitter and she swallowed. The taste was not too strange; a little like aspirin, with a slightly warming afterglow. It made the roof of her mouth feel dry, so she licked it with her tongue. But nothing in the room seemed different; even the temperature was the same, just as chilly as before, or was it just as warm?

She took another pellet. It seemed to her, with a recognized sense of the illogical, that the first pellet had done nothing, but the second was quite busy with her.

She did not know which of the worlds was turning, nor how many worlds there were. But only one of her worlds was at a distance, and it was the one she liked the best. She found it very pleasing, like a promise that had been kept, like a gift that turned out to be exactly what she wanted, the right size, the right color, the right everything. It was a lovely feeling.

I'm sliding down the night, she thought, as if the distance were a chute, down the far night.

And then the strange children arrived.

24

The children were misshapen, some had legs too long or heads too big, but most of them were strange because they thought they were alive. They danced around as if they *were* alive, they shouted and sang and made obscene gestures and tore at one another, drawing blood.

Sometimes they tore at her as well, but only with their voices, yelling that she couldn't act and that she acted the role of mother worst of all, and that murder and mother had the same number of syllables, they even sounded similar.

"Go die," one of them shrieked. "Why don't you go die?"

Death isn't the worst of things, somebody said, and it was Mr. Satin. She saw him clearly and identifiably, and could have described him to the authorities. He was tall and short, he was black and he was white. He started to distribute her among the audience. Who gets which part? he asked, for part meant role and part meant member. It hurt her to have the wrong role, and be dismembered. Mr. Satin laughed at that. Pain was comedy.

Then it became funny, how Mr. Satin sprouted the horns of a dilemma, but when one of them was goring through her breast, she cried out but could not bleed, and the lights started flashing, and somebody said for God's sake, it's an emergency, call a doctor, call *Variety*.

With all the hot arcs around her, she was ice cold and thought she would die of shivering. She fled back into the distance, got warmer and warmer, and then so hot that she did not dare to touch her skin. She fled again, indoors.

The stars were sharp and separate and they stung her eyes; each star a different punishment. But there was nothing that did not punish her, the gossiping wind, the false rumors carried by the river, and how far the emptiness went and never got there.

Then she saw Mina. Since there was nothing she could look at that didn't hurt, she cupped her hands and gazed into them, and saw the child running through her fingers. Stop, she called, stop.

Someone was cutting at her with a sound, hurting her ears and the pores of her skin with the laceration of the utterance. Go away, she cried, stop saying it, go away. Sometimes they did as they were told.

There was a special kind of suffering she dreaded, yet came to count upon. It was a vertigo of sorts, a dizzying and falling, but of a unique nature: she fell inward. It was like the slow collapse of a balloon that shrinks and shrinks and finally wrinkles itself into a little rubber skin.

Sometimes her eyeballs felt like burning coals; sometimes she could not clasp her hands because one palm could not fit the other.

One day, when Mina came, the child was grown up. She was fifteen, she said, and did not need any help; she could manage by herself. But she kept mispronouncing things and could not spell her name. Calla did not like her very much, and sent her back, and when the child was gone, she cried.

But when the daughter came again, she liked her even less. Why do you come here, she said to Mina, when we have nothing good to say to one another? Where should I go, the child said, where am I to go and Calla cried again. Then Mina went away and did not return for the longest while, and Calla kept calling her and calling her.

"Mina! Mina, come back! I didn't do anything—I didn't mean any harm—come back!"

Perhaps the child would never forgive her.

"Meee-naaa!"

After a while she couldn't endure how much it hurt, so she took to hurting herself, and she could not endure that either. Then there was nothing bearable, nothing, not a breath or a ray of light or the temperature of anything, or the certainty that one moment would be followed by another. Still, there was the dim, distant hope that she might be rescued, so she called to the search party and called and called, but only Mr. Satin came, and he was nobody.

Finally, when she thought she was beyond help, she started to hear voices. She heard Mamma Lorena's at first simply because it was audible, not demanding to be heard. She began to respond to what the black woman said, to bits of information, to small requests and casual touchings.

One day she recognized where she was: the orphanage. And she was holding a little boy. He was in her lap and she was fondling him.

"The boy is sick," Mamma Lorena said.

"Sick, yes," she replied, by rote. "How old is he?"

"Not yet two."

"Too young to be sick," she said.

Another time somebody was holding her hand and kissing it.

"Luke?" she said.

"Yes, Luke."

"Have you been here long?"

He smiled. "Longer than you."

"How long haven't I?"

"Five days."

"Is that all? It seemed a year."

"Yes, it did."

She had said a year, but was not quite sure what the term meant. She had no sense of time. She knew about light and darkness but was uncertain what they signified. Her only measure of chronology was Mamma, who told her when to sleep and when to awaken. She had come to rely upon the old woman for everything, and in everything Mamma was reliable. During the illness, she had fed and bathed the white woman, she had responded to her aberrations as if everything the actress did was explicable.

Calla was still not certain of the sequence of things when she became aware of Barney and Willi. With a start, one afternoon, she realized that they had come often, sometimes twice a day, and that Barney had been bringing her things to eat, ice cream and raspberries and little lemon squares that were half cake, half pudding. He treated her like a child, and she got a quiet pleasure from it.

As to Willi, it was as if Julo had never died. "He'll return," she said. "I haven't any doubt of it. Perhaps he'll come back in a form that others won't recognize. But I will. I'll know him the instant he appears."

Luke hated to hear her talk that way. And Calla realized that his bereavement was deeper than her illness had been. Add to which he was now, more than ever, anxious about the picture. And she had contributed to his anxiety. Her five days of absence had caused the film considerable damage. Luke would never upbraid her for it; his worry was a worse reproach. It was wearing him away; he did not know how to think anymore, or whether he could count on anybody.

"I'll be on the set tomorrow," she said.

He gently put his hand on her arm. "Tomorrow's Sunday."

"Monday, then."

He looked older than she remembered him. His skin had lost its color and his eyes were full of pain. She started to touch his cheek, but her hand shook and he saw it. He took her hand in both his own.

"You don't have to rush things, Calla."

"I'm quite all right—don't worry about me."

"But don't rush. We're finding things to do."

Not trusting himself to hide his misery, he got up quickly to return to the compound. As she watched him walk away, she wanted to call after him that it was useless to hide, she knew he was unhappy, she was now susceptible to all his feelings. Aching with grief and guilt over Julo, he also faced a specter of failure. He no longer had faith in her or in his screenplay or in his own skills, or in anything.

Calla yearned to help him. Desperately she wanted to go back to work tomorrow, tonight, this minute, to do anything he asked of her, to prostrate herself and beg his pardon, to crawl her way through the last days of the filming. If Barney's pellets had worked as well for her as for him, she would now be taking a dozen of them. Whatever she had lost as an actress, she wanted to find again, she desperately wanted to find it, not for herself any longer but for Luke.

She wanted to sleep with Lucas that night, but she was unaccountably shy about going to him. She was uncertain how to handle herself, and hoped that he would come to her and give her clues. But he did not arrive. Twice she started to leave Mamma Lorena's, but she was shaky about everything, and not sure how much was still the effect of the pellets. With a compulsive need to tell him she loved him, she was afraid he might think her fervor—at least the confession of it—was drug-generated. The possibility that it might be so, that she could not trust this goodness, this wonderful feeling she had about him, made her twice as lonely as before, but it angered her as well, which she took to be a good sign, and she began to enjoy the vigor of it.

The following day was midsummer in its most benevolent mood.

The faintest of breezes was blowing from the west, across the river and through the woodland. It was a homey afternoon, Calla thought, and Mamma Lorena's back garden had a moist smell of flowers freshly watered, recalling dooryard roses in Connecticut; and a single white cloud loitered in the sky, billowing like a bedsheet on a line.

Sitting on the porch steps, Calla could hear the children playing on the other side of the tall hedge, playing volleyball in the play yard, laughing, teasing. Closer, in the garden, the youngest orphan, the little sick boy, was sitting by a mound of sand, piling pebbles. In a singsong, playful with words, he counted them, "One-a, two-a, three-a." Three was as far as he could go. Nearly two years old, he should perhaps have gone further, but his illness had slowed him down. An unknown blood disease, Mamma Lorena called it, with unknown being a euphemism for deadly. Yet, there was no sign of mortality. His eyes were clear, his black skin gleamed like purple plums, and Calla thought how exquisite he was, the beauty, the sweetness of a promised life, not the sadness of default.

Slowly she got off the porch steps and walked to where he played. She knelt on the ground beside him and pulled some pebbles into his domain, from a place he could not reach. He methodically set them to one side; he was not ready to count the new ones, but he smiled at her and went back to his singsong:

"One-a, two-a, three-a—"

"Four-a."

Mamma Lorena came outdoors, carrying a white plastic bathtub. She placed it in the brightness of the sun. She was going to give the little boy a bath; he enjoyed it outdoors, she said, and the sun was good for him. Calla wondered aloud whether the air would be warm enough or the breeze too strong. Mamma smiled and said nothing would be too much or too little. She was running water through the garden hose into the tub. "You wanta hold this?" she asked.

Calla took the hose in her hand and enjoyed feeling the surge of water through the tube, and watching it gush through the nozzle.

"Would you like to give Lunny his bath?" Mamma asked.

Calla looked up. Mamma's head was against the sun, enveloped by a shine. How odd, she thought, that the woman had read the wish of her mind.

"May I?"

"Oh yes."

"Will it bother him?"

"Why would it bother?"

The black woman didn't linger to offer suggestions or to prepare the child, she simply went away. It was as if she consciously left Calla the privacy.

The water in the tub was not quite warm enough, she decided; she would let the sun shine into it. She sat down beside the child and helped him with his pebbles.

"One-a, two-a, three-a, four-a."

"Good," she said, and she laughed. He also laughed.

With her pale hand she touched the smoothness of his black skin and let her fingers remain there. It puzzled him a little but he did not move away. She said his name and he smiled, showing a few teeth, not many.

He wore an undershirt made of netting and a white cotton wrapping, much like a tiny skirt, which barely covered his privates and his bottom.

"Water time," she said.

Slowly she reached down and pulled his shirt up over his head. He giggled and made a silly noise with his mouth and tongue. She too giggled because he wanted her to. Then she lifted him so that he stood with his hands on her shoulders and his face in her face, and she untied his cotton wrapper, letting it fall to the ground. She arose and gave him her hand so that she could lead him to the bathtub, but as they walked together she had a need to carry him naked in her arms. Bending down, she lifted him. She could feel the softness of his buttocks on her forearm, and his unclothed body close to her breast. She kissed him on the forehead, then on one cheek and another. She clung to him, this warm black child close to her bosom, heartbeat and heartbeat, this something so real, so softly pliable to every touch and pressure of her love. Why couldn't the rest of her life be as warming and trustworthy, why couldn't love be as elemental as this?

She wanted to go on kissing the child, loving and rocking him, she wanted to continue feeling how tender he was in her own tenderness. When she stood over the bathtub, she held him a moment longer, then regretfully let him down, feet first into the tub. Still holding to her, he happily kicked at the water, enjoying it. Then quickly, with a plump, he sat down and let out a squeal of delight.

Sitting beside him on the ground, she watched him play awhile, splashing and giggling and pitching water at everything, including her. She laughed a little and smiled a great deal and kept gazing at him.

Then the noisy stage was over and he took to counting. His toes at first. One-a, two-a . . . He might be getting a little bored now, she thought, so she looked around for the soap. She found it on the other side of the tub and dropped it into the water. They played a game of finding it, letting it slip through wet fingers, and finding it again. At last that game too was over and she made a little lather on her hands. She smoothed his shoulders with it, then his back. He wriggled deliciously as she did it, but when she lathered his arms and armpits, he giggled and splashed and said no, no, but he didn't really want her to stop. Nor did she. So she washed the soap off and lathered him once again, the top of him, hesitant about going any further with the bath. Then, however, she washed his feet and legs and thighs. Soaping his buttocks, she did his anus as well, vaguely aware that she was murmuring to him and humming a little song she had heard Mamma Lorena sing, perhaps a childhood thing, something gentle and scarcely there. As she lathered the front of him, his testicles and penis, he took to giggling again, and lightly patted her face with his hand, and when his wet fingers touched her mouth she kissed them and took one of them between her lips and playfully nipped at it, and he giggled louder and pulled it away.

She had the sense that she was someone else, not Calla, but the boy's mother, whoever she had been. She was singing to her child, bathing and fondling and loving him in the most sensual way, touching all his precious parts with a pleasure of sweet possession, not wanting to stop, was being herself and someone else, departing and arriving at the same time, hearing her own voice in the voice of another, loving the little boy as if he were an infant and a man.

Then she heard the whirring sound. She looked up from the tub. The light was behind the figure. It was Lucas. He had a 16mm camera in his hands, and he was filming them. It seemed totally right that he should do so, not an intrusion. She had known in some hinterland of her brain, had been aware all along that he had been filming them, and she had not minded, had wanted him to do it. Then, abruptly, she knew why. Recalling the scene in the screenplay—the woman bathing the child—she realized she was simply actualizing something he himself had dreamed, he had invented her and the boy and the whole scene, as fiction invents life.

When she finished bathing the child, the whirring noise came to an end. She lifted the little boy from the water, dressed him and set him back to playing with his shiny stones.

She and the man exchanged a glance that said only one thing to her: He wanted her now, this minute, as she wanted him. Then he was gone. It didn't matter that he was gone; she knew they had made an assignation with each other, an immediate demand upon one another: come at once.

She could barely wait for Lorena's return. When the woman arrived, Calla thanked her profusely, embraced her, and said she would return for her belongings in a few days, she had been summoned to the company compound. Mamma smiled perceptively; she had seen Lucas, perhaps, and could guess what a Sunday summons might be.

It was over two miles to the compound. Calla hurried, running part of the way, walking to catch her breath, then hastening again. When she arrived at Luke's trailer, it occurred to her that it might be locked, but that was not unusual, she frequently arrived ahead of him, and knew where the key was, on the farthest windowsill. Unlocking the door, she went swiftly inside, into the shadows. Her eyes did not adjust immediately to the dimness; as they did, she wondered how soon he might arrive. He would be having things to do, she knew, the camera to dispose of, the orders to the men for the following day. She was bursting with desire for him, with a love she could scarcely wait to give him. So she started to undress, damning her sandals for having tight buckles and damning the buttons on her blouse. At last, naked and trembling, she turned his bed down, and debated whether to get in and be waiting for him, or simply stand and be there, so that he could take her unclothed body into his arms. She got into bed and out of it, in again and out. She paced and went narrowly to the doorway to see if she might watch him at a distance as he came.

There was no sign of him. There were, however, mistaken signs: every man who entered the compound was Lucas for an instant, but then was someone else. From somewhere on the river she heard the rolling call of a heron; from across the Bayou, the noise of the electric saw, and the vague, distant voices of the men. The laughing sounds were the loudest ones. She remembered, as a child, hearing her mother crying, and how she had confused it with laughter. At a distance, they were much the same, even at a short distance.

It was afternoon and dusk and early evening, and still he did not come. So, at last, she put her clothes on again, everything, all buttons buttoned, sandal buckles tight, and returned to her trailer.

There was a saying among the Gurries that a woman with a hunger to make love has a cougar in her belly. To them, the cougar, no longer extant in their woodlands, was the most treacherous of beasts. He was wanton and rapacious, he killed not only when craving food or beset, but with the lust for killing; he lewdly reveled in blood; he was ferocious beyond the natural cruelty of the forest.

Calla had a cougar. Walking from Luke's trailer toward her own, she suffered the claws of the animal as if it were real. No matter how she told herself that the beast was imaginary, she derived no relief. Then she struck upon another comfort; she was still feeling the hangover from the drug. It had been, among other things, she decided, an aphrodisiac; it had had a residual effect upon her, a temporary imbalance of metabolism and mind, releasing unruly energies; but it was exclusively a physical quirk, it would pass.

In the open air, it did begin to pass. She calmed down and slowed down, noticing things outside herself, that the summer daylight was over, the night was descending like a black lid.

In the compound, the two motors of the generator truck were pounding against each other angrily. A thick electrical cable, extending from the vehicle to the set site down the Bayou, swayed from the tallest treetop and looked as if it might fall. The lights along the compound, naked electric bulbs on strands of wire, flickered like butterflies. Distant hammer sounds kept time with the contest of the two motors, echoing along the river. An electric saw went off, screeching, tearing the fabric of the night, then died to silence.

Cold, it was getting cold again. She entered the trailer, hoping to find Willi there, but the place was empty. She had not eaten since she could not remember when, except for two oranges at lunch. I should be hungry, she thought, but I'm not. Still . . . the cougar. It's not a true hunger, she reassured herself, as if there were distinguishably true and false ones, and she tried to drive the animal away.

25

The filming of the picture was almost finished; there were only a few more scenes to do. One of them was a major sequence featuring Barney. They had delayed the shooting of it until the advent of another actor, who had not yet arrived in Mississippi. The other actor was a dog.

In the screenplay, Titus Macauley owns a mastiff. Although it is not a tracking animal, the hunter uses it as if it were a bloodhound, and the beast is hardly adequate to the task. The mastiff is an ugly monster, predacious on livestock, and mean in restraint. He is huge, with shaggy hair uncommon to the breed, an overshot jaw and a cruel hunting instinct. Man and beast are bound together, but they hate each other. One day, the dog turns rabid and springs at his master's throat. Titus fights with the mouth-foaming animal and kills him. . . . Luke had not expected any difficulty in casting a wild-looking dog that had been trained to follow command. However, the best the assistants could find, in Ashton and Memphis kennels, were a German shepherd who looked too tame and a Doberman who could not be trusted. Of the latter animal, the kennel owner said, "He ain't trained to pretend, he trained to *do* it—kill." When Luke had seen perhaps three dozen dogs, he had had to phone Harker's Zoo in Pasadena and rent a movie actor mastiff, tamed, trained and housebroken—$1,400 a day, plus expenses and fringe benefits.

The beast arrived in a cage on the back of an open pickup truck. His owner did not sit up front with the driver of the vehicle, but on an uncomfortable, rickety stool alongside the cage, to keep the creature company. The man was called Vergil Harker. He was short and dainty-looking with a pencil-thin mustache, and he looked as if he had been dressed by a confused designer to play in a Hollywood polo match:

whipcord jodhpurs stuffed into suede riding boots, a form-fitting khaki shirt with brass buttons and epaulets and a glaring, white pith helmet.

The mastiff's name was Darryl. As ugly and mean-looking as the part required, he was an old dog, and because his teeth had worn down, his canines were fitted with porcelain caps like the sheriff's, just as bright and gleaming. They'll show nice on camera, Vergil Harker said, we'll darken 'em down a bit. The poor beast had been sick on the airplane and sick on the ride from Memphis, and, what with tranquilizers and weakness and acid indigestion, he did not want to join the fuss. He lay half asleep, stirring to raise his massive head only long enough to see where they were, then he went flat again. His stomach was still upset despite the bottle of Pepto-Bismol that had been dumped down his throat, and even in the open air it was plain that he was flatulent. He had been left in his airline cage because of his incontinence of bowel, which Vergil assured everyone would no longer be a problem now that the dog was not flying. But from moment to moment, after they lifted Darryl's cage onto the ground, the animal continued to fart and grumble.

"I'm sorry he's a little windy," Vergil said. "But he's not as young as he used to be. And he's getting a little disillusioned about show business."

The trainer wasn't. He posed willingly for the still cameraman, he fingered his mustache and smiled and pursed his mouth as if for kissing. But he couldn't prevail on Darryl to rise to the occasion and say cheese.

"He'll be all right in a few days," Vergil pledged to the director. "When do you want to shoot?"

"Tomorrow."

"That soon, huh? Where?"

"A few miles from here—in the woods."

Vergil frowned. "More traveling." He turned to the cage. "Well, Darryl, another day, another dollar. To be or not to be—all the world's a stage. You can't teach grandma to suck eggs." Vergil too was windy.

In a convoy of three jeeps, a truck and a station wagon, they departed the following day, before dawn. The morning shots in the forest went quickly, for Darryl was indeed an old trouper. But at the beginning, he had little to do except run, lie down, stop and listen, jump over a narrow stream and growl loathingly at Titus, showing his false fangs.

In the afternoon, however, when he would have to do his death scene, he seemed to sense that the going would be tough. In the woodland clearing, the sun glared and the ground was hot. Vergil put fresh water in the mastiff's pewter bowl. "He's not used to this paralyzing heat," he said. "Pasadena's cooler than this, even in summer."

When the time came for rehearsal, the temperamental beast irrationally decided he wanted to go back into his cage. He had no interest in the mechanical rabbit his master wound up and sent scooting across the grass, nor in the dish of mashed-up Boston cream pie for which, in his old age, he had developed a carious sweet tooth. When at last the trainer teased him out, it was a long time before he responded to what Vergil called his warm-up exercise. All the old mastiff wanted to do was remain supine and unmolested.

"He's homesick," Vergil said.

At last he managed to coax the animal to its feet. But just as Darryl stretched, yawned and started his calisthenics, there was a noise. It was nothing more than the loud caw of a fish crow, but to Darryl it was a lion, and he was so smitten with fear that he scurried back into his cage, crawled to the farthest corner, stayed on his belly and tried to shut out the distant cawing that he took to be a roar.

"Easy, boy, easy," Vergil said. "Don't be scared, boy, daddy's here." Then, to the others. "He has this trouble with anxiety."

Angst or no angst, the dog was not to be pampered, Vergil said, because being tenderhearted with show animals softened their ferocity. But then he went to the door of the cage and treated Darryl like a puppy. He whispered dulcetly into the beast's ear, patted his head, rubbed his belly, his chest, his hucklebones. At last, placing his body in such a way as to hide the final intimacy, Vergil kissed the gray nose of his dear old darling. The animal mumbled a little, broke wind and arose. Slowly, he made his way out of the cage, as Vergil said, "Good dog, good old puppy."

The beast went through his warm-up paces, growl, lunge, roar, tear, rip, snarl, and in a while he was ready for his first rehearsal with the other actors.

"This is always the tough step," Vergil said. "So I have to use my gun."

His gun appeared. It was a siphon full of seltzer. "He hates it," the trainer said. "One shpritz in the eye, and he knows I won't take any more shit."

As Barney reached out to pat the mastiff, Vergil shook his finger at him. "Don't do that," he said. "If you're friendly with him, he won't even *pretend* to hate you. He's a very honest performer, you know."

The setup was being prepared. The special effects man was pouring cow's blood in the hollow plastic collar of the beast. Then he fitted the fingertips of Barney's left hand with sharp little nail caps. The plastic collar was extremely delicate, the effects man said to the actor, and Barney's nail caps would burst it easily.

"But when you do it, let's see the knife, Barney," Luke said. "As you're stabbing him with your right hand, keep the left hand buried under his head, so we don't see what it's doing."

The auxiliary arcs were ready, and Lucas explained the action. Calla had a single line of warning at the start of the scene, then the mastiff was to spring at the camera where Barney would presumably be standing. The rest would be intercutting to the hunter without a gun, to the animal, to the knife-and-jaws battle with the beast. In the course of it, Barney's hand would be mauled and his throat bitten by the mad dog, and the actor too would be fitted with blood sacs, one in his hair and a larger one under his shirt, both of which he himself would burst. Every step of the action, every movement had to be meticulously staged by the director, then translated by Vergil into commands that the animal would follow. Since the scene would be shot silently, without a sound boom, both the director and the trainer could shout directions to the beast and the actors, and to the two cameras that would follow the action.

The rehearsal went slowly. By midafternoon, the dog was still not obeying all his commands. And Barney too was off. His hands were unsteady, his reflexes slow. Calla watched him closely and knew what was unbalancing him; he was like a man recovering from a raving binge. She wondered if he had been so frightened of the scene that he had not dared take a pellet.

As the afternoon wore on, the mastiff got better, but Barney got worse. Sometimes he did not seem to hear Luke's shouts from the sidelines, sometimes he entirely missed his marks and left the animal prowling at loose ends. He was sweating profusely, his shirt had been replaced twice, and now Luke called for a recess so that his trousers too could be changed.

When the interval was over, Barney came back, asked for some coffee, turned away, and she knew he was taking a pellet. He took a long time finishing his coffee, set down the cup, walked away from the set, ran a hundred yards across the clearing, and back. On his return, his hands seemed restless and his head had an arrogant tilt.

"Let's go!" he shouted. "Mad dog, let's go!"

His excitement caught on. One of the crew let out a whoop. Vergil hurried to his beast, opened the animal's mouth, and with a pastry gun he squirted white sugar foam onto the tongue and about the chops. The dog sneezed and spat, making the froth look even more horrible.

"Let's go!" Barney shouted again. "Crazy mad dog, let's go!"

Luke yelled. "All right, let's take a chance—let's shoot it!"

One of the gaffers yelled, then an assistant: "Stand by!"

"Stand by."

"Roll 'em."

"Action!"

Rachel called the warning, "Titus, watch out!"

The hunter wheeled, saw the frothing beast, started to run, then fell as he was supposed to do. The animal leaped. The man rolled. He rose and ran again and the mastiff surged at him. Titus whipped the knife out of the sheath. The mad dog was at him and at him again. The blood spurted; the man's shirt reddened; the teeth snapped and bit at the air and at the face. The man's head and brow were bleeding now, but the knife kept flashing, striking, and the dog's neck became drenched with the redness. Again and again, the fake plunging of the knife, as the beast fell, tried to rise, fell again in a pool of blood.

But still the knife did not stop, it kept plunging into the animal, plunging, and the belly was open, pouring blood.

"Cut!"

The knife kept going, stabbing.

"Cut, I said! Cut!"

But the actor did not stop. The knife was real and the animal was real and the blood was real.

"Cut! Barney, for God's sake!"

The knife, still thrusting, and the crewmen rushing, and the trainer crying no, no, no.

"Barney—stop—Barney!"

It was over and the dog was dead.

"Barney!"

But he was gone. He leaped over the dolly track and raced to where the vehicles were parked. He hurled himself onto the seat of the pickup truck, the motor roared, and the tires screeched. Racing this way and that, not knowing which way to go, he found the tracks the convoy had made across the clearing.

"Barney!" she shouted.

Vergil stood over his dead beast, weeping no, no.

"Barney!"

When the company returned to the compound in the early evening, Barney was nowhere in sight. The pickup truck he had fled in was where it should have been, in the parking area, but he was not in it. Nor was he in his trailer. Luke assured Calla that Barney would come back. Although there was hardly any work left for the actor to do, and what there was could be done by a double, Luke was certain that Barney would feel compelled to finish his performance. There was little likelihood that he was on his way to the Memphis airport. None of the company vehicles were unaccounted for, no taxi had arrived to pick anybody up and nobody had seen him hitchhiking along the road. Then it occurred to both of them that he might have gone upriver by boat. But the rowboats were all there, and the motorboat was securely moored.

A half hour later, when Calla was alone in her trailer, Delia, the wardrobe mistress, came rushing in.

"He wants you, he wants you!" she yelled.

"Who—Luke?"

"Barney! He's in the wardrobe trailer."

"Get Luke," Calla called as she hurried outdoors.

"He says 'alone,'" the woman shouted.

Frightened, Calla slowed down. Then, grimly determined, she made her way across the compound. At the entrance to the costume trailer, she halted. She looked back at Delia, who stood there, outdoors, quivering in the night, her hands covering her mouth.

Inside, on the sewing table, a Coleman lantern gave all the light there was. Calla did not see him, saw only the hanging costumes, the hunting clothes, the cult apparel of Kono's followers, the brilliantly striped caftans, the beaded headdresses, and it occurred to her: what a strange place he had chosen to hide in, and yet how forlornly characteristic: another costume, another role to play.

But still she did not see him.

"Barney . . . ?"

She had a glimpse of something moving, a stir among the jackets that hung on the wooden rod. She knew he was behind them. How will he be dressed? she wondered.

The clothes separated and he stood there, hanging back in the dimness. The costume he wore was the one he had worn at the end of the scene. Nothing had changed. The false and real blood were still on him, on his forehead, down his cheek, his hands; and his shirt had dried to a bloody brown. Yet, while all the clothes were the same, the man himself had shockingly altered. The drugs had suddenly ravaged his face; it trembled as if it were falling apart. And his body quaked so that he had to lean on the sewing table.

"Is someone with you?" he asked.

"No."

"You're sure?"

"Yes."

"You came alone—you're not afraid of me?"

She tried the standard evasion. "Why should I be afraid?"

"I tried to kill you once."

"Kill . . . ?"

Her heart stopped. She would not be able to go through with this.

"No, not really kill," he said unhappily. "Uglify."

". . . Willi."

"No, not Willi—you." He suddenly put his hands to his ears as if he did not want to hear what she said, she was confusing him. He had, for an instant, sounded like a real person. Now he went back to being an actor. "You didn't suspect me at all, did you? There was nothing in my playing that made you suspect me, was there?"

She wasn't sure how much she herself was acting, but something made her resist surrendering totally to his scene. "Yes, I think I did suspect you a little."

"You didn't!" he said hotly. "You didn't! When? Not until today."

"Perhaps not until today."

"When I killed the animal."

"Yes."

"But not before then."

". . . I . . . should have."

"Should have? When?" His voice was getting more belligerent. "You had no reason! When?"

"When I saw the rushes."

"What about the rushes? What did I do?" He was suddenly eager, yet frightened of what she might say. And she was equally frightened of him.

"You were . . . fantastic."

"Yes, yes! But what? How could you know from the rushes? What did I do, what did I show?"

She wanted to tell him: you were violent, you were brutal. But she was too terrified, even too terrified to run.

He was insistent. "What did you see, Calla? That I could kill someone?"

". . . Yes."

"But I didn't!" As if fleeing from one turmoil to another, he was pleading now. "Cal, I didn't! And I didn't mean to hurt Willi. Honest to God, I didn't! It was dark—she was wearing your clothes, her hair was the color of yours, she was getting into your car. I didn't want to hurt her."

"Only me."

"I had reason!"

"Did you, Barney?"

"You wrecked my life! From the minute I met you, nothing—ever —! How could I ever make it, the way you did? How could I ever—? I was in your shadow! As good as I was, I was never good enough. I lost every chance. And then you killed Mina!"

"Oh, Barney—no!"

"Killed her!"

"I didn't!"

"She was the best part of my life—the best part! You killed her!"

"Barney—listen—"

"You listen! I never knew how good I was until Mina came along! Good, you understand that word?—good. Good as a man, not as an actor. She was making everything come in focus for me! She might have made things real! Real—me, Barney Loftus—real. She might have saved me! I might have become one person!"

The lie came before she could stop it. "You are one person."

"No, I'm not! But oh—I could have been, if Mina hadn't died! And you killed her!"

He was shuddering. She could see how ill he was, and wanted to comfort him. "It's been so many years, Barney."

"Years—what's that mean? Fade in, fade out, the end? What the fuck does that mean?"

He started to cry.

"Barney, let me help you. You're ill."

"I'm not ill! I've never been ill. I didn't have T.B.—I had drugs. I was fired out of Italy for drugs—not consumption—drugs. I've been on them since the Nazi picture. It's not a real sickness—nothing about me is real—it's drugs."

"Let me help you—please. If I can get you a good doctor, if you go somewhere—you could get off them."

"I don't want to get off them! I can play anything when I'm *there*." He was the actor again, proud of what he despised. "I can be so goddamn good that nobody can believe it. Nobody can even recognize me—not even you! Did you know me on the phone?"

"No, I didn't, Barney."

"There—you see? I played a lot of parts and you didn't know me in any of them. I was Mrs. Adams on the phone—the black man on the stairs—a Bronx operator—the voice in the woods—and none of them —you didn't spot me in any of them. Did you?"

". . . No."

"And the best of them—the Englishman! Oh God, am I proud of that one! Not ordinary. Not Limey, not Cockney, but something marvelous and special. A Cambridge type—very unusual—you've got to catch the music of it—a touch of the adenoids and a touch of the books." He was uplifted in a glory. "Did you hear the erudition in my voice? Did you hear the library, the turning of the pages? Did you hear that in my voice? Did I carry you into the book stacks? Did you smell the dust? Did you?"

"Yes, I did, Barney."

"Do you know how I *performed* that image? The educated bloke— do you know how I did him? I bought myself a briar pipe—an English briar. I didn't smoke it, mind you. I merely kept the pipe stem in my mouth, that's all. But every word I said, every syllable—it filtered through imaginary smoke."

"Yes . . . imaginary smoke."

"Imaginary—made up—crazy—the way I wanted to drive *you* crazy."

"And almost did."

"Yes—almost, almost! The *narco'* especially—I almost did it with the *narco'!*"

Abruptly he was overcome with everything. He uttered a terrible outcry. "Oh Christ," he sobbed. "Oh Christ!"

She started toward him in a motion of sympathy, but he quickly drew upon his resources, as if he were readying himself for an entrance, and he stopped weeping. The actor's self-discipline worked. He was calm. "I want you to know something else." He stood up straight. His voice had inordinate dignity. "I've always loved you, Calla. I never really changed. Even while I hated you, I never stopped loving you. You know that, don't you?"

"If you tell me . . ."

"No, you have to *know* it! You have to know I've always loved you. You were my best audience."

"Your best. . . . Yes."

"Absolutely my best! You always knew exactly what I was going for—and how hard it was to do—and how beautifully I achieved it. You knew all the joy and the pain that was in it. My best audience—the best I ever had. That's why I had to come back. After all those failures—I had to come back to my best. And you're my best, Calla. Why, look at you now. This minute—now—look at the way you're listening to me! Look at the expression on your face! My God, you look like you're ready to *applaud!*"

"Oh, Barney . . ."

"Applaud me, Calla—applaud me!"

"Barney—don't."

"Applaud me! Please—oh, please, applaud me!"

"Barney—"

"Clap your hands—clap—clap!"

She started to clap her hands.

"Louder!"

She smashed her palms against each other, weeping as she did. Louder, he kept yelling, louder, and her weeping was louder too. He stood there with his arms wide, accepting his ovation with a heartaching need for it, not needing any other comfort, not needing any caress, only applause. Suddenly, because she saw his desperation for it, she couldn't help joining his scene, and cried out:

"*Bravo!*"

It was the plaudit he had never heard, the one he lusted for. Laughing, crying, he ran past her, offstage. Shouting bravo, she ran after him.

As she pursued him in the night, she saw the other figures moving, Luke, Willi, many more.

Seeing them, Barney ran in the opposite direction, toward the river.

Abruptly, she saw his intention. "Barney!" she called. "Barney—come back!"

She heard the others racing after him. Someone, she thought, ran past her.

"Barney! Somebody, stop him!"

At the water's edge, he did not pause, but plowed in as though he knew precisely where he was going. When he was waist-high, he pitched forward into the current and started to swim.

They saw the creatures—a quick one and a more laggard one—giving chase in the water.

"Barney!"

Then other creatures.

At the riverside, nobody followed him. It would do no good.

She kept calling his name.

There were many animals now, fighting, beating against one another and flaying the water. The river spumed up and around them, violently in a whirlpool, and all the tails and arms and legs kept thrashing, making fountains of wetness in the dark current.

Barney, she kept yelling, Barney, Barney.

After a while, some of the creatures slithered to the farther bank, and a few swam downriver. The maelstrom disappeared, and soon there was no unusual whiteness in the water.

Shortly afterward, a number of small boats—rowboats and a couple of flatboats, perhaps a dozen in all—came skimming down the waterway. The shouting and splashing of the oarsmen put the croachers to rout. It was hard to see what other purpose they were meant to serve; certainly the boatmen did not collect any of Barney's remains, for nothing of the dead man was visible. Calla imagined that the search might be one of the rites of balance, to let the beasts know they had a grievance against them, and sooner or later would bring them to account.

As the boats started to drift away, downstream, Calla did not know why she still stayed there. Luke brought her a coat, but the chill went deeper. She did not recall that Mississippi nights were so cold; night chill, yes, but not so bleakly cold.

When only the two of them remained at the water's edge, and even the boatmen had disappeared, Luke begged her to come to his trailer and spend the night, so that he could keep her warm in the chilling darkness, and help to stop her shivering. She thought: how tender the man is, and she wanted to be with him. But she also wanted to be alone with Barney, to see him off.

Yet, by the time she got to her trailer, she could feel herself emptying, as if her heart had come unstoppered. As the state of nothingness set in, she suddenly dreaded the aloneness she had chosen, and hoped that Willi would be awake. Her friend, however, had apparently taken one of her sedatives, and she was deeply asleep. It was as if Willi weren't there. The space was empty.

And Barney's image filled very little space. She didn't know how to remember him. Although he had been dead only a few hours, her memory wandered between the clean-shaven young man she had married and the bristly-faced Titus Macauley. She tried to force her mind to store only one image of him, the happy, early one, the young lover when they were both young enough to love uncomplicatedly, the rambunctious Barney with the unexpected humors and the pretended awkwardnesses, the loony walrus flopping in the sea, the clowning stumblefoot. Or, before she had married him, the foster-father he had played in their first film together, the wonderful vulgarian full of high jinx and absurd obscenity. With a stab, she considered that he would want to be recalled as Mina's father, for the child had promised him himself, and reality. But Calla wondered if it might not ultimately have become a role in which he played Barney Loftus, a role for which he was miscast. He could never be anything other than an actor, and his last characterization, whatever it might be, would be his greatest. So he had died on ringing applause, an ovation. And with what a glorious role to make his final exit—The Slayer of the Mad Beast. Even if the beast was, like Barney himself, an aging actor.

All those parts, all those Barneys—she wanted to grieve, and it grieved her that she did not know which man to mourn. Mourn nobody, Barney might have said; applaud the exit of the actor, don't mourn the death of the man. Stand up and cheer.

But the cheers were only part of him. The rest was anguish. The loss of the vital throb, he had called it, with nothing to take its place except the mortal one. If only that were the answer for her as well. Pellets of madness and river serpents—no, the answer for her was to endure the life-guilt, whatever it might be—and hope that one day she could exorcise it—in her work.

Meanwhile, another scene to play, another try at Let's Pretend. What could she pretend to be, what could she pretend to want except what Barney wanted, the release of being someone else, the exhilarated escape in borrowed clothes, to cries of bravo.

26

The film was finished, yet it wasn't finished.

As they lay in bed, she felt Luke's restiveness. "Only a few pickup shots and then we can wrap it up," he said. "But I feel like the man who packed all his bags and flew off without his briefcase."

"What's in it?"

"That's just it—I don't know. Maybe it's empty. If there was something important in it, why would I forget it?"

"Is there anything in the script that you've cut and wish you hadn't?"

"No. . . . Maybe something I never wrote."

"Like?"

"I don't know. Some major scene."

"Tell me the story."

"What?"

"In one sentence tell me the story of *The Fabulist* and see if that's what you shot."

"Of all the simpleminded—"

"Come on, come on."

Mocking the notion, he recited like a schoolboy: "*The Fabulist* is the story of a woman who goes in search of her missing son, and when she—"

"Stop right there."

"Okay, why?"

"Goes in search of her son, you said. Does she find him?"

"You didn't let me finish the sentence."

"Finish it."

"She searches for him—and finds herself."

Calla ruminated. "But does she find her son?"

"No. She gives up the search."

"Why?"

"Because she's found something more precious—a man she was able to love—a new belief in herself—"

"Give me a hard fact. Why does she give up the search?"

"Because she believes Kono's story."

"The boy became a follower of the cult. When he became disillusioned, he deserted the religion. And Kono didn't kill him."

"No. If he's dead, God killed him."

"And Rachel believes that story."

"Not at first. But when she falls in love with Kono—yes, she believes it."

"Kono is not a murderer."

"Look, Calla, it's pretty late in the day to be questioning that."

"I'm not questioning it. I'm merely saying that if Kono hasn't killed her son, maybe he's still alive. Why doesn't she go in search of him?"

He was tempering his annoyance, but it showed. "Obviously, that *was* the thing to write. But the film isn't interested in that. The boy is merely a symbol. The audience has never seen him, doesn't know him, and after a while doesn't give a damn about him. All it cares about is Rachel's search for herself."

"But what does *she* care about?"

There was a long silence. He threw the blanket off himself but left it on her. She thought: He'll be chilly again in a moment.

"Lucas . . . I'm not trying to upset anything. I think it was bold of you to avoid the obvious, even if it was an obligatory-obvious. And maybe she shouldn't go in search of her son. But if she doesn't—why not?"

"I know what you're getting at—that she's afraid to do it," he said. "When Kono dies she wants to remember the best of him. And if she finds her son, she may find that Kono lied, that he did kill the boy."

"Well, that's what Titus thought. And for all the fact that Titus was a cruel bastard, he always nailed them with the truth."

"The audience will never believe Titus, they'll believe Kono."

"Whom does Rachel believe?"

"Kono, of course."

"Whom do you believe?"

He was silent again. And, sooner than she expected, chilly.

The following morning, even before dawn, Lucas was missing from bed, and there was an unusual stir in the compound. By daylight there was a hustle and bustle of activity. Every workman on the film seemed to be running in and out of the woodland. The two station wagons and one of the trucks rumbled back and forth, always on the point of colliding with one another on the narrow forest path.

"What's going on?" she asked Lucas.

"You're going on the search."

"To find the boy?"

"Yes."

"When?"

"As soon as I get things ready."

"Ready? What are you getting ready?"

"Obstacles."

"You mean you're going to make me sweat?"

"Worse, I hope."

"In what way, worse?"

He didn't answer. He started away.

"Wait!" she called. "Is he dead? When I find him, is he dead?"

At a distance, he turned. "How do you know you'll find him?"

"What? You mean I won't? Wait a minute! Luke—! You're not going to tell me what to expect?"

He didn't answer. Hurried into the woodland.

The work continued through the morning. Hardly anybody stopped for lunch. By early afternoon, there was still no indication when the workmen would be finished, and no summons for her to appear.

Toward four o'clock, without warning, Hubie arrived in one of the Jeeps and told her to hurry. They drove into the woods for perhaps a half mile. In a crowd of crew and assistants, Luke was giving last minute instructions. He barely noticed her. Person by person, he deployed most of the company through the forest. At last he turned to her. Putting his arm around her shoulder, he walked her away from the few assistants who remained.

"I don't know much more about this scene than you do," he began. "And nothing good may come of it. We're shooting it with only hand-held stuff, and there's no boom—the sound will be awful. There'll be a half dozen cameras along the way, and their stuff won't match. That may be all to the good. Anyway, for you it's like a treasure hunt— you don't know where you're going, you don't know what you're going to find. All you know is what you're looking for. You're going through every kind of obstacle. Try not to get hurt—be careful. But keep going deeper and deeper into the woods. You won't get lost. Whenever there's a choice, someone with a camera will appear ahead of you. Move toward it—treat the camera as a hope. In that direction, you'll find your son. Keep the hope alive—even when you're frightened—keep it alive."

He paused.

"Then . . . you'll come to the clearing in the woods. It's the same clearing where you looked for him before, and he wasn't there. This time, however, you think he has returned to the little lean-to he once built for himself. Perhaps he's alive, nothing wrong with him. Perhaps he's ill. Perhaps he's not there. As you move through the last hundred feet of woods, you realize you're approaching the open space. You can't stand it, how full of hope and terror you are. And now . . . step by step . . . you're there. You're in the clearing."

"What do I do?"

"Depends on what you see."

"What do I see?"

"You may see nothing. Whatever you find—it doesn't matter. All we care about is what happens to you when you come upon it. Anything that happens—that's fine. And if nothing happens—that's okay too. There's a tragedy in nothing."

He had come to the end of his directions. Suddenly he embraced her tightly; it seemed desperate to her.

"Go," he said.

She started on her search. It was not more than a pleasant walk at first, through lush woodland, through the summer cool of the damp forest, through the gossip of birds, and she got the feeling that the greenery was alive not as flora but as sentient animals, vigilant. She didn't mind their observation of her, and after a while, a long while it seemed, she enjoyed being there, so that when she caught sight of one of the cameramen with the whirring machinery at his shoulder, she resented being spied upon. She had an impulse to go in another direction, but she followed him and Luke's instruction.

Further, deeper in the woods, and she forgot that they were "taking" her. Taking, she thought, does it mean guiding or capturing? Unimportant; the search was everything. The search for what? Once, she had called herself a woman in search of a scream.

She came to a particularly serene place, and loitered. Don't stop, keep going, she urged. The woods were lovely, dark and deep, but she had promises to keep. No, she said, that was a wintry snow in a poet's New England, that was home, and this is a realistic woman in the South. Promises to keep . . . and searches.

Something lashed across her face. She felt it as a hand, as if someone had slapped her, but she realized it was a branch that had sprung loose from an imprisonment by other branches. The hurt passed quickly, but she had stumbled, bruised her knee. It was an odd thing to have happened, and she wondered if it had been staged, if the branch had been artificially tied in some way. She routed the thought: some things were natural.

She continued on for hundreds of yards, it appeared, and abruptly realized with disquiet that she had not seen a camera in quite a while. It occurred to her: I'm lost, or they are. While it worried her, it also gave her a perverse pleasure: I've outwitted them. I've given the voyeurs and the eavesdroppers the slip, left them behind, whirring away at nothing.

But then she saw another assistant, Elsie Rush, viewing her, ogling her with that black thing, watching every step, prying, gathering gossip.

She continued toward Elsie as she had been directed to do, trying to evoke the sense that the film was the hope of finding her son, but it didn't work; cameras were no longer guideposts, they were confirming themselves as intruders on her privacy. Closer and closer to Elsie, then further and further apart as the operator kept backing away and backing away until, all at once, the watcher was gone.

That way, then, I'll continue that way, she said, and suddenly—
She fell.

It was a trap, those bastards, they had strewn leaves and branches over a pit, a deadfall, and she was in it. It was wet, with an unpleasant funky odor, and moisture still oozing from its walls. She tried to lift herself out, but all she could cling to were a few weak tendrils and gummy earth that came away in her hands. There was something exuding from below; she thought it was water at first. She felt it over the tops of her low boots and then crawling upward on her legs, soft, damp, sticky, and she reached down, tearing them away, the clammy, creeping things, whatever they might be. Stop, she yelled upward out of the sumpy grave, stop, you bastards, did you have to go this far, did you have to do this, you bastards, you goddamn bastards.

Wrong dialogue. She was yelling things that had not been written for her. She was shouting at Lucas, who was directing the picture, but not a character in it. What she had called out wouldn't do. The curses and clamors would have to be wiped off the track . . . appropriate dialogue to be dubbed in later.

Meanwhile, she had to get out of the deadfall. Help me, somebody help me. But there was no rush of assistants and retrievers and gofers, no slaves to help the star. Get out of it yourself, she said. She clawed at the wet sides of the pit, cursed the crawling things, then with her hands she dug out footholds in the mucky walls. Inch by grabbling inch, she pulled herself to the surface. She lay there, tearing the slimy white things off her skin, the sluglike worms she did not recognize, furry and moist as caterpillars.

She walked and heard the rolling of camera film, soft, sneaky. She did not see the operator. But the machine became her steady companion, dim and distant at times, occasionally so close that she felt she could reach out and touch it. Yet, unseen. How did they manage it, she wondered.

She couldn't move. It had happened without warning. Impossible, she thought, that they had made this density, certainly not in one day, it seemed to have encroached from another era. Natural or artificial, old or new, she couldn't budge in it. Too many tendrils, too many branches, too many vines and briers and creepers; she felt bound hand and food, shackled by chains of greenery. There was no forward, no sideward, no return, and the more she moved the more the growth seemed to embrace her. We love you, Calla-Rachel, it seemed to say, love you, strangle you.

Suddenly, as she broke through, she felt the knives, hundreds of knives, piercing her skin, stabbing at her hands, her forehead, thorns as long as her fingers, help me, someone help me, I can't move in this, help me.

As she stopped shouting to catch her breath, she heard it: click. Another click, someone emptying a camera chamber, another click, the whirring sound. She saw the head behind the hedge and miraculously that was the way to free herself, and she followed it.

Free and walking, with the woodland beautiful again, she felt an exhilaration. She had endured bad things, and she could endure worse. Bring on your trials, she said, you bastards, bring on your tests and your out-of-town tryouts and your sneak previews, bring on your snakes, your wolves, your leopards, bring on all the beasts that have torn at me, bring them all on, you bastards, I'm alive and going to stay alive—and I will find my son!

She was ankle-deep in swamp. It smelled bad and she thought it was ordure, and wondered what poetic mind had put her nearly shin-bone-deep in shit, and she hated all of them, all who had such valiant imaginations for making viciousness and cruelty, and were frightened by a sonnet. You fucking miseries, she yelled, you fucking miseries. . . . Wrong dialogue again. Dub that one too.

Onward, and things were easier, and straightaway. Now there were no difficulties at all, everything seemed cleaner and greener, the earth was drier, there was a faint breeze and the trees made a soughing sound like the eucalyptus in her garden. All at once . . .

She had the sense, even before seeing it, that the clearing was there. It was there like the longed-for encounter with an old compan-ion, the friend was *there*—in the room behind the closed door, in the courtyard around the corner, the familiar one was waiting.

As the clearing in the woods was waiting.

She burst upon it in the dazzling sun. The sky was so bright ahead of her that everything was silhouetted, and the solar light was blinding. No delicate shadings, none at all, only a stark chiaroscuro of black and white—purple and scarlet, since this was Technicolor—of a lean-to nes-tled against the farthest edge of the open space, and almost in the mid-dle of the clearing, a wonderful and strangely formed great tree. She couldn't tell what sort of tree it was—oak because it was so mighty, or cypress because it was right for the terrain—but it was macabre, weirdly shaped like a cripple bending away from the wind.

Slowly, with her hand at her forehead as a shield against the sun, she approached it. As she came within its shade, she saw why it was dis-torted. It had been struck by lightning.

A great knife of fire had riven it into two parts. The fallen part lay dead upon the ground, leaves brown and black, those that remained on its branches, limbs dry and gone to tinder, crackling underfoot. As to the living part, it stood there with the gut of its trunk exposed, blackened by the electric burning, its sap still flowing like a gumming amber lymph. It was so morbid that it almost made her ill. . . . The black was airgunned, you fool, and the lymph is Vaseline.

Beyond it, the lean-to was not in ashes, only scorched. But there was a dismal incompleteness about the partial incineration; the insolent fire had not deemed that the house was worth the burning.

Then she saw the human body.

It was cleft in two. The guillotine of lightning had come down at an oblique angle and had sliced half the skull away, cutting diagonally through the chin, lopping off one shoulder, arm and breast. The excised part lay rotting on the ground, the eye already gone. The remaining eye was bizarrely open, staring, and the half mouth was open as well. It was ugly, vengeful, obscene. . . . A dummy, you fool, made by the property department, and cosmeticized by the makeup man.

She had found her son.

She screamed.

She had found her child.

She screamed and screamed.

It was Mina, cleft in two.

It was Mina, dying twice.

It's now and it's then. I'm here and I'm there. I'm Rachel and Calla receiving my child, and rejecting it once and for all. I'm Willi at the death of Julo. I'm Rachel and Willi and Calla! And all of us, all three of us together, are making a new entity, a child is being born of all of us, through the outcries and the ripping, searing pain, in the presence of a dead child's body, a child is being born. Oh God, let there be some splendor in it!

She ran round and round the carcass, the dead regenerative thing, screaming and tearing at her flesh the way the false thorns had torn them, rending through the agony to reach the joy.

I'm living and acting, both at once.

Cameras, are you getting this?

I'm being and seeing and feeling and pretending and dying and growing—all in the death of the moment, in its birth, in its heartbeat.

Are you catching me? Are you rolling?

She felt that her delirium was a dance, her vision an epiphany. Death and expiation, Satin and the exorcism of him. Resurrection. Her anguish, an ecstasy.

She screamed for the joy and pain of it. At last, her work and her life were speaking, crying, singing with one another.

Ecstasy.

She saw the cameras moving in upon her from all directions.

Are you getting this?

27

Slain by lightning. Not by a bullet or a beating, not knifed to death. By fire from heaven. It was interesting to Calla that the scenarist had blamed the death of Rachel's son on God. God was the romantic's whipping boy. She would have blamed it on Kono, or, more obviously, on Titus. But it was, in story conference vernacular, writer's choice. Fabulist's choice might be truer.

On the final evening of shooting, in the midst of a sober, muted wrap-up party, Willi disappeared. It was not unusual. Ever since Julo's death, disappearance was all Willi seemed to ask for. She did nothing in the company of others. She did not go to the dining tent, but had scanty meals in Julo's trailer. On the set, she retreated to the periphery, only stepping forward when she was called. She never talked to anyone, and hardly even to Calla. She went to bed before sundown and pretended to be asleep; in the morning, she vanished before sunup, and arrived on the set at the last moment. Her grief was a state of absence.

Calla could not bear to see her loneliness, especially not tonight, the last evening of the picture. So she followed her to Julo's trailer.

Willi sat on the edge of the bed. She seemed perfectly relaxed, with her hands gently folded on her lap, and her head loosely inclined forward. At first Calla thought she was merely staring at her hands, but then realized that her eyes were closed. For a moment she wondered whether Willi was aware that someone was with her. But she did not question it, simply stood there, at the doorway, trying not to stir.

The woman on the bed raised her head a little, but she still did not open her eyes. What was she perceiving? Calla wondered.

Unseeing, but seeming to divine her question, Willi spoke. "I don't want to lose sight of you." It was barely a whisper. "I'm watching you in that scene, I'm hearing you scream—and I can't stand how beautiful you are. . . . And how beautiful you have made me."

"Oh, Will . . ."

"Not on that one night we had together, wonderful as it was. But at the body of that boy—when you were Calla and Rachel and Willi." She halted to collect herself. "I never thought there was any joy in tragedy—"

"There isn't, Will. Only when we can imagine that it's art."

"It *is* art, Cal. You were . . . I'll never be able to get over it. And I never want to."

"It wasn't me—you know that. I didn't do it. Lucas did it—and then it happened."

Willi opened her eyes. She smiled. "I think it's called inspiration. It's a marvelous word. It means that someone . . ."

". . . breathed a life into me."

"Yes."

Slowly Willi got up from the bed, and as she did, Calla moved to her. Like a meeting of soft currents of air, they went into one another's arms. They held the embrace for a long time.

"I feel as though . . . today . . . we've had a consummation," Willi said.

Calla nodded. As they ended the embrace, as Willi turned away from her, Calla realized that she would never turn back again. The heaviness was more than Calla could support, she felt weighed down with losses and departures, she did not want to say good-bye again, not ever again, not in life or in a scene.

But Willi was managing. Already, she was busying herself. She had put all her African hangings on Julo's wall; now she moved the bed a little, and started to take them down. Carefully, picture by picture, she stacked them on the bed. Detaching the batik from its stretcher, she meticulously rolled it and fastened a rubber band around it. She did the same with the picture of the Masai warrior and the scarred Akarra woman. Finally she folded up the map of Africa. She was taking down her banners, dismantling her dream.

"I'm going away," she said.

"Where?"

Willi hesitated. "I'm going to Africa."

"Africa?"

"Yes."

"Even if . . . ? Alone?"

The word had escaped Calla's mouth. It was obvious that if she was actually going, she was going alone. But her query had quickened a response in Willi—alert, quizzical.

"If you really mean that question, Calla . . . No, I'm not going alone, I'm going with Julo." Her face lighted. "But I don't want to confuse you."

Calla was not confused by Willi, but by herself. Why did it seem absolutely right for Willi to say she was going with Julo, how had her mind accepted it? Perhaps her mind had nothing to do with it.

"Why are you going?" she asked.

"To find Gorá."

This was harder to accept. She knew there was no such country, as Willi knew. There was Uganda, there was Somalia, bitter wars on old frontiers, hunger in Ethiopia and the Sudan, turmoil, rages everywhere, as Barney had pointed out. Yet . . . there were savannas of beauty, and languages Willi might comprehend without knowing the words. She was a woman with intuitions she had not even begun to use, and perhaps in Africa she would use them. With different insights from Calla's, with her own and Julo's, she would see other vistas and have other visions. She was, after all, Willi and not Calla, and she would discover Willi's world.

But Calla would sorely miss her. "Does it have to be Africa?"

"It's where Julo wants to go. Or . . . let me say . . . it's where he'll be."

Willi seemed to be bracing herself to hear something that might hurt. When it didn't come, "Thank you for not saying he's dead."

"Only his body."

Willi's eyes filled. "Yes. But then his body never meant much to me, any more than mine meant to him. We never really discovered one another in that way. As to Julo *himself* . . . all I have to do is find him . . . lead him where he wants to go . . . or . . ." She stopped. She was in an unknown region. "I'm not sure about any of this, understand. I'm not as experienced at these things as Julo is . . . or as talented."

Calla warmed to the word. "Why do you say talented?"

"Everything takes talent, doesn't it?" She laughed. "Acting—cooking—how to walk without crushing things with your feet. How to find a spirit. I may not be as gifted as he is. And maybe even he is not gifted enough. After all, I don't really believe he's a god."

"Then, if he's mortal—"

"But not dead!" Then she added quickly, "And if he is, I'll go to Africa and give him a second life."

They both smiled. The logical illogicality cleared away the necessity to comprehend things. They did not need rational sentences.

"How long will you be there?" Calla asked.

"I don't know. I hope for always."

"How will you live?"

"You don't mean 'live,' do you? You mean food, clothing, shelter. But you don't have to worry about that—I'm competent. Don't you remember that I am? I'll find jobs, I'll work, I'll pay the rent. And it's no longer separate."

"What do you mean, separate?"

"I used to pretend that my livelihood was life—while I did my living in secret. Two levels, two lives—and ultimately—"

"—two faces."

"The double," she said. "I was a double in more senses than one. But I don't want to hide the important part of me anymore. . . . I have to find Gorá."

Whatever doubts Willi may have had about method and meaning, she had no doubt whatever about her vital need to quest. It was a luminous clarity for her; it gave her force and courage and hope.

Calla helped her to pack, because she would be leaving earlier than the others, at sunrise, to make flights for Washington and London, then a British Airways flight to Kenya. As she was closing her bags, she seemed her old capable self again, ready to deal practically and proficiently with gods, Gorás and airline schedules.

In the earliest of dawns, they clung to one another.

"If you ever want to come home . . ."

"I hope that wherever I'm going will be home," Willi said quietly. With a little embarrassment she delicately put her hand to her scarred face. "It's minor—and vain. But Julo says there are places where scars are beautiful. Home is where you're beautiful, I think."

They laughed gently, but there was pain in it. Always, on wrap-up day, the participants vowed to see one another again, to telephone, to write, to have dinner together; always, they knew it would not happen, even if they truly meant it to happen. Now, with Willi, there weren't even any pretenses. It was not farewell until we meet again, but the unmerciful good-bye.

"Oh, Willi, I can't bear it!"

She was weeping in Willi's arms, saying she couldn't bear it, she couldn't. Willi held her close and comforted her, and also wept.

"I love you, Cal," she said. "I've loved you since the very first day—I always have."

"I know, I know. And I love you too—you know that, don't you?"

"Yes, I do."

It was loss and loss again, and Calla knew she had not yet felt the depth of her deprivation; she would miss Willi all her life. But then, because leavetaking was unbearable, they pretended that by some manner or miracle they would get to see one another again, somehow, somewhere. I'll see you, they said, I'll see you, knowing it was not true, they would soon be vastly different people, it was wrap-up conversation after all, a palliative against the pain of departure.

When she was gone, Calla realized how much they had needed each other. Searching, the image makers always searching for images, seeking alter egos as she and Willi had sought one another, as Lucas had sought Julo, as Barney had sought every character he had ever played, never certain which was the principal and which, the double; never certain which was real and which, illusory. Find me.

Later, it was one of those clear days in which one could touch the other side of the world. Saying farewell to the Bayou and to Mamma Lorena, she had a whole morning of leavetakings and departures, and felt that the good-byes were robbing her of breath, choking her. Finally she couldn't stand it any more, and fled to Lucas and the car.

His stuff was stowed in the vehicle, and so was hers, all ready to depart. But he himself was not altogether ready. He still had the disconnected look of someone who had packed too hastily, and was sure he had forgotten something, had left something vital behind.

Julo, of course.

In the last days of shooting, they had been deeply happy together, except for the ache of mortality. While she felt that she had exorcised much of her guilt over Barney, she was certain that Luke was still afflicted with the enormity of having betrayed Julo. And guilt would give his grief its durability. She was certain, too, that in his habit of lightening himself as a burden to others, he concealed his suffering. One night, when she was sleeping more deeply than he, she was awakened by the sound of his almost silent weeping. She thought, at first, that the softness of the sound was his effort to keep it below the level of her hearing, but she realized it was worse: He could not give himself the relief, the forgiveness, of a great outcry. She would have done his weeping for him, if she could. In any event, she did weep for him, and loved him.

On the ride to Memphis, sitting close to him, she was already forgetting the farewell lines and the cues for farewell lines. The sadness was already starting to be a remembered one, less poignant than regret.

But she mustn't leave it so quickly, she told herself, not the beauty of the Bayou or the pain of Ashton. Stay awhile, she said, don't vanish altogether. She summoned up a vision of Willi and Lorena, of Julo's voice again, of Barney, and the sound of bitterns and the image of river gulls winging toward a far horizon until the sky swallowed them up, and the night mist on the marsh, and the touch of the sick child's hand when she bathed him. But the pain and the wanting to remember the pain fought with one another, and all the images, like phantoms, began fading again, behind the scrim of memory.

On the plane, high over the mountain, with Luke still beside her, she had a moment of nausea. As it passed, she thought: What if it's not air sickness as I'm supposing it to be, what if I'm pregnant?

She knew it was hardly likely, and when it didn't recur, she was sure it was only an indisposition of travel.

She had a pang of disappointment. And suddenly it occurred to her: Never, in all these years, had she wanted another child. And now, for the first time . . .

Excitement, a flush of excitement. The simple fact that she had wanted it—even if she never had another child—was like an unexpected gift. It was still in its wrappings; she had not yet opened them to gaze at it. But even hidden as it was, it gave her a tremulous joy.

She looked at Lucas. He was fast asleep. He seemed deeply tired, but momentarily at peace. Sleep, she said as if *he* were her child, sleep. She touched his hand gently. He barely stirred. Sleep, she said.

When he awakened, she debated whether to tell him about her fantasy of the child. It wasn't until they were just beyond the Rockies that she did.

He said nothing. He looked out the window before referring to the subject. Then: "Can you tell what the imaginary baby looks like?"

"Probably, if I put my mind to it."

"Does it look like me?"

"It has an even chance."

"Does it have my name?"

". . . Probably not."

"I'm asking you to marry me, Calla."

"Which of us? . . . Or both?"

She wondered whether he was actually mystified, or didn't want to understand her. Then she saw, by his disturbance, that he couldn't face the question.

"What do you mean?" he said.

"Rachel is dead, Lucas."

She hadn't meant to be cruel, and hadn't realized what a sore place she was probing.

"Don't say that," he murmured. "She'll always be alive."

"On film . . . that we'll probably be afraid to look at."

"I wasn't talking about film. Rachel's a part of you, just as she's been a part of me."

"So is Cordelia a part of me . . . and Susie McCord . . ."

"Those women in you, Calla—I'm in love with all of them."

"But you don't know them. And I've forgotten them. When they went out of the lights, they went out of focus."

"Rachel won't."

"Yes, she will, Luke."

"To you maybe."

"To both of us."

"You're giving yourself a bad name."

"How so?"

"You lose a part of yourself when you lose the lens."

"Well . . . I'm grateful for having it for a while. Most people never have anything to see themselves through. But I haven't found one that makes all the images come together."

"Maybe that's what marriage is supposed to do."

"It's a bad lens for two-shots," she said. "One or the other of us would always be out of focus."

"We'll find one so perfect—!"

She smiled softly. "Let's keep looking."

Yes, they would keep looking, she thought, but they didn't even know what to look for. Back in the city, there would be so many incalculables. Everything would affect their love for each other. Especially the fortune of the film. If it was a success, they might love one another more; if a failure, less. Or vice versa.

To her, the picture was already a success. Her whole life had changed for the better. It was not that she now knew more than when she had started the film. It was that she knew less.

She had started by being certain, at one time, that Lucas was a reactionary; but if he was, she no longer knew what a reactionary might be. She had thought that acting should be a conscious art, and that an actress should always be clear about what she was doing; yet, her most sentient work had been done when she didn't know whether she was living or pretending—the bathing of the baby and the finding of her son —and behold, the ecstasy. She had thought that sanity and derangement were categorically different, that flesh was distinct from spirit, that God and the devil, if they existed, were enemies. She had thought that no film was worth the death of two human beings, and she still believed it, but she wondered what Barney and Julo would have said on the subject.

All her life she had enjoyed barnstorming, with the security of knowing that after every storm of mind she would come out intact and sane. Spirit, however, was another thing, and lately she had had her fears. But now she had had a storm of the spirit, and come out free.